MW00613505

OUR LADY
CHAOS

THE BLOODLETTER
COLLECTIONS

III

ERIK HENRY VICK

RATATOSKR PUBLISHING

NEW YORK

RATATOSKR PUBLISHING
769 BROADWAY #1060
MANHATTAN, NY 10003

PUBLISHER'S NOTE: THIS IS A WORK OF FICTION. NAMES, CHARACTERS, PLACES, AND INCIDENTS ARE A PRODUCT OF THE AUTHOR'S IMAGINATION. LOCALES AND PUBLIC NAMES ARE SOMETIMES USED FOR ATMOSPHERIC PURPOSES. ANY RESEMBLANCE TO ACTUAL PEOPLE, LIVING OR DEAD, OR TO BUSINESSES, COMPANIES, EVENTS, INSTITUTIONS, OR LOCALES IS COMPLETELY COINCIDENTAL.

OUR LADY CHAOS / **ERIK HENRY VICK**. -- 1ST ED.
ISBN 978-1-951509-02-6

For Mildred Adicks, who with her kindness and generosity of spirit, started me on this path by walking me through a Scholastic Book Fair and helping me pick my first book, for Auntie Scrabble, with love, and last, but not least, for the best damn kid a father could ask for.

The haunting never fades, laughter's gone away
It's too late, when you've lost your soul
I left her everything, she only left my ring
My world is darker now than the blackest crow

—Dave Mustaine

Come now my lovely, won't you take a midnight stroll with
  me?
Through the misty air the things I keep I shouldn't dare
My garden's so inviting, and its deadly blooms are hiding
Be careful what you touch 'less the grave is what you lust
Draw the blinds, you're getting tired paralyzed
Don't close your eyes, gripped with fear,
Your dreams become nightmares from the deadly
  nightshade

—Dave Mustaine

I give, you take this life that I forsake
Been cheated of my youth you turned this lie to truth
Anger, misery…you'll suffer unto me
Harvester of sorrow… Language of the mad

—James Alan Hetfield, Lars Ulrich

I hope you enjoy *OUR LADY CHAOS*. If so, please consider joining my Readers Group—details can be found at the end of the last chapter.

Table of Contents

BOOK ONE:
BLACKEST
CROW

Chapter 1
1975

I

January 1975

Apsu moved through the thick black smoke as if born from it. And it made sense she did so—she had been, after all. Bright yellow flames danced across the back of the sofa and licked at the paneling, charring its surface and bubbling the clear coat protecting the stain that colored it. The carpet burned in places—an olive-green plain dotted with lakes of fire.

Behind her, the furniture and draperies in the formal living room went up with a *whump*, and the demoness grinned, satisfaction humming in her veins. The house's destruction whetted her appetite—a fine aperitif. She walked across the den and entered the hall.

In the back of the house, a baby wailed in terror, and a woman whimpered with fear. A sigh of contentment escaped her as the anticipation built. She'd been working toward that night for more than a year—twisting the man's mind with the subtle finesse of a master of human nature, letting his hatred build and build and build until he thought he would pop with it.

There had been other nights on the path to the fire she stood in, arguments that blossomed into slaps at first, then later into blows from a fist, and most recently into a beating that left the wife bloody and bruised. But after every such incident, Apsu allowed the husband to see what he'd done, to suffer remorse. She tolerated his promise to be better, to make it up to his wife with flowers and gifts, but always, always there was a bill to pay for such allowances—and the woman had paid each in full.

On one shame-filled night, she'd allowed them to create a child.

It hurt her to watch the wife's happiness bloom as the pregnancy developed, to see her glow in her husband's arms, and, as always, Apsu filed her grief away—a note to be called due at her leisure. She allowed the baby to come to term and gave the couple several months of bliss.

But the bride had made payments toward the balance of that bill of pain over the last several weeks. It wasn't fair that she had the propensity to bear children, not when Apsu could not.

She hated the wife—the husband, too, though he had his uses—for the affront of being fertile in the face of her own infertility. *But tonight…tonight I can finally show her how much I hate her. Tonight, she will know my wrath.* The thought excited Apsu and brought her anticipation to new heights.

She walked through the flame and smoke, allowing the baby's inchoate fear and the woman's direct dread of her husband to wash over her like hot magma. She savored the man's confusion, his pain at his own actions. Oh, he regretted setting the fire and tried to rebel, but it was far, far too late for that.

With a wave of her hand, she sent flames exploding through the den behind her, as though she'd tossed a can of turpentine or maybe gasoline onto the blaze. She couldn't feel the intensity of the conflagration—her own heat was too great—but she pretended the fire warmed her and drew comfort from that fiction.

Apsu turned and walked down the hallway, hurling flames into each room that opened off it. The last door in the hall was closed, and she sent a wave of fire splashing across its surface.

Behind the door, the wife screamed, and the baby screamed, and the husband yelled for silence. With a smile, the demoness raised a foot made only of flame and kicked the door from its hinges.

She stepped inside the master bedroom, and for the first time, she showed her true form to the family cowering before her. She smiled at them, and the wife lost her mind while the husband dissolved into a puddle of regret and self-hatred. The baby looked on in silence.

Apsu saved the child for last. Dessert, if you will.

2

March 1975

Dennis Cratchkin shuffled his feet, dropped his head, and muttered a few choice curse words into his chest. He hated math, and he hated Mr. Dubrovnik, his math teacher. To his mind, Dubrovnik needed a big dent between his eyes—one made by the short-handled sledgehammer Dennis had stolen from his father's toolbox.

"And what was that, Mr. Cratchkin?" asked Mr. Dubrovnik, except because of his accent, it came out: "Unt vat vas dat, Mister Crotchkink?"

That was why the braver kids in fifth grade called him Crotchking—one more reason Dubrovnik needed a dent in his forehead. *If I was bigger, I'd do it*, Dennis thought as he scuffed the sole of his new Converse All Star high-tops on the slick linoleum floor tile on which he stood. Dubrovnik always called on him—*always*—for the hard problems, even though Dennis never raised his hand.

He lifted his head and stared at the chalkboard half a foot from his face. Dennis didn't understand long division, and yet here he was, up in front of the class, muttering curse words and hating Dubrovnik all the more. *Who the hell cares what 258 divided by 43 is, anyway?* He grabbed a piece of chalk from the tray at the bottom of the chalkboard and rubbed his thumb along its length, pressing hard enough to break the long piece into thirds.

"Chalk is not free, Mr. Crotchkink. Do you wish to buy me a new box?"

Dennis sneered at the chalkboard and shook his head. He tossed two pieces back into the tray and lifted the other to the board. He dragged the chalk across the slate, making it screech and squeal—a proficiency he'd developed during his long tenure as Mr. Dubrovnik's student—he'd endured the third grade already the year before, but here he was again, repeating the grade, just as he'd repeated the second.

"Enough of that, if you please, Mr. Crotchkink."

The other boys who sat in the back row sniggered, and Dennis's cheeks flamed with anger and shame. He raised the chalk again and began to write as if he were working the problem. Instead, he drew a picture of Dubrovnik licking the ass of a horse. On top of the vinculum, Dennis wrote "FUCK YOU" and dropped the chalk into the tray. He spun on his heel and walked along his row, heading for his desk in the back.

The entire class seemed to have stopped breathing as he revealed his work on the board, and Dennis sneered at the goody-goodies sitting upfront. He lifted his gaze to the boys in the back and scanned their faces. Ari's face expressed surprise tinged with admiration, but Jasper's expression made Dennis smile. Jasper stared at him in open amazement, a small, crooked grin on his lips.

"Mr. Crotchkink!"

Dennis didn't stop walking toward his seat—though he had no intention of sitting. He intended to sweep his jeans jacket off the back of the chair, thrust his arms into it, and storm out the classroom's rear door. Dennis didn't intend to stop walking until he reached the hangout he and Jasper had built on the edge of the Thousand Acre Wood. He'd wait for Jasper and Ari there.

He was three quarters along the length of his row when Mr. Dubrovnik's hand fell on his shoulder like a lead weight and jerked him around. The teacher's face burned crimson, and his narrowed eyes blazed. The man had clenched his free hand into a fist so tight his knuckles shined white.

Dennis sneered at him. "Go ahead. Hit me, Dumbrovnik. Hit me and watch what happens." It made Dennis proud that his voice didn't shake, despite the fear tickling his belly. Dubrovnik's eyes widened at the play on his name, and his nostrils flared, but he did nothing more than stand there staring down at Dennis. "See something you like, Dumbrovnik? I gotta tell you, though, I don't roll that-a-way."

Dubrovnik snarled as he spun Dennis around and shoved him toward the rear of the room. "Read from chapter seven in your text!" he snapped at the rest of the class.

As Dennis walked past Jasper, he tipped him a wink and yanked his jacket off the back of the chair.

"Yes. Take your things, Mr. Crotchkink. I don't think you will be back before we return from the spring break."

"Fine with me, Dumbrovnik. I hate this damn class, and I hate your dumb accent almost as much as I hate the way you look."

Dubrovnik's hand again fell on his shoulder, his grip pinching and tight. "It would be best for you to keep silent, Mr. Crotchkink."

"*Cratchkin*, you dumbass! Not 'Crotchkink!' C-R-A-T-C-H-K-I-N. No fucking K on the end. No O in it at all!"

Behind him, Dubrovnik growled, and Dennis wrinkled his nose with glee, though he knew he had earned a paddling from the principal, a suspension for the cursing and disrespect, and that added up to an ass-kicking if his old man ever found out. But his father finding out wasn't likely, unless the principal could slip a note into the bottom of one of his Budweiser bottles.

Dennis knew his mom would help him hide the school trouble from his dad. They'd both learned that it was best to keep his father drunk and docile. Once the rage took him, there was no telling where his attention might fasten.

His old man, Dennis Cratchkin, Sr., needed a dent in his forehead, too.

3

April 1975

Eddie Mitchell's father came through the door with a big box in his hands. Grease and wet spots marred the otherwise unmarked cardboard, but it seemed sturdy enough to contain whatever rested inside.

"Kathy!" he called. "Come look at what I got for you."

"Ted? Is that you?" Eddie's mother winked at him and grinned. She enjoyed teasing his father that way.

"Well, of course, woman! Who else would it be?"

"Come on, Eddie. Let's go see what Daddy's brought home." She rose with a dancer's grace, and when Eddie got up from the floor, she took his hand and led him from the bedroom. Together they walked to the kitchen, smiling and jostling one another with elbows, hips, and shoulders.

When they reached the kitchen, his father waited next to the table, holding his hands out toward the stained cardboard box like a magician. "Go ahead, honey," he said. "Open it."

"What is it, Ted? It's not my birthday."

"Do I need a reason to buy my best girl a present?" He waggled his eyebrows in the way that always made Eddie laugh, and it was no less successful that time.

His mother stepped toward the crate, unfolded the top, and peered inside. Her whole face lit up the way it did when happiness overtook her. "It's gorgeous! Where on Earth did you find it? How can we afford this?"

Eddie's father spoke the words he always did in moments such as this, "Don't worry, Kathy. I got a good price." He winked at Eddie and showed his special smile—the one that suggested he held the world in the palm of his hand.

Eddie wasn't sure what "held the world in the palm of his hand" meant, but he'd heard his mother use the phrase with pride to describe his daddy when chatting with her friends. Whatever it might mean, it was a good thing.

Kathy smiled and reached inside the box. Eddie danced with a child's excitement, shifting his weight from foot to foot. His hands were up in front of his chest, folded as if in prayer, his eyes shimmered with delight, and a smile stretched across his face.

"You enjoy it when I bring Mommy presents, don't you, Son?" His father reached over and ruffled his hair, and Eddie nodded but couldn't tear his gaze away from the wondrous thing his mother lifted from the box.

His mom held a lamp with a colorful stained-glass shade and body over a brass base and beamed a smile of pure pleasure at her husband and son. The lampshade reminded him of the bottom half of an upended turnip. Short hunks of tinted glass composed most of the shade, beginning with a ribbon of rectangular glass pieces the color of his mother's pearls at the very top, then a stripe of teal, and then another ribbon of white. Below the stripes, the pieces of glass took on irregular shapes and a distinct shade of aquamarine. The artist had scattered smaller round fragments of red, dark teal, orange, and olive through the field of aquamarine. The white wings of dragonflies bordered the lowest edge of the shade, and the bodies of the dragonflies had been done in bright yellow. Between the dragonflies and the aquamarine chunks of glass were pieces of green and turquoise—but with the same small round bits of different colored glass. A mix of turquoise, aquamarine, and green irregular-shaped chunks of glass made up the body, and the lamp's base was bronze, as was the knob at the top, and the pull chains.

His mom's eyes shone with delight, and she flashed a broad, cheery smile at her husband. "Oh, Ted, it's perfect!"

His dad beamed at them. "It's a Tiffany."

His mother's eyes opened wide. "A *real* Tiffany? How?"

Their happiness made Eddie's heart sing.

His father put his hands behind his back and smiled wider. "Told you. I got a deal."

"But even with the best deal in the world, this must have cost a month's salary or more. How can we afford it?"

"Don't you worry about that." His smile faltered a touch. "I take care of us, right? Do we ever run short?"

"I didn't mean it that way, Ted." His mother set the lamp down on the table and walked toward his father, her hands held out to give him a hug.

Ted shook his head, a sour expression on his face. "Sometimes, Kathy, you don't appreciate what I do for you."

"But I do! I absolutely do, Ted. You are a great husband."

Somewhat mollified, Ted allowed the hug and gazed at Eddie. "Well, tiger? What do you think of it?"

"Pretty! I like the dragonflies."

"I knew you would, champ. The second I saw it, I got the feeling it was the lamp for this family. It was as if…" Ted stood for a moment, his gaze gone far away, his face slack, and his mouth hanging open a tad.

"Don't catch flies, Daddy," teased Eddie.

With a start, his father shook himself and grinned. "Where should Mommy put our new treasure?"

Eddie whirled and dashed into the living room, his regard flicking from the end table to the coffee table to the top of the small bookshelf and to the top of the Zenith console television set. He spun and trotted into the dining room, looking at the hutch and the serving cart. Then he turned and rushed back into the kitchen where his parents were hugging, and his mother was planting kisses on his daddy's cheek.

"In the living room," Eddie said. "We should put it on the end table on the side of the couch away from the dining room. Kind of in the corner."

Laughing, his mom nodded.

"Can I carry it?" Eddie rushed to the kitchen table and grabbed the lamp by its brass base and the pole of the same material between the body and the lightbulb. As he lifted it, something algid and greasy wriggled across the skin on the back of his hands. He cried out and let go of the lamp, leaving it tottering on the edge of the table. He held one hand with the other, up close to his chest as if it had stung him.

Ted darted forward and grabbed the lamp. He turned an angry stare on Eddie. "Watch what you're doing! This isn't a toy, Eddie. It's expensive! Do you understand what that means? It cost a lot of money, and I don't want you to break it with your carelessness."

Eddie stood there, shoulders slumped, his mournful gaze slithering back and forth between his mother and his father. It didn't pay to make his daddy mad—he would be grouchy and snappy for a month.

"You don't touch this! Do you understand me, Eddie? You *never* touch this!" Ted's voice ratcheted up in the way it did when his anger had gotten the best of him.

"I'm sorry, Daddy."

"Why are you so careless? When I was your age, I knew better than to touch things that didn't belong to me. Why haven't you learned that yet?"

"There's no damage done, Ted," his mother said in placating tones. "He didn't mean any harm. He's just excited." She put on a brilliant smile. "We are all just thrilled about this beauty."

"Why do you always coddle him, Kathy?"

"Let's set it up," said Kathy with a forced brightness to her tone that matched her radiant smile. "Let's not let this happy surprise go down the drain." She smiled at Ted and held out her hand. She stepped toward the living room, and after a moment, Ted picked up the lamp and took her hand.

"I'm sorry, Daddy. I won't do it again."

"See that you don't, Eddie," his daddy said in a cold voice.

Eddie followed his parents into the living room and watched as his father installed the lamp on the end table and plugged it in. He pulled one of the little chains, and light blazed through the stained-glass lampshade. Eddie sucked in a breath. "It's beautiful," he whispered.

"It's lovely!" said Eddie's mother in the same moment. She laughed and ruffled Eddie's hair.

Ted Mitchell smiled, but not as wide as he had before Eddie had almost dropped the lamp.

A lump formed in Eddie's throat, hard and cold. It seemed to have sharp edges, and it hurt when Eddie swallowed.

He always ruined everything.

4

June 1975

Kristy liked how the wind from the open window ruffled her blonde hair. She loved the springtime, especially when the weather stayed cool through June.

She turned thirteen in a few months—at the end of September—and sensed she was on the cusp of a life-changing event. Becoming a woman, she supposed.

She idled near her window, enjoying the evening air and waiting. Kristy felt a compulsion to wait there after supper.

She didn't understand it, but a thrill coursed through her standing in front of it—at least when the cute new boy next door sat at his window and stared at her.

Her mom chastised her for the behavior, telling her good girls didn't act that way, but the words rang hollow in Kristy's ears. And it seemed as though her mother might not *really* care if she did it.

Maybe he won't come to the window tonight. Maybe he's not even home.

"He" was the teenager that lived next door. Leif. Dreamy Leif. He was taller than the other guys his own age, let alone the boys in Kristy's grade. Leif had dark eyes and brown hair parted on the side that swept back from his face the way Shawn Cassidy's did. He wore cool clothes, too.

More than all that, though, he always smiled at her when she stood at her window and played in the wind. He appeared not to care about the difference in their ages, he didn't mind that she had only just graduated from middle school and he was older—a junior or senior at Oneka Falls High School, unless she missed her guess.

Sometimes, Kristy wondered if he would act the same way if she ever saw him out in public—which she never seemed to do. That was strange for a small town such as Oneka Falls, but true, nonetheless.

She peeked at her little alarm clock and watched it click to seven-fifteen. *Maybe he's out tonight. Dinner with his dad or something.* Only the two of them lived in the house beside Kristy—at least, she'd never seen his mom or any siblings.

She saw his father often enough—mowing the yard or enjoying a beer on the wrap around porch—and his dad grinned and waved at her every time. But in a cordial way, not a creepy way.

Kristy's mother appeared interested in the man next door. She invariably put on makeup and did up her hair when they strolled down to the little store on the corner of Mill and Main. Or even when they roamed around the block.

One of her more risqué daydreams involved her mom marrying the guy next door and Kristy having to share a room with the Shawn Cassidy look-alike—though it made no sense. As if her mother would ever allow that.

Kristy stole another glance at his window, and a little thrill ran through her belly as the light in the boy's bedroom came on. She glanced down and smoothed her green, long-sleeved T-shirt with the hot-air balloon emblazoned on its front. She had on matching green pants that flared to bell-bottoms. Her mom made her buy clothes from the Sears catalog, but Kristy thought the outfit looked cool, regardless. She imagined the guy next door would like it, too.

His drapes rustled, and there he stood, a lopsided grin on his face. Kristy lifted her hand halfway to her shoulder and gave him a shy wave, then ducked her face to hide her rosy cheeks.

When she raised her head to peek at him, the boy gazed at her in a way that made her belly tingle, and despite her deepening blush, she didn't break eye contact. He beckoned her, as though she could walk across the air twenty feet above the grass that separated their houses. She grinned and beckoned back, the safety of that space emboldening her.

His grin widened, he tipped her a wink—which sent another bolt of lightning through her belly—and made as if to climb out his window. Then he laughed, and Kristy joined him. He mimed walking down the stairs with his fingers and beckoned her again.

Kristy ducked her head. There was no way on God's green earth that her mom would let her go next door to hang out with an older boy. Still looking at the ground between the houses, she shook her head. *It might as well be a thousand miles between us*, she thought.

A low whistle drew her attention back to the boy's window. He stood there, as proud as Lucifer, as her mother would say, his shirt off and his pants unbuttoned.

Kristy's face burned as if it would burst into flames at any second.

But she didn't turn away. Not until his hand went to his zipper.

5

June 1975

Sean Walker had lived only seven years, but he knew a bad deal when he saw one. The enormous man in the car idling beside the sidewalk held the five-dollar bill out to him and cracked his lips in a toothy grin, which did more to freak Sean out than comfort him. The guy reminded him of a shark—all teeth, too-big mouth. "No, thank you," said Sean.

The man shifted in his seat, leaning away from Sean a little, and though his smile remained, his eyes went cold. "Go on, kid. Do it. Five bucks buys a lot of Now and Later candy."

That much was true, but they'd just had the "stranger danger" talk in the last week of school, and Chief Greshin himself had explained that some bad people tried to lure kids closer to their cars with money or sweets.

Sean took another step away from the car, shaking his head.

The man's smile faded and he squinted at Sean, the muscles around his wide jaw bunching and hardening. He leaned forward, and again, held the five-dollar bill toward the window. "I get it, kid. I surely do. Stranger danger, right?" The man laughed, and when he did, his belly shook. "It's great you listened to the police officer who gave that talk, son. Fantastic. Who was the cop this time? Officer Witherson? Or the young guy…Danny Jones?"

"Chief Greshin," said Sean.

"Oh ho! The Chief of Police, himself, huh?" The man's toothy grin resurfaced, and his eyes crinkled around the edges. "Like I said, good for you for listening. But it's okay. I know all of the officers in Oneka Falls. I'm in law enforcement, myself, y'see." He twisted in the seat and fished a black rectangle out of his pocket. "Name's Karl Munnur. Kanowa County Sheriff's Department." He flipped the leather wallet open to reveal a badge and a picture ID. "I'm off-duty, but I'm still a cop. What did Chief Greshin say to do when strangers approach you?"

"Go to an adult or a policeman."

The massive man chuckled. "And here you are, champ, talking to a policeman."

Sean relaxed all at once and grinned. "Hello, Officer Manner."

The big man in the car laughed. "It's Munnur, son. Deputy Munnur."

"Oh…sorry," said Sean.

Munnur waved it all away. "Don't worry about it, kid. What's your name?"

"Sean Walker, sir."

"Sir, is it? I like that. Your daddy's raising you right, isn't he?"

Sean's face crumpled around the edges, and he pinched his eyes shut. A lump formed in his throat—a lump of burning charcoal.

"Oh, son. I'm a great big idiot," said Munnur. "Vietnam?"

Sean could no more speak than he could fly. He settled for nodding, keeping his eyes squeezed shut against the tears.

"That damn war," the deputy fumed. "Listen, Sean, I'm sorry about your dad. I'm sorrier still I brought all that back to you."

Sean opened his eyes and glimpsed something on the big man's face—the same expression Dennis the Menace wore when he shoved one of the littler kids into a snowbank—but before Sean could even be sure of what he saw, it disappeared, replaced by a look of genuine sadness and pity.

"Only you and your mom these days then?"

Sean forced the lump away. "Yes. We're still a family, just a smaller one."

"That's right, isn't it? And things will get better."

Sean nodded in a distracted way, his gaze crawling over the deputy's face.

"Throw your bike in the back seat, Sean," said Munnur. "I'll run you home. It's getting dark."

Sean dithered, feeling he should trust the man, but the expression he'd glimpsed gave him pause.

"It's okay, Sean," said Munnur. "I don't bite." He bellowed laughter. "Not much, anyway."

Sean grinned, but it felt foreign.

"Come on, Sean. I'll give you a lift. You can keep the five dollars for having listened to Chief Greshin." He leaned across the big bench seat and pulled the passenger door handle of the green Impala. "I can meet your mother and tell her what a fine job she's doing."

"Well…"

"I'm safe, Sean. You can trust me, I promise. Do it, son. Do it, do it, do it."

Sean swung his leg over the seat of his bike and nodded at Deputy Munnur. He wheeled it over to the back door and opened it, putting the bike inside and leaning it against the backseat. Then he slid into the passenger seat and smiled at Munnur. "Thanks, Deputy Munnur."

"Think nothing of it, Sean," said Munnur. "And when we're alone together, you can call me Karl." He held out the five-dollar bill, and Sean took the money.

"Thanks, Dep—" Sean grinned. "Thanks, Karl."

"It's nothing, kid. You earned it, kid."

6

July 1975

With summer came longer evenings and a later bedtime, and both facts made Kristy happy. Most years she spent her time hanging out with her girlfriends—walking to the little store on the corner of Main Street and Mill Lane for candy or pops, chilling at BurgerWorld until dusk, or just strolling around the small town and talking. Always talking.

She suspected she would spend this summer another way, and though the idea excited her, regret tinged the emotion. The last week of school, she and Michelle Donnelly had fought—a small blow up—in the cafeteria. They'd flung hard words at each other with abandon, and even though both had apologized, Michelle still seemed angry. Or maybe jealous—the tiff had been about Kristy "always mooning about the boy next door" as Michelle had said it.

With an effort, Kristy forced the memory—and thoughts of Michelle—out of her mind and focused on what she was doing. She'd finished her dinner twenty minutes earlier and then showered before sitting at her vanity to try her hand at putting on sexy makeup. She had her door locked—her mother would definitely not approve of her plans for the evening—and had taken out the lipsticks she'd bought from different stores over the course of the previous week. So far, she liked the pink color best but thought red was sexier.

She had a special outfit in mind for the evening, and because of its nature, she could use whatever color eyeshadow she wanted. On her third try, she settled on a silky shade of blue and began to work on her lashes. With rouge on her cheeks, she sat back and cast a critical eye on her efforts before grabbing a Kleenex and wiping off the pink lipstick. Red was definitely better.

Finally, she was ready. She had saved her money for two months to afford the makeup, her special outfit, and a visit to the fancy grownup hair salon across town—a visit she'd made that afternoon. Her mother hadn't liked her changing her hairstyle, but she had said little, just frowned. Kristy took a moment and admired how her hair flipped back imitating Farrah Fawcett's feathered bangs. Kristy didn't have the thick hair Farrah did, but the stylist had added body with a special brush and a blow dryer. Her eyes drifted to a bag lying on the floor next to her vanity—the bag containing her brand-new round brush and the Conair hair dryer her stylist had recommended. Both together had cost her over twenty dollars, but she didn't care.

She took a lingering, final glance at the mirror before turning to her window and peeking through her blinds.

He was already at the window, doing nothing more than staring at her closed blinds, as still as a statue. Nervousness percolated in her gut, bringing a touch of nausea with it. With a deep breath to steady her nerves, she drew the blinds up with deliberate speed. The summer evening air washed across the bare skin of her belly, leaving goosebumps in its wake.

His eyes widened, and a slow smile spread across his cheeks.

The black bikini was perfect.

7

August 1975

Sean peeked out from his bedroom window as Mr. Munnur opened the passenger door of his big green Impala and offered his hand to Vickie. She said something, and they both laughed, but Sean's face was stony and hard.

The deputy and his mom stepped out together on a regular basis and had since the day he and Sean had met. He'd also been spending a lot of time with Sean—sometimes with Vickie in tow, sometimes just the two of them. Karl's schedule varied, and his days off occurred in the middle of the week more often than not, while Sean's mother worked Monday through Friday.

Outside, his mother laughed, and by the sound of it, Karl had gotten her drunk again. That meant Karl would sleep over.

Awesome, Sean thought.

Irritated lines settled over Karl's face as he glanced at the house. From time to time, Sean thought that Karl was only interested in his mother Vickie, that he'd only pretended to enjoy Sean's company to get points with her.

In one of the serendipitous moments that seemed to occur with increasing regularity, Karl glanced up at Sean's window and caught him looking out at them. He flashed an easy grin and gave him a small wave. Then he said something to Vickie, and they both giggled.

It's like he knows when I'm spying on him...as though he can hear my thoughts. Like he's got whatever Damien had in that scary devil picture he took me to last week. Karl had laughed all the way through it, and try as he might, Sean couldn't catch the humor of it. He still didn't understand how anyone could laugh at that movie.

Karl and his mother left the car behind and stood on the stoop. Munnur laughed, though neither he nor Vickie had said a word. As Sean watched, Karl turned toward his window and grinned as if they'd shared a joke.

Sean backed away from the window and crawled into bed. *He is a cop, that's all. He knows how people think and can imagine what's going on inside my mind.* It seemed plausible enough, but Sean didn't believe it.

A low murmur of voices began in the family room, and minutes later, the front door opened and closed as the babysitter left. The quiet rumble of Karl's easy laugh reverberated through the house as his mother and Karl walked back to her bedroom.

8

September 1975

The new school year rolled around all too fast for Dennis. Truth to tell, he did not understand how he'd passed the previous grade, but he felt grateful to whatever angel or devil had intervened. If he'd had to suffer through another year of Dubrovnik, it seemed a foregone conclusion that Dennis would've ended up in serious trouble.

Fourth grade would be different. He wanted out—out of the damn elementary school that tormented him daily. Out of school in any of its forms. Dennis couldn't wait until he turned sixteen so he could quit and never set foot on another school campus as long as he lived—unless it was to kick someone's ass.

He arrived on the first day of fourth grade wearing brown corduroys and his new favorite shirt. His mom had taken him to a Black Sabbath concert at the end of the previous school year, and he had the T-shirt to prove it. Solid black, with the band logo emblazoned across the chest in white, the shirt shouted cool. Below the emblem was a picture of the album cover which featured a weird mirror image of the band. His mother loathed the image on the album sleeve, but Dennis thought it was the coolest thing since Kool-Aid.

What made the shirt even cooler in Dennis's eyes was the disdain with which his father treated the band and the concert T-shirt. Anything his old man hated was surely solid gold.

Another gift from the concert: the plan for the rest of his life. Going on eleven years old, he already knew his impressions of the educational system were correct. He didn't need it—he was going to be a rock star, same as Ozzy Osbourne. Ozzy hadn't done well in school, and he had more money than God.

Ari waited on the top step, watching Dennis come sauntering up to the campus. The boy's eyes widened at the sight of Dennis's T-shirt, and he ran down the steps to meet at the edge of the sidewalk. "Cool shirt, Dennis," he said all in a rush.

"What? This thing?" Dennis glanced down at the shirt and smiled. "Yeah, it's righteous, right?" He raised his gaze to Ari's face. "But this year, call me Denny."

"Denny? Like the restaurant?"

Dennis grimaced and socked him in the arm, extending his middle finger to leave a nice bruise to remember the lesson by. "No, dummy! Like Ozzy."

"Oh." Ari twisted his head to the side and stared down at the sidewalk.

"You know who Ozzy is, right?" sneered Dennis.

"Yeah, I know."

"Then who is he?"

Ari half-turned toward the school. "C'mon. We're going to be late for homeroom."

"Who gives a fuck?"

Ari gasped, then giggled. "You said the f-word."

"Yeah, so? Now, answer my question. Who is Ozzy?"

Ari sighed, and his shoulders slumped. "Okay, okay. I don't know."

Ari was an okay kid, despite his penchant for pretending to know everything. "Just what I thought, Jewboy. You don't have to pretend to be a brainiac around me. I don't care about smart. I care about *loyal.*"

Ari nodded but didn't meet his gaze.

"Anyways… Ozzy Osbourne is the lead singer for Black Sabbath. They call him the Prince of Darkness, and when I turn sixteen, I'm going to be a rock star just like him."

"What instrument can you play?"

Dennis turned a look of withering scorn on his friend. "Well, duh. I *can't* play anything yet, but my mom said she'd save up and buy me a guitar or drums or something."

The tardy bell rang, and Ari jumped, then spun and started up the stairs. "We're late!"

"Who gives a fuck?"

Ari's attention bounced between Dennis's face and the school's doors. "It's the first day of classes, man."

Dennis cocked his head to the side and fished the pack of cigarettes he'd stolen from his dad's carton that morning. "You go ahead. I'm not sure I'm staying."

"But…" Ari's face scrunched up and, again, his gaze bounced back and forth between his friend and the brick building.

Dennis tapped out a cigarette and lodged it in the corner of his mouth as he'd seen his father do six thousand times. With his other hand, he dug for the matchbook in his other pocket. He squinted up at Ari. "You coming or going, Jewboy?"

"Don't call me that," said Ari, but his voice lacked conviction. "It's rude."

Dennis sneered as he folded back the cover and tore out a match. "Fuck that, Ari." He struck the match and held it to the tip of the smoke.

"Are those... Are those good?"

Dennis flipped his greasy hair out of his face and drew on the cowboy killer, hating the taste but determined not to let on. He'd grown his hair out all summer, and now, more often than not, it hung in his eyes. "Do you see me gagging and throwing it out? Of course it's good. You think all these people smoke 'em because they taste like monkey assholes?"

Ari took one final glance at the school and descended the steps to stand facing Dennis. "Let me try?"

Dennis squinted sideways at him through the smoke. "I don't know, man. You might consider it *rude.*"

Ari pursed his lips. "It *is* rude to call a Jew 'Jewboy,' and you know it, Dennis."

"Denny," Dennis said with a shrug.

Ari inclined his head. "Denny, then."

"Yeah. I don't mean nothing by it, Ari. You know that. You're my man."

Ari cut his gaze to the side. "Sure, Denny."

"Here," he said, holding the cigarette out to Ari. "Try a drag, but don't take too much. It'll make you cough like the dickens until you get used to it."

Taking the cigarette as if it were a live snake, Ari put it to his lips and puffed. His expression soured. "It tastes like monkey assholes, Denny."

Dennis chuckled. "At first, yeah. But you get to like it." He threw a glance up at the school. "Come on, my man. Let's beat feet before someone catches us."

"You're cutting the first day?"

"No, Ari. *We're* cutting the first day."

Ari took another drag on the cigarette and peeked at the doors before meeting Dennis's gaze. "Okay. What do you want to do?"

"Both your parents work, right?"

Ari nodded.

Dennis grinned and put his hand on Ari's shoulder. "Fine, then. Let's hang out there." He turned away from the school, dragging Ari with him. "Let's hustle. We can watch Dialing for Dollars from the beginning if we hurry. It's a monster movie today. I already checked the TV Guide."

"Monster movie? I don't know…"

"You'll love it, Ari." Dennis flashed a lopsided grin. "Trust me."

9

September 1975

Sean Walker watched Dennis pass the cigarette to Ari Abelman with little interest. Karl had told him how "coffin nails," as he had called them, caused mutations and junk like that inside a person's cells. When the two boys turned and walked away from the school, Sean couldn't contain his snort of derision.

"Something to add, Mr. Walker?" asked Mrs. Tyler.

Sean jumped and shook his head, feeling the blush creeping up his cheeks.

"Then perhaps we could pay attention to the happenings inside the classroom this morning."

"Yes, Mrs. Tyler."

"What's so interesting, anyway?" She walked to the windows, and as she did, Sean's stomach dropped out from under him. She looked out the window and frowned. "Do you recognize those boys, Sean?"

Sean squeezed his eyes shut. His day had just taken a left turn at bad and cruised on toward worse. "Uh…"

"That looks like…" muttered Mrs. Tyler, before she turned and fixed Sean with a freezing glance. "That was Dennis Cratchkin and Ariel Abelman, unless I'm mistaken."

Please don't force me to snitch, he begged in silence.

"Well, Mr. Walker?"

She won't let this go. If I tattle, Dennis will grind me to minced meat for sure. If I don't, I'll get in trouble, and Mom will no doubt tell Karl, and then I'll be in double trouble. He opened his eyes and sent a pleading look up at his teacher. *She's got to understand what happens if I squeal.*

Mrs. Tyler lifted her chin for a moment, then let it drop, and her expression softened. "I saw who it was, and I will deal with them later," she said. "But I'll take three hundred sentences from you by homeroom tomorrow, Mr. Walker."

Sean nodded, almost unable to contain a sigh of relief. He glanced around the room, and when his gaze came to rest, he'd locked eyes with Jasper Kent—another of Dennis's bully friends.

Jasper winked, and Sean's heart sank. He'd skipped ahead this year—bypassing third grade and continuing straight to fourth. It showed in his size and his strength. He didn't stand a chance against Jasper, even one-on-one, let alone with Dennis who'd already failed twice. Sean was eight, and Dennis was eleven.

What am I going to do?

IO

September 1975

Kristy climbed aboard the Oneka Falls High School bus for the first time and scanned the kids already seated, looking for Michelle Donnelly. The vacation had gone by at a breakneck pace, and she had seen little of her best friend that summer—she hadn't slept over at all, and Michelle hadn't stayed with her either. Leif—the boy next door—had taken most of Kristy's attention, even when she couldn't see him, she'd spent her time thinking and daydreaming about their next encounter.

Michelle sat halfway down the narrow aisle that ran between the benches. She stared out the window as if she didn't care whether or not Kristy saw her. Michelle sat alone in one of the bench seats but had her purse and backpack piled on the bench beside her, leaving no room for Kristy to sit next to her.

Kristy walked up the aisle, her stomach knotting up. She hated confrontations more than anything. She stopped by Michelle's bench and rested her hand on the seat back in front of it. "Hi," she said, intending it to sound cool and wincing at the croak that passed her lips instead.

Michelle turned her head and skimmed her gaze past Kristy. "Oh, hi." She made no move to grab her stuff.

"Can I sit with you?" asked Kristy.

"Do you have the time?"

Kristy cringed, her face screwing up into a grimace. "I…" She looked away, scanning the faces of the high schoolers seated behind them. Some stared at her, but most focused on their own conversations or sat with their heads back and their eyes closed. "I have so much to tell you."

Michelle lifted one eyebrow. "What's the matter? Your boyfriend couldn't drive you to school?"

Nausea began to swirl in her belly, and she wished Leif could take her to school that day, but it was an empty wish. "Don't be like that, Michelle," she murmured.

"Like what? Huh?" Blood suffused Michelle's cheeks, and her eyes blazed. "Like a friend you ditched for the last two months? Like a bitch? Or maybe like a snow cone? What?"

Kristy shifted her weight from side to side.

"Find a seat, miss," called the bus driver.

Kristy glanced toward the front of the bus, then looked at Michelle. "Can I just sit with you? Please?"

Michelle scoffed and scooped her stuff into her lap, but she turned her face to the window as Kristy sank into the seat. The bus lurched away from the sidewalk the instant Kristy's butt hit the seat.

"I'm… Shelly, I have so much to tell you. Aren't we still friends?"

"Friends?" Anger edged Michelle's voice. "I don't even know you anymore."

They rode in silence for a few minutes after that, Michelle fuming, Kristy wracking her mind for something to say that would make it all right again. The bus turned onto Mill Lane from Union, then pulled to the side of the road to pick up a handful of kids.

"Michelle, I'm sorry," Kristy said, reaching to put her fingers on her friend's arm, but stopping just shy of touching the girl. "You'll understand if you'll let me tell you what happened."

Michelle snorted. "You let him do it to you, didn't you? You let him stick his thing in you."

"What? No!"

"Sure."

Kristy withdrew her hand, anger beginning its slow burn through her veins. "Don't be jealous."

"Jealous?" Michelle whirled to face her. "Jealous? Of what? Of being a little slut?"

"I'm *not* a slut, Michelle Donnelly, and don't you call me one!" she hissed.

"So you didn't let him fuck you?"

Kristy jerked her head as if slapped. "Why are you acting like this?"

"Back to that? How am I acting, Kristy? Like a best friend who got shoved aside because of some boy? Like that?"

"He's not just 'some boy,' Shelly." Kristy sighed and let her shoulders slump. "Look, I know how I acted all summer. You have every right to be mad at me, Shell. I was a jerk, and I'm sorry."

Some, but not all, of the fire went out of Michelle's eyes. "It was supposed to be *our* grand summer, remember? We were going to spend every day together, looking through fashion magazines and getting ready for high school life." Her gaze skipped around Kristy's face, lingering on her eye shadow, her red lipstick, then bouncing to her new hairstyle and skimpy outfit. "I guess you did that without me."

Kristy blushed for what felt like the thirtieth time since she sat down. Everything Michelle said was true to the last detail. She looked down at her miniskirt and tight top, suddenly feeling every bit the hussy. "I'm sorry, Shelly. I don't know what came over me."

Michelle sighed and slumped in the seat. "You could at least act like a jerk so I could stay mad a while longer."

Kristy said nothing, not wanting to screw things up.

"What's his name?" Michelle asked.

"Leif Lawson. Him and his dad just moved into town, and they bought the house next door to us."

"Leif, huh? Why aren't you sitting with him? He's your boyfriend, right?" Michelle turned to scan the bus.

Kristy cleared her throat. "He doesn't go to school anymore. He works."

Michelle arched an eyebrow. "He quit?"

"No, no. Well, I mean, yes, but not the way you think. His dad worked for the government, and they spent most of Leif's life overseas. Grim places like Moscow and Beijing. There wasn't anything for Leif to do, so he did schoolwork year-round. He's already done with high school, so he doesn't have to go."

"That doesn't sound right."

"He's got a diploma and everything, Shelly."

Michelle tilted her head to the side and then back up. "Where does lover-boy work?"

Kristy winced and turned her gaze on her lap. "He goes to work with his dad. He does whatever needs doing—cleaning, cutting the grass."

"Oh, that sounds wonderful," said Michelle in droll tones. "I'm sure he'll be an excellent provider for the baby you will have in nine months."

Kristy blushed yet again and shook her head. "No babies. I… We didn't… I only let him *watch*."

"Kristy!" cried Michelle, eyes dancing for a moment before a sly expression stole over her face. "And you? Did he let you…watch?"

Kristy sucked in a breath and stared at her lap.

"He did! And you *looked*, didn't you?"

Head still down, Kristy nodded.

Michelle giggled, and everything felt as it had before the summer. "Tell me. Tell me *everything*."

II

October 1975

Dennis kicked the garbage can over, sending decaying leftovers and the other detritus of their lives scattering across the alley. One side of his face still burned from the slap his father had given him. His daddy had always been an asshole, but ever since Dennis and Ari had gotten suspended on the first day of school, his old man had turned everything up a few notches.

He thought of the short-handled sledgehammer he'd stolen from his dad and hidden in his hideout with religious awe. Sometimes he went there to hold the thing—the haft felt good in his palm and calmed him—but at that moment, he wanted to go to the hideout, grab that hammer up, and use it to put a dent right between his dear old dad's eyeballs.

Even thinking about the hammer made him feel better.

"Fuck this," he murmured and kicked the empty milk jug farther down the alley. He spun and sauntered away from the up-turned trash can. "I'm gonna do it, this time," he told himself as he stepped out into the street.

He never saw the big bald man watching him from the pickup across the street.

Dennis trudged with his head down, his mind on things other than his surroundings. He walked on autopilot, relying on his feet to get him to the hideout.

The fight that day had been about Halloween. Dennis wanted to go. Desperately so. But his old man had said no and wouldn't budge from his decision.

All because of that little twit Jasper had told him about. That Sean Walker kid. The one who'd drawn Mrs. Twitler's attention to the window.

Dennis still hadn't paid the kid back, and as far as he was concerned, he owed him for every slap, every punishment his dad had dished out over the last seven weeks. He owed him that *and* interest.

Maybe the hammer will work on a kid. The thought sprang into his brain as if from elsewhere, but Dennis smiled at the idea. *I could test the hammer on him. Learn how hard I can hit with it.* Dennis's smile widened. *I could see what type of dent it really makes in someone's forehead.*

Still smiling, Dennis lifted his head and whistled as he walked. Sometimes his ideas were so good he surprised even himself.

12

Halloween 1975

Sean smiled as he pushed through the doors and the cold air snapped around him. He loved the fall—especially sunny fall afternoons when it was cold, but the sun warmed his skin. He shoved his arms through his backpack and headed toward the pickup ramp. Karl had promised to pick him up and take him for hot chocolate and a cheeseburger at Jenny's Diner to celebrate the early snow and set the tone for the evening's trick-or-treating.

He strode past the bus ramp and rounded the corner of the school building, then stopped dead in his tracks. Fifty yards down the wet, icy sidewalk, Dennis stood between Jasper Kent and Ari Abelman, but they weren't looking Sean's way.

Sean spun and walked back toward the corner, hoping against hope that none of the three turned and recognized his back. He hunched his shoulders and tried to look shorter—maybe they would think he was a second-grader.

"There he goes!" growled a voice behind him.

He stole a quick glance over his shoulder, catching a glimpse of Dennis turning toward him, then hustled around the corner of the building. Three sets of winter boots pounded the sidewalk behind him, and an icy coldness that had nothing to do with the weather slid down his spine.

If he could get back inside, maybe he could duck into a classroom and sneak out after the trio passed him by. That, or he could go talk to a teacher about something. Anything.

He'd almost made it to the steps when a hand clamped around his right bicep and jerked him around.

"So, this is the little snitch," sneered Dennis.

Sean shook his head. "No," he whispered.

"Ain't that cute, boys? He wants to whisper. Bring him." Dennis let go of his arm and walked toward the corner that led around to the back of the school.

Jasper smiled at Sean and grabbed one of the straps of his backpack. "Come on, dude." Ari stepped forward and grabbed the other strap. With Jasper on one side and Ari on the other, Sean had no way to escape. He pulled back, but the two older boys just pulled harder.

Feet skidding on the pavement, Sean rounded the corner—right into Dennis's fist, and the air exploded out of his lungs with a *whoosh* as he doubled over.

"*That's* for getting Ari and me in trouble," said Dennis.

Sean couldn't speak. He could only stand there, bent at the waist, fighting for breath.

"But don't think that's the end of it. Ari, you want to take a poke before I get down to business?"

"I got suspended, you little sissy punk," growled Ari. "And I'm grounded for the whole term. I can't even do Halloween!" He stepped closer to Sean and shoved him up against the brick wall of the school.

Sean thought he might die if he couldn't catch his breath. Nevertheless, he tried to speak, tried to *explain*, but though his mouth moved, no air traveled past his vocal cords, and he made no sound beyond a whispery squeak.

"Lookit! He's a little mouse!" said Jasper, then laughed.

Ari balled up a fist and punched Sean in the mouth.

Colors exploded in his vision, and pain blossomed in his lips. They felt hot—as hot as if he'd burned them by gulping hot chocolate—and something welled up from his upper lip. *Bloody lip*, he thought.

Ari pulled his hand back to take another shot, but Dennis tapped him on the shoulder. "One's enough," he said. "After all, Jasper says the kid didn't tell on us. Twitler just caught him staring out the window."

Sean looked at him, hope dawning in him.

Dennis nodded. "Now, we're even for the suspension. Fair's fair, right, Sean?"

Sean nodded—if he could get out of this with only a bloody lip and a punch in the belly, he'd call it good.

A slow smile crept across Dennis's lips as he unslung his own backpack and let it fall to the ground at his feet. It hit with a *thud*. "Glad you agree. Tell anyone about this little talk, and you'll be sorry." He narrowed his eyes to slits. "I'll make you sorrier than you've ever felt before. I'll hit you so hard your mother will feel it." He stooped and unzipped the pack, then reached inside. "Now, we can move on to the rest of the bill. My dad didn't like me getting suspended. He's an asshole like that." He glanced at Sean and chuckled. "Oh, you thought we were quits for all and good? Nah." He pulled a short-handled sledgehammer out of his pack. "Nah," he repeated. "Your bill has a few more charges on it, Sean. Plus, there's the interest."

Jasper and Ari exchanged a silent glance. "Uh, what are you going to do with that maul?" asked Jasper.

"I'm going to maul someone, what else?" Dennis never took his gaze off Sean's face. He lifted the hammer and tapped the bricks beside Sean's head, laughing as Sean winced away.

"Is that a good idea?" asked Jasper, a small frown creasing his face. Ari had yet to say anything, but he looked a little sick to his stomach.

"Fuck yes, it's a good idea. This kid fuckin' *owes* me, Jasper. I can't do Halloween unless my mom sneaks me out tonight. Plus, I got bruises on my bruises. And anyway, I want to see what it'll do." Dennis tapped the hammer against his palm and grinned at Sean. "I think it'll dent his head. What do you think, Ari?"

"Denny, I…"

Dennis swiveled his head, narrowing his eyes at his friend. "You what, Ari?"

Ari snapped his mouth shut and shook his head.

"Dent? No dent?" asked Dennis.

Ari could only shrug, looking sicker than ever.

"You're no fun, Jewboy. What about you, Jasper? Care to make a bet?"

Jasper glanced at Sean, then twisted his gaze away. His face scrunched into a moue of distaste. "I don't know, Denny. I think it maybe'll kill him."

"Well, *duh*, Jasper. That's kind of the point of mauling someone, right? But will it make a dent? Smash his head like a pumpkin? What?" Dennis stared at Jasper as if his answer was the most important thing in the world.

Sean stood frozen, able to breathe again but petrified at the sight of the hammer. Dennis was a bully of the first order, but Sean didn't believe that even Dennis would hit another kid with a hammer.

When Jasper shrugged, Dennis turned away, frowning. "Jesus Christ, fellas. I thought you two had a pair, even if you had to share it between you. Out of all the rest of the kids in this school, I thought you two weren't such fucking sissies I could hang with you and not barf every other minute."

Jasper and Ari exchanged another glance.

Dennis hawked and spat. "Well, go on then, sissy-boys. Go off somewhere and pull each other's puds. See if I give a fuck." He smacked his palm with the hammer and cocked his head to the side, glancing at Sean. "I'll be damned," he muttered. "I think this fucker doesn't even believe I'll hit him." Before the sound died, he jerked the hammer back and up, then swung it with all the grace of a drunk ox. Sean shrieked, ducking to the side, and above him, slivers of brick exploded from the wall. Dennis's face clouded over and blood suffused his skin. He swung the hammer in a flat arc at Sean's side. Pain exploded from his left bicep, and before he could even scream, he doubled over and puked—

all over the Converse All Star high-tops Dennis wore. "Mother fucker!" Dennis yelled, trying to kick the emesis off his shoes.

Jasper and Ari turned and ran, followed by Dennis's laughter. "Go on, little fags!" Dennis yelled.

He turned back to Sean, a furious snarl spreading across his face. "Puke on me, will you? Let's see what this baby'll do to your skull."

Without thinking, Sean lashed out with his foot, connecting solidly with the bully's groin. As Dennis crumpled to his knees and dropped the hammer, Sean turned and ran.

He rounded the corner and sprinted for the car pick-up ramp. He ran faster than he'd ever run in his life, springing over splotches of wet snow, spinning around kids like a professional running back. He didn't look back, he ignored the shrieking pain in his arm, and he didn't stop when kids yelled at him.

Karl was waiting for him in his green Chevy. As Sean skidded around the corner, Karl took one look at his face and leaped from the car to run toward him. "What's wrong?" he called.

"I…" Tears flowed freely down Sean's cheeks, and he *wanted* to tell on Dennis, to get him in serious trouble, but Dennis's words circled in his brain: *I'll make you sorrier than you've ever been. I'll hit you so hard your mother will feel it.* He couldn't tell. He didn't dare—Dennis had already tried to brain him with a sledgehammer. What would he do if Sean ratted him out to a Kanowa County Deputy Sheriff? "I slipped on the ice and fell. My…muh-my arm… I think it's broken."

Karl looked at him for a moment, looked at him as though he knew *exactly* what had happened behind the school and needed to make up his mind whether to let the lie go. His gaze twitched to the corner of the building and then came back to rest on Sean's face. "Fell on the ice, huh?"

"Yuh-yeah." Sean nodded and winced at the pain that shot up from his arm. "I threw up, and..." Without warning, vomit sluiced into his mouth and he lurched to the side and threw up.

When he was finished, he found Karl squinting toward the bus ramp, a thoughtful expression on his face. Sean turned to look, and there he was—Dennis Cratchkin—trying to appear casual but staring at Sean. His backpack bumped against his back as he turned and walked the other way. The third time he glanced back over his shoulder, Karl grunted a laugh. "You sure you didn't have help falling on the ice?"

Sean dropped his gaze and shook his head.

"Come on, then. Let's get you over to Doc Hauser's place. And don't look so glum, Sean. It'll heal up."

13

December 1975

Eddie and his mother draped Christmas tree lights through the boughs of their Douglas fir. The decorations glittered in their boxes, twinkling as if they shared Eddie's almost uncontainable excitement. Smiling, his father bent and plugged the lights into the wall.

Even the beauty of flashing Christmas lights couldn't outshine the magnificent lamp. Eddie bounced his gaze from the tree to the lamp and back again, smiling all the while.

Everything was perfect.

But then the merry lights flickered and died. Eddie turned to his daddy in time to watch Ted's face go over red and blotchy—his angry face. He shifted his gaze back to the tree and frowned at the ice riming the boughs, making them droop and point at the floor.

He turned toward the lamp, concerned that the ice might damage it, but it seemed to shine even brighter than before—despite the layer of ice that coated the end table. Eddie looked at his father askance, hoping his dad wasn't looking at him as he did so. His daddy was staring at him with an even uglier expression than before.

Eddie was to blame for the mess. Eddie was always to blame for things turning sour.

With a crackle and a pop, the electricity in the rest of the house died—for everything except the Tiffany lamp. The warm air from the vents stopped, and frigid air raced in.

The wrapping paper on the gifts beneath the tree became brittle with ice, and Eddie's breath was visible in the stark cold. He drew a deep breath and gasped—he would have cried out, but the freezing air shocked his lungs. Eddie had never breathed air so cold. He twisted to ask his mommy why it had gotten so cold.

What he saw terrified him, made him forget all about the cold. His mother sat in her favorite chair—or at least her body did. Her skin had taken on a dried, mummified appearance, and her hair was falling out, but that wasn't the worst of it.

Light from the beautiful lamp cast dark shadows in the pits where his mommy's eyes had once twinkled. He could feel the scream thrashing within him, like a tiger he'd caught by the tail. His eyes darted toward his father, but Ted Mitchell lay on the ground, leering up at Eddie, his face frozen in the rictus of death.

Eddie opened his mouth to let the scream out, and—

"Come on, sleepyhead," said Eddie's mother. "It's time to get up, and we have things to do."

Eddie opened his eyes and began to cry.

"Hey there, kiddo," his mother crooned. "What's all this? What's wrong?"

"I had a nightmare," Eddie said between sniffles.

"Well, nightmares are only silly old dreams, Eddie. They can be scary, sure, but they mean nothing. You can set your mind to forget all about them." She bent over his bed and hugged him tight. "Put it right out of your brain, Eddie."

He tried to do as she instructed, tried to push the dream out of his head, but it resisted as if hooked on something. "But you and Daddy were—"

"Shush now, Eddie. Mommy knows best." She gave him another hug and then sat back, beaming her I-love-you smile at him. "Now, get up. We've got things to do if we're going Christmas shopping this afternoon."

Eddie loved Saturday mornings—it was a time he and his mom had to themselves. They had a routine of sorts—his mother woke him, and then they had a big breakfast full of his favorite foods: waffles with maple syrup, bacon, scrambled eggs, and toast with strawberry jam. By the end of breakfast, Eddie felt so stuffed he could barely move, but they spent the next part of the morning cleaning the house and that helped. They started with the kitchen and the ruins of breakfast.

He gathered the dishes from the table and took them to the sink. They didn't have a dishwasher—well they *did*, but it had broken the year Eddie turned five. His dad always said that Eddie was the new dishwasher. Eddie didn't mind—it meant more time with his mommy while his daddy went into the other room and did grownup things. He filled the sink with warm soapy water while his mother brought over the pans which had cooled while they ate.

"You wash, and I'll clean the stove."

Eddie nodded and dipped the first plate into the sink.

"Have you thought of anything? Something to give your father for Christmas?"

Eddie shook his head. He never knew what gifts to give people. He didn't have the knack of seeing a thing and knowing that someone would like it.

"Well, that's okay, Eddie. I have an idea or two I can lend you."

"Mommy, what do you want for Christmas?"

"You know I don't need anything."

"But I want to buy you a present."

"Save your money for something you decide, Eddie."

The conversation always followed the same track. "Mommy, I'm getting you a present. That *is* what I want. If you don't tell me what you want, I'll just give you coal."

She laughed. "I could use a pair of new earrings or maybe a key chain."

Eddie smiled to himself and nodded. "Okay." She always asked for the same two things. Earrings or a key chain.

They finished cleaning up the kitchen, joking and laughing. His mom had a way of making chores seem fun.

She handed him the dust cloth and ruffled his hair. "You know what to do, tiger."

"Can I use the Pledge this time?"

His mother shook her head. "No, we don't need Pledge this week. If we use it too much, it makes everything nasty."

She always said that when he asked for the furniture polish with the lemony scent. He wasn't sure why she even bought Pledge. He wondered if her saying no had something to do with him—if he used too much or too little. "Which room should we start in this time, Mommy?"

"I'll tell you what, let's have a race. I'll start in the dining room, and you do the living room. I bet I can finish before you."

Eddie grinned. The dining room had so much to dust, not only the furniture but all the dishes in the hutch. "You're on!" He darted into the living room and started sweeping his dust rag over the big Zenith television.

"Be sure you clean the screen. It's been looking dusty this winter."

He swept the rag back and forth across the screen, whistling to himself as he did. In the reflection, something moved behind him. Eddie twisted his head, looking over his shoulder, but there was nothing there. He smiled at how silly he was and turned once again to his task.

He pushed the cloth into the corners of the television screen, really going at it, and again, something in the room reflected on the screen moved. Eddie wriggled around on his knees, his head cocked to the side as though trying to solve a hard puzzle.

There was nothing there, just the chairs, the coffee table, the end table, and the beautiful lamp. The lamp seemed darker than it had before, but it *was* off. He stared at it for a moment before shrugging and turning back to the television screen.

The reflection of a mean woman's face leered at him over his shoulder. She was a thing of blackness, of midnight-blue-tinged shadows, and it veiled her dark eyes, but they whirled and spun, seeming to throw off midnight blue sparks, nonetheless. Her thick black hair writhed and twisted around itself, as if she had snakes for hair. Her mouth dropped open, and jagged black fangs filled it.

Eddie screamed and dropped the dust cloth. He lost his balance in his hurry to get up and get moving, and he staggered away from the Zenith, bumping the coffee table and sending a stack of newspapers careening to the floor. He fled to the dining room, crying by the time he reached his mother.

"Hey… Hey, there. What's all this?"

"There's a lady! She's in the living room! A scary lady!"

His mother's gaze lifted from his face and looked through the arch into the living room. When her gaze came back down to his face, she wore a smile, but she had a concerned expression in her eyes. "Look again, Eddie. There's no one in there."

He darted a glance toward the living room and then shook his head. "No, not out there in the open! I saw her in the reflection on the screen! You can't see her except in the television screen. Come see!"

"Okay, Eddie. Let's go check it out, but this is probably your nightmare coming back for a visit. Sometimes that happens. You dream something, and then something you see later in the day reminds you of it. And reflections play tricks on us, too."

"No! The scary lady wasn't in my dream, it was just you, me, and Daddy."

"And that was a nightmare?" His mother chuckled in that throaty way she had. "What, did your daddy take off his shoes?"

He knew she was trying to lighten the mood, trying to relax him with stinky-feet jokes. He tugged her by the hand into the living room, pointing at the big Zenith's screen. "See?"

His mother glanced at the television's screen for a moment, then looked around the room, making a show of looking behind the chairs. She turned to him and shrugged. "I don't see anything, Eddie."

"I told you, Mommy! You have to look in the television screen to see her. You have to *really* look!"

His mom stood facing the television and watching the screen. "Still nothing, tiger."

"I was sitting down right next to it. She peeked at me over my shoulder, leaning close." He shuddered and his hands wrestled with one another.

His mother hiked up her pants legs and squatted in front of the television. She peered into the screen before glancing at Eddie. "Nothing, kiddo. Only me."

Eddie went to her side, fear shivering through his body. He didn't want to look, he didn't want to see that face ever again, but when his mother took his hand, it lent him courage and he looked.

The screen was blank.

"You see? You're just being a silly goose." She ruffled his hair and then patted him on the shoulder. "It was leftovers from your nightmare, sweetie. Nothing to worry about."

"You promise?"

"I promise. And you want to know something?"

Eddie nodded.

"I will finish before you do. I'm winning the race!"

With one last glance at the television screen, Eddie picked up his dust rag and ran to dust the coffee table. He picked up all the papers from the floor and stacked them the way his daddy liked. It wasn't until he was dusting the lamp, that he noticed the colors in the shade had changed.

"Mommy! Come look!"

"What is it, Eddie?"

He could hear the frustration in her voice. "The lamp!"

His mom came into the room, her dust rag clenched in a fist that rested on her hip. She stole a peek at the lamp and then turned her gaze on Eddie. "What about it?"

"Don't you see it? It's changed colors!"

His mother gave him a strange look. "Stained-glass doesn't change colors, Eddie."

"But it used to be aquamarine! Now everything that *was* aquamarine is bright black." But that was wrong, and Eddie knew it as soon as he said it. The lampshade wasn't black; it was *almost* black, but the glass chunks were midnight blue and a dark, dark purple.

She looked at the lamp again and then turned her gaze back on Eddie's face. "You're starting to worry me, Eddie. That lamp's always been dark blue."

The lampshade still resembled an upended turnip, but *all* the colors had changed. The teals, turquoises, and aquamarines were all gone. So, too, were the dragonflies and the smaller, bright-colored round chunks. The bands of white had become a wide, jagged line of bright, arterial red. Beneath the red, the primary colors were midnight blue and dark purple, and those chunks of glass were so dark, they appeared more black than blue or purple. Fish, done in bright shades of royal blue, swam against the almost-black background, and when the lamp was lit, they glared so bright it hurt to gaze at them too long. The bottom edge of the shade looked sharp enough to cut a little boy's fingers if he strayed too close. The body of the lamp had changed as well. Gone were the chunks of colored glass, and in their place was a brass serpent that stretched from the lamp's base, up into the shade. The pull chains ended in lumps of brass that looked like babies.

Unbidden, the memory of that face leering over his shoulders flashed before Eddie's eyes. As hard as he tried, he couldn't dispel the idea that the woman's hair had been the same dark colors as the lampshade—midnight blue and dark purple. Shades that were closer to black than anything else.

The house seemed colder than it had at breakfast.

14

Christmas Eve 1975

The evening usually crawled by—sitting through a "dress-up" dinner with her mom and whatever family was in town, forced to eat clam chowder which she hated with a passion, and then a church service despite the fact it was the only time all year her mother set foot in a church—but that Christmas Eve turned the evening into torture. Try as she might, Kristy couldn't focus on anything. Not dinner, not conversation, not singing the hymns.

She had Leif on her mind. Leif, and his suggested present. Part of her craved giving him what he wanted, but the thought of it petrified most of her. She recalled Michelle's taunts on the first day of school with utter clarity. *You let him do it to you, didn't you? You let him stick his thing in you,* she'd said. She accused her of letting Leif *fuck* her—the crudity of it still made Kristy flinch. Later, she'd said she hoped Leif's job would support a baby.

A baby.

Kristy wanted Leif's baby about as much as she wanted nails driven through her eyeballs. Babies were for later.

Babies were for when she got married, and as cute as Leif was, Kristy wasn't getting married any time soon. Plus, her mother would kill her dead if she got caught having sex with Leif. Well, with anyone.

But Leif *really* wanted to do it. He said it made him hurt below the belt just thinking about it. He'd said she should consider it torture, letting him look but not touch.

And if she were honest, watching him do his thing while he looked at her turned her on. A lot.

She shook her head and forced her attention to return to the Christmas Eve sermon—anything but imagine doing it with Leif. Her cheeks already burned with both shame and lust.

"Why are you here?" the minister thundered. "Why have you come to God's house with impure thoughts?"

Kristy dropped her gaze to her lap, sure the minister spoke only to her and that everyone would see what a slut she had become.

"Thoughts of presents! Thoughts of candy! Don't you think God can see what's in your heart? Don't you realize this holiday is about more than Santa Claus, presents, and good food? We are here tonight to celebrate God's grace. We are here to celebrate the birth of the Messiah! Santa doesn't figure into it."

Kristy's mom grabbed her hand and squeezed it. "We should have gone to Saint Genesius' instead of this tripe," she whispered.

Kristy managed a weak smile, full of doubts, brimming with shame at what she'd been thinking about.

"Let's get out of here, sugarplum."

Kristy nodded, and they made their way to the back of the balcony. At least they escaped the minister's ire without drawing too much attention to themselves. She wasn't sure if she believed in God or not, but she was almost sure she didn't believe in ministers and church. But even so, his words rang in her mind, chasing each other around the way dogs chased cats.

Outside, her mom gave her a stiff hug. "Let's walk home. I'll come back for the car tomorrow."

Kristy zipped up her parka and looked up into the gently falling snow. "I don't want to get all wet. Plus, it's cold, Mommy."

Her mother cocked her head to the side. "Hot date tonight?"

Kristy dropped her chin and shook her head. "I don't date, Mommy. You know—"

"Let's not lie to one another, sugarplum. Don't think all those evenings up in your room going through fashion magazines have gone unnoticed. The hairstyle, the makeup, the clothes." Her mother smiled. "It wasn't very long ago that I was your age. It wasn't so long ago I can't remember what high school is like."

Kristy held her tongue and stared at her feet. "Can we take the car?"

Her mom laughed. "We can if you tell me his name."

Kristy dared to meet her mother's gaze. "You're not mad?"

"Mad that you're becoming a woman? Mad that you have a perfectly natural interest in boys?" She laughed again and linked her arm through Kristy's. "No, I'm not angry."

You would be if you knew what I was thinking about during church.

"I'll never be upset about you liking a boy, sug. Just don't be stupid. Don't get yourself in trouble." She unlocked the passenger door of their beat-up old Chrysler, then opened it. As Kristy moved to get in, her mother stopped her with a hand on her shoulder. "You know what I mean by that, don't you Kris?"

Flames seemed to lick Kristy's cheeks—it seemed that all she did was blush and duck her head. "Yeah. We did a unit of sex-ed last year, remember?"

Her mom lifted her chin an inch, then let it drop. "Yes. I will make you an appointment, I think."

"An appointment?"

"With the girly doctor." Her mother's face lost a touch of its previous jocularity. "To get you on the pill."

Kristy had never dropped her gaze as fast as she did at that moment. Again, her stupid cheeks blazed. "I…" She shook her head once.

"I'd rather suffer through that appointment than the one where the doctor tells me you're pregnant."

Kristy stood frozen in the cold wind and the falling snow. She couldn't think of a single thing to say, couldn't make her muscles work.

"Hear what I'm telling you, baby girl?"

Kristy swallowed hard and nodded.

"Good. Then we shouldn't have to talk about it again." She patted Kristy's shoulder. "I'll have that appointment set up as soon as they can fit you in. In the meantime, you *be smart.*"

"Okay." It sounded lame to Kristy, but it was the single word her mind came up with.

"Then let's go open presents!" Her mom walked around to the other side of the car and got in.

Kristy stood in the wind and snow for a moment more, then sat in the passenger seat. She'd decided.

Leif would just have to wait until *she* was ready.

Chapter 2
2007

Chapter 2
2017

I

Greg followed Mason Harper's van—the one containing the only other survivors of Herlequin's attentions that he knew of. Toby Burton, Shannon Bertram, and Benny Cartwright had not only survived, but they'd also found a way to rid the world of the Demon King once, and hopefully, for all. Mike Richards and Scott Lewis both slept in the back of the cherry red 1965 Pontiac GTO Greg had inherited from his grandfather—both injured after encounters with what Toby called "a new demon."

The old Goat rumbled along East Lake Road just west of the border Pennsylvania shared with New York. Toby had said there was a safe place they could rest and recuperate in Erie, and they'd traveled on crumbling surface roads—and the smaller the better, it seemed—from Lake Genosgwa, driving through the afternoon. It wasn't far, a little over one hundred and twenty miles, but the pair of cops in his backseat hadn't seen more than five miles of the trip.

Ahead, the van slowed and its right turn signal blinked to life. Greg followed it down the arrow-straight two-rut track that penetrated the trees separating Lake Road from Lake Erie and pulled up in front of a large house built close to the edge of the cliff, leaving the engine idling. Toby climbed out of the van and stretched. He motioned for Greg to kill the GTO and turned to unlock the door using a key on his key ring.

Greg glanced in the rearview mirror as the V8 died, but neither man in the backseat so much as twitched. He got out of the car and scanned the front of the house. It looked empty and well maintained, but not quite as well maintained as Preston Peters had kept his place on Lake Genosgwa—the little he'd seen of it. Still, if the condition of the GTO was an example of how he maintained Greg's lake house, he had no doubt it was in perfect shape.

Shannon and Benny got out of the van, both appearing to have just awakened. Benny beamed at him and drew in a deep breath. "Don't you love how fresh the air smells on the edge of the lake?"

To Greg, the place stank of algae and fish, but he cocked his head to the side and grinned back.

"Algae and fish?" asked Benny with a smirk playing at the edges of his mouth. "Man, Florida must smell like roses."

"Not all the time. And it depends on where you are, as with everywhere else." Greg wrinkled his nose over a smile. "Speaking of which, this isn't Erie."

"No?" Benny lifted his eyebrows and then squinted for a moment before his features relaxed again. "Oh. Erie's twenty minutes west. Close enough." He turned and gazed at the house, then whistled. "Toby's *rich*."

"Nah," said Toby from the front door. "I got a deal."

"Wait, you *own* this mansion?" asked Shannon.

Toby treated Greg to a wink that Shannon couldn't see. "Yes. And?"

"Then why were we driving all the hell over the state back home looking for a place to stay? Won't the demons—LaBouche in particular—find us here?"

"I own this *house*, but not under a name I've ever used in New York. In fact, I haven't touched this identity since before med school, other than to buy and keep this place."

"Where did you…" Greg bit off the end of the question, but Toby only smiled wider.

"Don't worry, Greg. It won't offend me. Where did I get the money?" He wagged his head to the side. "Having a bunch of identities comes in handy. I did nothing that hurt anyone." His gaze slid to the GTO. "Let's leave it at that. Scott already has enough problems with me."

Greg turned his attention back to the house. "It's nice. Will it concern the neighbors that we showed up unannounced?"

"I'll call the groundskeeper in a minute. He's the only one who should be out here, anyway." Toby strode to the garage and punched a code into the keypad there. The door rumbled upward, and Toby made a gesture as if inviting them inside the garage. "Let's get these vehicles out of sight. I have another car in the other garage we can use."

"You should look at my passengers," said Greg. "Check them out."

Toby nodded. "On my list."

"A girl could start to believe you have a thing for cars, Toby."

"Can't ever have too many means of escape." He grinned. "Or cool rides."

2

"Put me down, you giant purple motherfucker!" Mason screamed above the shrieking wind.

Dan Delo rolled his glowing azure eyes but kept his mouth shut. It would serve the squirming idiot right if he agreed to his demand—but the drop would be fatal from the altitude at which he flew. And LaBouche had been specific about his instructions—Mason Harper's life was important in the general scheme of things. *It's a mistake, all these demons becoming attached to their pets. These humans are nothing more than over-indulged meals, and my 'betters' would do well to remember that.*

Mason began pounding his fists on Delo's taloned feet.

Dan shook his head and increased his flight speed. The sooner he dropped off Brigitta's baggage, the better.

3

As soon as the car stopped rolling, LaBouche sprang out of the back and ran to Brigitta's side. Brigitta glared at him as he approached, her face impassive, but something terrifying in her eyes. Nicole Conrau lay at her feet, but from the look of her, she was no more than anesthetized. The old Oneka Falls Police Department cruiser reserved for the chief of police rested on its side in the trees beside the gravel road, a crushed, smoking ruin. Ricky Fast stood with his hands on his knees near the wreck, head hanging. There was no sign of Dan Delo or Chaz Welsh.

He inclined his head in Brigitta's direction. "I came as soon as I heard. Did the hunters escape?"

Brigitta's eyes narrowed, and LaBouche had to fight the urge to step back and drop his head. At times, she reminded him of home—his *real* home—and not in a good way. "They escaped," she said. "Chaz failed me."

LaBouche turned his gaze away, pretending to search for the big pearly asshole. "Again."

"Yes!" Brigitta snapped. "Thank you for pointing it out. The fact had evaded me." Her voice contained a snap to it he hadn't heard there before—a promise of eternal pain, perhaps.

LaBouche dropped to one knee. "Forgive me."

Brigitta scoffed and stomped her foot. "Oh, get up, you yellow buffoon. You are my only general, now. I won't have you seen in such a weak pose. From this moment on, you must carry on the work I gave Chaz. In addition to your own tasks."

Joy surged through LaBouche's mind. Again, he peered around.

"You won't find him," said Brigitta. "I sent him home."

"Back to Oneka Falls?" he asked, not daring to hope.

"*HOME!*" Brigitta roared.

LaBouche backed away a step before he could stifle the impulse. "Yes, my queen," he murmured. The sudden surge of fear overshadowed the joy he'd felt moments before, but a kernel of irrational happiness remained. He would celebrate later—in private.

At their feet, Nicole Conrau moaned, and they both looked down at her. "She allowed the hunters to incapacitate her," said Brigitta in a toneless, enervated voice. "I'd hoped for more from her. Perhaps I should—"

"She's young, Brigitta. And Chaz—and his sloppiness—no doubt wore off on her. If you allow it, I can redeem her. I'll set her back on the right path."

Brigitta looked at him askance, her expression unreadable. After the space of ten breaths, she nodded and turned away. "They stole something that belongs to me. A human killer they call Abaddon. I believe you've met Mason Harper? I do not sense his presence."

The kernel of joy expanded, and LaBouche couldn't stop his freak-show mouth from curling into a smile. "I have, Brigitta, but I don't think the hunters have him. If they did, Dan Delo's body would be here somewhere, and as stupid as he sometimes is, I've no doubt he would have taken at least a couple of the humans out before he fell."

"You sent him here? To retrieve Mason?"

LaBouche dipped his chin. "I did."

"Why would you do such a thing? I didn't sense any of this until after I'd dismissed you."

Deep inside, something ugly bristled at her choice of words, but LaBouche kept that part of himself well-hidden in Brigitta's presence. He lifted his hands to his sides and shrugged. "I guessed at his importance to you. The way Owen Gray mattered to you, perhaps. I acted incorrectly regarding Owen, I wanted to ensure I didn't make the same mistake again. I ordered Delo to bring Harper to Oneka Falls and to keep him there until either you or I give him further orders. This place is..." LaBouche swept his gaze across the scene. "Scotty will notify the authorities the first chance he gets. They are probably on their way here, sirens blazing."

A ghost of a smile touched Brigitta's lips. "You've done well, LaBouche." She glanced at the quick-silver demoness lying at their feet. "As a reward, you may have her. But!"

She lifted her head and stabbed the air with an imperious index finger. "I will hold you responsible for her future failures." Brigitta's gaze traversed his body, and she sniffed. "Take her as a mate if you wish, but do not allow her to rule you. It's in her nature to try."

LaBouche bowed his head. "Thank you."

Her gaze flicked over his shoulder in the direction of the smoking OFPD cruiser. "And get that idiot out of here before the human authorities arrive. You are no doubt right that your former partner has blown Mason's little love nest."

"Leave it to me."

She cocked her head to the side and gazed into his eyes. "You've done well, LaBouche. It may be that you and I should spend more time together."

"It would be my honor," he said. He peeked at Conrau's unconscious form.

Brigitta laughed. "You may still have her. You may even *have* her if you wish. I'm not jealous about who you fuck." She cocked her head to the side and looked him over, her fearsome expression relaxing a little as she did so. "Not yet, anyway."

LaBouche smiled. "Please tell me if that changes."

"Trust me, LaBouche. You *will* know." Brigitta smirked and disappeared with a telltale pop.

4

Tom Walton parked his car into a spot outside the emergency room of the hospital in Cuba, New York. The woman from Mason Harper's place sat in the seat next to him as quiet as a church mouse, as still as if carved from stone. She hadn't said a word to Tom since he'd pulled her out of Harper's van. "Here we are, miss. You're safe, and as soon as I get you inside, I'll call the State Troopers. They'll be able to protect you much better than an old geezer like me."

As if moving against resistance, she turned her gaze away from the windshield, let it crawl across the dash, up the steering column to his hand, and then down his arm and up to his face. Her lips twitched in a gruesome smile, then quivered. "I…" she croaked.

"It's all right," he said. "Everything will be okay now." He opened his door, and she jumped. "Let's get you inside where they can help you. The quicker we do that, the quicker I can put the troopers on Harper's trail."

"He had a…" She shook her head, tears springing into her eyes. "He had a mask. He made it from someone's skin, someone's face! He…he…he kept coming to the van and…and…and—"

Tom's face fell into the expression he'd cultivated over years of law enforcement—grim, stern, yet caring. "It's all over now, miss."

She turned her head to gaze at him. "It's Debbie. Debbie Dillis."

Tom nodded once. "Let's go inside, Miss Dillis."

Her lips twisted into a smile of sorts. "It's just 'Debbie.' For you, it will always be Debbie."

"Fair enough, Debbie. I'm Tom. Tom Walton."

She nodded and closed her eyes in a long blink. "Who were those others? The woman, those men?"

"Come on inside now, Debbie. Let's get you checked out by these fine doctors and nurses."

Again, Debbie nodded, but again, she made no move to climb out of the car. Tom slid out and closed the door gently. He circled around and opened the passenger side door. Debbie turned her gaze on him. "He didn't even…" She shook her head. "He just scared me again and again. Why did he…"

"Some things, Debbie, defy understanding. These kinds of people are broken inside. They're not human anymore. Harper has been…" Tom grimaced, memories of Harper's life in Genosgwa flashing before his mind's eye. The occasions he'd responded in such weird ways—situations from before he'd perfected his act, his mask—the peculiar way he'd acted back in 1986. The funny looks, the weird way Tom had felt around him. "Well, Mason Harper has been a strange egg from the very beginning."

"Those others. They talked about…about demons."

"Come on, now, Debbie. Let's get you checked out."

She inclined her head, then lifted it slowly, and this time, she swung her legs out of the car. "I was so scared, Tom."

"Anyone would have been. Had a moment there, myself." He held out his hand, a gesture out of history, but one that felt right.

She looked at him then, her gaze assessing him, judging if he had lied to her. With a faint smile on her lips, she took his hand and allowed him to help her out of the car. "My husband…"

"Give me his number. I'll call him and let him know where you are. Get him directions."

She smiled and then hugged Tom hard. "Thank you," she whispered in his ear.

When she stepped back, Tom nodded once, as his friend Joe Canton had always done. Somehow, it just felt right.

5

LaBouche pulled the car into the handicapped parking spot near the glass door of the Oneka Falls Town Hall. With a glance at the liquid-silver features of Nicole Conrau, he grunted. She remained unconscious but had been twitching for the past fifteen minutes. "Come on, now," he said. "Wakey-wakey."

Nicole groaned and rolled her skull on the headrest.

"Snap to, Chief Conrau. We're going to need our Chief of Police."

Her head slumped to the side, and she made no other sounds of coming awake.

LaBouche blew his breath out in frustration. He got out of the car and stomped into the building. Sally McBride stood behind the reception desk, wringing her hands. LaBouche snapped his fingers at her. "No time for sniveling, Sally! Get Chief Conrau inside and wake her up."

Sally bobbed her head. "Where's... Is Chaz..."

Lee rolled his eyes and let loose another irritated sigh. "He's gone. Brigitta sent him home."

"Home..." She glanced around the lobby.

"Yes, yes! Home. All the way home."

"All the way," she murmured, and her eyes filled with oily tears.

"Christ on a stick!" snapped LaBouche. "Hop to, McBride! Your grief is unbecoming, and we have things that need doing. Who was Welsh's right-hand?"

"Right-hand?"

"Yes, yes! His second-in-command?"

Sally's shoulders twitched as if she'd suppressed a shrug. "Red Bortha is as close as he got. Well, until Nicole."

"Right. Go carry her in from the car. Wake her up." LaBouche stared at her as her eyes glazed. "Get moving!" he snapped.

Sally jumped and strode toward the door.

"And I want the keys to that blue monster in the parking lot."

"Chaz's BMW?"

"No longer," said LaBouche with a self-satisfied smile. "Everything that belonged to Chaz now belongs to me." He leered at her with a slow smirk distending his face, his shark-like teeth glistening.

Sally gulped and turned away.

6

"No! I want to talk to Chaz!" Mason yelled.

The big man—the fat *fucking* cop—seated across the desk grimaced and squeezed his eyes shut. "Mr. Harper, listen to me. Chaz gone. Chaz no come back. Never." His eyes snapped open and bored into Mason's. "Get it now? Have I said it in simple enough language?"

"Where? Where has he gone?"

He sighed and raised his hands out to his sides before letting them thump on the surface of Chaz's desk. "Brigitta tells me you are of use, but I'll be damned if I can figure out what she sees in you. From where I sit, you seem incredibly stupid."

Mason leaned back in the armchair and sneered.

"Chaz is dead. In this world, and in all likelihood, in the next one as well. Do you understand? Where Chaz has gone, you can't follow." He swiveled his chair—Chaz's chair—to the side and released another lungful of air. "I'd send you on to search for him yourself with joy in my heart, but it would not please Brigitta if I killed you."

"Give me a car. I want to go home."

The thick cop shook his head. "All that is blown, Mr. Harper. My ex-partner was among the humans you met back there, and if I know Scotty, every member of the New York State Police already knows your name."

Mason glanced at the badge lying on Chaz's desk and the cop flashed a lopsided grin. "Yes. I'm a State Trooper, but more importantly, I'm Brigitta's second-in-command. My role with the troopers is to safeguard others of my kind."

"Demons."

The trooper chuckled. "And our friends."

"And you go by Lee?"

"I prefer LaBouche. It just fits better, but in this culture, everyone has to have a silly little moniker stuck on the front."

"LaBouche, then. So, if I can't follow Chaz—" He raised a hand to stop LaBouche from interrupting. "—and I can't go home to finish my work, what am I supposed to do?"

LaBouche tilted his head to the side and lifted his hands. "We'll find you somewhere to live here in Oneka Falls. We will take care of you here—hide you from the authorities. I'll do what I can from within the State Police to lead them away, but for now, you'll have to lie low, to curtail your…*activities*. There is still an investigation going on in town, so it's important you follow me." His stare bored into Mason's. "No hunting. If you must kill, we will bring you someone. Do you understand?"

Mason sat and fumed for a moment. He'd never done well with authority. Finally, he nodded but did not meet LaBouche's gaze.

"I heard Red Bortha and Chaz Welsh spent a lot of time with you—teaching you, guiding your development."

"And?"

"It may be possible to continue that tutelage, albeit under my wing. Would you like that?"

Mason turned his gaze on a guise he knew to be false. That was okay with Mason; his face was also a mask. "Sure. That sounds great."

7

It seemed as if ten elephants had sat on her skull, and her arms and legs ached as though abused beyond measure. Nicole Conrau opened her eyes and then shut them at once. The afternoon sunlight burned and made her brain throb. Her brain processed the glimpse, and she realized she was back in Oneka Falls, in the single-room police department, slumped in the corner like a bag of garbage.

Raising a hand to block the light, Nicole opened her eyes the merest of slits. The last thing she remembered was being up above the forest, glassing the battlefield through the scope of her rifle, when something hissed and spat right below her. She had the vague impression of falling to the earth through the branches of the tree, and then, nothing.

She shook her head. Whatever had happened, Chaz must have brought her back to town. He would have dealt with the hunters—either that or Dan Delo dispatched them.

She never considered that the humans may have won. That would be preposterous.

"Oh, good, you didn't die."

The contempt-laden words pounded at her ears, and Nicole winced. "McBride," she whispered.

"Yes, McBride. I expect it satisfies you. I hope you are pleased with yourself," Sally sneered.

Nicole shook her head. "Get out of my grill, McBride. I'm in no mood. Is Chaz in his office?"

"No, you silver bitch! Chaz is *not* in his office."

Nicole suppressed the urge to backhand Sally with two of her fists. "When?" she grated.

"When? When what?"

"When will he return?"

Sally's expression froze in a grimace of hate and pain. "When will he return?" she parroted. "How about *never*? You saw to that with your…with your perky tits and tight little stomach!"

Nicole sighed and rubbed her temples with one set of hands. "What are you talking about, McBride?"

"He's *gone*. Brigitta was so incensed at your failure, and at his…his…*puppy love* for you that she banished—" Sally sobbed and turned away.

"She sent him home?" asked Nicole in a soft tone.

Sally nodded and snuffled, reminding Nicole of feeding pigs.

"Who has taken charge?"

"LaBouche," said Sally in a monotone voice.

"Oh," said Nicole. "How delightful." Sally whirled to face her, and Nicole raised a single index finger. "You wouldn't survive it," she hissed.

Sally huffed and stomped out of the room.

"That one is tiresome," Nicole murmured to herself. "Her lack of control is dangerous." She stood for a moment, thinking hard, then smiled. She knew just what to do.

8

"Has he settled down then?" Brigitta asked.

LaBouche tilted his head to the side. "It seems so. We brought him a…playmate."

"That should appease him." She turned in the seat of the blue BMW that had, until recently, belonged to Chaz Welsh. "For a time. If I know Mason, he believes he's playing you. He has some plot going in his brain, some intrigue."

"And I play a central part, no doubt. Though he says otherwise, he seems to have taken a dislike to me."

"You don't say," said Brigitta around a tight-lipped smile.

"Yes, it perplexes me, too. I'm such a likable fellow." LaBouche spread his hands. "Kind. Humorous. Friendly."

Brigitta chuckled low in her throat and patted his arm. "It's because you are a cop. Mason hates all cops on principle."

"I explained all that."

"Doesn't matter to one like Mason." She sighed and leaned her head back. "You drive this car with much more care than Chaz did."

"I appreciate fine automobiles. Chaz…" He shrugged.

"Yes," she said and closed her eyes.

LaBouche watched her from the corner of his eyes. Her recent behavior perplexed him. It seemed...out of character.

"And Nicole?"

"Sally is watching her until she wakes."

Brigitta lifted her face and opened her eyes, turning to stare at him. "Sally?"

"McBride is easily cowed."

Brigitta tilted her head, a small smile playing at the corners of her mouth. "She has...hidden depths. Don't dismiss her."

Lee shook his head. "The shit she let Chaz get away with..."

"Yes, but still. She has been here for ages. She was one of the first to arrive. She came across with my father."

LaBouche glanced at her, eyebrows raised. When Brigitta nodded, he said, "Things must have changed between then and now. She was my pawn, she was Chaz's whipping girl, his dupe."

Brigitta smiled, and the sight of it chilled Lee to his core. "It would be a mistake to underestimate her. She served *her*, you know. That's why she came across so long ago."

Lee's eyebrows shot upward. "She's a *ji*—"

"Don't say it," said Brigitta, putting her hand on his arm. "Don't even think it."

LaBouche turned his attention back to the road, his mind racing, recalculating. If what Brigitta implied was true, Sally could be of immense value to his plans.

9

Mike groaned and stretched, moving carefully to avoid pulling out his stitches. He sat in one of the overstuffed recliners that faced the floor-to-ceiling window overlooking the shore of Lake Erie. A warm glow of relaxation and contentment coursed through him.

To Mike, it seemed as if the events of the past week had zipped by in a blur of color and sound. He'd moved from being a drunk—incredibly unhappy, one hundred percent in the closet, and about as lonely as a person could get—to being…happy, content. Surrounded by two out of three of his best friends from childhood, and new friends such as Shannon, Greg, and Scott. Only one thing was missing, and Mike had made do without romantic love for his whole life so far.

Besides, who knew what fate had in store for him—for all of them.

Toby came down the stairs, yawning and stretching.

"Good nap?" he asked.

Toby turned his head, his gaze resting on the golden-pink reflection of the sunset on the water. "It's marvelous, this time we've all had to rest and…"

"Reflect?" asked Mike.

"Yeah. Sit up so I can look at your wounds."

"Wow. That's a great bedside manner you've got, there, Doc."

Toby grinned. "Most of my patients aren't so sensitive."

"Or so alive."

"Or that," said Toby. "There are benefits to being a pathologist. Now, shut up and let me check you out."

Mike grinned and tilted his head to the side and dropped the footrest of the recliner. "You're pushy, you realize that?"

"Am I? Lift your shirt and turn around." Toby flashed a crooked grin at him.

Mike chuckled and turned away from Toby. "How long do we stay here? How long will we be safe here?"

"Good questions. Let me know when you figure it out."

"Yeah. Those are the easy ones, though. Aren't they?"

"What do you mean?"

"It doesn't seem as if we've done much since we burned the old tree. Ran around and got people hurt for the most part."

Toby stopped prodding him but said nothing.

"I didn't mean that as an accusation, Toby. But I've been thinking about what—"

"I get it," said Toby in a quiet voice. "It seems like every time we believe we are being smart, we're only making things worse."

"How…" Mike shook his head.

"No, go ahead."

"How can we fight them, Toby? How can we hope to make any meaningful progress? Getting rid of them one at a time is—"

"Can I suggest something?" asked Greg from the door to the kitchen.

"Sure," said Mike.

"Trying to stop water running through a hose is easiest when you first turn off the spigot."

Toby drew a deep breath and blew it out. "I've been thinking along those lines, myself. As long as they can come through the Passage—or however they are really moving here—at will, it doesn't matter how many we send back."

"That's it," said Greg.

"But—"

"The problem, Greg, is that we don't understand how they are coming here. We interrogated a demon, but he told so many lies and half-truths we don't understand what's real."

"I've been thinking about that. Do you know what I do for a living?"

"No," said Toby.

"I'm a software developer."

"Okay…" said Mike, pulling his shirt back down over his bandages.

"We lack information, correct?" asked Greg.

"Yeah. Desperately."

"Right. We need to sort through all the falsehoods, all the stories, all the reports of paranormal occurrences. We need a method of culling the lies from the truth."

Toby nodded. "That will take decades. We have descriptions of demonic activity in this area going back thirty or forty years. We lived—"

"More," said Greg. "There have been rumors of the supernatural in this area for centuries."

"Great," muttered Mike.

"If we go back that far, we'll all be old men before we have even a guess as to the truth of it."

"Yes, using the methods you've employed to date. Using just the members of this small group."

"You have got a better idea, then?"

"Have you ever heard of the human search engine?"

"Human search engine? Like Google?"

Greg nodded and came into the room. "It's a way of solving big problems by harnessing the brainpower of a ton of people and the material on the Internet. A human search engine relies on hundreds and thousands of individuals over the Internet, each one doing what they do best, then passing the information on. The next person grabs the data and does what *they* do best, et cetera."

Toby nodded, a small smile on his face. "I've got this website—"

"I've seen it. What I'm thinking of goes way beyond a forum for people to tell stories. I'm talking about setting up an *organization*."

"What? A company?"

Greg lifted his hands. "Maybe, but not necessarily. What if we formed a not-so-secret secret society? On the surface, it would look like a bunch of crackpots, but under that obfuscating layer—"

"We could have one of those human search engines."

"Right."

Mike tilted his head to the side. "How do we keep the crackpots out of the underwear layer?"

"Always with the jokes," Toby said with a grin.

"That would be the secret part. I don't know how we select people—I do software—but once they're selected, they'd have access to a level of technology and data beyond what the public sees."

"Secret meetings?"

Greg shook his head. "Nah. You're thinking too analog. Think digital. Think global."

"Think *software*," said Toby, eyes dancing.

Greg smiled.

10

"I will need the two of you, working in concert, to find them. It is of the utmost importance that we put a stop to their meddling. Once and for all."

Nicole nodded, as LaBouche knew she would, but Mason didn't move. He'd been staring at Nicole since she'd entered the house where LaBouche had stashed him. She hadn't bothered with a visage.

She hadn't bothered with clothing, either.

It amused LaBouche. Her dress—or lack thereof—had been a calculated tactic on her part. She used her sexuality as a whip, and a strong lash it was, but she'd underestimated LaBouche. Many did, but he didn't mind. It made dominating them all the easier.

"Wake up, Mason. Haven't you seen tits before?" he asked in a wry tone.

The situation would've embarrassed most human males, but not Mason. He shook his head as if it hadn't been a rhetorical question. "Not silver ones. Not perfect ones. Not like hers."

LaBouche flashed his alligator smile at Nicole, who had turned to glare at Harper.

"No offense," Mason said. "I think you are the most beautiful thing I've ever seen. Perfect." He grinned at her in dazed amazement.

Nicole turned her gaze back to LaBouche, then rolled her eyes. "I eat your kind, human."

"So do I. I'm an artist. I'd love to show you my work, but…" Mason's face fell.

"Mason is our guest until the authorities grow distracted," said LaBouche.

"They will take my whole collection. They'll ruin it."

"No doubt," said Nicole.

Mason dropped his gaze to the floor.

"But you must start anew," she purred, and Mason lifted his head and smiled at Nicole. "Perhaps I will help you."

"That would be…" He floundered for a word, eyes zipping from place to place in the small living room. "That would be *awesome*!"

Nicole turned a lopsided grin at LaBouche. "But before we even consider that, we must do as LaBouche asks. We must find these 'hunters.' The men and women from your house on the lake. We should work…*closely*…with one another."

"Yes, we should," he said, his excitement plain in his voice. "I'm real good at finding people. I used to do it for Chaz all the time."

"And, as I understand it, you've already tracked the ringleader once. Drew Reid also known as Toby Burton." LaBouche tilted his head back and stared down at the man. "For Chaz."

"Yes, but Chaz put too many constraints on that search. He said to look in Rochester only, but they weren't there."

"Obviously."

"They were on their way to Genosgwa by then."

"Yes," said Lee. "How will you find them?"

"We can start with a few Internet searches. It won't be easy, but with perseverance comes success." He paused and glanced down at his shoes. "Red taught me that."

LaBouche jerked his head toward Mason, his gaze locked on Nicole's.

"And what shall I teach you?" she asked in a voice silkier than the night sky.

Mason shivered.

II

"You're kidding," said Scott, looking down at his brand-new Pennsylvania driver's license.

"Why? What's yours?" asked Mike, his smile stretched wide. "Mine is Richard Michaels."

"Louis Scott." He grimaced. "Very creative."

Benny came to the table. "I want to see what you came up with for me. I can't imagine anyone would believe Cartwright Benjamin would be real."

Toby shook his head and handed it over.

Benny laughed and tapped the card against his palm. "That's a good one. Say, you know I can't drive, right?"

Smiling, Toby said, "You may have mentioned it."

"So what is it, Benny?" asked Mike.

"Tobias Benjamin. At your service." Benny made a slight bow.

"And yours, Shan?"

She blushed and dropped her gaze. "Bertie."

"Bertie what?" asked Mike, grinning like a little kid.

"Bertie Benjamin," she murmured.

"You *married* us?" Benny asked.

Toby chuckled. "Why not? You already act married. I just thought it would be more believable that way."

"And me?" asked Greg from where he stood behind them.

"I didn't know much about you, so I had to ask Benny," said Toby, holding out a driver's license. "We named you after your grandfather and your dad. Joe Stephens."

Greg nodded and took the card, staring down at it.

"What's your new name, Toby?" asked Shannon.

"No new name for me. I own this house, remember? But here in Erie, I go by Ben Withers."

"Oh," she said. "Now that we're new people and all, what do we do?"

"Greg, Mike, and I talked that over yesterday. Greg has a great idea, and we should run with it." He pulled out a stack of photocopies and passed them out to each of his friends. "We will all be principles in a new non-profit organization called SEMPRe. Greg and Mike will—"

"SEMPRe?" asked Benny.

"Society for Extrasensory, Metaphysical, and Paranormal Research. Each of us will hold an executive position or board seat—that'll just help with the IRS. It will justify your incomes. In addition, though—"

"Incomes?" asked Scott, a sour expression on his face.

"Yes. I have plenty of money—more than I could ever spend. I've amassed it over the years against a time when I might have to run. I'm sharing it with you. I had my lawyer set up two blind trusts to funnel the money into SEMPRe, and you will all get paychecks. Nice and legal."

"Except it all comes from hacking."

Toby shrugged. "Not all of it. I stole some money from the demons I killed."

Scott closed his eyes and clicked his tongue.

"Anyway. Greg says we need a software company, too. To build the infrastructure for SEMPRe. It's—"

"Infrastructure?" asked Shannon.

Toby sighed and shook his head. "I'd be able to describe this faster if you guys would stop interrupting me to ask me questions about what I'm going to explain in the next sentence."

Shannon rolled her eyes but made a shooing gesture at Toby.

"SEMPRe will have a private layer. On the top, a bunch of crackpots, but members of the secret society outside the public view will work on sifting the Internet and old histories, trying to discern the truth from the lies in the records of supernatural activity around here."

"And so, we need an infrastructure to support that," said Greg. "We don't want to rely on public investigations. The people in Oneka Falls could track that."

"We'll build something to allow private inquiries?"

"Yeah, think of it as an Internet below the Internet. Plus, the job requires huge databases and user interfaces for those—"

"Okay, so we require a software company," said Scott. "Besides Greg, who actually works in the field, the rest of us just hang around all day doing nothing?"

Toby shook his head. "No. I bet SEMPRe will have something that will interest you."

"Doing what?"

Mike smiled at Toby and the two shared a laugh. "Investigating things."

"Oh," said Scott. "Well, okay, then."

12

"I'm glad to hear from you again, Brigitta," said Chris Stanton.

"Yes, it's been awhile, hasn't it?"

"Twenty years." His voice shook with strong emotion. His eyes ravaged her body. "You haven't changed a bit."

Brigitta smiled. "Of course I have, silly."

"You haven't aged." He glanced down at his middle-aged body, at the paunch bought by too many meals on the run, too little exercise, and he shook his head.

"Chris," she purred. "I need a favor."

"If it's about the foundation's accounts, I can assure you—"

"No, it's not about that."

"What kind of favor?"

"I'm looking for a friend. We've lost touch."

"I'm not sure how I can help with that, Brigitta. I'm just an investment banker, not a private investigator."

"But that's what I need. My friend was an avid investor."

"I see."

"I need someone who understands this financial stuff. Someone who can trace the money."

"Trace the money," Chris repeated.

"Yes. My friend… Is this conversation being recorded?"

"Uh, let me call you back from my mobile phone. Is this number good?"

"For the next twenty minutes, yes," said Brigitta.

"Will I…" Chris's voice broke.

"It can't be that way again, Chris. Not while you are seeing my aunt."

"Abby is your aunt? I never—"

"Call me on your cell phone, Chris."

"Brigitta, I've never understood why you…" He trailed off as he realized the line was dead. With trembling hands, he grabbed his cellphone and jogged to the elevators. He had a feeling the conversation he was about to have was not one he should have in the office—not even on his private mobile phone.

<u>Chapter 3</u>
1976

I

February 1976

The monster stood in front of the remains of a teenaged girl and leered at Sean. The massive thing looked similar to a cross between a banana and a giant monkey but had the mouth of a great white. His smile stretched and stretched and stretched until Sean thought the monstrous head would split in half and topple off the beast's neck.

Sean wanted to scream, to cry out, to raise the alarm. Oneka Falls had its very own monster lurking among the inhabitants, feeding on the residents. He leaned to the side, attempting to catch a glimpse of the girl's face past the big yellow monster's girth, but all he saw was blonde hair.

The thing hissed at him, drawing his attention. "I didn't want you to see me like this, Sean," the yellow fiend said. He held up one thick, claw-tipped finger and shook it at Sean. "You shouldn't meddle in my business."

Sean wanted to answer, but all the moisture had drained out of his throat. He couldn't swallow, couldn't unstick his tongue from the roof of his mouth, couldn't even make clicking noises. He stared into the thing's alligator eyes, as if mesmerized, his arms going limp, his shoulders slumping. That voice…it's so familiar, *Sean thought but couldn't place it.*

The yellow miscreation stretched a long, ape-like arm behind him, and when he pulled his fist back to the front, a bursting, sucking sound accompanied the movement. He gripped one of the girl's forearms in his massive fist as if he held nothing more awful than the drumstick from a Thanksgiving turkey.

Sean sucked in a breath to scream, his eyes watering at the pain caused by ripping his tongue from the roof of his mouth. He half-turned away from the appalling spectacle.

"No, son," said the beast. "No screaming, no carrying-on. I'll not have it."

That voice reminds me of... Sean bit down on the thought, not wanting to complete it. Not wishing to face what his mind wanted him to show him. He rocked his head from side to side, squeezing his eyes shut.

"Yeah, that's a good idea, kid. I didn't want you to see me like this." The monster chuckled—the harsh, basso sound of a lugging lawnmower engine. "Not yet, at least."

Sean awoke with his heart pounding and his sheets soaked in sweat. He felt enervated, drained of his will, and sad for reasons he didn't understand. Not one bit.

The voice of the monster... It belonged to Karl Munnur.

The front door opened, followed by the storm door, and then both snicked shut. Steeling himself against the chill, Sean threw back the covers and slipped out of bed. He almost gasped at the shock of his bare feet hitting the ice-cold oak floor. Almost.

Karl must've decided to go home rather than stay and sneak out in the early morning. It amused and disgusted Sean in equal parts that his mother and Karl thought he was so easy to fool.

He tipped-toed to the window and peered out from behind the curtains. Karl stood naked in the drive next to his big green Impala, looking up at the midnight sky. His head swiveled toward Sean's window.

With an almost physical shock, Karl met Sean's gaze, despite the fact that he'd only twitched the drape aside to peek out, despite the fact that he stood in near-perfect darkness. Sean sucked in a breath. He didn't dare let the curtain fall back into place, but something in Karl's demeanor frightened him.

No way he can see me, Sean thought.

In the driveway, Karl's face distended with a lopsided smile that seemed grotesque. He lifted one of his big hands and extended his index finger. He shook it at Sean in the same manner the monster in his dream had.

Sean couldn't breathe, couldn't move, couldn't cry out.

Karl winked at him and opened the door of his Impala. He got in and started the car.

It wasn't until after he left that Sean's ability to draw breath returned. It wasn't until after Karl left that Sean realized he hadn't taken his clothes, his shoes...as though Karl had tried to mimic the monster in his dream... *How did he know what I dreamed*, Sean wondered and shivered, but only partially from the cold.

2

March 1976

Eddie didn't see the scary woman again for what seemed a long time to him, but when he did, it scared him more than ever. He *had* dreamed of her multiple times, but dreams didn't count. They were just *dreams* after all.

His mother and father had fought more and more regularly between December and February. On Spring

Break from Cottonwood Vale Elementary, the arguing and shouting grew particularly bad, and Eddie couldn't decide what to do. He tried to make them laugh, but more often than not he succeeded only in making them angrier.

"Eddie!" his father shouted. "Eddie, get your butt down here, now!"

Eddie got up at once and ran to the kitchen but stopped at the top of the cellar steps. "Yes, Daddy?"

"I said *down here*, Eddie."

Eddie hated going in the basement, and his dad knew it. Something about the musty-smelling room spooked Eddie in ways only his nightmares, and the image of the scary lady's face could. "Daddy…"

"Don't make me come up there, Eddie." Ted's voice slid up from the cellar like an angry serpent's hiss.

Eddie stepped down to the first tread, and his dread stepped up a notch.

"Ted! You know it scares him down there!" shouted his mother from the living room. "Why do you want him down there in the dark and dust?"

In the basement below him, Eddie's father growled something under his breath. Eddie thought he had said the F-word. "Kathy, you keep out of this!" his father boomed.

Kathy got up and walked into the kitchen, her hands already resting on her hips. "No, Ted. I will not stay out of this. What are you doing down there, anyway?"

"Do I have to clear every tiny thing I do? I don't think so, Kathy. I wear the pants in this family, no matter what your Libber friends in the Garden Club have to say about things."

Eddie put his back to the wall and stood on the top step. Though a tight little smile formed on his mother's lips, she rolled her eyes up at the ceiling.

"Come on, Eddie. If your father wants to do something in the basement, more power to him, but you don't have to go down there."

"Goddammit, Kathy! Don't you countermand me! I said *get down here*, Eddie, and you better believe that's what I meant!"

Eddie didn't know what to do. He wanted to obey his mother more than anything, to stay out of the basement, and to avoid his father's anger, but disobeying his father would not make things better. He lifted a pleading gaze at his mom and held out his hands as if asking for a hug.

"Don't you ignore me, Ted!"

"And don't you butt into my business, Kathy!"

His dad came into the splash of light at bottom of the basement stairs and glared up at Eddie. *Why are the lights off down there? What can he be doing in the dark?*

"I'm going to count to three, Eddie, and if you're not down here at the bottom of the steps by the time I say three…" The threat in his dad's voice was clear. Eddie's stomach fell, and he turned and descended a few steps.

"Eddie, come back up here to Mommy. Your dad's just being a grouchy-bear, and as long as he is, he can stay down there in the basement. *In the dark.*" She said the last sentence words as though it tasted bad and she needed to spit them out. She held out a hand to Eddie and smiled at him.

He glanced down to the bottom of the steps. His father's face had gone a deep crimson, and his lip was curled, but he wasn't looking at Eddie, he was glowering past him at Kathy.

"Come on, Eddie," said his mother. "I won't allow your father to punish you."

With another glance at his father, Eddie turned and obeyed his mom. At the bottom of the steps below him, his dad made a strangled, angry sound, but that only inspired Eddie to move faster. Something moved, off in the shadows of the basement, and Eddie's mind supplied the image of the scary lady, leering up at him from the darkened room.

At the top of the stairs, his mother rested her hand on his head and smiled at him. When she shifted her glance down the steps, though, an ugly expression transformed her face from a thing of beauty into a thing of terror.

Eddie hated it. He detested the atmosphere that had blossomed within his family over the course of the last few months. His father had always been volatile, quick to anger, but his mom had always been able to soothe him.

Not anymore.

What was worse, though, was that his mother no longer seemed capable of calming *herself*. It was as if she no longer *wanted* things calm.

"Run along and play, Eddie," she said. "Your father and I need a moment to discuss things."

"Goddamn *right*!" his father snapped.

He went into the living room and sat on the edge of one of the overstuffed chairs. His gaze fell to his hands in his lap—they were trying to strangle each other again.

"I won't have it, Kathy! I'm through coddling the boy because of you! It's time he started to grow up!"

"Keep your voice down, Ted," his mother snapped. "He's just in the other room."

"Think I don't know that?" His father thudded up two steps. "You think I don't get what you're doing here?" His father's tone had gone ugly and grated with suppressed violence. Until that point, they had limited themselves to hurling insults and slamming doors, and as awful as it had been, it was nothing compared to what his father's tone promised. "Do you think I don't see you're trying to turn little Eddie against me?"

In the living room, Eddie's gaze snapped up, and he stared at the short hall that led to the kitchen. He felt as though he was going to throw up, the way he had felt when Jack McGregor had punched him in the belly the day before Spring Break had started.

"And what is it I'm doing to turn him against you, Ted?" his mother sneered. Her heels clacked on the linoleum.

Eddie pictured her stepping toward the door to the basement. His imagination painted her face in the ugly shades of hate, vehemence, and rage.

"You know what," his father growled. "Don't play coy." He ascended another couple of steps, his boots pounding the treads. His breath rushed in and out like one of Uncle Gil's bulls. His mother sighed, and his father imitated her sigh but made it somehow nasty. "Keep it up, Kathy... You go right on ahead and keep it up."

"And what? What are you going to do, big man?" Her heels clacked again, and Eddie thought he'd imagined it right—she was at the top of the stairs, glaring down at his father, daring him to come up the steps.

Ted growled with anger, but there was no sound of him coming up the steps.

"You just stay down there, Ted. Go ahead and live down there until you've got a hold of yourself. You've already made quite an ass out of yourself today. Is this how you prefer for Eddie to remember you for the rest of his life?"

Something flickered at the edge of Eddie's sight. Something black, something that brought cold, bitter wind to his mind. He didn't want to turn his head, but it turned as if by its own accord.

A lady's face hung in the corner behind the midnight-toned lamp emblazoned with bright blue fish that seemed to wriggle and swim in the black glass. Black smoke—or maybe just shadows—surrounded the woman, and he couldn't see any more of her. The skin on her face was dusky, and the bones of her skull seemed pressed against the inside of her flesh as though barely contained. At first, the light couldn't penetrate the dark mist that occupied the corner, but as the seconds ticked by on his mother's cuckoo clock, the light bled into the shadowy corner, as if the shadows grudgingly allowed it entry. The woman's skin was the color of desert dust and gleamed in the colored light cast by the lamp. Eyes like blackened pits glinted at him from the depths of the shadows, whirling and whirling, and with every harsh word coming from the other room, her irises pulsed with blue-tinged light. Her lips stretched in a smile that chilled Eddie down to the bone. As with when he'd first seen her reflection in the television set, her thick hair writhed like a mass of blue-black snakes. Black smoke permeated the area between her chin and the floor, making her appear to be a decapitated head floating in space.

Her eyes twitched toward the hall that led to the kitchen, and her smile widened at the thudding sound of his father's footsteps as he climbed up from the dark cellar. Her lips parted, revealing jet black teeth that looked more like the fangs of the werewolf he'd seen in last Friday's Creature Feature. In the light cast from the lamp, her jagged fangs appeared to drip with blood.

Her gaze drifted to Eddie, and when their eyes met, her smile grew even wider, and Eddie vomited all over his thighs. When the deluge of emesis stopped, he screamed, and his mother came running.

3

April 1976

The afternoon had warmed up from the chilly temperature the day had started with. The gray morning clouds had rolled away without dropping rain, sleet, or snow—Kristy considered it a minor miracle. Michelle Donnelly had invited her to go shopping at the mall, and she sat at her vanity putting on her lipstick as if getting ready for an evening with Leif. Over the previous few months, she'd taught Michelle everything she'd learned about makeup—and male anatomy.

She finished her makeup and pulled on her skin-tight Jordache jeans. With one last glance at the mirror, she ran downstairs and out into the beautiful afternoon. She had no bike, so she had to hoof it over to Michelle's house by two o'clock, or she'd miss out on the mall.

"Hey, sexy," said Leif's voice.

She looked around but couldn't see him. "Leif?"

"Up here," he said with a chuckle.

She gazed up into the boughs of the maple tree that had always decorated their front lawn, and there he was, sitting on a branch, dangling his legs. He wore Levi's, a green T-shirt, and a Cheshire grin. "Hey there," she said in the voice she considered sultry.

He wrinkled his nose and smiled. "Where are you going all dolled up?"

"Well, I'm supposed to go to the mall with Michelle Donnelly. You know her, right?"

He shook his head. "I don't see any girls but you."

She fought the urge to roll her eyes. "Schmoopy, today, are you?"

"In this weather? With a sexy blonde standing beneath me? Who wouldn't be?"

"A woman."

"Yeah, you say that now, but if we reversed roles—"

"Then I wouldn't need to say anything at all. You'd already be climbing up to me."

Leif laughed, and it sent a little thrill coursing through her veins. "That's true. How could I resist that outfit?" He patted the branch next to him. "Come on up. It's an easy climb."

Kristy glanced down the street in the direction she should be walking. "Okay," she said after a moment. "But only for a minute or two. Michelle's mom has a thing about punctuality. She won't wait for me." She grabbed a bough and hauled herself up, then looked for a path that would take her to him.

"What's so important about the mall today? Going to Frederick's of Hollywood to buy me a present?"

"In your dreams," she said. She climbed onto his branch and slid out next to him, swinging her feet a little. "Besides, I'm going shopping with Michelle. She's my best friend, and I ignored her all summer for you."

"Yeah, I understand. But you have to admit I'm pretty cool." He pretended to comb his hair back.

"Yes," she said, letting the word slither out between her teeth the way she'd seen Brooke English do on *All My Children*.

Leif slid closer and slung his arm around her shoulder. "You sure you want to go shopping?" As she opened her mouth to say yes, he leaned in and kissed her.

She never even made it to Michelle's house, let alone the mall.

4

May 1976

"Well, look-it there. There's our friend, Sean Walker. Should we say hello?" asked Dennis.

"No," said Jasper in a firm voice.

Dennis sneered and laughed. "Pussy."

"I have to fly," said Ari into the silence. "My mom has me doing piano lessons."

"Pussy," Jasper said in a near-perfect imitation of Dennis.

"How come you have to go every time we're about to do something fun, Jewboy?" Dennis tilted his head to the side the way his dad did when he was grilling Dennis about some supposed wrongdoing.

Ari hunched his shoulders and half-turned away. "My mom's coming down on me, man."

"Ah, poor baby," sneered Dennis. "Move on then, Jewboy. Run home to mommy."

Jasper's face twisted up, and he shifted to the side.

"What?" demanded Dennis. "Am I being mean to the Jewboy?"

"What's your problem?" asked Ari.

"Me? Oh, nothing. I'm just wondering where my friends Ari and Jasper went. It's like you two got replaced by one of them pod people."

"Pod people?" asked Jasper.

"Yeah. From that old movie from the fifties. Invasion of the Body Snatchers. Don't tell me you haven't seen it."

Jasper shrugged and crossed his arms. "Nope."

Dennis sighed, dropping his chin to chest. "My, oh my. I can't believe you two sissies are my friends."

Ari rolled his eyes. "Got to book. Catch you putzes on the flip side."

"Backatcha, Ari," said Jasper.

"Well, I'm not going to hang here with you two goons, anyway. Not when there's a perfectly good opportunity to smack the shit out of that little narc." Without waiting for a reply, he walked away.

"He didn't narc!" called Jasper.

Dennis crossed the street and fell in behind Sean. His cast had been off for months, but the kid still held his arm out as if it were glass. He caught up to Sean and made a fist, extending his middle finger knuckle a bit. He stepped to the side and socked Sean hard.

"Ow! What the heck, Dennis?"

"You know what that's for. Don't freak out, little narc."

"But I didn't—" He snapped his mouth shut as Dennis thwacked him again.

"Don't argue with me, Hong Kong Phooey."

Sean shook his head, his nose wrinkled, and his lips cocked in a lopsided grimace. "What does that even mean?"

"Jesus Christ, does no one in this shitburg watch television?" Dennis slung his arm around Sean's neck as though they were lifelong pals. "What are you doing this afternoon? Jasper and Ari flaked out, so it's just you and me."

Sean looked at him askance.

"Now, don't look at me like that, kid. We're past all that, right?"

Sean rubbed his bicep and lifted his shoulders.

"Let's go hang out in Thousand Acre Wood. I'll show you this cool path I found."

Sliding out from under Dennis's arm, Sean shook his head. "Nah. I don't want to. Sorry."

Dennis smiled at him crookedly. "That's what I like about you, freakazoid. You don't even bother to lie." He tapped Sean's bicep with his middle knuckle. "Maybe we should hang out more. Unless I'm not good enough to hang out with you."

Sean didn't reply, he just kept on moving with his head down and his hands in his pockets.

"Nothing? Nothing to say at all?"

Sean shrugged, and Dennis laughed.

"Well, okay then," said Dennis. He stopped walking but stuck out his foot. Sean tripped over it and fell headlong to the sidewalk. "Whoa, sorry, dude!"

Sean rolled over, hatred blazing in his eyes. "Just leave me alone, Dennis Cratchkin. I never did anything to you, so *leave me alone.*"

"Whoa! I almost believed you had a pair. For a minute." With a nasty smile, Dennis turned and walked the opposite way, leaving Sean sitting on the sidewalk, fuming.

5

June 1976

Apsu moved through the cool hallways that smelled of antiseptics and sickness. She spent a lot of time in hospitals, lingering near expectant mothers, looking through the window at the newborns, but no one ever hassled her.

No one ever *saw* her. Not unless she wanted them to, and when she did, it was too late for them, anyway.

Her foul mood wafted off her like heat off asphalt, and though no one could see her, they sensed her on a subconscious level as evidenced by how they jumped to clear her path. Some shivered and crossed themselves as she passed, and if it was a pregnant woman, Apsu stared at her for a moment longer than the others. More often than not, the women she paid special attention to miscarried.

She reached the neonatal ward and stood in front of the huge window, longing to break it, to send shards of shattered glass rattling amongst the babies on the other side. Hatred burned in her soul, cauterizing any weakness she might feel at their little faces, their tiny digits.

Apsu *hated*. She loathed the cruel fate that had made her sterile. She scorned the human ability to reproduce at will— among her kind, it took *effort*, not that Apsu had ever succeeded regardless of how much effort she put into the attempt. Apsu hated what she couldn't have. Apsu *hated*.

She stood for a long while, looking down at the spiteful symbols of her failure. Apsu longed to sweep the nurses aside and to crush those little heads.

She didn't do it. She *never* did it. Instead, she vented her choler in other ways, usually on other targets.

But that afternoon, she sowed sickness and death in the air on the other side of the glass, spawning billions of tiny bacteria—Mycobacterium tuberculosis, to be specific. She smiled, thinking of the panic and pain that would follow, and left the hospital, giving an old woman brain cancer on her way out.

She'd learned that trick from her mistress.

6

June 1976

Doctor Erikson steepled his fingers and tapped his index fingers against his front teeth. "Tell me again about this woman, Eddie. You told me she shows up when your parents are fighting and appears to enjoy their arguments?"

Eddie looked away, looking glum and feeling worse. "She just shows up. I don't have anything to do with when she comes."

"I didn't think you did, Eddie," said Doctor Erikson. "But it's important that we talk about her."

"But why? She never does anything. Well, except scare me."

"How does she scare you, son? You told me she only looks at you. Why is that scary?"

Eddie hiked his shoulders up around his neck, uncomfortable under the doctor's intense gaze. "I don't know. She's... Her eyes... She's always hard to see. She wears shadows the way Mommy wears her coat."

Doctor Erikson jotted something down in his little pad. "And you mentioned her irises twirl at you from the depths of those shadows? They whirl and throw off blue sparks?"

Eddie went back to watching his hands wrestle with each other in his lap. "Like windmills," he muttered. "And the shadows are made of smoke. Black smoke."

"And her mouth?"

"I know it's weird, okay? I can't help it. I can't help how she looks."

"It's okay, Eddie. Tell me about her teeth."

"Her fangs are all black. And sharp. Like a—" Eddie snapped his teeth together.

Doctor Erikson looked at him in that way adults had. The way that said, "you haven't told me enough yet."

"A werewolf," Eddie muttered. His gaze met Doctor Erikson's, as if daring the man to contradict him or laugh, but the psychiatrist only nodded as if it was a perfectly normal thing to say. "She's... Her skin is dusty. Tan."

"Tan the way a woman gets at the beach?"

"I've never been to the beach."

Doctor Erikson smiled. "Okay. Do you ever watch the news with your parents?"

Eddie grimaced and tilted his head.

"What channel do you watch?"

Eddie flopped his hands to his sides. "Daddy likes CBS."

"Have you seen the weather girl on the local news?" asked Erikson.

"Sure."

"Is the scary woman's skin tan like the weather girl's?"

"No. Not really. It's more like when my Uncle Gil makes Auntie Margo run the combine, that dust that the combine kicks up as it eats up the field. Her skin's not shiny and pretty, like that woman on the news. It's..."

"Is the woman who visits you covered in dust?"

Eddie shrugged. "Don't think so. Her skin is the color of dust, and looks…kind of the way an abandoned house does after a while."

Erikson wrote something down on his pad. "Does she ever talk to you?"

Eddie shook his head. "No, she just stares at me and smiles sometimes. But…"

"Go on, Eddie."

"Well, her smile isn't the same as a normal person's. Not like when you grin because you're happy or something's funny. It's…a mean smile."

"I understand." Doctor Erikson jotted something on his pad. "And you say you see her when your parents are having a fight?"

"Not the first time," said Eddie. "That time I was dusting."

"Interesting."

That was the word Doctor Erikson used when what Eddie said wasn't interesting at all. "She comes because of the lamp."

"The lamp?" Doctor Erikson looked at Eddie over the top of his glasses. "Oh, yes, the Tiffany lamp your father gave your mother."

"Right. I… I told you about that, right? That the colors changed?"

Doctor Erikson flipped back a few pages in his little pad. "No, I don't recall you saying that. Tell me more."

"When my daddy first brought it home, the shade was mostly aquamarine and had pretty dragonflies around the bottom of the shade. But now, since that lady's been showing up, it's so dark blue and dark purple that it seems black unless the light is on. Instead of dragonflies, bright blue fish that move."

"They move?" Doctor Erikson leaned forward in his chair and then wrote something on his pad. "Tell me more about that."

"Yeah. They wriggle and flop around the way real fishes do."

Erikson's pen jittered across the page, then he tilted his head and looked Eddie in the eye. "And where it was once aquamarine, it's now blue and purple?"

"*Dark* blue and dark purple—almost black. Yeah. Like a big bruise, except the red on the edges and the blue fish." Eddie watched Erikson write a flurry of words on his pad. "The body changed into a snake made of bronze. Oh! The chains…"

"Go on, Eddie."

"The pull chains used to end in little bronze balls. Now, they are babies."

"Babies?"

"Yeah." Eddie slouched back against the couch. He didn't know why talking about the lamp got him riled up, but it did.

"And your parents? Have they noticed these changes, too?"

"I've never talked to my father about the lamp," said Eddie, looking down at his lap."

"Ah. How about your mom?"

Eddie shook his head. "The lamp changed. It *did*."

Doctor Erikson dipped his chin toward his chest. "Your mother disagrees?"

"Yeah, she said it's always been the new colors, but even more than that, the pictures on it became something new and she says they haven't."

"Pictures?"

"Yeah. The dragonflies and the fishes."

"Go on."

"Go on? That's the end. That's how the lamp looks now. Fishes instead of dragonflies."

Doctor Erikson flashed a balmy smile at him "Yes, Eddie. I meant go on with telling me about the fish."

"Oh, why didn't you just say that? I already said they are bright blue, and they flop around."

"And do the fishes' eyes whirl in imitation of the woman's?"

Eddie shook his head. "No, it's only a lampshade. They aren't real fishes."

The doctor smiled again.

"Anyway, I don't get what the lamp has to do with the scary lady."

"Neither do I, Eddie. Why do you believe the woman comes because of your mother's lamp?"

Eddie looked at him askance. "Because she didn't show up until after Daddy brought it home."

"Ah. I understand." Erikson wrote on his pad, the pen making disgusting little scratching noises as the nub twitched across the page. "But you didn't notice the lampshade had changed until after you started seeing the woman."

"So?"

"You don't find that significant?"

Eddie tilted his head to the side and looked at Doctor Erikson with interest. "What do you mean?"

"Maybe something happened to you, Eddie. A thing that altered how you perceive things."

Eddie scratched his ear. "What do you think happened to me?"

"The question is this, Eddie: what do *you* think changed?"

Eddie lifted his shoulders and let them drop all in one fast motion, more like a twitch than a shrug. "Dunno. I think it just changed. Because of the scary lady."

"So, the woman appeared because of the lamp, and the woman's presence changed the shade?" Doctor Erikson smiled and put down his pen. "Does it strike you as funny that since your parents have been fighting, you've been seeing a woman that no one else can see, and that the lampshade has changed to grim shades?"

Again, Eddie lifted his shoulders and let them fall. "What's grim mean?"

"Harsh. Threatening. Scary."

"Oh." Eddie's hands started their annoying dance in his lap.

"It seems to me, Eddie, you associate this lamp and the scary lady's visits with the start of your mom and dad's arguments."

Eddie shook his head. "No, they—"

"You told me they argued on the day your father brought the lamp home."

"No, I almost broke Daddy's expensive present. That's all, they didn't argue. I almost broke Mommy's new lamp. I'm a klutz."

Doctor Erikson nodded. "Would you believe me if I told you sometimes adults are arguing, and their children don't know?"

"Dunno."

"Well, you can believe me, Eddie. It's true. But even if they were not arguing on that day, didn't you say mother seems less inclined to calm the situation since then?"

Eddie's attention drifted over Doctor Erikson's shoulder. After a heartbeat, Eddie's gaze dropped to the floor between them.

"That's okay, Eddie. Remember what you tell me is between you and me, and no one else will ever know."

Eddie pumped his head up and down but didn't look at the psychiatrist.

"It's part of the oath I took when I became a doctor. But, more importantly, I made you the same promise when we started, and I always keep my promises."

Eddie nodded but shrugged at the same time. He'd heard something similar from his daddy on many occasions. But Ted Mitchell didn't keep his promises.

"Let's get back to the scary woman. Why do you suppose she comes to visit you?"

Eddie shook his head. "She doesn't come to visit me. She just shows up whenever she wants. I don't have anything to do with her visits."

Doctor Erikson released a slow breath. "And yet, Eddie, she only shows up when no one else is in the room."

"That's not true. She shows up sometimes when my mommy and daddy are in the room, but they don't see her."

Erikson nodded and wrote something in his pad. "I understand. Does she do scary things when your mom and dad are with you?"

"She looks at me and smiles." Eddie tilted his head to the side, and his gaze drifted over Dr. Erikson's shoulder again. "Sometimes she only stares at me."

"But you find her staring at you scary, right?"

Eddie grimaced. "She has a mean smile, but it's somehow worse when she doesn't."

Doctor Erikson leaned back in the chair and steepled his fingers again. "And does anyone else ever smile at you in a mean way?"

"Yeah. Jack McGregor at school."

Erikson's pen went *scratch, scratch, scratch* on his pad. "And Jack is a friend of yours?"

Eddie rocked his head side to side. "No. I *hate* Jack. He picks on me."

"Ah. Jack bullies you?"

"Yeah."

"Have you told your teacher? Or your parents?"

Eddie looked at his shoes. "I told my parents, and Daddy said I should learn to fight. Mommy disagreed." His shoulders again hitched up and down in rapid succession. "Just another argument I made them have."

"Eddie, you can't make them have arguments. They have arguments, that much is true, but having an argument is a choice. You don't cause these tiffs."

Eddie looked out the window and then at the clock. "Seems like I do."

"I understand." Erickson treated him to a nod and a smile. "But believe me, Eddie, it's not your fault."

Eddie pursed his lips and threw a glance over Erikson's shoulder. "Is it time for me to go?"

Erikson glanced down at his watch. "Yes, our session is up for today."

Eddie relaxed for the first time since he'd come into the office.

"I want you to practice a few things in this next week, Eddie. First, try ignoring the woman when she comes to visit. Don't look at her or get up and leave the room—pretend you don't notice her. Can you do that?"

"I don't know. Sometimes I get all frozen up, staring at her."

Erickson leaned forward. "I understand. Try your best. Okay?"

"Okay. Is that all?"

"One more thing. Does your bathroom have a big mirror?"

Eddie bobbed his head.

"Good. At three different times during the day—so maybe before breakfast, when you come home from school, and right before bed—I want you to go into the bathroom and look at yourself in the mirror. Smile, and say: 'this is not my fault.' Can you try now?"

"This is not my fault." Eddie grinned. "Easy."

Erikson smiled and nodded. "Each time you practice this, please say the words five times. And if you begin to feel as if it is your fault when your parents are arguing, just get up and go into the bathroom, close the door and say the phrase five times. Okay?"

Eddie pistoned his shoulders up and let them drop. "Yeah, okay."

"Next week, we'll talk more about the scary lady and the lamp. Why don't you spend a few minutes over the next few days trying to memorize a few more details about this lampshade of yours?"

Eddie grinned and wagged his head with enthusiasm. He *enjoyed* looking at the lamp when the scary lady wasn't around. Sometimes he heard a melody while he stared at it—a melody unlike any he'd ever heard—and the song stayed with him for a long time afterward.

He got up and trotted toward the door, ignoring the woman dressed in black smoke standing behind Doctor

Erikson's coat rack with as much deliberation as an eight-year-old could muster.

7

June 1976

Sean walked down Union Street—Main Street was no longer safe for him. Even in the relative safety of Union, Sean didn't relax—*couldn't* loosen up—and kept his head scanning back and forth across the street, using his eyes to explore places where Dennis might hide, ready to turn tail and run at the slightest sign of danger.

Cratchkin wouldn't let it go. He'd never get past it, and Sean despaired of ever being rid of the bully. At least Jasper and Ari seemed scarce that summer. He ran faster than Dennis, and he'd gotten away almost as many times as Dennis had caught him.

I will have to do something, he thought. *Like what? What can I possibly do to Dennis Cratchkin?* He walked with his head down, his vigilance forgotten.

"What's got you down in the dumps, dude?" said a boy.

Sean jumped, his gaze flitting here and there.

"Up here," said a girl's voice.

Sean's gaze followed the trunk of the maple tree in the yard next to him. They sat midway to the tree's leafy crown, legs dangling. Sean blushed and turned away as soon as he realized the girl wore a denim skirt. He didn't want her—or her boyfriend—to assume he was looking up her skirt.

The guy laughed. "He's shy, Kristy."

"Hmm. I think he's just polite. I *am* wearing a skirt, after all."

"I hadn't noticed," said the boy, but he said it flirty. "Hey, kid. I'm Leif."

Sean looked up and met the older boy's gaze, then ducked his head again. "Sean."

"Hear that, Kristy? His name's Sean."

"It's a skirt, not earmuffs."

"Ear-whats?"

"Don't be crude, Leif," she said, but again, it had the feel of well-worn schtick.

"Hey, Sean, look up here a second."

Sean lifted his face toward the couple, and as he did, Leif flipped Kristy's T-shirt up, then laughed. She wasn't wearing a bra. A hot blush scourging his cheeks, Sean looked away.

"Leif!"

"Ever seen a pair as nice as that, Sean?" said Leif in a conspiratorial tone. "Great, ain't they?"

Sean couldn't come up with a single thing to say. He didn't know if he should apologize to the girl or not. *He* hadn't done anything.

"The kid's flushed, Kristy. That means he liked them."

"Don't tease him, Leif. It's not kind."

"Kind? A kid his age doesn't get to look at tits often—if at all. I was being *nice*."

"Maybe. But talking about his embarrassment isn't so nice."

"Eh."

The way the boy spoke seemed familiar. It wasn't his voice, Sean had never spoken to him before, and yet…something he couldn't quite place tickled his mind.

"Show him your panties."

"Leif!" Kristy laughed. "What's gotten into you?"

"All boys should've had a look at a girl's panties by the time they hit middle school. Call it education."

"How do you know he hasn't already seen someone's underwear?"

"See that blush? He hasn't. Trust me. Plus, you enjoy showing yourself off."

His accent? wondered Sean. *Nah. It doesn't seem it's very strong. But still.*

"Up here, Sean," said Kristy.

For a moment, he considered turning and running home, but…well, he *wanted* to see. He looked up but didn't catch a glimpse of her panties.

She wasn't wearing any.

8

August 1976

Dennis stomped into his room and slammed the door as hard as he could. Too hard for the hollow-core door to latch as it turned out. Instead, it bounced back at him, and he slammed it again. He trudged to his bed and threw himself down before reaching under the far side. He lifted his school backpack, lay it on the mattress next to him, then unzipped it. He reached inside and closed his eyes. Resting his hand on the cold metal head of the hammer calmed him.

Jasper and Ari were avoiding him. They had been all summer, and the fury that evoked built and built until just seeing them buying candy together in the little store on the corner of Mill and Main had sent him into a near-uncontrollable rage. He'd wanted to run up on them and start swinging, but he hadn't taken his backpack that day…

I should have brought it! If I had, things would've been different, and that Jewboy and his pussy, dick-loving friend would've paid the bill for ignoring me. He pulled the hammer out of the pack and held it by the haft, turning it back and forth. He watched the summer sunlight streaming through his open window and dancing back and forth across its head. *Might need dents in their foreheads. Both of them.*

He didn't much care that they'd once been buddies, and he didn't much care that they didn't seem to be friends anymore. That they would dare shun him rankled like sandpaper in his underwear.

I can't let this stand. They have to pay their bill, same as anyone. He smiled as an idea came waltzing into his mind.

He knew how to make them pay.

9

September 1976

"Sugarplum, what's wrong with you?"

To Kristy, the world seemed gray and lifeless. The food she ate had no taste; her stuffed animals grated across her skin like sandpaper. She'd taken to showering less often, and she no longer put on makeup or got dressed up after dinner. She thought about death in almost every waking moment. "I'm okay, Mom," she lied.

"You can tell me anything, sug. You know that, right?"

Kristy blew out a breath, making her bangs dance. "I said I'm all right!"

"Yes, Kristin, you did, but you haven't been to school in a week, and by the look of your hair, you haven't showered in that long. You don't do anything but sit on that couch and stare at the television blathering on like the idiot box it is." She crossed the room and snapped the RCA off, then turned to face her daughter. "You don't even disappear upstairs after supper to talk to Leif."

Lethargy enshrouded her at the sound of his name, and it felt as though ten thousand pounds pinned her to the sofa cushions. A broken-hearted sigh escaped her, and her eyes swam with tears.

"Oh, I see," said her mom. "Boy-trouble."

It wasn't a question, but Kristy dredged up the energy to nod.

"Trust me, sugarplum." Her mother crossed the couch and sank into its warm embrace. "I'm a good listener, and I know a thing or two about assholes."

"Yeah," whispered Kristy. "But..." She bent her head and clamped her lips together against the sob that threatened to escape.

"Come on, Kristy-poo. Tell your old mother what Leif did."

"Do you remember what we talked about at Christmas?"

Her mom nodded. "You didn't miss a pill, did you?"

Kristy shook her head. "No, I never do. But it wouldn't matter if I did." She looked at her mother sidelong, cutting her gaze away. "I...I never..."

Miriam tilted her head back. "Oh, I get it."

"He said..." Kristy no longer had the strength to hold her despair at bay, and tears soaked her cheeks. "He said that I'm selfish, that I teased him all the time and wouldn't…" She burst into sobs and lunged into her mother's arms.

"Let me guess," Miriam breathed. "He broke up with you because you wouldn't have sex."

Kristy sobbed harder. "I don't… I mean, I should've…"

"Shh, sugarplum. I'm proud of you for sticking to your guns. You aren't ready, and you know what? That's okay. It's okay that you choose to wait. It's okay that you don't want to rush into being a woman." She stroked Kristy's hair. "You did the right thing. *Are* doing the right thing."

"But now Leif—"

"Listen to me, sug. Are you listening?"

Kristy nodded.

"Any guy that tries to pressure you to do something you don't want to do isn't worth your time. Any guy who does that doesn't love you—no matter how many times they say it. Any guy willing to break up with you to push you into doing anything is a scumbag, and you, my dear, are far too precious to waste your life on scumbags. I've done enough of that for both of us. I'll bet entire busloads of boys down at the high school are dying for a chance to treat you better." She pulled away a bit and looked down at Kristy's face. "Hey, I've got an idea. Your birthday is coming up, right? Why don't we have a big party? You could invite all the boys you want. We'll play records, and you kids can dance all night."

Kristy could do nothing but cry. It was true, what her mother said, plenty of boys at school paid attention to her.

But none of them were Leif.

10

September 1976

The yellow-scaled ape came toward him, moving inexorably forward, yet with an easy stride, arms swinging back and forth as if he were just out for a walk. Sean sprinted ahead of him, pumping his fists and pounding the hot pavement with his bare feet.

"Where are you going?" the thing asked in Karl's voice.

Sean had no air to answer, even if he'd known what to say. His legs ached, his soles burned, and his breath rasped in the back of his mouth—in and out, in and out. His parched throat hurt as much as the time he'd had Strep, but he didn't dare stop running.

Not with that brute chasing him.

He threw a panicked glance over his shoulder and faltered, almost tripping over his own feet. No yellow-scaled gorilla thundered along behind him. Only Karl chased him, an anxious expression on his face, and fear clouding his eyes. "Sean! Quit it!"

Sean wanted to stop, but his muscles wouldn't obey him. It was as if they didn't trust what his mind told them, that they still believed the thing behind them was the gorilla monster and not Karl Munnur.

Sean groaned and opened his eyelids, the crust coating his lashes crumbling away. His throat burned as if he'd swallowed live coals, and his tongue lay swollen and dead in his mouth. He shifted to the side, and as he did, Karl stirred in the chair in which he slept.

Sean let his lids drift shut, but the pain in his throat wouldn't allow him to return to his dreams. "Thirsty," he croaked, craving ice-cold water.

"Here, baby," said his mother.

He turned his head toward the other side of the bed. Vickie leaned close, holding a plastic mug with Scooby-Doo cavorting on its surface. Sean accepted the cup and sipped—it wasn't water, it was Dr. Pepper, a treat reserved for when he was very sick. He grimaced as he swallowed, the cold liquid going to war with the hot-coal, pins-and-needles sensations that ravaged his throat. He drew another sip and sighed as the sugary sweetness slid across his tongue.

"Karl's been with you every minute, Sean. He's such a fine man."

Sean nodded, knowing his mother had never left his sickbed either.

"Look who's awake," said Karl in a rough, sleep-slurred voice. "I was starting to think you'd dream away the whole weekend."

Still sipping from the mug, Sean shifted his gaze to the other side of the bed. The big man dwarfed Sean's little desk chair, and he seemed about as comfortable as an elephant in a Volkswagen Beetle. Karl grinned at him, and Sean moved the drink for a moment—just long enough for a quick grin—then took another sip.

His mother's cool hand came to rest on his forehead. "He's still got the fever, Karl."

Karl's gaze cut to Vickie, and his eyes narrowed a little. "We can take him to Rochester. Or Cuba—it's closer."

"How do you feel, Sean?" asked his mom.

"Throat hurts," he said. "Tired. Hot."

"I don't know what to do, Karl."

"Maybe moving him will make him worse. We should just let him sleep."

Sean turned toward his mother, awaiting her decision. He drained the remaining Dr. Pepper from the Scooby cup. "More?"

"That's a good sign, isn't it, Vickie?" asked Karl. "The other times he woke up, he wasn't with it enough to even drink soda. Now, he wants more."

"Yes, I suppose," said Vickie Walker, but her voice didn't ring with confidence. "What about it, Sean? Do you feel better than before?"

He shrugged. "Don't remember."

"I'll fetch him another cup of Dr. Pepper. Karl, take his temperature again?"

Karl grunted and turned to get the thermometer from Sean's desk. He handled the mercury-filled glass cylinder as if it might explode at any moment, and Sean smiled at him as Karl slid the cold-tasting tube under his tongue.

When Vickie came back with another Scooby-sized dose of Dr. Pepper, Karl withdrew the thermometer and squinted down at it.

"Well?" asked Vickie.

"I…" Karl blushed. "I can barely read this damn thing, but seems it's come down a degree."

Vickie handed the cup to Sean with one hand and held the other out for the thermometer. She stared at it for a moment, then grinned. "One hundred and two. That's down two degrees since last time."

"Let's all get some rest. We can check him again in the morning."

Vickie's gaze slipped away from Sean's eyes. "You go ahead, Karl. I'll stay in here."

Sean had another sip of his Dr. Pepper, then held out the cup. "Sleepy, again."

Vickie took it and patted him on the shoulder. "Go to sleep, silly."

Sean's eyelids had already drooped closed. In moments, he'd fallen asleep.

Sean walked down Union Street, casting frequent glances behind him, keeping his eyes peeled for Dennis Cratchkin. The bully was after him. Again.

He crossed to the left side of the road and stepped up on the sidewalk. Cratchkin won't let this go, *he thought.* I will have to kill him. *He shuddered.* Where did that come from?

He walked under the boughs of a large maple tree, a strange déjà vu overtaking him. He looked up, expecting to find a teenaged boy sitting with a pretty girl, but instead, a yellow-scaled gorilla swung from one of the upper branches, something flapping behind him in the wind of his passage. Sean peered upward, trying to identify the flapping garment as it seemed of critical importance. He lifted a hand to shield his face from the suddenly too-bright sunlight.

"No fair peeking, Sean," growled Karl Munnur's voice.

Sean stumbled back a step or two, still peering up. But the sun had moved in the sky to silhouette the gorilla's shape. He dropped his gaze to the dancing shadow of the thing and the strange bit fluttering behind it.

"It's her skin, kid," said the gorilla in Karl's voice. "Kristy's. I took it for a cape. Do you love it?"

Sean skittered back, unbalancing himself and falling on his ass. He didn't want to look, but his head raised on its own, and his eyes swiveled up in their sockets until his gaze rested on the gorilla's chest.

The beast had knotted the cape around its thick throat. Two strap-like sections hung over his shoulders, and after a moment, Sean recognized them and gagged.

The straps were the skin from a girl's arms.

"Don't carry on so, kid. She's a trollop. Do you know what I got her to do? Plus, even you've seen her pretty bits naked."

Sean rocked his head from side to side with such violence that his neck muscles screamed in protest. He squeezed his eyes shut.

"Dude... What the hell's wrong with the kid?" said a stranger's voice.

Sean turned and peeked. A bright red shape rested in the road, about as tall as Karl. It looked as if made of wax, but an intense heat had warped and melted it around the edges. Three tentacles sprang from its top, a single, bone-like talon at the tip of each. Its eyes reminded Sean of the enlarged photographs of insects they had in the school library, of honeycombs, of imagined alien invaders. But the worst things had to be its mouths—three triangular-shaped openings, rowed with sharp, hook-shaped fangs.

Sean opened his mouth to scream, but before he could, Dennis Cratchkin stepped from behind the red thing, tapping his short-handled sledgehammer against his palm. "Bill's come due, Sean. Time to pay up," he said.

Sean scrabbled back like a crab, only the heels of his hands and the soles of his feet touching the concrete sidewalk. He hadn't forgotten about the yellow-scaled gorilla—not exactly—but he had lost sight of the thing.

When the scaled yellow hand fell on his shoulder with the weight of mountains behind it, Sean screamed and...

...sat bolt-upright in bed, his heart thundering in his chest. His mother slept twisted in an odd position in the dining room chair she'd pulled next to his bed. Gasping for breath, Sean turned his head.

Karl perched in the little chair that went with Sean's desk. His gaze rested on Sean, his eyes narrowed to slits. A peculiar expression twitched on the man's face—suspicion, irritation, or perhaps something darker. "Nightmare?" he asked.

Sean dropped his gaze, unable to continue to meet Karl's hostile stare. "Yeah."

"We should talk about your imagination, kid," said the deputy. "It might just get you in trouble someday."

II

September 1976

Kristy *did* feel better than before, but she didn't feel *good*. She wasn't happy, and being unhappy at her birthday party made her a little sick. Her gaze kept straying toward the side windows that looked out on Leif's house.

If she were honest with herself, she had hoped Leif would've relented by her birthday, but she hadn't seen him. She still harbored a twisted hope that he would crash the party, that he would come and apologize, that he would take her back.

She didn't share that wish with anyone. Not her mother, not even Michelle.

The guest list had swelled and swelled and swelled, and it seemed as though people stood elbow to elbow in the living room. True to her word, Kristy's mother had made a space for a dance floor of sorts, moving the dining room set out onto the back porch, and the dining room was full of bouncing, twisting, cavorting bodies and thumping to the rhythms of David Bowie, Elton John, and the Eagles. To Kristy, the dancing kids looked as though they were having sex with their clothes on.

But then again, sex had been on her mind almost every waking moment since the fight with Leif. She stood alone, a subtle gap of space between her and her guests. She wore an outfit Leif had called "hot," and she wore it as if born to it. The boys she'd invited stared at her with lust in their eyes, and while that stroked her ego…they weren't Leif and never would be.

With a suppressed smile, she walked to the window and peered up at Leif's bedroom. Unchanged since the day he dumped her, the shade blocked the window with no telltale border of light surrounding it. She hadn't noticed his lamp on since that horrible night. She'd neither seen nor heard from him in the previous weeks, and that ripped at her heart.

Why does he have to be this way? *Why is he being so fucking mean*? The two questions had become a refrain of sorts—chasing each other through the hallways of her mind like Tom and Jerry. Her mother said he'd acted like a child and shown his "true colors," but Kristy didn't believe that. She'd played her part in the drama. She'd acted the fool that night, too—screaming at him to leave her alone, to go find a slut to fuck.

Kristy hated to think of it, despised the memory of how she'd felt: vicious, mean, wanting to sting him. She regretted it. She'd acted like a child, and though he'd hurt her with what he said, she knew he hadn't meant the jibes. The situation had frustrated him, that's all.

"Come dance, Kristy!" called Michelle, who'd been dancing with the same sophomore all night. *He's cute*, she thought. *But he's no L—* She cut that line of thinking dead. She'd been thinking it too much, too often. Watching television—*Erik Estrada was adorable, but he was no Leif.* She sneered at how simple she'd become. She measured everyone and everything against the perfection of Leif.

Michelle pointed at her date's friend and tossed a wink at her. Kristy tilted her head to the side and looked the boy over. He wore a KISS concert shirt over Levi's. The tight jersey showed off his body—he was in great shape—and his face was pretty enough. She winked back at Michelle, nodding and holding up her index finger. She took one last look up at Leif's window.

The shade was up, the light was on, and Leif stood in the window, looking down at her, a small grin playing on his lips. She smiled a little, bittersweet smile.

"Happy birthday," he mouthed, and she heard his voice in her mind. His silky, sexy voice.

She nodded up at him and paused for a moment, frozen with indecision, before glancing at the boy Michelle had pointed out. She turned her gaze to Leif's window, and his expression had fallen. He looked so sad, so heartbroken, and she knew what she wanted. What she'd wanted all along.

She lifted her arm and beckoned him, and his face broke into a radiant expression of joy. He disappeared from the window, and Kristy's stomach danced with butterflies as they had the first night she'd caught him watching her.

She smiled at Michelle and the boys she stood with, but instead of joining them, she went out the front door to meet Leif on the lawn. They would talk for a few minutes, then go in and dance.

She wanted to ask him for a special present, one only he could give her. They would dance until the party ended, and then he could give it to her. She hoped his dad wasn't home and they could use Leif's bed.

Kristy didn't want her first time to be in a flower bed.

12

Halloween 1976

Excitement bubbled in Dennis's brain like the bubbles in soda. Each little bubble contained a vision of torment with either Jasper or Ari as the target. He'd been working on his plan, ironing out details and testing ideas since his epiphany in the week before school started.

And the day of his revenge had arrived.

But what if I get caught? asked a whiny voice in his mind. *Dad will* kill *me if I do.*

Dennis grimaced and pushed the voice away—it was the least of his worries. He bent his mind to his task, focusing on the last few details. *They'll never catch me. The plan is perfect.*

After tonight, one of his so-called friends would be dead, and the other would be charged with his murder.

Perfect.

He left the house, his backpack slung on his shoulder, dressed in black pants, a black T-shirt, and a black nylon windbreaker. Inside the pack, he had a few necessary items, one of which was a black balaclava.

"Hey, Denny," said Ari as he and Jasper came up the sidewalk. "Ready to have fun?"

Dennis plastered a grin on his face and nodded. "I hope you two are ready for some freaky-deaky hijinks."

"Hijinks?" asked Jasper with faint signs of amusement twisting his lips.

"I thought for sure you'd flip over 'freaky-deaky' yet here you are asking about 'hijinks?' Sheesh, Jasper, get with it." Dennis broke into a wide grin to hide his feral rage.

"So, what's this big plan?"

"It's a killer, man, but you'll have to wait a little longer to hear the details." Dennis made a show of tapping his ears and looking around. "No telling who's listening."

"Come on, dude. Spill."

Dennis grinned. He had both of them hooked and neither suspected a thing.

"Yeah, man. Tell us. Will it take long? I want to have time for candy tonight."

Candy, Dennis thought with derision. *Fucking clowns don't know what's coming. Idiots.* He pasted a smile on his face and winked at Ari. "Oh, we'll be getting candy, all right. Trust me. There will be tons of it. But first, we have to set things up."

"Wait. What?"

Dennis smiled and winked, though it made him want to puke. He'd much rather be swatting these two bugs with his hammer. "Yeah. We're going to have a fake haunted house. We'll lure the little kids there and scare the shit out of them. They'll drop their bags and boogie, and if they don't, I'll be hiding in the dark, and I'll *steal* the bags from them as they run away."

Jasper looked him up and down. "Hence the black."

"Hence? Hence?" Dennis sniggered.

"Hey, if you can use hijinks, I can say hence."

"You're using it wrong, bozo," said Ari. "Not supposed to use it at the beginning of a sentence. You should say 'thus,' instead."

Dennis and Jasper shared a glance then brayed laughter.

"Well, you should," said Ari, but that only elicited more laughter. "Fine. Be uneducated brutes all your lives."

Dennis let his laughter peter out and slapped Jasper on the shoulder. "Let's go get this thing set up, you uneducated brute."

"Let's do," said Jasper in his snooty butler voice. "Thus, we will be ready to steal candy when the time comes."

"Thus, Ari will quit crying about grammar."

"Assholes," Ari said, but he laughed as he said it.

"Where do we set up this master plan?"

"At our old hideout."

Jasper twitched his head back. "How do we get kids to come into the woods?"

"You look like a chicken when you do that," said Dennis with a long-suffering air. "And your question is stupid. We'll tell them we're giving out whole candy bars."

Jasper pursed his lips and looked up and to the right. "That should do it…if my math is right."

"It is," said Dennis.

"I concur," said Ari.

Dennis twitched his eyebrow at Jasper and the chortling started anew. The three boys walked into the woods, laughing and joshing one another as boys will do.

When they reached the tumbledown shack they called their hideout, Dennis stopped and said, "Okay, it'll work like this. One of you, and it doesn't matter which, waits inside for the kiddies to show. The other hides in the woods, and when the kiddies go in for their candy, you run out making monster sounds and beat your fists on the outside of the shed. The guy there makes as if he's scared, that there's a werewolf or something out here."

"And what will you be doing?" asked Ari.

"I'll be hiding in the woods, too, ready to snatch any plastic pumpkins or candy bags they manage to keep ahold of." He reached into his backpack and withdrew the balaclava. He slid it on and grinned. "What do you think?"

"Do you have more of those for us?" asked Ari.

"No, but you don't need it."

"Why's that?"

"The kiddies will only see the guy inside, and if you act scared enough, they won't realize you're in on it."

Jasper made a face. "I don't know. That part seems risky."

Dennis smiled his most winning smile. "You're the outside man, then."

"Hey, wait a minute," said Ari.

"You snooze, you lose," said Jasper with a grin for Dennis. "Get inside, Ariel. And act scared when I do my thing."

"Won't they see I don't have any candy?"

"I've got that covered," said Dennis, reaching into his pack again. This time, he pulled out a Snickers display box. "It's empty, though, so keep the lid closed."

Ari grinned. "This could work."

"Of *course* it will work," said Dennis. He turned and jogged into the trees. "Get ready, guys."

"But who will bring the kids here?" called Jasper.

"I'm going to put up signs at the end of the path. Don't worry! I considered everything." He slithered into the woods and butterflies of nervousness and excitement tickled his belly. He slipped his hand into his pack for the third time, but this time, he withdrew the sledgehammer.

Finally get to see if you'll make a dent in someone's forehead, he thought at the hammer. *I bet you will.*

13

Halloween 1976

Sean dressed in beige pants and one of Karl's long-sleeved white shirts. He left the shirt unbuttoned and had his mother's bathrobe belt to tie around his waist and hold the shirt closed. He had an arm's length of aluminum pipe that he'd spray-painted Day-Glo green.

Karl looked him over and tipped him a wink. "You make a good Luke Skywalker, Sean Walker."

"Cute," said Sean with mock severity. "It'll cost you five bucks, though."

Karl grunted, then grinned at him. "You sure you don't want to trick-or-treat around your house?"

"Rabbit Run will have better candy."

The big man looked at him in that way he had, and Sean pretended not to notice. "You know, Sean, if that bully is—"

"No, it's fine. I mean no one is bothering me."

"I can teach you to—"

"Karl, it's *Halloween*."

"Right. Message received." Karl chuckled.

"Thanks for taking me."

"No bother. Gets me out of doorbell-duty. I hate getting the door on Halloween." He turned down Neibolt Street and passed the park, peering into the gloom to make sure no skells hung around in the darkness.

"Halloween, Karl," said Sean.

Karl chuckled. "Busted. You can take the man out of the cops, but you can't take the cop out of the man."

"Nerd."

"Brat."

"Goof."

"Goober."

Sean rolled his eyes.

"And I win again. Undisputed heavyweight champion of the world!" Karl crowed.

"I let you."

"Did not."

"Did too."

"Don't lie to a cop, son."

"I'll count that as a win."

Karl twitched his big head to the side. "Fair enough." After a moment of silence, his expression turned solemn. "Sorry he's not here, Sean."

"Who?"

"Your dad. He would have been here if he could. He'd have loved this."

A crushing, unreasoning sadness wrapped its arms around Sean and squeezed. For a moment, he had to fight for breath, but then it passed. "Yeah," he murmured. *Why does he always do that?* he wondered. He glanced at Karl out of the corner of his eye. The gargantuan deputy sheriff was looking at him with a scary intensity—like he wanted to eat him. Sean shuddered, and Karl turned his gaze to the front.

"You want me to walk around with you or wait in the car?"

"I'm not little anymore, Karl," Sean said.

"Nope, but I don't mind going around with a big kid. I'm one myself." His grin was infectious, and despite the dollop of melancholy the comments about his dad had evoked, Sean smiled back.

Sean peered out the window at a gaggle of kids striding down the pavement dressed as various creatures of the night and imagined just running up to them and joining their group. He knew a few of the boys from school, though he never sat with them at lunch or played with them during recess. His mind painted the scene for him—the boys laughing and strolling away from him, leaving him standing alone in the middle of the street.

He turned back to Karl, and for a heartbeat, Karl's voracious face scared him, but then the shadow left the deputy's face, and with it, the nasty expression. "Yeah," he said. "Maybe you can get me extra candy."

Karl laughed and tousled his hair.

14

Halloween 1976

Dennis circled wide around their hideout—*his* hideout. Neither of the two pussies he was with deserved that place. Not that they would be able to come back after that evening, anyway.

He'd ditched his pack after donning a pair of gloves and wiping the hammer down with care. The gloves felt awesome. In fact, his all-black outfit felt a little…sexy. A broad, aggressive smile had warped his expression since he'd left the others, and his cheeks ached. Even so, he didn't gentle his expression; he had nothing benign in his heart or mind anymore. Inside, he felt as he imagined a hunting lion felt—powerful, ruthless, *murderous*.

He slowed to a walk, not wanting to alert Jasper to his presence. Dennis aimed to come up behind the boy and scare him, then smash his head in during Jasper's moment of shock and fear. *The perfect blitzkrieg*, he thought. *The perfect ambush. And after he's down...Ari's turn. The perfect crime, and the perfect patsy.*

A shadow moved ahead—Jasper, no doubt—and Dennis slowed even further. His gaze stuck to Jasper's silhouette as if welded there, and his heart beat so fast he feared it might explode before it was all over. He'd spent many a night practicing this moment, practicing moving through the woods like a stalking cat, and Jasper never heard him.

When he stood within arm's reach of the other boy, Dennis cocked the hammer over his shoulder and said, "Hey, pussy." His voice sounded strange, even to himself— deep, resonant, and spine-shivering. Jasper jumped and spun around, creating a hell of a racket.

Dennis swung with every bit of his strength, putting his entire weight behind the majestic hammer, adding the power of his hatred, his anger, his scorn. The short-handled sledgehammer impacted Jasper's forehead with the tone of splitting rock, and the boy collapsed as though every muscle in his body had turned to jelly. He hadn't made a sound— no scream, no grunt, no nothing.

Dennis froze at the end of his swing, a powerful emotion, a powerful joy, raping its way through his body and mind. He shivered with the power, the majesty, of the ecstasy, almost to the point that he feared a seizure was about to grip his brain in a tight embrace. In slow motion, the events of the last few minutes replayed in his mind's eye again and again, and as each hammer blow struck, a jolt of pure electric pleasure struck his mind like lightning. Even so, he didn't drop the hammer. No, he held it tight.

After a short time, the emotions, the memory of what he'd done, let go, leaving a hole in its place. Dennis wondered if that hole had always existed, and he'd never noticed, or if the potent emotional experience of killing Jasper had burned so bright that it left a cavity in its wake. He shivered as though someone had walked on his grave.

He stood over his former friend, without bothering to check if he was alive or dead, trusting in the hammer's brutal efficiency. *And now I have to give it up.* The thought rocked him, and he shifted his gaze to the hammer, smiling a little smile at the blood that coated the head. *Maybe I can work this so I can keep it*, he thought, but even as he did, he knew the thought was a lie. The plan hinged on Ari's fingerprints being on the haft. He couldn't substitute a rock or something for the hammer—the cops would see right through that, and if they did, the whole plot would fall apart.

No, he thought. *As much as I love this thing, I have to let it go. This's the price for tonight.* He peered down at Jasper and grunted. A huge dent decorated Jasper's forehead. *I knew it! Even if it does seem more like a moon crater than a dent in a car door.*

Again, he looked down at the short-handled sledge with longing. *There are other hammers*, he told himself.

He shook his head and let his fist drop to his side, the hammer thumping him on the thigh like a goodbye kiss. He had to concentrate on relaxing the fingers of his right hand to allow the haft to slide through them. It hit the ground with a *thud*, and Dennis turned aside, tears stinging his eyes.

Maybe I won't be a rock star, he thought. *I could do this forever. I could live in New York City and do hits for the Mob.* He forced himself to step away from the hammer, to walk toward the hideout's only entrance. He pulled off the balaclava and shoved it into his jacket pocket.

The next part of the plan was critical, and he did something he never did: he let his tears slide down his cheeks. He stopped outside, gathering himself. *It has to look real.* He recalled dropping his hammer in the woods. He imagined the police taking it and keeping his sledge locked away forever. He thought about never being able to touch the cold steel again, and a sob escaped him.

He bashed the door open with his shoulder, and inside, Ari shrieked as a little girl might. "Denny! You scared the shit out of me, man!"

Dennis rushed in and grabbed Ari by the shoulders. "*HE'S DEAD!*" he screamed.

"*What?* Who? What are you talking about, Dennis?" Ari tried to pull away, but he couldn't break Dennis's grip.

"Jasper! Someone *killed* Jasper!"

"This isn't funny, Denny," said Ari in a tremulous voice.

Dennis scoffed and dragged Ari out the door. He shoved him toward Jasper's body. "See for yourself!"

Ari stumbled to a stop, then looked back at Dennis. "This *really* isn't funny, Dennis," he said in a cold tone. "Me and Jasper will never play with you again after this."

"*JASPER'S DEAD, YOU DUMB FUCK!*" Dennis screeched.

Ari gazed at him for a moment, his expression going from one of pique to one of abject terror in a few heartbeats. He spun toward the woods. "Jasper?"

Behind him, Dennis shifted his gaze to the ground, looking for the fist-sized rock he'd brought from the brook on the edge of Thousand Acre Wood earlier in the day.

Ari took three steps toward the tree line, then stopped again. He glanced over his shoulder. "Aren't you coming?"

Dennis shook his head. "I don't... I don't want to see him that way again." He pretended to shudder.

Ari turned his gaze back toward the dark trees. "What if the murderer is still out here?"

Dennis rolled his eyes and suppressed a sigh. "I was just in there, and I'm alive, so whoever did this isn't in the woods anymore." His gaze came to rest on the rock. He must have kicked it as he ran into the clearing. The stone rested three giant steps from Ari, off to his left. "Go on, Ari. The cops won't believe only me."

"The police?"

"Yeah, dummy! The police! Do you think we're just going to leave him to rot in the woods?"

Ari nodded and strode into the trees. Dennis listened to his footfalls for a moment, then swooped toward his rock and swept it up, holding it behind his back. He stepped to the edge of the clearing and stopped.

"Oh, fuck!" said Ari in a whispering, fluttery voice. "Ohmygod, *ohmygod*!"

Dennis smiled a heartless smile as the sound of puking filtered through the trees. All that remained was for Ari to find the hammer. "Make sure you're not stomping all over evidence in there, Ari!" he shouted.

"What? No, I'm... Oh my god! Dennis! There's a... It's a hammer." Ari was silent for the space of five breaths, while Dennis held his. "Denny? This looks *exactly*..."

Fuck! Dennis strode into the woods, hoping Ari had picked the goddamn thing up. "What?" he called.

"Uh... Denny, did you leave your hammer at the hideout?"

"No way. Mine's in my backpack same as always."

"I think... Dennis, I'll go to the police department. To take this hammer to them and tell them about, uh, Jasper. You, uh, you stay here. To, um, to sec—"

With a sickening crunch, Dennis put Ari's budding fears to rest.

Maybe for good.

15

Halloween 1976

Munnur slid behind the wheel of the Impala and put his key in the ignition. He looked at Sean sidelong, wondering if he should bring up the kid's dad again. The depth of Sean's sadness stirred a wave of gluttonous greed in Munnur's soul. *Too soon,* he decided. *He already suspects something on a subconscious level. I'd better watch it; I don't want to kill him and his mother. Not yet.*

Sean rustled through the sweets in his orange plastic pumpkin, then grinned at Munnur.

"A nice haul?"

"The best I've ever gotten! I'll have candy until Christmas!"

Even this boy knows how to preserve the food he likes most. Surely, I can do as much. Despite the thought, he almost asked the kid if it was better than when his dad took him out on Halloween. Almost. "Ready to go home? Or do you want to hit somewhere else?"

Sean glanced at him, then ducked his head. "Could we run down Main Street? The kids said the shop owners put on big shows and give out whole candy bars."

Munnur threw back his head and laughed. "Sure we can, Sean. Whatever you want." He started the Impala's engine and goosed the accelerator a little to shower the side of the road with twin plumes of dirt and gravel.

When they turned on to Main, it was as festive as the school kids had led Sean to believe.

At least until Dennis Cratchkin ran up the street screaming bloody murder.

Chapter 4
2008

I

"What do you mean you can't find them?" LaBouche roared. "We've bought you every damn thing you've asked for. I've allocated tens of thousands of dollars for your trips, your *investigations*! They *did not* disappear into thin air, Mason. They are out there, right now, putting all of this, all of us, at risk. Don't waltz in here and tell me you haven't found them. Don't sashay in here and say they can't be found!"

Mason shrugged, doing his best to hide his boredom. "I don't know what else to do. I've *scrubbed* the data on Toby Burton, Drew Reid, Mike Richards, Shannon Bertram, and Benjamin Cartwright." He rested his hands on his knees and leaned forward. "Toby was a muddy mess even before everything went down last year. His records say he was in Millvale State Hospital, but he wasn't. And this Drew Reid character?" Mason blew his bangs straight up and rolled his eyes. "How could you have missed that he appeared out of the ether in 1995? Don't you cops do thorough checks?"

"Don't turn this back on me, Mason," said LaBouche with an air of weariness. "We aren't here to talk about what may or may not have happened before these hunters killed Herlequin."

"They must've split up," said Mason. "Must've had escape plans waiting. Identities, travel arrangements." He turned his head to the side but glanced at LaBouche out of the corner of his eye. "I mean, maybe I could do a better job with someone helping me."

LaBouche sneered. "No."

"This type of investigation gets boring, Lee," Mason said, leaning forward. "It takes hours and hours and hours of staring at data on a screen. It's just easier with a partner."

LaBouche stood and paced behind his desk. "Didn't we bring you a playmate the other day?"

Mason nodded. "A week ago. But that's different, though. That scratches another sort of itch."

"Nicole has other things to do. Besides, she said when she's there, all you do is put the moves on her." LaBouche winked at him. "Don't you know that humans can't compare to the hammers demons swing? She's not interested."

Mason looked away. "Still."

"Still," mimicked LaBouche. "Let me tell you about 'still.' Brigitta *still* wants these people found. Brigitta *still* wants you kept alive, but I sense she's getting impatient. You are *still* at her mercy, and if ever she tires of you, your heart will become *still*."

Mason wagged his head to the side. "No need to resort to threats, Lee. I'm with you guys. Red, Chaz, and Brigitta have been more like family to me than my own flesh and blood, and now that the State Police has plastered my identity all over the place..." He raised his hands and let them drop. "I'm stuck. I don't have any ideas of what else to do, where else to look."

LaBouche stopped pacing and twisted to face him. He opened his mouth but closed it without saying a word. He turned and gazed out the floor-to-ceiling window behind his desk. "Okay," he said. "But it won't be Nicole."

"That's all right," said Mason. "I just need someone to bounce ideas off. Someone to talk to." He smiled at

LaBouche's back. "Besides, I still have those pictures from when Nicole posed for me."

Lee spun around, eyes blazing, until he saw Mason's smirk. He scoffed and chuckled. "One day, Mason Harper, you may pull the wrong joke on the wrong demon."

Mason only grinned at him.

"Now get out of here. I have things to do."

2

Tom opened the front door and gazed at the nerdy-looking guy standing on his stoop. "Not interested," he said and started to close the door.

"Wait, Chief Walton. My name is Dan Delo. I'm an intern at the Democrat and Chronicle."

"Yes?" Tom squinted at the diminutive man, marking his features.

"I'm down here for my editor. She said I need to ask you about the three kids who survived being kidnapped by Owen Gray in the 70s."

Tom shook his head. "Wrong town. Besides, you weren't even born then, were you?"

"I'm older than I look." The nerdy guy smirked. "And anyway, Mrs. Magerite remembers it well."

"I guess," said Tom. "But why bring all that up again?"

"Owen Gray comes up for parole next year."

Tom scoffed. "That asshole? He's never getting out."

"I agree, but Mrs. Magerite says it's better to raise awareness than report a tragedy."

"She's right about that, at least." Tom looked the young man up and down, marking more features. "Might as well come in, I suppose. My wife, Janet, is visiting our grandkids, so the place is a bit of a mess."

"Doesn't bother me," said Dan. "I'm a confirmed bachelor."

Tom stepped back and waved Dan in. "How can I help you, Mr. Delo?"

"Call me Dan. Mr. Delo reminds me of my father."

"Okay. Then you'd better call me Tom. I haven't been chief of police here for years, anyway."

"Tom, then." He stuck out his hand.

Tom shook it and got the strangest impression of strength from the skinny man. "What can I tell you, Dan?"

"For starters, I was hoping you might have contact info for Toby Burton, Ben Cartwright, or Shannon Bertram? I need background information about the investigation, but Mrs. Magerite wants an interview from one of the survivors."

Tom shook his head. "Can't help you there. They weren't from Genosgwa. They were from Oneka Falls."

"Oh, yes, I understand, but with the tragedy that befell the Oneka Falls P.D. at the time, and the disappearance of Chief Richards, information in Oneka Falls is pretty sparse. Plus, I heard from a source in the State Police that you were instrumental in Abaddon's identification, and that the three survivors had helped you rescue Abaddon's final—"

"No, you're wrong, son," said Tom. "Let me stop you there because you've got your facts mixed up. It's true that I identified Mason Harper as Abaddon, and that I rescued his last intended victim, but it was only me."

Dan scratched his head and peered at Tom from the corner of his eyes. "I realize that's the official story, Tom, but my source at the State Police—"

"Doesn't know what he's talking about."

Dan held up his hands in surrender. "Sorry. Just passing on what my source told me. Can you tell me anything about the investigation in 1979? I understand that there was a victim from Genosgwa?"

"All of that is ancient news, son. And none of it pertains to Gray's parole hearing. We never charged him in the Genosgwa kidnapping. No evidence."

"No, I suppose you are right, but for the story we plan on running in the D and C, it's germane."

"Maybe, but an old man's memories some thirty years later? No, for all of that information, I suggest going through what the papers ran back then."

"Fair enough," said Dan Delo. "I would love to speak to the survivors, though. Their experiences are—"

"Sure, sure," said Tom. "But as I told you, I can't help you there. They weren't from Genosgwa."

"You've said." Dan cast a shrewd glance at Tom. "Are you sure you haven't seen them since 1979?"

"Since 1979? I don't recall ever seeing them, Dan. As I said—"

"Yes, yes!" snapped Dan. "They weren't from here. But, I've got to tell you, Tom, my instinct says you are hiding something."

Tom laughed and opened his mouth to reply, but when the phone rang, he held up an index finger and walked into the kitchen. "Walton," he said into the receiver.

"Tom? It's Benny Cartwright."

"Why, hello. What can I do for you today? I'm pressed for time. I've got a reporter in the other room asking about that mess over to Oneka Falls back in '79, so we'll need to keep this short."

"He's no reporter, Tom. He's one of the demons from the fight at the lake house. Get out of there. Get out now."

"Message received. I'll drive over there as soon as I can. Could you call me back at some point, though?"

"Go to a hotel or something, Tom. Somewhere outside of Kanowa County. I'll call you there."

The line went dead before Tom could say anything else, and he cradled the receiver, staring at it for a moment. *How did he have my number? Hasn't been listed in the directory since the late sixties.* With a shake of his head, he turned.

Dan Delo stood in the doorway, watching him.

Tom smiled. "Sorry, Dan. I need to cut this short. Could we pick this up later?"

"Sure. If you could just let me know where those survivors are."

Tom froze, staring into the young man's eyes. His face hardened into the familiar lines of the expression he'd worn when dealing with problems as police chief. "I guess we've been miscommunicating, son." His voice crackled with authority, and he expected Dan to apologize, to back off, but he didn't.

Instead, Dan Delo took a step closer and narrowed his eyes. "I guess we may have, Tom. I guess we may have."

Tom's hand flew to his hip—the same hip on which he hadn't worn his .357 Magnum for years and years. He cocked his head to the side and narrowed his own eyes. "I'm not sure what you hope to accomplish, Mr. Delo, but let me assure you: I've dealt with far more intimidating men without buckling. You're wasting your time." Tom shrugged. "And besides, I really don't have the answers you want."

Delo's face slackened, losing all traces of expression. He stood stock still for a moment, then lifted his chin. "You've never *dealt with* anything like me, Walton," he hissed.

Tom laughed and relaxed. "Son, do you have any idea how many people have said that or something similar over the years?" He backed up until his butt rested against the leading edge of Janet's fancy countertops. He lay his palm on the cool stone surface. "Look, Dan. I don't know where those three kids have gotten off to. It's been *years*, and I wasn't lying when I said I never even met them back in 1979."

Delo hitched his shoulders. It was a peculiar motion, as if he were stretching invisible wings. Tom slid his hand along the counter, closer to the block of knives Janet kept near the stove. "We can set up a time to talk about the investigation. If it will help with the article, I mean," said Tom.

Dan cocked his head to the side, staring at Tom's face.

"If I remember anything about those three kids, I'll jot it down. But there's a matter I have to attend to, and it won't wait." Tom lifted his hand from his hip and gestured toward the front door. After a moment, Delo nodded and turned away, and as he did, Tom drew one of the carving knives out of the block and slipped it point-down into his back pocket. "Give me a ring later in the day, and we can set up something for later in the week."

"Sure, sure," muttered Delo. He walked to the front door, and, without waiting for Tom, opened it and stepped through, leaving the door swinging open.

By the time Tom reached the door, the young man had disappeared. With a shake of his head, Tom closed and deadbolted the door, though he had no expectation that a mere deadbolt could stop Delo from coming in if he wanted. Not if Delo was a demon.

Tom turned and jogged to the master bedroom where the first thing he grabbed was his .357. He packed a bag, and ran to the garage, not bothering with the trunk, but slinging the suitcase on the passenger seat. He lay the big pistol on top of the bag and hit the garage door opener.

Half of him had expected to find Delo there, blocking his exit with a vehicle or something, but the drive was empty. Tom threw the car into reverse and backed out into the street.

He didn't notice the large hawk circling his house.

3

"And what about Sally?" LaBouche asked. "Have you wormed your way into her good graces yet?"

Nicole sighed and stretched her right arms over her head. Her left arms stroked LaBouche's chest and cheek—a sensation that had taken a while to get used to but now soothed him the way a mother's caress could soothe an infant. "She's a tough one," she murmured in his ear.

They lay together in the giant custom-sized bed LaBouche had commissioned years earlier but had ordered moved from Rochester to his new house—the one Chaz had occupied—in Oneka Falls. He nodded and sighed as the muscles in his neck relaxed.

"Yes," he said. "And she has hidden depths, concealed strength. You must be careful."

Nicole laughed. "As you may have mentioned sixty billion times."

"I'm serious, Nicole. She's far older than she appears, and despite her—"

"LaBouche, I *know*. You've told me before. Plenty of times."

He grunted but let it go. He *had* told her a million times before, and one more time would neither help nor goad her into being more careful. "I worry," he said.

"Yes," said Nicole, her husky breath tickling the hole in the side of his head that served him as an ear.

LaBouche shivered at the sensation.

"Now, pay attention to *me*, LaBouche," Nicole whispered and slung her leg across his thick torso.

After a moment, she was all he could pay attention to.

4

"Tell me, Sally. How are things progressing in Oneka Falls?"

Sally shrugged, then see-sawed her hand in the air. "LaBouche is making progress, but as far as finding the hunters, I get the feeling he and his minions have hit a wall."

Brigitta's expression hardened, and Sally inclined her head.

"It's not for lack of trying. He has Harper working long hours, and he sent Dan Delo out to speak with the old police chief, but those efforts have produced nothing worth noting."

"This distresses me."

"Yes, Mistress," said Sally.

"LaBouche is not without merit."

"No, Mistress. He's good at what he does."

"Then they've either fled or are better at hiding than we are at finding them. At any rate, I have other resources looking at the problem."

"Yes, Mistress." Sally grimaced. "Nicole continues her pathetic attempts to draw me into her confidence."

"And you shall let her, Sally," said Brigitta.

Sally shuddered and twisted her face away. "Is there no other way? I detest her—she reeks of sex and LaBouche all the time. How can you—" She snapped her mouth shut.

Brigitta chuckled low in her throat. "LaBouche isn't my lover, Sally. He's a sperm donor. I don't care what he and Nicole get up to—provided she never conceives."

Sally nodded.

"Or if she does, as long as she miscarries."

Sally smiled. "I promise you that, Mistress."

5

When his mobile rang, Tom fumbled for it, almost swerving into the wrong lane. He snatched it as it tried to slide off the bench seat, then spent a few seconds tapping the "accept" button that wasn't really a button, but a swipe thingy. "Goddamn piece of crap!" he hissed as he raised the phone to his ear. "Walton."

"Chief, it's Benny again. Try not to freak out, but the demon who called on you at your house is following you."

Tom's gaze snapped to the rearview mirror, but the road behind him was empty of traffic in both directions. "Not certain where you're getting your information, Mr. Cartwright—"

"Plain old Benny will do, Chief."

"—because no one is following me. No cars on this road except me."

"Yeah, but he's still following you, Chief. He's above you."

Tom pulled the phone from his ear and looked at it, then pursed his lips and put it back to his ear. "As I recall, Benny, you spent a few years in Millvale."

Benny laughed. "Yes, I did, but I did that to hide from the demons. Mike Richards is here with me. Would you rather talk to him?"

Tom shrugged. "No, I guess not." He leaned forward, searching the part of the sky visible to him for helicopters, but saw nothing.

"Tom, listen to me. You won't be able to perceive him. He's a demon, and he's tracking your car from the air, but he's blurring your perceptions."

"Blurring my perceptions."

"Yes. They can manipulate our senses—except with Toby. He can pierce their best efforts."

"Okay," said Tom. *Maybe this one should still be in Millvale, demons or aliens or whatever notwithstanding.*

Benny chuckled. "I understand why you might think so, Chief, but—"

"Think what?"

"You were just thinking I should be back in Millvale. Don't worry; I'm not offended. And whether they are demons in the biblical sense or aliens out of a sci-fi horror show doesn't matter. What matters right now is your safety."

"My safety," Tom repeated.

"Yes. That particular demon has frustration issues. Mike says to tell you the last time we frustrated him he dropped a tree in front of Mike's car."

"Uh...okay."

"His name is—"

"Claimed he was Dan Delo, a reporter or intern for the Democrat and Chronicle out of Rochester."

"Yes," said Benny. "And that is his real name—at least the name he uses when he thinks of himself. Delo is a winged demon, what Toby calls a 'traditional,' though he's purple instead of red and has—"

"Benny," said someone on his end of the line.

"Right. Chief, we can help you, but we need time to travel to your area. What we want you to do is drive around without a particular destination in mind, but so you're able to jump on I-86 in Alleghany in about an hour. Can you do that?"

"Are you asking me to lead a demon with frustration issues on a wild goose chase, Benny?"

"It will take time to get there, Chief."

Tom squinted at the sky ahead of him. "I don't know." All he could think about was Janet and the grandkids.

"I understand. But before we can get your family to safety, we need to provide for your physical safety. We've already dispatched a team." The line hissed and popped for a few seconds. "Besides, nothing actively threatens them at present. You, on the other hand..."

"I understand," Tom said, putting on his turn signal and slowing to take the next right. "But, son?"

"Yes, Chief?"

"Please get out of my head."

"Sorry. Occupational habit. I'll call again as we draw near."

"Anything else?"

"Mike says not to stop, not for any reason. If Delo throws a tree, swerve, he says."

"Got it." Tom thumbed the disconnect button and lay the phone to the side of his pistol, then went back to fruitlessly scanning the heavens as he drove.

6

Chris Stanton sat surrounded by LCD panels of all sizes. Each screen showed real-time trading data from all over the world. Take-out containers littered the floor around him, and an air mattress and pillow lay strewn behind him.

His eyes burned, but that was nothing unusual. His once-tan skin had first paled and then gone sallow, and the yellow tinge he now detected when he bothered to look at himself hinted at jaundice or worse. He'd lost the paunch that had troubled him when Brigitta called, but not by exercising and eating right. He did have an original diet plan guaranteed to cause weight loss, though. *Should write a diet book*, part of him thought. The other part, the *smart* part, focused on tracking a series of suspicious trades.

He'd been at it for eleven months. He almost never left the office, and when he did, he returned in short order. Atrophy had taken its toll on his muscles, and poor nutrition had taken its bite, too.

At least he didn't have to spend much time with Sammy. *She's probably glad*, he thought. *Bitch*.

He opened his eyes wide and shook his head to clear the irrelevant thoughts from his mind. *Focus! Almost got him this time.*

To his employees, he'd taken on a sort of Howard Hughes mythos. They all believed in his ingenuity, in his ability to forecast the markets with a scary percentage of profit. They thought his obsession with the markets lent him the vision, the understanding. They assumed he was the next Warren Buffett.

He wasn't. Brigitta's friend was the genius. Chris watched his trades and mimicked them, betting heavily on the guy's past success rate. So far, it had earned him and his clients millions.

But he'd come no closer to identifying the anonymous genius.

The man traded through the same houses for a while—just long enough that Chris thought he'd caught up to him—but the guy always switched to another trading house, another market, as soon as Chris got close. Then it took Chris anywhere from a few days to a few weeks to even find the guy's new trades.

Whoever he was, it appeared as if he had the ability to read Chris's mind. As if he had the power to predict the future.

7

Mike drove east through Allegany on I-86, then pulled off on St. Bonaventure's first exit. He turned left on Fall Road, then swung around and parked on the shoulder. "Okay," he said to Benny.

Benny saluted, a cell phone pressed to his ear. "Okay, Tom. We're ready. Timing will be critical, so make sure you tell—" He paused and peeked at Mike in the rearview. He pointed toward the highway. "Yes, we're on our way now. Once we get back on the interstate, though, we can't slow down and wait." He switched the phone to the other ear. "Yeah, okay."

Mike glanced at Shannon next to him. She reclined in the seat, her head against the headrest. As if she could feel his gaze, she nodded. Mike hit the accelerator, ignoring the stop sign at the end of the road and piloting the SUV under the interstate. He gunned it up the on-ramp for the west travel lanes.

"Yes, go ahead and jump on, but stay in the slow lane and let us overtake." Benny reached from the backseat and squeezed Shannon's shoulder. "No, Tom, trust me. He won't be able to stick with us once we get close enough." Benny smiled. "Yes, 'that beautiful woman will pull one of her tricks again.'"

8

Dan Delo watched the old police chief merge into westbound traffic on I-86 and grinned. *Finally, he's tired of all this fucking around.* He did not understand why the man had driven in circles—there was no way he could be aware of Dan's presence, and there was no sign of the hunter, the one who could see past their visages.

He flew a thousand yards above and behind the old man's boat of a car. His excitement mounted.

Off to the side, a bird shrieked and veered toward him, and Dan dropped his wingtip to curve away. It happened from time to time when he traveled as a bird—he invaded a local predator's territory or attracted a mate. He glanced at the hawk and shifted his visage to that of a bald eagle, but instead of driving the thing off, the bird shrieked a challenge and dove at him, talons extended.

Dan swerved to meet the attack head-on; he had nothing to fear from a hawk, after all. He reached for the bird, planning on crushing its skull in his fist and letting the bird drop onto the travel lanes. Hopefully, he would hit a truck and cause a big accident.

But the hawk flew right through his outstretched hand.

"Oh, no," he muttered. He turned his attention back to the interstate. The old man's car had disappeared. "That tricksy bitch!" he screamed. "LaBouche is going to kill me."

9

It frustrated Mason beyond measure. He'd tried—he'd worked hard to find the five people LaBouche had named, but it seemed as if they'd walked into a different dimension. He'd asked LaBouche to send someone to talk to Tom Walton—half in the hope that Tom would let something slip and half in the hope that at least Tom's murder would entertain him.

He'd given up watching the hunter's properties in Rochester, had given up trying to catch him paying the mortgages. He was far too slick.

But not Tom. Tom Walton is old, tired. Plus, he wasn't all that bright even in his heyday.

Even so, there had been no word, and boredom had latched onto Mason's mind. He flipped his laptop open and opened a Google page. He typed "demons" in the search box and hit the enter key. It was something he did to pass the time—a habit almost as old as the Internet itself.

He skipped past the videos of songs about devils and evil, past the dictionary entries and Wikipedia pages. He skimmed past the biblical references—he'd combed through those before—scrolling rapidly until he started seeing the interesting pages. Pages with titles like "Monsters are REAL!" and "Demonic possession—it really happened!" He enjoyed reading the "true" accounts of demons almost as much as he enjoyed reading speculation about Abaddon and why he'd disappeared.

For the last few months, Mason had loved getting on the forums for various sites claiming to be the authority on all subjects paranormal and starting flame wars. Most of the time, it was easy pickings—he'd just pick a thread in which the poster claimed to be an expert and reply with a preposterous fiction about the author's sex life. His screen name was Abaddon, of course.

It wasn't art, but it *was* fun.

He skimmed the list of sites, reading the titles of threads and checking the web addresses of the sites themselves. The sites came and went, seemingly with the tide, and there was always something unique.

His gaze stopped on a fresh listing and his heart skipped a beat. He clicked on the link and the site opened. "Society for Extrasensory, Metaphysical, and Paranormal Research" blazed in large letters across the top of the page. He scanned the menu—they indeed had public forums, and his mouse pointer hovered over the link. But there was something interesting about the page itself, so he right-clicked to bring up the source code. One look told him the code was generated—delivered by a server-side process when he clicked the link.

Pretty sophisticated for a fly-by-night paranormal website, he thought. Most used pre-built pages and plugins, plus cheap software ran the forums, but not the SEMPRe site.

Mason leaned back in his chair and tilted his head. *Where would be a perfect place to hide?* he asked himself. *I'm hiding in plain sight. Granted I have help from LaBouche and friends. I need not pay bills or go to work. The town of Oneka Falls shelters me from outside eyes.*

He didn't know why his thoughts had taken that turn, but they had, and Red had taught him to listen to his own intuitions. After a moment of staring at the screen, Mason got busy.

10

Tom Walton shook his head. "I can't sit here while Janet and the kids are at risk."

Toby held up his hands to stop him. "Tom, we've put people on the ground in Minnesota and in California. They are watching out for your family while we get everything arranged."

"People?" asked Tom.

"Scott Lewis, himself, flew to Minnesota to take command. He'll call us as soon as he's spoken to Janet. He still has his NYSP credentials. She will trust that, right?"

Tom tilted his head to the side and then brought it back upright. "Yeah. But—"

"You've met Scott. You know what he's about, what he's lost to the demons. He'd die before he lets anything happen to your wife, kids, or grandkids."

"Yeah, but if he does, so do they. Right?"

Shannon leaned forward and patted Tom's fist. "There's nothing you can do, Tom. Even if there was, we can't get you there before Scott gets them under cover."

Tom squeezed his eyes shut. "Demons," he scoffed. "Have I lost my mind?"

"No, Tom, you haven't," said Mike. "We knew they would take an interest in you, eventually. Benny's been watching over you."

Benny nodded. "Your family, too."

"I've never seen you in Genosgwa." Even to himself, Tom sounded surly.

"I haven't been back there since the day we met."

"Benny doesn't need to go somewhere in person to keep watch."

"Right, right. ESP," said Tom, a crease between his eyebrows.

"Yes," said Toby. "Exactly."

Shannon reached her hand out, and Tom took it. "Tom, you've witnessed what I can do. Right?"

Tom twitched a shoulder up and down. "I've watched you concentrate, but I don't know what happens." He dropped his gaze to the table in front of them.

"Tom, look at me," she said.

He lifted his head and gasped.

Shannon let her illusion fade. "What did you see?"

"The…" He shook his head. "I saw a woman…a *dead* woman with black, sagging skin."

She squeezed his hand. "I'm sorry for that shock, but I needed you to understand what I do. I can put any image I want in your mind; I can make you believe that I look however I choose. I can do that for myself, for you, for anything I please."

"Who…"

"That was a class of demons Toby calls 'undead.' Brigitta, the woman who haunted Greg at Lake Genosgwa, is an undead demon."

"The Lady in the Lake is *real*?"

"Yes, but she's no more limited to Lake Genosgwa than you are," said Benny. "She goes all over the place. She can teleport."

Tom shook his head. "All these years… I believed Stephen Canton was insane. The things he talked about—"

"Yes," said Toby. "Tom, I've been hunting these monsters for years now. I've dispatched almost seventy of them—sent them back to Hell, or so they say. Their tricks don't work on me."

"Shannon does what they do, doesn't she?"

"We don't think so. Our experiences in Oneka Falls—and Greg's in Genosgwa—awakened something within us," said Benny. "Each gift is different, but we can develop each one. Enhance it."

Tom turned to Mike. "Your gift?"

Mike shook his head. "I didn't get snatched the way these three did. I didn't get tortured, chased, whatever triggers the change. No gifts for me."

"Yet," said Benny, then laughed.

"Yet?" asked Tom.

"An old joke between us," said Mike. "At the start of it all Benny pretended he could give me 'superpowers,' but try as he might, he can't do it."

"Yet," said Benny again.

Mike chuckled.

"Then you truly can get in my head?" asked Tom.

Benny's expression grew solemn. "Yes, Tom. At first, that's all I could do well, and I had to be close to do it." He grinned crookedly. "But as I said, we can improve our talents."

"What else can you do? I mean, how has your gift developed?"

"Well, for one thing, Benny can read the demons now. From afar." Shannon glanced at her lover and smiled.

"He's also getting a knack for predicting the stock market," said Toby.

"I think that's reading a kind of gestalt deal. The group-mind of all the investors and bigwigs out there in la-la land," said Benny. He turned his attention back to Tom. "You understand? I was watching out for you, but not in person. I was watching out for you by keeping psychic tabs on Genosgwa."

"Watching for demons?"

Benny shrugged.

"You can see them?"

"No, but I can feel their nature. Their thoughts are…" He shivered.

Tom's face turned red. "Then you've all been sitting here, doing nothing while…while demons stalk New York? Sitting here, living like kings!"

"You don't realize the scale of it, Tom," said Mike. "And we're not relaxing here doing nothing. Not at all."

"Then—" Tom closed his mouth as Toby's mobile rang.

"Hello? Good. Let me hand the phone to Tom Walton. Repeat for him what you told me." Toby extended his arm, his phone set to speaker.

"Hello, Tom. This is Scott Lewis. You remember me?"

"Yes," said Tom.

"I've got a few people here who want to say hello." There was a pause and a noise like sandpaper being dragged across the phone's microphone.

"Tom? Tom, is that you?"

Tom sagged back in his seat and released a long-winded sigh of relief. "Yes, Janet, it's me."

11

LaBouche drew a deep breath in through the slits that served as his nostrils and held it while he counted to ten in his head. Rage coursed through him, but he didn't know why. *It's not as if I didn't realize this big purple idiot wasn't a genius.* He glanced at Nicole and found her malachite gaze. She flashed him a grin and a wink, and something inside him relaxed. He chuckled, and Dan Delo flinched, which made LaBouche laugh all the harder. "So, let me get this straight. You went to the old fucker's house and got him to bug out. Then you followed him by air, but a little bird scared you off?"

"No! The hawk didn't scare me away, it *distracted* me. But it wasn't a bird anyway, it was the tricksy bitch, and she did it on purpose!" Dan fidgeted at the foot of the overlarge bed, his gaze dancing around the room—anywhere but at LaBouche.

"Of course she did, you giant Fruit of the Loom reject!" snapped LaBouche.

"Fruit of the Loom?" muttered Delo, but after one look into LaBouche's crocodile eyes, he slapped his lips together—wisely—and returned to examining the walls.

"They set you up, Dan," said Nicole. "That's why Walton drove around in circles, to give them time to get the trickster into position."

LaBouche smiled at Dan, but it was a smile tinged with anger. "So, once again, you allowed a key person to disappear, but at least this time you learned something."

"Learned something?"

"Yes," said Nicole. "This afternoon's debacle tells us that wherever they are, it takes them less than an hour to get to Allegany."

"But, how..." For a moment, Dan's azure eyes glowed brighter. "Oh!"

"I'm glad you finally understand," said LaBouche. "Now, get out."

<u>Chapter 5</u>
1977

I

January 1977

Dennis scowled at the school from a block away. The last thing he wanted to do was attend class with the ugly purple and black shiner his dad had given him, but it was colder than a witch's tit that Monday morning, and he didn't want to freeze all day, either.

He slowed to a halt, standing in a slushy pool of dirty, salty water that had gathered at the edge of the road. The plow had created a baby snowbank beside the road as Father Winter had given them a miserly amount of snow to play with that year. His mom said it was because of the cold, but that made no sense to Dennis.

Pulling off his right glove, he shoved his hand into his front pocket and pulled out the pack of cigarettes he considered just compensation for his eye.

He'd been compiling an accounting of slights, of black eyes, of bruised ribs, ever since Halloween. Ever since he'd learned how much power rested within him, waiting for a chance to come out and dance. The bill his old man had already amassed was a long one. When he called that bill due, his father would pay for each and every item on his list.

Thinking about that day calmed him, took a bit of the shame and disgrace about his black eye away. He lit a cigarette and stood staring at the school. *Should go*, he thought. *I don't want to fail, again.* Then again, an unforeseen side effect of murdering Jasper and leaving Ari a vegetable whom everyone assumed had murdered Jasper was that the teachers cut him slack. A lot of slack.

He hadn't had a single detention, not one suspension, not even a note to his mom since Halloween week. His lips spread into a lopsided grin. *Should've killed someone earlier.* He chortled, releasing a lungful of smoke, and turned away from the school.

All he had to do was find a warm place to spend the day. Going home was out of the question; his father was out of work again. The hideout was off-limits, and his allotment of friends had dwindled to zero. He cackled again.

Maybe he could locate an empty house to break into, and if he didn't, well, he'd been cold before.

He took the long way around the shitburg's pitiful little downtown area. The cops didn't share his teachers' feelings about cutting him slack. That fucktard Greshin always looked at him through squinted up eyes as if he was a motherfucking Kreskin and knew everything there was to know about Dennis Cratchkin. *Fuck that guy.*

He walked down the middle of Union, looking left and right for a suitable house. He never heard the car until it pulled up behind him. With a sinking feeling, he turned, expecting to see a cop car.

Instead, an old pickup truck idled in the street. The driver was the biggest man Dennis had ever seen. He sported a cue-ball hairstyle that brought bikers to Dennis's mind. The giant tilted his head and watched Dennis.

He lifted a hand in a way he hoped the giant man would take for an apology and turned toward the sidewalk.

"C'mere, kid."

Dennis looked over his shoulder. The man had his arm out the driver's side window, beckoning. The stranger danger bullshit Greshin put them through every year flashed through his mind, but he sneered at the idea. He reversed direction and approached the truck. "Yeah?"

"You're Cratchkin, right?" The burly man seemed to wear the rig rather than ride inside it. "The one whose friend murdered your other buddy with a hammer?" Incongruously, the guy smiled as he asked the question.

Dennis nodded, more than a little unsure whether or not he should bolt.

The giant waved his hand as if he knew Dennis' thoughts. "Name's Red Bortha, Cratchkin. There. Now, we know each other, and you can stop thinking about that bullshit Greshin filled your head with at the end of school last year. Besides, boys ain't my thing." Bortha shivered. "Colder than a witch's tit out there, kid. Want to climb in here in the heat?"

Dennis stood for a moment, staring up at the big man.

Bortha shrugged and made to as if to roll up his window.

"Wait," said Dennis.

Red stopped and gave Dennis his full attention, waiting.

"Why do you want me to get in?"

"I like what I hear about you, kid. You seem to have your shit together."

"And?"

Bortha laughed, and his laugh matched his appearance—large and loud. "Listen up, Cratchkin. I understand you, see? Like calls to like. I can help you, teach you." He glanced around, and seeing no one, leaned farther out the window. "You got lucky last Halloween," he stage-whispered. "You think your plan was perfect, but there were ninety-five thousand things that could've gone wrong, and you might've ended up in juvie until you hit eighteen and they transferred you to Attica." He withdrew back into the cab. "That would be a waste." He turned his gaze to the front. "Get in, kid."

Dennis hesitated only a moment before trotting around the truck and climbing inside. *Finally*, he thought. *Someone who knows something I want to learn.*

2

March 1977

Sean pulled back against the tide of students rushing out the school's doors. He'd spotted Dennis Cratchkin loitering by the bus ramp and didn't want to risk running into him. That kind of thinking had kept him free of bruises and worse the whole school year so far, and he didn't want to sully his record.

"Get a move on, Walker," said Ivan Parra—who had the distinction of being the only Hispanic kid in Oneka Falls Elementary. Ivan was tall, even among the boys his own age, and he towered over Sean.

"I forgot something," Sean murmured.

"Then move out the way. I don't want to miss my bus."

Sean shrugged and danced to the side, pressing himself against the announcement board no one ever read. Ivan gave him a funny look, but then he was gone, swept on by the tide of nine- and ten-year-olds rushing to get to the busses and home.

As the deluge of students slowed, Sean stepped away from the bulletin board and glanced out. Dennis stood over a third-grader, glaring down at him and holding out his hand. The skin on the boy's elbows looked like someone

168   ERIK HENRY VICK

had taken a cheese grater to them, and tears ran down his pudgy cheeks in torrents. Dennis said something, and the third-grader ducked his head, digging through his pack. He pulled out a little change purse decorated with beads—no doubt made at summer camp the year before—and Dennis cackled as he snatched it out of the kid's grip. He shook the coin purse and waved it around as though doing a girly dance. The kid on the ground slumped and buried his face in his hands.

Karl always said he should stand up to bullies, but Sean didn't think a big man like Karl Munnur had ever had to stand up to a bully half as tall again as he was, who outweighed him by thirty percent of his own body weight, and who was older and more experienced. He doubted Karl ever had to stand up to anyone. He doubted the world contained anyone stupid enough to pick on Karl.

Sean watched, frozen with indecision. Dennis was distracted, focused on his latest victim. Sean might sneak out and loop behind the building without Dennis noticing him. He dithered, shifting his weight from foot to foot and back again. On the other hand, Dennis might see him and come on the run. The bully might think they had unfinished business—their last encounter around the rear of the school had ended with Sean kicking him in the balls, after all.

Outside, Dennis ripped the coin purse open, not even bothering to catch the cascade of coins that rained down. He only wanted to destroy the kid's coin purse.

It angered Sean, but what could he do? *Someone should help the kid. Somebody should tell Dennis to leave him alone.*

No one would. No kid, at least.

Twelve-years-old and still in the fourth grade, Dennis might as well have been an ogre. As big and brutish as he was, with an ugly personality to go along with it, he had the run of the school, and for some reason, the teachers were letting him get away with murder that year. They sometimes stopped him bullying someone, but it ended there. He never had detentions or got paddled or anything. Not since Halloween.

Dennis turned the purse inside out and said something to kid. When the kid didn't respond, Dennis laughed and ripped the purse apart, throwing the torn leather halves in the kid's lap. He dusted his hands as if he'd just done a good work and lifted his head.

His eyes met Sean's for a moment, and Sean expected the worst, but Dennis only raised a hand for a short wave and smiled. Then he shifted his gaze away and sprinted after another hapless victim.

Sean turned, sure a teacher stood behind him, and that was who Dennis had smiled and waved at, but the hall was empty.

3

March 1977

"If you want to evoke terror, kid, randomness is the key," said Red.

"Randomness? What the hell does that even mean?"

Red's smile twitched on and off like a faulty neon sign. "Randomness means you don't do the same thing every time. You have to be unpredictable."

Dennis thought about it for a moment, lips pursed, brow furrowed. "Unpredictable?"

"Sure. If you always pick on the third-graders, the fourth-graders will see, and they might fear you a little, but they'll recognize they are safe from your attentions for that day. But, if you choose a kid at random and go ape-shit on him, no one will know who's next. Randomness."

Dennis grinned and bobbed his head. "I get it! Eenie-meenie-minie-moe."

"What?" asked Red, his face scrunching in confusion.

"Never mind. Picking kids by chance."

"Oh. Yes. But it's more than just the choice of the victim. That is...if you want to cause *real* fear."

Dennis stepped forward, eyes burning. "I do. I really do."

Red nodded as though he'd expected nothing else. "Then listen close, Cratchkin. Dread comes from the uncertain; complete terror develops from the completely erratic." He looked at Dennis's face and sighed. "What I mean is, it's good to choose your target in an arbitrary manner, but what's even better is to pick the kid *and what you do to him* at random."

"So, like, I pick a third-grader and stomp his guts out today, but tomorrow, I pick a fourth-grader and push him into the thorn bush?"

"Sure," said Red. "But consider this: how scary would you be if some days, you picked a kid and did something *nice* for him? Treated him as a friend, protected him from a wanna-be bully?"

Dennis's face screwed up in a grimace. "Why would I do that? I want to stomp his ass, right?"

Red lifted his head and stared down his nose at Dennis. "Is that what you crave? I thought you wanted to be *feared*."

"But I do. How... Why would they fear me if I don't kick anyone's ass?"

"I didn't say that, Cratchkin. I said, 'sometimes you pick a child and be nice to him.' That's the key. You don't even want the kid who gets picked on to have any idea what the fuck you will do next. You want to crush their expectations, leave them hanging out in the rain. Don't give them any clue what you're doing. Don't allow them to discern a pattern or sense your mood. Hide your true self deep inside. You control what others perceive about you. Only let your victims know the real you, and never for long."

Dennis dipped his head with each point, a look of near rapture on his face. "I can do that," he said. "I think."

Red laughed and a strange clicking noise accompanied it. "I will teach you, Cratchkin."

4

April 1977

"But, Leif, I feel stupid," said Kristy.

"Please? You know what it does to me."

"There isn't even any music."

"Pretend you hear some." Leif batted his eyelashes at her. "Come on, Kristy. Please?"

She tilted her head to the side and favored him with a long, calculating look. "What will you do for me?"

"Anything you want." His eyes lit up. "Oh, hey! I forgot. I've picked up something guaranteed to light you up like a Christmas tree. Dance for me, and I'll get you high."

"High?" she said, her fingers playing with the buttons of her blouse.

"Yeah. I've got something you'll love."

"I didn't enjoy the beer." She stopped unbuttoning the blouse half-way down.

"This isn't beer."

"What is it?"

"Trust me, Kristy."

She tilted her head to the side. "Deal." She pulled her shirt off then kicked out of her jeans and started to dance for Leif.

5

April 1977

"Eddie," called Mrs. Butterworth, looking up after scanning the note a runner had brought. "They need you in the front office. But don't worry, you're not in trouble. There's someone here to see you, is all."

"Who, Mrs. Butterworth?" asked Eddie.

Eddie didn't know it, but his life was about to crumble.

"Well, you'll find out up at the office. Now, get a move on, Eddie."

Mrs. Butterworth smiled to take any sting out of the words, but she seemed upset about something to Eddie. He stood, putting his pencil in the pencil holder slot at the top of his desk and sweeping his jacket off the rear of the desk. "Will I be back to eat, Mrs. Butterworth? My mother packed me a special lunch."

The expression Mrs. Butterworth flashed at him brimmed over with compassion, pity, sadness. Eddie didn't understand the look; he didn't know why she would be sad.

"Take it with you, Eddie," said Mrs. Butterworth. "In fact, take all your things. You won't return this afternoon."

Eddie stared at her a moment, confused, but then he blinked a few times and packed his stuff into his little red backpack and slung it over his shoulder. "Well, I hope I can come back. I don't want to miss the skits after lunch."

Mrs. Butterworth smiled at him and inclined her head, but the smile appeared strained, quivery even to a kid.

As he left Mrs. Butterworth's classroom, she lay her hand on his upper back and then rubbed the spot between his shoulder blades. "Remember that you have friends, Eddie."

Eddie had no idea how to respond to that. He settled for a nod and then skipped through the door. He jogged down the long central hallway of the old school building, smiling and whistling to himself.

When he reached the front office, his smile faded. The principal stood waiting, and next to him, a huge man wearing the dark navy-blue uniform of the Cottonwood Vale Police Department. He looked familiar, but Eddie didn't recall his name. The policeman's gold badge gleamed in the bright fluorescent lights. Eddie understood that meant something—a gold-colored badge—but he didn't remember what. The man's shoes were black and super-shiny. White powder, similar to the sugar they coated doughnuts with, dusted his shirt under his right shirt pocket. A bronze-colored tag that said, "John Morton" hung above the pocket. Another bronze tag hung under the badge pinned to his left pocket, and it read, "Chief of Police." When Eddie read that, he sucked in a breath.

"Now, don't you worry, Edward," said the principal.

Chief Morton shot the principal a look that Eddie didn't understand—the big man's expression was a mixture of anger and disdain—and then he lowered himself to a squat, putting himself at as close to eye level with the nine-year-old boy as possible. "Eddie, I'm John Morton. I'm the chief of police of Cottonwood Vale. Do you know what that means, son?" The big man smelled of Old Spice, but his breath stank of old coffee.

Eddie nodded while he fought to swallow past an obstruction that swelled to fill his throat. "You run the cops," he croaked.

Quick as a whip, a small smile bloomed and faded on the chief's lips. "Yes, son, I guess that's right. I do run the cops. Part of that job is great fun. But another part isn't great. I'm sorry to say, son, that what brings me here to speak with you this morning is the part of the job that isn't so great." He looked up at the principal. "Do you understand what I mean, Eddie?"

Again, Eddie gulped, forcing his throat to swallow past the obstruction. Fear tickled his belly, and icy fingers twiddled in his guts. "I…I guess so," Eddie murmured, and his eyes fell to his own shoes. There was a spot on the toe of his left sneaker. Something brown and greasy.

Chief Morton put a big, meaty hand on his shoulder and gave him a little squeeze. "Something's happened, son. It's not good news, I'm afraid."

Without looking up, Eddie nodded.

"Do you have any family here in Cottonwood Vale? Beside your folks, I mean? I don't recall any other families named Mitchell living in town."

Again, Eddie bobbed his head without raising his gaze from his sneakers.

The principal cleared his throat and took a small step forward. "His aunt and uncle live out on Salt Road. The Rathersons."

Morton glanced over his shoulder at the principal. "You might want to notify them, then. And you might've mentioned this earlier." The chief's tone was what Eddie's mom would have called "a mite surly."

"Yes," said the principal. "I guess I should have."

"Why don't you go call them now?"

"Yes." The principal spun and took a stride toward his office.

"It might be best if Eddie and I continue our conversation in the privacy of your office, Principal Skinner."

The principal paused mid-step but didn't look back. "Yes, of course."

The chief turned to Eddie once more, and again rested his hand on his shoulder. "Come on, son. Let's go in Principal Skinner's office." As he rose, his knees popped like firecrackers, and he gave Eddie's shoulder another squeeze, then led him toward the principal's office.

He closed the door to the office behind him and guided Eddie toward one of the two chairs that stood in front of Skinner's big desk. The big man sat in the chair next to him and leaned forward. "Now, Eddie, I've got bad news. Terrible news, but we are going to take care of you, so I don't want you to worry. Cottonwood Vale is a small town, and we don't let our own fall to the wayside." He cleared his throat, and the harsh sound made Eddie cringe. Morton eyed him for a moment and then glanced away. "I'm sure your aunt and uncle will be here soon. It might be best if we wait until they arrive."

Eddie looked up into the big man's face and shook his head. "No, sir," he said. "I have to know. *Before* Uncle Gil gets here." He didn't *want* to learn what had happened, but something inside his mind screamed and screamed and screamed. He wanted to shut that screaming voice up.

"Are you sure?" The police chief pursed his lips.

Eddie nodded.

"Well, then. I don't care to share this kind of news with anyone, let alone with a nine-year-old, but you have a right to the information, same as everyone else." The chief leaned back in the chair and ran his hands through his hair, letting a sigh gust into the space between them. "Your mom and dad... There's no easy way to tell you this, son. There are no words to soften this. Your parents are gone, and I'm sorry as all get-out, but they are. I'm sorry to be the one who has to explain it to you, but as I said before: it's part of the job." He wound down, and silence settled between them.

Eddie stared up into the big man's face. "Gone?"

John Morton nodded.

"But... Where?"

Morton's eyes closed, and he gave his head a little shake. "I'm sorry, son. I meant your parents are gone, but not gone on a trip or anything."

Eddie cut his gaze away. "You mean *gone* gone. Gone the same way as my grandma and my uncle Davie."

The police chief sighed. "Yes, Eddie, I suppose that's right. Gone like your grandma and your uncle Davie."

"Gone to heaven?" Eddie gazed steadily into the policeman's eyes. Even at nine, Eddie could see a lie in a person's gaze.

Chief Morton looked away. "Your mother, Eddie, I'm sure she's there."

"And my father?" Eddie's gaze didn't waver.

The police chief made one of those little shrugs people make with their heads—tipping it first to the right, and then back to the left—the kind of gesture that said, "I don't believe what I'm about to say." He leaned forward and rested his elbows on his knees. "Yes, Eddie, I'm sure of it."

Only then did Eddie let his gaze drift away. His attention waddled around the room, drifting from item to item, from place to place, from book to book, until he'd seen every little thing in the principal's office. One shelf contained knickknacks: trophies, small plastic toys, a baseball, two Revell models of muscle cars, and three books standing between two bookends carved from dark wood. Eddie's eyes snagged on the toys for the briefest of moments, then traveled to the models, and went to the books last. A hundred hands had worn the leather on their gilded spines, but Skinner had allowed no dust to gather on them.

Chief Morton had lied right then. Eddie understood that by the way he glanced away and the little head-shrug. Eddie was only nine, but he wasn't stupid.

"Do you have any questions, son?" asked Morton in a quiet, somber voice.

"How?" That's all he wanted to know. Eddie felt numb on the inside—empty, as if someone had taken an ice cream scoop and scooped his feelings out along with all his innards.

"Well, now," murmured Morton. "Son, I've been doing this a long time. Sometimes it's better to remember our loved ones as they were most of the time, rather than in the last moments of that life."

Eddie shook his head but didn't take his attention off the gilded spines of the principal's books. "How?"

Someone knocked, and the chief sighed with relief. "Come."

Principal Skinner poked his head inside the door. "Gil and Margo Ratherson are on their way up." His gaze tracked toward Eddie's, who had finally looked away from the books on the shelf. "Everything all right in here?"

"Ayup," said John Morton.

"Anything I can help with, Chief?"

"No, we'll wait for the aunt and uncle."

Eddie dropped his attention to his feet. Aunt Margo was his mother's sister, and she was okay, but Uncle Gil... Uncle Gil hated Eddie. He always called Eddie names such as "brat" or "rug-rat" when they were alone together. He *never* called him by name.

Eddie didn't want to see Uncle Gil. Not with...*things*...being what they were. But Salt Road wasn't that far from the school.

Eddie's eyes darted to the principal's door as Skinner began to close it. "I could just leave," he said.

"No, son," said Morton. "A time such as this...you need to be with people who love you."

Eddie dropped his head, and Morton's gaze snapped up to Skinner's. He raised his eyebrows, asking a silent question. Skinner shrugged.

"Don't you care for your aunt and uncle, Eddie?" asked Skinner.

Eddie stood for a heartbeat before shrugging.

"Is there... Has anything ever..."

Eddie twitched his head to the side. "No stranger danger, Principal Skinner."

"Well. Okay, then." Skinner pulled the door closed with a gentle click.

"Don't get along with your aunt?" asked Morton.

"No, Aunt Margo is just fine."

"Ah. Your uncle then?"

Eddie cocked his head, marveling at how much the news of his parents' deaths *didn't* hurt. "Calls me names," he muttered.

"Ah, son." Morton scratched his eyebrow. "Some people show affection by teasing. I had an uncle that—"

"He's not teasing. He's *never* teasing."

"Oh. Sometimes it's hard for a kid to recognize when an adult is pulling their leg."

Eddie half-turned and returned his eyes to the spines of those leather-wrapped books. The titles were in a language other than English. "What does 'Über das Pathos der Wahrheit' mean?"

"Son, you got me there. I never learned German, and even if I had, I doubt this Nietzsche guy would be someone a cop would read."

"It must be about war. Something about the path to war."

"Why would you say that?" Morton asked.

"'Pathos der Wahrheit.' Sounds like 'path to war' to me."

"As I said, I don't speak German."

"Hmm," Eddie breathed. "What about 'Die Geburt der Tragödie?' Got any idea about that one?"

"No, son."

"Principal Skinner likes weird books."

"Yeah, I'd go along with that. But just look at those muscle cars!"

One of the models was a 1970 Mustang, painted metallic sky blue with white stripes. The other was a big, black convertible.

"What's that one?" asked Eddie, pointing at the convertible.

"Ah, now, son, that shows you appreciate fine automobiles. That right there is a 1966 Lincoln Continental. Ain't she a beaut?"

Eddie shifted his attention to the big police chief.

"That particular model car has what's called suicide—" Morton closed his mouth with a snap and a small shake of his head.

"What?" asked Eddie, turning toward him. The cop's face blazed red, and he wouldn't meet Eddie's gaze. *Ah*, thought Eddie. *Suicide. Both of them?*

Eddie knew what it meant. He didn't know how, or why he did, but the word made him think of his father's brother, Uncle Davie, and conversations overheard through his parents' bedroom door.

"Well, see the back doors don't open the way a regular car door does. You see, hinged at the front, opens at the rear?"

Eddie grunted.

"On that model, the rear doors hinge at the back and open from the front. They got a bad nickname along the way because in the beginning, they had a tendency to come open during accidents. But never mind that."

"Did my mom die of suicide?" Eddie asked, watching Morton's face.

The chief's eyelids slid shut. For a heartbeat, he seemed angry, but only for a moment, and not at Eddie. He shook his head as if exhausted. "No, Eddie," he said. "Your mother did not commit suicide."

"My father, then? He committed suicide?"

Chief Morton looked as if he wanted to be somewhere else. Anywhere else. "Should we wait for your aunt and uncle?"

"No," said Eddie in a lifeless voice. "No. Tell me."

Again, Morton's eyes slid shut for a brief time. He opened his mouth, but before he spoke, the door banged open and Eddie's aunt charged through it.

"Oh, Eddie!" she cried and wrapped him a huge hug.

She smelled a little of the barn—of cattle and cow manure and hay and dust—and Eddie had to suppress a sneeze. "Hi, Auntie Margo," he managed.

"Oh, Eddie!" she said in a mournful voice. "I'm so sorry! I'm just so sorry!"

"Hey, kid," said Uncle Gil from the doorway. He hadn't changed from his work clothes, and straw dust covered him. Muddy boots covered his feet.

"Hi, Uncle Gil."

"This is quite a mess, eh, kid?"

"Yeah." Eddie nestled his head on Aunt Margo's shoulder. "Yeah," he sighed. The numbness that had protected him so far was fading. Terror gripped him—he didn't want to feel anything, not today. He believed he might die if he did.

"Chief," said Uncle Gil, by way of greeting.

"Mr. Ratherson."

"Ted did it, did he?"

"We should talk about it in the hall. Let Mrs. Ratherson and Eddie mourn in peace."

"Oh, sure," said Uncle Gil, sounding surprised—as if the idea Eddie did not want to hear all the details about his parents' deaths had never crossed his mind.

But Eddie *needed* to hear those details. He waited as the two men left the office, still wrapped in his aunt's arms. "Auntie Margo, what happened to my mommy and my daddy?" Eddie whispered the words in her ear, and as he did, she sucked in a breath.

"Never mind, sweetie." She hugged him tighter.

"But I want to know, Auntie Margo. I *need* to know. I think…I think Daddy committed suicide. But I—"

"Who told you that?" asked Auntie Margo. She pulled back, but kept her hands on his shoulders, kept him right in front of her.

Eddie lifted his hands out to his sides.

"Did Chief Morton—"

"No, Chief Morton wouldn't tell me anything."

"Then why would you say that, honey?"

Eddie lifted his arm and pointed at the model of the 1966 Lincoln Continental convertible. "Suicide doors."

"Do you even understand what the word 'suicide' means?"

Eddie dropped his gaze to the carpet.

Margo's face crunched up, the way his mommy's had when something upset her. "How did you learn such a word, Eddie? Little boys your age shouldn't know words such as that."

"Uncle Davie…"

"Your father's brother? He died in the war, didn't he?"

Again, Eddie shrugged. "I heard Mommy and Daddy arguing one night. Daddy was crying, and he said something about Davie and then Mommy said 'suicide.'"

"Well. I'm sorry you had to hear that." Margo's face hardened. "No child should know things like that at your age."

Eddie looked at his shoes.

"You didn't do a thing wrong, dear heart. I just hate that you've heard that ugly word and know what it means." She pulled him close and smothered him in the musky odor of the barn and her shampoo. She rubbed his neck and made crooning noises in the back of her mouth. "Oh, Eddie, what are we going to do?"

It seemed she was crying, but Eddie couldn't tell for sure. An ache formed deep in his throat, and his stomach began to hurt. If he let it continue, his mind would betray him, and his body would follow. He couldn't allow that to happen. Not now. He had to stay in control, to keep his grief at bay.

I wish there was a big hole in my middle. A huge hole that I could shove…everything in it. With that thought, came an icy calm.

"Do you know how much your mother loved you, Eddie?" Margo sniffed and rubbed his back all the harder.

Eddie nodded against her shoulder but kept his mind on that gap in his middle. He imagined it was so deep that he couldn't sense the bottom, that all he could see was a velvety blackness. His eyes drifted to the fancy leather-bound books on Principal Skinner's shelves. His gaze caressed the model muscle cars, the plastic toys. He examined the baseball, his gaze lingering on the red stitches and the scuff mark on the side. The trophies didn't interest him much, but the way the light glinted on the faux-gold cups *was* interesting.

"Your father, too, I guess."

Deep inside, a powerful emotion stirred within Eddie. He snapped his gaze away from the trophies. When it reached the carved wooden bookends, something within him quivered with excitement. The scene carved into the old dark wood looked like a snippet of time right out of *Little Red Riding Hood*—a huge wolf with drool dripping from his jaws twined around a child.

"And you know I love you, Eddie."

Eddie lifted his chin but kept his mouth shut and his eyes on the carved bookends.

"I hope we can keep you. I believe we can raise you how your mother would have liked. But…" Margo hitched her shoulders, and her rough work shirt rubbed against Eddie's cheek—not an unpleasant sensation, but a *different* sensation. "Well, you know how your Uncle Gil is. He… He…likes everything his own way."

Again, Eddie stood in her embrace, as silent as a mouse, and his eyes caressed the spines of those leather-bound books again.

Margo pulled back and gazed into his face. "You believe that, don't you, Eddie? You understand that if I had it my way, there would be no question. Right, Eddie?"

Eddie knew he was supposed to respond, that Auntie Margo was waiting for him to answer. But his insides felt locked up, frozen. He guessed it was part of the cold numbness, and because of that, he didn't try to unlock them.

Uncle Gil opened the door and stepped inside Principal Skinner's office, closing it behind him. His gaze skimmed past without meeting Eddie's and came to rest on his wife's face. "Margo, we should talk out in the hall."

"Gil… We can't just leave the boy by himself, not today."

Uncle Gil's expression clouded over as though a thunderstorm gathered, darkening the sky. "Now, Margo. We *need* to talk."

Auntie Margo's upper lip trembled. Her gaze met Eddie's and then darted away. She gave him one final squeeze and stood. "Gil, the boy's been through quite a lot. I think—"

"No, you don't. You don't think." Gil's voice was nasty, and his face was all scrunched up in a sneer. He took a step and made it seem menacing.

Eddie couldn't stand the sight of him. He had never seen it before, but Uncle Gil was cut from the same hateful cloth as his father, only Uncle Gil didn't hide it. *How have I not noticed that before?*

"Outside, Margo," commanded Gil. "Get outside now."

Eddie glanced at his aunt's face. The tremble in her lip had become a quaver, and a small muscle above her eye began to twitch.

"Yes, Gil." Margo hustled toward the door, but as she reached for the knob, Gil grabbed her wrist and his knuckles went white with the strength of it. "Gil," said Margo in a voice most people would take as calm, but in the icy coldness of his numb emotions, she sounded terrified to Eddie.

Gil released her with a glance in Eddie's direction that again didn't meet his gaze, then snapped the door open. He took Margo by the elbow and ushered her out. "We'll be right back, kid."

As the door snicked shut behind them, Eddie looked around. The quietness of the office seemed oppressive. On the wall across from the knickknacks, hung a print of the painting depicting a golden angel staring up into the face of a red-winged devil. The memory of the scary lady flashed through his mind, and Eddie shuddered and looked away.

He didn't want to think, he didn't want to imagine what Gil was saying to Margo out in the hall, but he couldn't help it. They hadn't seen Gil and Margo very much, despite living in the same town, despite living close enough to walk to their house in twenty minutes. Only on holidays, and not even all of them.

Auntie Margo always made an excuse, but Eddie understood the truth. He tried to tell Chief Morton, but the man hadn't gotten it. Uncle Gil *hated* Eddie. There was no other answer—at least, not one that Eddie could dredge up.

He felt bad. He didn't like the idea that his mother and her sister hadn't been able to spend time together because of him.

I ruin everything!

The strong emotions that he kept pushing into the velvety black hole inside of him pushed back hard and threatened to run wild. He fought the tears, both those of anguish and frustration, and he turned his gaze to the knickknack shelf. When he got older, he was going to buy a Continental identical to the one on the shelf. One with suicide doors.

What am I going to do? Where will I live? Who will make me dinner? Where will I sleep? Icy fingers of dread pawed at his guts. He tried to shove those questions into the black hole inside of him, but they wouldn't go. Maybe they didn't fit with all his other feelings already in there.

He went to stand by the door and pressed his ear to it. It was a trick he learned a year ago, when his mother and father were talking about Uncle Davie behind the closed door of their bedroom. His mother had called it "eavesdropping" and had told him it was impolite, but Eddie didn't care. He had a right to know what Gil was saying about him.

The voices in the hall were muffled, indistinct, as if they were having a heated argument in whispers. But, even so, he heard Uncle Gil say "no" several times.

In the vast empty space at his center, his feelings stirred and thumped, fighting to get out. For the first time that day, tears squelched into his eyes. The lump in his throat was back, the cold sickness in his belly, too. Strong emotions lurched and thrashed in his guts, banging against the lip of the crater within him. He imagined ugly purple tentacles slithering up over the edge, grasping at anything nearby and pulling tight.

In his mind's eye, the velvety blackness inside the hole bulged and squirmed as though it were a black cloth over a jar of snakes that were all trying to escape. He fought it. He fought it with all his psychic strength. He didn't want to be at the mercy of those emotions, not after adding his feelings about Uncle Gil and Auntie Margo to the mix.

In the hall, Auntie Margo gasped, and it sounded like a gasp of pain. Then, he clearly heard Uncle Gil say, "Now, why'd you make me do that?" It was something he'd heard his father hiss at his mother many, many times over the past year. Most often when he was drunk, and there was no more beer in the refrigerator. The next day, his mother would have a bruise on her upper arm or on her cheek, but she never said a word about it. Not even when he asked her, she would just shake her head and hold up her hand in that way she had that told him to stop asking.

He didn't want to be there anymore. Not in Principal Skinner's office, not in school, not in Cottonwood Vale, not in Western New York, and not on Planet Earth. *Suicide*, he thought, and as he did so, the thing lurching around in the hole inside of him broke free.

His throat burned as if he'd swallowed hot coals, but in his belly, winter reigned. He fought nausea; he fought the urge to expel his breakfast all over Principal Skinner's carpet. His eyes darted around, looking for the trashcan…looking for somewhere to puke.

Powerful emotions—the horrible, gut-wrenching sadness, the fear of being abandoned—hit him full force. He imagined it hit him the way one of those category five hurricanes descended on the west coast of Florida where his grandma and grandpa had lived. His emotion threatened to drown him, to pull him under into a watery grave. He stood very still, struggling to contain his emotions, fighting the sob that wanted to escape his lips, battling to keep the tears in his eyes and off his cheeks. He rested his hand on the doorknob, leaning on it for support while he gasped for breath.

When he lost the fight against his tears, he turned the knob without deciding to do so. He flung the door open, his feet already moving, and he raced past a surprised Uncle Gil and Auntie Margo. Margo was crying, but quietly, oh so quietly. Gil's face reminded Eddie of Jack McGregor's—the school bully who'd been held back twice in the first grade and was so huge compared to the other kids in his class. Margo's hand reached for him, but it was a moment too late.

He burst into the public part of the front office, his eyes taking it all in in one quick snapshot. Principal Skinner's expression of surprise, and the concern that painted Chief Morton's face. The two men stood between him and the door to the outside world.

"Eddie—" began Principal Skinner, but Eddie was already shaking his head.

He tried to run between them, but John Morton, the huge policeman, scooped him up with one massive arm and hugged him tight in a great big bear hug. "It's all right, son. It's okay to cry. Don't you worry none." His voice was soft— warm and kind—and it brought Eddie's mother to the front of his mind.

At first, Eddie struggled, but Chief Morton's strong hug didn't relax one single bit. The man didn't seem to mind that Eddie was kicking and shoving at him, trying to get away, trying to push the man away.

"It's all right, son. Everything will be good again, just give it time. You'll see I'm right. In the meantime, you just cry. You get it all out."

Gradually, Eddie relaxed into the big man's embrace. Through tear-filled eyes, he saw the scary lady smiling at him from the shadows in the vestibule.

6

May 1977

Sean loved Friday afternoons. Especially in the late spring. He reveled in the feeling that coursed through him as the last bell rang, the excitement about the coming weekend, the anticipation of seeing what the two school-free days had in store for him. He bounced down the hall with the other students, his mind a thousand miles away. Sean didn't notice as the noise level of the mob dropped to almost nothing. When someone tapped his shoulder, Sean jumped.

"Hi, Sean," said Dennis Cratchkin. "I've been meaning to catch up with you."

Sean's head spun side to side, looking for an escape, for a teacher, for anybody who might help him. There was nowhere to go and, as usual, there were no teachers around when he needed one. As far as anyone helping him, no one would even glance his direction. He sighed and slumped his shoulders. "Look, Dennis, I didn't—"

"No, no. Wait a minute, Sean. Look, I owe you an apology. All that junk back then... Well, I was having a hard time. I'm really sorry about that stuff behind the school, and I've let all that go."

"I…" Sean stopped walking, and Dennis stood next to him. *Smiling.*

"Listen, Sean. I realize you don't have any reason to forgive me, but I was hoping we could be friends. Losing—" Dennis choked up and looked down. "Last Halloween changed me, man. It's been tough, but it made me take a hard look at myself, at what Jasper, Ari, and me used to do." He wiped his hand across his eyes, still staring at the floor. "Anyway. If you can forgive me, I'd be in your debt. If you want to be buddies, just tell me. That's all I wanted to say."

Sean stood there, too stunned to speak, and after a moment, Dennis shrugged and walked away. The crowd of students streamed by as well, and still, Sean stood there staring after Dennis.

7

June 1977

"Leif, I want more," slurred Kristy from the couch she lay on. Her unbuttoned blouse fell to either side, showing off her flat belly but still covering her breasts. She wore panties, but nothing else.

Leif came to stand over her, looking down with assessing eyes.

"What?" she asked. His stare made her feel like a bug, like something he didn't give two shits about.

"It's almost time," Leif said.

"Time for what?"

He gave no answer. Instead, he turned and walked to the cabinet where he kept his stash. He brought out the small, black leather bag that looked so much like a doctor's kit she'd used to tease him about it. She didn't tease him, though. Now, the sight of the bag excited her.

"Are you too far gone to cook this yourself?" Leif asked.

"But I'm so comfortable here…"

He shook his head but chuckled. "Fine, sleeping beauty. I'll cook it. I'll even stick you, but it will cost you."

Kristy shifted her position so she could spread her legs. "I'll pay. Gladly."

Leif winked at her and set about cooking the heroin and setting up the needle. In the beginning, she hadn't liked the needles, but now, as with the bag, the sight of it sent shivers of anticipation roaring through her.

Kristy waited until he turned back to her to lift her butt off the couch and slip out of her panties. "I'll pay you twice?" she asked, a smile playing on her lips and unadorned lust dancing in her eyes.

8

June 1977

Owen Gray bellied up to the bar next to the stunning young woman. He wore faded blue jeans with worn-out knees, a black T-shirt, and a pair of once-white Converse high-tops. She wore black. Black leather skirt, black silk blouse, black three-quarter length coat—even though it was summer, and the evening was warm. Her nails were painted black, and to Owen's mind, it was the perfect contrast to her swarthy skin and dark eyes. Her raven-black hair cascaded down her back in heavy, luxurious looking strands. "Mmm," he said, drawing her scent into his nose.

She glanced at him—just once, and only a nanosecond long. "No."

Owen dimpled. "Now, don't be that way. I meant it as a compliment." She rocked her head to the side and peered at him from under a curtain of thick black hair, and to Owen, her gaze danced across his nerves like a low-voltage current applied to his testicles.

She squinted at him for a moment, then half-turned on her barstool to face him. "What's your name, cowboy?"

"Cowboy, eh? I kinda dig that." He flashed his best smile. "Call me Randy."

She arched a perfect eyebrow at him and drew her head away, as though she were farsighted and wanted a better look at his features. She crossed one leg over the other and smirked as Owen's gaze descended for a quick peek at her lower half. When he looked up again, she grinned at him and winked.

"Barefoot? I dig that." Owen chuckled. "I'd go shoeless if I had the legs to get away with it. Then again, I'm a guy, so that would never happen."

She favored him with a slow blink, tilting her head as though about to be kissed.

It was then that he noticed her hair was more than black, it appeared to be a dark hue of blue. His gaze slid to her tiny, elfin ears, then continued down the side of her neck, lingering over her carotid artery as if her pulse were visible.

"Are you a vampire, Randy?" she asked in a husky voice as erotic as pure sex.

"What? No, I'm not a bloodsucker, but I do love nuzzling a beautiful neck."

"A girl might think that's fresh." A slow, lazy smile touched her lips. "But you never answered me."

He scrunched his brow and leaned his head to the side. "What didn't I answer?"

"I asked your name."

His grin returned, and his forehead smoothed. "Oh, that. Maybe you didn't hear me with all this noise. Call me Randy."

She shook her head in a small way, almost not moving at all. "No. Your *name*."

Owen pulled his face away, his forehead wrinkled in his confusion. "But I—"

"*No*," she said with iron in her tone.

How can she know? he asked himself. "Randy is my—"

"No, it isn't. If you won't share your name with me, I guess I'll go back to my cocktail." She tilted her head, letting her glossy black hair drape down her neck. "My *solitary* drink."

He swallowed hard and stared around as a ferret looking out for a badger would. "Don't do that," he whined.

"Then tell me."

"How..." He twitched his head to the side—only once, but in an abrupt motion that spoke of confusion. "How do you know?"

She smiled and winked at him. "Oh, the list of things I know would delight you." She uncrossed her legs and let her knees drift apart a few inches. "The things I can do," she crooned.

Owen swallowed hard, and, after a moment of keeping his gaze on her face to show he respected her, dropped it to her legs and followed the gentle curve of her inner thigh toward her crotch. "Owen," he breathed when he discovered she wasn't wearing panties.

"Well, hello, Owen," she said in a voice that made promises directed at his libido, while at the same time struggled to contain her mirth. "Are we going to be friends?"

"You…" Owen gulped. "You can't tell anyone. I'm…" Again, he looked around like a rodent. "I'm lying low."

She lifted her chin, and her eyes danced. "That doesn't appear to be true, *Randy*. Not at all."

His cheeks burned, and he ducked his gaze away from her. "Sorry. It's just…"

"I remind you of someone?"

"Yes, and no." She laughed, and for a moment, Owen thought the strands of her hair twined about each other like snakes. Her teeth faded to black and sharpened into fangs, but only for a heartbeat, then everything was back to normal. Owen shook his head, his mind rambling through time to Vietnam, to the jungle.

The woman leaned forward, and her musk almost stole his feet from under him. "Her scent lingers on you, Randy."

"Wh-who?"

Her lips stretched in a knowing smile. "I can smell…this 'Candy' girl you bedded."

Owen had the idea that she'd been about to say something else and was about to call her on it when she spread her knees a little more. His pulse slammed in his veins like a racehorse coming out of the gate. "Who *are* you?"

"Call me Abby," she said with a grin and leaned closer to him, nipping his ear lobe and brushing her breasts against his chest.

The irony of her phrasing was not lost on Owen, but he simply didn't care.

9

July 1977

Warm night air wafted across the back of Dennis Cratchkin's neck like a mother's loving caress. He again wore his balaclava, his black clothes, and his backpack. Crouched at the edge of Thousand Acre Wood, he stared at Mr. Dubrovnik's house as the lights went off one by one.

Almost time, he thought. *Got to be careful, got to do it just the way Red taught me.* He'd skipped the evening's fireworks show—he had his own fireworks in mind. His hand strayed to the set of lock picks the big man had given him and trained in their use. He winced at the ache in his shoulder—the latest "lesson" his father had wanted to teach him. *Why couldn't Red be my dad?*

He shook his head, shaking away errant thoughts. He shouldn't need the lock picks, but as Red always said, better to have and not use them than need and not have them. Dennis peeled the cuff of his long-sleeved shirt back and read the phosphorescent dial of his new Timex—another gift from Red. He reset the shirtsleeve, covering the watch, and raised his gaze to Dubrovnik's home once more.

Nothing moved inside the boxy residence, and not a single light remained on. Dubrovnik lived alone with only a little yip-yip dog for company. Dennis figured he was gay or a creeper or something.

It wasn't the first time he'd sat in that very spot, watching Dubrovnik's house. Red insisted that he learn the man's routine and that he prepare for all possibilities. Dennis drank Red's wisdom in, reveled in it.

Right on cue, the bedroom lamp snapped on. Then the hall light, followed by the den, and finally, the spotlight above the deck. The slider opened, and the little yip-yip fucker came trotting down the steps to the small plot of grass. Dennis smirked, anticipating what was to come. Dubrovnik kept the same schedule every night—he went to bed and then ten minutes later got up to let the dog out. It had happened each time that Dennis had watched his house.

If he'd never met Red, he'd never have had the balls to try what he would pull off that evening. If he'd never listened to Red, he'd have been in the middle of the yard when Dubrovnik came outside...and that would've spelled disaster.

The yippy mutt stepped on the leg trap and screeched as its steel jaws snapped on the dog's foreleg. Dennis's smile grew vicious. He *hated* little dogs like that. Red hadn't told him to do it, but Dennis had spent a few hours preparing the trap. A few hours' labor had made the device *special*, had ensured the dog would die from the encounter.

The dog panicked—and why not? Dennis had sharpened the jaws of the trap and beefed up the spring, so that not only would it trap the mutt, it would break its front leg and cut it to the bone—maybe even amputate the limb. The dog yelped and screamed, jerking its injured limb—and the trap—to the extent of the chain Dennis had used to secure the trap to one of the posts holding up Dubrovnik's deck.

The slider opened. "What is it, Beauty? Is there a fox?" called Dubrovnik as he raced for the stairs, except it came out sounding like: "Vat is id, Beaudy? Is der a fucks?"

Dennis sneered and wrinkled his nose. *Stupid fuck should learn how to speak English.*

Dennis's former math teacher pounded down the steps, his fat belly jiggling. He was barefoot and dressed in his boxers, as Dennis knew he would be. The dog's cries grew weaker and weaker, its frantic struggle to free itself from the trap devolved into nothing more than feeble tugs at its leg. As Dubrovnik hit the grass, the dog keeled over on its side and whimpered.

"Oh, my Beauty! What has happened?" Dubrovnik ran toward the dog and made it a few steps before setting off one of Dennis's big bear traps. "Holy Mother of God!" the man screamed.

That's my cue, Dennis thought. Moving silently as Red had taught him, he left the cover of the woods. He carried the instrument of Dubrovnik's doom in his hands. It had cost him three months' worth of chores and allowance, but it was worth it.

Dubrovnik had bent over to examine his trapped leg—putting his head in the perfect position for a killing blow from the splitting maul.

10

August 1977

"How can you even ask me that, Leif?" asked Kristy. She swung her legs off the bed and fished in the dark for her jeans.

"Oh, come on, Kristy. It's no big deal. Haven't you ever heard of 'free love?' I bet your mother has."

"Leif!"

"I'm joking!"

"About the whole thing?"

"Yeah, it was just a joke."

Kristy huffed but stopped feeling around on the floor for her clothes. "Not a hilarious one."

"I guess not," Leif said. "Let me make it up to you."

"How?"

He sat up and rubbed her shoulders. "I've got something fresh."

"New?"

"You'll love it."

"Better than the heroin?"

"Much better than horse. Ever heard of LSD?"

"No. What's that?"

"People call it 'acid.' Trust me, you're going to worship it. No needles. You just put a bit of jelly under your tongue and away you go."

"Then what?"

"Then, we do whatever you choose to do."

"Even if we don't…"

"Whatever you want, Kristy."

"Okay."

"You forgive my stupid joke?"

"Okay," she repeated.

Leif crawled out of the bed and went into his bathroom.

"Hey, Leif, where's your dad been all this time?"

"What?"

"Where's your dad?"

"Oh. Government shit. Don't worry about him, he won't come home anytime soon."

"Oh," she said.

Leif came back into the room holding a tiny plastic bag. "This will make you feel like the queen of the universe."

"Good," she said, accepting a square of gelatin under her tongue. "Now what do I do?"

"Just wait."

Kristy shrugged and put her arms behind her head. "Nothing's happening."

"It is, trust me. Think of something fun—flying, floating on a cloud, whatever you want."

"Okay..." she said, sounding anything but convinced. But twenty minutes later, she sat up and looked at Leif, wide-eyed. "Oh my God."

"Right?"

She giggled. "This is..."

"Yeah, it is." He came to sit next to her on the bed. "So, what do you want to do?"

She rolled her head toward him. "What do you think?"

"That's my girl," he said with a laugh. "Be back."

"Where...are you...going?"

"I'll be right back. Don't worry about a thing, Kristy."

"Yeah," she said with a sigh. The acid blurred her mind, painting pretty pictures on top of reality.

The bedroom door opened and closed. Someone got into bed with her, and she slid under them. She didn't realize it wasn't Leif—didn't recognize that it was a grown man—until it was over, and even then, she hardly cared.

The drug didn't let her.

II

August 1977

Toby frowned as his mom's new boyfriend carried box after box into their house on Mill Lane. The home wasn't a big one, and though Randy had pretended to be nice to him when Toby's mom was around, he'd hinted that things would change once he moved in.

"Come help, Toby," said Candy from the front step. "There's not much more."

Toby didn't move, didn't answer her.

"Say now!" said Randy. "Show some respect for your mother, boy."

"It's okay, Randy. He's getting his hormones is all."

Randy and Candy, Toby thought with derision. *How goddamn cute. I think I'll just puke.*

Randy approached him, his face hidden from Candy's view and twisted with sullen anger. "Toby!" he snapped. "I'm speaking to you." He dropped a hand on Toby's shoulder and squeezed, fingertips digging into Toby's flesh. "Don't stand there and sneer at me when I'm talking to you."

Toby stared up at him, unable to keep his emotions buried, and Randy squinted down at him, not bothering to hide his anger. His mom came up behind Randy and lay her hand on his arm.

"Let's not let him spoil it, Randy. He's just jealous that he doesn't get me all to himself anymore."

With a laugh for Candy's benefit, Randy released him, but the expression he wore promised they'd return to the conversation in the future.

Toby ducked his head to the side, not wanting to show fear. For half a heartbeat, he glimpsed a woman made only of fire standing in the corner staring at him.

Staring at him and *smiling*.

But then the image disappeared, and the corner held only cobwebs and shadows.

"Toby, it'll be a change for all of us. My living here," said Randy. "But we'll work on it. We'll make it work out, won't we? For your mom's sake?"

Toby nodded because he knew she expected it of him. Something about Randy wasn't right, but Toby was only ten, and he didn't know what it was or how to tell his mother even if he did.

Dread settled into his belly and put down roots.

12

August 1977

Eddie's stomach lurched when he saw Uncle Gil's Dodge pickup parked in the handicapped space in front of Doctor Erikson's office, and his feet slowed to a stop. Auntie Margo picked him up most of the time. He didn't want to spend the car ride home trying to turn invisible, crammed up next to the door staring out the window. *Why couldn't Auntie Margo come?*

Eddie winced as the Dodge's horn blatted. He peeked at Uncle Gil and grimaced. Gil sat glowering at him from the driver's seat. His mouth moved—probably calling him names. He had hesitated too long and angered Gil. *Great. Now he won't ignore me on the ride home.*

His uncle waved furiously and punched the center of the steering wheel of his old truck. This time, he held his hand there, loosing a blatting, continuous claxon in the quiet afternoon.

Eddie blushed to the roots of his hair and dropped his gaze. He started himself moving again, but not fast enough for his uncle.

Gil opened his window and stuck his head out. "Get a move on, brat! You think I've got all day to waste? You think I don't have things to do?"

Eddie looked at his feet as he trotted to the passenger door. He tried to open it, but it was locked. He stood there for a moment, his hand lying on the truck's door handle, not daring to look through the window. After a moment he pulled the handle again without success.

With a sigh, Eddie raised his eyes. Gil sat cocked to the side in the driver's seat, back resting against the door, his arm stretched over the back of the seat. He glowered at Eddie.

Eddie lifted his hand off the handle and rapped on the glass. The expression on his uncle's face didn't change. Gil's gaze never left his own, and the man just sat there, staring. Eddie turned his face away and knocked again. Gil still didn't unlock it. Sometimes he got that way—to make a point or something. Eddie knocked a third time. "Please, Uncle Gil."

"Pwease, Uncle Gil," he mocked.

Eddie shook his head. *Great. That's real grown-up of you.*

"No, sir!" snapped Gil. "You don't shake your head at me, brat. You understand me?"

If only Doctor Erikson could see him this way. Then he would stop trying to teach me how to talk it out, how to meet

Gil halfway. As if Uncle Gil was interested in meeting *anyone* halfway. "Sorry, Uncle Gil."

"Sowwy, Uncle Gil."

He almost did it again. He had already turned his head to the side when he realized what he was doing and stopped. He tried to play it off, to pretend that he was just looking into the parking lot.

"Do you think I'm teasing? You think I didn't mean it when I tell you not to shake your head at me?"

"No, sir." Eddie dropped his gaze to the asphalt. "I don't always—"

"I don't guess I care to listen to your excuses today, rug-rat. You've wasted enough of my time."

Then unlock the stupid door, jerk. Eddie tried to keep his face flat, a slab of stone.

"And whatever it is you're thinking, you can just shove it up your tight little ass, brat." With sharp, angry movements, Gil lunged across the cab of the truck and pulled the lock. He sat there stretching across the seat, glaring at Eddie through the window.

Eddie stared right back, keeping his face as still as if cast from bronze. *I'm not stupid. I'll never open this door with you sitting there waiting like a snake.*

As if he could read Eddie's mind, Gil cocked his head, a butcher's grin on his lips, then moved across to the driver's side. He settled himself in front of the steering wheel and treated Eddie to a slow wink and a smug smile.

Eddie watched him for a moment, then opened the door, but he didn't get in right away. "Sorry, Uncle Gil, that I kept you waiting. I was messing around with Doctor Erikson. Sometimes I pretend to be a shrink, and he..." Gil's face scrunched with impatience, and Eddie knew better than to keep going. "Anyway, I thought Auntie Margo was coming for me today, and she's always late."

"From the mouths of babes," said Gil with a chuckle. "But don't let your Auntie Margo hear you saying something such as that. She might fricassee you like a chicken. We wouldn't want that."

Eddie flashed him a tentative smile and grabbed the edge of the cushion to pull himself up into the cab. "No, sir. I try to avoid being fricasseed whenever I can."

"Oh, he's got jokes."

Eddie slid into the passenger seat and reached for the door to draw it closed.

Quick as a snake, Gil's fist shot across the cab and slammed into Eddie's arm below his shoulder.

"Ow, Uncle Gil! That hurt!"

"Oh, quit your whining. It was a little tap, all in fun." Gil turned to Eddie, the smug smile stretching across his face. "Besides, you made me wait."

"But I said I was sorry!"

Gil shrugged and laughed. "Oh, is that all it takes? Well, I'm sorry, rug-rat."

Eddie rubbed his arm, looking straight out the windshield and grinding his teeth.

Gil chuckled in his nasty way. "Yeah, I don't think much of your apologies either, brat. Now close the damn door, so we can get out of here."

Life under his uncle's roof had become one horrendous nightmare after another.

Anger simmered in Eddie's blood as he reached for the door and slammed it shut. He tucked his arms across his chest and stared out the passenger window.

Gil chuckled again. "Don't think that silent treatment cuts bait with me, boy. Margo used to try that crap, and as you may have noticed, she don't do it no more." Gil cranked the ignition, pumping the gas pedal, and after a moment, the pickup roared to life. He backed out of the parking space and into the cloud of nauseating blue smoke.

Eddie coughed and covered his mouth and nose with his hand.

"Stinks, don't it?" asked Gil. "Maybe if we didn't have to spend all our money taking you to doctors, I could afford a truck that didn't burn oil. Maybe if I didn't have to shell out for food and clothes and every other damn thing under God's great blue sky, I wouldn't have to work so damn hard just to keep a ratty old pickup truck running." Gil glanced at him as he pulled out onto the main road. "What do you think about that, brat?"

Eddie kept his mouth shut and stared out the window.

"Nothing to say?" Gil rolled down his window and spat through it. "Maybe all them people are wrong. Maybe snot-nosed kids can learn respect."

Eddie sneered at the buildings rushing past the glass.

"That fancy mind shrinker teach you that? The respect?"

Eddie froze, except for his face. He didn't want to be sitting there with a sneer frozen to his lips when Gil looked over to see why he was being so quiet.

"Well, shit. I guess that bastard is worth the money after all."

Unbidden, the conversation he'd had that day with Doctor Erikson scrolled through his mind. They'd talked about the scary lady, but only a little. She hadn't been around much in the past few weeks.

Or if she *was* around, Eddie hadn't seen her.

It was the longest stretch without her that Eddie could remember since… Well, for a long time. Erickson said it was because Eddie was learning to deal with his "stressors" and "emotional triggers"—whatever the heck that meant. Eddie wasn't so sure. He thought she might have just gotten bored.

"Are we sulking now, kid? I'm gonna have to toughen you up, aren't I?"

Eddie started to shake his head but stopped himself in time. "No, sir," he mumbled.

"Are you a mouse or a man? If you're a man, talk like a man."

"No, sir," Eddie said with more volume.

"'No, you aren't pouting,' or 'no, I do not need to toughen you up?'"

Bastard sounds as if he's having fun. Anger roiled in Eddie's guts. "No to both."

"Ah." Gil switched on the radio and then punched through the presets, leaving no chance to hear what was playing on the stations. With a grunt, he snapped the radio off. "Damn radio stations never have nothing good. Too busy sucking on the corporate tit." He shot Eddie an alligator smile. "Suppose we'll have to chat since the radio's a waste of time." He swung back to watch the road. "So, what do you say to that headshrinker, anyway?"

"Doctor Erikson said I don't have to tell anybody what we talk about."

"Oh, ho… I guess *Doctor* Erikson will feed you and clothe you and raise you up from now on? I guess I'm free and clear of the boat anchor that is your life?"

"What?"

"What? What?" Gil said in a mocking tone. He cackled his mean laugh, and Eddie's stomach fell. "Does Mister Doctor-Headshrinker get to override the fellow who puts food in your belly for nothing? The fellow who puts up with you, puts up with your moods, your bullshit? Is Mister Doctor-Headshrinker in charge of me now?"

Eddie didn't know how to answer, so he didn't do anything, he just stared out the window watching the scenery blur by.

"Whelp, I guess I don't care what Mister Doctor-Headshrinker says you do or don't have to do. Know why?"

Eddie wracked his mind, trying to come up with a plan to defuse what was turning into an ugly situation at the speed of light. Doctor Erikson always said he should try to see things from Uncle Gil's perspective. He came up with nothing.

"I can tell by the way you're sitting there with your thumb up your butt that you don't have any idea why. Good thing I'm here, because I know why, and I don't mind sharing. The reason I don't care what that snooty college boy says is because what he thinks means absolutely nothing to this old farmhand. Counseling, psychiatry." Gil snorted an ugly laugh. "All that's just coddling for the weak. Nonsense. Garbage that the Libs think will solve the world's problems, when what we need is someone willing to kick a little ass. I don't mind telling you, they're mistaken about all that. Well, I guess they've got most everything wrong." Gil grinned to himself and nodded.

Eddie tried to disappear into the truck's upholstery. *You get that I'm nine, right, dummy?*

"I'm waiting," said Gil. "Don't you know better than to keep me waiting?"

"We talk about the scary lady most of the time."

"That again?" Gil sneered. "Haven't I told you a thousand times to let go of that?" He scoffed. "I've heard of kids having invisible friends, but I've never heard another kid having an invisible…an imaginary bogeywoman or whatever she is to you. You need to just stop all that nonsense, then maybe we'll have a few dollar bills to rub together."

"He also says that I don't understand you. That I should try to see things from your side."

"I'll be damned. College boy's not half as stupid as I thought." Gil leered at him from the driver's seat.

"In fact, he said it might help if you were to come along for one of the sessions."

Gil scoffed and spat through his open window. "So much for having one or two brain cells. What the hell do I need to see a child psychologist for?"

"It's not for you—well, I guess it is sort of… He thinks that if we can talk in a neutral setting, that maybe we can work things out."

Gil turned his head to stare at Eddie, his face turning to stone. "Work things out? What in the hell are you telling him?"

"What?"

"You heard me. What do you tell him about me? What are you telling him about our family?"

"Nothing! I just—"

"Didn't I tell you that there were things you don't say nothin' to nobody about? Did I not?"

"I didn't, Uncle Gil! I promise—"

Gil slapped him on the back of the head. "Maybe you need not see that headshrinker no more. Not if you can't follow my rules, brat."

"No, sir! I didn't say anything! All I talked about was how I can't do anything without making you mad. He said… He said that I was just—"

Gil slapped him again. "What do you mean you can't do anything without making me mad? That makes me sound as though I'm as crazy as a loonie bird. Is that what you're trying to do in there with Mister Doctor-Headshrinker? Trying to get me in trouble?" Gil's voice had doubled in volume.

"No, Uncle Gil! I didn't make you out to be anything! I just told him I keep making you mad, same as I did my daddy, that it…bugs me."

"I ain't nothing like your old man, boy. Don't you ever compare me to him! Do I look like some damn weak-willed sack of guts?"

Should've kept my mouth shut. Should've sat there and let him rant at me. Should've lied, said we talked about school or something. Eddie sneered at himself. *Sure, think of all that now—now that it's too late.*

Gil was still staring at him, his eyes blazing, veins over his temples throbbing with every beat of his heart.

Eddie shook his head. "No, Uncle—"

Quick as a whip, Gil hit him for the fourth time, using his fist and winging his knuckles off the back of Eddie's skull. "I told you! I told you not to shake that head at me, you little brat! Did I not?"

Eddie winced at the volume of the shout and cringed away, pulling his hands up around his head. "I'm stupid! It's all my fault, Uncle Gil! I said it bad! I didn't mean to shake my head!" He snuck a peek at Uncle Gil. *Why can't I ever say the right thing? Why do I always make things worse?* The man's cheeks blazed red, and the veins in his temples throbbed to a staccato rhythm. He'd pulled his lips back in a parody of a smile, but hate and anger reigned in his eyes. *Why do I make him so furious? Why did I make Daddy so mad all the time? What's wrong with me?* Eddie glanced in the rearview mirror, and his breath caught in his throat. He twisted to stare over his shoulder and out through the rear window.

The scary lady stood in the bed of Uncle Gil's pickup, facing forward, her arms out at her sides as if she wanted to hug Eddie and Gil. For once, there were no shadows for her to hide in.

Her long black hair glinted in the afternoon sun, and for the first time, Eddie saw that her hair wasn't black. It was a deep shade of midnight blue, with dark purple highlights…the same colors that his mother's Tiffany lamp had adopted once the scary lady began visiting him.

As he watched, her hair started to writhe and twist, moving like a nest full of snakes. Her skin was dusky, but in the sun, it shined like gold. She wore a long, black leather dress that was slit up the side all the way to her waist.

Shadows buried her eyes. Her lipstick was dark blue or black. She met his gaze and smiled, sharing her grisly onyx fangs with anyone who cared to look. She turned her face up toward the sun, smiling as if she wasn't some freak straight out of a horror book, and the shadows covering her eyes burned away like the morning mist. Her eyes whirled and spun like miniature Ferris wheels. In the sunlight, he could see the color of her eyes. They weren't black, after all.

They were midnight blue, same as her hair.

At least they were until she burst into flame.

Chapter 6
2010

I

"And you are sure?" asked Brigitta in a tone that would have frozen magma.

"Yes, Mistress. Quite." Sally tapped her snout. "Say what you will about my situational awareness—Chaz always did—but there's no fooling this nose."

"I can't accept this! I can't believe LaBouche would choose her to mother his child over me!" Brigitta's eyes narrowed to mere slits, and her mouth curled into a grimace. "This can't stand."

"No, Mistress. LaBouche has always shown a lack of…" Sally shrugged. "A lack of respect."

"Indeed. You can handle the matter without Apsu?"

"Of course, Mistress," said Sally.

"See that it's done as soon as possible."

"And the mother?"

Brigitta lifted a hand to shoulder height and flapped it as if shooing away a fly.

"As you command, Mistress."

"And Sally?" Brigitta cocked her head to the side and smirked.

"Yes, Mistress?"

"Enjoy yourself."

Sally smiled.

"But I'm not finished with LaBouche, yet. Let him live."

Sally ducked her head to hide her disappointment. "As you wish."

2

Nicole rubbed her belly and smiled at LaBouche. "I'm sure, LaBouche."

He grinned at her, eyes dancing. "Do you…"

"Know anything more? No, not yet."

"And how long?"

"My kind quicken in a shorter span than most."

"And will it be a single birth or a clutch?"

Nicole shrugged. "I was a single, but my mother gave birth to clutches both before and after my birth. Your genes dictate the answer."

LaBouche nodded, a huge grin on his face. After a moment, he sobered. "This has to remain hidden."

"We keep it secret?" Nicole couldn't seem to resist rubbing her belly.

"Yes." LaBouche grimaced. "Brigitta has…"

Nicole sniffed, her smile fading. "I am aware."

"Then you understand the need for secrecy. She will view this as an affront."

Nicole grimaced, her eyes closed to slits. "She would find me a unique adversary should she choose to act."

LaBouche sighed. "There are things about her lineage you do not know. But she'll send someone else first. A more mundane demon. We should prepare."

Nicole lifted her chin. "Who?"

LaBouche shook his head. "I have no idea, but whoever it is, they will be formidable."

"They will need to be," said Nicole in a fierce tone of voice.

3

Sally drove home smiling for the first time in decades. She turned the radio to a station she thought of as "pop bullshit" and hummed along to a few of the tunes. She considered herself well-suited for the task Brigitta had assigned her.

Many demons given such a job would attempt a physical confrontation, but not Sally. She hadn't survived as long as she had by being stupid.

Once home, she assembled her materials: a bit of her own blood, a few strands of sable hair she'd plucked while dealing with the unconscious Nicole Conrau, a vermillion swatch of cloth, a chunk of LaBouche's flesh from his silly fight with Chaz in the Bertram woman's apartment, a frog, and a fistful of ashes from Herlequin's clearing. She brought out a clay bowl, filled it with water, then added her blood and Herlequin's ashes to the bottom. She knelt in the middle of her kitchen floor, broke a sprig of cottonwood, a sprig of birch, and a sprig of yew and arranged them to make a small fire.

"*Lilu, utukku-šū abāru,*" she chanted as she held a match to the wood. A green flame erupted from the birch twig, then danced to the yew and cottonwood. Sally nodded to herself.

She added the strands of sable hair—a few to the contents of the pot, a few strands to the flames. "Nicole Conrau *atmu-ša dâku.*" She took up the chunk of LaBouche's flesh and bit it in half, spitting the flesh from her maw into the bowl and adding the rest to the fire. "LaBouche *atmu-šū dâku.*"

The concoction in the basin began to smoke and hissed like a viper. Sally drew spit into her mouth and spat it into the bowl. She plucked up the vermillion swatch of material and rubbed the remains of her blood into it with her thumb. "*Kalbatu lišānum-ša eqēqu*." She tossed the cloth into the dish with a flourish of her hand.

She stared into the pot, watching, waiting. The ash and blood mixture from the heart of the bowl swirled and bubbled up around the edges of the clay vessel, then swooped toward its center all at once. The concoction swarmed over the vermillion cloth and dragged it down to the bottom of the bowl.

Sally smirked. *One more curse*, she thought. *Then my work is done.*

She picked up the frog and gripped its body in her left hand. With her right, she took the frog's head and twisted it until blood flowed into the bowl. "Nicole Conrau *balāṭu-ša šarāqu, šagapīru gallû!*" she screamed. Her voice echoed around her kitchen, sustained by the power of her spell, until the words seemed to overlap, to fight one another for dominance.

The twigs exploded, chunks of flaming wood showering over Sally, and the clay bowl cracked, its contents flashing to steam that dissipated in an instant.

LaBouche meant to dominate me, Sally thought as she climbed to her feet. *He believed me petty and small. An irritant, a tool to use and discard.* She paused, her right hand dripping frog blood over the knob of her back door. *Chaz, too, if I'm honest. Neither of them ever knew me. Neither of them cared to look deeper than the Sally McBride visage. If they had…* She shook her head. *I will survive them both, like I survived Hera and all the others since then.*

She grinned as she opened the door and flung the frog's carcass out into the darkness.

4

Greg sighed and scrubbed his hands through his hair. The digital clock on his desk claimed it was one in the morning, and Greg had lost most of another night to minutiae. Running International Datawerkz had turned into much more of an executive position than he'd ever dreamed it could. He hadn't touched the codebase in months. With one more sigh, he pushed himself away from the desk and stretched, his stiff joints crackling and popping. He threw on his jacket and flicked the lights off on his way out of his office.

He stuck his head in the development war room as he strolled by. As usual, a number of software developers and database architects had decided to work late and hash out this detail, that feature request that had filtered in from SEMPRe's human search engine.

"Don't stay too late," he called.

"Goodnight, Mr. Stephens," one of them called back.

He waved and continued down the hallway, passing the huge server room, and enjoying the blast of cold that came of the glass wall protecting the machines from dust and people. He smiled and waved at the guys manning the security desk and pushed out through the front doors.

The night air was crisp, even if it was a touch too cool. Winter was on the way, but on the whole, Greg enjoyed the weather on the shores of Lake Erie. Everyone thought he was crazy when he said he *preferred* the climate of the northeast over the weather of Central Florida, but that was only because they'd never been to Florida in August.

He walked toward his grandfather's GTO—it had gotten a new identity two years before as well, but it was still the same cherry red jewel his granddad had loved so much. Greg cherished it, too, and not just because his grandfather had.

He slid his key into the door lock, but before he turned it, footsteps rang on the asphalt behind him.

"Well, hello there, Greggy."

The voice, more than the words, froze Greg in place. *Mason Harper? How?*

"Denny, bring the van, would you?" asked Mason.

"Why not bleed him here?"

"Where's the artistry in that?"

"*Fuck* artistry."

"Go on, please, Denny."

Greg turned the key in the GTO's lock and jerked the door open.

"Now, now, Greggy. Let's not be rash."

Greg slid into the driver's seat, slammed the door, and slammed his fist down on the lock post. Mason stayed near the front of the car, smiling. Twenty steps away, another man Greg didn't recognize stood watching.

"Denny, the van, please."

The other man sneered and walked off.

Greg shoved the key into the ignition and turned it but nothing happened. The starter didn't emit even a click.

Mason cocked his head to the side and grinned. "You didn't think I'd leave this to chance, did you?"

5

A noise woke LaBouche from a deep sleep. He reached to the side where she'd been sleeping but found nothing. He sat up and the sound came again—a rhythmic knocking not unlike a beast in its death throes.

LaBouche sprang from the bed in a fluid motion and hit the ground running. He raced toward the master bathroom's double doors. "Nicole!" he cried. He flung the doors open with enough force to rip one of them from its hinges.

White light blazed from the bathroom fixtures, reflected from the white marble counters and the white granite floor tiles. White granite tiles tinged green by Nicole's lifeblood.

She sat, cocked against the big whirlpool tub's enclosure, one knee up, the other splayed at an angle. Emerald green blood pooled from her crotch. It surrounded her, coating her silvery legs.

"Nicole!" he cried.

He slid to his knees beside her, gathering her into his arms. "Nicole!" Her head lolled to the side, her once-malachite eyes gray and lifeless. "Nicole!" he cried.

He lay her flat on the ground and tried to revive her, but it was no use. He scrubbed his face with his hands, smearing her blood everywhere, wishing he could cry.

Nicole Conrau was dead, and his child along with her.

6

"Guys! Guys!" Benny shouted as he ran from room to room in Toby's big house on the cliff. He pounded on bedroom doors as he went. Shannon came behind him, bleary-eyed and disheveled.

"What is it, Benny?" asked Mike as he stepped into the hall.

"Greg! Greg's in trouble!"

"Scott! I need you!" roared Mike, stabbing his legs into his jeans.

7

Greg stared at Mason through the windshield of the GTO, still turning the key, still trying to get the engine to start, despite the fact that nothing worked—no lights, no starter, nothing.

Mason smiled at him as if they were old friends, then shook his head. "It will not start, Greggy." He ran a loving hand across the GTO's smooth, cherry red paint. "Such a beautiful car. It's too bad we must leave it."

Greg convinced his hand to let go of the key. He sat back in the driver's seat, watching as Mason Harper walked toward the driver's window. "What... What do you want?"

Mason grinned and tapped on the glass. "Can't we have a civilized conversation?"

· Greg slammed his thumb on the switch mounted to the left of the ignition. Nothing happened.

Mason cocked his head to the side and grinned. "I'm a little bit offended that you think I'd miss a panic button. I *am* a professional, you know." He twirled his hand as if rolling down a window. "Come on. Let's palaver."

Greg shook his head.

"Fine," Mason sighed. Moving with a lazy grace, he pulled a short-handled sledgehammer from the backpack he wore looped over one shoulder. "I learned this trick from my new friend Denny. You might want to look away." When Greg didn't move, he shrugged and swung the hammer, smashing the driver's side window to smithereens. "Let's talk about art, Greggy."

Chapter 7
1979

I

September 1979

After dinner, Eddie sneaked down the basement steps to the damp cellar that had become his refuge. Nothing about Uncle Gil's farm was fancy, and the cellar of his house was no exception. The small space had a dirt floor and packed walls of raw, black earth. But all that worked in Eddie's favor, and he liked that shovel marks still showed in the musty earthen walls from when the pit had been dug.

Auntie Margo spent very little time down in the dark, and when circumstances required her downstairs, she never strayed from the base of the stairs, standing between the two shelves full of homemade canned goods and canning supplies. It was as if she feared the gloomy basement as much as Eddie once had. He grinned at the thought of an adult scared to go into any darkened space.

The furnace stood in the exact center of the dirt floor, forming a wall between the base of the steps and the far end of the basement. On the other side of the heater was a dark, damp space that smelled of wet earth and dust, and that was where Eddie kept his collection.

It was his very first collection, and it wasn't great, but it was *his*. He stored it on a scarred wooden desk so scratched up and dented it looked as though it had lost a fight with a threshing machine. When he could, he sneaked downstairs and played with individual pieces of his collection.

Eddie's new life was a lonely one.

It'd only been three years since that day in the principal's office, the time he'd first seen the collection that had sparked him. His collection seemed nothing like that one…nothing as good as Principal Skinner's. He had no old books, no shiny trinkets, no cool models of muscle cars, but he *liked* what he had. He enjoyed brushing their artificial hair, dressing them, posing them, and he enjoyed telling them whispered stories based on what had happened at school—and sometimes stories of what he wished had occurred, instead. His collection contained a beautiful array of—

"*Dolls!*" shouted Uncle Gil.

Eddie started, his heart racing, and then he froze, his arm straight out almost touching his black-haired Barbie, the one with the pretty red dress.

"Are you playing with *dolls*? Why in the hell would you be playing with that shit, rug-rat?" Uncle Gil's voice filled the basement, seeming to suck all the air out of the room and dropping the temperature at least twenty degrees.

Eddie stared at the black-haired Barbie just beyond his fingertips. It didn't matter to him that one of her hands was messed up—melted as if someone had left her too close to the stove or a hot plate—or that the dress was smudged with dark and foul-smelling gunk. None of that mattered.

What mattered was that she was his.

"Edward James Mitchell!" Uncle Gil's voice cracked like a whip. "You better stop ignoring me, brat, or you know what happens next."

"It's… It's my collection. They are… They are my friends." He said the last bit only a hair's breadth above a whisper.

Uncle Gil stomped toward Eddie, his thick-soled work boots sending up clouds of odor from the dark, rich earth.

Eddie didn't turn to face his uncle; he didn't want to see Gil's expression. It would be an ugly one, hateful.

"Look at me, brat!"

Eddie sensed Uncle Gil looming over him from behind; he imagined the man's baleful glare heating the back of his neck like a sunburn. His mouth dried out, and that scratchy pressure that meant tears wanted to get out burned in his eyes. "It's no big deal, Uncle Gil. I didn't spend any money on these."

"Are you telling me you *stole* these dolls, you little bastard?"

"What? No! No, no. I don't steal, Uncle Gil. No, I found these in the dumpster out back of the toy store."

"In the trash? You got into their garbage and slogged around like a hobo? You dug into their junk and took things they threw out, the crap that even that moneygrubbing Don Wiseman didn't think were worth anything?"

Eddie turned halfway toward his uncle, just enough to steal a quick glance at Uncle Gil's face. As expected, he didn't think much of what he saw. "They were throwing them away anyway. And I—"

Uncle Gil wrapped Eddie's bicep in a grip of iron and jerked the boy to his feet. "You look at me when you're talking to me, brat," he hissed.

"Suh-sorry, Uncle Gil." He turned his face toward his uncle's, but he couldn't quite make his gaze lock on to the older man's.

Uncle Gil gave him a brisk shake to punctuate his meaning.

"Sorry," said Eddie, despising the tinge of whinging that laced his voice but unable to banish it. "I didn't think it was hurting anybody if I took the stuff that they were throwing away. I didn't think it mattered if stuff was in the trash. That's not stealing, right?"

"Girly toys?" said Uncle Gil in a tone that rang like hot iron trapped between a hammer and an anvil. He gave Eddie another hard shake. "*Dolls*?"

"People collect these figurines, Uncle Gil. They can be worth lots of money." Across the basement, the shadows twined and whirled as though a sudden gust of wind disturbed them.

"Dolls?" Gil's face hardened like a slab of stone, slick and cold. His grip on Eddie's arm tightened until his hand turned dark with trapped blood.

"I'm not playing with them! I... I *collect* them."

Gil laughed, but it wasn't a pleasant sound—it was more akin to a rusty saw blade grating against bone.

"I'm not! I enjoy looking at them. *Appreciating* them." That was a word Auntie Margo had taught him the previous week. It was what she called standing in the dining room and looking up at the fine china she had taken from his mother and father's place.

Gil laughed again, and again it sounded more charnel house than comedy club. "Don't bandy words with me, you little brat! Don't pretend that you're smarter than me...because let me advise you, boy, you *ain't*."

Eddie stood and waited—there was nothing more to do now, nothing more to say. Gil had already decided to punish him, probably before he'd said word one to Eddie.

"Nothing else to say?" Gil lifted an eyebrow. "And they say you can't teach an old dog new tricks. I'll tell you this for nothing, Eddie, that's the smartest thing you've done all night." He punctuated the paragraph with another quick jerk of Eddie's arm.

Gil shifted his gaze from Eddie's face to the scuffed and marred desk and the figurines arrayed there. They weren't all Barbies, a Ken doll, and two G.I. Joes also gazed up at him with plastic innocence. One of the G.I. Joes had Kung-Fu Grip, but the two middle fingers on his right hand had gone missing. Everything in his collection had at least one flaw—they *had* come out of a dumpster after all—and Eddie supposed one of the wealthy families across town had returned them, that a rich kid had decided they weren't good enough to keep around and had ditched them in favor of a new and perfect version.

Gil's eyes swept down the line and then right back up it. As his gaze came toward Eddie, his lips were moving as if he were counting under his breath. "Fourteen, brat? It's bad enough that you're playing with dolls, but fourteen of them? Why in the hell do you need fourteen? Ain't the shame of a single doll enough for you? Ain't dumpster-diving for *one* doll bad enough? Stealing a lone doll wouldn't embarrass me enough down to the Elks?"

Eddie's eyes tingled and burned. His belly started to ache the cold way it always did when something terrible happened, and his throat stung as if he'd swallowed broken glass.

Gil shook him again. "Boy, if you think this silent treatment cuts bread with me, you are in for a shock." Despite the vicious abuse he laid on Eddie's arm, Gil's voice sounded calm, uninterested.

Eddie opened his mouth to say something, though he didn't have a clue what, but as if Gil had been waiting for him to do so, the man snapped his arm back and forth at that moment, hard enough Eddie thought his shoulder would pop. Eddie's teeth slammed together on his tongue, and tears flooded his eyes from the pain of it.

"Gotcha there, brat. Didn't I just?" Gil snickered like the biggest, meanest bully in school.

Eddie thought he tasted blood, and his wounded tongue throbbed to match the diesel engine in Gil's old tractor. His eyes smarted, but he'd decided that he'd be damned before he'd let Gil drive him to tears. He remembered standing in Principal Skinner's office, about that hole he'd imagined being inside of himself, and as in many instances since, Eddie shoved his fear, his rage, and his sadness into that big hole.

Uncle Gil watched his expression as a cat might watch a bird. As Eddie began to feel calm and numb—the way he wanted to feel—Uncle Gil's eyes lit up. "Don't you do that, brat. Don't you do that thing you do! I'll make it *hurt* if you do, and I can do that without losing a wink of sleep."

Eddie looked up and met his gaze, feeling an icy numbness rolling through his body. His eyes no longer felt hot and itchy, his throat was no longer scratchy, and his stomach no longer hurt. He could almost convince himself he didn't care what Uncle Gil would do.

"Ah, now. Now you done it, brat. You look at me that-a-way, there's gonna be some tap dancing. You *know* that."

"Gil? Are you down there?" asked Auntie Margo. She trod on the top step of the stairs but came no further.

"I am."

"Well, what are you doing down there?"

Gil's already tight grip on Eddie's arm grew even more uncomfortable. "The kid and I are having a discussion."

Auntie Margo descended another step, as timid as a young girl. "Gil…" There was no sound in the basement besides Uncle Gil's bull-like breathing. "Gil, he's only a kid."

"He's twelve!" Gil's eyes never left Eddie's, and his voice was as cold as a stone in winter. "Man enough to mad-dog me with his eyes."

"Yeah, but—"

"I will be busy with the kid for a little while longer." Gil's tone had gone even colder, but his anger seethed beneath it. "But I can make the time after that for another discussion— you and me. Would you prefer that? Should I pencil you in for an appointment?"

Everything quieted for a moment, as though even the house held its breath. "No," whispered Auntie Margo.

"Then I'll thank you for getting your ass back upstairs and do them dishes." Gil's voice had taken on a more conversational tone, but menace still lurked there like a shark beneath the waves.

"Yes, Gil." Auntie Margo's steps retreated through the basement door, and she closed it behind her with a soft click.

Gil stood still for a moment, his gaze on the stairs and a self-satisfied grin on his face. Eddie shifted his weight from one foot to the other, and the spell broke. Gil's gaze settled on him like a vulture alighting on a carcass. "Now, where were we?" He gave Eddie a little shake by the arm.

"Dolls," said Eddie, enervated and uncaring.

"Ah, yes. The dolls… The girly toys you stole from the toy store. The baby dolls—"

"I *didn't* steal them."

Uncle Gil's eyes widened, and his lips twitched as if to smile wider. Without saying another word, his other hand came whistling around and impacted the side of Eddie's face. "That's for smarting off. Should we go for another just the same as that? One to grow on, mayhap?"

Eddie stood as still as a statue, staring at him, and Gil's self-satisfied smile faded a little. Eddie didn't even lift his hand to his cheek.

"I'm not going to have no nephew of mine playing with dolls, and I ain't going to have no faggot living in my house, either."

The last accusation confused Eddie, though it also made him feel guilty, and he cut his eyes away. He had a vague idea that it was bad from having heard the older boys use it at school to pick on other kids, but he didn't understand what it meant. He shook his head, just once, but once was enough for Gil.

His hand came whistling back for a return visit, this time rocking Eddie's head to the side. Eddie's anger burbled deep in his chest, but he shoved that into the hole, along with his other emotions.

"Didn't I tell you about that, rug-rat? Did I not mention what it would cost you to shake your head at me?" He leaned closer, his foul breath on Eddie's cheek, in his nose. "Did I not teach you this lesson already?"

Eddie stood frozen, and Gil shook him hard by the arm.

"Cat got your tongue, orphan boy? Answer me proper."

"Yes, sir, Uncle Gil."

"Yes, what?"

"Yes, Uncle Gil, you told me not to shake my head at you; you told me that every time I did, I'd earn a smack in the chops."

"That's right, I did, didn't I? And yet, here you are doing it again. Maybe I didn't tell you *hard* enough last time, eh?"

"I…"

"Well, brat? You what?"

Eddie hitched his shoulders up toward his ears and then let them drop.

"I don't want it said that I don't give you a chance to speak on your own behalf, brat. If you got anything to say, say it. It's a free country."

Eddie started to shake his head but caught himself in time. "No, sir."

"No, what?"

"No, sir, I don't have nothing to say."

Gil stared at him for the space of five breaths, eyes squinted almost shut, his mouth pursed as if he were trying to find an excuse in Eddie's expression, in Eddie's manner, that would justify a sterner punishment. Then his grip relaxed a teensy bit around Eddie's bicep, and he opened his eyes. "Well, that's okay, then." His gaze swept across the wooden desktop. "Then let's get back to these dolls you stole." He turned his face to Eddie's and glowered at him.

"Yes, sir," said Eddie. *But I didn't steal them.*

"That's better, boy, but I know what you're thinking. You're thinking you didn't steal them and that I'm a moron for insisting that you did. Am I right?"

There was no safe answer, no way for Eddie to defend himself. It was almost as if Uncle Gil could read his mind.

"Almost got you there, didn't I?" Gil said with a nasty smile.

No, you didn't, thought Eddie. *I am smarter than you, Gil. You are a moron.*

"Well, I don't suppose I can fault you for your thoughts, boy." Gil tipped him a wink. "But let's get back to them dolls. Let me tell you why going in the toy store's dumpster and taking these out *is* stealing. That dumpster is on that store's property, right? And what's in that dumpster belongs to that store, right? It's not trash until it gets pushed out at the dump, and even then, all of it belongs to the county since they own the dump. Get it, boy? You see how that is stealing?"

"Yes, sir," said Eddie, fighting to keep the sullenness out of his voice.

Uncle Gil flashed a tight little smile. "You're getting good at that, brat." He spun Eddie toward the desk. "So, tell me what possessed you to *steal* these dolls from the toy store. What kind of faggot are you?"

Almost involuntarily, Eddie shrugged. "I don't even know what that means," he whispered.

Gil laughed, and again, Eddie heard the butcher's bone-saw in it. "It means the guy who wants to sleep with guys, Eddie. Now you know what it means."

It perplexed Eddie. He knew about sex, but he wasn't sure if just sleeping with someone was having sex. It seemed that if that was the truth, then all those sleepovers he'd been to meant... He never had a sleepover at a girl's house. *Maybe I am a faggot.*

Gil laughed again, and his eyes twinkled. "Come on, brat, you're *twelve*. Don't tell me you don't know what 'sleeping with someone' means."

"You mean a sleepover?" Eddie tilted his head away from his uncle. *Can you really read my mind, asshole?*

Gil's laughter died, and the twinkle left his eyes. He stared at Eddie for another moment, as if he were unsure whether Eddie was making fun of him. "Girls play with dolls, Eddie. Girls and faggots. So, which are you?"

Eddie's gaze slid away from Uncle Gil's and to his collection arrayed on the desktop. His eyes lingered on the G.I. Joes and the Ken doll.

"Them G.I. Joes is okay, but that Ken doll...he's just a sissy, anyway. Yeah, he's a man doll, but he's a man doll *for girls*." He gave Eddie a little shake, but compared to the ones at the start of the conversation, it hardly registered. "Which are you? Are you going to answer me, brat? Girl? Faggot?"

"I'm... I'm your nephew."

Again, Gil's bone-saw laugh rang in the basement. "But you ain't my blood, boy. Ain't nothing in you that came from my family. You came from your mama and your daddy, boy, and we both know how weak your daddy was." He glanced up at the floor above his head. "And we both know how weak—and stupid—both your mama and your Auntie Margo is." He shook his head. "Sometimes I wonder how I let that woman trap me. She can't even have a kid." He made a disgusted sound in the rear of his throat and then turned his attention to Eddie. "Weakness, Eddie. That's what we're talking about here. Playing with dolls, lusting after other men. Hiding down here in the dark. All that's nothing but weakness, boy."

Eddie couldn't help it, he shrugged. He expected another brisk shake, maybe another one hard enough to make him bite his tongue, but Gil only laughed.

"More weakness, boy. Indifference, apathy, weakness. So, I'll ask you again, and mind me now, this'll be the last time I ask using my mouth. Girl? Faggot? Or..."

"Or?"

Gil grinned. "Well, it just struck me. You could prove you don't want to be a girl, and you could prove you don't want to be a faggot. Know how?"

Eddie shook his head.

"You could show you're not weak, boy. You could *prove* it."

"How?"

Gil's free hand swept from one end of Eddie's collection to the other. "You could take all these here dolls outside into the dooryard, and you could burn them. I've got lighter fluid, and we can take a match from Auntie Margo's kitchen box. It wouldn't take but a minute."

Eddie's gaze fell to the floor and then climbed up the leg of the desk, traversed the top, and landed on the black-haired Barbie with the melted hand. Something inside him writhed and screamed, and he wondered if mind-reading Uncle Gil heard it, too.

A horrid, slimy thing crawled out of that big hole inside him. It felt like a monster, evil incarnate, but Eddie knew what it was.

Pure hatred.

He kept his eyes out of Gil's line of sight, sure that if his uncle saw the look in his eye, the man would see that hatred. He might sense it, but as long as he didn't see it or hear it from Eddie, Gil would still be unsure.

"Well, boy? Are you a faggot or do you want to prove otherwise?"

Without looking up, Eddie bobbed his head.

"Which?"

"I'll prove I'm not."

Gil's grip on his bicep relaxed. "No going back on this, Eddie. I don't want any bawling up in that dooryard when it comes time to strike that match."

Again, Eddie nodded, his eyes on the dirt floor between his shoes. Inside, the black hatred of Uncle Gil seethed and gnashed its teeth.

"Well, okay then." Gil took a step backward and handed Eddie a wooden apple box. "Let's get to it. I want to finish this foolishness in time for Jeopardy."

Eddie took the apple crate and set it on the desk. One by one, he picked up the pieces of his collection and placed them inside the box as though fragile. The last doll he put in was the black-haired Barbie in the red dress. The monstrous rage inside him cavorted and danced.

With his whole collection piled in the apple crate, Gil frog-marched him up the stairs, past the swirling shadows, past Auntie Margo, out through the kitchen, and into the dooryard that stretched between the house and the barn. Uncle Gil squirted starter fluid onto the pile of dolls and handed Eddie a box of safety matches. Gil stood there flashing his pearly-whites as Eddie struck a match and dropped it into the crate full of his treasures. With a *whoosh*, it was done.

Gil's smile stretched wider as the first wisps of black smoke twisted up toward the sky. He smiled and smiled, and Eddie stood there, stone-faced.

Inside, though, Eddie boiled the way the lava had seethed in that volcano they'd watched the film about in school. The blackness that had crawled out of him down in the basement lingered in the back of his mind. His hatred for Gil grew unabated, it grew and grew, until Eddie thought it would fill the entire world. *I wish I could burn you, Gil.*

Across the dooryard, in the deepest, blackest shadows that inhabited the barn, a faint *pop* slithered from the darkness. Peering into those shadows, Eddie saw a feminine shape. One that smiled at him and winked.

The image scared him. Doctor Erikson had said the Scary Lady was all in his head—that Eddie imagined her in times of stress. He'd said it didn't make Eddie crazy, but it showed how much stress Eddie had endured during his parents' fights.

Compared to life under Uncle Gil's thumb, their frequent fights had been nothing. *Nothing.* They'd kept him out of it, most of the time. Sometimes they'd argued *about* him, but they'd never made him the object of their anger.

Not like Uncle Gil.

He didn't want to see her again. Not ever. *I've got to get out of here*, he thought. *Get real. Where can I go?*

He stared at the plume of black smoke that rose from the flames consuming his prized collection. His *treasures*. His stomach turned cold and began to hurt.

If you stay there, Uncle Gil's going to kill you. The idea slipped into his mind like smoke through a screen. He didn't recognize the voice, but he knew it for his own. He had never allowed himself to think it, but he had sensed the shape of it as he lay in bed, night after night, imagining ways to hurt Gil. To cripple him... Maybe even kill him.

With a start, he realized Jeopardy's theme song blared from inside the house. He peeked beside him. Uncle Gil had left him with only the foul smoke of Eddie's sacrificial pyre.

Without another glance into the barn's darkness, Eddie turned and walked inside. He didn't care if the fire grew wild and burned down the whole farm.

Part of him wished it would.

He walked to his room and sat on the edge of his bed. He stared out the window and let his mind wander. Eddie never even heard Auntie Margo come to check on him. He wasn't aware of her questions, her caresses.

She no longer mattered. Auntie Margo had watched the whole thing from the kitchen window.

And said *nothing*.

He practiced shoving his emotions into the hole at his center. He practiced not thinking about hurting (*killing*) Uncle Gil.

Eddie practiced ignoring the world for three hours. Long enough for Uncle Gil and Auntie Margo to retreat to their bedroom on the other side of the farmhouse. Then he waited another twenty minutes for them to fall asleep.

Finally, he stirred.

2

September 1979

Abby stood in the shadows, watching the couples laughing and caressing one another in the parking lot next to the park at the head of Lake Genosgwa. There were so many young lovers to choose from, but none of them were *right*. Her project in Cottonwood Vale had drawn to an end—at least for the parents. She suspected the boy might offer additional amusements.

Behind her, the air popped, and Abby drew a deep breath in through her nose, sampling the aroma of the new arrival. "Brigitta," she breathed by way of a greeting.

"Hello, Sylou."

Abby shook her head. "It's Abby, now."

"As you wish," said the demon behind her.

"What do you want? I'm busy."

"Yes, I can see that," said Brigitta in dulcet tones that still conveyed her amusement. "You are involved with a man—"

"I smelled you on him."

Brigitta stepped forward to stand at Abby's elbow, all deference. "I need him again. My father—"

"Herlequin is not your only parent!" Abby snapped.

"—wishes to play in Oneka Falls. I need *my* man again."

Abby drew another deep breath in through her nose. "You *want* him." The statement was flat, devoid of emotion, but at the same time, damning.

"I..." Brigitta drew a deep breath. "He's one of my favorites."

"And yet you left him to wander alone."

"My father—"

"Don't refer to him as your father again in my presence! After what he did to your mother—"

"Yes, Mistress. Herlequin called me away from Owen. I did not wish to leave him."

"Then, why did you? You have nothing to fear from one such as Herlequin—even if you insist on the pretense you are no more than he!" Abby snapped. "Besides, Owen entertains me. What I might motivate him to do to the human woman he lives with intrigues me."

Brigitta held her tongue for a moment, then drew a deep breath. "The woman doesn't matter. My fa—*Herlequin* would use his unique skills. My...association with him seems to be the best avenue to achieve the goal."

Abby turned and squinted down at Brigitta's black, sagging flesh. She curled her lip. "There's no reason for you to adopt that form. Your mother—"

"*Abandoned* me. This is how I honor Herlequin."

Abby drew her head back as if Brigitta had slapped her. "She did no such thing! And Herlequin looks nothing like that—not his real shape. It demeans you to play among the low caste—whether others choose to do so or not. The quality of your breeding—"

"She abandoned me! She came *here* and left me alone! And this is how he thinks of me, so this is how I am! How I remain! If my mother wishes something different from me, let *her* come to me. Let *her* tell me."

Abby darted a glance at the cars in the parking lot, but no one seemed disturbed by Brigitta's outburst. "Keep your voice down, or I shall take it from you."

Brigitta dropped her head. "Yes. Of course, Mistress."

"Oh, Brigitta," sighed Abby. "You've always been as a daughter to me. How can I make you see that your mother had as little choice—"

"Let's not speak of my mother," grated Brigitta. "I'm here to ask you to release Owen. I marked him first, after all, and our conventions dictate—"

"Don't speak to me of the meaningless rules of the untouchables, girl." Abby's quiet tone contained a promise of pain and more than a hint of iron.

"He was mine before you laid eyes on him," snarled Brigitta. "He *is* mine!"

"Is he?" The ire had left Abby's voice, replaced with melancholy. "Why do you care so much for a meat animal?"

"Owen's more than that. He has unique talents, abilities." Brigitta crossed her arms over her breasts, and a woman built from pure fire reflected in her green eyes. "Not all humans are fit only for food. Some desire to be like us— and Owen is one such. I would change him myself, had I the power."

"Then it's good you don't!" snapped Abby. She crossed arms of flame over a chest burning bright in the night, unconsciously mimicking Brigitta's stance. "Your mother would not find it pleasant to hear you say that."

"As if my mother has even heard my voice in centuries."

A sigh escaped Abby. "Child, why do you continue this way? You could be so much more than you are."

Brigitta sneered, but then her expression softened. "She doesn't want me. She never has."

"That's not true. She—"

Brigitta chopped her hand through the air. "Enough of this. We have the same discussion every time we meet, Syl—*Abby*. And between our conversations, my mother continues to turn her gaze away from me, to ignore my very existence."

"Let us hope you never understand the burdens—"

"Yeah, I've heard that before, too. Will you give Owen back to me or not? Your heat is uncomfortable in this form."

Abby raised an eyebrow of flame. "Then change."

Brigitta refused to meet her gaze. "Owen? Yes or no?"

After a moment, Abby sighed and forced herself to relax. She had fed on Owen in her own way, had inspired him to greater cruelty than he might have reached otherwise, but she had no real vested interest in him. "He's yours, child. He always has been. I did nothing to change that—he amused me, is all. I ask, though, that you complete my work with his...*family* in Oneka Falls."

"Thank you, and I promise he'll kill the skanky bitch before all is said and done," said Brigitta without looking up. "My fa—*Herlequin* wants to play with the child, so he will suffer more than you plan him to in any case."

"One more thing, Brigitta."

"Yes?"

"If ever I want one of your conquests..."

"Of course. Ask, and he will be yours." Brigitta's voice was distant, cold. "I'll leave you to tonight's amusements."

Abby lifted a hand, but the air popped next to her and it was too late. "Don't go," she whispered.

3

September 1979

Eddie climbed out his window into the yard, and with the acrid smoke of his doll collection still lingering in the depths of his throat, Eddie hunched against the wind and walked away from Uncle Gil's farm. *For the last time*, he promised himself. *I'm never coming back here. Never.* Not *ever.*

Eddie had a blanket, a bit of bread he'd tiptoed into the kitchen and stolen from the bread box, and a change of clothes in the school backpack slung over his shoulders. He didn't have any money, and no way to get any, but he had the perfect place where he could sleep.

It had come to him while he stared out the window.

Uncle Gil had wanted to sell it, of course, but Auntie Margo wouldn't let him, despite the black eyes and the days of limping her refusals had earned her. Gil had been livid for weeks, and Eddie had hidden his grin with care, but the deed required Auntie Margo's signature, and she'd refused to give in no matter how dire Gil's threats had grown.

Eddie had a key. That had been simple. His aunt and uncle had kept the keys in the little wooden bowl with a carved duck for a handle on the lid. It had been easy to steal the key. He'd done it a year ago after Gil had forgotten about the house and its key.

Once Auntie Margo had refused to allow Gil to sell it, his uncle had lost all interest in it. The place sat empty—Gil didn't care to rent it, he'd wanted the lump sum from selling it for yet another get-rich-quick scheme he'd read about in one of his magazines.

The way Eddie saw it, *he* owned that house, and he had every right to possess the key.

Even in the frigid fall wind that seemed to announce the coming of winter, the walk would take less than twenty minutes. Eddie wore his wool hat and a thick coat. He had on a pair of brown cords, and he wore his work boots. Eddie reckoned he'd stay warm enough.

He hoped so because it was doubtful that the furnace had heating oil or that the pilot light was lit.

Anyway, that's why he had the blanket.

Hiding out in his parents' apartment wouldn't keep Gil from finding him, but then again, he didn't believe Gil would mind that he'd run away. Auntie Margo might, but she was Gil's creature through and through, and if he didn't care to look, he wouldn't let her come looking either.

The town was dark, as it often was after ten o'clock at night, especially once the weather started to turn cold. A few early fall leaves skittered across the road like massive bugs, and the shadows seemed to loom from the yards of the homes he passed, but no one spoke to him, no one accosted him. No one saw him.

No one made him go back to Gil's farm.

He hadn't been home since the day his father... Not since his parents had died. Not even to pick up clothes or toys. Auntie Margo had taken care of all of that. Gil had gone along "to help." *As if*, thought Eddie. *He probably came to look for jewelry or cash or something he could sell to make money. That's all the man cares about.*

Eddie let a sigh of relief gust out of him. It felt good to be out from under Uncle Gil's thumb. It felt good to be free. He could collect dolls now if he chose. Who would be there to stop him?

No one, that's who.

He turned onto that familiar street, and a dark thing stirred in his belly, something that tasted the same as fear or maybe dread. He still didn't know what had happened that day, and he wasn't sure he *wished* to, but from the way people talked—or rather *stopped* talking when he came into the room sometimes—it must've been horrible. Eddie's father had committed suicide, no one had ever disputed that, and despite what Auntie Margo had said about kids not needing to learn that word, people had no qualms about using it in front of him regarding his father.

At times, curiosity about how his mother had died vexed him. He didn't believe that she had suicided. That wasn't in her. *No, Daddy did something to her,* he thought. *Something bad. Daddy and Gil—two peas in a pod. At least Gil hasn't killed Margo…yet.*

He shook himself, chilled, but not from the cold wind. Ghosts weren't real, so there was no issue with him being inside the building where his father had… Where his parents had died. No, the only danger came from the neighbors, and only if they called the police.

The house crouched before him in the darkness, a barren skull, its uncovered windows glaring into the street. He stood in front of it, staring into the impenetrable blackness that wrapped the interior. The yard had gone to seed, as had the planting beds his mom had always maintained with meticulous care.

A twitch of pain at the sight of the flowerbeds shuddered through him. He and his mother had spent many hours weeding those beds, planting new annuals, and maintaining the perennials. They had laughed and thrown dirt at each other, they had shown each other silly faces, silly grins, and hugged.

His eyes began to sting and itch.

Eddie shook his head, trying to force the emotions away and then sighed. He trudged up the drive, almost dragging his feet along, allowing the thick soles of his work boots to scuff against the asphalt. He walked around to the side of the house, to the door closest to the free-standing garage. The door his mother had always called "the garage door," although it opened on the dooryard rather than the garage.

He stared at the outbuilding for a moment, as though trying to peer back through time, to see the events of that fateful day that had ended with his father hanging by an old rope, knotted from the rafter above the hood of their car.

Gil had told him that, and he couldn't help but picture it. A chill raced through him again, causing goosebumps to shiver to life. *No such thing as ghosts, Eddie*, he thought. *It's only a building. An empty building, now.*

He slid the key into the lock of the side door and grinned as it turned with minimal effort and the bolt clicked free. Eddie tore his eyes away from the garage with a grimace. He pushed the door open, but then stood staring into the darkness that blanketed the house. Now that he was home, it seemed…almost disrespectful to his mother's memory to go inside.

But then warmth spread from his chest toward his limbs, akin to a hug from his mother, and he sighed at the memory of his mother hugging him and smiled at the feeling of welcome. He mounted the steps and closed the garage door behind him, pausing a moment to turn the lock.

The air smelled musty, disused, and a thin layer of dust covered everything. His mother never would've abided that, and Eddie supposed he would have a lot of cleaning to do once the sun came up and he could see better. He tiptoed through the murky house, traveling by memory, and made it to his bedroom without bumping into one single thing.

He took that as a sign.

Winter gripped the inside of the place like a dark promise. It would be a long night if he didn't find a way to keep warm. He set down his backpack and walked back toward the kitchen. He stood there a moment, just taking in the pleasant emotions of being in his mother's kitchen again.

My kitchen, I suppose, he thought.

He opened the basement door and flicked on the light switch, hoping against hope, but to no avail. There was no electricity in the house, and he'd forgotten a flashlight. Still, his father had kept one on the shelf next to the bottom of the steps.

He wondered for the umpteenth time where his mother had died. *How* she'd died. The idea that she had died alone down there in the basement's dark shadows surfaced and he couldn't sink it again.

He walked down the steps, ignoring the spiderwebs that swept across his face. At the bottom, he stretched out his hands for the shelves that still stood there, finding them at last, right where they should have been. He found the flashlight and flicked the switch. A watery yellow beam stabbed through the darkness of the basement, and for a moment, he pretended it was a lightsaber straight out of Star Wars.

He had no doubts the pilot was out. Same as Gil would've shut the electricity and the heating oil deliveries off years before. But he had to check.

He walked over to the hulking heater and bent down to open the little metal door that hid the pilot light. *Is that… Do I smell oil?* he asked himself. He drew a deep breath in through his nose, his heart throbbing in his chest, hoping the oily odor he thought he detected was more than a mere trick of his mind.

But he smelled nothing, and no blue flame flickered from the little opening. He heaved a sigh but wasn't ready to quit yet. Eddie reached up to the top of the old heater and patted around for the box of safety matches his father kept there. He withdrew a match and struck it, then held it inside the opening.

Nothing happened. No *whoosh* as the pilot light ignited. No explosion, either.

No nothing.

Behind him, something shifted the stale air trapped in the basement. He whirled, stabbing at the dark with the beam of the flashlight, and for a microsecond, he was sure someone stood in the shadowy corner. A woman.

He flicked off the light and squeezed his eyes shut, almost daring a ghost or a zombie or a monster to come get him. But that was silly. *No such thing as ghosts or zombies or monsters*, he told himself. *And I am alone in this basement*. He took a deep breath and opened his eyes.

Nothing lurched out of the velvet blackness that wrapped the basement tight. He flicked the switch on the flashlight, and the beam stabbed across the room. On the floor beside a stack of sealed-up boxes, sat his mother's Tiffany lamp. Dragonflies populated the bottom edge of the shade, and the predominant color was aquamarine.

He breathed a sigh of relief and smiled to himself. He'd always liked the dragonflies. *Tomorrow, I'll clean up that lamp. Take it upstairs and put it in the corner of the living room, where it belongs.* He yawned so wide his jaw creaked with it.

He climbed the stairs, exhausted and wrung out. All he wanted to do was sleep, so he made his way back to his bedroom, spread out the blanket he had brought from Uncle Gil's, lay down on it, and folded it over himself. He was asleep almost instantly.

For once, his slumber was free of nightmares. He dreamed his mother was alive, and they cleaned up the Tiffany together.

4

September 1979

Sean walked down Union, whistling to himself. Earlier, before the deputy had gone to work, Karl had slipped him a few dollars for "an after-supper treat." He did that from time to time, and it had become a secret they shared—one they kept from Vickie.

The small convenience store on the corner of Mill and Main had a big sweets aisle, and Sean intended to make full use of the money. As Karl often said, every boy Sean's age needed candy.

Ahead, a green Impala turned onto Union and cruised down the street away from Sean. For a moment, he thought it must be Karl, but the driver was too small, too slight of build. Even so, it *looked* like Karl's Impala…

Sean broke into a jog to follow, but the car turned into a driveway and rolled toward the back. His gaze crawled over the house, but he didn't know who lived there.

The home next door, though… A tree stood in its front yard, and the sight of it made him feel both embarrassed and randy at the same time. It was the tree where Kristy had shown him…*everything.* Even after all those months, Sean's face burned with the memory.

He jogged to the end of the driveway the green Impala had disappeared down and peeked around a shrub.

The car still idled, but as he watched, the driver put it in park and killed the engine. Both front doors opened, and the teenaged boy from the tree exited on the driver's side. A man Sean didn't know got out the other side.

"You will love her, Dennis. Trust me," said the kid. "She's cherry."

The other man scoffed. "No whore is cherry, Leif."

That was the name! That's what Kristy called the boy.

Leif laughed and swatted the roof of the car, and unease gripped Sean. Karl did the same thing when he wanted to emphasize something.

"I'm telling you, Dennis. She's… Well, you'll see in a few minutes."

"She better be as tight as you promised, or I ain't paying full price."

"Oh, she is," said Leif. "She's broken in, but she's as tight as a girl can be."

The boy and the man circled around the front of the car and met at the steps that led to the back door of the home. Leif held out a hand to stop the man. "Before we go in, you got to pay me."

The man only looked at him for a moment, then laughed and reached for his wallet. "Two hundred?"

"Yep," said Leif. "Cash or drugs, I'm not picky."

The man handed a wad of bills to Leif, and the two climbed the steps and went inside.

Something inside Sean uncoiled and slithered around in his guts. Not fear... Anger. Without thinking about what he would do if the two older guys caught him, he sprinted the length of the drive and mounted the steps behind them.

Peeking through the window in the rear door of the house, Sean watched them climb the stairs to the second floor. The doorknob turned in his grip, and he sneaked into the kitchen, leaving the door ajar.

His heart thundered in his ears, and Sean wanted nothing more than to run, to return to his quest for sweets from the corner store. But Kristy had been *kind* to him, and something in Leif's manner struck him as...*wrong.*

Sean tiptoed up the steps, listening with all the energy he could spare, ready to turn and sprint down the stairs and out into the night at the first sign the men were coming back.

The lights were off, but soft light outlined a door at the end of the hall. From behind the door came the muffled sound of Leif's voice and that oh-so-familiar speech pattern, then the tinkling of Kristy's slurred laughter.

Sean crept to the door and pressed his ear against it.

"I don't know," said the older man. "She seems strung out, kid."

Leif laughed. "Who cares? She fucks like a bunny."

"How old is she? You said she was seventeen, but she looks younger. Closer to my kid's age than seventeen."

"And how is young Master Cratchkin?"

Kristy mumbled something Sean couldn't make out.

"Look, dude, you've already paid me, and the house policy is no refunds. Might as well take a swing. Younger's better, no?"

"If I require a refund, kid, you'll give it to me."

"No, I don't think so." The voice's timbre was too high, but Sean had no doubt that Karl had said the words. Somehow. He put his hand on the knob.

"...*don't want an old man!*" Kristy mumbled.

"But you need more acid, don't you? Come on, Kristy. Do it. Do it, for me, okay?"

"No, Leif. I don't want to be with anyone else. Just you."

"But you're going to be with this guy, Kristy. Come on. This isn't anything new. You've done it with other guys."

Again, the volume of Kristy's voice dropped until Sean had to struggle to make out her words. "...*tricked me...*" she whispered.

The unmistakable sound of a slap was her only answer.

"I can do rough," said the man, lust lacing his tone. "Let me in there, kid."

"*No!*" shouted Kristy.

Without planning to, Sean turned the doorknob and pushed the door open. The hinge creaked as it swung inward, and the two males spun to face him.

"What's this?" asked Dennis. "I don't want an audience."

"I'll tell," said Sean. "I'll tell Chief Greshin."

"Sean!" said Leif. "Get the fuck out of here. This is adult stuff."

Sean shook his head.

Dennis took a step toward Sean, wrapping his belt around his fist. "Seems to me your dad didn't teach you any manners, kid." He smelled of beer and farts, and Sean backed away from the doorway.

"I'll run and call the cops!" he shouted.

Leif squinted at him, his face expressionless, hands loose at his sides. "Sean, go home," he said.

Sean shook his head.

Dennis took another step, and Leif put out his hand. "Stop right there, Mr. Cratchkin. He's a kid. Nothing to worry about."

"He threatened to go to the cops. I can't have that."

Behind them, Kristy swayed to her feet and stooped to grab her jeans off the floor.

Leif tightened his grip on the older man's arm. "Come on. You came to fuck. Get to fucking." Something in his voice froze Sean's blood.

Kristy darted between the two men, bouncing off the frame of the door and into the hallway. "Run, Sean!" she slurred.

Sean turned and ran for the staircase, Kristy stumbling along the hall, weaving from wall to wall. Behind them, Cratchkin made an enraged sound in his throat and thudded after them.

"Go!" yelled Kristy.

"Fuck!" shouted Leif as he joined the procession to the stairs.

Sean pelted down the steps, taking them two at a time, then spun in the kitchen door. Kristy stumbled down the staircase, Cratchkin closing the distance, his knuckles white around the wide leather belt. His fist shot out and clipped Kristy on the side of the head. Leif stood at the top of the stairs, staring down on the scene with the same hungry expression Karl wore when he spoke of Sean's dad.

"Karl!" shouted Sean.

Overbalanced by the drugs and the blow, Kristy spun and fell, tumbling down the steps. Mr. Cratchkin smiled at Sean. "You next, kid," he said.

He sounded mean, same as his son.

As he made to step over Kristy, she kicked upward, and Mr. Cratchkin shrieked in pain, clutching his groin. She slithered out from beneath him and came down the stairs on her ass. At the bottom of the steps, she got to her feet and looked around as if unsure where to go.

Sean lifted his hand. "This way!"

Together, Sean and Kristy sprinted through the kitchen and out into the night. "Mom!" Kristy yelled.

As they crossed into her yard, Sean threw a glance over his shoulder. Leif—or Karl—stood next to his Impala, staring at Sean with furious eyes.

5

September 1979

Eddie awoke to sunshine streaming in through his bedroom window and a fresh coat of snow on the ground outside. He'd always enjoyed that early sunlight penetrating his room in the morning. Grinning, he rolled from the blanket into the patch of warmth and yawned.

The light revealed just how the house had fared in two years of abandonment. Dust bunnies lived in every corner, and there were rat droppings, too, but Eddie would see all of that put right.

He sighed and stretched, a loose smile on his lips. It was the first day since…since everything had happened that he wouldn't have to face Uncle Gil. His stomach growled, reminding him that all the stretching and sighing and smiling wouldn't keep him alive.

He sat up and pulled on his thick-soled boots, shivering a little at the cold. The fresh snow out in the yard looked pristine, pure. The ugly, unkept lawn he'd seen in the night had disappeared. He couldn't see the garage from his bedroom window, and it gladdened him.

He got up, pulling on his coat against the morning chill. The first thing he'd have to do is check if any heating oil remained, and if so, figure out how to get the pilot light lit. His father had always cursed and grumbled as he did the job, but it hadn't seemed that hard to light the furnace.

He stood right inside his bedroom door, his hand resting on the knob, imagining he heard the scrape of a wire whisk against the sides of a pan, that he smelled eggs and frying bacon and coffee and toast. His stomach growled, and the spell broke.

He opened the door, and for a moment, only a moment, he could have sworn the wire whisk sounded again. But there was no such thing as ghosts, and no one lurked in the house except Eddie, so he supposed his imagination had run a bit wild.

Even so, he stomped his feet and took his time getting to the kitchen.

He hadn't thought to check if the City had left the water running. He hoped so because his parched throat burned after his exertions of the night before.

A thin rime of dust covered the counters—the same counters that his mom had always kept clean enough for surgery. Eddie shook his head and added it to the list of tasks he would have to do that day. He didn't think it fair to the memory of his mother that all the things she had loved and worked hard to keep nice had been left to rot.

One more reason to hate Uncle Gil.

He crossed to the faucet and pushed the lever up. The pipes rattled beneath his feet, but after a moment, water gushed from the nozzle, splashing into the dirty sink. With a little grin, he bent forward and drank from the stream of water, slurping it as fast as it came. His mother would've never let him get away with that and, abashed, he pulled back and swallowed the water in his mouth.

He checked the cabinets, but only dust lingered in them. Auntie Margo had taken everything not nailed down. He pursed his lips and glanced at the faucet again, but one more thing remained to check. His mother had kept a sheaf of paper plates and a stack of plastic cups in the cellar. "For emergency cookouts," she had always said. Eddie smiled at the memory.

He crossed to the basement and pushed the door open with his pinky. The hinges creaked like the lid of the casket in a vampire movie. Eddie shivered again, this time not from the cold. He climbed all the way down the steps before he remembered that he'd taken the flashlight up with him.

Shaking his head, he glanced back up the stairs, but it was *his* house. His first home, the house he'd grown up in, and he knew the proper place for each item inside it, dark or not. He was safe there, and basements no longer scared him at any rate.

He peered into the stygian shadows of the basement. They seemed to close in on him, to beckon, to reach for him. He shivered and rubbed his arms. *Don't be a baby*, he thought. *There's no such thing as ghosts or monsters or vampires or...or* anything.

He tiptoed forward into the gloom, and something across the room clattered. Eddie froze. His imagination painted leering faces, smirking, black-fang-filled faces, onto the shadows. He shook his head, unwilling to picture *her* face—not down there in the gloomy shadows and cobwebs. *The place is empty. No such thing as ghosts, remember?* With great deliberation, he strode away from the penumbra at the bottom of the stairs.

Holding his hands out in front of him as a blind man would, Eddie shuffled farther into the dark vault. His imagination kept right on painting those faces into the shadows, kept right on making him think the sound of scuffing footsteps on the concrete floor approached him from behind, but Eddie knew what all that was: just nerves, and he didn't have time for nerves.

He found the metal racks at the far end of the basement, and they were shockingly cold under his fingertips, and slick, as though iced over. Eddie patted his way across the contents of the shelves, the old paint cans, his mother's stock of cleaning supplies, the ancient cardboard boxes, and the bags of rotted holiday tissue. He stared at the wrapping paper for a moment, and his dream—his *nightmare*—about Christmas resurfaced in his mind, bringing the icy-tang of fear with it.

Everything is normal, he thought. *Just normal junk.*

He wondered what treasures lived in that basement, what extraordinary things his mother kept down there in the dark. His fingers crawled across the shelves like spiders, but Eddie hated bugs of all kinds, so he pushed that idea away.

From behind him came the distinct sound of someone breathing. Eddie whirled toward the sound, his eyes wide, and his hands rising to shoulder height and balling into fists out of pure instinct.

But there was nobody there.

Of course there isn't, he chided himself. *I'm the only person here, and there's no such thing as ghosts. You know that, Eddie, so just stop it.*

He couldn't shake the feeling someone watched him from the shadows as he swung back to the shelves and continued his blind man's search for plastic cups and paper plates. He found them after a few more minutes, and tucking the stack of plates under one arm and carrying the cups in his other hand, he turned back to the warm, welcoming light shining down from the kitchen.

With a grin at how silly he was, he took a step toward the staircase. Something shifted in the blackness behind the steps, and this time Eddie stared right at it when it moved. No way he could convince himself it hadn't happened, no way to tell himself it was just nerves. He froze as if all his muscles locked up at once. There was only one possibility...

The scary lady!

BOOK TWO: NIGHTSHADE

<u>Chapter 1</u>
1979

I

If you haven't already read the novella The Devil, now would be a great time. It is featured Devils: A Collection of Devilish Short Fiction, which you can find here: https://ehv4.us/4devils, and is also a welcome gift for joining my email list, which you can sign up for here: https://ehv4.us/join.

September 1979

Eddie wanted to tear his gaze from the cold darkness behind the steps, and he told himself, again and again, to look away before *she* could lean out of the shadows and burn him down with her black-toothed grin. His heart lurched into high gear, and he pulled his arms tight to his sides. The thing hiding in the darkness beneath the stairs sighed like Auntie Margot did whenever she "appreciated" his mother's fine china.

Get out of here, Eddie! a voice in his mind screamed. *Move feet! Move!* But his legs didn't even twitch.

In the darkness, she tittered, and the sound made his blood run cold. He gulped a lungful of basement air, rich with dust and mold. He coughed it back out a second later, accompanied by another low, rasping chuckle.

Eddie lurched back a step, and small noises followed him from the shadows—as though she'd slid her foot forward to follow. "Who... Who's there?" he whispered. He'd intended to shout, but a whisper was all he could manage.

She didn't laugh, and silence echoed from the concrete walls and floor. Eddie listened with an intensity that hurt his brain. When the sound of a single footstep broke the stillness, his legs unlocked. He shot up the treads, refusing to look over his shoulder, refusing to check the cone of washed-out light at the bottom of the stairs to see if a troll-shaped thing stood smirking at his retreat into the world of light.

In the kitchen, he slowed to a walk, staring out the window and refusing to shift his attention from it. He set the stack of paper plates down on the dusty table and, without looking, closed the door to the basement a little too hard, wincing at the booming racket it made. He heard a noise down there in the dark. *More laughter?* he asked himself. *Or was that creaking on the steps?*

He shook himself like a dog shaking the snow off his back. *Get ahold of yourself, Eddie. No such thing as monsters. Well, they exist, but they look like Daddy and Uncle Gil. You imagined all that down there. Or it was a mouse moving scrabbling around in an empty box under the stairs. The scary lady is* not *real. Dr. Erikson said so.*

He shook his head at his own silliness and crossed to the faucet, filling one of the plastic cups. Eddie gulped it down, ignoring the thin streams of cold water that snaked down his chin from the corners of his mouth. He refilled the cup and downed its contents too, all while staring out the window over the sink. The morning light showed him the side of the garage, the peeling white paint reminding him of skin after a bad sunburn.

What happened out there? What did you do, Daddy? Why did you do it?

He curled his lip at his own weakness. It didn't matter why. It didn't matter what happened. Death had taken them, they were *never* coming back.

He turned away from the window, and just for a moment, a flash of red danced in the little window on the side of the garage. *Was that Daddy's red hat?* He shook his head. *No*, he thought. *Only your imagination, Eddie.*

He let his gaze wander around the small kitchen, remembering all those Saturday mornings—breakfast, dishes, and cleaning the house with his mother. A bittersweet smile creased his face until his gaze brushed by the door to the basement. He hadn't grabbed his mother's cleaning supplies while he was down there. He hadn't even taken a rag.

Stupid.

As he stared at the door, a step behind it creaked as though someone stood on the other side of the door shifting from foot to foot. His gaze fell to the doorknob, hoping against hope that he had locked the door without thinking, but he hadn't.

Heart racing, he slid his boot toward the door, and the stairs creaked again. He froze in place. *Standing here like a goober will not help if there's somebody behind that door. Or* something. *Which there isn't, because there's no such thing as ghosts or monsters or werewolves or vampires or anything else you can muster up, dumbass.*

No scary lady, either.

Grimacing at his fear and stupidity, Eddie forced his other foot to move, to lift from the ground in a normal step. He forced himself across the kitchen floor and grasped the cold doorknob, tensing to bolt away at the first sign of one of those things that didn't—that *couldn't*—exist.

Nothing happened. No more creaking stairs, no more breath sounds, no laughing, no nothing.

See? he thought as a sigh of relief gusted out of him, and he shook his head, rolling his eyes at his own silliness. *Nothing there.*

He relaxed his grip, then froze, heart lurching in his chest. *Did the doorknob just move? No, it couldn't have. There's nothing there, remember?* But it sure seemed like the handle had rotated a tiny fraction. The knob warmed beneath his flesh— heated up like a living thing. He jerked his palm away from the doorknob and stared at it. *It's only a doorknob. A dusty, dirty doorknob. If it warmed up, it's because of your own body heat. Stop being an idiot.*

He willed himself to grab it and turn it, but his hand didn't want to obey. His arm seemed frozen. He glared at his fist, telling it to move, to grab the doorknob, but it refused to listen. When he returned his gaze to the doorknob, the light reflecting from its surface shifted a mite, as if the knob moved the tiniest bit...as though someone had been turning it and then let go right before he looked at it.

Without planning to, he took a step back, his rebellious hands still refusing to obey him. His heart raced, and his breath came in gasps. He waited like a doomed man, taking shallow breaths and swaying from foot to foot.

The doorknob didn't turn, and the stairs didn't creak.

With a deep sigh, Eddie forced himself to relax, shaking his hands as if to wake them up after they'd fallen asleep. "You're so silly, Eddie," he murmured. He stepped closer to the door and reached for the handle. He laid his hand on the doorknob, and it was ice-cold again.

Someone pounded on the door that led to the dooryard, and Eddie jumped, a small shriek escaping his mouth. He turned toward the side door and froze.

No one should be knocking on that door, he thought. *No one knows I'm here. They abandoned the house, right?* The knocking paused, and Eddie held his breath. *If I keep quiet, whoever it is might go away.*

After the space of five heartbeats, the knocking began again, and Eddie sighed. After a moment, Chief John Morton's face appeared in the kitchen window above the sink. The chief grinned and gave Eddie a jaunty little wave. He pointed to the side door and mimed turning a lock.

Eddie stood frozen, staring at the cop as if he were an apparition or a zombie returned from the dead. *Too late to hide*, he thought.

Morton waved toward the door, his smile faltering a little. "You're not in any trouble, Eddie," he called through the window. "This is your house, after all. Or at least your Aunt Margo's until you turn eighteen." He pointed at the side door again. "Come on, Eddie. Let me in. It's freezing out here."

Eddie plastered a smile on his face and waved. *So much for no one ever finding me here*, he thought. He walked to the side door and thumbed the deadbolt. He opened the door. "Hi, Chief," he said.

Chief Morton beamed at him. "Hey there, Eddie. Thanks for letting me in." He stomped his big feet on the top step of the stoop, dislodging the wet snow from the treads of his boots. His eyes never left Eddie's face while he did this. "Colder than a witch's tit out there this morning. The house isn't much better. Rough night?"

Eddie licked his lips. "It was warm enough. I brought a blanket." He cleared his throat and examined the chief, looking for a red woolen watch cap or a scarf or anything. "Were you…" He shook his head.

"What, Eddie?" asked Morton softly. "Was I what?"

"It's stupid." Eddie blushed and ducked his head.

"Nah. Come on. Ask old John. I don't bite."

"It's just that I… *Maybe* I saw a flash of red. Out in the garage. Anyway, I thought you might have a red hat or something and…" Eddie wound down, feeling three kinds of foolish.

"Nope. I'll go check it out if you want, but it was probably an old blanket flapping in the wind."

Eddie's blush deepened, and he shook his head.

"It's no skin off my nose to go out there, Eddie. It's my job, you know." He put a thick hand on Eddie's shoulder.

"No, it's stupid. Just my mind playing tricks. Seeing things that aren't there."

John Morton stepped into the house and pulled the side door closed behind him. Morton looked at him for a moment, assessing him. Then he smiled and ruffled Eddie's hair. "Geez, son, your breath freezes even inside there. Don't you have the heat running?"

Eddie shrugged again. "Pilot light's out."

"Well, let's get that sorted out," said Morton. "It's been a few years, but if I remember, the cellar door is in the kitchen. Am I right?"

Eddie's throat went dry, and he imagined the lining of his esophagus cracking the way wet sand in the desert did as it dried. He settled for a nod and pointed toward the basement door.

With his eyes on Eddie's face, the chief turned the deadbolt and then looked at the vault door. "Are you sure you have heating oil, Eddie?"

"I… Maybe." Uncle Gil or Auntie Margo would have had to pay to have the tank filled, and part of him hoped that they had, but another part of him doubted it.

"What, did your aunt and uncle let the utilities drop?" The big man unzipped his shiny municipal jacket with its patches and badge and walked into the kitchen.

"They…they didn't tell me one way or the other."

Morton made a noise that was half amusement, half scoff. "I'm having trouble imagining your Uncle Gil parting with the money to keep this place warm."

Eddie chuckled. "You don't know the half of it, Chief."

The chief turned and peered at him, his face serious. "I suppose it's been hard."

It wasn't a question, but Eddie found himself nodding anyway.

"Worse of late, I bet."

Eddie couldn't meet his gaze and looked at his feet, nodding. *He* shouldn't be the one feeling guilty, yet he did. Somehow, it didn't seem fair.

"Guess that's why you're here." Morton's footsteps boomed across the kitchen, and he put his hand on the door's knob.

"Wait!"

Morton turned to look at Eddie, arching his craggy eyebrows.

Feeling foolish, Eddie dropped his gaze again. "I was… I mean, I went down there earlier… I needed a cup, and my mom… My mom used to keep a few down there for… For impromptu cookouts, I guess. I…"

The chief chuckled, an amused but understanding expression splashing across his face. "More mind tricks, eh? Well, don't you feel embarrassed. Old, empty houses can be creepy, son. But don't you worry, the police are here."

Eddie peeked at the chief's face and then away. The chief wore a huge smile, and Eddie folded his arms in front of him.

"Don't worry, son. We all get spooked from time to time. Even big fat police chiefs." With that, he turned the knob and descended into the basement. "If you only knew the calls I get, you wouldn't waste any more energy on embarrassment."

With his heart in his throat, Eddie walked to the top of the staircase and looked down, just in time to catch Chief Morton leaving the cone of luminance at the bottom of the stairs.

"Dark as the devil's asshole down here, Eddie," said the chief. "Turn on the overheads, will you?"

Eddie shook his head and reached for the switch, then grimaced at his own stupidity. "Electricity's off."

In the shadows at the bottom of the steps, a figure moved. But it wasn't the right shape to be the chief's shadow. And the way it moved... *Like* she *used to—how an insect moves.* Eddie shuddered and squeezed his eyes closed, hoping it would go away.

"Course it is, your Uncle Gil being who he is and all. Of course, the electricity's off." Eddie heard the distinctive sound of knurled metal rasping against plastic. "Good thing I brought my Maglite." A bright white beam stabbed into the darkness below, flickering across the shelves, across the empty space, and then froze on the hulking mass of the heater. "There she is."

"I tried to light the pilot last night," said Eddie, his gaze going to his own flashlight standing like a lone soldier on the counter next to the sink.

"No joy?" The chief chuckled. "Obviously not. Sometimes I'm a tad slow, Eddie."

"No, you're not, Chief."

The chief chuckled again. "Well, thank you for the vote of confidence, but from where I stand, I'll have to disagree with you."

Not knowing what to say, Eddie shrugged.

"Oil tank down here, son?"

"Yeah," said Eddie. "To your left."

The white flashlight beam flickered to the chief's left. "Yup, I see 'er. I'll take a look." As he turned, a shadow detached itself from the corner. A shadow that the Maglite couldn't pierce.

"Be—" Black smoke spurted up the stairs in the space between Eddie's heartbeats. He had a mere moment to move, and he wasted the time gawking. The plume of smoke formed itself into an almost human shape, and, as if the thing opened eyelids made of smoke, two orange eyes gleamed at him from where the face should have been.

Eddie's throat closed as though a strong man had wrapped his hands around it and squeezed. The eyes whirled and twirled, like pinwheels in a strong wind. They spun so fast, Eddie found himself listening for the *clickity-click* his brain insisted must be there.

"What was that, Eddie?" called the chief. "Didn't catch what you said."

While he stared into those spinning eyes, the thing of smoke disappeared in a snap. Eddie cleared his throat, the harsh sound echoing in the vault below, and he cursed himself for a major dweeb. "I said: 'Be careful.'"

"Don't you worry, son. Everything is in hand."

The basement stairs creaked, as though someone was shifting their weight from side to side, right below where Eddie stood. His heart froze in his chest, and though his mouth opened, he couldn't say a word. A shadow hid against the wall of the stairwell, pressed flat like a ninja—a shadow of a woman.

"Ah! Someone turned off the valve."

An ice-cold object brushed against Eddie's cheek. It felt like the most frigid hand in creation rested against his cheek, patting, caressing, but he couldn't see anything, not even a shadow. He tried to shout for the chief, but his voice betrayed him. He croaked out a string of unintelligible syllables.

"You say something, Eddie?" called the chief.

Eddie parted his lips to speak, but that freezing object left his cheek and invaded his mouth, coating his teeth, gliding over his tongue. "Ugmmmph!" he grunted, trying to keep the cold—to keep *her*—out of his throat. He pulled his head back, but the pressure didn't abate. He stumbled back until his butt bumped into the cabinets under the sink.

"Don't be shy, son." The police chief stepped over to the bottom of the steps, and Eddie imagined him standing there in the penumbra at the bottom of the stairs. "I got the oil turned back on, son. We'll have this heater going in two shakes."

Eddie tried to shake his head, but he couldn't move. He tried to shout for the chief—for help, or as a warning—but he couldn't even make the unintelligible sound that he made before. His chest began to hurt, to ache as if he'd been underwater too long.

"I'll be right back, son." His big feet thumped on the concrete, getting farther away.

Eddie's tongue felt as though someone squeezed it with tongs made of the coldest metal imaginable. He tried to lean back over the sink, tried to lift his arms to ward off whatever the thing was. He thought his chest would explode if he didn't get away from whatever had him.

The scary lady wants to do more than watch this time, a tiny voice in his mind whispered. Eddie's eyes rolled side to side. *So this is how she always hid from my mom and dad. She turned into a shadow or turned invisible.* He twisted his head to the side, and a fraction of an inch outside the rays of the morning sunlight, a shadow hunched. A shadow with an arm stretched toward Eddie's shadow.

In the basement, the clank of the pilot light door sounded. "Eddie? Do you have any…oh. Here they are, right in front of my nose." A match scratched away down there in the darkness, and the heater *whooshed* to life. "That got her, son. Head on over to the thermostat and set a nice, warm temperature."

The shadow faded as though the light making it had gone out, and the pressure on his tongue, the ice-cold invasion of his mouth disappeared.

Maybe nothing was ever there, he thought. On shaking legs, Eddie walked to the hall to set the thermostat. Behind him, the chief thumped up the stairs. "It'll be warm as a pizza oven in here in a few minutes," said the chief.

"Uh-huh," Eddie croaked, his mind racing, ideas fluttering around like mad hummingbirds in a tornado. *What was that? Did I imagine it?*

*Was that the scary lady? She seemed…*different *somehow*, the small voice in his mind whispered. *That was way worse than the other times the scary lady paid me a visit. She's never touched me, not in any of her previous visits. Why did she touch me*—attack *me*—*this time? And why were her eyes different?* The small voice had no answers, or if it did, it didn't want to share.

"Well, then." The chief settled his bulk into one of the dusty kitchen chairs. "Did you see that beautiful Tiffany lamp down there in the basement? Didn't your Auntie

Margo want that out to the farm where she could appreciate it? How do you suppose they got the glass that bright-red color? It's almost as if the lamp is on, even though the thing's not plugged into any socket I can see."

Red? Eddie turned the thermostat to seventy-three degrees and tapped it with his finger the way his mother always had.

"Can't say I appreciate the picture much. A Garden of Eden thing? That ugly willow tree with orange leaves, that orangish-brown snake with the red spots… And that weird bird! Not my style at all. Did your mother *like* that shade?"

My mother never saw that shade, Eddie thought. *When daddy brought it home, it was as I saw it last night, but when the scary lady started to come, it changed to the dark background and bright-blue fish. It's never been red.* He wanted to say the words aloud, but even at eleven, Eddie knew better than to say things such as that to a cop.

He turned, glancing at the kitchen visible from where he stood. A part of him wanted to go down into the basement and look at the new lampshade, but he didn't believe he'd ever go down those steps again. Not without someone dragging him.

"Why don't you come back in here, Eddie, and we'll have ourselves a little chat?"

"Coming." With a gentle sigh, he turned away from the thermostat and walked back to the table in the kitchen. Eddie chose the chair across from Chief Morton's and sat, resting his elbows on the table. After flicking up to the chief's face, his gaze rested on Morton's bronze name tag.

"Eddie, I know it's hard." The big man cleared his throat, but in a much more polite way than Eddie had a few minutes before. "It must be, it must be hard to deal with…well, what you have had to deal with. I don't imagine your Uncle Gil makes it easy, either."

Eddie pursed his lips and turned his head away.

"But there has to be something good in all this."

Eddie darted a quick peek at the chief's broad face.

"Your Auntie Margo is a nice one. Don't you enjoy being with her every day? I mean, it's better than a stranger, right?"

Eddie fidgeted with the zipper on his coat and leaned back in the chair.

"It can be hard, a boy your age and a man such as your Uncle Gil. I imagine he's a hard taskmaster. Hard to please. High expectations."

Eddie ducked his head.

"But is that all of it, Eddie?" asked the chief, leaning forward and resting his elbow on the table.

Eddie glanced up into the chief's face, met his concerned gaze, but said nothing.

The chief looked uncomfortable for a moment, rubbing the back of his neck. "Your aunt…" Morton shrugged again. "Well, there's been rumors. A small town such as Cottonwood Vale… People talk, and when the little old ladies at church glimpse bruises under your aunt's shawl… Well, you know." The chief reached for his neck again but stopped and dropped his hand to his lap.

Eddie raised his eyebrows.

"I can help, Eddie. If there is something going on, something not right, all I need is for you to tell me what it is."

Eddie cut his gaze away.

"Eddie, look at me," said Chief Morton, but it wasn't a threat the way Uncle Gil always said it.

He brought his gaze back to the chief but stared at the end of the chief's nose instead of looking him in the eye.

"I *can* help, Eddie. There are laws. It's not how it used to be. If your Uncle Gil is getting up to no good, all you have to do is tell me."

Eddie tried to swallow the sudden pain in his throat, unable to speak even if he wanted to. For a moment, he imagined that cold pressure on his tongue kept him from making a sound, but there was no pressure, no tightness around his throat or deep in his chest. He pictured that big black hole in his middle and shoved all that pain and fear into it.

Morton sighed and flopped his big hand on the table. "Okay, then. Tell me why you are here in this cold house. Why did you leave the farm last night?"

Eddie closed his eyes for a moment and took a deep breath. "I… I collect things. Gil…he…he doesn't want me to collect things. He…" Eddie shook his head.

"Go on, son," said the chief in a voice just above a whisper.

"I was collecting…" Eddie's gaze darted up to meet the chief's. "I had these…these figures, and Uncle Gil…Uncle Gil… He *hated* them."

"What, action figures?"

Eddie licked his lips and cut his eyes to the side. "I had two G.I. Joes—one with the Kung-Fu Grip."

"I can't imagine anything wrong with that, son. A boy your age."

Eddie squinted at the chief. "I also had… Do you know what a Ken doll is?"

John Morton nodded. "Yes, goes with a Barbie, right?"

"Yeah, I had a Ken doll and a few Barbies, too."

"Barbies, you say?"

Eddie swallowed hard. "As *collectibles*. They're going to be worth real money in twenty years. Everyone says so."

Morton grinned and lifted his shoulders. "If you say so, son." His face grew serious. "I'm still not seeing it, Eddie. I still don't get why your Uncle Gil should get upset about this collection."

"He...he called me a bad name."

"Because of the Barbies?"

Eddie nodded, and John Morton pursed his lips and sighed. "Son, some men..." He shook his head. "Some men are a little uncomfortable with the idea that someone in their family might be different."

"He called me a *faggot*," Eddie blurted.

"I'd guessed that, Eddie. Do you understand what the word means? It's an ugly word, for as much as it gets used these days."

Eddie tilted his head to the side and looked off into the corner. "I think so. Men that..." Eddie blushed to the roots of his hair.

The chief leaned toward him. "Yes, men that love other men."

"I'm not—"

"No, no. Playing with dolls doesn't make you gay, son. If it were that simple, I don't reckon there would be any gay men."

"Then why did Uncle Gil—"

"To get at you a little." The big man put his hands on the table between them and stared at his palms. "To make you feel small. Weak."

"I don't understand." Uncle Gil always called him weak and made it sound like a bad thing. *Why make me feel weak, then*?

The chief glanced at him, meeting his gaze. "If your Uncle Gil is the type of man that he seems to be, Eddie, there's a lot about him that's hard to understand. It's a weakness that some men have, a broken part deep inside that leads them to do bad things to the people they love."

Eddie thought about the way Uncle Gil treated Auntie Margo, about the bruises she wore from time to time, about how he cowed her into doing whatever he wanted. He thought about how mean Uncle Gil had been to him over the years, how he had made Eddie burn his doll collection, and he bobbed his head.

The chief nodded back. "I see you understand. As far as I'm concerned, that's another nail in your uncle's coffin. All you have to do, Eddie—all you *ever* have to do—is ask me for help, and I'll be there. I know how to stop a man who's bent up inside like your Uncle Gil, to stop him cold. You just tell me."

Eddie squirmed in his chair. *I told you about Uncle Gil*, he thought. *I told you he didn't like me. I told you he called me names. How many times do I have to tell you?* But he said none of those things, and so, nothing changed.

2

December 1979

As they walked toward the park, Sean summoned the courage to take Kristy's hand. She winked at him and licked her glossy lips, sending his pulse racing.

"Come on," she purred at him. "Let's go for a hike through the woods."

"A hike?"

She tipped him a wink. "Yeah, silly. You and me, all alone in the trees where no one can see what we do."

Something stirred in Sean's belly as he nodded. Kristy was seventeen, and he was only twelve, but he didn't care. He wanted *her*.

She led him off from Main Street, following a serpentine path. She peeked at him often, smiling her sexy smile and giving his palm a squeeze. "You will love this, Sean. I promise."

Sean gulped and tore his gaze away. He'd never even kissed a girl, let alone—

"Ah, there it is," Kristy said. She lifted her free hand and pointed at a ramshackle collection of cast-off boards hammered together with all the skill of school children.

Sean's stomach dropped. He recognized the shack—it was where Denny Cratchkin said Ari had murdered Jasper with a hammer. He stopped walking in the middle of the trail.

"Come on, Sean," crooned Kristy. "I'm going to make you see the face of God." She winked and pulled on his hand.

"Don't you know what that place is?"

"Sure, I do. What could be more fun? We can find the exact spot where Jasper bled out, and you can lie down where he died. I'll climb on top of you and—"

"No!"

"Oh, come on, you little narc. Get your freak on."

While Sean had seen Kristy's lips move, the voice was Denny Cratchkin's, and he…

…bolted upright in the bed, his heart thundering in his chest.

Something's wrong, he thought, though he couldn't say why he believed it. *Kristy's in trouble!*

3

December 1979

Denny strode down the sidewalk next to Union Street with the studied casualness Red Bortha had drilled into him. He had no doubts Red had changed the course of his life for the better, so even if the favor Red had asked for hadn't seemed fun, he would have done it.

But it *did* seem fun.

A rapacious grin stretched his lips, and given the cover of night, he didn't feel compelled to hide it under a mask of normalcy. What Red had called a "little favor" had Denny's heart pounding and his blood up.

Without glancing around, Denny turned up the driveway of the house neighboring Kristy's. He acted as though he had every right to walk up the drive, he pretended he owned the place, and if he performed up to Red's expectations, he *would* own the house—and soon.

He mounted the steps that led to the kitchen and slid the key to the door into the lock. The deadbolt opened with a solid *thunk*, and he stepped inside the silent home. Red had a specific scene he wanted set, and Denny aimed to please him.

4

December 1979

Karl Munnur sat hunched behind the wheel of his "new" automobile, though the seventeen years of service the machine had seen in Western New York had robbed it of its new-car luster. He missed his Impala, and he missed his old life, but he'd gotten sloppy, and his present situation was his just dessert.

Miriam Benchly had made a single phone call that evening back in September, but with the kidnappings, the mass shooter, and all the rest, Leif had garnered little attention from the Oneka Falls Police Department, and given the murders within its ranks, Munnur didn't expect much of an investigation into a drug-pushing teenaged boyfriend—the charges of pimping notwithstanding. Even so, he'd had to leave the house next door to Kristy Benchly, and worse yet, he'd had to abandon all the work he'd put into the girl. And that *rankled*. He'd intended her to become a mobile buffet, someone whose shame and guilt kept her by his side for further debasement.

His mind turned down a well-worn path through his psyche, one littered with signposts that read "why," and "how." Karl had no answers to those questions. Sean Walker had somehow done the impossible. *How in the blue fuck did he recognize me? Have I become so slothful, so* slothful, *that an eleven-year-old can breach my visage?*

He sat watching the Walker residence, waiting for Sean to appear. All Munnur had to do to ensure Red's plan would succeed was to keep Sean away from Kristy's house for the next few hours.

The blinds covering Sean Walker's bedroom window twitched, and a small peephole emerged. *Why, hello there, Sean,* Munnur thought. He considered giving the window a jaunty wave, but until he could figure out how in the hell Sean had seen through his disguises, he'd decided to treat the boy like an archenemy.

But, if Red's project went off the way he'd claimed it would, his archenemy wouldn't survive the evening, and he'd share what remained of Kristy Benchly with Red. The alpha's strategy relied on simplicity, where the complexity of Munnur's exotic plan had led only to mistakes and missteps.

Simple, he thought.

Karl pursed his lips and clenched his fists at the memory of all the effort he'd wasted cultivating Kristy, of the time he'd squandered courting Vickie Walker just to be close enough to Sean to dine on the boy's crushing sadness when he was peckish. In hindsight, his ideas seemed…juvenile and naive.

At least he wasn't the only demon who'd suffered setbacks. Herlequin himself had pulled up stakes and moved to the forest close to Lake Genosgwa. The rumor mill said three of his prey had seen through the game Herlequin played with them and escaped.

Munnur shook his head. Something in Oneka Falls had gone cockeyed, and it had cost him a well-established identity and a job he'd enjoyed.

And his Impala.

5

December 1979

Not for the first time since the ugliness with Leif in September, Kristy lay awake well past when she should have been sleeping. Frigid cold ruled the darkness in her mother's house, and though she needed to pee, Kristy didn't want to leave the comfort of her warm bed.

The preceding three and a half months had been hard on her. As the haze of the steady diet of drugs—drugs Leif had fed her—withdrew from her brain, memories of their evenings together had returned, and shame ruled Kristy's mind and heart.

The things I've done...

Kristy grunted and rolled to her side, pulling the covers over her face. She'd lost count of the number of sleepless nights she'd spent trying to make sense out of everything, struggling to understand what Leif had done and why.

She and Sean Walker had become friends, despite the five-and-a-half-year difference in their ages. The boy seemed smart and thought with almost adult maturity. He said Leif wasn't a teenager, not really, that he was the same person as a middle-aged guy Vickie Walker had been dating, but that made little sense when you knew Leif's anatomy as Kristy did.

She hadn't seen Leif Lawson or his father since the night Sean had burst into Leif's bedroom and stopped Leif and that pig, Dennis Cratchkin, Senior. Without his intervention, the evening would have ended with a gang-rape at the very least. She'd read that in Cratchkin's eyes, but as time wore on, she'd come to believe the expression had also shone in Leif's eyes.

No question about it, she thought. *I owe the kid.*

6

December 1979

Denny climbed the stairs in silence, practicing what Red called his "ninja walk." The house rang with emptiness, but he practiced as much as he could because Red said it was important.

As he walked down the upstairs hall, he picked a door at random and opened it. A stale odor pervaded the air inside, the scent of dust bunnies and old air. The room was vacant except for a bent wire hanger on the floor of the closet. Denny shrugged and opened the door on the other side of the hallway. It, too, was empty.

A slow smile drifted across his cheeks. *Kristy the dink*, he thought. The image of Kristy in her black bikini accompanied the idea, and lust stirred his blood. *Soon*, he said to himself. *Soon you can play with Kristy as much as you want, and there won't be any goddamn swimsuit getting in your way.*

He walked to the door at the end of the hall—the only upstairs room Red's friend had used—and slipped inside. The blind was down, but Denny could still make out the details—a cheap stereo, a twin bed, albums stacked against the wall, clothing strewn on the floor. If nothing else, he had to admit that the bedroom gave off a convincing appearance.

He'd had his eye on Kristy for some time—the gorgeous blonde who put out for drugs. She'd always sounded like Denny's very idea of fun, but Red had forbidden him from touching her. He'd said to leave Kristy alone, that someone else had taken an interest in her.

But, no longer.

With a feral gleam in his eye, Denny stripped the sheets from the mattress and twisted and tied them into bonds that would soon hold Kristy in place while he had his fun.

7

December 1979

Sean hooked his index finger through a space between the slats of his blinds and twitched a peephole into existence. He peered out, staring at the white Ford Galaxy parked a block up the road. He'd seen the car before but never the driver.

His instinct said Karl Munnur sat behind the wheel, despite the figure there being half the size of the deputy and having the wrong color skin. Leif had looked nothing like Karl either, but Sean *knew* they were one and the same. *If he can do it once, he can do it again*, the boy thought.

Thinking back, Sean had seen the Galaxy many times over the past few months. Outside the school, parked on the side of Mill Lane a few blocks from the store, and cruising down his own street in the evenings. He peered between the slats, trying through sheer force of will to penetrate the gloom inside the car, trying to pierce whatever magic Karl used to camouflage himself.

"Come on, come on," he muttered, pressing harder with his mind and opening his eyes wide. He pushed until his pulse pounded in his temples and his eyes burned as if he'd stared at the sun, but though the darkness seemed to recede a bit, he could see the driver no better.

With a sigh, Sean let the peephole close and turned away from the window. He snatched his jeans off his desk chair and shoved his legs into them. *There has to be a way to see who Karl really is. Has to be.* He grabbed the T-shirt he'd worn the previous day and pulled it over his head. *If he can…what? Project? If he can project whatever he wants me to perceive, how would I ever know if I saw the truth?*

Instead of pulling on his shoes and socks, Sean returned to the window and pierced the blinds with his index finger once more. The car still waited down the street, swathed in shadow. *I know Karl. I've spent a lot of time with him. I should be able to pierce his illusion.*

He sensed Karl's gaze on him, despite the darkness inside the Galaxy, despite the fake face that stared straight out through the windscreen. Again, he opened his eyes wide and did that thing he did inside his head that felt like pushing. He maintained the effort past when his pulse started to pound, past when his eyes teared up from the ache of not blinking. He clenched his fists and hunched toward the window, pushing and pushing and pushing.

He let his pulsing eyes slide closed, and just before they closed all the way, he glimpsed something yellow in the driver's seat of the old Galaxy. Something yellow that resembled one of those silverback gorillas Jane Goodall lived with. The thing had a broad, V-shaped mouth filled with the teeth of a great white shark. The vision came to him for only a split second.

He remembered his nightmares of the yellow monster chasing him, wearing Kristy's skin as a cape. Sean remembered how the thing had spoken in Karl's voice, how uncomfortable those dreams had made him.

He recalled the fever dreams he'd had when he was eight. Karl had stayed by his bedside along with his mother—and he remembered awakening during one nightmare to find Karl staring at him with a peculiar expression on his face. Karl had stared at him as though irritated by the nature of his dream—and Sean hadn't told him a thing about the dream. *We should talk about your imagination, kid*, Karl had said. *It might get you in trouble someday*. But they'd never spoken of the incident again.

Was that my subconscious? Were those dreams my mind trying to warn me about Karl? Sean snapped his eyes open and stared at the car. *If my subconscious mind can see the reality of him, then so can my conscious mind. Right?*

Behind the steering wheel, the driver shifted his position—leaned his head back against the headrest and rested his wrist on the door, letting his hand dangle in the night air.

Sean started to turn away, but a flash of yellow caught his attention. He returned his stare at the car but could pick out nothing yellow. He turned his head to the side again, and when he caught the flash of color, he froze, resisting the urge to roll his gaze on the yellow flash.

Watching from the corner of his eyes, Sean moved his head a little at a time and Karl's pure form—the yellow scaled flesh, the bulging gut, thick musculature, chartreuse alligator eyes—became apparent as his vision shifted over the man's frame.

The man's *frame? Karl is no man*, he thought. *Karl is a monster. A real-life monster.*

Sean moved his hand away from the blinds, letting the peephole close again. Karl could smash him like a gnat on the windshield of a big rig. *A baseball bat to the noggin probably wouldn't even faze him.*

Even so, Sean had to move. If his dreams about the yellow monster were real, then his latest dream about Kristy most likely contained some truth to it.

And that truth is Denny Cratchkin is after her. With that thought, Sean turned and tiptoed toward the back door of the house, carrying his shoes and socks in one hand.

8

December 1979

When he'd prepared everything, when he'd set the prefect scene for the night's theater, Denny stood back and smiled at it. Red had told him the story, how Denny's pervert of an old man had tried to bed Kristy but hadn't been able to get it up. Red told him how Kristy had belittled the man, laughed at him for being small and impotent, and despite Denny's hatred for his father, rage seethed within him as he recalled the tale.

The old man's an asshat, but no one's going to get away with mocking him... Or with mocking me through him. Denny nodded to himself, his unfettered expression gone savage in the darkness. *She'll see just how us Cratchkins take care of business tonight,* he thought, wrinkling his nose at the primitive nature of his own smile. *She's going to learn her lesson. And right fucking now.*

He spun on his heel and retraced his steps through the dark house. Denny drew a deep breath on the top tread of the back stoop, then jumped down, landing with both feet on the gravel drive, imagining the sound came from bones shattering beneath him.

He turned and dashed down the gutter of space left between the two houses, bent a little at the waist as he imagined those Killer Kane motherfuckers had run in Nam. Those bad asses ran hunched over their guns.

Denny didn't have a gun, but he had a new hammer.

9

December 1979

Sean shifted the curtains open a mite and dragged one of the kitchen chairs to sit in front of the stripe of the dark night. He sat and pulled on his socks.

A still silence reigned in the backyard. Nothing moved against the backdrop of fresh snow, nor could he see any footprints marring its surface.

Shoes on and tied, Sean sat for a moment, reflecting about what he'd seen in the Galaxy across the street. *No wonder he gave off such a weird vibe at times. He's a monster...a real-life monster. A demon, maybe.*

But if that's true, why didn't he eat me?

He got up and fetched his winter coat, wool cap, and gloves. Big, wet flakes of snow still fell from the sky, and he didn't know how long he'd be out skulking around in the darkness. He didn't know if he'd have shelter from the snowstorm or whether he'd have to sit in the tree in front of Kristy's house until dawn. Whatever he had to do, though, he wanted to be warm.

He returned to the slider and stood staring out into the snow-covered yard, his breath fogging the glass a touch as he exhaled. Nothing moved out there. He turned back toward the coat closet and found his baseball bat.

Warm and ready for anything, he thought.

Sean slid the door open just wide enough to allow him to squeeze out and stepped outside. He closed the door behind him, then froze, scanning the backyard for telltale puffs of breath, listening for soft footsteps or the mere shifting of weight from foot to foot.

He took a step away from the house and scanned the yard from the corners of his eyes—just like he'd done to see Karl's actual shape. Satisfied no one spied on him from the shadows, Sean stepped from the deck into the snow and slogged his way to the stockade fence that stretched across the rear of their property. Trees buffered the backyard from the noise of Main Street, but Sean had the idea they might also cover his exit.

Karl was out front, and if he went through the woods, Sean could get away clean.

10

December 1979

An unfamiliar noise awakened Kristy. She let her eyes drift closed again, hoping sleep would return. She'd fallen asleep thinking about Sean Walker again, about her debt to him, as she often did. Kristy didn't know how to repay him—the first idea that came to mind was always *Leif's* preferred method of payment, and that would *not* happen.

No matter what other debauchery Leif had talked her into, she wasn't going to bed a twelve-year-old. She shook her head in the darkness and rolled to her side, drawing the blankets closer. Winter was often colder in Oneka Falls than other parts of Western New York, but that year had been super-cold. She considered a mad, freezing dash to the thermostat, even imagined the scent as the heater stepped it up a notch, but she never so much as twitched the covers. No matter how great turning up the heat seemed in the middle of the night, the image of her mom's disappointed expression brought her back to reality.

Since that evening in September, the truth had come out. The drugs, the sex, the nude dancing, all of it. Kristy had told her everything, and true to her word, her mother hadn't shouted at her, hadn't punished her, but the disappointment in her eyes had cut Kristy to the quick.

Downstairs, something *thunked*, and Kristy's face wrinkled. She'd quit thinking about the sound that had awakened her. She'd put it out of her mind, but that *thunk* wasn't right.

Kristy cocked her head, pulling the covers down to expose her ear, and listened hard. The house creaked and sighed the way it always did. They had no grandfather clock, so the only ticking Kristy heard came from a cheap K-Mart alarm clock on her nightstand. Strain as she might, she detected nothing out of the ordinary. Chiding herself for a kid scared of the dark, Kristy forced herself to relax, to lay back and get comfortable.

Then the loose third step of the staircase creaked.

11

December 1979

He froze as the tread beneath him creaked. *Nothing I could do about that one*, he told himself, but even so, part of him imaged Red's disappointment, and shame soured his stomach. The house remained quiet, despite the noise he'd made, though, so Denny pressed on.

Without putting more weight on the loose step, he shifted toward the wall—where Red said stair treads would have the most stability—and felt a blush creep up his neck. He climbed the rest of the stairs at a slower pace, testing each tread as he ascended.

At the top of the steps, he took a second to orient himself. He knew Kristy's bedroom was across the gap between the two homes from the room where Denny had set up his scene. The place where Kristy had mocked his old man.

A grin stretched his lips as he turned right, turned toward Kristy's room. He crept toward her door, staying close to the wall, one gloved hand skimming the plaster, the other fondling the haft of his short-handled sledgehammer.

He stopped at the door with a big wooden K hanging from its center. His cheeks hurt from smiling, and he moved his jaw back and forth, trying to loosen the muscles, but the moment he relaxed, the rictus grin returned.

He dropped a hand to the doorknob and withdrew the hammer from his belt with the other. He sucked in three deep breaths, then flung the door open and charged into the darkness beyond.

12

December 1979

Sean pushed the ajar front door open wider and peered into the darkness of the Benchly home. He'd seen the open door first thing and understood what it had to mean on a cold winter night. He tiptoed into the house, closing the door with as little noise as possible and throwing the deadbolt.

Sean had visited Kristy many times and was familiar with the layout of the first floor. He passed the couch where they'd spent so many evenings watching Jeopardy. He stepped beyond the arch that led to the formal dining room, where he and his mother had shared Thanksgiving leftovers with the Benchlys the day after Turkey Day. Sean glanced through the pocket-door into the kitchen as he ghosted past it, but he didn't waste time searching the room. He knew Denny's destination, and it wasn't on the ground floor.

Sean made his way back to the staircase and climbed, stepping over the loose step he knew was there. Two steps shy of the second floor, he stopped and peeked around the corner. At the far end of the hall, a black-clad figure flung the door with the large wooden K on it open and charged inside the darkened room.

Without making a sound, Sean ascended the rest of the staircase and rounded the corner to the right.

13

December 1979

Denny charged into the dark room and stumbled over something. He fell headlong into the darkness. Rolling to his back, he swept the hammer at whatever had tripped him.

The hammer smashed the cardboard box, and inside, glass tinkled as a tchotchke broke. *What the...* Denny whirled to his knees and glared around at the boxes stacked in towers spread throughout the room. No bed, no nightstand, no vanity, only stacks of cardboard boxes.

Denny glanced at the shade-blocked window and crawled there on his knees. He pulled the blinds back and peeked out on the bedroom where he'd set up in the neighboring house.

This is the right room... He looked around. *But at the wrong time.* His face settled into grim lines. He could call it, wait a few months, and come back to finish later. *Yeah, that's the safe choice. The other option is to search room by room until I find the bitch, then drop the hammer.* At the moment, he didn't know whether that meant he'd kill her or take her next door and teach her a lesson. *Maybe it means both.*

14

December 1979

Sean stood in the dark, waiting for the sound of footsteps. Or for the rattle of the doorknob that opened the bathroom door to the hall.

He hid in a tiny space, sandwiched between where the open door would stand and the wall of the linen closet. At that moment, the truth about Kristy's room kept him from worrying. She and her mother had switched her bedroom to one right next to Miriam's.

One that lay to the *left* of the staircase.

He strained his ears, listening for footsteps, but only the sound of his own heartbeat reached him. He held his bat in front of him, almost like a shield, choked up to where the meat of the bat swelled to treble the size of the handle. The wood felt cold beneath his gloves, but Sean sweltered in his coat, gloves, and hat.

He lowered the bat and leaned it in the corner behind him, then he stripped the wool beanie from his head and threw it on the counter across from him. Sean peeled the gloves off as well, then unzipped his coat with as little noise as he could. He skinned out of it and tossed it into the tub.

The zipper hit the side of the porcelain bathtub with a hollow *thunk,* and he winced, cursing himself for his stupidity.

15

December 1979

Her mind supplied the image of Leif creeping down the hall toward her old bedroom, his little black bag tucked under one arm. For a moment, Kristy hoped it *was* Leif, hoped he had his bag of tricks, hoped for the bliss therein. But only for a moment.

Her mother wasn't the only person disappointed in the depths of her depravity.

She heard someone else on the stairs, a light tread on the steps. *Who could that be?* Leif had had no sidekick.

Except for Kristy.

At the far end of the hall, a door creaked open followed by a thud. Kristy rested her palm on the doorknob. She'd taken a moment to pull on a pair of jeans, but she still wore the extra-large T shirt she slept in, and her bare feet ached with the cold coming off the hardwood floor in waves.

She peeked over her shoulder at her bifold closet doors and lifted her hand from the latch. It rattled a bit as she stepped away from it. She opened one side of the closet and bent to find a pair of warm socks and her boots.

Behind her, the door slammed open, and she couldn't help it.

Kristy screamed.

16

December 1979

The doorknob rattled, and Denny froze, listening hard. Someone stood on the other side of the door, listening and breathing.

Waiting.

Kristy, he thought, and almost sighed with the elation that piggy-backed it. He leaned close to the door and heard a rustle—like a woman walking. His rictus-grin stretched broader still, and he grasped the doorknob, ready to throw the door open and charge inside.

He heard a strange creaking noise that took a moment to identify. *Folding closet doors! Oh, isn't that sweet? Kristy-poo thinks she can hide from me in her closet.*

He drew a deep breath and crashed through the door. Kristy kneeled across the room, pawing through a pile of clothing, and Denny stiffened where he stood.

Their gazes met, and she screamed.

Denny lifted his hammer and sprinted toward her, not shouting, not making a sound, but charging her as Red had taught him—in eerie silence. Her eyes widened, but true to Red's teachings, she quit screaming and didn't move.

He shifted the hammer into a two-handed grip and flung it high over his shoulder. All thoughts of teaching Kristy Benchly a lesson, thoughts of rape, thoughts of a beating, all that had disappeared into a mist of red rage and bloodlust.

He was almost within range when the hand of God clubbed him in the back of the head.

17

December 1979

After Kristy screamed, Sean sprinted to her new bedroom, bat raised. Denny Cratchkin ran at Kristy, who knelt at her closet door. Sean's eyes widened as Denny switched grips on the short-handled sledge.

He dashed forward, moving his grip on the bat for maximum reach. He hoisted the bat around to his right and leaped at Denny. At the apex of the leap, he swung with all his strength. Denny dropped like a sack of stones, and Sean swung again, this time shifting his aim at the sledgehammer, sending it spinning under the bed.

Kristy stared at the bat, and Sean followed her gaze. Blood dripped down its length from where it had smashed into the back of Denny's head. He ripped his gaze away from the blood. "Come on, Kristy. We have to get your mom." He forced one hand to let go of the death grip he had on the bat and held it out to her.

"You're…" Kristy's voice broke, sounding like the croak of a frog. She sat for a moment, her throat working. "You're making quite a habit out of saving me, Sean."

"Come on," he said.

18

December 1979

Somewhere out on Main Street, a siren whirred to life, and Karl started out of his revelry. He peered at the Walker house, but it remained dark, asleep. Sean hadn't peeped out at him in a while, and Munnur figured the boy had gone to sleep.

Red and blue sweepers revolved on the roof of an Oneka Falls Police Department cruiser as it roared past the intersection. Out of habit, Munnur reached for the switch controlling his own red and blues, but he no longer had a car equipped with lights and a siren. He no longer had a job in law enforcement, no position that allowed him to satisfy his curiosity by joining the call in progress.

Munnur let loose a deep sigh and dropped his hand. He didn't even have a scanner yet. *Well, that's one point I can control. I'll get over to RadioShack tomorrow and buy one. And there's another thing I can do.* With a final glance at the Walker place, Munnur started the shitpile Galaxy and drove to the end of the street. He looked both ways on Main, then pulled out.

He had no idea where the cruiser had gone, but in a town as small as Oneka Falls, finding them again wouldn't be hard. Munnur sat at the town's single traffic light, right across from the town hall, and considered his options. The likelihood someone on Rabbit Run or Deer Vale had called the cops paled in comparison to the streets on the other side of town, the other side of Main Street.

Munnur smirked to himself and drove through the intersection against the red. If they had a felony call, both police cars assigned to night patrol would respond. *Another benefit of small-town life.* He turned right on Union and let the old Galaxy advance at idle until he rounded the bend.

Red and blue lights reflected in the window glass of the homes toward the other end of Union, near where the road took another sharp, ninety-degree bow in the street. A sour taste flooded Munnur's mouth. The house he owned as Martin Lawson stood around that bend.

The place where Red's protégé had planned to deal with Kristy in his own crude way.

As he approached Saint Genisuis' Sanctuary of the Holy Mother, a towering figure stepped out of the shadows and held up a hand. *Red*, Karl thought and pulled to the edge of the street.

The huge demon came to the car, seeming to float an inch or so above the snow and leaving no footprints. Right before he opened the Galaxy's passenger door, he flung his three tentacles over his head and slammed his three horn-shaped talons together.

The big red demon wedged himself into the Galaxy and glared at Munnur through the honeycombed eyes of an insect. "You sure screwed the pooch on this one, Munnur."

Karl drew his face away from the demon. "How so? Sean Walker is at home in bed."

Red blew three simultaneous raspberries from his three mouths and waved a tentacle at the street ahead of them. "At least pull up so we can watch."

Munnur did as Red instructed, pulling across the road to the curb after rounding the bend.

Two Oneka Falls Police Department cruisers sat parked at odd angles in front of the Benchly house, and all the lights in the home blazed into the night like a ship on a vast white sea of snow. "What the hell went wrong?" asked Munnur.

Red shifted his bulk, crowding and leaning toward Munnur. "What went wrong? What went wrong was me trusting you at all after the way you managed your affairs. What went wrong was you *falling asleep*."

"I didn't fall asleep!" sputtered Munnur. "And I promise you that Sean Walker is at home…" He let the sentence fade as a uniformed officer came out the front door of Kristy's place. His hand rested on the bicep of a boy of about fifteen, dressed in all black. Blood trickled down the back of his neck.

"Do you see?" hissed Red. "My project, being led away. He'll be in juvie for years, all because of you."

"No," said Munnur. "A thousand things could've gone wrong. Miriam Benchly might've heard a noise, maybe she was up reading. Hell, even—"

"Look again."

Munnur glanced toward the house. On the porch stood the other patrolman, Miriam and Kristy Benchly, and…

Sean Walker. Munnur sat frozen for the space of ten breaths, then turned to Red. "But that's impossible. I followed him home at dinner time. I staked the place out all night, and no one left!"

Red sneered and waved all three tentacles in a flurry of anger. "And yet, there he is!"

Munnur glowered at Sean. "Yes," he said in a faint voice. As he watched the boy, Sean's movements became furtive. He approached the other policeman and said something. The cop lifted his head and stared right at the Galaxy.

"Oh, for fuck's sake," breathed Red.

"Don't worry. I've got this."

Red looked his direction but said nothing. He also didn't get out of the car and run away, so Munnur counted it as a win.

As the cop approached, he rested his hand on the butt of his sidearm and pulled his Maglite out of the ring on his belt.

He rolled down the driver's window. "Evening," he said. "I'm on the job."

The policeman peered at him and shone his Maglite into the front seat. "Karl? Karl Munnur?"

Munnur smiled and offered a little nod. "That's me. Can't figure out who you are because of the flashlight."

The cop turned the light on Red and grunted. "Deputy," he said.

"My partner," said Munnur. "Devin Deen."

The cop switched off the Maglite. "Sorry about the light. I'm Ross Dolen."

"Hey there, Ross," said Munnur. "What's going on?"

"B and E—a teenage punk who thinks he's a badass. That other boy clocked him with a bat." Ross's gaze traversed the Galaxy.

"Surveillance vehicle," said Munnur, keeping a smile plastered on his face.

"They spare no expense, eh?" Dolen's lips twitched with a suppressed grin.

"Imagine it's the same everywhere," said Munnur. "How'd the call come in?"

The cop tilted his head to the side. "Nine-one-one. Say, Karl, we've got this APB out on you. Seems someone at the State Police wants to talk to you."

Munnur forced a laugh. "Yeah, that. I got it all straightened out this evening. That APB will come down tomorrow."

Dolen stared into his face for a moment, then issued a slow nod. "I'll take you at your word, Karl."

He left the rest unsaid, *and if you're lying to me, I'll be knocking on your door in the morning*, but Munnur heard it loud and clear. He winked at Ross Dolen and started the old Galaxy. "Well, Ross, we've got to get back to our post. We just saw the lights on our dinner break—"

"BurgerWorld?" asked the OFPD officer.

"You know it. Best burgers in the county. Anyway, we thought we'd check if you guys needed a hand, but it looks like you've got it covered."

"Sure," said Ross with a little salute. "We're always happy to see the Kanowa County Sheriff's Department on the prowl. Don't pull a muscle sitting there watching people sleep."

"Might need a massage," grunted Red.

Munnur waved and pulled away from the curb. He turned around in the street and headed back the way they'd come. "Shit," he murmured.

Red laughed. "That puts the last coffin nail in your identity. You know that, right?"

"Yeah, yeah," grumbled Munnur.

"I could never figure it out."

"What?"

"The name."

Munnur turned toward the other demon and grinned as wide as he could, showing off his shark-like teeth. "Karl Munnur. Short for *hákarl munnur*."

Red rolled his honeycomb eyes. "And?"

Munnur shrugged. "It means 'shark mouth' in Icelandic." He flashed his broad smile again. "Get it?"

Red blew out breath from each of his three triangular mouths. "Oh, boy."

"Funny, right?"

The red demon turned to stare out the windshield. "Perhaps you can come up with something just as funny for your next identity. The troopers will be all over Munnur, so ditch the *whole* thing."

Hmm. New York State Police. That could be a fun gig. All I need is a new visage and a cool name. I wonder how you say 'mouth' in French…

Chapter 2
2010

I

LaBouche sat across from Nicole Conrau's husk. She shouldn't be dead...that's not how it worked with demons. She should either have disappeared as she traveled home, or life should have dribbled back into her body. But neither thing happened. Instead, her flesh gave up its heat to the surrounding air.

He felt numb as if someone had immersed him in gelatin. He stared at her, his mind adding twitches and small movements where none existed. Her blood faded to black as it cooled.

LaBouche had no doubts who bore responsibility for whatever had befallen Nicole. *Brigitta*, he thought. *She must have sussed out the pregnancy somehow. Nicole must have let it slip. But what in the fuck did Brigitta do? How is Nicole dead?*

As her body lost its heat, Nicole's quicksilver skin clouded like oxidizing metal. Her scarlet tongue lolled between her golden tusks, which now looked more similar to old, desiccated bone than ripe wheat fields.

Brigitta has powers beyond those most of us can summon. Maybe it's something— LaBouche shook his head. *No. No, demonic power has limits, even if the rumors of her parentage were true. Whoever her mother was, Herlequin was her father—according to both her and Herlequin—and he was of the same ilk as me.*

He stared into her eyes, once such a beautiful malachite color, now as gray and lifeless as old stone. Emotions warred within him—anger, grief, hopelessness—circling and circling each other, whirling like kids on a merry-go-round.

He recalled the conversation he'd had with Brigitta. The one about Sally McBride. *What had she said?* 'It would be a mistake to underestimate her. She served *her*, you know.' *Then I started to ask if McBride was a jinn, and Brigitta shushed me.* 'Don't say it,' *she said.* 'Don't even think it.'

LaBouche cast his gaze around the once-white bathroom without seeing his surroundings. Nicole's blood had dried to black in many places, but there were no footprints, no signs that anyone had been there with Nicole.

He snarled and swung his massive fists through the air as if affronted by its presence. He sprang to his feet and took two steps closer to Nicole. Gazing down on her, LaBouche could no longer lie to himself that she might return.

His grief threatened to overwhelm him, to mire him in despair and inaction, but his fury infused him with murderous energy. With one last glance at the corpse of the erstwhile mother of his child, LaBouche gave in to his outrage.

Turning his back on the bathroom, LaBouche swept his gaze across the room that had become his sanctuary. In two strides, he crossed the room and swept his mobile phone off the nightstand. His stare strayed to the bed, to Nicole's side of the bed, and stuck there for a time.

If it's true… If McBride is a jinn, then she fooled all of us. Not just me, but Chaz, Red, all the alphas. He pinched his lips and frowned until he thought his skin might split. *Herlequin must have known if Brigitta knew. Why would he keep her secret? Why would he allow a jinn in our midst? Why would he chance it?*

LaBouche swept the room one last time, then spun and stomped toward the garage. He grabbed a five-gallon can of gasoline and came back to the bath. He didn't look at Nicole's corpse, didn't linger near her, only splashed the fuel throughout the room and into the bedroom. LaBouche coated the bed, the carpet, and the draperies with gas, then he returned to the garage and found a box of safety matches.

As he struck the first, a question occurred to him. *If McBride is a jinn, then what is Brigitta?* Thunderstruck by the idea, the match burned down to his fingers and went out without his notice. His mind swam with possibilities, and none of them struck him as worthwhile. *If jinn are among us,* here *with us, then how likely is it we've escaped the gaze of...* He killed that line of thought but shuddered at the implication. *And if Sally* is *a jinn that means one of the old superstitions is true: the jinn can create visages we can't penetrate—the way the trickster does.*

He glanced around him, feeling watched, pursued, hunted, for the first time. The human hunters didn't scare him, but the *jinn*? They evinced a class of terror beyond his ability to ignore.

His gaze tracked to the open door of the bedroom he'd shared with Nicole for the past few years. The room in which they'd mated, produced offspring... His rage swelled within him. If the *jinn* walked among the denizens of Oneka Falls, no safe place existed, and his kind had escaped nothing by running from home.

His hands shook as he struck another match and threw it into the gasoline puddling on the bedroom floor. The fuel ignited with a *whoosh* and a *thump*, and LaBouche turned and ran.

He recalled Nicole's beauty as he climbed into the Monaco-blue BMW. He replayed a memory of her laughing, head thrown back, malachite eyes dancing, vermilion tongue forking at the air, and his rage burned away all traces of his fear.

If the jinn are here, if McBride is one of them, then I will make them all pay.

He backed away from the burning building as flames began to lick out of the bedroom window, but he sat in the road, the BMW's V8 burbling, and stared at the house, watching the paint peel from the siding, watching the shingles curl.

His phone vibrated in the console, drawing his attention from Nicole's impromptu pyre. A text blazed on his lock screen. A text from Mason Harper.

A ferocious grin split LaBouche's face as an idea burned in his mind.

Revenge, he thought and put the BMW into gear.

2

"*Dammit!*" cried Benny as they piled into Mike's Cadillac CTS-V.

"What?" asked Scott.

"They've got him! Abaddon has Greg!"

For a split second, silence reigned, and everyone but Benny froze in the middle of whatever they were doing. Then, as if someone threw a switch, they all sprang back into action.

"Where are they?" asked Mike. The Caddy roared to life, and as soon as the last door *thunked* shut, Mike hammered the accelerator. "Tell me where to go!"

"They were in the parking lot at International Datawerkz."

"And now?" asked Scott. He held a Remington 870 between his knees, the butt of the scattergun on the floor between his feet.

Benny closed his eyes for a moment. "In a van...headed...east..."

"Back toward New York," muttered Toby. One of the new dart guns rested in his lap. SEMPRe had recruited gunsmiths to its ranks, and after a year of trial and error, they had produced a semiautomatic tranquilizer gun with extended range and better muzzle velocity.

Mike raced down the long driveway, the eight-cylinder engine roaring, and the tires spitting gravel.

"Clear right," said Scott.

The Caddy slewed out onto the pavement, tires shrieking, but Mike held it steady and let it slide. "Where?" he snapped. "Where, Benny?"

"It's a dark color...Ford, maybe..."

"Benny, *where*?"

"They've turned south...headed toward Highway 20 or one of the interstates."

Mike took the next left and accelerated down the narrow two-lane road.

"Any demons with them?" asked Toby.

"I don't..." Benny pursed his lips, a grimace of disgust on his face. "They've handcuffed Greg to a metal bed in the back of the van...right up against a corpse. Harper is teasing him about being squeamish... There's...there's someone else with them. He seems familiar, but..."

"Great, great, but *are there any demons*?"

Benny shook his head. "Not with them. At least, I don't think so."

"Shannon, hide us!" snapped Toby. "If we can catch up to them, hang back until I can get set up, Mike."

Mike threw a glance at Scott. "Tires?"

Scott nodded. "If I can get a shot that won't kill everyone."

"Get us there, Mike! Get us there now!" Benny slumped in the back seat. "*Hurry!*"

Mike's gaze jerked to the rearview mirror. "What do you think I'm doing?"

3

His phone rang, and again, Chris Stanton ignored it. He was deep into a Gordian knot of trade routing, but he was close, and he knew it. He'd been ignoring the cell all night.

Stanton unraveled another layer of misdirection and grinned. He thought he had the location where the trade had originated. His fingers rattled across the keyboard. Behind him, something popped and warm air wafted past his face. He hunched closer to the screen, keying more instructions to his spider bot.

A golden glow appeared on his primary monitor, and Chris grunted with annoyance. "Close that damn door!" he snapped, sure that Sammy had come—against his expressed wish to be left alone—to see if he was hungry yet. "I'll eat when I fucking want to, woman!"

He peered at the screen, but the glare didn't go away. Ire rose in him like a whale coming to surface for breath. "Do we need to have the talk again, Sammy?" He tore his gaze from the screen and spun in his chair.

His mouth dropped open as if he had more to say, but he said nothing and only stared at the woman made of fire standing between him and the closed door.

"Chris," she hissed.

"Abby, is that you?"

"You shouldn't ignore me."

"No, of course not! I—"

"I want you to buy some real estate. An entire neighborhood."

"Real estate is risky, Abby. And where? Nothing down near Genosgwa is worth anything, except on one of the lakes. No, let me put together a package—"

Abby streaked across the room and held a burning finger—but no, that wasn't right...there was no finger, only flames—a quarter of an inch from his nose. The heat baked his face, and tears sprang to his eyes.

"You've enjoyed my acquaintance, correct?"

Chris leaned away from the fiery finger, but the woman made of fire leaned closer. "Yes, Abby. You know I have! Brigitta called and—"

"Shut up!" Abby snapped. "I know what my sister has—"

"Sister?"

"—asked of you. She wouldn't approach you without speaking to me first. You will do as I ask, Chris, or our acquaintance is at an end, and the repercussions of that..."

Chris didn't need her to elaborate. For a moment, he wondered if he'd gone insane... He understood Abby was more than the woman she pretended to be, but... He didn't even know the word for what she appeared to be.

"*Ifrit*," Abby breathed. "A demon of fire."

"Yes." Chris turned his gaze away. "What properties did you want me to acquire for the foundation?"

Abby straightened, and the heat lessened at once. "That's better."

4

"Won't this crate go any faster?"

"Relax, Denny," said Mason Harper. "No one even knows we have him."

Dennis Cratchkin pressed his lips into a thin, bloodless line. "I've got a funny feeling, Harper."

Mason lifted a hand from the van's steering wheel and flopped it side to side. "Funny feeling? Are you kidding me?"

"Red taught me to listen to my instincts, and my instincts shout that we're not out of the woods yet."

Mason rolled his eyes. "Hear that, Greggy? Denny thinks your friends are coming for you."

Greg lay in the back, chained to the metal bunk that ran along one side of the van's box. He shared the narrow mattress with the moldering corpse of a twenty-something-year-old woman. A shop rag filled his mouth, tasting of gasoline and ancient oil, held in place by a band of black duct tape.

"Oh, I know you can't speak yet. Denny said we needed to keep you quiet, lest you yell out at a stoplight and Johnny Q. Do-gooder hears you and calls the cops. But don't you worry, Greggy. We'll catch up when we get back to New York." Mason tsked, then chuckled. "I can't believe you hid so close, so…out in the open." He sucked his teeth and chuckled again. "But I can't argue with your success."

Greg's gaze danced from spot to spot in the rear of the van, looking for a weapon or a tool that would help him escape. The short-handled sledgehammer Mason had used to smash out the window of his car rested on the floor between the two front seats. Every now and again, the man Mason called Denny dropped his hand to it and stroked the metal head of the sledge with his index and middle finger. So far, Mason hadn't seemed to notice.

The van lurched, and the woman's corpse fell against him once more. Greg squeezed his eyes shut but refused to make a sound—he didn't want to give the assholes up front the satisfaction.

Denny laughed. "She's hugging him again."

Mason glanced at the rearview mirror which he'd adjusted so he could see the bunk. "Making friends back there, Greggy?" Denny cackled again and stomped his foot. "If you get horny, have at her. Denny and I have already had a turn, and we don't mind sharing."

Bile burned in Greg's throat, and he shook his head. Denny had turned to watch him, and his cackle filled the van again, drawing an irritated glance from Mason. Greg stared at Denny, trying to keep the revulsion off his face.

"She's not his type, Harper. I bet he bats for the other team."

"Greggy? No, I don't buy it." Mason's gaze found him in the rearview mirror. "You're not light in the loafers are you, Greggy?" Mason's laughter joined Denny's, and Greg turned his head away.

He hadn't been following the mental exercise plan Benny had devised for him. Who had time for exercises when running a business? More to the point, he'd been neglecting his gift, but he had to try.

Greg squeezed his eyes shut tight. One hand couldn't get more than four inches from the headboard of the bed, but he reached toward the cab of the van with the other. He blocked the sound of their voices, ignoring the road noise, the corpse pressed to his back, concentrating with all his energy on setting Denny ablaze.

If he succeeded, Mason might crash the truck, but Greg would rather die in a wreck than at the hands of Mason Harper.

Or the demons.

5

"I've completed the task, Mistress."

"Ah!" Brigitta beamed at the other demon. "All of it?"

"The child and the mother."

"That's wonderful, Sally!"

The heavy-set woman raised her chin. "Sally no longer, Mistress."

Brigitta cast a glance at her, her eyes narrowed a little. "Is it so?"

"Please call me by my name, Mistress."

"Your…" Brigitta pursed her lips. "Your *true* name?"

"Yes, Mistress. I've hidden too long behind this visage of weakness."

Brigitta squinted at her. "Do you wish to return to my mother then?"

The image of the heavy-set woman known in Oneka Falls as Sally McBride first wavered, then faded. A creature emerged from the darkness in her place, a creature with the body of a woman from the waist up and the long, thick tail of a snake from the belly button downward. Her black-scaled tail coiled beneath her, and her torso swayed atop it, arms crossed under her breasts.

Brigitta drew a deep breath. "This will cause much concern in the ranks of demons in Oneka Falls, Lamia."

Lamia, the *jinn* who had hidden behind the mask that had been Sally McBride, uncrossed her arms and flashed a warm smile. "Let them thrash, Mistress. But to answer your earlier question, no, I do not wish to return to your mother. I serve you now, Naa—"

"No!" whispered Brigitta. "Not even in private."

Lamia bowed her head. "As you wish...*Brigitta*."

"What do I tell them? How do I explain..." She swept her open hand at Lamia's length.

"Shall I adopt another visage, Mistress?"

Lamia's tone was bland, innocuous, but Brigitta understood the question was not an idle one. *It's a test*, she thought. She covered her eyes with her hands, massaging her forehead with her fingertips. "Why did those damn hunters have to kill my father? Everything was—"

"A deception," said Lamia. "Everything was a lie. Herlequin orchestrated the drama, but it was a lie, nonetheless."

Brigitta sighed. "A comfortable lie, though. One in which we were able to act as we wished. Free of the bonds of caste and the expectations that go with it."

Lamia shrugged, yet the tip of her tail lashed back and forth. "We still are. We always have been."

Brigitta flapped her hand in the air. "Have we? Why did you maintain the fiction for such a time? I can't believe you never tired of these gloating fools."

"I…" Lamia's forehead puckered. "Had Chaz not been here, I'm not sure how long I would have hidden here. Apsu has often chided me about it."

Brigitta nodded. "And me. I honored my father by pretending to be one of his kind."

"How can it be, Mistress?"

"You know better than anyone how—"

"Not that. How can it be you do not know the truth?"

Something oily and cold twisted over in Brigitta's guts. "Don't be a fool!" she snapped.

Lamia reached out and touched Brigitta's cheek with a tenderness her mother had never shown her. "Does this self-deception serve a purpose, Mistress?"

Brigitta turned away. "I have no idea what you mean." Behind her, Lamia sighed.

6

When he had burned the demon at the hospital, Greg had experienced an ethereal flow between him and the corpse just before the fire erupted. He felt nothing now, no ghostly surge, no flames, no intense wash of heat.

"What are you doing, Greggy?" asked Mason.

Greg released his pent-up breath and dropped his hand. "Nothing. Don't call me 'Greggy.'"

"Aw, why not? It's such a cute little moniker."

"Why are you doing this? Why are you doing any of this, Mason?"

Harper's gaze tracked to the rearview mirror, and even his reflected aspect felt cold and dead on Greg's face. "You know, Greggy, this existence isn't what most people think. Humanity isn't a homogenous sea of souls. There are sides, and in life, you either choose your side or someone chooses for you."

"What?" Greg swallowed, then gulped again. His throat was dry, and summoning spit took real effort. "Sides? There are no—"

"There *are*," said Denny. "Only idiots buy that all for one and one for all bullshit. That shit's old and tired, man."

"And, Greggy, it's even more pronounced, once you know the truth. You learned that truth that summer back in 1986."

Greg closed his eyes. "How did you…"

"I've been a part of it all along, Greggy. Since before you even met her, I have served her and her kind."

"But why? Why serve monsters intent on eating your own kind?"

Mason chuckled. "That's where you are wrong, Greggy. I have far more in common with my friends than I do with humanity. I've never suffered the weight of judgmental gazes on my back when I'm around demons. I can be myself, my *whole* self, and no one thinks less of me. No one says I should be in the nuthatch with your dad." Mason glanced at the side mirror and grunted. "How is the old man, anyway?"

"Did you ever stop to think that they accept you because they can feed off your victims' emotions?"

"You don't get it," said Denny.

"Do you see this, Den?" asked Mason in a low voice.

"The truck?"

"Yeah," said Mason. "Watch it for a minute."

"Why? It's just a guy driving his route."

"No. Watch, okay?"

Dennis looked at Mason with a flat expression for a moment before swinging his attention back to the side-view mirror. "This is… Oh. Yeah, I see it."

"Right?"

"The tricks the woman can do?"

"That's my thinking."

Denny peered at the passenger side mirror and made a peculiar sound—half-grunt, half-chuckle. "Let them come." He turned toward Mason. "Find a gloomy road or a dark parking lot and pull over."

"No, I don't think so. They may be armed."

Denny laughed. "So? Red taught me a few tricks, and I'm sure he taught you some, too."

Mason hitched one shoulder. "We'll allow Greggy to decide." Once more, his gaze found Greg in the review. "What do you say, Greg? Should we stop and swat your pesky friends now, or should we lead them into a nest of waiting demons?"

7

"Back off, Mike!" snapped Scott. "You might as well have a bright-red flag on the hood."

Mike grunted but didn't lift his foot. "If they see us, they will pull off to stop us."

"Or they'll kill Greg outright and be done with it," said Scott.

"We don't want to *follow them*, Scott. We need to intercept them."

"Yeah? And when they pull over and come at us? Do you think they'll leave Greg alive in the back of the van while that happens?"

Mike lifted his foot and allowed the van to pull away. "Okay," he said.

"We need a plan."

"They've seen us," said Benny.

"Shit!" muttered Scott.

8

"See there, Denny? They're falling back."

"Yeah. But now what?" Denny's hand strayed to the floor between the bucket seats and found the short-handled sledgehammer. He grasped the haft and lifted the hammer to his lap.

"Now, we wait and see."

Dennis scoffed and ground his teeth. "I thought you were a man of action, Harper."

"Oh, I am. I most certainly am. *Cratchkin.*"

Greg watched the interplay between the two men with a practiced eye. While running a company, he'd learned how to smooth over rough spots between his employees. He imagined the reverse of that worked just as well.

"Why do they call you Abaddon?" he asked.

Harper's gaze flicked to the rearview and then back to the side mirror. "You know why."

"Yeah," said Greg. "But what I meant is *why Abaddon?*"

"Don't you read your bible, Greggy?"

Denny scoffed.

With a glare at the passenger seat, Harper said, "Abaddon is the Angel of Death, Greg. Says so in Revelations."

"Oh. I guess that makes sense, what with you being a serial killer and all."

Mason peered at him in the rearview, a smirk decorating his face. "Are you trying to piss me off, Greggy? Don't bother. No one has riled me up for...I don't know, two decades or so."

"No offense," said Greg. He turned his gaze on Denny. "What do they call you?"

Denny grunted and licked his lips.

"Oh, come on. Don't be shy. The press has a name for you, too. Right?"

The man gazed down at the hammer in his lap.

"He doesn't have a nickname, Greggy. Nobody knows about him."

"What? That can't be right. Do you just help Mason out, then?"

Denny stared at Mason, a sneer distorting his face.

"No, no. It's true," said Mason.

"That's right," grated Denny. "No one knows about the things I do, because I never leave *anything* behind to hint at a crime. Red taught me—"

"Oh, not that again," murmured Harper.

Denny grimaced, and cords stood out of his neck. "Red taught me to create a plausible story for the cops to believe." He grinned with half his mouth. "That's not quite true. I always thought that way, but Red refined my way of thinking. Perfected it." He tilted his head toward Mason. "Now, I can do whatever I want, and there's never a hint of trouble. *I* haven't been kicked out of my own house."

Mason threw a hateful glance at him.

"What's more," said Denny. "No one survives an encounter with me. No one ever ran to the cops because I *made sure* they could never run again."

Mason clicked his tongue. "Yeah, yeah. But everyone knows *my* name."

Denny narrowed his eyes and glared at Mason as the trees blurred by.

"Still, you have got to have a nickname. Maybe they don't know who it is, but they'd have a name for your…exploits."

Denny turned a flat glare on Greg. "It's time for you to shut up, Greggy."

"No offense!"

Cratchkin tilted his head and caressed the hammer in his lap. "You don't want me to come back there."

"No, no," said Greg. "I'm curious, is all. I don't mean anything by it."

The man leaned toward him, draping one arm over the seat. "*Shut up.*"

"Better do it, Greggy. I won't save you if you provoke him, even though both of us will be in trouble if we don't bring you in alive." On the console between the two front seats, a cell phone jittered and buzzed. "Could you grab that for me, Denny?"

With a low growl, Cratchkin scooped up the cell phone and peered at it. After a moment, he swiped it with his thumb and lifted it to his ear. "Yes?" He cocked his head to the side and glanced at Mason. "I'm sitting right next to him, Delo."

Mason squinted at Denny through slit eyelids. "What—"

Denny chopped his free hand through the air. "The line's shit, Delo. I can hear you, but understanding is a different thing." After a moment, he nodded. "Yeah, that's better. I'm answering Harper's phone because he's driving and we—"

Mason sighed and waved his hand at Denny, who ignored the gesture.

"No, listen a second. The hunters are behind us." Denny listened for a moment. "Oh, sure." He pulled the device away from his ear and looked at it with a puzzled expression on his face.

"What?" asked Mason.

"Speaker?"

"Gimme it." Harper snatched the phone away when Denny touched his palm with it. He took a rapid glance at it and mashed the screen with his thumb. "There."

"Okay?"

"Yes, Dan. You're on speaker."

"Dan?"

"Whatever," murmured Mason. "What do you want?"

"Change of plans. We've got word the hunters are—"

"They're right behind us."

The line hummed for the time it took to take three slow breaths. "Good. That could be good."

"I don't see how," muttered Denny.

"Ambush. You will lead them to us, but we have to switch meeting places. We'll need privacy, but if all goes as I think it will, we can end this tonight."

Mason nodded. "Okay. Where do you want us?" He listened to the instructions and grunted. "Easy."

"I'll expect you soon."

"Five or ten minutes. We're close."

9

A grim, angry smile settled on LaBouche's features. Brigitta had thought to exclude him from her plans for the evening, and that underscored her role in the plot that had taken his child from him. If it hadn't been for Mason's compulsive need to gloat and show off, LaBouche wouldn't have known about the trap Brigitta had laid for the hunters.

Her time will come, he thought. *I will return her betrayal tenfold.*

10

Greg slit his eyelids as the din from the engine compartment changed, and the rear tires of the box van shrieked as the brakes locked. Both he and the corpse he shared the bunk with flew forward against the limits of their bounds.

"Jesus!" shouted Denny. "What the fuck are you doing?"

Mason held the steering wheel in a white-knuckled grip with both hands, staring into the darkness through the windscreen. "Oh, relax, you big pansy," he said through gritted teeth. He cranked the wheel, setting the van into a skid.

The rear tires skipped across the macadam, and the truck leaned precariously to the side. Denny slammed one hand against the door, and the other hammered the roof. The short-handled sledge slid from his lap to clang off the door, before thumping into the passenger footwell.

Greg grabbed the metal frame of the bunk with both hands and tried to tip it, hoping that in the confusion, he might twist things to his advantage, but it wouldn't budge.

Mason fought with the wheel as the vehicle left the asphalt, loose stones clattering against the rear of the van. He twisted the switch on the dash that turned off the lights.

"You trying to kill us all?" asked Denny in a low, angry tone.

"Relax. No time to baby you." Harper leaned forward over the steering wheel, peering into the darkness ahead. The van jounced and bumped over a rutted track that led between the trees. "Shut up and let me concentrate."

In the back, Greg twisted his legs underneath him and pushed himself onto the cot in a seated position. His eyes scanned the dark cargo box, again and again, looking for anything he might use as a weapon. If he didn't do something soon, either Mason or the demons would kill him.

II

"What's he doing?" asked Toby as the van slid side-to-side ahead of them. "Watch it, Mike!"

"Not his fault," muttered Shannon. "I made them think we'd fallen way back."

The truck ahead dove off the side of the road onto a twin-rutted track that snaked off through the trees, sliding in a wide arc.

Mike kicked the CTS-V's brake pedal. "Hold on!" he cried. He twisted the wheel to follow the vehicle into the woods.

"Give him space," said Scott. "And Shan? Make them think we drove by!"

Shannon nodded, never opening her eyes.

"They... Someone called them... Change of plans... They...the demons know we are following and told Harper to divert to another location." Benny's skin wrinkled between his eyebrows. "But..."

"But what?" asked Toby.

"Something feels...wrong."

"Should we back off?" asked Mike. "Try to pick them up after the swap?"

"No." Benny's tone left no room for doubt. "No, it feels off, but it's Harper who's being deceived. Harper and...*Dennis the Menace.*"

"Dennis the Menace?" asked Shannon. "From Oneka Falls Elementary?"

"The very same," said Benny, opening his eyes. "He's the other one in the van. Harper, Dennis, and Greg."

"Who's lying to them?" asked Scott.

Benny swallowed and rubbed his temples. "They think it's the big purple pain in the ass from Greg's lake house."

"But you don't?" Scott turned in his bucket seat to look at Benny.

"We'll find out soon enough," said Mike. "They're stopping."

Ahead of them, the rutted track widened into a clearing—a clearing of overgrown summer grasses that threatened to swallow the van whole. Mike brought the Caddy to a smooth stop. "Anyone see anything?"

Harper and Dennis Cratchkin climbed out of the cab, and Dennis faced the sliding door and pulled it open. Mason turned and surveyed the meadow.

"Don't see anything," Denny said.

"This is the place. This is where Delo said to bring our guest. You heard the instructions as well as I did."

Denny grunted and said nothing, disappearing inside the cargo compartment for a moment. When he reappeared, he held Greg's cuffs by the short chain that connected the bracelets. "So…what now?" he asked.

Harper pursed his lips and paced ten steps beyond the front of the van. "He said he'd beat us here. He said—"

"Well, someone had to make sure you weren't being followed." The giant, winged demon stepped from the woods opposite Mike's car.

Mason peered into the trees. "Where are the others?"

The demon strode forward, exuding confidence. "Had to leave them in place to avoid raising suspicion."

"Suspicion? Whose?"

Benny straightened. "That's not Dan Delo! That's—"

The purple fiend bellowed and swatted Mason Harper five feet into the air and off into the timbers. He pivoted toward Cratchkin and Greg and closed the space between them with blinding speed. Two swipes with his massive arms and Dennis lay at his feet, unmoving. Greg turned and ran.

"Wait!" said the winged monster, holding out a hand.

"*That's LaBouche!*" said Toby.

Scott's eyes widened, and he whirled to throw the door open. He sprang from the car, racking the slide of the shotgun as he came to his feet.

"Scott! Wait! He's—" A blast from the 12 gauge drowned out Benny's pleas.

The purple demon staggered back, and the image of the winged beast flickered and died, replaced by the human visage of Lee LaBouche. Another volley from the shotgun sent LaBouche reeling, and the visage dissolved.

Scott took a step and fired for the third time, then racked the slide. He stepped forward again and pulled the trigger again. A fourth emptied shell spun into the darkness.

"He's trying to *help*!" yelled Benny.

Scott moved forward, firing as he went—step, fire, rack the slide, step—and LaBouche seemed to dance backward across the wild meadow, arms pinwheeling for balance, but he never tried to defend himself. He never fought back.

"Stop him! Mike, stop him!"

"Benny, there's no stopping this," said Mike. "There's nothing we could say—"

Scott racked the slide, took a step, leveled the scattergun, and pulled the trigger, but no blast followed. LaBouche teetered where he stood, his blood black in the moonlight—or perhaps black in any light. His mouth worked, but the shotgun had wrought devastation in his chest, and he seemed devoid of the breath required to speak.

He racked the slide again and pulled the trigger. When no concussion followed, Scott ran forward and slammed the butt of the shotgun into LaBouche's face, and after the banana-yellow demon sprawled on the ground at his feet, he hit him, again and again.

"Now, we can stop him," said Mike. He slid out of the driver's seat and strode to Scott's side. He put his hand on the trooper's shoulder, but Scott shrugged it off and continued pummeling LaBouche. "Scott, leave off." He grasped Lewis's shoulder again. "Come on, buddy. He's dead."

Scott flung the shotgun to the ground and hunched over his knees as if he might lose the contents of his stomach. Tears slicked his cheeks and mucus dripped from his nose.

Mike squatted next to him and threw an arm around his shoulders. "It's okay, Scott. You got him," he whispered. "LaBouche is dead. You got him."

Scott wretched and shook his head. "Not enough," he croaked.

"I know," murmured Mike. "Come on; you'll be more comfortable in the car. Let Toby and Benny mop this up."

"I want him to pay! I want…" Scott gazed away into the shadow-shrouded forest surrounding them. "I want them back, Mike."

"Shh," said Mike. "I know you do, Scott." He stood, helping Scott to his feet. "Come on now." He led the man back to the silent Cadillac. Greg stood next to the passenger quarter panel, a stricken expression dominating his features. "I'll get those cuffs in a minute, Greg," said Mike.

"Don't worry about me."

As they passed him, Greg lay a hand on Scott's shoulder, but Scott didn't seem to notice. Mike guided Scott into the passenger bucket seat and snapped in his seat belt, then gently closed the door. He jerked his head at the three in the backseat, then turned to remove Greg's handcuffs.

"What about Mason and that other guy?" asked Greg in a whisper.

"I'll cuff them to the van. We'll call the state police after we deal with LaBouche."

"About that," said Benny.

Mike glanced at him, one eyebrow arched.

"He isn't dead. I mean, he *is* dead, but he won't stay that way if we don't drain his blood and dispose of the flesh."

"We understand that, Benny," murmured Toby.

"Yeah. But…" Benny peeked over his shoulder at Scott. "Maybe we should let him reanimate."

"Benny, don't be a—"

"No, listen! LaBouche set up this ambush to *help* us get Greg back. He laid both Harper and Dennis the Menace out with a couple of swipes of his arm. Do you think he couldn't have done the same to Scott? Didn't you see that he never even tried to defend himself—and we all know that if he'd wanted to fight back, that shotgun wouldn't have done the trick on its own?"

Across the meadow, LaBouche sucked in a breath and groaned. All eyes turned toward Scott, who stared at LaBouche's twitching form. Mike ducked his head and fished out his keys. "I'll get the trunk. We've got ammo."

"No," said Scott as he opened the door. "Benny's right."

"Listen, Scott, no one would blame you—"

"As much as I wish it weren't true, I know Lee LaBouche about as well as anyone. Benny's right. We need to hear what he wants." He gazed at each one of them. "*Then* I'll kill him again."

Chapter 3
1982–1996

I

1982

"I mean, Eddie, it's just…just a little weird. All right?"

"Well, I don't care. It's just something I do. It's part of who I am. Why should I care what somebody else thinks?" Eddie sneered and said the whole thing at once, all in a rush.

"Well, if that's how you want it…" Pete pushed himself up from the lunchroom table that they had all to themselves.

Eddie didn't want him to leave, not now, not ever, but he pushed those feelings into that hole he kept inside himself. He peeked at Pete from the corner of his eye, and by the expression on Pete's face, he felt the same as Eddie. "Look, Pete… I… I collect things. It doesn't matter what. It's almost as though I don't care what, as long as it's *something*. The cars… Do you remember Principal Skinner from the elementary school?"

Pete let the strap of his backpack slide down his arm, and the pack fell to the floor, but he didn't sit. "Skinhead Skinner, sure."

Eddie grimaced. "He wasn't all that bad."

Pete flapped his hand, shoulder height. "Whatever, dude."

"Anyway, in his office, he had this…this shelf. A shelf full of his treasures—you could tell by how he kept it so clean that they were his treasures. On it he had a couple of old books with titles in a foreign language. I don't remember which. And he had trophies and crap such as that, but what was cool were these models of old muscle cars. They were…"

Pete slid into the plastic lunchroom chair. "They were what?"

Eddie licked his lips and looked down at his lap. "They were cool, that's all. They had so much detail. And the paint jobs…my God, the paint jobs were similar to *real* cars. And there wasn't a speck of dust on any of it."

"Yeah." Pete looked around the cafeteria and retook his seat, crossing his arms. "But…"

"But what's all this got to do with my cars?" asked Eddie. "You remember I told you about how my parents died when I was ten? About how I live with my aunt and asshole uncle now?"

Pete uncrossed his arms and began to toy with the plastic spork he'd used to wolf down his school lunch.

"Well, the day my parents died, I got called up to the office. There was this cop… the chief of police, Chief Morton."

Pete's gaze tracked up to Eddie's face.

"The cop and I got to use Principal Skinner's office. And right in the middle of Morton telling me that my parents were dead, I saw the shelf. Skinner's shelf full of treasures. Looking at those things on that shelf made me feel better. Especially the model cars." Eddie wrinkled his nose and scratched his chin. "I don't understand why, but there it is. His collection comforted me somehow."

"Yeah, Eddie, but we're fourteen, now, and if you carry around Hot Wheels in your backpack that way, people will think you're even weirder than you really are." But as he said it, Pete flashed a smile, and everything was okay.

"Yeah," laughed Eddie. "I wouldn't want that."

The bell signaling the end of lunch rang, and both boys scooped up their backpacks and slung them over their shoulders. Neither boy picked up his Styrofoam tray, though they glanced at each other and grinned.

They parted company in the hall outside the lunchroom, as Pete had World History on one side of the school next, and Eddie had Algebra I on the other. They didn't have very many classes together, because Pete, despite all of his social failings, was still a good student, and Eddie...

Well, Eddie was not.

He trudged toward class, his head down, and his hands shoved deep in his pockets, trying to ignore all the other students that thronged the hall. He didn't care for the other students, and the crowded hallways of the school delighted him about as much as a pocket full of cow manure would.

Middle school had been bad, but high school... *Man, high school is hell*, he thought as he dodged a gaggle of giggling freshmen girls. Eddie wasn't big; in fact, he was downright short. Add to that the fact that gaining weight seemed beyond his capabilities, and he was the perfect target for all the jocks, all the bullies, and they made sure he knew it.

He thought about Pete's reaction to the handful of Hot Wheels cars Eddie always carried with him in his backpack. He had more, secreted around the farm, but the thirteen cars he carried were *special*. True treasures. He had the Dixie Challenger. He had the Peterbilt Tank Truck. He had his '37 Bugatti. And those three were brand-new and *rare*. Luck had been on his side the day he'd found each one of them.

He also carried the Three-Window '34, the Hiway Hauler, the Super Scraper, a reissued Warpath with the new color, a Porsche 911, and a blue Hot Bird. The seven others were all older models: the Chief's Special—and that one always brought John Morton to mind despite it being a fire chief's car—the Mighty Maverick, the Sand Drifter, the Super Van, a Boss Hoss Silver Special, a Ferrari 312 P, and an electric green copy of The Demon.

Those thirteen cars were his pride and joy. He valued The Demon as if it were the king of all Hot Wheels. But they all meant something. They all had...*personalities*. He wanted them close; he liked the weight of them in his backpack, or, in the winter, in his coat pocket. It didn't matter to Eddie that other boys had given up their Hot Wheels a year or two before. It was different for Eddie.

Everything was different for Eddie.

Ever since Uncle Gil had made him burn his doll collection, Eddie had kept all of his treasures a secret. He had to enjoy them in the dark, or when he knew Uncle Gil was busy in the fields, or the barn, or down to the Elks. He didn't dare hide them in the house, because Uncle Gil had a way of finding things that Eddie or Auntie Margo wanted to keep hidden.

Eddie shook his head to clear the thoughts of home from his mind. The last thing he wanted before walking into Algebra was to focus on all the crap that Uncle Gil put them through daily. *Talk about pouring gas on a fire...*

No, the incident with his doll collection had taught him something, although not what Uncle Gil had expected him to learn. The biggest lesson he had learned that night was not to trust adults. Sure, he knew that Uncle Gil was a piece of work, but Auntie Margo...she had played her part in his betrayal that night. She could have stopped it, she *should've* made Gil stop, but she'd chosen not to.

Oh, he knew that Gil beat her, and Eddie knew that she feared his uncle, but still…still, he expected her to stand up for him. She had promised to take care of him.

Eddie shook his head to clear out the negative thoughts, and behind him, a chuckle that turned his stomach sounded. Jack was behind him in the hall.

Jack McGregor, King of the Assholes.

"Anything rattle up there, Mitchell?" asked Jack. All around them, boys and girls laughed.

Jack wasn't much of anything in high school—not as he had been in middle school. But it was his first year, and though he was a year older than the rest of the kids in his class, he didn't have much confidence when it came to the juniors and seniors. That didn't stop him, however, from plying his trade on the freshman and sophomores, but *especially* the freshman with whom he'd gone to middle school.

"What's the matter, Mitchell? Nothing to say?"

Eddie shook his head and hunched his shoulders.

"Aw," crooned Jack. "Are you having a bad day, widdle Eddie?"

Eddie hunched his head deeper between his shoulders and plowed on through the mass of humanity in the hallway.

"Well, isn't that just rude? Don't you want to be friendly, Eddie? Aren't we friends?" Sarcasm dripped from Jack's voice. "I mean we been to school together forever, right?"

Eddie kept his lips shut and kept right on walking.

"He doesn't seem to like you, Jack," said one of Jack's cronies.

"No, he doesn't act like he does. Not one bit," said Jack. "That's downright hurtful, don't you think?"

"Seems that way to me, Jack."

The moment Eddie had been dreading—the moment where he either stood up for himself or became the butt of yet another string of jokes—was at hand, this time would be no different from all the others. He sighed, feeling helpless, feeling alone.

His backpack jerked as if he were crawling through the brush and a branch had snagged the loop at the top of the pack. Eddie knew what it was—Jack, pulling on his backpack to slow him down.

"Don't you want to be my friend, Eddie? You don't want us to be enemies, do you?"

Eddie shook his head, hoping that this time he'd come up with the right combination of words or gestures that would defuse the situation. "No, Jack," he began, "I'd rather us be friends, but you always seem—"

A horrible ripping sound came from behind Eddie, and the tugging sensation on his backpack ceased. He began to turn when the sound of it—his precious Hot Wheels, raining to the linoleum floor, sounding like ice chips on concrete—reached his ears.

Panic sank its fangs into Eddie's guts. He spun side to side, his eyes trying to track thirteen small toy cars scattering underneath the feet of the stampeding students headed for fourth period. "*No!*"

"Aw, isn't that just cute," said Jack. "Eddie brought his toys to school."

Eyes darting left and right, Eddie fell to his knees and started scrounging for his treasures. He didn't even hear Jack and the other boys laughing. He grabbed the cars close by and shoved them into his front pockets, his eyes dancing to find the others.

"What the hell is wrong with you, Mitchell?" Jack's voice no longer held any pretense of good humor, but Eddie paid him no mind. If he had, he might have sensed the warning signs…the way Jack's voice resembled Uncle Gil's in mid-rant.

So far, he'd only found the Peterbilt Tank Truck, the Hot Bird, and the Sand Drifter, but there was a glint of electric green toward the left wall—The Demon—and Eddie scrambled toward it on his hands and knees, ignoring the comments of the other students as he got in their way or shoved them out of his.

"That kid's crazy."

"No, he's just an asshole!"

Eddie's focus was laser-sharp, and the people around him had faded into nothingness. He reached for his electric green Demon but just before he wrapped his fingers around it, a foot stomped on the back of his hand, and another foot kicked The Demon farther down the hall. As he watched it scoot away, the black, slimy thing that he'd first noticed when Uncle Gil made him burn his doll collection crawled out of the hole in his middle.

Hatred. Rage. Lividity. These three emotions sang within him, boiling his blood, cooking his brain as thoroughly as if he'd put it in a microwave. Eddie twisted his hand under the foot that had stomped on it and latched on to the sole of Jack's Converse High Top. He surged to his feet, jerking the foot into the air, shoving Jack off balance, lifting his leg as high as he could.

Someone was shouting something—no, not shouting, more like roaring. Eddie slapped his other hand over the toe of Jack's shoe and wrenched Jack's foot counterclockwise. Jack screamed in pain, and Eddie's mouth opened in a rictus grin.

Someone slammed into Eddie's side, driving him into the wall of lockers, and he lost his hold on Jack's foot. He looked down at one of Jack's cronies, pressed into his chest. Eddie lifted his arm high above his head, as John Travolta had in that disco movie, and then brought his elbow down as fast and as hard as possible, right in the middle of the other boy's neck. His elbow shrieked with the impact, and the other boy squealed the way Gil's pigs did when slaughtered. The pressure on his chest, the force that held him up against the lockers, disappeared in an instant.

A roaring filled Eddie's ears, a roaring similar to the surf at the beach on a windy day. Space had opened in the crowd of kids headed toward fourth period. Inside the ring of staring faces, stood Eddie, and Jack. Jack's crony was in the ring, though he wasn't standing, he was on his hands and knees shaking his head like a stunned animal.

Eddie's eyes strayed around the circle of leering faces, coming to a stop only when he saw a dusky-hued woman standing behind the ring of students. She grinned at him, her sharp black fangs glinting in the florescent lights, and as she did so, her locks of blue-black hair writhed and twined around each other, the bright blue and purple highlights dancing in the bright fluorescent lights that marched down the ceiling of the hallway.

Jack's face was purple to match the highlights of the scary lady's hair, and his mouth was a flat, thin line, but his eyes blazed like spotlights in the dark. At his side, his hands were curled into tight fists—so tight that his knuckles blanched. "What the hell are you doing, Mitchell?" he grated.

Eddie had nothing to say, but his rage did. He stepped forward, eyes still on the scary lady, and swung his foot into the midsection of the boy on his hands and knees, kicking as hard as he could. Her grin stretched broader, and she nodded at him. She stretched her arms wide, and there were too many of them—like the goddess Kali. Then, and only then, did his gaze track to Jack's. His face had gone hard as if carved from stone, all except for one muscle underneath his left eye that had started to twitch.

"Stop it!" shouted Jack.

Eddie pulled his foot back and kicked the other boy again, putting his full weight behind it. The boy on the ground collapsed, his arms wrapped around his belly, rocking back and forth and making a mewling sound as a kitten might. Jack took two steps forward, and his hands arced out, lightning-quick, one impacting each of Eddie's cheeks. The blows were hard, and Eddie knew they should hurt, but they didn't. It was as if he wore the thickest wooden armor ever made. He stepped over the boy on the ground and punched Jack in the throat with all his strength, turning at the waist and throwing his shoulder behind the blow. Jack made a retching sound, but Eddie didn't care. He punched him again, this time with his left hand, right in the nose. Blood exploded down the front of Jack's shirt, and he squawked like a chicken.

With a lesser foe, the fight might have ended right there, but Jack knew how to fight. He brought his hands up to block his face, then snapped out his right, punching Eddie in the left eye. His other hand followed a burning arc through the air, a massive haymaker, and slammed into Eddie's right ear, and Eddie saw stars for a moment, staggering back into the lockers behind him.

He shook his head to clear it, much as he had in the moments that had started the fight, then tucked his chin down and charged at Jack, sprinting, pumping his legs as fast and as hard as he could. He slammed into the older boy, his head ramming into Jack's solar plexus, and the breath exploded from Jack's mouth. The crowd erupted with noise as Eddie drove Jack back into the group of watching students.

Over the noise of the crowd, Eddie caught *her* voice. "Don't let him get back up, Eddie," the voice said. "Don't let him *ever* get back up." Her voice rang with passion, the way the women on Uncle Gil's porno movies—the ones he pretended no one knew about—sounded.

Together, Eddie and Jack fell, Eddie on top, Jack slamming his head into the linoleum floor when they hit. The forest of legs shifted around them, widening, giving them space.

Eddie put his hands on Jack's collarbones and pushed himself into a seated position, straddling Jack's belly, his knees in Jack's armpits. He lifted his arms and drove them down into Jack's face, in the way a silverback gorilla pounded the ground. He pummeled Jack without mercy, all the while hearing the woman roar and laugh and cheer. Again and again and again, Eddie lifted his arms and then drove them into Jack's head and face.

Around them, the kids had gone quiet, shocked at the level of violence Eddie had brought to the fight. Beneath him, Jack whimpered.

The sexy woman laughed into the silence. The scary lady.

"Stop it! Stop it, Mitchell!" someone shouted.

But Eddie didn't stop. His muscles began to burn as if they were on fire, and still, he didn't stop. The silence of the people watching didn't stop him. The scary lady's laughter drove him on, fueled his rage, his hatred. Jack's crony—the one he had kicked twice in the stomach—shouting his name didn't stop him.

"Someone get a teacher!"

Up and down. Up then down. Up. Down. Up. Down, a sickening crunch rattling up through the bones and joints of his arms each time he brought his fist down on Jack's face.

Blood slicked his fists, ran across the linoleum floor, and still, he lifted his hands high and brought them down, thinking of asteroids slamming into the Earth.

Jack no longer whimpered, no longer tried to keep his hands in front of his face, no longer rocked from side to side trying to get out from under Eddie. He just lay there, shuddering with each impact, twitching a little, and bleeding.

"Mitchell! You stop this right now!"

Someone grabbed him from behind and pulled him off Jack. Eddie whirled bringing his blood-slicked hands up in front of him, ready to fight.

The scary lady cackled with glee, but it faded away—as if she'd walked down the corridor and turned a corner.

"Mitchell!" shouted Coach Randall. "What's gotten into you, boy?"

Eddie stood there, gasping for breath, and then his gaze fell to the floor and began to search for his other treasures. He dropped his hands, almost sighing with relief as his burning muscles relaxed.

"You there! Stevens!" said Coach Randall. "Get down to the nurse's office. Tell her we need her out here right now. Jesus Christ on a crutch. Tell her we might need an ambulance, Stevens."

One of the onlookers turned and started to walk up the hall toward the office.

"Dammit, Stevens! You *run*!"

Eddie heard all of it, but it didn't seem as though he were an integral part of events. To him, it didn't seem that he had ever been a part of any of it. He glimpsed electric green out of the corner as eye and whirled toward it.

"Where in the hell do you think you're going, Mitchell?" asked Coach Randall. "Get back here, boy."

Eddie ignored him, shoving his way through the crowd, and then stooped and picked up The Demon, running a finger across its top, leaving a streak of congealing blood. He put the car in the palm of his left hand and curled his fingers around it and felt better—calmer, more relaxed. With a slight smile, he turned to search for more of his missing treasures, and the bitter, stygian hatred retreated into the hole in his middle.

Eddie pushed and elbowed his way through the crowd, his eyes turned downward, darting this way and that, looking for gleaming metal and bright colors. The other students in the hallway stepped away from him when he came close, and the eerie silence that had fallen over them during the fight continued unabated. No one said a word as he pushed past them, no one shoved back.

A heavy hand fell on Eddie's shoulder. "I asked you where the hell you're going, Mitchell?"

Coach Randall was the football, wrestling, and weightlifting coach for the high school. He also taught biology, but that didn't matter as he squeezed Eddie's shoulder with his formidable strength. The coach must've carried three hundred pounds of muscle, although he had a bit of middle-aged paunch around the waist. He stood six-foot-four-inches tall, and he loomed over Eddie's five-foot-four scrawny frame.

Eddie weighed ninety-seven pounds with a five-pound weight in his hand, but despite the difference in their weights, Eddie shrugged off Coach Randall's hand as if it were nothing.

He didn't do it out of anger, not even out of irritation or pique, he did it because Coach Randall's hand kept him from continuing his search. White noise filled his head, and nothing penetrated it.

Behind him, Coach Randall squawked with outrage, but Eddie ignored him. Out of the corner of his eye he'd caught a flash of bright orange. It might be his Dixie Challenger or his Super Scraper. In either case he *wanted* it.

He pushed his way toward the glint of orange, but Coach Randall's hand fell on his shoulder once again. With his other hand, Coach Randall grabbed Eddie's upper arm and spun the boy to face him.

"Have you gone crazy, Eddie Mitchell? Have you lost your fool mind?"

Eddie looked at him, his expression empty, his mind blank—filled with an impenetrable white noise of no-thought—took a breath and then turned his head to look for the flash of orange again. He tried to take a step, but Coach Randall held him fast.

"Are you on drugs, Mitchell?" Randall hissed.

Moving as slow as molasses in winter, Eddie turned his face back toward the coach. The questions Coach Randall was asking him made little sense to Eddie. *Can't the man see what's going on here?* Eddie tilted his head a little bit to the side and shook it. *It's blazingly apparent what's going on here. Any fool can see it.*

"Answer me, damn you, Mitchell!" Coach Randall punctuated the statement with a small shake of Eddie's shoulders.

Eddie shook his head again. His eyes strayed, back to where he'd seen the flash of orange, and Randall shook him again, harder.

"What's the matter with you, Mitchell? What's gotten into you?"

"Coach Randall?" The girl that had spoken seemed familiar to Eddie, but he didn't remember her name.

Coach Randall sighed with exasperation. "I'm a little busy, Miss Fox."

"I–I understand that, Coach. It's… it's about all this," said the girl. She spread her hands as if to encompass all the students in the hall.

"Well?" snapped Randall.

"Jack started it. He *always* starts it. He's a bully, and he's not happy unless he's picking on someone. Him and his friends were picking on Eddie. They ripped his backpack and scattered his stuff all over the place. And Eddie…" Her gaze settled on Eddie, as light as a feather. "Eddie was just trying to get his stuff back. Jack and this bozo jumped him. Eddie was just defending himself." She smiled at Eddie, and it warmed him like the first rays of spring sunshine after a long, hard winter.

"Has everyone lost their fool minds?" muttered Coach Randall. "This is a little more than just defending himself." He jerked his head to where Jack lay bleeding. The boy still hadn't moved or made a noise.

Eddie turned in the direction of his nod, and his gaze settled on Jack's face. There was blood everywhere, coming from Jack's torn lips, his nose—wrenched to the side. Both of his eyes were already starting to turn that sickly green shade that meant deep bruises were in his future and swollen almost shut. Beside him, two teeth gleamed from the linoleum. Eddie rolled his face away, back toward the flash of orange he'd seen, and he writhed in the big coach's grasp.

Coach Randall shook him, harder yet again. "You cut that out, Mitchell."

"He just wants his stuff, Coach," said the girl.

"Yeah? Well, he can just damn-well wait." The coach peered around and then stole a peek at the Hot Wheels Eddie held in his hand. "Toys? This is about toys?"

In Eddie's mind, Coach Randall's voice took on the tenor and pace of Uncle Gil's, and the rage that had calmed itself by bashing Jack's face in came roaring back. Eddie shoved The Demon into his pocket and balled his fists.

Coach Randall looked at him with wide eyes and a mouth that hung open. "You've gone nuts, son. I don't think you have any idea what you're doing anymore."

Eddie squeezed his fist so tight that his tendons creaked. He wanted to hit the man, he wanted to do to him what he'd done to Jack, but he hadn't completely lost his mind—not like Coach Randall said.

"You can't just…" Randall shook his head. "You can't just *do* that to someone, Mitchell. There are rules, no matter who's picking on you. No matter what they do, there are rules."

Words surged into Eddie's mouth like hot bile. "Yeah," he sneered. "Yeah, there're *rules*. There are always rules unless somebody is doing something to me. *That* I'm just supposed to take. *That* I'm just supposed to ignore. Tell me, Coach Randall, how much did *you* put up with in high school."

The coach shook his head and sighed. "Mitchell, it might surprise you. I wasn't always big, you know." His gaze drifted to Jack. "Where the hell's that nurse?" He murmured.

"Jack… He took my things! He ripped my backpack. He scattered my *collection*, I'll lose most of them. And these are my *best ones*. These are the ones I always carry with me. *I can't lose them!*" Eddie jerked out of Coach Randall's grasp and dove toward the spot where he'd seen the flash of orange.

"Mitchell!"

There it was. It sat on its side, its wheels pressed up against the wall as if it were driving on the wall surface. The Dixie Challenger. Something in Eddie's chest felt warm as he wrapped his fingers around it.

"Make way there! Let the nurse through," boomed Coach Randall. The big man turned back and spared a glance for Eddie. He lifted one heavy hand and pointed at him. "Don't you move, Mitchell. I mean it." With that he turned and began moving the students out of the way so the nurse could get to Jack.

Eddie peered through the forest of feet and legs, looking for reds and blues and silver. *Five*, he thought. *Eight more. I'll never find them all.* Despair weighed him down.

He crawled on his hands and knees, tapping people on the leg with a bloody hand when they didn't get out of his way, his gaze sweeping back and forth, back and forth. He didn't know how far his precious collection had scattered as the backpack ripped, but the fight might have spread them even farther.

"Are these…Eddie, are these yours?"

It was the girl, the one who'd stood up for him. He'd already forgotten her name, but he'd never forget her face. His gaze slid from her face down her arm and to her hands that she held together in front of her. Resting on her palms were his Boss Hoss Silver Special, his Three-Window 34, and Warpath.

Tears sprang into his eyes as he looked at the toys, and then he turned his gaze to her face, and she smiled. The day seemed less ugly; the world less beastly. She held the cars out to him, still smiling. He took them one by one and slid them into his front pockets. His eyes never left hers.

"I'll help you find them all, Eddie," she said.

The lump in his throat stopped him from answering. It was the first time since his mother had died that anyone had stood up for him.

Half an hour later, Eddie sat in the back of the police car, his hands cuffed behind his back. Other students from the high school stood on the bus ramp staring at him, a few pointing, others whispering to the person standing next to them.

The ambulance sat in front of the police car, and they were just now getting Jack loaded into the back. A pang raced through Eddie as they wheeled Jack by on the gurney. His face had been so…bloody, broken.

Did I do that? Eddie wrinkled his nose. *Could I have done that?* His memory of the fight had already fragmented.

The principal walked behind the gurney, talking to the nurse and Coach Randall. Every now and again, he darted a glance at Eddie.

The cop who had put him in the car was not John Morton. He had been a little rough as if he were mad at Eddie or something. Eddie had no idea why. *It's not as though the cop and Jack even know each other.*

After putting Eddie in the car, the cop had disappeared back into the main building of the school. Eddie had thought he'd been going in to speak to the principal, but the principal stood by the ambulance, and yet the cop did not appear.

Eddie bit the inside of his cheek.

The cop had taken his Hot Wheels and had put them into a big brown grocery bag along with Eddie's backpack.

He had better not lose them, Eddie thought. The girl—Melanie—had found more of his cars before Coach Randall had made her quit looking.

The coach hadn't allowed her to give them to Eddie, so he didn't know which cars she'd found, or even how many, but at least she'd found some. He hoped the cop put them with the other vehicles.

The paramedic closed the ambulance's rear doors and walked around to the front. The principal, the nurse, and Coach Randall, all stood in a little knot, their backs to Eddie. He stared at Coach Randall's profile, and the man's face was red. A vein throbbed over his temple.

Coaches never liked Eddie. *Too small*, he thought. *Too much of a wimp. Wonder what they'll do to me.*

At the end of the sidewalk, the scary lady appeared in the shadow of one of the brick pillars that supported the roof over the bus ramp. He was looking right at her as a shadow with the consistency of smoke spewed up from the sidewalk and solidified into her human shape. Her eyes lingered on Eddie's and didn't stray. A small smile played on her lips. Unlike before, she didn't hide in the shadows wrapped in black smoke—she wore a shiny, black leather dress that fell to her ankles, with the slit he remembered running up to her waist on the side of her right leg. Her feet were bare, but immaculately clean—as if the dirt of the world daren't touch her. Her hair writhed as if the strands had a life of their own. Her midnight-blue eyes spun and spun as she watched him.

As he watched, another plume of smoke shot up behind her. Eddie shook his head; his gaze never wavered. The second plume solidified, and he glimpsed bright red hair and shining orange eyes set in pale skin.

Great. Another one.

Another police car turned into the school parking lot as the ambulance's engine roared to life. The police car had "CHIEF" painted on the front quarter panels, and Eddie's stomach sank a little more. The idea of seeing Chief Morton filled him with dread. He didn't want to see the chief's expression—his disappointment in Eddie.

The chief pulled into a space and got out of his car. His gaze strayed to Eddie in the back of the police car and then snaked away toward the knot of school officials. As the ambulance pulled away, Chief Morton approached the principal and said something.

At the end of the sidewalk, the scary lady and her red-headed friend stepped behind the brick pillar, as if John Morton's presence scared them. *She's not real*, he thought. *Neither is the new one.*

Yes, they are! insisted a small voice inside him.

No, neither of them is there. Erikson said she sprang from my mind's attempt to deal with unmanageable stress. He wondered what Doctor Erikson would say about the day's events.

He'd looked the terms up in the library. *Hallucinations. Schizophrenia, maybe.* Though with what he'd just done to Jack, maybe there was a psychotic component as well. He supposed his father had had to be psychotic to have murdered his mother, so at least he came by it naturally. And judging by the appearance of a second smoke-woman, he was heading in the exact opposite direction of a healthy, *normal* teenager.

The principal shook his head, and Coach Randall turned and spat onto the asphalt. Morton spared the football coach a dark glance, and his expression was blank, but Eddie read the glance as evidence the chief thought little of the coach. The principal shook his head again, in response to something Chief Morton said and then crossed his arms over his chest. Morton gazed at Eddie and heaved a sigh before walking toward the car in which he sat.

Shaking his head, Morton opened the door closest to Eddie. "Well, Eddie, you've kicked over the shit bucket this time. Come on out of there."

For the briefest of moments, Eddie considered not getting out, but he knew that wouldn't solve anything, and he'd have to face John Morton one way or another. He slid out of the car with all the grace of a drunken baby elephant, and Morton studied him as he stood.

"If I take off those cuffs, you're going to act like a gentleman, right?" Eddie nodded and Chief Morton spun him around and removed the cuffs. "What got into you, son?" he asked as Eddie turned to face him.

Eddie's hands tried to kill one another in front of him, his face set in a sullen rictus, and he stared at Chief Morton's shoes.

"No, no, son. You don't get to play that with me. You're better than that." Morton sighed and raised his hands out to his sides before letting them drop. "You're better than all this...this *bullshit* you pulled today. You and I both know that."

Eddie shook his head. "No, I'm not."

"Oh, I see. It's time for self-pity. I wasn't aware. And here I didn't bring my violin. Should I let you get back into the car where you can have your own little pity-party?" A little heat had edged into the chief's voice. "Or maybe you can just tell me what got into you."

"I don't know." Eddie kept his gaze on the asphalt.

"You don't know if I should put you back into the car and let you have your little pity-party all by yourself, or you don't know what got into you today?" Morton shifted his weight, and the boots he wore scuffed across the black asphalt. His voice had a snap to it that Eddie had not heard in their earlier conversations.

Before he could stop it, a sigh erupted from Eddie. *This is it*, he thought. *This is when Chief Morton washes his hands of me.* His chin trembled. *It's what I deserve.* He glanced at the students lined up on the bus ramp and then turned his gaze back to the asphalt. "They think I'm weird. I *am* weird."

Morton waited for Eddie to continue.

Eddie opened his mouth and closed it without saying anything. He shook his head.

The chief took a step closer. "You hurt that boy, Eddie. Hurt him *bad*. You might've broken his cheekbones, his orbits, and you broke his nose for sure. Knocked out two teeth, too, according to the nurse." The snap had left Morton's voice, replaced with something that seemed like concern.

Eddie shoved his hands into his front pockets to stop their eternal war.

"What do you have to say for yourself?" The snap was back. "Why in the world would you attack that boy?"

"He attacked me," Eddie murmured in a sullen voice. "I only fought back after he started it."

"Self-defense, is it?" Chief Morton grasped Eddie's chin and lifted his head, turning it to the left and the right. "Let's see…no broken cheekbones, no broken nose, no split lip, no missing teeth."

Eddie jerked his head away. "Then arrest me!" he growled.

Morton took a deep breath and let it out in a slow stream. "Is that what you want, son? Do you understand what would happen to you? Something as serious as this?"

Eddie shook his head.

"You might catch a serious charge for this, Eddie. Fourteen or not, that boy is seriously hurt, and there's no question that *you* did it." Morton took another deep, slow breath. "My question is *why*. You're not that type of kid."

Eddie's feelings threatened to come surging out of that hole in his middle, and he had to fight to keep them contained. In the meantime, he just stood there, not moving, not talking.

"You want my help or not, son?" asked the chief, irritation creeping into his voice. "Because if you do, then you'd better stop with the hard, silent routine. I've seen it from tougher men than you, and it didn't impress me then, either. You'd better talk to me, Eddie."

"I'm sorry," said Eddie in a voice just above that of a whisper. "I have to… It's hard… I have to fight so hard, just to keep everything inside me. I—"

"Keep everything inside? What makes you think you have to keep everything contained? What kind of idea is that?"

Eddie shook his head. "Anyway, Jack is a big bully. Always has been. He—he—he ripped my backpack!" As he spoke, Eddie's voice gained volume, gained heat. "He flung my collection, my Hot Wheels, all over the place. When I went to…when I tried to pick them up he…he…he—" Eddie snapped his mouth shut.

They were out. His emotions were out, and they almost drowned him. He looked around, expression wild, fighting the lump in his throat, fighting the burning and itching in his eyes, looking for a place to run, a place to hide.

Morton put a big hand on his shoulder. "It's okay, son. It's okay."

"No, it *isn't*," hissed Eddie. "It's not okay. It's never okay. It's never *been* okay, not since…not since—"

"Shh, now, son." The chief sighed, eyeing the students ogling them from the bus ramp. "Let's get you out of here. They've gotten enough of a show this afternoon." He guided Eddie to the front seat of the chief's cruiser and opened the door. "I don't need to put you in back."

It wasn't a question, but Eddie felt compelled to shake his head. "No, sir. Never."

"I know, son." Morton applied subtle pressure to Eddie's shoulder, and he sat and pulled his legs in the car. The chief closed the door with a solid sounding *thunk*.

As the chief walked around the front of his cruiser, the principal shouted something Eddie couldn't make out, and Chief Morton replied, "I'm the goddamn Chief of Police, Terry, not you. Mind your business!" He got into the driver's seat and started the car. "You'll have an uphill fight, son." After a brief staring contest with the principal, Chief Morton piloted his cruiser out of the high school parking lot. "The principal wants me to arrest you. He wants me to take you to jail and throw away the key. That isn't what you need, Eddie." He turned to Eddie. "Am I right?"

Eddie looked down at his lap and nodded.

"No, Eddie, that's not good enough. You need to tell me. Right out loud. You need to make me a promise."

Without lifting his head, Eddie peeked at the chief's face. Morton kept darting glances at him, splitting his attention between the road ahead and Eddie. "What promise?"

"You need to tell me that what happened today won't happen again. You need to promise me you will keep your temper in check. That you will ask an adult for help if someone is bothering you."

"And if I promise you that, where will you take me?"

The big police chief flashed a thin smile at him. "Home. Where else?"

Uncle Gil will love this. Eddie sighed. "Okay, Chief Morton. I promise." As they passed the brick pillar that the scary lady was hiding behind, Eddie looked for her, but she had disappeared again, and so had her friend with the Kool-Aid red hair.

Gil kept his act up until Chief Morton left, backing down the long gravel drive to the macadam of Salt Road. Then, Gil glared at him and fingered his belt buckle. He shook his head and glanced at Margo. "Well? You going to defend the brat this time?"

Auntie Margo shifted her gaze from Eddie to her husband. Her face came over white, and she pressed her lips into a thin line. "I…" She shook her head. "No, Gil. I can't defend this behavior. Anyway, I've got dinner to start."

Gil grunted, sounding like a primate at the zoo, and Margo blanched. She turned her head and met Eddie's gaze. "Brutish behavior like that is unacceptable. You need a lesson in how to act."

Eddie's gaze and his stomach raced to see which could get to the ground fastest. *Don't know why I ever expect anything different from her.*

"Ayup. Fighting is one thing, but to keep beating the boy after he's beaten, well, that just don't sit right." Gil turned his blazing attention to Eddie. "Well, brat? What do you have to say for yourself?"

Something inside Eddie turned over, something hot, something angry. "Will it matter?" he demanded. "Does anything I ever say make any difference to you? Does it matter to you that Jack has been picking on me for *years*? Does it matter to you—"

A stinging slap rocked his head to the side, and he staggered a step. "I don't understand why you believe that lip will help you, brat," said his uncle. "But, hell, you just keep right on going." He sounded almost pleased. "Lord knows, I can keep right on going, too."

"Gil…" said Auntie Margo. The man scowled at her, and that's all he needed to do. She turned and walked into the kitchen, letting the swinging door close behind her.

"Now that Margo has had her whine and I've dealt with it, we can get back to the bullshit you pulled in school. Oh, and keep on cracking wise, we can make this lesson a twofer." Gil took a step closer, breathing loose and carefree, his hands hanging at his sides. "You know what, rug-rat? You and I should go on out to the barn. Yeah, our talk might go over better out there. Any objections?"

Eddie just stood there, staring at his toes, his cheek burning.

"Yeah, I didn't think you'd object. Let's get on out there." Uncle Gil's hand fell on Eddie's shoulder like an axe blow and spun him toward the barn. "What? Nothing more to say?"

Eddie opened the door and looked out into the cold November afternoon. He stood, waiting in silence.

"You might be learning, brat." Gil shoved him, and Eddie sprawled in the gravel that covered the dooryard, face first into the hard, cold ground. "Get your ass up, boy. Get your ass into that barn."

Suppressing a sigh, Eddie got to his feet and trudged toward the barn. Gil followed close on his heels, undoing his belt buckle as he walked.

Once Uncle Gil got started, he went on and on and on, until Eddie thought Gil was going to beat him to death. The beating began with the leather strap of Uncle Gil's belt, then progressed to the belt buckle, and ended with Gil's fists. Gil took occasional breaks, breathing hard with his hands on his knees while he glared at Eddie. After an eternity, nursing his skinned knuckles, Gil hawked and spat, then turned and walked back into the house. "No supper, brat. Not for a week or two."

Eddie didn't respond, wasn't able to respond.

But three hours later, with his left eye swollen shut and a path of dried blood reaching from his nostrils down his chin, Eddie stood in his dark room, shoving clothes into his old backpack.

Margo had stayed in the house during the entire beating. Of course she had.

But as the blows had rained down on him, Eddie had promised himself something. He promised that as soon as he had recovered enough, he would get the hell out of there. He would leave Uncle Gil and Auntie Margo in his dust.

They deserved each other.

The black rage had quivered inside him during the entire beating, but he knew he was no match for Uncle Gil, rage or no rage. He kept it contained, hidden far away from Gil's sharp eyes, but now his hands shook with it.

Can't go to the house, he thought. *Not after last time. That will be the first place Chief Morton looks.* Eddie shook his head and walked to his closet. He squatted and pried up the floorboard under which he'd hidden a few dollars.

It wasn't much, not even thirty dollars, but it was all he had. He inspected his closet, looking for anything that he had to have, but the things he really wanted were inside a brown grocery bag in the back of the policeman's car. *Can't stay here—not even one more minute. I'll start a new collection when I get where I'm going.*

Eddie pushed to his feet, grimacing at the ache in his mid-back. Gil called it a "kidney punch," and it hurt like hell for days. He looked around his room, his gaze roving over the top of his dresser, his bedside table, the straight-backed wooden chair draped with dirty clothes. He shook his head, feeling nothing. It was amazing how much stuff he had that he cared nothing about.

Slinging his backpack over his heavy coat, he strode to the window and pried out the nails Uncle Gil had put in after he ran away the last time. He'd already loosened them, but he put them back just in case Gil looked. He couldn't stop himself from glancing over his shoulder when he thought of Gil, half sure his uncle would be in the doorway glaring at him.

But his door remained closed. He slid the window open, grimacing at the grating noise it made. Frigid air invaded the room, stinging his cheeks.

Unbidden and unwanted, the memory of his hallucinations invaded his mind. The scary lady. He remembered how the caress had left his cheek numb when Chief Morton had been down in the basement of his parents' house lighting the furnace, how the cold had swarmed over his teeth across his tongue and down his throat into his chest and shivered, imagining her arm down his throat. Maybe the one with hair the color of a cherry snow cone and eyes the color of fire would be hot.

Shaking his head, Eddie swung his leg out the window and then ducked through. He pulled his other leg through the window and lowered himself to the ground. Looking up, he wished he could close the window, sure that Gil or Margo would feel the chill and come to investigate, but there was no way he could reach it from the ground.

OUR LADY CHAOS   363

With a blank expression, Eddie turned his back on the house in which he'd spent the last four years. He turned his back on Auntie Margo and her failure to protect him from her monster of a husband. He turned his back on Gil's sadism and abuse. Eddie turned his back and walked away, vowing never to set foot on that farm again.

He seemed to grow lighter with each step he took. He remembered his thoughts from a few moments before, the thing about starting a new collection as soon as he got where he was going

All well and good, but where am I going?

Where should an almost 15-year-old boy go? Obviously, nowhere in Cottonwood Vale. There had been a place in Oneka Falls, something for kids, but he didn't remember what the place was. *Might be a church for holy rollers*, he thought. *Or maybe a reform school.*

It didn't matter. After what had happened to those four or five kids in Oneka Falls a few years back, no kid in their right mind would go near that town, even if the place for kids hadn't closed. He believed they'd caught the psychopath who'd caused all the trouble, the guy that shot up the town, but the memory of the spree still made him uneasy. *No, somewhere else.*

He needed a place big enough that he could disappear. Someplace where no one would look twice at a kid on the street.

Someplace such as New York City.

He nodded once to himself. *New York City. The Big Apple. Plenty of room for me there.* Plus, there were a lot of stores there, and a lot of *dumpsters* behind them. *Bet I can find a lot of great stuff there.* He started walking, head down, stride determined.

2

1982

Two days and thirty-eight miles later, Eddie's grand escape ended in a town named Hornell. The cop—Officer Ray Quinlan—had caught him sleeping in the park at the center of town.

Eddie closed his eyes and tuned out. *It's finished. I'm not going to New York City. I'm going right back to Gil. Wonder if he'll kill me this time.*

If I'm lucky.

He might've dozed, or he might've been so zoned out that he didn't hear Quinlan, but when the cop's hand came to rest on his shoulder, Eddie jumped.

"Sorry, kid. The chief wants to talk to you." Quinlan held the phone receiver toward Eddie.

Eddie considered refusing, but Morton had always been kind to him, and it wasn't his fault Eddie's life sucked. He reached for the phone with his handcuffed hands and grimaced.

"Oh, let me get those off you."

Eddie held the receiver to his ear as Officer Quinlan unlocked the cuffs. Something had changed in Quinlan's demeanor. "Hello?"

"Eddie? Eddie, is that you?"

A dank, dark depression stole over Eddie as he heard the chief's voice. *Probably should push that into my pit.* Somehow, Eddie didn't have the energy. "Yeah, Chief Morton. It's me."

"Good, good. You okay? You don't sound yourself."

"Tired is all."

"I'll bet. Did you walk the whole way?"

"Most of it. Nobody wanted to give me a ride. I'm a bloody, beat-up mess."

The line hissed and popped. Eddie could hear Chief Morton breathing on the other end.

"Bloody? Beat-up?"

"Yeah." Eddie squeezed his eyes shut, wincing at the tight, painful way the skin around his eyes stretched. "It is what it is."

"Is that why you ran away?"

"What you think?" Eddie winced at the acrimony in his voice, and again, the line hissed with silence.

"Was it your uncle?"

"Who else?"

"I dunno. I thought maybe…Jack's family…"

Eddie laughed—he couldn't help it. "Jack barely even knows my name. I doubt his family even knows I'm alive."

Chief Morton cleared his throat, and it came across the line with the bluster of an artillery barrage. "Well, perhaps. I bet Jack's family knows your name after the other day."

A smile slid across Eddie's face. "Yeah."

The chief cleared his throat again, and Eddie winced at the volume. "You remember when you ran away the first time? When I told you that all you ever had to do was tell me your uncle Gil was up to no good and that I would help?"

Eddie smile died stillborn. "Yeah."

"Son, why didn't… I said I would help. All you had to do was say something."

Eddie sighed, and this time he was the one sending the artillery barrage. "Yeah."

"Why didn't you… With all that I know, this isn't the first time he's tuned up on you if my guess is right. Why didn't you tell me?" Chief Morton sounded more than a little hurt.

Again, Eddie sighed. "I did, Chief Morton. Not in so many words...hell, maybe not with words at all, but I *did* tell you. I told you on that day...that day when you came to tell me my dad killed my mom." Behind him, Bonnie Quinlan, the town's dispatcher, gasped. "I told you that day I ran away, I told you in the car the other day. I told you, and I told you, but you didn't listen to me."

The silence stretched, punctuated by the hisses and pops of the phone line. "I didn't understand, Eddie. I didn't catch what you meant. I'm sorry."

"Yeah," sighed Eddie. "I know."

"Eddie, I need you to tell me now. I need you to use words and tell me all of it. Tell me about your aunt, tell me about you."

"Chief, I don't want—"

"You have to, Eddie. You must be explicit. I need you to tell me everything."

"Why? It won't help. Nothing helps." The blackness inside him threatened to overwhelm him, and his eyes burned with unshed tears.

PUSH IT BACK! I have to PUSH IT BACK!

"This will help, Eddie. I promise. I will help you. It *will* end."

"How?"

"Well, I'll tell you, son. I'm sitting at my desk back in Cottonwood Vale. On the blotter in front of me, I have an arrest warrant. At the top of it is the name 'Gilbert Ratherson.' All I need to execute it is the details, Eddie, and a judge's signature. You give them to me, and I'll make sure you never see Gil again."

Even though Gil was a bastard, a lump formed in Eddie's throat. "I don't—"

"Trust me, Eddie. This is the right thing to do."

The chief had never lied to him. Every time they'd spoken, Eddie had walked away feeling stronger. John Morton felt more like a relative—a grandfather—than Gil ever had. Eddie nodded to himself.

He told Chief Morton everything.

At the end of the story, Chief Morton grunted. "I'm sorry, son. I should never have left it go this long. I should have—"

"I should've told you. With words."

The line popped and hissed for a moment, and then Chief Morton coughed. "Well, let's leave it that we both should have done something other than what we did. In a minute, I'm going to ask you to give the phone back to Officer Quinlan. Then I want you to take it easy, to *rest*. I'll come after you myself, but I've got to get the warrant taken care of first. So, you just rest and wait for old John."

"My auntie Margo—"

"Don't you worry, Eddie. I'll tell her you're okay. She'll see you soon enough, anyway." Chief Morton cleared his throat, but this time, he covered the receiver with his hand. "Now, hand the phone back to Officer Quinlan."

Eddie started to comply but then put the phone back to his ear. "Chief?"

"Yeah, Eddie?"

"It's…it's about my auntie Margo…" Eddie wound down, unsure of what to say next.

"Yeah?"

"Well, you said I should tell you."

"Has she been hitting you, too?"

"No, nothing like that. But…she *knew*. She knew what Gil was doing, and she let him do it. She—"

"Eddie, listen to me, now. Your auntie Margo is as much one of Gil's victims as you are. She's been with him a long time. Something happens to a woman—hell, to anyone—when they're subjected to systematic, long-term abuse. It's as if their will erodes. They know it's not right, but they lose the ability to fight back, to do anything other than what their abuser tells them to do."

"Really?" Eddie was as close to dissolving in tears as he had been since his parents died.

"Yes, Eddie. I've seen it time and time again."

"Then… So, Margo didn't help me because she *couldn't*?"

"That's right, she couldn't. Gil beat that part of her into submission first, or else she'd have clocked him with an iron or a frying pan."

"Oh," whispered Eddie.

"She loves you, son. Things will be different once Gil is in prison. Trust me, okay?"

"Okay," mumbled Eddie.

"Okay. Now go ahead and hand the phone back to Officer Quinlan, please."

Eddie bobbed his head and handed the phone to Quinlan. He sank back in his chair, half-listening to Quinlan's side of the conversation but thinking about what Chief Morton had said for the most part.

He thought about all the times Margo had tried to rein Uncle Gil in, the look on her face when Gil shot her a glare or offered to discuss it with her in private. Eddie thought about how her face would blanch to the point she looked as if she were on the verge of fainting.

Quinlan put his hand over the receiver. "Bonnie? Do we still have film for the Polaroid?"

"Yes. I picked a box up from the drugstore the other day."

"Chief Morton wants us to document the boy's injuries. Can you bring the Polaroid in here and take pictures of this boy's face?"

"Of course, I can."

Eddie closed his eyes and pretended he was somewhere else while the Polaroid snapped and clicked and spit pictures out into Bonnie's hand.

"Don't worry, son," the woman crooned. "You'll be back in your family's loving embrace soon enough."

But it hadn't happened that way at all.

Thank God for small favors.

3

1986

The campus was huge, and Eddie loved it. But he didn't love the sick feeling in his stomach every time he thought about the tuition, the books, the meal plan, and the required freshman housing. The Morton's didn't have a ton of money, and both the Chief and Mrs. Morton had told him not to worry about it, but still.

He stood with his backpack hanging from one shoulder, his head tilted back, the rays of the sun caressing his cheeks. It felt good—no, scratch that; it felt great. Ninety-seven miles separated him from Cottonwood Vale, and that made Eddie smile—except when he missed his step-parents.

The distance was one of his most substantial reasons for going to college. If he didn't, he'd have gotten stuck there in Cottonwood Vale, working a menial job—at the grocery store or the feed and tack—and he'd see *them* all the time.

He didn't want that. He *never* wanted to see Gil or Margo again. Unbidden, the memory of going "home" after the chief arrested Gil came flooding back.

Margo had been so angry. Livid. Spitting mad. She had screamed at Eddie the moment he came through the door. *Cursed* at him. She was furious that Eddie had told on Gil because Gil was going to prison.

Chief Morton had stood behind him, with one hand on his shoulder, his face a study in incomprehension. Without saying a word, he had turned Eddie around and taken him back out to the car. He hadn't said a word as he started the car and drove away from Gil and Margo's farm, but when he pulled into the driveway of a white clapboard house on the other side of town, he'd told Eddie not to worry, to put Margo and Gil out of his mind.

That was how he'd come to live with John Morton and his wife, Izzy. They treated him as the grandson they'd never had—their only son had died in Vietnam. They'd raised him like family, provided everything he needed and more.

Margo had been so vindictive… She'd sold his parents' house two weeks after Gil's conviction and transfer to the Gowanda Correctional Facility. She'd never given a dime to the Mortons for Eddie's care. As far as Eddie knew, she never even asked about him. She'd sold everything in the house. Of *course* she had. She called it an "estate sale," even though Eddie was alive and well.

Gil had gotten out of prison two months before the day Eddie left for college. It seemed beating your nephew to a pulp wasn't that big of a deal to the Department of Corrections. He was "rehabilitated."

Sure he was.

It seemed Margo didn't consider it a big deal, either, as she allowed Gil to move back into the farmhouse. John said he'd expected it, that Margo hadn't had enough yet.

With a sigh, he put the thoughts of Gil and Margo away, shoving both the memories and the emotions that came with them into that empty, purpose-built hole he kept inside himself.

He was excited about the upcoming year. It was an opportunity he'd never imagined he'd have. He had no idea what he wanted to do yet, what he wanted to study, or even what he was interested in majoring in, but the course catalog was chock full of classes that looked fun. The only required class in his first quarter was a class called Freshman Orientation, and if he didn't get a move on, he'd never make it across campus in time for the first meeting.

With a smile on his face and a full, confident stride, Eddie set out from the dorm, traversing the "Brick Mile"— a long, straight sidewalk bordered by brick buildings. Even the sidewalk had an inlay of bricks in the middle, laid in a herringbone pattern. The buildings, the inlays in the pavement, all of them contained the same color red with the same bone-colored mortar gluing them all together.

It followed a long, straight line all the way from the dorms to the administration building in the dead center of the campus. He didn't think the Brick Mile would be much fun during the frequent fall windstorms and winter blizzards, but in early September, he enjoyed the walk.

He walked with his head up, smiling at other students going the other way. It struck him as weird, to smile at all the strangers, but college made Eddie happy. Not that the

Mortons hadn't made him happy, they had…but to express happiness in *public*, that was something new.

He didn't know anyone at the school, but that had been another of his main criteria for picking a school. He hadn't had many friends at Robert Jackson High School back in Cottonwood Vale. His friendship with Pete Paulson had faded after their freshman year—not out of any animus, their schedules just had nothing in common.

His relationship with Melanie Fox, on the other hand, had lasted throughout school. He'd taken her to senior prom, driving Mrs. Morton's Oldsmobile Delta Eighty-Eight, but Melanie hadn't minded that at all. In fact, she'd enjoyed the back seat after the dance. And so had he.

Melanie had made it clear she expected their relationship to last through college, and perhaps the rest of their lives. And to be honest, Eddie had given it significant consideration, but Melanie didn't have the grades for college, and more to the point, the Fox family was dirt-poor, and Melanie didn't have anyone to pay her way as the Mortons did for him. Instead of starting college that September, Melanie had started her third month working at the knife factory in Franklinville.

It had hurt her when Eddie had told her he wanted to be "free to experience college life." He'd seen the pain in her eyes, but she hadn't cried. Her three and a half years of dating Eddie had taught her he didn't respond well to negative emotions. They drove him into "his cold place," as she put it. The pain had floated in her eyes for a few moments, but then she'd forced a smile to her lips, and after another few moments, the smile had reached her eyes too.

Eddie shook his head to clear those memories from his mind as well. She'd given him the opportunity to experience college life, and he would take it.

He had a chance at a new start. No one at the college knew him as "that poor boy whose father murdered his mother and then hung himself in the garage," nor "that poor boy whose uncle beat him half to death." Eddie's smile stretched wider at the reality of his anonymity.

He walked on, gripping one strap of his backpack, enjoying the warmth of the sun on his face, just one more face in the crowd of young people traversing the Brick Mile. Chief Morton had taught him ways to meet people. They'd done a lot of role-playing, a lot of pretending they'd never met.

Eddie hoped the preparation would pay dividends. His track record in the making-friends department stank like a pig farm.

He made it to class with a few minutes to spare and took a seat in the middle of the room. A few students had arrived as early as Eddie, including a stunning brunette who sat at the front of the class, tapping her pen against her thumbnail. He wondered what her name was.

Two minutes before the scheduled start of class, a skinny man wearing sandals, shorts, and a black T-shirt came in and walked to the podium. He didn't look old enough to be a professor to Eddie.

The class filled up in those last few minutes until a freshman sat in every seat. To Eddie's left sat a guy who reminded him so much of Jack McGregor that Eddie turned in his chair, putting his shoulder and back between himself and the guy on his left.

That gave him a better view of the girl sitting to his right. She also wore shorts and sandals, but unlike the professor, she wore them as though she owned the very idea of them. She had long, tan legs, Kool-Aid red hair that gleamed in the classroom lights, and startling green eyes that made him want to faint when she glanced at him, and a smile crooked her lips.

No time like the present to try out what John taught me, Eddie thought. *God hates a coward.* He opened his mouth to speak, but before he could say anything, the girl leaned toward him.

"That guy's too young to be the professor, right?" she whispered.

Eddie grinned. "I just thought the same thing. How old do you suppose he is?"

She darted a glance at the man behind the podium, and her hair shimmered as it moved. "No idea. Late twenties?"

"Yeah, maybe." Eddie turned his attention back to her. "My name's Eddie." The girl was a knockout—all except the hair. It reminded him of something he'd seen somewhere, but he couldn't recall what, except that it made him nervous.

"Well, hello, Eddie. My name's Amanda. Are you a freshman here?"

Eddie chuckled and nodded. "Freshman Orientation, remember?"

Amanda blushed and dipped her head. "Oh yeah," she murmured. "Real ditz move, huh?"

Eddie chuckled. "Don't worry about it, Amanda. Happens to the best of us. I just asked someone in the hallway outside my dorm room if he went to school here."

Amanda laughed, and it was a beautiful laugh. "No, you didn't," she said. "But I appreciate the effort to make me feel better."

"No, I did," said Eddie, grinning.

Amanda laughed again and reached across the space between their two desks and patted his hand. "You're sweet, Eddie."

That made it Eddie's turn to blush.

The guy at the front of the class cleared his throat and tapped the podium. "If I can have your attention, please," he said.

"Oh my God, he sounds just like Michael J. Fox," whispered Amanda, putting a hand over her mouth to stifle her giggle.

Eddie had never liked Family Ties, so he didn't think he could discern Michael J. Fox's voice from Michael Jackson's, but Amanda was cute, so following that age-old male-female calculus, he nodded and smiled.

"My name is Professor Keaton." The professor paused as if he expected something to happen, and after a few moments, the class erupted in laughter. The professor flashed a lopsided smile at them and raised his hand. "Okay, so now we have the obligatory Michael J. Fox joke out of the way. My real name is Andy Jackson, and that *isn't* a joke." He smiled at the class, revealing brilliant white teeth. "Welcome to your Freshman Orientation. Why don't you take a minute and greet the students sitting around you?"

Eddie didn't turn to his left. Instead, he grinned at Amanda and held out his hand. She slid her dry palm across his and smiled back.

And that was all it took.

That day marked the start of the relationship that would bring him to the verge of flunking out that first quarter. He spent a lot of time with her, hanging out in the common area of the girls' dorm, and when she had something else she had to do, he'd spent most of his time day-dreaming about her. She captivated him, ensorcelled him, so much so he found it hard to breathe in her presence.

It hadn't been that way with Melanie. Not even close. Things with Melanie had been...cooler, less immediate.

There was nothing wrong with Melanie—she was a great girl, and she loved Eddie a lot…

But she was no Amanda.

Except for Freshman Orientation, Eddie's classes were a snooze fest most of the time, and most of his professors were old—thirty-five or forty—and did not understand how the real world worked. Most of them had never suffered through a bad day in their lives.

Eddie couldn't see the point in learning English grammar or American History or Algebra. He couldn't imagine a future in which he would need any of those things. He relished his computer class, however—at least the parts of it that taught him about writing programs. Eddie didn't think all the algorithms and all that other bullshit had much value—not in the real world—but he enjoyed being able to make the computer do what he wanted it to do. And last, but by far the worst, Art Appreciation and History… A worthless class, to his way of thinking.

Even though he didn't enjoy most of his classes, Eddie still attended every scheduled meeting. The Mortons were paying for his education, and he would get their money's worth.

Every cent.

Amanda was the icing on the cake, though. Funny and creative and sweet and smart and beautiful. And sexy. Lots and lots of sexy.

He couldn't believe his luck.

4

1986

To his surprise, Amanda stood outside the locked glass doors as he trotted downstairs to the dorm's lobby. She wore her thickest coat but shivered as if she were freezing. She flashed a little wave at him, and her face dimpled.

Laughing, he went to the door and opened it. "What are you doing here, crazy-girl? Don't you know what time it is?" He waved at the dawning light breaking across the sky.

She looked him up and down, moving her head in a slow, methodical manner. "Seems to me, you are ready to go, too, *crazy-boy*."

Eddie laughed and pushed his arms into his coat. "Guilty. But what are we going to do until the mall opens?"

Amanda grinned and patted her stomach. "Mama's hungry," she said with a saucy grin.

"Then we better get you to a Denny's. Stat!" He threw his arm around her shoulder, and Amanda snuggled against his side.

"This will be a fun day, Eddie," she said. "I can feel it."

"Yeah," he said, thinking every day had been fun since they'd met on the first day of classes. She was perfect. All except for the hair. It looked like a bunch of strawberry licorice. *Why would she want hair that color?* That hair confused him and made him uneasy.

But bright-red hair or not, Eddie couldn't believe a girl as great as Amanda liked him, that she wanted to be his girlfriend. She could have any man she wanted.

She caught him staring at her and thumped him in the ribs. "What?"

"Nothing. I can't wait to see this mall is all. Have you been there?"

"For the three thousand nine hundred and eighty-fifth time, no, Eddie, I have not been there." She said it with a laugh and squeezed him around the waist. "You're like a little kid about this place."

"What can I say? Going to an antique store is just my idea of perfect fun. Going to a mall full of them with the cutest, nicest girl in the world? Nirvana."

She squeezed him around the waist again. "Kind of a schmoopy dork, aren't you?"

Eddie laughed. "I'm whatever you want to call me, Amanda."

Suddenly shy, Amanda ducked her head. "What if… What if I wanted to call you my boyfriend?"

"If a girl like you wants to call a guy like me her boyfriend, it means one of two things: either you're stark raving mad, or I am the luckiest man on Earth."

They walked in silence for a minute, lost in mutual embarrassment at the sappy turn their conversation had taken. After a dozen steps, Amanda hugged him yet again. "Schmoopy dork."

"As long as 'schmoopy dork' means 'boyfriend,' I'm happy to answer to it."

"Can you hear me rolling my eyes?" Amanda said.

"I can! You'll want to see a doctor about that. Either that or squirt a little WD-40 in there."

The second they emerged from the walkway between two buildings into the parking lot, the full force of the frigid wind buffeted them again. It ruffled Eddie's hair and twisted Amanda's candy-apple-red locks around her head, covering her eyes, infiltrating her mouth.

"That's a good look for you, but I didn't know your middle name was Medusa." He grinned, but something inside him twanged like an out-of-tune guitar.

She swatted his stomach. "You don't have any idea what my middle name is, mister, and if you don't want your middle name to be mud, you'd better straighten up and fly right."

Eddie laughed. "Kind of weird early in the morning, know that?"

"Dork."

"Medusa." Eddie said it with a grin, but a dark, smoky memory lurched within him. He squeezed his eyes shut for a moment and practiced one of the refrains Dr. Erikson had taught him.

They reached her car, and she disengaged to unlock the door of the little silver Nissan Maxima. She sank into the driver's seat and hit the power locks.

Eddie got in the car and whistled. "Nice wheels." He didn't have a car—he allowed himself to infringe on the Mortons' generosity only so far.

Amanda laughed. "You don't have to say that *every* time I give you a ride somewhere, Eddie."

Eddie looked at her and waggled his eyebrows. "It's not what I *want* to say, anyway. At least not the 'wheels' part."

Amanda blushed, but her smile dazzled him. "Well what is it you want to say?"

Eddie looked out the passenger window to hide his embarrassment. "Oh, you'll just call me a schmoopy dork." He waved his hand in the air. "Or punch me hard."

Amanda chuckled and rested her hand on his shoulder. "Well, now you *have* to tell me."

Heat blazed in Eddie's cheeks, and he hoped he wasn't as red as her hair. "Well, it starts with nice…"

"Nice seats? Nice steering wheel? Nice to meet you?"

"No, no, and no."

"Nice breath? Nice doggy?"

Eddie shook his head, a pit yawning where his stomach had been. "I don't think I should tell you."

Amanda dropped her hand to his side and tickled him. "Well that's not fair, so I'm not starting this car until you tell me, mister."

"Can we just forget I said anything?"

"Nope."

Eddie relaxed back into the seat but kept his gaze directed out through the passenger window. "I'll tell you, but you have to promise not to be mad."

"Mad? Now you really have to tell me."

"Nice…" He fidgeted with the zipper of his coat, looking down at his lap. "Promise not to be mad?"

"Okay, okay. I promise not to be mad at whatever schmoopy-dorky thing you're scared to tell me." Amanda laughed and tickled him again.

"The thing I always want to tell you every time I see you is…" His voice trembled a little, and he let the sentence linger in the air.

"Oh, come on, Eddie. Don't be a tease!"

Eddie looked at her askance. "I want to tell you that you have nice…breasts."

Amanda burst out laughing. "'Nice *tits*?' That's what you want to say every time?"

It felt as if Eddie's cheeks were on fire, but he nodded.

Her laughter slowed and ended with a grin. "Well, thank you, Eddie, but you haven't even seen them." She cocked one eyebrow at him. "Not yet…" She tipped him a wink and started the car.

As Amanda reversed out of the space, Eddie took a deep breath and said, "So…you still want to call me a schmoopy dork?"

"As long as it means boyfriend." Amanda didn't look at him. "Maybe now more than ever," she murmured.

Eddie grinned, he couldn't help it. "Good, because I love being *your* schmoopy dork."

They split a Grand Slam breakfast and drank carafe after carafe of coffee. They sat in a Denny's booth looking out the plate-glass window as the sun rose. Eddie insisted on paying the check when it came, even though they both knew it would cut into his food budget.

"I wish you would let me pay, Eddie."

Eddie shook his head. "You're paying for gas."

"Cash, grass, or ass," she said with a lopsided grin. "Seriously, though—"

"It's okay."

Amanda laughed without looking at him. "Yeah who wants to eat, right?"

Eddie patted his stomach and sat back in the booth. "After this breakfast, who *needs* to eat?"

The antique mall opened at nine, and they were the first ones in line as the doors opened. The place smelled like dust with a nasty odor underneath it—like cow manure or vomit.

The mall had about as much in common with a shopping mall as deer did with seaweed. More like a flea market, ramshackle stalls filled the interior instead of shops. The building itself was a giant rectangle, with steel siding like a warehouse, though there was linoleum on the floor.

"I go antiquing with my mom back home," said Amanda. "It's a lot of fun, though I don't care about the antiques all that much. It's all about the journey."

Eddie stood inside the door, just looking around, taking it all in. "It's *wonderful*. Look at all these *treasures*, Amanda."

Amanda looked around as if she hadn't noticed all the junk and then returned her gaze to his face. "Yep. That's a lot of stuff. What do you want to start with?"

Eddie tore his gaze away from the thousands of items populating the stalls that he could see and looked at Amanda. "*All of it*."

Amanda laughed and patted his arm. "Well, that is the idea of coming here." She glanced around again. "I meant, what do you want to look at *first*?"

Eddie turned his head, taking in the enormous open space surrounding them. Flimsy walls or hanging banners, and in many cases by nothing at all, separated the stalls. "I… I don't know where to start. It's so big!"

"Yeah, *thousands* of vendors." Amanda grabbed his hand and pulled him to the left. "When in doubt, follow the wall."

"What?"

Amanda laughed again. "It's one of my mother's rules for antiquing. When in doubt how to get around, follow the wall."

Eddie looked at the center of the floor. "But…but all that stuff in the middle…"

Amanda laughed all the harder. "Yeah. Follow the wall and then work your way toward the center."

"I think I might love your mother."

"Eww, that's gross. Besides, you are mine."

He snapped his gaze back to her face and arched an eyebrow at her. "Am I? It's official?"

Amanda scoffed, but not in a mean way. "I'm not asking *you*, Eddie. I mean, I've dropped all the hints I can come up with."

"I…"

"It's the guy's job to ask, the girl's job to answer. Didn't your high school girlfriends teach you that?"

Eddie dropped his gaze to the floor. "Only one."

"Only one? One what? One question?"

"No. Only one high school girlfriend. And I never asked her to be my girlfriend. We just sort of…"

"Well," said Amanda. "If you want this girl to be your college girlfriend, we're not going to 'just sort of.' You will have to ask."

"I…" Eddie shook his head, feeling helpless.

"What, you can tell me I have nice tits, but you can't ask me to be your girlfriend?" Her eyes danced with mischief.

An old woman overheard what Amanda said, and she shook her finger at Eddie.

Eddie only grinned. "Amanda Medusa Hawthorne, a question burneth in my hearteth. Pray telleth, wouldst thou be-ist my girlfriendith?"

"Not good enough, Eddie." She grinned at him and winked.

"Young man, it's not a time for joking," said the old woman. "You better get it in gear before another young man beats you to the punch and snaps this young beauty right off the market." She looked at Amanda. "But Heavens, girl, what have you done to your hair?"

Amanda smiled at her. "My mother asks me that very question every time she sees me."

"Okay. Amanda, I don't want to see anyone but you. I have no interest in other girls. Do you feel the same way?"

"I don't want to see any other girls either," said Amanda with a grin.

"Oh, missy, if he can't joke, neither can you," said the old woman, though she wore a smile on her face. "Fair is fair, after all."

Amanda shrugged. "I do feel the same way, Eddie."

"Then would you do me the honor of going exclusive?"

The old woman rolled her eyes and turned away, flapping her hand at Eddie.

Amanda stood up on her tiptoes and kissed him on the lips. "We will work on the whole asking important questions thing, but my answer is yes. We are officially a couple."

"Yes!" he shouted, but Eddie couldn't help it. His gaze strayed over her shoulder and began to slide over the treasures in the next stall.

5

1986

John Morton laughed when he saw the amount of stuff Eddie had set out to take home over the Christmas break. Boxes and boxes of things waited arrayed on the curb, ready to load into the car.

"Did you bring this much stuff with you when you moved up last fall?"

Eddie hunched his shoulders and looked away.

Morton arched his eyebrows over a wide grin. "Let me guess, you found a place that sells...*treasures.*"

Glancing up at the man who had taken him in, Eddie returned his smile. "Amanda finds the best antique shops."

"Maybe I should make Amanda haul all this stuff back to Cottonwood Vale." Morton said it with a smile, even as he opened the trunk of his cruiser and loaded in the first box.

"She's already gone home." Eddie laughed and loaded another box into the trunk.

John Morton's expression fell, giving him the look of a comically disappointed grandfather. "I was hoping to meet her this time."

"Her grandmother was coming into town early. Her grandma's been sick."

"Ah." Morton looked between the stack of boxes remaining on the curb and the full trunk. "Son, we might need to buy you a van." He chuckled and carried the next carton to the rear door of the car and loaded it into the back seat. "See if you can get that bastard to close."

The trunk wouldn't close until Eddie removed one of the boxes. He took the box to the other rear door and loaded into the back seat without looking at his stepfather.

"I know you take pleasure in your treasures, son, but we might want to have a talk about restraint. That or the joys of self-storage places."

Eddie licked his lips and kept his eyes down as he retrieved the next box.

"Now, Eddie, don't be that way. I was just teasing you. I don't care how many things you want, how many things you own. You know that."

Eddie looked at the chief askance. "I just collect things—"

"Eddie," said John softly. "I was only kidding."

Eddie smiled, and they loaded the rest of the boxes into the cruiser. He climbed into the passenger seat and closed the door.

John sank into the driver's seat, grunting as he did so, and Eddie noticed how stiff he was, how much effort it seemed to take him to do the simplest tasks, and his eyes began to itch and burn. *He's getting old. Mrs. Morton, too. What will I do when they...* He shook his head to clear those thoughts away and shoved his emotions into that bottomless black pit at his center. Not for the first time, he wondered if everyone had such a cavity.

Morton got settled and put on his safety belt. He sighed with what sounded like relief. Then he put a smile on his face and turned toward Eddie. "Excited about being home for Christmas?"

"Yeah," Eddie said in a near monotone.

"Well, don't sound so enthusiastic, son. Your excitement will distract me from driving." He rolled his head toward Eddie and gave him a look.

"Sorry, it's just that..."

"It's just that Amanda doesn't live in Cottonwood Vale." Morton chuckled as he started the cruiser's big engine.

Eddie grinned.

"There's plenty of time for women, son. Mrs. Morton is looking forward to seeing you. She's missed you."

Eddie swallowed hard. "I've..."

"You don't have to say anything, Eddie. We know how you feel—even if it sticks sideways in your throat."

"I do want you to meet Amanda. You will love her."

"I'm sure we will, Eddie. But there's time. You two are young yet. Enjoy your time alone together. Enjoy this time away."

Eddie cleared his throat. "How's the department? How's Cottonwood?"

John grimaced and pressed his hand into his abdomen just below his ribs on the left side. "Well, son, you'll learn this soon enough, but even a job you love can sometimes be a big pain in the ass."

"Trouble? The City Council?"

"No, no. Nothing like that." Morton burped, and his face twisted into a tighter, meaner grimace. "You remember all that brouhaha over in Oneka Falls?"

"You mean when I was a kid?"

The chief nodded.

"Vaguely. I can't remember any details, if I ever knew any to begin with. Gil wasn't much for the six o'clock news."

John stared straight ahead, and his knuckles blanched on the steering wheel. "Yeah. Well, four kids got kidnapped by this ex-Marine who went a little nuts. He was a Vietnam vet—a Force Recon sniper—and he shot up the whole damn town. One of his victims was Bobby Jefferson, the best damn Sheriff Kanowa County has ever had—they named your high school after him when he was…" He waved his hand in Eddie's direction. "Never mind all that. You don't need to know the details. Anyway, similar shit kicked off over to Lake Genosgwa last summer, and I've got to testify about one of the bodies they found the first week of the new year. The States Attorney's been grilling me on my testimony. I've been in a lot of ass-numbing meetings about the damn thing."

"Oh," said Eddie. "That sounds like it sucks."

"Ayup. She went missing so long ago…" Morton nodded, a faraway look in his eyes, and a silence descended on them. After a mile or two of silence, the chief forced gaiety into his voice and said, "So, this Amanda…Mrs. Morton and I are dying to hear all about her."

Eddie blushed, but he wasn't sure why. "She's great. Funny, smart. Bright-red hair."

John arched his eyebrow. "Nothing wrong with a redhead."

"Yeah, well. It's not the same red as a redhead. It's red like a cherry snow cone or something."

John chuckled. "Oh, Mrs. Morton will *love* that." He reached across the seat and thumped Eddie's shoulder without much force behind it. "It sounds as though you two have been spending a lot of time together, clown-colored hair or not."

The night they'd spent together before Amanda had gone home for break flashed through Eddie's mind. "Yeah."

John laughed. "It's only a few weeks, Eddie."

Eddie chuckled. "But it already feels as if it's been a few weeks, and it's only been two days."

John hit him with a quick glance. "Are you excited to hang out with Melinda when you get back home?"

It seemed such an innocent question, but to Eddie, it was a punch in the gut. His stomach dove toward the floorboards. The truth was, he hadn't even thought about Melinda Fox in weeks, maybe months. "Is she… I mean, does she still come around?" He dropped his head to watch his hands try to strangle each other in his lap.

"Oh yes. Almost every Sunday afternoon, she's over to the house, helping Mrs. Morton with whatever project's taken her fancy. Sometimes they bake, sometimes they paint, but fair warning, Eddie, they *always* talk."

Eddie's stomach sank even farther. "Yeah." He turned and watched the miles race by the passenger side window. "Chief, I…that is, I don't know how to…"

"Don't worry, son. Mrs. Morton knows how you feel about Amanda. I wanted you to know how Mrs. Morton feels about Melanie."

Eddie shrugged. "But... How do I, you know, talk to Melanie?"

"In my experience, Eddie, honesty is always the best policy. From the way you talk about Amanda, it seems to me that you've moved on in your life, and that's wonderful for you, but keep in mind that Melanie may not have. She may need a bit of delicate handling."

Eddie cleared his throat. "But I tell her, right?"

"Well...yes, but not right away. You can let her down easy."

"How do you mean?"

"Don't just come out with it—you don't just say, 'hey, I'm seeing this wonderful, great woman for whom the Earth stops spinning when she asks.' You can just tell her how great it's been to be away at college. How much you're enjoying your classes. Maybe you can emphasize how being up there without a girlfriend back home has been good for you."

"All that is true, Chief, but still...it doesn't sound...honest."

"Why not? It's all true, right?"

"Yeah, but the reason I don't want to hang out with Melanie—at least not in a girlfriend-boyfriend kind of way—is because of Amanda."

Morton pursed his lips. "Eddie, you should always be honest, but sometimes telling the *whole* truth is just hurtful to people."

"Okay."

"If the subject comes up, you just tell Melanie that you don't want to renew your relationship. Tell her that freedom is important for your college experience and that the time away has also given you the opportunity to consider things."

"Oh, I get it. I tell her that what we thought would last forever in high school, might not be what either of us needs as adults."

"Something like that," Morton said with a shrug. "Before you do anything, though, have a chat with Mrs. Morton. She might have an insight or two."

"Has she made Bernice's Bars yet?"

John laughed and swatted Eddie's thigh. "Well, you know her. She's been baking for days, but she didn't put the Bernice's Bars up until this morning as I was walking out the door."

"Blueberry pie?"

"Check."

"Sugar cookies with raisins?"

"That's a ten-four."

Eddie giggled. "All my favorites, then."

John returned his grin. "And some of mine, son. And more. You might gain fifty pounds before you head back to school."

They spent the rest of the ninety-seven-mile ride chatting away like two old men in the barbershop. Eddie enjoyed it; there was no pressure to act or think in a certain way just John's unconditional acceptance.

His unconditional *love*.

They drove through Cottonwood Vale, John lifting his hand off the steering wheel to wave at people on the street from time to time. The town looked very much the same as when he left—which made sense since he'd only been gone for three months.

As they turned onto Route 243 from 19, Eddie saw Margo as she entered the small convenience store on the corner. He grimaced and turned his head away while his hands took to trying to kill one another.

"You're going to see her, Eddie. Gil, too. He's been very visible since he got out, and I should warn you he's got a chip on his shoulder. The bastard's got a few people in town all wound up about how I framed him, about how I abused my power as police chief so that Mrs. Morton and I could get you under our thumbs." He waved a big hand. "General bullshit such as that."

Eddie shook his head and sank down in the seat.

"Now, don't worry, son. There's nothing we can do about Gil or the vile bullshit he spews, so there's no sense wasting one second on the bastard. He's a despicable man that craves attention and likes to play the victim. The only thing that we can do is go on with our lives and ignore him. Don't you waste another second of your life thinking about him." Morton piloted the police cruiser the few miles between the center of Cottonwood Vale and the old farmhouse he and Mrs. Morton had lived in for all of their married life.

The place Eddie now called home.

"Think about Amanda, instead," said John as he pulled into the drive.

Using that maternal ESP that all women seem to be able to access, even if the child isn't their blood, Izzy Morton stood on the stoop waiting for them as they pulled into the dooryard.

She looked older, frailer.

She waved with both hands and danced down the steps. Eddie got the seatbelt off half a second before she ripped the car door open and pulled him out, before she wrapped him into a huge hug and rained kisses onto his cheek.

He supposed it should embarrass him, but he wasn't. He *liked* it. "Hi, Mrs. Morton," he said.

"Hello, Eddie. Welcome home!" She treated him to a few more motherly kisses. "Let's leave all this stuff in the car and head inside. I've got a surprise for you, and it's hot out of the oven." Her gaze strayed to the boxes in the back seat, then darted to Chief Morton's face, one eyebrow lifted.

"I know it's a lot of stuff, but it's all *good* stuff," Eddie said.

Izzy patted him on the shoulder. "I bet it is, Eddie. You can tell me all about your new treasures as you eat a nice big piece of blueberry pie. Or do you fancy a Bernice's Bar, instead? They're nice and cold, just how you like them."

They stood there grinning as if they were a real family.

The crunch of tires on the gravel drive shattered the moment. Eddie looked over his shoulder, and his stomach dropped like a stone at the sight of Gil's old Dodge truck. Margo was in the passenger seat, but she had her eyes on her lap. His uncle's gaze rested on his as the rasping vehicle slowed to a halt, and then Gil's face knotted up in a rictus of anger.

"Go into the house, Eddie," said John Morton in his cop voice. "You too, Izzy."

"What do they *want*?" asked Izzy.

"Never mind that. Go into the house. Take him inside, Izzy."

Eddie just stood there staring into Gil's malignant face, as if his uncle's gaze had rooted him to the spot. A strange melody danced on the breeze. The music sounded strange in his ears—he didn't even recognize the instruments. Mrs.

Morton also seemed unable to get moving toward the house, though her hand fluttered along Eddie's forearm.

The driver's door of the old Dodge truck creaked open, and Gil stepped out. Eddie's gaze darted to Margo, and she grimaced at him. Gil stood for a moment, hands on his hips, stretching his lower back and gazing out at the old barn and the fallow field beyond it.

With a shake of his head, he turned. "Not much of a farm," he said without taking his eyes off Eddie.

"What do you want?" demanded Chief Morton.

"A little civility, for a start." Gil's gaze snapped to the chief. "After all the bullshit you put me through, Morton, it's the least you can do." He returned his gaze to Eddie's face, and he winked. "At least until the civil suit comes out in my favor. Then, I imagine I *will* turn this into a farm."

"I'll burn every bit of it to the ground before you touch it!" snapped Mrs. Morton.

"Why, Isabel, that isn't very neighborly."

Mrs. Morton scoffed and took a protective step closer to Eddie.

The music grew a little louder, more insistent. Eddie wanted to look at either of the Mortons, to find out if they heard it, too, but he couldn't seem to move his gaze off his uncle's malignant face.

Gil laughed and waved his hand at her. "Even as a man, brat, you're still looking for a woman to protect you, huh?"

"I'll ask you one more time, Ratherson. And believe me, this is the last time I'm asking you. What do you want?"

Gil's gaze slithered over to Chief Morton's. "Well, I'll tell you, John…if this was any of your damn business, I'd be happy to answer you. But since it isn't, why don't you fuck off and go do something productive. *Police* work, mayhap."

John Morton was getting up there in years, but he was still a bear of a man, and when he took a step forward, there was something about it that made Gil take an involuntary step back. "Now, let me tell you something, Ratherson. I don't give two happy fuckalls—" John darted a glance at his wife and grimaced. "I don't care a whit about why you are here, what you want, or what you believe you're entitled to. To be honest, Ratherson, I don't care whether or not you continue to draw breath. If you've got the mistaken idea you can come over here and cause trouble, let me correct you on that bad assumption. In fact, let's just end this conversation here. Get your scrawny ass back into your beat-up old shitbox of a pickup truck and go away."

"And don't you ever come back here, Gil Ratherson," said Izzy.

Gil hawked and spat. "You two done?" His gaze came to rest on Eddie's face, and as it did, the music flared, as if an invisible conductor had called for a flourish. Eddie imagined Gil's gaze felt like worms crawling over his cheeks. "I don't give two fuckalls about either of you. I've got lawyers for that. I come here this afternoon to talk to my nephew, and I'm *going* to talk to my nephew."

"He doesn't—"

"If you've got the idea I care what he does or doesn't want, Morton, let me correct you on that bad assumption. In fact, why don't you and the missus go inside and moan about what a bad man I am?"

Chief Morton grinned, and the sight of it was enough to freeze Eddie's blood. "Listen to me, you flatulent coward." As hot as his voice had been a moment before, it had turned bone-chilling cold, enough that Eddie expected to see frost. "Get out of here. While you still can."

Gil didn't move, except to tilt his head back and laugh.

"Izzy, go inside and take Eddie with you. Call dispatch and tell them to send over an ambulance and have Brad roll this way."

Gil laughed again and held his hands out to the side, shaking them like a circus performer. "Oh, scary." His laugh grew louder. "Hear that, Margo? We're going to have dispatch send over an ambulance."

In a flash that belied John Morton's size, his Colt 1911 moved from the holster on his hip to his hand held straight out in front of him. His thumb moved to the hammer and rested there.

"You going to shoot me?" sneered Gil.

Morton's gelid grin widened into a dreadful smile that showed all his teeth. "If you don't get back into your truck and get out of here, I guess we'll find out."

Mrs. Morton and Eddie stood frozen where they'd been when Gil pulled up, but Eddie disengaged Mrs. Morton from his arm and applied gentle pressure to her shoulder, pushing her toward the house. "Go on in. Do as the chief asks."

Mrs. Morton looked at him through wide eyes.

The forbidding black rage that lived within Eddie was out, and he could feel it twisting his features, shifting his expression into something alarming, monstrous. "It's okay, Mom," he said in as gentle a voice as he could. "Go on." The music twisted—almost convulsed—into a creepy key. It made Eddie think of desert sand and hot sun.

Her eyes misted, but the endearment wasn't enough to settle her fright at what she read in his face. "Make him leave, John. Make him leave. *Now.*"

In the drive, Gil cackled anew.

John took another step, a single step, the big .45 caliber pistol still extended, still aimed at the scrawny center of

Gil's face. It was enough to rob Gil of his laughter. "You're not as stupid as you look, shitheel."

Eddie applied more pressure to Izzy's shoulder. "Go inside, Mom. Please." The tempo of the creepy music accelerated, the beat hammering in time with his heartbeat.

She shook her head.

Eddie took a step away from her but glanced back and said, "I don't want you to see me this way." His voice shook with the strength of the black tempest of rage whirling inside him

Gil chuckled. "Hear that, Margo? The brat doesn't want his fake mommy to watch him throw a fit."

Eddie turned his gaze on Gil, and there was something about Eddie's expression that made the smile sour on his uncle's face. "Dad, I can take care of this." The music had grown so loud, Eddie's ears rang with it.

"No, Eddie. I want you to go inside with your mother. *I* will take care of this bit of road trash." He flashed a nasty smile at Gil. "After all, I've done it before."

From the passenger seat of the rusty old Dodge pickup, Margo screamed, "She's not his mother!"

Deep inside Eddie, at a depth he didn't even know existed, something snapped, and it seemed even his organs rebounded from the force. His gaze snapped to Margo's. "More than you ever were! My *mother* wouldn't be able to stand the sight of what you've become!"

"Let me handle it, Eddie," said Chief Morton.

Eddie took another step forward as if the chief hadn't spoken. The melody cavorted up and down through the register, the tempo wild, the rhythm harsh and demanding. His hands shook, though he kept them by his side, open and loose. Stringed instruments clashed with cymbals and drums. He remembered the day he had fought with Jack

McGregor back in high school. Something that reminded him of a flute wailed over the strings, bending the main melody into an inverted counter melody. He remembered feeling out of control but *reveling* in it, and the freedom of it. The rhythm twisted again and again, and things began to flash at the edge of Eddie's vision as if someone danced just out of site. He felt a little like he had that day in high school, but the fury was so much deeper this time, so much more *alive*, that the idea of what he might do scared him.

"Eddie," said Morton.

Gil glowered at him. "Better listen to your fake daddy, boy."

Eddie smiled again, but it wasn't a pleasant smile. The melody and countermelody of the music melded in a crashing cacophony of crescendos. His jaw muscles bunched, twitched, and spasmed beneath his skin, and his teeth ached with the force with which he ground them. Eddie took another step, and his shaking hands curled into tight fists. "It won't be the way it was when I was twelve, Gil." The instruments on the wind faded until only drums and cymbals remained.

"God, I hope not." Gil grinned a death's head grin. "But if you want to dance, brat…" He held his hands out to the side as if to say, "here I am."

"Izzy! Take Eddie in the house."

"Yeah, brat. Better go inside with your mommy."

"She's *not his mother*!" screamed Margo.

Gil didn't bother to look at her, he just pointed at her, and she whimpered and sank down in the seat.

Eddie took another step, and a harsh, uncaring coldness settled over his mind, but it wasn't the same as when he shoved his emotions into the pit inside of him. Not at all.

This time the coldness came part-and-parcel with the raw, rampaging rancor that raged within him.

Sneering, Gil took a step forward, mimicking Eddie, his face twisting with derision.

"Ratherson! Get your truck and get out here. Last warning." Chief Morton took two steps forward, but his eyes followed Eddie, not Gil.

"I'll go call dispatch," said Isabel Morton.

"Take Eddie!"

"John, he won't come." Izzy sounded exasperated, but even so, she took a step toward Eddie.

"Eddie!" John's voice rang with authority, with the confidence that no one would dare ignore him.

But Eddie didn't even hear him. The melody had started anew, albeit at a faster tempo. He saw nothing other than Gil; he heard nothing but Gil. He advanced another step, and as he did, the muscles in his shoulders and hips bunched, shifting his weight. His arms swung up, hands curled into rock-hard fists.

"Oh yeah," sneered Gil. "Look, Margo! We got ourselves a *fighter*."

"You idiot!" snapped John. "Don't you remember what he did to the McGregor kid?"

"I do, John. I hope he'll try it on me."

"Has the entire fucking world lost its mind?" John walked forward, gun no longer covering Gil, but pointed at the sky. "Gil Ratherson, I'm placing you under arrest for criminal trespass, disturbing the peace, and assault. Get your hands on the hood of that truck."

Gil laughed and sneered at the chief.

Eddie's advance quickened, and the rhythm of the melody on the wind matched his pace.

He was lost, by then—at least the parts of Eddie that anyone would recognize—displaced by the berserk juggernaut of his enmity. The irate rictus of wrath that distended his face deformed his features more and more with each step, as unfettered fury displaced parts of his personality, and his face ached with it.

Behind him, the door to the house opened and closed, and Eddie was glad. He didn't want Mrs. Morton to see him in that state, to watch what the mindless rage wanted to do to Gil, and the will, the power to stop it, eluded Eddie.

"Hands on the truck, Ratherson," said John. "Do it now, or I'll see you back in that prison for a parole violation. "

"*Idiot*. Do you think I'd be here if I was still on parole?"

After everything else, Gil calling John Morton an idiot was the one small step beyond what Eddie could take. With a bull-like roar, he dropped his head and charged.

"Eddie, no!"

He slammed into Gil, his head snapping up into his uncle's chin, driving the man's head back with an audible snap. Eddie screamed, and the monster he'd hidden within himself all his life shattered the last of his restraints and lunged free. His fists rocketed out, pummeling Gil's face, neck, head, and cymbals crashed with each and every blow. His furious onslaught drove Gil to his knees, as surely as the butcher's hammer dropped cattle.

With each blow, a shriek of pure rage erupted from Eddie, and in each scream, rang years of hatred, years of anger, of pain. Visions of life with Gil flashed before him. Margo with a black eye, his doll collection melting and sizzling and popping, the petty meanness, the beatings, all of it, came roaring back, and Eddie was as powerless to stop those scenes from replaying in his mind's eye as he was to stop his fists.

His hands felt petrified as if they would never uncurl again. The muscles in his neck, shoulders, and upper arms felt like river rocks, hard and cold. His knuckles ached with each impact.

Thick arms wrapped around Eddie from behind as Morton lifted him bodily away from his uncle. John took five steps, holding his writhing adopted son against his chest. When he set Eddie down and took a step back, he wrapped his big hands around Eddie's bicep's and held him there.

"Let me go! Let me go!" Eddie hadn't been aware until that moment that he'd been yelling the words at John Morton ever since the chief had picked him up. He blushed with shame and snapped his mouth shut. He listened for it, but the music no longer played with the wind.

"No, Eddie." John's voice rang with calm, quiet authority. "You need to stop this, now. Let me handle him."

Eddie's gaze zeroed in on John's face, and the sight of his adopted father's expression was enough to push part of the rage away. Behind John, Gil staggered to his feet, his face a mask of vindictive anger, dripping blood and snot.

"You'll go to prison for this, brat!"

"I doubt that," said John without taking his eyes off Eddie's face.

"You'll see!"

John sighed as though he were the weariest man in the world. "Just go away, Ratherson. Haven't you done enough?"

Gil sputtered with anger and stood his ground.

"Go away."

"And die," rasped Eddie in a harsh, hateful voice that even he didn't recognize.

Gil squawked and sprinted toward Eddie, his hand going for his belt buckle.

Eddie's gaze drifted from his uncle to his adopted father's face, and then with a move any martial arts master would be proud of, he shifted his weight and twisted his arms until he was free of John's grasp. He faced his uncle and raised his hands again.

"I'm warning you, Ratherson!"

Gil came on, ignoring John as much as Eddie had moments before. He closed the distance to Eddie, stripping his belt from his belt loops. When he was three steps away, he ratcheted his arm back as he had so many times in the years that Eddie suffered under his wrath, slinging the wide leather strap behind him like a drover readying his whip.

"Oh, for fuck's sake!" said Morton, once again pulling his gun.

Two steps away from his nephew, Gil began to bring the belt forward, the strap whistling through the air.

Eddie didn't move out of the way, he didn't protect himself. He just stood there.

Waiting for it.

The belt slapped over his shoulder and snapped against his back. As if that had been what he waited for, Eddie lurched forward and grabbed his uncle by the neck, fingers digging, digging, digging into the older man's throat.

Gil abandoned the belt and started swinging his fists. He stepped forward and hooked his leg around Eddie's, shoving him hard and breaking his grip. Eddie fell to the gravel, banging his head. Like a cat leaping on a mouse, Gil dropped on him, straddling his torso with his knees, and began raining down blows.

Morton took a single step, and Gil froze as the .45's hammer clacked back into firing position. "Give me an excuse," the chief hissed into Gil's ear. "Please, I'm begging you…"

Eddie's ears rang from the assault, but he heard what the chief said as plain as day—and his uncle's whimper.

"Now, Ratherson, what we're going to call this is mutual combat. No jail for you, no jail for Eddie. But don't mistake this for weakness, because I'll tell you right now if you *ever* come back here, if you *ever* bother Eddie again, I'll see you back in prison. And this time, you cowardly son of a bitch, I'll make sure you stay for a good long time. Even if I have to manufacture the evidence to make it happen." Morton took a single step, his face contorted with rage. "Now, get up off of that boy, or heaven help us both, I *will* pull this trigger!" His icy voice seethed with hatred.

Gil got up, his hands up, his movements slow and deliberate. "I got witnesses to what you just said, Chief."

"So what? Who do you think people will credit more? The chief of police or an asshole skell who's already been to prison once? And for beating the boy, you just assaulted?"

Eddie sat up without the berserker fury that had ruled him moments earlier. He rubbed his jaw. A calm, a cold detachment separated him from the fight. He looked up at John.

"It's okay, Eddie," said Morton. "Why not go on into the house now?"

With a nod, Eddie stood and dusted himself off. He glared at Gil, but the man wouldn't meet his gaze.

"So, Ratherson, you ready to leave?" Morton's big .45 remained pressed behind Gil's ear, and Gil's hands were still up in the air. He nodded. "Then go."

Eddie stared at Gil's pickup truck. Through it all, Margo hadn't moved. Her angry gaze tracked Eddie as he walked to the house but froze on the steps.

On the roof above him, stood the scary lady, her face writhing with pleasure.

6

1989

The phone rang, jarring Eddie from a deep sleep. He rolled over, fumbling for the cordless phone that he kept on the nightstand. It was Thursday, the one day a week where his obligations allowed him to sleep in. He only had a lab, and it started at three-thirty in the afternoon.

He found the phone without having to open his eyes—which was a plus toward going back to sleep after he ended the call. Eddie thumbed the on button and pressed the phone to his ear. "Yeah?"

"Hope I woke you up, brat. Hope I woke up that pretty new wife of yours, too."

Eddie's eyes flew open, and he pushed himself up on one elbow. "Gil?"

"Your Auntie Margo always said you was a smart one."

Eddie pinched the phone between his shoulder and ear, freeing his hand to scrub the sleep from his eyes. There was no way he was getting back to sleep after talking to Gil. "What do you want?"

"I want you to tell me who the hell you think you are sending this letter to Margo. I want you to tell me where you get off making demands of us after all you've done."

Ire sang its sickly sweet melody in the back of his mind, sounding similar to something he'd expect to hear in a Middle Eastern coffee house. "After what I did to you?"

Gil chuckled, and it was a nasty sound. "Hell, yes, you little bastard. What you did to us. Me in prison, your auntie Margo left alone to struggle, no help from you. No, you are off in your perfect little life without a second's consideration about us."

Eddie growled in the back of his throat. *I should just hang up.* He threw back the covers and swung his legs out of bed, wincing as his feet struck the cold hardwood floor. "I did all that? Little old me? And to think all those years you said I wouldn't amount to anything."

"Are you sure you want to get smart with me?"

"You'd prefer me dumb, wouldn't you Gil? Too bad for you I'm not dumb, and I was always smarter than you—as much as you railed against it." Eddie suppressed a sigh and shook his head. *I shouldn't let him bait me.*

"You sure about that, brat? I mean you always *thought* you were so smart, but I seem to recall me always getting the better of you and not the other way around."

"What do you want, Gil?"

"I've said, haven't I? I want you to answer those two questions."

Eddie sighed and closed his eyes, counting to ten in his head. "First, I didn't send Margo any letters. It was—"

"There you go again. There goes that smart mouth."

"Do you want answers or not?"

Gil sighed, and it sounded like an explosion in Eddie's ear. "Go on then."

"I didn't send you any letters. As to the second question, anyone with a pulse can figure it out—even you, Gil, with your limited intellect—I am within my rights to demand the money Margo made by selling my house out from under me."

"Well, ain't you just all that." Gil's voice had taken on the nasty edge, that edge that Eddie always associated with danger. "Don't we deserve repayment for all the money we spent on you? All the money taking you to waste time with that headshrinker? For the extra food? For the clothes?"

"I don't seem to remember you doing much of anything for me, Gil. And, my attorney happens to be very good at his job, and he says you owe me the money."

"I guess I had you figured right. I guess you are the type of man to let everybody else fight your battles." Gil cackled, and it sounded mean. "Even way back when, I knew you'd never be the sort of man that would come talk to me face-to-face. Lawyers!"

"Don't call here again, Gil. It's not as if you're going to say anything that will surprise me. And, unfortunately for you, I'm no longer a twelve-year-old with no place to go. I no longer have to *listen*."

"Is that so? Let me say something that won't surprise you, then. That money is *gone*. You won't get one red cent from either Margo or me. Waste your time all you want, talking to lawyers, writing letters—it won't get you one penny from me. We got nothing for you."

Eddie stood, his hands shaking with anger. "Ha. Congratulations. You said something correct at long last."

"You got a smart mouth—"

Eddie thumbed the disconnect button and threw the handset on the bed.

"Your uncle?" asked Amanda.

Eddie spun on his heel. Amanda stood in the doorway, one hand on the door frame on each side. She had on a paint-stained T-shirt and a pair of cut-off jeans. Paint speckled her cheeks and her blonde hair. "Didn't you have class today?"

"Want to talk about it?"

"Your class?"

She grinned and stepped into the bedroom. "Do you want me to smear wet paint all over you?"

"Interesting idea…"

"You shouldn't let him bother you, Eddie."

Eddie flashed her a thin smile. "I know all too well what Gil's motivations are. You should've heard what went on in my head—that I should just hang up, that I shouldn't let him get to me."

She cocked her head to the side. "You're a smart guy, Eddie. You should listen to yourself more often."

He waggled his eyebrows. "Should I? Even now?"

"Is that all you ever think about? You just woke up. Your breath no doubt smells like a truck stop pisser."

He felt a grin to match hers stretch across his lips. "It wouldn't take me but a second to brush my teeth."

"I'd love to test that theory, but as you can see, I'm covered in paint, and I have class in a half-hour."

"It seems to me, the solution to all of our problems is in the bathroom." He ticked his points off on his fingers. "Toothbrush. Shower." He winked. "We could kill two birds with one stone."

"You *are* a smart man." She pulled her T-shirt off over her head. "Race you."

Fifteen minutes later, Eddie sat down at the kitchen table wearing a pair of running shorts, a loose T-shirt, and a smile. As he shoveled a spoonful of Cap'n Crunch into his mouth, Amanda swept into the room, dressed for class, her hair up in a ponytail.

"You should tell Roger about the phone call."

Eddie nodded and grinned around his mouthful of cereal.

"I'm serious, Eddie. Roger can probably do something, and if he can't, Daddy can." Having a father-in-law who was a partner in a large law firm had its benefits.

Eddie swallowed. "I will. I promise I'll call him as soon as I'm done eating."

She kissed him on the top of his head. "I've got to go, or I'll be late."

"No flirting with the guy sitting next to you."

She batted her eyelashes at him. "Maybe I will, maybe I won't. Either way, you'll never know."

"Oh, no? What makes you believe I don't have my spies in your classes?"

"What makes you so sure I'm not flirting with your spies?"

He chuckled. "Touché. Though it would be nice to win one of these exchanges before I die."

"Plenty of time for that, but if that's in your bucket list, you better increase your game." She strolled out the door before he could think of a comeback.

Eddie finished eating and put his bowl in the kitchen sink. With a sigh, Eddie turned, and his gaze drifted to the cordless phone handset standing on the counter. As he recalled his conversation with Gil, his expression soured. *Won't I* ever *be free of him?* Another sigh slipped between his lips.

He picked up the phone and dialed Roger Stein's number. Roger worked for Al Hawthorne—Amanda's father.

The receptionist put Eddie straight through to Roger's office, and he picked up on the second ring. "Hello, Eddie. How are tricks?"

"How do you do that?"

Roger laughed. "How do I answer the phone with such grace and aplomb?"

"No. How do you always know it's me?"

"Geesh, Eddie. Would you ask a magician to reveal his tricks? The receptionist tells me."

"Oh." Eddie's cheeks grew warm, and he could imagine the rosy color they must have.

"What can I do for you today, Eddie? Besides educating you on the wonders of modern telephony."

"My uncle called this morning."

Roger's voice lost its jocular tone and became all business. "Gil Ratherson called you this morning?"

"Yes. He called to yell at me."

"Yes, I understand. Al told me that in the past, your relationship was less than…"

"Yes. He beat me on a regular basis."

"And he did time for it, correct?"

"Not very much, but yes."

"I understand. I will draft a restraining order and get it filed this afternoon. He called you at home?"

"I'm not sure that's a good idea. It might just make him angrier."

"Are you worried his behavior may escalate?"

"I'm not twelve anymore, and the last time we had any interaction, it didn't go as he planned at all. Then again, he's vindictive. He might do something sneaky—something to the house, or the cars. I don't want him to—"

"You don't want him to mess with Amanda? Of course not. I can include a distance limitation for both you and Amanda in the court order."

"Okay. But you should talk to Al. He knows the history. Plus, Amanda is his daughter. Whatever Al wants to do is fine."

"Done. Tell me about the call."

Eddie sighed and then blushed again at the sound of it through the phone. "Well, it was just more of the same old same old. Although he said I'd never get a penny from him. Does that mean we can go ahead right away?"

"No, we still need to wait out the waiting period we put in the letter. But I don't want you to worry about all of this. It might surprise you how many times defendants say something similar but then the day before the waiting period expires they pay in full. Or, at least file an answer."

"I doubt Gil will pay—no matter how much time we give him."

Fabric rustled as Roger shrugged. "He may answer the complaint."

"Okay," Eddie said.

"I'll speak to Al in a moment about the restraining order, but while I've got you on the phone, let's assume that your aunt and uncle answer the complaint. Given this phone call, I want to reiterate, and perhaps underscore, that it would be best if you didn't attend the trial."

"You'll get no argument from me. If I never see them again, it will be too soon."

"Good. Though, as I said in our first meeting, there's an excellent chance we may get a summary judgment, and there won't even be a trial. Of course, we'll have to wait for their answer to the complaint before we know, but it's black letter law. Your aunt will breach her fiduciary responsibility to the trust if she refuses to distribute the proceeds from the sale of your house and the goods inside by the end of this waiting period."

"If there's anything Gil can do to make this process more difficult, he will do it."

"I understand. There's not much he can do. If they could claim legitimate expenses in your upbringing, they might have a legitimate defense, though. Do they have anything such as that?"

"He mentioned something like that today, but I can't imagine what they could claim as legitimate expenses."

"It sounds as though he's been to see an attorney, then. Still, it's nothing for you to worry about. Let me do the worrying."

"Okay, sounds good. After you speak to Al, can you call and let us know what you two decided? I may not be here, but you can leave a message on the answering machine."

"Will do," said Roger. "Oh, there's Al. Let me run and catch him before he leaves."

"Okay, go. Thanks, Roger."

"It's why I'm here. Talk to you later."

Eddie disconnected and put the phone down on the corner of the kitchen table. He didn't want another phone call from Gil, so he packed his backpack and headed to the library to get a little studying done before his lab.

7

1989

They didn't hear from Gil again—the restraining order that Roger filed was enough to scare him off. The next few months rushed by in newlywed bliss, and, to be honest, Eddie didn't even think about the lawsuit. So when Al Hawthorne called and invited Eddie and Amanda to dinner, he thought nothing of it.

They were to meet at a steakhouse on the shores of one of the Finger Lakes, and it was one of the dressier establishments. Eddie wore his dark blue suit, and Amanda wore a stunning blue dress.

Despite arriving five minutes early, the maître d' treated them to a fake smile and ushered Amanda and Eddie back into the dining room. Eddie's mouth dropped open when he saw John and Izzy Morton seated at the table along with the Hawthornes.

"Surprise!" said Al Hawthorne with a broad grin.

"What's all this?" asked Amanda, though she wore a mischievous grin.

"I guess you are in on this?" Eddie asked her.

Amanda just grinned and took her seat next to her mother.

"Of course, you were." Eddie sank into the seat next to his wife.

"It's time to celebrate!" said Izzy.

"Celebrate?"

The maître d' brought Roger Stein to the table, and he was all smiles. He glanced at Al and asked, "Have you told him yet?"

"No. We were waiting for you."

Roger chuckled. "My mother always said I'd be late for my own funeral."

Al snorted, then waved at Eddie. "Why don't you do the honors?"

Roger leaned back in his chair and widened his smile. "Today, I had an appointment down in Kanowa County. An appointment at the county courthouse, Judge Robert R. Abernathy presiding."

"It was today?" Eddie mumbled.

Roger gave a slow nod. "It was today." He shook his head but kept his smile. "I knew your uncle was a piece of work, but there's nothing as telling as meeting the man in person to underscore what a louse he is."

"You can say that again," said Izzy, and both she and John leaned toward the table.

"As soon Judge Abernathy as took the bench, your uncle started in on him—claiming the judge had a bias, demanding that Abernathy recuse himself, accusing the judge of colluding with our firm, with Al...you name it. Judge Abernathy was less than impressed, but by looking at your uncle, you'd have thought he'd won arguments in front of the Supreme Court."

"The man is...delusional about his own intelligence," said John Morton. "I'm surprised, though, that he would say all that in Judge Abernathy's courtroom after Abernathy dressed him down and dismissed his lawsuit against me." John smiled like the Cheshire cat. "Said it was frivolous."

"Ah! I'd wondered what all that was about. When he responded to Mr. Ratherson, he used the word frivolous about thirteen times. Your uncle looked as though he'd have a stroke."

"If only," muttered Eddie. Under the table, Amanda put her hand on his leg and gave it a comforting squeeze.

"Abernathy asked me to present my case, which I did. It took all of five minutes and a copy of the trust agreement. Abernathy asked your uncle's lawyer if they had any defense, and right off the bat, Ratherson spews one vile conspiracy theory after another. Everything from Abernathy being drinking buddies with the chief here, to Al playing golf with Abernathy every weekend." Roger spread his hands on the tablecloth in front of him and lost his smile. "It would be funny if I didn't think the man believed every bit of it."

"Yes, Gil Ratherson has a…*unique* view of things," said John.

"Well, the outburst cost him."

"Contempt?" asked Al.

"You bet. If he would've left it alone, Ratherson would've gotten off paying a fifty-dollar fine…"

"But he couldn't leave it alone," said Eddie, in a cold, flat tone. Amanda squeezed his thigh again and grinned at him.

"Of course he couldn't," said Izzy. "The man has no sense."

"He isn't the sharpest tack in the bunch," said Roger. "He actually said to the judge, 'I don't care if you charge me five times that much, it wouldn't show the amount of contempt I have for you.' Of course, Judge Abernathy raised the fine to two hundred and fifty dollars without batting an eye."

"Naturally," said Al.

"Would you believe me if I said Ratherson didn't leave it at that?"

John Morton chuckled. "I'd find it harder to credit if you said he did."

Roger nodded. "I guess you know the man better than I do."

"How much?" asked Eddie.

"Another citation. Another two hundred and fifty dollars." Roger shook his head. "Ratherson's attorney seemed dumbfounded. I don't believe he understood what he was getting himself into."

"John McCarthy?" asked John.

"Yes."

John nodded and crossed his arms over his chest. "He knew. He's known Ratherson for years. Represented him God knows how many times in frivolous lawsuits in the years since he got out of prison. Suits against his neighbors, the owner of the feed and tack, you name it."

"Ah. Well, the judge asked McCarthy if the Rathersons had any plan for a *legal* defense. He even stressed the word legal. McCarthy seemed a little flummoxed for a moment but then admitted that their defense had no basis in the law."

"No defense at all?" asked Al.

"They claimed several things that went beyond the conspiracy theory nonsense Ratherson started with. They claimed that they'd spent all the money on expenses, but they couldn't produce a single receipt to back anything up. They claimed that I shouldn't be representing Eddie because of our relations, and—"

"Related?"

"Yes. I explained that I worked for your father-in-law, but your father-in-law recused himself in this case, and that was the end of it."

Eddie shook his head.

"Next, they tried to claim that the trust agreement wasn't legal. Abernathy interrupted him in the middle of his spiel with a single word, 'frivolous.' I thought your uncle would explode right there, but your aunt kept him under control." Roger took a sip of water and then winked at Eddie. "Five minutes later, it was all over. Abernathy had already read the trust agreement, and since the Rathersons couldn't even drum up a defense in any way related to case law, he rolled in our favor."

"So, it's finished?" asked Amanda as she took Eddie's hand.

"I'm sure there will be more shenanigans coming," said Roger with a slight frown. "But we now have a legal judgment that orders a surcharge in the amount of one hundred and seventy-three thousand dollars. The Rathersons have thirty days to pay in full, or Abernathy has instructed the Kanowa County Sheriff's Department to seize their property and hold an auction."

"I didn't…" Eddie shook his head. "I don't want them to lose their farm."

"Don't you worry about that, Eddie, "said Izzy.

"That's right," said Betsy Hawthorne. "The things Amanda told us they did… Anyway, that money belongs to you and always has. If they spent it…" She shrugged.

Eddie hung his head and stared at his hands, which were trying to strangle each other in his lap.

"Don't, son," said John softly.

An uncomfortable silence settled around them for a moment, and Eddie turned his head away. Across the room, a woman sat with her back to him. Her hair cascaded down her back in a crimson wave. It was the color Amanda's had been the day he'd met her, and *that* memory brought a smile to his face.

But the woman's posture drew his attention. She sat in a funny way, an unnatural way—almost as though she weren't human. The longer he looked at her, the more uneasy he grew.

"Eddie," said Amanda. "This resolution a good thing, and I won't let you feel guilty. I *strictly* forbid it." She grabbed one of his wrestling hands and held it still. "Do you hear me?"

Eddie's gaze stuck to the back of the red-haired woman's head. She hadn't moved, not to shift position, not to smooth the hair out of her face—he wasn't even sure if she had breathed.

"Eddie, look at me," said Al.

He continued to stare at the woman until Amanda squeezed his hand. Then with a little shake of his head, he turned toward Al.

"It's natural, what you're feeling. Even more so in a case where both litigants are family. But, and I want you to listen close now, that man doesn't deserve a second of your pity. Trust me, I'm a lawyer, and I know these things."

Betsy Hawthorne rolled her eyes, and Izzy laughed. Just like that, the tension broke, and Eddie smiled.

8

1991

The grimy shop window let in a modicum of weak fall afternoon light. The blubs lighting the shop's interior flickered as if in the middle of a brownout, but the light in that shop never rose above dim. The shop owner had rigged the lights to emit soft, watery light so that customers could not see any scratches, dings, or dents on his merchandise.

"Mr. Mitchell! It's been a while since I've seen you. Where have you been?" asked the shop owner.

"Well, my wife…you know how it is." Eddie lifted an empty hand and let it drop.

The shop's owner treated him to a knowing smile, nodding in sympathy. "Short leash?"

"You better believe it," Eddie said with a chuckle. "I'm just a browser today. Not a buyer."

"Looking is always free. And besides, you've been such a good customer over the years, who could begrudge you a day of window-shopping?"

They were all the same, the junk shop owners. They always made it seem as though they were doing Eddie a big favor to even let him in the store, even though he'd *poured* money into their hands.

Eddie smirked, his eyes straying past the shelves to the little living room scene set up in the back corner of the shop. Staged as a display for antiques, he eyed the grungy stuff with disdain.

But then his gaze drifted to the Tiffany lamp on the end table. It was a new addition to the shop, and yet it seemed familiar. He didn't remember ever having seen a lamp similar to it, but there was something about the aquamarine lampshade with dragonflies bordering the bottom...

He shivered and turned away.

"Catch a chill?" asked the shopkeeper.

Eddie shook his head and rubbed his hands up and down his arms. "No, just déjà vu, I guess. That Tiffany lamp seemed so familiar."

The shopkeeper cocked an eyebrow at him. "Déjà vu? Well, the lamp is new to the shop, but you have been here about sixty-eight million times. Doesn't everything here seem familiar by now?" He chuckled.

Eddie tilted his head to the side and grinned, but he didn't join in on the laughing. His gaze had crawled back to the lamp like a beaten dog to its master.

It had an ornate brass base, and above that, stained glass in the colors turquoise, aquamarine, and greens made up the body. He shook his head. *Why should that seem so familiar? Where have I seen a lamp matching that one before?*

And why am I scared all of a sudden?

"I know you said you're only looking today, but I can make you a deal on that lamp. Today only, mind, but I could let you have that for…let's say three-fifty."

"Just looking." The answer came to Eddie's lips without effort, as though someone had programmed the words into his tongue. "That's such a nice shade. Whoever made that was a real artist." His gaze stroked the lampshade with relish, like a lover's caress. The dragonflies' wings made up the bottom edge of the shade. With bright-red bodies and white wings, the dragonflies seemed to call to him, to demand he remember them. Eddie shook his head. "It seems so familiar."

The shopkeeper fastened an empty gaze on the lamp. "All Tiffanys seem familiar to me. My mother had several as I was growing up."

That's it! My mother's lamp! The one Daddy brought home before they started to fight all the time. Before Daddy— Eddie cut that thought off in midstream. "Yeah, my mom had one, too. Except my mom's was…" Eddie scratched his head. "I think my mother's wasn't as cheery as that. Dark colors—midnight blue and purple—predominated."

The shopkeeper wagged his head as if he couldn't care less. "Take a look at it. It's a beauty, and as I said, I'm willing to deal today." He turned and walked back to the small rolltop desk that served as the shop's counter. He stepped behind it, and when Eddie glanced his way, he pasted a smile on his face to cover a look of avarice. The shopkeeper waved toward the small living room setup. "Make yourself comfortable. Take your time."

Eddie repressed a sneer. Guys like the owner always pretended to be friendly but seemed to look down on him.

You'd think with as much money as I spend in shops such as this, they'd treat me like royalty.

He strolled through the shop, taking his time, walking up and down each aisle, examining anything that caught his eye. It was a game he liked to play, prolonging the anticipation, putting off looking at the thing he really wanted until he could hardly stand not to.

The shop's inventory put the "junk" in "junk shop," one step above dumpster-diving, but a tiny step. A layer of grime coated almost everything. The shop owner's clothes were not in great shape, and to Eddie's practiced eye, he looked like a slovenly man—which his merchandise reflected.

Hell, I've got better stuff than most of this junk. Eddie had a lot of things—too much stuff if you asked Amanda—but he never settled for cast-off trash. He never bought something just to buy it. It had to be a real treasure to make the cut.

He made his way to the back corner and eyed the dirty couch with suspicion. He wanted to sit down, to take his time and admire the lamp, but sitting on that disgusting couch seemed like an invitation to get fleas or worse.

The lamp had brass pulls, one on each side, to control the bulb. Eddie reached out and pulled one of the chains. The lamp made a clicking noise but didn't light. Eddie peeked over his shoulder, sure he'd see the shop owner hovering, but to his surprise, the shop owner wasn't even looking at him.

"Hey, does this lamp work?"

The shopkeeper pointed behind the couch. "It's not plugged in." He stepped out from behind the rolltop desk and took two strides toward Eddie, and then the light flickered on. "Oh. Maybe I plugged it in, after all. Maybe the bulb needs replacing." He turned and went back to his work.

Eddie turned his gaze back to the lamp and sucked in a breath. It was *beautiful*, throwing soft aquamarine light on the wall behind it. The dragonflies; red bodies and white wings stood out from the rest of the shade, but in a pleasurable way that drew the eye.

He caught himself smiling. *Looking, not buying*, he reminded himself. *She would kill me.* The money from the judgment had gone to pay off the house, and while he was in graduate school, Amanda had taken a low-paying job near campus. *We can't afford this.*

His eyes danced across the lampshade, and he felt like a little kid again. He reached out to touch the shade but jerked it back before his fingertips brushed the edge. *I shouldn't touch it.* It was a silly thought, but it roared through him with the force of one of God's commandments, and he jerked his hand away.

He extended his hand, and this time he allowed his fingertips to brush the bottom edge of the shade, delighting in the tactile difference between the smooth glass and the lead edging, between the heat of the lightbulb behind the glass and the coolness of the lead.

Someone came up to stand next to him, but he didn't look, thinking it was just the shop owner. "Just looking today, as I said."

"That's a shame. That lamp should go to someone who would appreciate it."

Eddie startled at the contralto voice and twisted to gape at the woman standing next to him. She was the spitting image of his mother—not as his mother *would* look if his father had not murdered her, but as she had looked when

Eddie was a child, even down to the cut of her dress and feathered hairstyle.

She looked at him and grinned. "Close your mouth, you're drawing flies."

Eddie snapped his mouth shut and shook his head. "Sorry. Sorry. It's just that…"

"I remind you of someone."

It wasn't a question, but Eddie found himself nodding in answer, regardless.

The woman cocked her head, her eyes roving over his features. "Someone special."

Eddie swallowed hard, his heart beating fast. "Yeah. Yes. My mother."

The woman laughed. "That's not exactly what a woman hopes to hear a man say."

Eddie blushed and lifted his shoulders and let them fall. "She's… My mother passed when I was a child. But…and I mean no offense, but your dress, your hair…that's how she looked back then."

The woman tipped back her head and laughed even louder. "Me, too," she said with a mischievous twinkle in her eye.

"I'm Eddie." He held out his hand.

The woman put her small, dry hand in his. "Call me Kathleen." She shrugged. "Kathy."

It felt as if someone had punched Eddie hard in the stomach. He had no air, but choked out, "You're kidding?"

The woman's smile faded, and she shook her head. "That is my name. Are you sick? Here, sit on the couch, tiger."

Eddie's eyes darted to the couch, and he shook his head. "I'll be okay in a minute." He took a deep breath. "Kathy was my mom's name."

"Getting your arguments ready?" asked the shopkeeper.

Eddie started and tore his eyes away from the woman next to him. The shopkeeper stood a few steps behind and to his left, a sly grin stretching across his face. Eddie looked at Kathy, but she only grinned. "What?"

"For your wife. Are you getting your arguments ready?"

"Arguments?"

The shopkeeper chuckled. "Any man who comes into my shop and stands around talking to himself while he stares at an item is buying that item. I've learned that much after eighteen years in the business."

Eddie lifted his eyebrows at Kathleen and then turned to the shopkeeper. He jerked his thumb in the woman's direction. "I'm not talking to myself."

The shopkeeper's smile faltered. "Well…are you talking to me?" He glanced over his shoulder at his workstation across the shop. "Because if you were…"

"No, no, no. I was—" Eddie tilted his head at Kathy, and she held a finger up across her lips. Her eyes twinkled with mischief, and she shook her head. He snapped his mouth shut.

"Um." Memories of the therapy he'd endured the last time he told people about a woman only he could see came flooding back.

He turned back to the shopkeeper, fighting his confusion. The shopkeeper's shoulders tensed, and his face was hard, worried. Eddie put on his best smile and tilted his head to the side. "You caught me."

Nonplussed, the shopkeeper took half a step back. "Caught you what?"

Eddie forced a chuckle. "Oh, it's as you said. I was having a pretend conversation with my wife." He twitched his shoulders. "But I felt foolish."

The shopkeeper didn't seem convinced, but he seemed less fearful. "Oh. Yeah."

"I bet you see it all the time."

"See what?" asked the shopkeeper.

Eddie forced another chuckle. "People. People in here talking to themselves, either trying to talk themselves out of buying something or trying to justify their purchases to someone else." Eddie shook his head. "And then when you catch them at it… Well, I didn't want to admit I was talking to myself."

The shopkeeper nodded once, but his gaze darted away as though looking for an exit. "Is there anything you want to ask about the lamp? Anything I can help you with?"

Eddie shook his head. "No, as I said before, my mom had one of these."

"Okay. Well, once you've decided, come on over, and we can discuss the price."

Eddie shoved his hands in his pockets, and the shopkeeper walked away, sparing a quick glance over his shoulder. He turned back to Kathy, confusion written across his face in large letters.

Kathy patted his arm. "It's been hard for you. You miss her."

"My mother? Of course, I do." He'd been about to ask her something… Something she'd said a moment ago had startled him, but talking to the shopkeeper had driven it right out of his mind.

"Remember that time when you ran away? You were, what, eleven, twelve? You ran away to the house your parents had owned?" Kathy asked the three questions in a rush.

Eddie shook his head and took a step away from her. *How could she know that?*

Kathy just smiled and took a step forward, again closing the distance between them. "Don't you remember, tiger? The lamp—your mother's lamp—was in the basement." Kathy waved her hand toward the lamp in the display. "Your mother didn't own a lamp *like* this one, Eddie. Your mother owned *this* lamp. This very lamp."

Eddie's mind flashed back to when he was twelve. He'd been in the kitchen and had heard something creaking on the basement steps behind the closed door. John had been there, too, and when the police chief had descended into the basement… "Oh my God," Eddie murmured, his gaze flitting to her antiquated hairstyle, her years-out-of-fashion dress, and her cork-soled wedge sandals.

Kathy flashed her mischievous smile and winked.

Eddie took another step away from her. "That was…"

"Yes, that was me." She took another step forward, again maintaining the intimate distance between them. "Something scared you, and I came to protect you—as I always did."

"That really happened?" he grated. He didn't remember anyone coming to protect him but John. There had been a scary presence, something that had grabbed his tongue with ice-cold fingers, but *John* had scared whatever it was away. "I thought that was… I thought that was just my imagination. The overactive imagination of a twelve-year-old boy."

"No," Kathy said. "It all happened, and as you remembered it. You don't remember me because I didn't show myself to you. It scared you enough already."

"Oh."

"I fought that foul thing off you, though." She waved her hand at the lamp, her smile seeming a little forced. "You need to buy this lamp, Eddie."

"Are you..." He couldn't say it. Not out loud.

She turned to face him, smiling. "You know who I am, tiger."

"No, that's not possible. *Ghosts* aren't..."

Kathy laughed again. "Ghosts, spirits. Why do we have to invent such names? I'm not a ghost, not a spirit. I am just a woman in a different state of being than yours."

"But...Daddy killed you." Eddie's expression was grim, and his face paled to the color of old bone. "I mean, my dad killed my mom when I was ten."

"I know, Eddie." Her gaze drifted to his, and she laid a feather-light hand on his forearm. "I was there. I'm so sorry I had to leave you."

"Are you... It... How can you be here? How can—"

"Shh, now, Eddie. None of those questions matter. What matters is that I am tied to this lamp. If you want me in your life, you need to buy this lamp. If you do, and if you take it home and put it in a prominent place, I will be there with you until the end."

Eddie gulped, and his gaze drifted to the brightly colored lamp. "Yes."

"It's important. You mustn't allow this lamp to get away again. *Honor* it. You mustn't put it in the basement to gather dust."

Resolve firmed inside him. "No, of course not." His thoughts turned to Amanda, and her prohibition of new purchases, but he brushed them aside. She would understand. She would understand this time. "I'll be back." As he turned to walk away, Eddie thought he glimpsed a hungry expression on Kathy's face—his mother's face—but when he turned back to her, she wore a sweet, smiling expression.

He crossed the store with a determined stride. The shopkeeper looked up at him as he approached, and after scanning his face, the shopkeeper's expression transformed into one of greed. "I've decided," Eddie said.

"Excellent. I can tell by how you walked over here that you want the lamp. As I said before, if you buy it today, I can let you have it for three-fifty."

Eddie chuckled and shoved his hands in his pockets, half turning away. "You and I both know it's not worth three hundred and fifty dollars. I might've been born at night, but it wasn't *last* night."

The shopkeeper sneered. "I've always hated that expression. Make a counteroffer but make it *reasonable*."

Eddie looked over his shoulder, expecting to see the woman—his mother—smiling back at him, but she was standing in front of the lamp, looking the other direction. "Well," he said, turning back to the shopkeeper, "It's nice, but I don't have to have it. I could go one-fifty, cash."

The shopkeeper scoffed. "Can't do that, I've got more into it. Three hundred."

"No. How about two hundred? One fifty in cash and I'll write you a check for the other fifty."

The shopkeeper stroked his chin, staring into Eddie's face. "If I have to take a check, let's split the difference. I'll sell it to you today for two-fifty and take a check for one hundred dollars."

Eddie looked back at the lamp. *Amanda is going to kill me*, he thought. *And if there's anything left after she's done, she's going to kill me again.* He reached for the check he kept in his wallet for emergencies, pulling it out and unfolding it before he pulled out a hundred, two twenties, and the ten with the other. "Deal," he said.

He turned to smile at Kathy, but the woman had disappeared.

9

1991

Eddie brought the lamp home from the little junk store in a greasy cardboard box and plugged it in right away. He smiled as he pulled the little brass pull on the right side. His smile stretched as the lampshade lit from within.

He stood there for God knows how long, just staring at it. *Amanda will love this,* he thought. *She won't mind that I broke the rule for this...this beauty. I'll tell her about my Mom, about Dad bringing the lamp home way back when. She'll understand why I had to buy this.* A frown threatened his face the way dark clouds threaten a sunny day. *But do I tell her about Kathy? Do I tell her about my mother's ghost?*

When his feet started to hurt, he crept backward and sank into the chair he knew was there without looking. The pile of newspapers he kept next to the chair crinkled and avalanched to the floor as the chair rocked taking his weight, but he didn't hear the noise. His gaze centered on his new lamp as if glued to it. His new *treasure*.

Amanda will be home soon. The thought of his wife coming home from work made his stomach feel a little sour. *She might appreciate the lamp, but she won't appreciate the fact that I took a shopping trip today—no matter how many fairy tales I tell myself. She will hate it that I spent two hundred and fifty dollars on a lamp that was worth only half that.* Eddie sighed, but he didn't take his eyes off the lamp. He didn't get up and straighten the stack of newspapers, even though Amanda hated having the papers spread all over creation. He just sat there, staring at the lamp.

"Are you there?" he asked the empty room. "Kathy?" She didn't appear, and no one answered him. "Mommy?"

He tilted his head to the side and gazed at the colors shining on the wall behind the lamp. Aquamarine, turquoise, and green spots seemed to dance across the wall and ceiling. *So beautiful,* he thought.

At the limits of his hearing, he imagined he heard a melody on the wind. It was eerie, almost mournful. Drawn out dissonance and clashing, jangling chords washed over him, but unlike the haunting, driving music he heard when he fought, this melody relaxed him instead of setting his nerves on edge. *Am I asleep? Dreaming all this?* The tune grew a little louder, and his pulse quickened. Though no one sang along, he could almost hear lyrics in the spectral lament. But the words... They sounded Middle Eastern— Arabic, maybe. *Those jangling chords are the aquamarine,* he thought and then shook his head at the nonsense. *Pull yourself together, Eds.*

But he *was* together. As silly as the thoughts were, he couldn't find fault with them. If music had color, the jangling chords *did* sound as though they would be aquamarine. *And the reedy, wailing part...that would be turquoise.* The song grew louder yet, and Eddie stopped thinking, stopped analyzing what he heard. His eyes drifted closed, but something about the song stirred his desire to watch those spots of color dancing and swaying across the wall, and he snapped his eyes open wide. The colors seemed to move in time with the rhythm of the song. *They are* part *of it!* he thought. Then the melody overrode his thoughts, and he became a receptacle for the song, the colors, the dancing spots on the wall.

When Amanda came home, Eddie still sat staring at the wall. She came in through the garage door, which wasn't a surprise since no one could enter through the front door anymore—too many treasures. She put a bag of groceries down on the kitchen table, the only surface in the kitchen that was still clear of junk. "Honey?" she called. "Eddie?"

Eddie didn't answer—he heard her speak but didn't understand the words. Her words weren't colors, they weren't wailing melody. He sat, head cocked to the side, a smile stretched across his face, though drool ran from the corners of his mouth. He stared and stared at the beautiful lamp and the colors that danced on the wall.

Amanda bustled into the dining room and the smile on her face faded. Her buoyant expression soured and fell. Eddie viewed it all through the corner of his eye, but his smile didn't fade, and he didn't acknowledge her presence.

She took a visual tour of the room, her face settling further into the angry grimace that she'd worn more often than not in the past year. "Did you go shopping?" Her sigh gusted into the air like so many others—thousands of sighs, it seemed—that had come before this one. Her eyes blazed with repressed anger, frustration. And again, her eyes swept the room. "What is it? What did you buy this time?" Her eyes came to rest on the lamp. "A lamp? A Tiffany lamp? Where did you find that? How much did it cost? Why did you buy a lamp?"

"Honey, relax. It wasn't—" he croaked, mouth so dry that the inside of his cheeks stuck to his teeth. *How long have I been sitting here?*

"Don't you 'honey' me! We *agreed*, Eddie! Do you even remember? The agreement, I mean? Do you even remember the conversation?"

"Amanda, I remember." He held up his hands, palms out. "I *do*. But you're blowing this out of proportion."

"Out of proportion?" She scoffed, her expression darkening. "Look around you, Eddie! Have you seen the house lately? *Really* seen it? When was the last time you connected with reality?"

"I'm sorry, honey, but it's not that big of a deal. It's just one lamp. And it's *special*—"

"Just one lamp," she sneered. "And how much did this '*one lamp*' cost?"

Eddie turned away. His eyes roved around the room, across the junk-strewn carpet, at the pile of junk beneath the window that had reached the sill, but his gaze crawled back to the lamp and landed there.

"Eddie! *Earth to Eddie*! Are you listening to me?"

Eddie tried to suppress the sigh before it passed his lips, but he failed.

"Oh, I get it. I'm being 'unreasonable' again. Silly old Amanda, gone off around the bend, yet again. *Blowing it out of proportion!*" She threw up her hands, and they settled at her temples, where they began massaging in circles. "Eddie…"

"Two hundred dollars. It cost two hundred dollars, Amanda." The little lie slipped from his lips without conscious thought, without planning, without intent. "I had a hundred cash, and I wrote a check for the other hundred."

Amanda's hands fell toward her waist as if she'd forgotten she had them. Her face was a mask of incredulity. Her mouth opened in a tiny O-shape, and tears welled in her eyes. "*Two hundred dollars*, Eddie? And you wrote a check for *a hundred*?"

"Yeah, babe." Eddie hitched his shoulders up toward his ears and let them fall. "This lamp is *special*."

"You get that the check will bounce, right? If it doesn't, it will make our insurance payment bounce. Don't you even *think* about our budget anymore?"

"When I came across it in the store, but... But this one is special, worth breaking the budget for. It's my mother's lamp, Amanda. The lamp my Dad bought when I was a kid. The *exact* lamp. Can you imagine?" His voice had taken on a dreamy quality, and his gaze had tracked back to the colors on the wall. "And that song... Can you hear it?"

The tears overflowed her eyes and ran down her cheeks, cutting swaths through her makeup. "Eddie..." her hands fluttered up to hover out from her sides, palms up, fingers curled. "Eddie."

"I know, Amanda. I promised, and today I broke that promise. But I didn't break the promise for junk, not the way I did before. I mean, *look at the lamp.* Can't you see how special it is? Can't you see that it would be special even if it wasn't my mother's lamp? Can't you hear the melody?"

"Eddie." His name gusted out of her like a sigh. Her hands fell to her sides, enervated, lifeless. "Eddie."

"Stop saying that, Amanda. Stop saying my name as if I'm some kind of murderer. I'm sorry. I... I just thought... I hadn't planned to buy anything. I... I... I just stopped in to look. There's no harm in looking, right? I went to that store up on Ridge. You remember the one, the one that's just junk. I didn't consider that there might be something there I'd want. I didn't... I...didn't think I'd find anything that I had to have... But this—"

"Oh, Eddie," she said, and her shoulders hunched forward as though she bore the weight of the world. "Do you have any idea how many times you've said something like that to me in the past two years? How do you know your mother owned this exact lamp? You were, what, six when your dad brought home that lamp?"

"Yeah, I know, Amanda. It *seems* unlikely, but it's *true*. I *know* it's true because—"

Her sigh sliced into his heart like a butcher's knife. "Eddie..."

"Amanda, I'm sorry, okay? But it represents the last part of my childhood that was happy."

Another sigh gusted past Amanda's lips. "Eddie, are you hearing yourself? You always told me that the day your dad brought home the lamp was the day your family—your *life*—started its long slide into the toilet. That bogeywoman you imagined, all the fighting, your aunt and uncle..."

Eddie waved her words away, grimacing. "I don't remember saying that, but it doesn't seem true. Not anymore."

Amanda shook her head, her hands twiddling with her skirt as if she didn't know what to do with them, while Eddie's hands tried to kill each other in his lap.

"I'm sorry, Amanda, I am, but can't you understand how much this link to my past means? The last time I saw it was when I ran away to my parents' house, after Gil made me burn my first collection. Don't you get how much this lamp means to me?"

She stood there staring at him as if she had never seen him before. "The lamp, Eddie?" Her voice had gone as cold as a February night.

"Yeah, honey. The Tiffany lamp I bought, remember?"

"Yes, Eddie. I remember the *fucking* Tiffany lamp!" As enervated and lifeless as she had seemed a moment before, now she seemed full of life, full of energy—full of rage. "Yes, Eddie. I remember all the things like this *goddamn* Tiffany lamp!"

"Honey—"

"Oh, shut up, Eddie!" Once more her eyes traversed the room, lingering on the piles of treasures Eddie had accumulated over the short span of their marriage. Her eyes scrabbled across the floor stacked with old newspapers, old magazines, cardboard boxes full of knickknacks, boxes full of loose electrical components. "Eddie, we *agreed.*"

"But this lamp—"

"Oh, shut up, Eddie!" Her eyes snapped back to his face, and there they seemed to take an inventory of his features. "It'll never be different, will it, Eddie? This…this *junk* is worth more to you than anything in the world, isn't it, Eddie? This junk means more to you than *I* do! Doesn't it? Eddie?"

"No, Amanda! You are the most important thing in the world to me. How can you even think all this stuff is more important? Anyway, we picked a lot of this stuff *together* on our weekend treasure hunts."

Her gaze sharpened on his face, and a small, crooked smile blossomed on her lips. "Then you don't mind?"

"Mind? Mind what?"

"You don't mind if we clean up? Right? Since I am more important to you than the stuff…"

Eddie's eyes tracked across the piles of things in the room. His *treasures.* He hadn't meant to turn away, it just happened. When his gaze returned to Amanda's, she was no longer looking at him. She'd turned halfway back toward the kitchen.

"Two hundred dollars," she muttered. "Pick me, Eddie. Why can't you pick me over this *stuff*?"

"Amanda, I—"

She turned the rest of the way toward the kitchen and stepped through the doorway. As she did so, her shoulders hitched in a sob.

"Honey! I'm sorry!" called Eddie, but his eyes had already returned to the Tiffany lamp, to the melodic colors dancing on the wall. In the kitchen, Amanda made a noise that reminded Eddie of a rabbit clutched in the paws of the cat. "I'm sorry, Amanda! I won't do it again. You mean more to me than *anything*!" His eyes traced the shape of the lampshade, lingering on the bright nuggets of shimmering electric blue glass that defined the fishes swimming in a field of midnight-blue and dark-purple chunks. He marveled that such dark blue and purple pieces of glass could make such beautiful shades of blue and purple with the lamp turned on.

In the kitchen, Amanda began unpacking the bag of groceries she brought home. *Next, she will start dinner. Maybe she'll want to do chili, and we can cook together, though it will be filled with uncomfortable silences. She will go to bed early—she always does when she's put out with me—but tomorrow, things will start to get back to normal.* That had always been the pattern of these kinds of fights before, and Eddie didn't see how this latest fight would differ.

His eyes caressed the colors, joining in their majestic waltz on the surface of the wall. It was almost as if someone had snatched pieces of the night sky and put them in his lampshade. His *treasure*. Eddie grinned as the colors moved on the wall—as though the lamp shade itself were moving.

He almost missed it.

He almost missed the sound of the door to the garage closing. "Amanda?" he called. He shot to his feet, but his eyes remained on the kaleidoscopic colors on the wall. *Wait a minute… Wasn't the lamp a different color when I bought it? Aquamarine and turquoise?* He shook his head. *Impossible. Stained glass can't change colors.* The last thought rang with déjà vu, but Eddie dismissed it.

The garage door rumbled up, and Amanda's little car started in the garage. Panic seeped through his mindless infatuation with the light on the wall. He turned and ran to the garage door, heart in his throat. *I should have gotten up, should have hugged her.*

Eddie dashed into the garage in time to glimpse Amanda's tear-streaked face as she backed out. He waved at her, but she just shook her head and continued down the driveway. "Amanda!" he shouted. "Forgive me! I'll make it up to you!" Panic throttled his heart. *I should have offered to clean up! That's what she wanted, right?*

At the end of the driveway, Amanda shook her head and dashed away her tears with the heel of her hand. She turned her head toward the street and drove away.

Eddie stood in the garage, not quite believing it. Not quite believing what had just happened but pushing his emotions into that pit of despair he curated within. *I'll just clean up. She'll be back, and when she comes back, she'll understand how sorry I am. She'll see that she means more to me than my collections.* Even as he thought it, he recalled the haunting, yet beautiful melody that the lampshade made as its colors danced on the walls. But then the memory of Amanda's tear-streaked face replayed. *I can be better than this.*

Even so, it seemed his life was spiraling out of control. Again.

I've got to get it together. He turned and trudged back inside and got to work on the dishes piled in the sink.

By the time Amanda came back home, the kitchen was spotless, and there was a bouquet of wildflowers in a vase on the table. Eddie stood in the door to the dining room, eyes down. "I'm so sorry, Amanda," he said. "Please forgive me. We can clean it all up. I'll do the work; you just tell me which collections you want me to pack away. To... To get...rid of."

"Oh, Eddie. You schmoopy dork," she murmured. The phrase caught in her throat. "Perhaps I overreacted, as you said."

"No, you didn't. I'm an ass, and I'm sorry."

Her gaze darted over his shoulder. "Is it..." She heaved a sigh and walked over to hug him. "Is it the same lamp?"

He thought about how he'd imagined the lampshade had been aquamarine and turquoise with dragonflies around the bottom edge when he bought it, and how it had "changed" to dark colors and bright-blue fish that seemed to swim around the shade. "Yes, it is. I..." He didn't want to tell her about seeing his mother's ghost in the store. How she'd told him he had to buy the lamp and keep it so she could be near him. *That's... That just sounds* crazy.

"What? You what, Eddie?"

"Oh, nothing. I remember the shade is all."

"How did they get the fish to seem so alive? And is the shade black? The background, I mean."

"No, it's midnight blue and dark purple. It's easier to tell when it's turned on."

She pulled back and looked up into his face. "Eddie, you scared me earlier. You asked me if I could hear the song the lamp was playing."

"I..." Eddie shook his head as if to shake out the cobwebs. "I think I'd fallen asleep before you came home. Maybe I had a dream about the lamp, that it was a different color—that the lampshade had changed. In the...dream, there was this song going, like a Middle Eastern sort of thing that reminded me of the desert. It..." He chuckled. "I've always dreamed the weirdest shit."

"That's because you are a weirdo," she said. She glanced over her shoulder at the flowers. "Whose yard did you pillage to make my bouquet?"

Eddie flashed her a sheepish smile. "Do you like them? I made them myself out of moonbeams and cinnamon toast."

She turned her face back to him. "You are so weird, Eddie."

"Good thing," he said. "Because you *love* weird."

Just like that, everything was okay again.

10

1992

Eddie lay in bed, enjoying the crisp air and the sound of birds outside the bedroom window. He hadn't checked the time, but the quality of light peeking around the blinds pointed at a little before six. Predawn light washed the bedroom with gray light. Like most times when the silence was oppressive, Eddie imagined he heard a mournful dirge on the wind.

Amanda lay next to him, snuggled under the blankets with only her face showing, and he smiled. Things had gone well since the day he brought home the lamp. He had tried very hard to make things easy, to make the most of what they had. The only thing that bothered him—besides the restricted budget for buying treasures—was that she didn't seem very enthusiastic about antiquing anymore.

Eddie had kept things together, kept most of the rooms in the house clean—cluttered, but clean. He'd even curtailed his buying—a little anyway—but it didn't seem to matter. It was as if he had crossed an invisible line, and Amanda couldn't get past it. She was *different*, less...open to silliness.

He still asked her to go with him every weekend, but it was a rare Saturday when she got in the car with him. And even when she rode along, she held herself stiff, not as willing to play around as they had before the lamp incident.

That was still how he thought of it: "the lamp incident." If he were honest, he'd have to admit that he was still a little irritated at how far out of proportion Amanda had blown things, how long she'd carried the grudge. Then again, he figured that was what marriage was about: letting go of the little irritations in favor of the good times.

He lay there wondering if Amanda would go with him that morning, letting his gaze drift around the room lazily. His attention meandered from the things scattered on the top of the dresser, to the old photograph in an antique frame hanging on the wall between the closet and the bathroom doors, then to the chair they sometimes sat in to put on their shoes to the old cherry wardrobe. The corner between the wardrobe and the dresser was particularly dark that morning. The shadows were dense, almost solid.

The tenth time his eyes flitted past the corner, his heart lurched in his chest. *Is there someone standing there? Watching me?* He strained his eyes, trying to penetrate the thick gloom. *There's something there*, he thought. *But is it a person? Or just something Amanda moved into the corner to get it out of the way. A stepladder? A coat rack?* The volume of the song on the wind increased.

Stop being an idiot, Eds. Get back into that lazy Saturday morning state of mind. He had such good memories of Saturday mornings—at least during the early part of his life. And in fairness, since he'd known Amanda, Saturday mornings had been delightful in their marriage. She was just that kind of woman, everything they did together was fun.

Or it had been before the lamp incident. The mental voice that uttered the sentence in his mind didn't sound like his own.

He shoved that idea aside, replaying the memory of their first antiquing trip, how they'd both been so excited they'd gotten up early, and then had to sit in Denny's *forever* waiting for the antique mall to open. That had been the first time she'd called him a schmoopy dork. *Her schmoopy dork.*

With a silly grin on his face, he set his gaze adrift. He put his arms behind his head and sighed with contentment. He loved Saturday morning.

When he caught the movement in the corner of his eye, Eddie almost leaped out of his skin. He came up on his elbows and stared at the murky soup of shadows in the corner. *Something moved,* he thought. *I didn't imagine that.*

Don't be frightened, tiger. The words seemed to ride the wind to his ears, lilting with the same rhythm as the creepy little ditty. Eddie recognized that voice. *Kathy. The woman who told him to buy the lamp. Or the ghost, whatever.* He darted a quick glance at Amanda, but she hadn't stirred. He'd last seen the woman almost a year before—she had made no other appearances since he'd purchased the lamp.

"Kathy?" he whispered. "Muh-Mother?"

"Who're you talking to?" asked Amanda, sounding a lot like a drunk Chinese woman.

Kathy stepped forward, but she no longer had the appearance of a woman ripped straight out of the eighties. She wore a dark dress—black or dark blue, he couldn't tell in the early morning light. Her hair was dark, as well, and seemed to blend into the shadows. Her eyes locked on his face, and she held a finger to her lips and shook her head.

"Go back to sleep, honey."

"Mmmph." Amanda snuggled deeper into the blankets and sighed.

Eddie folded back the bed clothes and swung his feet onto the cold wooden floor, his gaze riveted to the woman standing in the corner of his bedroom. He beckoned her to follow him, but she made no move to do so. *Is she even real?* He shook his head and pulled on a T-shirt and a pair of wool socks. The apparition in the corner hadn't moved. She just stood there, staring at him—he wasn't even sure if she had blinked. Armored against the early morning chill, Eddie pointed at the door to the hall and beckoned again. Again, she made no move to follow him, and with a shrug, Eddie turned and left the bedroom.

He pulled the door closed behind him, making as little noise as possible. *Maybe Erickson was right... Maybe all these female apparitions are just hallucinations. Bogeywomen.* He shook his head. It just didn't seem plausible that he would hallucinate such intricate images, hear what the hallucination said, the funny little song—all of it—and not have any other symptoms. It didn't fit with what he understood about mental illness.

He padded into the kitchen, glancing out the window over the sink. The backyard had a spectral quality, cast in grays and blacks by the predawn light. He turned to the cabinet and got out thick ceramic coffee mugs and set them on the counter. He looked out the window again, as he turned toward the coffee machine.

The black-clad woman stood under the old maple tree in the corner of the yard. It had just suffered the explosive greening of early spring, and it cast deep shadows across her features.

Eddie paused a moment, staring out the window, and then he shook his head and turned back to the coffee machine. He added a coffee filter and coffee, then grabbed the coffee pot and turned toward the sink to fill it with water.

He'd already grown tired of the game the woman—or hallucination or whatever—was playing, and he didn't want to contribute, but he peered out the window, nonetheless. She still stood under the boughs of the tree but had moved forward out of the deep shadows. She grinned and tossed a little wave at Eddie as if they were lifelong friends.

Eddie shook his head and looked down to watch the water tumble into the coffee pot. *Let her appear inside this coffee pot if she wants me to look at her.*

Oh, come on, tiger. Her voice seemed to whisper with the susurrations of the wind across the eaves of the house. The creepy song grew louder, more insistent.

Eddie sighed and poured water into the coffee machine, then replaced the pot. He flicked the switch to brew the coffee. *Next, breakfast.* He turned and took a step toward the refrigerator.

The window over the sink rattled, and Eddie looked up and started. The woman stood right outside the window with her nose pressed against the glass and a goofy smile stretching across her lips. The rattling sound came from her fingernails drumming against the upper pane of glass.

He dropped his gaze. *I don't want to see you anymore. Perhaps I should go see Erickson again…*

"No need to resort to savagery, tiger. Anyway, you spend enough time in that idiot's office." She spoke aloud that time, her voice muffled by the glass.

"Who *are* you?" He kept his gaze down, but half-turned toward the window. "Why don't you leave me alone?"

"You already know who I am, and I can't leave you alone—you own the lamp."

"What are you? A *jinn*? Trapped in a lamp?"

She laughed, and the sound of it made Eddie shiver.

"Tell me the truth. Are you the woman that used to scare me when I was a kid?"

"You know who I am. You've always known who I am."

Eddie shook his head and glanced at the kitchen window, but she'd disappeared. He heard her voice as plain as day, and if he heard her even when she wasn't close… *A hallucination, then.* Again, her nails-on-a-chalkboard laugh ground against his eardrums, but this time he suppressed a shudder.

"I'm no hallucination, Eddie Mitchell. I never have been."

Her voice sounded close as if she was speaking into his ear. He could almost feel her breath in his ear. "No? Then what are you?"

"As I said back in the junk store, Eddie: I'm just a woman in a different state of being from you. I'm no ghost. I'm no *jinn*. Just a woman."

Eddie scoffed and shook his head. "Somehow, you don't fit the definition of 'woman.'"

"No?" This time, she seemed to speak into his other ear.

"No. Women can't appear wherever they want, turn invisible, or appear to me and not to anybody else."

"Then what am I, Eddie?" She sounded amused, but a hint of iron rang beneath it.

"If I knew that…" He opened the refrigerator door and took out the eggs and bacon. *I'd know how to get rid of you.*

"Now, that's not very nice." Her voice took on a pouting quality. "Besides, you don't want to get rid of me. You bought the lamp just to make sure I'd stay close."

"So, all I have to do to get rid of you then, is to get rid of the lamp?"

She didn't answer, not with words, but as he took an egg out of the carton to crack it into the frying pan, the egg shot away, exploding all over the front of the cabinet next to the stove.

"Great. Just great. Not only do I have to put up with an invisible woman, but one who enjoys playing adolescent pranks."

"And why not? You're a young putz."

Eddie held his tongue. He grabbed a fistful of paper towels and cleaned up the mess. "Can I go on with fixing breakfast? Or should I wait down here to clean up the rest of the eggs?"

There was no answer for the space of five breaths, but Eddie remained where he was. After a moment, an egg rose out of the carton and floated toward the frying pan. It cracked itself on the edge and dropped the shell's contents into the pan. Then the empty shell floated toward the garbage can, the lid came up, and the shell sank inside.

"Let's change the subject, shall we?" she said.

Eddie stood and threw away the wad of paper towels he'd cleaned up the raw egg with. "You might as well become visible."

A knock came from the door that led to the garage, and Eddie opened it. She stood outside as if she had to go through the doors to enter the house. She wore a black leather dress, and her luxurious, sable hair hung to her shoulders. Her olive skin almost glowed under the kitchen light. Strangely, she was barefoot.

"May I come in?"

"So a vampire instead of a *jinn*? You've never needed my permission to come in before."

She laughed, setting Eddie's nerves on edge. "I'm nothing so mundane as a vampire, Eddie. It's just polite to ask, once we've become friends." She tilted her head to the side. "My mother taught me that."

"So did mine." He stepped back from the door and motioned her inside. She lifted her perfect, bare foot to step up into the house from the garage, and for the first time, he noticed her toenails glistened like chrome. His eyes tracked up to her hands, and her fingernails were the same, and they drew to sharp, vicious points. "How in the world do you scratch an itch with those nails?"

She laughed once more, and it was harsh, grating—the sound of a garbage disposal chewing up a fork. She turned and closed the garage door.

"Do you even need to use a door?"

She shrugged with one shoulder. "No. I can go where I please."

"As I thought." He went back to fixing breakfast, stirring the scrambled eggs and turning the bacon. "Do you eat?"

"Of course. All living things consume things that sustain them, don't they?"

"Then you're a living thing?"

She drew her lips into a pout. "You've got a nasty streak, this morning."

A sigh gusted out of him. "I'm frustrated."

"Don't worry, Amanda will come around. She enjoys antiquing just as much as you do. And she calls my lamp 'pretty' in her mind. But she's into playing the bitch right now. You'd do well to put her in her place."

Eddie shook his head and turned toward her, crossing his arms over his chest. "Amanda isn't the person who's frustrating me. I screwed that up, and I will fix it in time. And don't you dare call her a bitch."

"Using my great powers of deduction and using the process of elimination, I guess you find me frustrating."

"You could say that."

"And what is it about me that frustrates you?"

A chuckle burst from Eddie. "It would be easier for me to tell you what doesn't irritate me. You could also start by telling me your name. I figured out you're not…my mother. You're not 'Kathy,' either. I don't understand how I know that, but I do. You just used that—you used my mother's image, and you used her name."

She held up her hands next to her cheek and treated him to a golf clap. "Well, I'm glad you figured all that out. I don't care for the styles of the eighties."

Eddie scoffed and turned back to the eggs. "So, we've established that you eat… Does that mean you want eggs?"

She shook her head. "No. You wouldn't enjoy what I eat." Her voice rode the thin edge between sarcastic and downright nasty.

Eddie peeked at her over his shoulder, arching one eyebrow. "Vegan, huh?" That earned him one of her God-awful laughs, and he grimaced.

She sobered. "Do you want to understand who I am? Truly?"

"Yeah, I always find that that's a good place to start. Although our place to start was a long time ago, right?"

One of her eyebrows twitched.

"More than a year."

"Abby. You can call me Abby."

"Huh. Somehow I didn't figure you for an Abigail."

"That's good." She grated out a laugh that sounded anything but amused. "In my case, Abby is not a diminutive for Abigail."

Eddie stole a glance over his shoulder, and her expression sent a chill down his spine. "No offense."

Abby sniffed and turned her head to gaze out the window. "Dawn approaches."

Eddie laid the bacon on paper towels to absorb the grease and took the eggs off the fire. "Are you sure you won't have an egg?"

"I've said, haven't I?" Her teasing tone of voice had departed, and her voice had grown frosty instead. "Besides, your woman will arise soon."

"And you know this, how?"

"It is enough for you that I know. She shouldn't meet me. Do not tell her of me. Not yet." She looked at the door that led to the cellar stairs. "Perhaps we should meet in the basement from now on.

Eddie shuddered, recalling the amount of time his father stood down in the darkness of their basement in Cottonwood Vale. Alone, but carrying on a conversation. He took a deep breath, turned off the burners, and put his back to the stove. "I've been racking my brain, and I can't come up with another name."

Her gaze drifted back toward him. "Another name?"

"Another name that shortens to Abby."

"You haven't heard of it."

"Okay. So…Abby, then?"

"Yes." She sniffed again and looked toward the hall that led to the back of the house. After a moment, the sound of Amanda getting out of bed reached Eddie.

"Will she be able to see you?"

Abby's expression darkened, and the corners of her mouth pulled down. "Do you prefer that she does?" Her eyes narrowed, and Eddie wanted to be anywhere else but in their focus.

"I... I'm not sure. Would it—"

"No. I have decided. She will not see me. It is too soon."

"Why...why is it that no one else can see you?" Fear settled in Eddie's guts.

Abby turned her face toward Eddie. Her expression was cold, hard. "Why, indeed?"

"Are you... Doctor Erikson would say that you are a hallucination."

"Would he? And this Erikson knows everything about the world?"

"When I was a kid, I used to see...um, a woman who you remind me of. Her face... She freaked me out."

"Did she?" As if from stone, the planes of her face hardened and froze, she didn't blink, she didn't smile.

"Y-yes."

"And why was that?"

"I... I was just a kid, but there was something... I don't remember."

"It couldn't have been all that bad then, could it?"

Eddie shook his head.

"Remember the cellar," said Abby. "And don't tell her about me. Tell her, and I'll kill her."

"I—"

"Eddie? Who are you talking to, hon?" called Amanda from the bedroom.

"Just talking to myself, Amanda." Eddie glanced toward the hallway and then turned back to Abby.

She'd disappeared.

"Yeah, crazy people do that, Eddie."

He forced a laugh past the constriction in his throat. "Yeah."

"Hey, we haven't done it for a while, but how about we go antiquing today?" Amanda came into the room, a big smile on her face.

"That would be great. I was hoping you'd want to come along earlier."

Amanda's gaze settled on the skillet full of scrambled eggs and the bacon in the paper towel. "Well, stop hoping and start feeding me."

Eddie chuckled, though he didn't feel like it. His gaze traveled around the room, but there was no sign of Abby.

II

1993

Eddie stood as still as a statue while the doctor delivered the news. He couldn't speak, hell, he didn't even feel capable of blinking. An angry swarm of raw emotion swirled and thrashed within him like a category five hurricane. He tried to push it all away, to build his walls, to bury it all in the hole within him, but this time… This news was too much, too big to contain.

He didn't know what to do. Amanda would be fine, but the baby…

And if he understood the doctor, there would *never* be another baby.

Eddie stood frozen, stuck. He knew he should go out into the waiting room and tell the Hawthornes and the Mortons the bad and the good news, but it seemed he'd lost the ability to move his own limbs while the doctor spoke.

"Mr. Mitchell? Are you all right?" The little doctor looked at him with apprehension, as though worried Eddie might fall on him. He wore green hospital scrubs and still had the funny little hat that surgeons wore to cover their hair.

Eddie stared at him without blinking, but he managed a slow nod.

"Is there someone... Would you please sit down? Can I get you something? A soda? Water?"

Eddie shook his head.

"You don't look well, sir. I understand this is a shock, but I don't want you passing out. Here... Sit over here."

Eddie followed the doctor with his eyes, and after a moment, he lurched into motion and sank into one of the chairs next to the little man. It seemed like the hardest thing he'd ever done. "How..."

"I'm sorry to say that there was a problem with the delivery." The little man cleared his throat. "As you already know." The short doctor raised his hands out to his sides. "We performed an emergency cesarean, but I'm afraid the baby was stillborn and your wife hemorrhaged. These things sometimes happen, which is no comfort, I understand. There are things that we just don't understand well enough to prevent one hundred percent of the time. This is one of those things."

"And Amanda..."

"She's recovering from the cesarean and the concurrent hysterectomy I performed to stop the bleeding. I will take you in to see her in a moment, but first, I need your permission to do an autopsy of the baby."

Eddie shot out of his chair and swayed on his feet, fighting dizziness. "Why?" Without waiting for an answer, he lurched toward the hall. "I have to get to Amanda."

The doctor stood and moved to intercept him. "I understand, Mr. Mitchell. But in cases such as this, it is important that we determine the cause of stillbirth. The only way we have of doing that is to examine the body of the child for causal factors. The results can help to determine the likelihood of future problems with pregnancy."

Eddie's gaze swiveled down to the doctor's face. "Hysterectomy. You performed a hysterectomy."

The doctor blushed. "Forgive me. I misspoke. Yes, the cesarean hysterectomy was necessary to save Mrs. Mitchell's life. Perhaps we should include Doctor Hawthorne in this discussion?"

The last thing Eddie wanted was to discuss this with Betsy Hawthorne. Not now, maybe not ever. "You have my permission to do the autopsy. I have to get in there now." Eddie moved to step around the doctor.

"One moment, please, sir. There is a form to sign—"

Eddie stepped around the doctor. "Bring it to me, and I'll sign it." He walked out into the hall and turned in the direction from which the doctor had come.

He halted and stared at the other end of the hall. Two women stood with their backs to him. One had Kool-Aid red hair, and the other...the other had thick blue-black hair with locks that writhed and twisted around one another.

Abby! Eddie stopped breathing, stopped moving, and just stared.

"Mr. Mitchell, please." The doctor took him by the elbow and pulled him in the other direction. "Your wife's room is this way."

One of the women reached for the doorknob at her side and opened the door. The one with the red hair said something, and both women laughed. Without turning, both women went into the room, and the door closed behind them.

The sound of their laughter stayed with Eddie, echoing in his mind as though he were a vast cavern. Empty and dark.

A sudden fury tickled the backs of his eyes.

"Mr. Mitchell?" asked the doctor.

"Thanks." Eddie said, tearing his gaze away from the closed door. He turned and allowed the little man to lead him, putting his brain in neutral. "Can you...can you please tell the Hawthornes and the Mortons? You'll find them sitting together in the lobby. The nurses wouldn't let them stay in the waiting room with me. I don't understand why. But it's—"

"Yes, hospital policy. Sorry about that. I don't notify the extended family in cases such as this. I will have them brought to Amanda's room."

"But you won't tell them?" Eddie looked down at the little doctor, feeling his face distend and morph as his expression darkened.

The doctor sighed and dropped his gaze away from Eddie's. "I will speak with Doctor Hawthorne. In private. She may tell the others."

Eddie shrugged and stepped out of the hall into Amanda's room. Her head lolled toward him at the sound of his footsteps. Her gaze swam toward his face but then veered away before meeting his gaze.

"Oh, Amanda..."

Amanda burst into tears at the sound of his voice.

Eddie lurched to the side of the bed and wrapped his arms around his wife as best he could with him standing and her lying in bed. She seemed so frail, so small. "Oh, Amanda..."

"I'm so sorry, Eddie," she sobbed.

In the corner on the other side of her bed, black smoke seeped in through an electrical socket, dripping down the wall like a viscous liquid.

The whirlwind of emotions pulsed and throbbed. The lump in his throat had reached epic proportions, and it hurt to swallow or speak past it. Eddie shook his head. "Not your fault, Amanda."

"I'm so sorry!"

The smoke accumulated with increasing speed, multiple streams pouring out of all the room's empty sockets.

"Shh, honey. It's not your fault, there's nothing for me to forgive." Eddie stroked her hair the way she liked and tried to keep his eyes on her face instead of watching the smoke invade the room.

There was a noise behind him, and Eddie glanced over his shoulder. His parents and his in-laws stood behind him in the door to the room. Izzy's cheeks were wet, and her eyes were red, but her complexion had turned as gray as a headstone. John and Al both looked gutted. Betsy had her professional face on, and hers and Eddie's were the only dry cheeks in the room.

Eddie dropped his gaze, not wanting to see the pain in the eyes of Izzy and John. He turned back to Amanda, fighting to ignore the woman forming from the pillar of smoke in the corner.

Amanda sobbed, holding his hand to her cheek. "I'm so sorry, Eddie."

"None of that, love. The doctor said there was nothing anyone could have done." Eddie's eyes strayed to the corner. *She* stood there, gloating at him...Abby.

In the distance, he thought he heard the clashing, discordant voice of a buzuq, the sweeping tones of a qunan seeming at war with the buzuq, and the sweeping reedy, breathy wailing from a nay taking the countermelody. He thought he smelled the spicy aroma of the desert. *No. That's just a reaction to stress as Doctor Erikson always said. Abby isn't real.* Can't *be real.*

Can't I? asked a voice in his head.

John stepped up behind him and lay a thick hand on his shoulder. Izzy joined her husband and then sank down next to Eddie. She took one of Amanda's hands and kissed it, eliciting fresh sobs.

Almost as if he had no control over his eyes, his gaze crept to the side of the bed and then beyond. It skimmed across the ivory linoleum floor and swept in toward the corner. The volume of the eerie song that only Eddie heard increased, as if the musicians were approaching from a distance. His gaze skittered to a stop when he came across a perfect bare big toe. The skin on the toe was the golden color of desert dust in the wind. The chrome toenail was perfect—shapely and trimmed. He followed the toe to an ideal bare foot. A sea of black leather with a slit up the side all the way to her hip hid perfect legs.

Eddie took a deep breath that hitched in his throat. He didn't want to see her face, but he didn't seem to be able to look away. He held his breath as his gaze climbed her torso.

The skin of her neck seemed to glisten as if moist. His gaze continued its inexorable rise, drifting over her chin, and, when he reached her lips, he squeezed his eyes shut, not wanting to see her mouth, her teeth…her black, werewolf fangs. He didn't want to see the scary lady's face on Abby.

After a moment, he opened his eyes and found her midnight-blue gaze resting on his own. Her hair twisted and threshed around the edges of her face, moving like serpents. "Hello, tiger," she said.

Eddie gasped, and John squeezed his shoulder, mistaking his fear for grief. Abby's hair stopped moving for a moment as if watching the scene.

"It'll be okay, son," said John in a gruff voice. "It'll be okay."

Eddie couldn't take his eyes off Abby, who, for her part, stood in silence as she had during his childhood, a small smile on her face. She nodded as though he'd asked her something, and then, still smiling, pulled her lips apart. Behind them, onyx black fangs glistened. Eddie bit his lower lip to keep from screaming.

12

1996

Eddie awoke sullen and angry. It wasn't unusual. It was the status quo in the months and years since… But he didn't even want to *think* about that. A dark depression had settled around him, and for the first time in his life, the hole in his middle had failed him.

His emotions no longer fit into that hole, no matter how hard he pushed. Something in there...*resisted*. He didn't know how to be a human, how to be kind, how to deal with his anger, his bitterness. Without the hole, vileness poured out of him without warning.

Amanda didn't deserve what he had become. *If I had any guts, I would end this. I would let her off the hook and put myself out of this misery.* But even as he thought it, something inside rebelled. *Fear. I am a coward.*

He pulled himself out of bed and peered at the clock with watery, stinging eyes. He'd slept past noon. *Again.* His mood descended further into the depths of his despair. "Amanda?" he called.

Silence reigned in their little house.

He believed it was Saturday, but to be honest, he didn't pay much attention to the days of the week anymore. *Maybe it's still the middle of the week. Thursday?* He stumbled toward the kitchen, scratching through his scraggly beard. He wore his boxers and a sweat-stained T-shirt. *What's the point of getting dressed?*

In the kitchen, he found a note from Amanda. "Going to Mom and Dad's," she wrote. "You'll sleep half the day, anyway. I'll be home for dinner."

He crumpled the note in his fist and threw it in the corner. "What? No 'I love you?'" He considered having a bowl of cereal, but as usual, he had no appetite. Food no longer brought him pleasure. He scoffed, sneering at the note. *Nothing brings me comfort anymore.*

After standing for a moment, staring at nothing, Eddie turned on his heel and walked back into the living room. He saw the lamp and felt calmer. He turned it on and smiled at the colored spots that danced on the wall. "What? No song today?" He backed up and sat in the recliner behind him without so much as a glance. "Abby?" Only the sound of silence answered him. "No one loves me today." He picked up the remote and ran his thumb across the buttons before dropping it to the arm of the chair. He sighed and had to fight to keep it from turning into a sob. "Well, Eddie, what are you going to do today?" he asked himself.

He stared at the dark blues and purples that dotted the wall above the lamp, then he brought his gaze down to the bright-blue fish swimming on its shade. If only he could find another treasure similar to the lamp. *That's it! That's what I should do...a little antiquing.* He considered calling the Hawthornes and seeing if Amanda wanted to go, but they'd had a doozy of a fight. *Another* fight.

We never used to fight. Not before... Anyway. He turned to the lamp. *Well, except for one time when I bought the lamp.*

You're too good for her, said a voice that sounded as empty as the desert wind.

No, Abby. You're wrong about that. He stood, but instead of going into the bedroom to get dressed, he stared at the spots of color on the wall and listened to the twisted little song that only he seemed to be able to hear. When he couldn't hear the song, he sometimes thought it was creepy. But when he heard it again, he didn't understand why he thought so. "Might as well think the colors dancing on the wall are creepy. Come to think of it, why do the spots of color seem to move on the wall? The shade's fixed, and it's not as though the lightbulb can move around in there...inside the shade." He scratched his ear. "The wall isn't moving, so how can the spots of color move?" he muttered into the silence.

He came back to himself with a start, with no sense of time having passed. But his feet hurt, and his knees had stiffened. "What are you doing, Eds?" A smile slipped across his lips. "Talking to myself, I guess."

He crossed the room and turned off the lamp without looking at the colors on the wall. The song continued, but it seemed...quieter, less *present*. He wrinkled his nose and left the room.

He peered at the alarm clock on the nightstand. *Lost a couple of hours standing there in the living room staring at the wall like a moron.* With a half worried, half disgusted self-mocking grin, Eddie got dressed without showering and headed out to go shopping.

He had a bit of fun that afternoon, and he found several new treasures to add to his collections. He didn't even remember that Amanda had said she would be home by dinner time. Not until dusk turned to dark as he was driving from one store to another.

He considered going to the store anyway, but something inside him rebelled at that idea. Amanda wasn't his enemy, as much as Abby's voice in his head screamed the opposite, and she didn't deserve his contempt. He turned the car around at the next traffic light and headed home.

Amanda's car was in the garage when he got home. He got out of the car, feeling like an asshole and headed inside. She was sitting at the kitchen table, along with the remains of her dinner and his empty plate.

"Sorry, Amanda. I just lost track of time, and it didn't even dawn on me that it was dinner time until I realized it was dark."

"And I suppose you were antiquing?" Her tone was mild, but her eyes never left his empty plate.

"Yeah, when I woke up, I just didn't want to sit around here watching television."

She inclined her head, toying with her fork. "And I suppose it didn't cross your mind to come over to Mom and Dad's?"

Eddie winced as he shrugged. "Ah, Amanda... My head's bothering me today. My company would've brought everyone down.

"But not bothering you enough to keep you from going shopping." Her gaze drifted from her dinner plate up his torso but stopped shy of his chin.

"Come on, Amanda. It makes me feel better."

A wry grin spread across her lips. "Don't I make it better anymore, Eddie? Don't I make you happy anymore?"

"It's not that way, honey. You're the best thing that's ever happened to me. I've been having a hard time lately, is all. You know, with the headaches and always worrying about Gil..."

"Gil," she scoffed. "Dad asked about you today."

Eddie almost sighed with relief at the change of subject. "How is he doing?"

Amanda waved it away with her fork. "His question was...more specific."

"Oh?" There was a strange tickle in Eddie's belly. It was almost the way he felt around Jack McGregor before...

"Yes. He wondered if he should intervene."

Eddie's cheeks burned with hot blood. He half-turned away from her, staring at the kitchen sink. "Intervene?" His voice sounded enervated and weak, even to him.

"Yes." Amanda's tone matched his own. "He wonders if it's time to... To get you help."

An unreasonable, irrational anger surfaced in Eddie's mind. *Why can't people just leave me alone?* He knew it was an unjust sentiment, but he couldn't quite dispel it out of hand.

Here it comes, Eddie. What I've been warning you about all these years. She'll say it's for your own good.

Eddie sneered at Abby's voice hissing in his head and chopped at the air with one hand.

"Eddie. Look at me."

For a moment, Eddie didn't move. The muscles across his shoulders and neck went rock hard. He turned but didn't face his wife. He glanced at her out of the corner of his eye.

"Eddie. *Look at me.*"

He turned his chin toward her and met her gaze. He thought anger would shine from her eyes, but instead of being hard and insistent, they were soft, confused. Worst yet, they filled with tears, and Eddie's heart ached to see it.

"Eddie," she said again, and this time it almost sounded like a sigh. "Is it? Is it time I let my father draw commitment papers for you?"

"*Commitment papers?*" He tried to keep his voice even, calm. He failed.

"Eddie. Don't be that way. If you are...*ill,* then it's for your own good." Though her voice was flat, unemotional, her face crumpled, and tears streaked her cheeks.

Did I not tell you?

Something dark and hateful had slithered out of the hole in his belly. He fought against his rage monster but lost. "Why does it always come back to this?" he demanded. The light in the room seemed harsher, brighter, and a hot, sweaty pallor wrapped him.

"Eddie. Please—"

"Stop saying my name that way! Stop saying it like I'm a psycho!" His face ached, and he had no doubt his expression had crumpled into a gruesome mask of hatred, but he had no control. Not anymore.

Amanda closed her mouth and raised her hands in a lifeless shrug. She shook her head, and it was…mournful, hurt.

"For the last time, Amanda, I'm not crazy!"

"Okay. Okay, Eddie." The calmness had left her voice, replaced by a glacial quality. "You don't need our help, do you, Eddie? *My* help?"

"No! Not that type of help." He snapped his head away from her, so he didn't have to see her cry.

"Fine. I'll make sure I tell my Dad not to worry about you. Because that's what it is. Worry. Mom and Dad care about you, Eddie. I—" Her voice broke, and she pushed her chair back from the table. "I *love* you, Eddie. It doesn't seem as if you know that anymore."

"Amanda…" But what could he say? How could he undo the way he'd mistreated her? She didn't deserve that. *I should end it.*

"What makes you happy?"

No, Eddie, said Abby. *You should end her!*

Eddie jumped and dropped his gaze to the floor. "What? What do you mean? I don't know. What makes *you* happy?"

Amanda sighed, sounding like a scythe cutting through wheat. "You, Eddie. You used to."

His ire stepped forward in his mind. "I *used* to? Oh, I see. You mean before. *Before!*"

"Oh, Eddie."

"That wasn't my fault! The doctor said so!" He looked at her askance, just in time to see her shake her head. "Don't you shake your head at me!"

That's it, Eddie. Show her who's boss.

She stopped her head moving and seemed to crumple within herself. "Whatever you say."

"Damn right. Things are going to change around here, Amanda. I'm tired having blame for every little thing that happens around here heaped on my shoulders! I'm tired of being accused of mental illness every other minute!"

Step closer to her, Eddie. It doesn't appear she's listening.

He stepped closer, looming over her.

Amanda nodded. "Yes. Yes, you're right, of course, Eddie. Things need to change."

"Oh, come off it! You're only saying that because I just said it. Tit for tat?"

Just like the bitch she is.

She shook her head, eyes averted. "No. No, you are right." She just stood there, slumped like a teenager, staring at the ground between them.

His heart softened a touch. "I don't mean to be so angry, Amanda. I can't... I used to... I had this pit..." He wound down, not knowing what to say and feeling helpless.

"Yes," she said.

"I'm... There is something wrong with me, Amanda. My father murdered my mother. My uncle abused me, and my aunt let him."

"Yes," she repeated.

"My life has been *hard*, Amanda."

She nodded instead of saying "yes" again. "Your childhood was hard, Eddie. You suffered terrible things at the hands of your family, and I'm so, so sorry that you did. But you're forgetting a few things."

Don't let her disrespect you in this way!

"Oh, am I? What am I forgetting?" Without meaning to, his tone had gone angry again. Angry and mean, just as Gil's had always been, and Eddie *hated* it. He just couldn't seem to control it anymore.

"I mean, you've forgotten John and Izzy Morton. You forgot all about Melanie Fox. You've forgotten *me*, Eddie. And my family. But most of all—"

Fear and anguish swooped down on him. "You're wrong." Eddie swiveled to face her. "I haven't forgotten you, Amanda. I—"

Oh, for fuck's sake, Eddie! Don't puss out again!

Amanda's arm snapped up as if she were a cop directing traffic. "No. You don't interrupt me, Eddie. Not in this. You need to listen to what I'm saying to you. You need to *hear* what I'm saying."

Hit *her, Eddie! Teach her to* "hear" *what you are saying!*

Eddie closed his mouth. *Here it comes.*

"What I was thinking about most when I said that you'd forgotten things is this: *you survived*. Your childhood was miserable, horrible, but you survived it, Eddie. More than that, you *thrived* despite it. Despite your goddamn uncle. Despite your father, and the bastard he must've been. You thrived, Eddie. You grew up with great people, and John and Izzy loved you as if you were their own flesh and blood. You stood up to your uncle, got out of Cottonwood Vale, and went on. College, graduate school, *marriage*. Why isn't all that enough?"

Don't listen to this drivel, Eddie! screamed Abby in his mind.

Eddie stood there, mouth open. "What..." He swallowed hard, wincing at the way his throat ached. It seemed as though there was a lump of ice in his stomach, but fire everywhere else. "What can I do?"

YOU FUCKING PUSSY!

"Oh, Eddie."

Oh, Eddie, sneered Abby. *I think I'll puke. You are such a disappointment.*

He'd never heard Amanda's voice like that, the sorrow, the pain, and it wrenched at him. He sank to his knees before her, head down, tears dripping on his jeans. "You…" He had to fight back a sob because if he let one out, he didn't believe he would ever stop. "I don't deserve you."

"Oh, Eddie." She sank to her knees and grabbed one of his hands. "You *do*, Eddie. You deserved John and Izzy. You deserved my mom and dad. You deserve me. You deserved a child—" Her voice broke, and she slumped forward.

He caught Amanda and wrapped his arms around her.

You do *deserve a child, Eddie, and she can never give you one. Do you understand me? NEVER!*

"You deserve to be with someone who can give you a child, Eddie. Not me. I'm…broken inside."

See? Even she agrees!

"You're not broken!" Eddie said. Inside him, the membrane that covered the pit of his unwanted emotions stretched and distended as if struggling to contain something that now wanted out instead of keeping him from shoving his feelings in. He looked at Amanda and knew that if he turned frosty and numb at that moment, she would walk, and he couldn't blame her for that.

You can't blame her? Eddie, Eddie, Eddie! Can't you see that she's the architect of your suffering?

SHUT UP, ABBY! My suffering started when you appeared. Eddie stood, pulling Amanda with him. "Let's get out of here for a while, Amanda. Let's not even pack a bag, let's just go."

She looked up into his face, eyes swimming in tears, and reached for his hand.

Turn your back on me at your peril, Edward James Mitchell.

Abby's voice seethed with hatred, with the promise of pain and worse, but Eddie ignored all that as he bundled Amanda into his car. He backed into the road, put it in drive, and drove like hell.

Let it be on your shoulders, then.

They spent the next week in a honeymoon suite overlooking Niagara Falls. On their return, Eddie and Amanda boxed up the lamp and put it in the basement.

When they sold the house two months later, they left the box in the basement.

Abby never said a word.

Chapter 4
2010

I

LaBouche groaned at the fire burning in his chest and rolled to his side. He hawked and spat clotted blood from deep in his throat, wincing at the pain the motion evoked. His face throbbed and burned, and he lifted a hand to explore the damage. "Hamburger," he mumbled. He tried to open his eyes, then let his fingers explore further. "Popped my eyes, did he?" he muttered.

"You'll heal," said Toby Burton. "We need to understand why, LaBouche."

"Why? Isn't it obvious? I'm changing sides."

"*The fuck you are!*" bellowed Scott.

LaBouche shook his head and winced at the pounding in his head that accompanied the movement. "Scotty, I—"

Three quick steps approached and something cold and hard pressed under his jaw. "Call me that again," Lewis hissed.

LaBouche sighed and let his shoulders slump. "I deserve that."

"I don't know what game you're playing—"

"Is that you, Chief Richards?"

"Chief no longer."

"Sure. Police chiefs in Oneka Falls tend to die." He snapped his mouth shut against the heartbreak that threatened to choke him. "I… Trooper Lewis, I understand, now, what I did to you. I understand it in a way I never could have before. Brigitta… See, I mated with Nicole Conrau, and she quickened. Got pregnant. Brigitta had someone kill her, and my offspring died with her. I understand what—"

The cold, hard metal pressed into his throat. "You should stop now," Scott said in a flat, horrible voice. "Stop or by God, Lee, I'll splatter your brains on the grass behind you."

LaBouche leaned forward, pressing the gun into his throat. "If only that would kill me, Scott, I'd beg you to do it."

The meadow fell silent, but Scott pulled the gun away. LaBouche's breath trickled out of him, and a dark depression wheezed into him.

"What do you want, LaBouche?" asked Toby.

"Same thing Scotty does." Lewis growled, and LaBouche lifted his hands in surrender. "Sorry, sorry."

"Quit fucking around. What do you want?"

"Vengeance," he said. "I'll help you beat the demons in Oneka Falls. I'll give you Brigitta gift wrapped and wearing a bow. Anything you want. All I want in return is help killing Brigitta and the one who took my Nicole from me."

"And who would that be?" asked Mike.

"Sally McBride."

"Sally?" That came from mousey Shannon Bertram, though by all reports, she'd outgrown her shyness.

"That's not her real name, of course. Can't be," said LaBouche. He gasped as a splitting, burning pain stabbed through his left eye socket. "Christ that stings."

"Poor baby," sneered Scott.

"What is *your* real name, LaBouche," asked a man he didn't recognize.

"I don't want to tell you that yet. But there's one more promise I need from you."

"Promise?"

"Why should we—"

"Enough!" roared LaBouche. "I *will* tell you my real name when the time comes. After we've dealt with Brigitta and McBride—probably a *jinn*, if the legends about Brigitta's mother are true—then I want you to kill me."

"Wait...*jinn*?" asked the unfamiliar voice.

"I'll kill you every single day for the rest of my life, LaBouche," growled Scott.

"That's it?" asked Toby. "After we 'help' send Brigitta and this McBride home, you want us to send you home?"

"No. I want you to *kill* me and to make me stay dead. I know it's possible, now. Nicole is...*gone*. They didn't send her home; they gave her true death." LaBouche shrugged against the pain in his breast and his eye socket. "And that's what I want: true death."

"If Sally McBride is a *jinn*, what is Brigitta's true nature?"

"Who are you? I don't recognize your voice."

"I'm Benny Cartwright."

"Of course you are."

"Are you going to tell me?"

LaBouche sighed. "I don't know for sure."

"Guess!" snapped Scott.

"Herlequin always said Brigitta was his daughter, and that they left her mother back home. But knowing that a *jinn* has lived in our ranks for so long...like a fucking fox in the hen house, there's no real telling. She has powers most among my kind don't." LaBouche scratched his cheek beneath his growing eye. "She turned me into a bird, you recall. She didn't give me *the appearance* of a bird, mind. She *made* me a bird."

"You keep saying *jinn* like it means something," said Cartwright.

LaBouche frowned. "You don't know much about us, do you?"

Scott growled deep in his throat.

"We are a hierarchical race," said LaBouche. "We base our hierarchy on power and sometimes birthright. For example, I'm considered an alpha among the demons in Oneka Falls. All that means is that I've enough strength to defeat most of the others."

"But *jinn*?"

"No. *Jinn* are..." LaBouche sighed. "Your kind remembers so little. I belong to a race called *mazzikim*—we live as you do. We require places to live, sustenance. The *jinn* live only to serve. They do not need sustenance in the same way *mazzikim* do. They often serve an *ifrit* or one of the higher castes—"

"I'm sure you'll fill us in when we have time," said Toby. "What do we do with these two kidnappers?"

"Leave them. They will awaken and believe Dan Delo attacked them. They will return to Brigitta and tattle like school children. It will sow discord."

"Fine. And you?"

"I will also return to Oneka Falls, but I do so as your agent, your provocateur."

Scott stepped forward, chest thrust out, fists clenched. "And if I *ever* suspect you've lied to us, you'd better run, Lee."

LaBouche cocked a lopsided smile on his face and grunted. "Scotty, Scotty, Scotty," he said with a sigh. "Don't you see? I *want* you to kill me. I *want* to die. What I don't want...what I *will not* abide, is to be sent home." He ran a hand across his forehead, scales rasping against scales. "You don't have to threaten me, Scott. I've seen the error of my ways. I never thought about you back then, about your family, I only thought about myself. My needs."

"No fucking shit, Captain Obvious!" snapped Scott. "I do not forgive you, Lee. I'll never trust you again. You showed me who you *really* are, and I'll *never* forget it."

LaBouche cocked his head to the side. "Only a moron would forgive and forget what I did, Scott. You are not stupid."

Scott sucked at his teeth and stomped away to stare into the woods.

"Come on," said Toby. "We need to get out of here before these two wake."

"Yes, go," said LaBouche, allowing his shoulders to slump. "But how do I contact you?"

"SEMPRe," said Toby.

LaBouche curled his lips. "No, that's out in the open, now. Harper sussed it out. That's how he found you."

A deep frown creased Greg's face as he stepped forward. "No. He never got close. My people were on him. The plan was to draw him out." He glanced at Mason's slumped form. "It worked. Maybe a little too well."

"Reckless," said LaBouche. "Still, how does that keep him from telling Brigitta all about SEMPRe?"

Greg's smile could have curdled milk fresh from the teat. "Easy. He only saw the top layer." He pulled a card out of his pocket and scribbled something on the back. "This is your access code for an app you can download from the link written below it." He held out the card. "*Don't* visit that link in Oneka Falls. *Don't* follow it from anywhere your demon pals associate you with. Nowhere they control. Buy a burner to run the app."

LaBouche took the card and read it. "You have *an app*? You've got to be kidding."

Greg's smile widened. "Not one bit."

LaBouche threw back his head and cackled into the night.

2

Eddie Mitchell grimaced at the sunlight streaming through the cheap blinds. He'd fallen asleep while reading again, and his Kindle had spent the night jabbing him in the armpit.

And he'd had the dream.

Again.

The dream. That merciless mind-fuck of a dream. Amanda didn't feature in it, but the nightmare always left him knowing two things: first, Amanda was dead, and second, Eddie had caused her death—maybe even killed her himself.

He clenched his teeth and flipped the Kindle away from his side. *It's relentless,* he thought. *Fourteen years of the same dream is... Well, I don't know what it is, other than fucking ridiculous.* He rolled on his side. Amanda had already gotten up, and her side of the bed felt cold beneath his fingers.

His mind played one of the creepy melodies he used to hear while watching the colored light dance on the walls above the damn Tiffany lamp. He often heard the songs after having the dream, but only *inside* his head. No melodies playing on the wind. He couldn't understand how he'd ever *enjoyed* the songs, the strange instruments, the crashing melodies. But he had to give them credit for being the ultimate earworm.

He stretched and groaned, flipping to his back to stare at the ceiling. *Why do I dream I killed her? I've never wanted that. I've never even said it in anger.* He clenched his teeth and swung his legs out of bed. *Maybe I should find a shrink.*

He pulled on a pair of jeans and went into the kitchen. Amanda sat at the table reading a magazine, a stack of mail forgotten at her elbow. "Hey schmoopy dork," she mumbled.

"Oh, no. Not another Cosmo quiz. I beg you, dearest, do not subject me to that."

"After you failed the last one in such a memorable manner? You'd be *lucky* if I let you do another one."

"Breakfast?"

"If you're cooking, I'm eating."

He grinned as he leaned down to kiss her cheek. "Your wish."

"My command," she said before turning to catch his kiss on the lips. "Now, get to work or no more sugar for you."

"Yes, mistress," he said with a mock bow. His eyes skipped across the envelopes spread next to her. "Stanton Growth Fund? Do we have shares in that?"

Amanda put down her magazine and frowned at the mail. "No. I'm not familiar with it."

"SGF is big news these days. They say the modern Howard Hughes is at the helm." He pointed, and Amanda worked it out of the pile. "Official-looking envelope. Open it while I get the bacon going."

"Yeah," she muttered, working her thumbnail along the seal. Paper rustled as she emptied the envelope. "I don't understand this."

"What?" he asked, dabbing butter into the frying pan.

"It's a check and a thank you note."

"A check? Has to be a scam."

Amanda whistled. "Looks legit. It's for three hundred and twenty-six thousand dollars."

"What?" Eddie slid the pan off the fire and crossed the room in three strides. He stood at her side and skimmed the letter. "This note is thanking us for 'accepting their offer to buy the house.'"

"I know."

"What offer?"

"I'm calling Daddy. Something is wrong here."

Eddie shook his head. "Let's hope he can fix it. I *love* this house."

Amanda nodded, already dialing her father's cell.

3

LaBouche sat in his office in the Oneka Falls Town Hall, shoulders slumped, staring out the floor to ceiling window at the maple tree. Dawn had come and gone, and the maple still glowed with its colors.

Nicole, he thought and winced at the burning ache that filled him. Demons didn't fall in love—at least not the way humans defined love—but sometimes they came to depend on one another during the mating process. The dependence often faded after the offspring emerged, but LaBouche felt Nicole's loss like an amputated limb. The lost potential of the child or children ate at him.

A soft knock drew his attention away from the tree. "Come," he called. Brigitta and Sally stepped into the office, each wearing mournful expressions. LaBouche closed his eyes on the image of them, fighting to control his temper.

"LaBouche," said Brigitta. "Nicole is gone. I'm so sorry."

Keeping his eyes closed, LaBouche leaned toward them, putting his elbows on the desk. "I know," he hissed.

"Of course." Without waiting for an invitation, Brigitta advanced into the room and took a seat across the wide desk from him. Sally stood outside the door, watching him from behind veiled eyes. "What can Sally and I do?"

You've done enough! LaBouche sighed and spread his hands. "What is there to do?"

Brigitta made her mouth into a grim line. "I fear nothing."

"She…" LaBouche sighed and steeled himself. "She is *dead*, Brigitta. She didn't go home."

"No, she didn't."

The calmness with which Brigitta spoke the phrase boiled his blood. "How *the fuck* is that possible? She's not gone home, and yet she's not coming back. Because of the pregnancy?"

Brigitta's gaze twitched to the right, and then LaBouche understood the truth. *Sally did this.* The idea burned in his mind as though accompanied by a splash of acid. His gaze left Brigitta and tracked to the piggish demon standing outside the door.

"The time for pretenses is over, Lamia," said Brigitta.

Lamia! LaBouche's muscles tensed as one, as if a full-body tonic convulsion struck along every nerve pathway, activating every muscle fiber at once. His mother had used the legend of Lamia to keep him in line.

Lamia stepped into the room and closed the door with a quiet thump. She faced him with serenity, meeting his gaze with a frank expression. After a slow blink, the image of Sally McBride wavered and faded.

LaBouche's gaze crawled from the tip of her long black-scaled tail, up her belly, across her perfect breasts, up her long neck, and locked on her chiseled features. "Well. You've fooled us all, haven't you?"

Lamia shrugged. Her hair caught the light from the window in greenish tints and highlights but still appeared black. Her eyes glowed a putrid green, and her skin seemed tinged with it. Her crimson lips, however, seemed to promise blood would soon flow. "My power allowed it. My birthright."

LaBouche found it necessary to rip his gaze away from her, staring down at the desktop. "*Jinn* birthright." He said the words as though grinding them to dust.

"It is so," said Lamia.

LaBouche snarled and clenched his fists.

"LaBouche," said Brigitta in her too-calm voice. "Look at me."

He didn't lift his gaze, didn't unclench his fists, didn't relax.

"LaBouche," Brigitta repeated. "Look at me."

He drew a calming breath into his lungs and lifted his head, careful not to let his eyes wander toward Lamia. He fought to keep his expression neutral—*safe*—but by the expression in Brigitta's eyes, he judged the effort a failure. "*She* did it."

Brigitta lifted her chin and narrowed her eyes. The room seemed becalmed, frozen in the moment, the only sound the harsh breath rasping from LaBouche's throat. Then, Brigitta completed her nod, and the spell broke. "It is true," she said. "But fate required it."

LaBouche turned his face to the side, keeping himself from lunging across the desk and gouging at Brigitta's eyes by sheer force of will. That and the knowledge that a jinn watched over her, which made Brigitta one of the *ifrit* at least.

LaBouche knew his own strength, his own power, his own intelligence, and how inconsequential an *ifrit* would find all of it. But still...*Sally McBride*? Without looking at her, LaBouche muttered, "How much of the Sally persona was an act?"

Brigitta sighed. "Come on, LaBouche. Don't be this way. Don't throw your life away." She huffed and crossed her legs. "And don't make me waste you by sending you home as I did Chaz."

4

Mason Harper grimaced at the sunlight streaming through the boughs of the trees above him. His head thumped with each beat of his heart. For a moment, he had no idea where he was or why he'd slept out in the open, but then it came rushing back...the kidnapping, the pursuit, diverted to another meeting place... The demon who'd attacked them. The purple, winged beast.

Dan Delo, you son of a bitch, he thought, his sneer deforming his face into foul lines. *Why?*

He sat up and looked around. His van sat in the overgrown meadow a few yards away, and with a groan, he pushed himself to his feet and sauntered toward it. Near the rutted track that led back to the road, he saw evidence of another car…and of murder, by the looks of it.

Spent shotgun shells littered the ground around a matted circle of tall grass and weeds. Blood that appeared quite black in the early morning light coated the vegetation.

Did the demon kill Greggy? he wondered. *But why would Delo attack me only to kill him? It's what I would have done after Brigitta gave the okay.* He closed his eyes. *Brigitta. That's why the purple asshole did this. He's betraying Brigitta. Switching sides.* Behind him, someone groaned, then cursed under his breath. "Wakey, wakey, Denny," Mason said.

"Fuck you."

Cratchkin sounded the worse for wear but didn't sound dead, so that was a plus. "Come on, Denny. We've got to get back."

"What the fuck happened?"

"Dan Delo happened. Looks like he murdered Greggy."

Denny stumbled to his feet and staggered over to stand by his side. "My head feels like a bag full of assholes."

"You have Dan Delo to thank for that."

"Never liked that prissy little bitch." Denny sucked in a breath and blew it out hard, wincing as he did so. "He cracked one of my ribs."

"We've got to get back to warn Brigitta."

"Warn her?"

"Think about it as I get us back to the blacktop. If you haven't figured it out by then, I'll walk you through it." Mason strode through the long grass and climbed into the van.

Denny stood staring down at the blood until the van's engine roared to life. Then, with a groan, he joined Mason in the truck.

5

"Daddy's people will look into this. He said not to cash the check."

"Wasn't planning on it," said Eddie with a grin. "Whatever this is, I'm sure it'll work out."

"Famous last words." Amanda walked over to the stove and leaned against his back, her arms snaked around his middle. "Smells good."

"You say that even when I burn the bacon."

"That's because food someone else cooks always smells great to me."

Eddie chuckled. "Burning food counts as cooking it?"

"It does when someone else is cooking. Duh."

Worry laced her otherwise jovial tone. "What else did your dad say?"

"Not to worry."

"And you are ignoring him because…"

"I don't know. I've just got this feeling of impending doom."

"That's because you are making me cook breakfast. Burned bacon, burned toast, and runny eggs."

Amanda laughed. "No, all that sounds perfect."

"Let's go for a drive after breakfast."

Amanda nodded against his shoulder blade. "Do you…"

"Do I what?"

"No, never mind."

"This isn't anything to worry about, honey. Honest."

Amanda wagged her head a little. "It's not that."

"Then what?"

"Do you ever revisit that night?"

Eddie pursed his lips and drew a deep breath.

"I mean, do you ever think about what almost happened?"

"As little as possible," he said. "You shouldn't, either. Yeah, it happened, but we survived it. We overcame all that."

"We did," she said. "But I had such evil thoughts." Her voice fell to just above a whisper as she spoke.

Abby. The name sprang into his mind like flames on dry kindling. "Evil thoughts? You?"

"It was as if I had an evil cheerleader in my head, goading me. Telling me to…"

"To hit me?"

Amanda gasped. "Slap you, yes. How did you know?"

"Food's done," he said, and Amanda stepped back. He held his tongue until he'd plated the food and set it on the table. "There's something I never told you about the lamp."

Tell her, and I'll kill her. The memory of her words flashed through his mind like the shock of immersion in ice water.

"About the lamp?"

Eddie pinched his lips together. He hadn't seen or heard from Abby in years, but her leash still held him. Plus, there was the dream. The dream that Amanda died, and it was always his fault.

"Tell me," Amanda said as she took his hand.

"There's a…" He rubbed the back of his neck with his free hand. "I'm not sure I should tell you. I'm not sure it's safe."

Amanda sat back and blinked at him. "Safe?"

Eddie nodded. "You know how I have that recurrent nightmare? The one where…"

"Where I'm gone. Yes."

"It's my fault in the dream. That you're…gone. I don't know why or how by the time I wake up, but I'm left with the fact it's my fault. Sometimes… Sometimes I—"

"Eddie, it's a dream. I don't believe dreams are prophetic. They are only random firings of neurons while you sleep."

Eddie bobbed his head. "Yeah, but…" He cleared his throat. "There was a threat."

"A threat? To me?"

"Yes." Eddie ducked his head. "Someone said that if I told you anything, you'd die."

"Who said that?"

"Don't ask me," he whispered. "Please."

Amanda cocked her head to the side, her expression a mask of concentration. "Your scary lady? The one from when you were a kid?"

Eddie thought he could see lines of concern wriggling around her eyes. "I can't say."

"You've seen her since you went to live with the Mortons? Since you escaped Gil and Margo?"

Eddie smoothed back his hair and picked up his fork. "We shouldn't talk about it."

"This concerns me, Eddie."

"I…" He forked a heap of eggs into his mouth. "I sometimes wonder if it was a mistake to get rid of that lamp," he said around the eggs.

"What does the lamp have to do with…*her*?"

Tell her, and I'll kill her. Eddie couldn't say whether someone spoke in his mind, or if it was only memory. "Eat your breakfast before it gets cold."

"Eddie, tell me."

He dropped his gaze to his plate. "I'm… I'm so scared, Amanda."

She leaned toward him. "There's nothing we can't handle together. Right?"

Eddie thought about midnight blue and dark purple. He reflected on eyes that could throw bright blue sparks as they whirled and twirled. The image of black werewolf fangs smothered his other thoughts.

Tell her, and she's dead, Eddie. I promise you that. The voice in his head burned as though a hot poker had pierced his skull.

He shoved himself away from the table, eyes wide. He tried to look everywhere at once, but his gaze kept returning to the cellar door. Eddie took a halting step in that direction, and behind the door, on the *cellar-side* of the door, a board creaked as though someone stood there on the stairs, shifting her weight from foot to foot. *Abby?*

"What are you doing, Eddie?" Amanda's tone swam with worry.

The memory of when he ran away—the presence that invaded his mouth, held his tongue, while John Morton got the furnace relit—burned through his mind like a runaway forest fire. He stepped to the door and put his ear to it. His gaze fell to the doorknob, the shining, fake-gold knob. He lay his hand on it, and it was so cold it burned his palm, but he didn't take his hand away.

"Think you can hold it, Eddie?" The whispered question came through the wood of the door. "Think you can keep me locked in the basement? Think you can get rid of me by leaving my lamp behind?" Standing on the dark steps, Abby laughed. "Think leaving the box down your old cellar unsupervised for months was a good idea? Are you sure you didn't bring the lamp with you after all? Maybe someone changed the label."

Eddie's guts froze solid and fear locked his mouth shut, locked his mind. Beneath his palm, the doorknob jiggled. *Amanda! I have to get Amanda out of here!*

Abby's laughter rang in his ears, loud, raucous—even through the wooden door.

"What the hell is that?" asked Amanda, coming to her feet in a rush. Her chair toppled over behind her.

Something thumped against the door, but not hard enough to shake it in its frame. Again, the stair tread creaked. He gripped the doorknob with both hands and squeezed hard against its rotation, ignoring the burning pain, the almost electric shock of the intense cold. For a moment, he didn't think he could hold it against Abby's strength, but then the pressure on the knob relented, and a faint pop sounded behind him.

"Hello, Amanda. My name is Abby."

Dread settled in Eddie's core, and though he knew where the path would lead him, he shoved his fear into the yawning pit in his middle. The icy numbness descended on him like a balm, like a salve for his ice-burned palms.

Ever so slowly, Eddie relaxed his grip on the doorknob. The fear that circled his mind like a raging tornado was that he held the door against nothing, that Abby was no longer on the other side of the door.

He turned his head and screamed at what he saw.

6

"We'll double security," said Greg.

Mike shook his head. "We can post ten times the security. If they send one demon, you're dead."

Greg made a moue and looked out at Lake Erie for a while. "Who's to say we are safe here?"

Toby shook his head. "Harper penetrated the outer layer of SEMPRe, but LaBouche didn't leave me with the impression that he knew it was anything but a website. Besides, we insulated this place from SEMPRe, too."

"But I *enjoy* running International Datawerkz." Greg sighed. "What am I supposed to do now?"

Scott clicked his tongue. "Welcome to my world, buddy," he muttered.

"I sent a memo you'll be working from home for medical reasons. After a few weeks, we'll put you on indefinite leave."

"That will cover the window dressing, but it doesn't answer my question."

"Come on, Greg," said Mike. "You know it's too risky, now. Plus, you've been dripping acid in my ear for months about how you want to be a coder, not an administrator."

Greg turned his face away.

"Plus, it gives us more time to hang out here," said Mike in a low, silky tone.

Greg sighed and took Mike's hand. "That part will be nice."

"No more late nights."

"At least not late nights apart."

Mike chuckled deep in his throat, then seemed to remember the others in the room and blushed.

7

Mason put the van in park and sagged back against the seat. "God, what a night."

Denny grunted, opened the door, and climbed out of the van. "Come on, Harper."

Mason nodded and got out. His gaze scanned the parking lot. LaBouche's blue BMW stood a few spots away, along with Sally McBride's beast of a car. It was too early for anyone else. "At least we don't have to interrupt LaBouche and Nicole."

"I thought you liked that part," sneered Denny.

"I'll look at her tits any chance I get. So will you, and you know it."

Denny grunted and pulled the glass door open. "Come on."

The town hall building rang with early morning silence, but the air already blew from the vents and blessed coolness embraced them as they crossed the lobby.

LaBouche's door was closed, but the murmur of voices came from within. Mason knocked.

"Come!"

Mason opened the door and froze for a split second, his gaze bouncing from LaBouche to Brigitta to something straight out of Greek mythology—a thing with the body of a woman on top of a black-scaled snake's tail. From their expressions, he and Denny were interrupting a serious conversation.

Harper plastered a grin on his face and held up his hands. "Sorry for interrupting, but I've got something you need to hear."

LaBouche squinted at him and sneered. "Well?"

"Dan Delo is a traitor," said Mason. "He diverted us from the meeting place, then we think he murdered Greg Canton."

"*Maybe*," said Denny. When Mason glared at him, he lifted his shoulders. "Why would a demon that big need a shotgun?"

"Shotgun?" asked Brigitta, turning an icy stare at the pair of them.

"Delo attacked both of us, and when we awoke this morning, there was a kill scene near the van. Blood everywhere, surrounded by shotgun shells."

LaBouche grimaced and turned his face away. "Where is Dan Delo?" he asked. "And why did you have Greg Canton to begin with?"

"I sent him to capture the hunter," said Brigitta in melancholy tones. "Why would Dan Delo do this?"

Mason twitched his shoulders. "Betrayal?"

"He *is* unstable," said LaBouche. "I've said so all along."

Brigitta turned her cold glare on him. "Then why haven't you sent him home?"

"Unstable doesn't mean un-useful." LaBouche tilted his head to the side. "Plus, while I knew he was unstable, I didn't know he was fucking insane."

Sally scoffed, and LaBouche glared at her.

"Something to add…*Sally*?"

McBride squinted at Mason. "This story seems…*contrived*." She turned to face Mason and Denny. "It seems like a story weak humans might make up to cover for their mistakes."

Mason smiled his best smile—one that would've sent a human woman running for a cop—and took another step into the room. "I'll take anyone interested back to the scene.

Perhaps my *inexperience* led me to a false conclusion that someone as *lofty* as Sally McBride might pierce."

Sally returned his smile, but *hers* gave *him* pause.

"Come now, children," said Brigitta. "I'm sure Sally didn't mean to offend your delicate sensitivities, Mason." Brigitta swiveled in her chair to glance at the other demon. "You didn't, did you, Sally?"

Sally pursed her lips and crossed her arms over her ample bosom. "No, of course not."

Mason glared at her. "Are you sure? I can show you, up close and in person."

Sally turned her head away, but Mason thought she might have been grinning.

Grinning.

"Stop wasting time measuring your dicks," snapped LaBouche. "We need to deal with Delo."

"Indeed," muttered McBride. She turned to Brigitta. "Your command, Mistress?"

Brigitta lifted the index and middle fingers of her left hand and flicked them toward the door. Then she stood, looking as though she bore the weight of the universe on her shoulders.

8

"Run, Amanda!" Eddie cried. He spun and swept up a chair from the kitchen set.

Amanda sat at the table, staring at Abby, frozen to the spot as surely as if she were a rabbit gone tharn. She still held the check in her hand.

Eddie took three quick steps from the cellar door and smashed the chair across Abby's back. The chair disintegrated as though he'd smashed it against a wall of granite, though Abby didn't so much as a twitch.

"It's so nice for you to meet me, Amanda. You don't know how long I've dreamed about this day." Abby's cold tone turned nasty as she spoke, and spittle flew from her lips.

Eddie grabbed her from behind but yelped and snatched his hands away as though he'd touched fire.

Abby glanced at him over her shoulder. "For fuck's sake, Eddie. You've even *seen* my true form in the back of your uncle's pickup!"

For a split second, Eddie thought he saw raw, golden flame swirling in her eye like a tornado. She showed him her black fangs in a vicious grin. "What did I promise you, tiger?"

Eddie met Amanda's gaze. "I love you, Amanda. I always have." Then he stepped around Abby and stood between her and Amanda, holding up his fists. "Run!" he screamed.

Abby laughed.

9

As Lamia and Mason argued, LaBouche held Chaz Welsh's mobile phone under the desk and swiped it open. The phone wasn't a burner, but no one knew he had it. He'd found it under the driver's seat of the BMW.

Using the claw of his thumb, he typed "Dan Delo" into the recipient field of a text message.

Next, he typed: "Get away. Brigitta on the warpath. Sending LaBouche to capture you."

As he thumbed the send button, he fought to keep a feral snarl from his face.

10

"Coming, LaBouche?" asked Brigitta. "He's your underling, after all."

LaBouche tilted his head to the side, then leaned back in his massive chair and licked his lips. At the same time, he flicked the mobile into the briefcase he'd taken to carrying. "Yes, yes," he said. "Wouldn't miss this for the world." He snapped the case closed and picked it up.

Brigitta rolled her eyes and turned to the humans. "Mason and Denny will come with us."

With a grin, Sally moved to stand beside them, putting one hand on each man's shoulder. "Yes, Mistress. Of course, they're happy to serve."

11

Amanda lunged to her feet, scattering the mail across the linoleum, sending her chair skittering into the wall. "What do we do? Eddie!"

Abby glowered at her over Eddie's shoulder. "Simple, hon. You die." As one would swat a fly, Abby slapped Eddie, and he crumpled to the ground. "Most of the time, I allow the husband to do this part, but Eddie's been a naughty boy." She glanced at him where he lay, then returned her gaze to Amanda. When their eyes met, Abby's narrowed, throwing electric blue sparks. "Come here, you little bitch!"

Amanda lunged away, keeping the table between them. "Eddie! Eddie!"

"Eddie! Eddie!" Abby mocked. "Quit whining! I let you get pregnant the one time." She grimaced, and it grew into a gloating smile. "Though in the end, I came to my senses and killed it before your brat drew breath."

Amanda had moved the length of the table while Abby spoke, but she stopped and straightened. "What?"

Abby's glowered at her. "Didn't you hear me?" She hunched her shoulders, extending her neck to thrust her face in Amanda's direction. She opened her mouth, exposing a double row of obsidian fangs. Her jaw kept dropping until her mouth gaped impossibly wide. Mocking baby noises came from deep in her throat. Her mouth snapped shut, then she yelled, "*I killed your baby, bitch!*"

Amanda drew her head back as if slapped, then cocked her head to the side. "Is that…" She blinked and frowned. "Where is that music coming from?"

Abby threw back her head and laughed. Her laughter seemed to fill the room, and neither she nor Amanda noticed Eddie slipping into the cellar.

12

Anger simmered in Dan Delo's blood. He'd wasted an entire night flying in lazy circles above a pack of idiots parked out in the middle of nowhere. Brigitta had said Mason Harper would bring them Greg Canton, but Harper had never arrived.

When his mobile phone buzzed, Delo almost fished it out of the fanny-pack he wore and threw it with all his strength. But before he did, he glanced at the screen and read the text message displayed there.

Without another glance at the demons milling around below, he veered away, descending until he skimmed the tops of the trees. His gaze danced back and forth, trying to see everywhere at once.

Brigitta eliminated Chaz, he thought. *Brigitta sent him home, and she has no reason to lie about that. So who sent this text?*

He had no satisfactory answers to that question. He didn't even have satisfactory guesses at those answers.

Even so, he didn't want to be sent home.

13

"*Motherfucker!*" yelled Scott as he slammed his bedroom door open. "He's *private messaging* me now?"

Mike arched a lazy eyebrow but didn't lift his head from the back of the couch. "Who?"

"Fucking LaBouche, that's who!"

Mike sat up. "LaBouche? What does he want?"

Scott made a disgusted noise and threw the cell down on the couch. "Read it yourself." He slammed his bedroom door on the way back through.

"It'll be hard for him, working with the demon that killed his little girl," said Benny from the kitchen doorway.

"Benny, you have a gift for understatement." Mike grinned at him to take away any sting.

"Yeah." Benny jerked his chin toward the phone. "What's it say?"

Mike picked up the cell and swiped away the lock screen. "Don't you already know?"

"I could pick it out of Scott's brain, but he'd consider it rude."

"True enough. The whole message is two words: 'Want her?'" Mike paused, thumb poised over the screen. "What do I say? Ask him who 'she' is?"

"No, that much is obvious," said Benny.

"Yeah? I can think of a good answer."

"Brigitta," whispered Greg. "The Lady in the Lake."

Benny made a finger gun and shot at Greg with it.

"Yeah," muttered Mike. "I guess that makes sense." He typed a short burst of letters, then looked up. "Sent."

"What did you say?" asked Greg.

"I channeled Scott. I said 'Duh. Stop messaging me, asshole.' Then I gave him a link to my account in the app."

"Good. Toby and the others should be here before you reply to the next one."

"Go round everyone up," said Mike. "I've got the feeling LaBouche is under the gun."

14

Eddie *hated* leaving Abby and Amanda alone, but if he didn't find something to use against her, both he and Amanda were dead. He knew that for a certainty. *My entire fucking life before John rescued me proves that point. Gil hasn't killed Margo, but if he hadn't gone to prison... Who knows what he would have done?*

A discussion he'd had with Dr. Erikson kept repeating as though on a loop. Erikson had asked him about the lamp, about how it had changed, and why Eddie believed Abby's appearances to him as a child had brought about the changes to it. He remembered the doctor saying that something had happened to Eddie to change his perceptions of events. He hadn't considered it at the time, though he'd returned to the idea many times as he'd gone on with his life. *What if Erikson was right, but for the wrong reason? What if Abby started coming because of something that happened to me rather than because Daddy bought the lamp?* He sneered at himself and descended into the darkness of the basement. *Cognitive psychology will not help me get rid of Abby!*

Standing in the darkness at the bottom of the cellar steps, he reached for the rechargeable flashlight. He'd hung the charger right at the bottom of the staircase, and he always put the flash back into it, so the charge remained fresh. He stretched his fingers wide and brushed the charger with his pinky, then latched onto the light and pulled it free. The body of the flashlight felt cold and slimy against his palm. The sensation was so visceral, so immediate that he paused and stared at the thing in his fist.

The lamp! Eddie thought. *When Daddy brought it home, I almost dropped it on the kitchen floor.* He didn't understand the importance of that memory, nor did he have any idea why he'd remembered at that moment.

Eddie flicked on the light, the bright white beam piercing the darkness with ease. He flashed the beam into all the dark nooks and corners of the cellar. If the far corner, boxes still packed from their move stood in a leaning tower. Written on the side of one the boxes in indelible black ink were the words: "Tiffany Lamp—DO NOT MOVE." Someone had scratched a single black line through the label.

Think, Eddie! he railed at himself. *Think!* He swept the light back and forth in the basement, seeing nothing that could help, coming back, again and again, to the old cardboard box in the corner.

How could we have missed that? How many times have we been down here, either alone or together? I mean, it's right fucking there!

Something thumped against the floor over his head, and Eddie jumped, stabbing the flashlight beam straight up as if that would help anyone. The barrel of the light felt so greasy, so...

"Holy fuck!" he hissed. *The lamp! Erikson was right, something* did *happen to me that changed things!* He bolted across the cellar and knocked the leaning tower of boxes over. Squatting, he ripped open the one marked "Tiffany Lamp—DO NOT MOVE" with the single black line refuting it.

What he'd forgotten, what had seemed so inconsequential, had happened before any fights, before any faces leered at him from the reflected room in the television screen, before the lamp had changed. What he'd forgotten had happened the very first time he'd touched the lamp. *It felt like this damn flashlight! So cold against my skin, so greasy...* The memory replayed again and again as he stared down at the lamp.

"Can I carry it?" he'd asked with the excitement of a *seven-year-old. He'd rushed to the kitchen table and grabbed the lamp by its brass base and the pole of the same material between the body and the lightbulb. As he lifted it, something algid and greasy wriggled across the skin on the back of his hands. He cried out and let go of the lamp, leaving it tottering on the edge of the table. He held one hand with the other, up close to his chest as if it had stung him.*

The lamp *had* stung him, and Abby was the stinger.

15

"Why in the hell is Delo posted way out in the middle of nowhere?" grumbled LaBouche.

"It's about halfway from where we grabbed Greggy," said Mason. "It seemed to make sense at the time. Enough distance to spot any pursuit, not so far as to risk an interception."

The cell phone in LaBouche's pocket vibrated once, but he didn't reach for it yet. Instead, he turned to Mason. "And yet they intercepted you."

"Yeah, but only because Dan Delo switched sides."

"If he did that, he wouldn't be at the meeting point any longer," said LaBouche. "And this would be a wasted trip."

"He's there," said Lamia. "I asked a friend before we left."

Hunching his shoulders, LaBouche turned toward the window, pulling his cell from his pocket. Using his body as a shield, he read the message from Scott and smiled. Lewis was so easy to predict. He only wished he could be there to taste the man's emotions. LaBouche tapped in the new number and sent a quick message, then turned the phone off.

He couldn't risk any more incoming messages from the SEMPRe app.

Whatever happened next was in the hands of the hunters.

16

Above his head, Amanda screamed, but the sound cut off as if Abby had stolen her breath away. Eddie peered down into the box, shoving aside old newspapers, ripping old rags out of the way. He dropped the flashlight, and it rolled in a third of a circle before coming to rest pointing at the cellar steps. He shoved both hands into the wrapping and froze when his fingers rested on something bone-chilling and slick. A burst of loud music slammed through him as though he stood in front of the speaker wall at a black metal concert. At first, he could discern nothing, no melody, no rhythms, but then the eerie, wailing strains of music coalesced in the music of the desert sun stalking across baking dunes, of sandstorms, of howling pestilence blown on evil winds.

Amanda shrieked in pain and something upstairs shattered. He locked his fingers around the body of the lamp and jerked it out of the box, flinging rags and paper all over the floor.

The lamp seemed to writhe in his hands, as though it were a living thing. A quick glance told him the colors of the shade—midnight blue and horrible dark purple. The electric-blue fish seemed to stare at him, and the brass serpent of the lamp's body seemed to wriggle beneath his palms. The volume of the haunting music swelled until his brain hurt, as though physical contact with the lamp gave the music direct access to his mind. He swayed to his feet, made dizzy by the volume, woozy by the melody itself. The music rang in his head like thunder, like an artillery barrage at point blank range. He never heard the silence fall upstairs. He never heard Amanda whimper, then cry.

Eddie turned toward the stairs, and the volume increased again—growing so loud he wanted to vomit. The door to the kitchen stood open, and Eddie couldn't remember if he'd closed it behind him. The flashlight at his feet still pointed at the steps, but after a moment it flickered and died. The lamp stopped moving in his hands, perhaps content to abuse him with the music. He glanced down at it and gasped. All of the bright-blue fish had turned to stare at him, and the bronze-cast serpent's eyes had turned merciless electric blue.

When he raised his head, a scream escaped him. On the top of the steps stood a pair of dusky-hued bare feet. Flecks of blood decorated the ankles. The toenails gleamed with the light of the kitchen. The left foot lifted, then descended to the second step and Eddie stopped breathing, rooted to the spot.

17

"Seems real to me," said Toby. "Benny?"

"I sense no deception, Captain Picard."

Toby flashed a lopsided grin at him. "You discovered Star Trek: The Next Generation, at last, I see."

"We can't go in there blind," said Mike.

"Or under-manned," said Scott. "I don't like this. What's keeping LaBouche from setting us up?"

"If he wanted us, he could have had us last night," said Toby. "Instead, he let you empty a shotgun into his chest."

"But—"

"Scott, he didn't defend himself, didn't move. He stood there and took blast after blast to the chest." Benny put his hand on Scott's shoulder. "Then he allowed you to bash his face in until he was dead. Plus, I don't read deception from him. He's sitting in a car with Mason Harper, Dennis Cratchkin, Brigitta, and someone he thinks of as 'Lamia...'" Benny squinted into the distance. "But there's something funky around Lamia. His emotions are all confused when he thinks of her—fear, contempt, surprise, and respect."

"And where are they heading?"

"As far as LaBouche knows, they are heading to the address he sent Mike."

"Why has he killed the app?" asked Mike.

Benny shook his head. "He turned off the whole phone. He's concerned the others might hear the notification or otherwise catch wise."

"Are we doing this, then?" asked Scott.

Everyone turned toward Toby, and he lifted his head and nodded. "Yes, but we need to have a plan. We can't expect to go against Brigitta alone without massive firepower and support, let alone wade into a pack of demons."

"Damn right," said Scott. "Let me mobilize my response teams. They can hit the demons while we try to take Brigitta down."

Benny cleared his throat. "Remember that LaBouche will work on our side, but whether he will act against the other demons in the open, I can't say. He won't attack the six of us, but that might not apply to anyone else."

"LaBouche is a traitorous, manipulative bastard," grated Scott. "There's no guarantee he will leave us alone."

"Right," said Toby. "We'll take three teams. Each of your teams has a combat medic, right, Scott?"

"Yes. The six of us can take a spare Suburban." He looked at each of them in turn, his expression one of infinite weariness.

18

Abby descended the stairs, as regal as any queen, moving with studied deliberation, revealing herself by inches. Her pace was slow but relentless: step down, pause a heartbeat, lift her other foot, and then repeat it all again.

Eddie couldn't seem to move; he stood there watching his death descend those steps, unable to look away. His grip on the lamp tightened until his fingers blanched. He would have choked the damn thing to death if possible, but it was a lamp of glass and bronze, and it had no life to give up— no matter how much it wriggled.

The darkness in the cellar seemed oppressive—hot and bitter cold at the same time. The shadows seemed to press in on him, to restrict his breathing, to shove at him, to encapsulate him with doom. His heart raged against his ribs. His pulse pounded in the blood vessels of his neck, throbbed in his temples.

"What are you doing with that, Eddie?" Abby asked in a voice that ripped at him like a hot saw blade.

Without meaning to, Eddie looked down at the lamp in his hands. The shade was changing, the dark midnight colors receding before a brilliant red, the fish morphing and bleeding electric blue into the air.

"Do you think you can harm me with a lamp of this world? Don't be ridiculous."

An orangish-brown figure wriggled at the very edge of the shade, undulating like a snake. Eddie wanted to drop the lamp, to dash it against the concrete, but his arms refused to obey him.

"What can you be thinking of, Eddie?"

Outside, a car horn blared.

Eddie ripped his gaze from the Tiffany lamp, his head jerking from side to side, flashing back to Abby every few heartbeats to mark her progress. *Can't get out that way,* he thought. *Can't go through her, and if I get close, she'll kill me for sure.*

The horn sounded again, and like a siren's call drawing a ship onto the rocks, it pulled his attention to the part of the cellar behind him. He turned his profile toward Abby, then stole a glance at the shadow-strewn cellar.

His workbench stood against the wall beside the unpacked boxes, and a sliver of light peeked from its edges. *The outside bulkhead!* They'd blocked the stairs with his workbench—a poor man's burglar alarm, he'd joked.

"Eddie, Eddie, Eddie," sighed Abby. "Put my lamp down and step away from it. I might let you live if you do."

"Wuh—why? I thought it couldn't hurt you."

"Eddie," she whispered, sounding too close.

He darted a glance over his shoulder and gasped. Bright golden flames had replaced the dusky-skinned flesh of the legs descending the steps. She was more than halfway down, and her hips, her sex, were exposed. All of it burned and writhed—pure fire.

The horn blew a third time as Eddie turned toward his workbench and let go of the lamp with one hand. He grabbed the bench and flung it away, then bolted up the steps to the wooden doors. He burst through them, smashing them from their hinges, driven by stark terror.

Amanda idled the car at the curb, her face stark white, blood dribbling down her cheek from a cut at her temple. Her expression relaxed for a heartbeat as he burst from the cellar. Eddie sprinted to the car, watching her face. Her face blanched further, and her lips moved, and Eddie knew Abby had given up the regal progression in favor of running him down like a dog.

He ripped the back door of the little car open and dove inside. "Go! Go!" he cried.

Amanda floored the accelerator, and the little car shrieked away from the curb, momentum slamming the rear door. Eddie put the lamp on the floor behind the passenger seat and sat up, craning his neck behind him.

Abby was there, too close, running a series of steps then leaping high into the air like a springbok. As he watched, her eyes twitched to meet his and a grimace of fury settled on her fiery features, and she poured on hate-driven speed, gaining on them.

"Faster! She's gaining!" he shouted.

"This is as fast as this piece of shit will go!"

Abby smiled and narrowed her eyes.

19

As Lamia pulled the car into the parking lot, LaBouche roused himself from his dreams of revenge and glanced out the window. Six lesser male demons stood in a loose circle, none willing to stand close to the other. Though he craned his neck, LaBouche couldn't find Delo flapping around overhead. *Finally did something right*, he thought and grinned.

"I don't see him," said Mason.

Lamia opened the door and got out. She seemed to have grown taller to LaBouche, riding higher on her tail. She turned toward the demons, and one of them sneered at her, recognizing Sally McBride but not the changes in her.

Lamia waved her hand. "*Balāṭu-šū šarāqu*," she chanted. The demon who had sneered convulsed and fell to his knees. After a single heartbeat, he sprawled face-first on the macadam, thick purple blood running from his eyes and ears.

LaBouche tensed at the sound of the ancient language of the Akkadian Empire. He knew the meaning of the words: "Take his life." Visions of Nicole, broken and bloody, flooded his mind. Rage bubbled in his blood. He recalled her lifeless, once-malachite, now-gray eyes staring past him into eternity. Fury drummed in his ears. He remembered how the overhead lights had reflected in her blood without end.

Brigitta rose from her seat in the car and turned an icy glare on the remaining demons. "Behold Lamia. Behold Mormo. Behold Poine. Behold Ker." She stepped to Lamia's side. "Behold this *jinn* and tremble in awe and fear."

"Come on, I want to see. Gonna get out or what?" asked Denny Cratchkin.

Without taking his eyes from Lamia, LaBouche flicked his claws through Denny's throat, then sat and allowed the hot blood to shower over him. On the other side of Denny, Mason Harper scrabbled for the door handle, then launched himself face-first into the parking lot.

LaBouche leaned against the door, and that was all it took. The door popped off, its hinges ripping and tearing chunks out of the car's body. Brigitta turned an expression of irritation his way, then froze, staring at him.

Moving with methodical care, LaBouche extended his legs and stood. He glared at Lamia for the space of a hummingbird's heartbeat, then roared and charged her, claws bared, mouth spread wide to expose all of his teeth.

20

"Where do I go?" Amanda cried.

His gaze locked on Abby's, Eddie laughed.

"Eddie?"

"She's out of gas! She's like an alligator, only built for short distances."

"*Where do I go?*"

"As far from here as you can get. Head out of town."

"Shouldn't we go for help? To the police or something?"

Eddie shook his head, grinning as Abby stopped running. She stood in the middle of the road behind them, arms akimbo, and glared after them. "Do you think they could help? I don't."

Abby grinned and held a hand up next to her cheek, waving. She blew him a kiss and disappeared.

"Oh, shit," muttered Eddie.

The tires screeched as Amanda hit the brakes hard and swerved toward the middle of the road. Eddie thumped against the door, and his face passed within inches of Abby's body.

Amanda fought for control as Abby lunged toward the car.

21

The drivers of the first three trucks in the convoy of heavy sport utility vehicles knew their business. They seemed to drive as one, hauling ass down the two-lane back roads, driving within inches of the vehicle in front of them. Their passage was like that of a snake on amphetamines, litter and leaves whirling in their wake.

Toby pointed through the windscreen. "Demons!" he cried.

As they pulled into the parking lot, the SUVs separated, moving to encircle the cars and a small knot of demons. Brakes squealed, and tires shrieked as they came to a halt. Doors opened and the attack units deployed.

Toby pointed at the lesser demons standing dumbstruck, watching LaBouche claw and hiss at a strange, unfamiliar beast—one with the torso of a woman and, from the waist down, the tail of a snake. "Take them!"

Without question, Scott had trained his men well. They moved in like three SEAL teams, weapons covering the group of demons.

"LaBouche! Stop this!" screeched Brigitta as she circled the pair of demons rolling on the ground, fighting and slashing each other.

Toby pointed at her. "Brigitta!" He jabbed his gun toward LaBouche. "LaBouche and someone I don't know. Leave them be and focus on bringing the bitch down!"

At his command, Brigitta cocked her head and turned to glower at him. "You won't find me as easy to bring down as my father!"

Toby snapped up his dart gun and began to fire and advance. Scott fell in to one side, Mike on the other. The three moved in a line, firing a steady stream of darts as they went, two of them pausing and providing covering fire while the other reloaded. Benny, Shannon, and Greg stood by the Suburban, trying to see everywhere at once.

One of the lesser demons broke from the fray and sprinted toward the woods on all fours. Benny snapped up his hands and pulled them back toward him as if pulling a rope. The fleeing demon first slowed, then came to a halt. "Got him!"

Greg focused on the demon and held out his hands as if to warm them over a campfire. His face tensed, his lips contorting with effort. He inclined his head, breathing hard, and after a few agonizing heartbeats, the demon in Benny's snare erupted with blue flames, giving off a wave of volcanic heat.

Brigitta snarled and charged at Toby, claws extended. Darts riddled her loose black skin, but they didn't seem to slow her, let alone put her out. Mike and Scott stepped away from Toby, building a flattened triangle, firing without pause.

LaBouche roared and dove at Lamia, jaws snapping. She twisted away, striking at him with her black-scaled tail as he rushed past her. LaBouche stabbed his claws into the flesh of her tail and latched on, pulling them both back down to the macadam.

The four remaining lesser demons banded together and charged one of Scott's teams, ignoring the other two groups of men. They slammed into the group of five men, ignoring the multitude of darts, paintballs, and lead slugs striking them from all sides, and began to rend flesh from bone. The shrieks of the men echoed through the trees.

Benny stepped toward them, but Shannon put a hand on his arm. "Help Toby! I'll fix these motherfuckers!" She stepped past him, concentration settling on her features like a well-worn mask. Greg grabbed at the air, staring at one of the lesser demons, then flung his hand away, and the demon lifted off his feet and flew into the trees like a discarded toy.

Mike and Scott encircled Brigitta in a classic pincher movement as Toby backpedaled. She ignored the two former cops, focusing on Toby with a hate-filled countenance. Brigitta blinked, and the air popped as she teleported to within inches of him. She slashed at him with cracked, bone-colored claws. Mike and Scott trotted forward, firing dart after dart into her back until she looked like a queer specimen of porcupine.

LaBouche and Lamia rolled on the macadam, hissing and spitting like a pair of tomcats. The *jinn* had muttered a spell and a couple of fangs poked from her gums, growing as if shown in time lapse. Venom glistened from the tips of the eight-inch fangs. She lunged forward, mouth wide, and LaBouche raised an arm to fend her off. Her fangs impaled his forearm, and he screeched, writhing in agony as whatever she used for venom hit his bloodstream.

Brigitta pressed Toby back, slashing at him with her claws, kicking him, biting at his face. He fired his dart gun dry and reversed it, to club her with it. Mike and Scott glanced at one another, and, as though by mutual agreement, dropped their tranquilizer guns on their straps, reaching behind them for their Remington 870 shotguns.

Shannon stood twenty feet from the gaggle of lesser demons. She held out her hand, fingers splayed, and squeezed her eyes shut.

"The Trickster!" one of them shouted.

Greg flung the demon into the air, grinning as the beast slammed back to the asphalt with a sickening crunch. He took a step forward and extended his hands toward the broken form, his face writhing. Harsh blue flames exploded around the broken demon, thick black smoke twining into the sky.

Shannon bent her head toward the remaining two lesser demons, and they cried out, holding out their hands as if blinded. They whirled to and fro, slashing the air with claws and fangs, more often than not striking one another. A smile settled on Shannon's face.

Benny ran forward as Brigitta swept Toby's legs from under him, slamming him to the ground. "No!" Benny cried, then skidded to a halt and lifted his hands. For a moment, Brigitta froze stock-still, but it didn't last. She writhed against his telekinetic hold on her, then disappeared. After a heartbeat, she reappeared behind Benny, lifting both hands above her head clasped together into a single, massive fist. Benny spun toward her as she brought her hands down, clubbing him on top of the head. He collapsed, falling into a heap like a puppet with its strings cut.

Shannon stared at the two lesser demons, twisting their perceptions toward darkness, silence. She spent all her focus on the task, allowing Scott's teams to pour firepower into them.

But she'd forgotten the demon Greg tossed into the trees—everyone had. He burst from the trees, charging Shannon in a quadrupedal gait, arms swinging like those of a great ape. He bowled into her, lifting her from her feet and slamming her into the Suburban at her back. She screamed as he raked his talons down her ribs, splattering her blood on the hood of the black Suburban. Freed of Shannon's illusions, the two lesser demons vented their anger on the teams accosting them, and blood and bodies flew.

Greg reached for the demon attacking Shannon, and though he grunted and strained with effort, couldn't budge him. He lashed out, whipping psychic energy across the thing's back, but still, the thing ignored him. It hacked at Shannon's body, flinging blood in wide arcs. "Help!" Greg shouted. He leaned toward the demon, extending one hand as though grabbing a thick book from a shelf, then squeezed his fingers together. He screamed as he did it, and blood vessels burst in both eyes and gouted from his nose.

Scott charged at Brigitta as she bent toward Benny, slamming into her side and barging her over. She twisted as she fell and grabbed him lightning quick by one arm and the throat, pulling him down with her.

LaBouche wrenched his arm away from his body, pulling Lamia to the side. He rolled on top of her, keeping her head pinned with his impaled arm. He pounded her face with his other fist while her tail lashed his lower body.

He kept lifting his fist and bringing it down, channeling his absolute hatred of the *jinn* into each blow. As he struck her, he screamed, "Nicole!" again and again.

Toby rolled to his knees, dizzy and nauseous as Mike charged across the parking lot to help Scott. The men fighting the pair of lesser demons dissolved into chaos and confusion, firing at the whirling dervishes in their midst without thought for crossfire. Greg cried out as he lifted the demon into the air, but he didn't have the energy to throw him around as he had the others. He had to settle for walking backward, dragging the demon away from Shannon.

They'd all forgotten Mason Harper.

22

The car careened back and forth across the road, shedding speed accompanied by the shriek of tires.

"Go! Go!" Eddie cried as Abby lurched at the back door of the car.

"I'm trying!" Amanda got the car pointed in the right direction and hammered the gas pedal. The little four-cylinder engine moaned, but the car leaped forward.

Abby screamed as the car sped out of her reach, then disappeared again. When she appeared, she stood in their path as if daring Amanda to run her down.

Amanda wrenched the wheel to the right, and they slid sideways, the light back end of the car lifting. Abby grinned and raced after them, seeming to stretch and grow as she ran.

"What do I do, Eddie?" Amanda cried.

In the backseat, Eddie's gaze dropped to the lamp. *There has to be a reason she broke off her fight with Amanda to come after me when I found this. But what and how can I use it?* He bent and scooped it up, grimacing at the slimy sting of the brass against his skin. "Coming up front," he said as he wedged himself between the front bucket seats.

"*What do I do?*"

"Keep driving."

Amanda stole a glance at him as he settled in the seat. "Why do you have that? I thought we left it at the old place."

Eddie grimaced and fastened his seatbelt. "Abby changed the label on the box. It's been in the cellar all along."

Ahead, Abby appeared with one flaming foot on either side of the yellow center line.

"Why?" Amanda returned her focus to the road and twitched the wheel to the left, the tires drubbing on the shoulder, throwing gravel and garbage into the vortex of their passing.

"Something about this lamp is important. I don't know what, but when I picked it up, Abby stopped fighting you and came to the cellar."

Amanda opened her mouth, but closed it, shaking her head. "Smash it!"

"I don't know if that's the right thing to do. What if smashing it releases a binding or something like that?"

"A binding?"

Abby blinked into existence to their right, just beside the front wheel. She slammed her fist down on the hood.

"Jesus!" cried Eddie, slamming his hands to the dash, dropping the lamp to his lap. The back of the car surged upward.

Amanda hit the brakes hard and, when the car settled back down, punched the accelerator again. "How the fuck do we get rid of this bitch?"

"I wish I knew," said Eddie. "I've been trying my entire life."

23

LaBouche's fist ached. His other arm burned and tingled in alternating fits as Lamia's acidic poison ate away at him. His fist still rose and fell, rose and fell, and each impact with the *jinn's* face sent a shock wave of agony racing up his arm.

He no longer had the breath to shout Nicole's name as he struck. His vision had narrowed to twin points straight ahead of him, and his breath seemed ripped from his chest.

Lamia's face was a bloody mess of torn flesh and broken bones. Her eyes had ruptured, destroyed by the violence of his assault. Her fangs still penetrated his forearm, but they seemed brittle, dead.

He smashed his fist into the ruin of her face and lacked the strength to lift it again. LaBouche slumped from where he sat straddling her belly, wrenching Lamia's head to the side with a sickening crunch. He'd beaten her.

He'd beaten a *jinn* in single combat.

Too bad she wouldn't stay dead. *Not unless the demon hunters help me send her home.*

24

Brigitta wrapped her legs around Scott's middle and squeezed with all her strength. She pummeled his face and neck with her fists, hissing and growling like a pissed-off mountain lion. Scott couldn't bring the shotgun or the dart gun to bear and had abandoned both. He'd pulled his .45 caliber Glock and had fired that dry, point-blank into her chest. He threw himself side to side, trying to break her hold on him, trying to get away. Mike ran toward them full speed and without slowing, he kicked Brigitta in the head, putting all his momentum behind the kick.

She yowled and disappeared with a pop.

"Fucking hate that," muttered Scott.

"Come on," said Mike, holding out his hand.

A faint pop sounded near Toby, and Brigitta was back, reaching for the man's eyes. LaBouche stumbled past Mike and Scott, weaving from side to side, one arm hanging at his side. "Brigitta!" he roared.

She lifted her gaze, an infinite contempt in her eyes. "You fucking idiot!" she hissed.

"Couldn't leave it be, could you?" he demanded. "You couldn't let happiness stand, couldn't allow us to have children."

"While I remain childless?" She stepped away from Toby, shoving him over as she did. "Don't be stupid, LaBouche! You knew what I wanted. Why did you waste your seed on such a lesser demon as that silver hussy?"

With a sound somewhere between an enraged shout and a groan, LaBouche lowered his head and charged her.

Greg held the demon that had attacked Shannon a few inches from the ground. "Shannon? Shannon, are you okay?" The beast thrashed in his grip, flailing in midair and squawking like a trapped animal, and Greg staggered from the force of it.

The fight between the two lesser demons and Scott's troops wound on behind him, the air ringing with gunshots and shouts. Every few seconds, the wet sound of a dead human hitting the ground punctuated the battle.

Greg struggled to hold the demon, burning through his reserves of energy and concentration at an alarming rate. He dragged the beast farther away from the Suburban, darting quick peeks around the parking lot, looking for someone to call on for help, but everyone fought a demon or lay on the ground bleeding. The fiend slipped in his imaginary fingers as if a viscous oil coated them. Panic worried the fringes of his mind.

"Well, hello, Greggy," said Mason Harper as he slid a knife into Greg's back. He lifted his other fist and brought it crashing down, and Greg dropped like a felled tree.

With a strangled cry, the demon Greg had been holding dropped to the ground and sprang at Shannon again. The Suburban rocked on its springs at the force of his return.

Mason watched the demon set to rending the flesh from Shannon's bones and smiled.

25

Scott was standing bent at the waist, trying to catch his breath when he caught sight of Mason Harper stabbing

Greg in the back. He'd started to run as the serial killer struck Greg in the back of the head, crumpling him like an empty can. He reloaded as he ran, cursing in a continuous stream. As Harper bent over Greg and lifted a short-handled sledgehammer, Scott stopped, steadied his aim, and fired. The .45 caliber slug took Mason Harper in the forehead, snapping his head back. His smile dissolved into a slack-jawed leer as he flopped to the side.

Scott glanced at Greg and didn't like what he saw. He took a step toward him, then one toward Shannon. In his entire career, Scott had never felt lost during a battle, but he did at that moment. He stole another glance at Greg. "Sorry, Greg," he said. He turned, lifted his Glock, and fired two rounds into the demon's back.

With a grunt and a howl, the demon spun and charged. The fiend hit Scott like a cement truck, sending him flying. Growling as a rabid dog would, the fiend followed him.

Scott landed on his side, hard enough to snap his wrist and the Glock skittered away. He tried to get up, tried to run or at least meet the demon head on, but time for trying ran out and the demon dove atop him. It dug four-inch talons into Scott's upper chest, curling them around his collarbones. The demon threw his weight back and snapped Scott's bones like twigs.

The demon grinned down at him. "You're dead, you just don't know it yet."

"Fuck you," grunted Scott.

The demon threw back his head and laughed while Scott struggled to roll away. Then the demon leaned forward and snapped his jaws on Scott's throat, his chuckle gurgling through the spouts of blood.

26

LaBouche slammed Brigitta into Lamia's car, half-spinning the vehicle in a circle. He held her by the feet and swung her like a club, pounding her into the ground, the car. With each blow, Brigitta shrieked like a teakettle.

"I'll kill you for what you did," he rasped.

Brigitta's loose, black skin tore and sloughed off her shoulders. Beneath it, red flames raged.

27

"Scott!" wheezed Toby.

Mike followed his gaze, just in time to see the demon end Scott Lewis' life. His hand flew to his hip, landing on his pistol.

"Too late." Toby lurched to his feet, his face twisting. "Shannon…" He stumbled toward her.

Mike passed him at a full sprint, his stare welded to Greg's body. "Help Shannon!" he shouted over his shoulder. He slid on his knees next to the man he loved. Blood pooled underneath Greg as Mike checked for a pulse. "Medic!" he shouted.

He looked up, looking for the support team. "Help me!"

28

Benny groaned and lifted his head. He had no memory of what had happened to him, and no memory of being knocked unconscious. He cracked his eyelids and winced at the brightness of the light.

LaBouche sat astride a woman made of red fire, piles of shredded black skin littered around them both like fall leaves. The yellow demon's scaled flesh sizzled and popped as red flames licked hungrily at his legs. He didn't seem to notice. He seemed lost to a berserker rage as he slashed at her with claws that cracked from the heat.

Benny glanced in the other direction, his gaze tracking first to the battle between what remained of Scott's troops and the three lesser demons, then to where Mike kneeled over Greg, and finally to where Toby stood next to one of the Suburbans. As he watched, Toby turned his head and met Benny's gaze, his expression dire, his eyes streaming. Benny got to his feet and took a step toward his friend.

Then he saw the blood splashed all over the truck.

He snapped his gaze back and forth, scanning the battlefield. His gaze lingered on Scott's broken body for a moment, but... *Shannon?* he sent. *Shannon, where are you?*

He staggered faster, stumbling toward Toby, still looking for his love. Mike glanced at him and shouted, "I need help! Benny, get the medics!"

Benny nodded to show he'd heard. *Medical teams needed!* He sent the thought toward the squad leader of one of the units. *Check with Mike!*

He turned back to Toby.

And he saw her.

His knees went weak for an instant, and then he was running. He ran faster than he'd ever run before—faster even than when chased by Herlequin.

29

Killing her lay beyond his abilities, his power. As her skin came off, he knew the truth of her nature. Brigitta wasn't of his kind, wasn't even a *jinn*.

Brigitta was an *ifrit*, and compared to hers, his power wasn't even an irritation. For all his strength, for all his plotting... He could never beat Brigitta in the long run.

Not without help.

She's always said she is Herlequin's daughter, but how can that be possible? How could an untouchable like Herlequin father an ifrit?

Beneath him, Brigitta opened her eyes and snarled.

30

Toby's heart had broken when he'd seen the horrible damage done to Shannon's flesh. Blood still flowed from her wounds, and if she had any chance of surviving, they had to break away and get her to a level one trauma center.

And even then...

Toby hung his head, and the tears came.

31

Benny skidded to a halt, shouldering Toby out of the way.

Alive! *She's still alive!*

His gaze danced from laceration to puncture, from compound fracture to dislocation. He knew in an instant what chance she had.

"We've got to—"

"She needs a trauma center," Toby said. "Life Flight." He looked over his shoulder. "Greg, too, if he's still alive."

Benny started to turn toward Greg, but couldn't take his eyes off his love. *I NEED A MEDIC FOR GREG!* He sent the thought with enough psychic force to make Toby stagger two steps back.

All around them, the fighting paused as if someone had called a time-out, but it was a short pause.

GET THE FUCK OVER HERE! The power of his mental command grabbed everyone in the parking lot, and everyone who could, took a step toward him, but no medics came running.

Rage leaked into his brain like an insidious poison. He clenched his fists and spun to glower at the lesser demons and the squads engaging them. With a wave of each hand, the demons exploded skyward, slamming into the trees beyond the parking lot. They stuck there, twenty feet in the air, as though nailed to the trunks.

GET OVER HERE!

The teams ran toward him, and he pointed to Greg and to Shannon, then whirled to face Toby. "And you!" he snapped at him. "You *save* her, Toby!"

Toby grimaced. "Let one of these guys take the lead, Benny. We trained them in trauma, in battlefield medicine. I did one four-week rotation through an ER that wasn't even busy."

"Toby, I—" LaBouche screamed at the other end of the parking lot, and Benny turned his head in that direction.

Brigitta stood holding the yellow demon aloft with one hand, raking claws made of red flame across his torso with the other. She'd doubled in size. LaBouche screamed again.

"We've got to get out of here!" one of the squad leaders screeched. The man threw away his weapons and bolted toward one of the SUVs.

NO! Benny waved at him and sent him flying. *Help Shannon, help Greg! Then we will leave.*

Brigitta laughed. "No one will survive this meeting!" she boomed in a basso voice.

The rage that had been seeping into him became an unstoppable torrent. Benny picked out medic patches from the remaining men and pointed first at Shannon and Greg. Then he turned without a word and faced Brigitta.

"Be careful, *boy*," she said. "I chased you with my father. I know your weaknesses." She flung LaBouche aside like a forgotten rag doll.

"Doubtful," Benny muttered. He gave into the rage and stretched out his hands. He screamed and sent a wave of force at her.

Brigitta staggered under the onslaught, falling back step after step. Wisps of red flame peeled and fluttered away as if playing on the wind, only to sputter and die a moment later.

Benny kept pushing, and Brigitta kept stepping back, her hands up as if to ward off a blow. As more and more flame left her mass and withered, she shrank, returning to her average size.

Brigitta planted her feet and leaned toward Benny, glaring at him with sudden hatred. Darkness leeched in from the edges of his vision, leaving him blind.

"Benny? Where are you?" It was a child's voice, and one Benny hadn't heard in decades. It was his little brother's voice, the one Herlequin had attacked during their aborted trip out of the state. *Billy.*

"Yes, Benny. Where are you? Where am I?"

Not real, thought Benny. *Billy is decades dead.*

"I'm not, Benny. I'm not dead. I'm right here. Come to me."

Even if he were alive, he'd be a man, not a kid.

Benny's vision returned, but instead of a parking lot surrounded by the remains of a battle, he stood in a dense forest, one populated by trees with boughs that seemed to knit a canopy overhead, denying the light. *Herlequin's forest. Thousand Acre Wood.* He glanced down at himself. He wasn't a man...he was only eleven years old. *What?*

"It was a trick, silly," said Billy. "They made you believe you grew up, that you could kill them, but no one can kill them."

Fear grabbed Benny by the balls and squeezed.

"Fuck you, bitch," growled LaBouche.

A horrendous crash sounded, and Benny opened his eyes, staggering at the jarring discordance between the terrible forest of his youth and the hot parking lot.

Across the macadam littered with bodies, spent rounds, and blood, LaBouche stood next to the smoking remains of a beat-up old car. He stood leaning to one side, one eyelid torn, burned in vast swathes across his body. He looked at

Benny. "She won't stay down for long," he grated and collapsed.

"Come on, Benny!" said Toby, sprinting toward the ruined car. "Can you do the thing Greg does? The fire?"

Benny shook his head. "She's made from fire. I don't think that will work."

Toby drew up short. "If she's made of fire, then…"

Benny nodded. "No blood. No flesh—at least not real flesh." He looked at Toby a moment, then turned in Shannon's direction. "We don't have any idea what to do with her, and we don't have time to figure it out. Greg and Shannon can't spare it."

Toby glanced at the smoking heap of twisted metal, then at LaBouche, then back at Benny. "Right. Time to go. Can you get LaBouche into one of the Suburbans?"

32

It had been twenty minutes or so since Abby last appeared in the road. Amanda drove a little slower, her attention focused on the road. Eddie stared out the windscreen, wondering why the flaming bitch had let them go.

The car bucked and hitched. "Oh, no," whispered Amanda.

"What? What is it?"

"Gas," she said in an enervated voice. "We're out of gas."

Eddie pointed at the state park sign on the opposite side of the road. "Duck in here. Maybe someone has a spare can."

"What if…"

"We'll worry about her if she shows up again."

"'When,' you mean."

"What?"

Amanda sighed, and the hopelessness in the sound broke Eddie's heart. "You said, 'if she shows up again.' That's wrong. It's not an 'if,' it's a 'when.'"

Eddie grimaced and gazed down at the lamp. "I suppose that's right." The lamp shade had turned a shade of cherry red that both sickened and scared Eddie. The orangish-brown snake with the red spots had wriggled its way from the bottom edge of the shade to its center, and a weird bird had joined it. A strange-looking sapling grew next to the bird. "What the fuck?" he muttered.

Amanda slowed and turned into the parking lot on the left. She stood on the brake with both feet, and the car screeched to a halt.

He glanced at her, then followed her gaze. A fight had raged in the parking lot. A *war*.

A war between guys in black uniforms and…and things that looked like…

"Are those demons?" Amanda asked in a tremulous voice. "Have I gone insane?"

Eddie dropped his gaze to the lamp. The tree grew and grew like a strange time-lapse set in stained glass.

33

Toby advanced on the car, his tranquilizer gun pointed at the sky. "Who are you, and what do you want?" he shouted.

The blonde woman driving the car looked at him as though he were crazy. She threw the car in reverse, but the man rested his hand on her arm. He rolled down his window. "I'm Eddie Mitchell, and this is my wife, Amanda." His gaze traveled past Toby's shoulder. "Are those..." He swallowed hard and scratched his ear. "This sounds crazy, I know, but are there strange...*things* in this parking lot?"

Toby stared at the man. "You can see them?"

"Well, yeah. Can't you?"

"Describe them."

Eddie glanced at his wife. "Well, there's a big yellow one over there on the ground. He's got scales but looks like a big gorilla, and he's had his ass handed to him by the look of it." He turned his attention to the middle of the lot. "There's something that looks like a cross between a woman and a black snake, and—"

"Enough," said Toby. "Besides myself, you are the only person I've ever met who can pierce their illusions, Eddie."

"I can see them, too," said Amanda. "But listen, we need your help. There's a woman made of fire who..." She stared at Eddie and frowned. "I'm not telling this right."

"We have this lamp," said Eddie. He held it up, staring for a moment at the red glass shade. A large tree with a huge brown snake around its base stood on the field of red, and a crazy-looking bird stood nearby, staring outward at Eddie. "It's changed again," he murmured.

"What's with the lamp?"

"There's a...a genie tied to it. Or something. Something bad."

Toby nodded. "She said a woman made of fire. Was it red fire?"

Both of them shook their heads. "More golden. Yellowish."

A vague tickle started in the back of Toby's mind.

Eddie lowered the lamp. "But listen a minute. The genie is bad news—"

Amanda snorted laughter.

"Okay, she's the fucking devil, and she's after us. She's been after me since I was seven. She makes people do bad things, things they'd never do."

"Abuse," said Amanda. "Hatred. I think..." She looked down at her lap. "She makes happy people hate each other."

Toby grimaced. *What is it about a lady made of fire...* Then he remembered. His mind flashed back to the day Randy Fergusson had moved in, how he'd picked a fight with Toby and in the middle of it, Toby had thought he'd seen a woman made of fire standing in the corner and smiling. "Oh, shit," he breathed.

"Listen, uh..." said Eddie.

"Toby." He shook himself and focused on Eddie's face.

"Toby, right. You look as if you've been through a war and all, but we can't hang around. We're out of gas, and Abby has—"

"Abby?"

"She says that's her name," said Amanda.

"She's following us. Coming for the lamp, I guess. We've got to get out of here." Eddie pointed at the row of black Suburbans. "Do you have any spare gas?"

Toby pointed to the side of the macadam lot. "Park there. You'd better come with us. We can fight them."

Amanda's eyes tracked to the men with guns, the bodies. "Uh…"

"We're your best chance," said Toby. "And now that you can see them, now that you've acted against this Abby out in the open, they will all be after you."

"There are more?" asked Amanda, eyes wide.

"Lots." Toby jerked his head to the side. "Park there. Ride with me." He turned on his heel and jogged back toward the trucks, slowing as Benny came around the back of one. "Benny, you're never—"

"I heard," said Benny. "You can stay and help LaBouche if you want, but I'm getting Shannon out of here. The medic says it's now or never."

Toby looked at LaBouche's slumped form. "How much do you think he weighs?"

"Are you coming?" snapped Benny. "I drive like shit, you know."

34

They had Shannon and Greg stretched out in the back, two medics crouched back there working on each of them. Mike and Benny sat in the backseat, watching the medics with sharp eyes. Eddie and Amanda Mitchell sat wedged in the passenger bucket, the weird lamp on the floorboard at their feet. Toby put the truck in reverse and, with a last look at the men trying to get LaBouche into one of the other vehicles, backed toward the road.

"One of you get on the phone," said the medic working on Shannon. "Tell them we need Life Flight and ask where to meet them. Then get us there about ten minutes ago."

A woman of golden fire popped into existence next to the Mitchells' car.

"That's her!" yelled Amanda. "That's Abby!"

Abby turned and looked at the Suburban, then turned her gaze on the men working with LaBouche. She said something, but they couldn't hear what over the rumble of the Suburban's V8.

At Eddie's feet, the lamp lit up as if someone had plugged it into a live circuit. Evil red light bathed the interior of the Suburban. A high-pitched whine started inside the lamp. Outside, ugly storm clouds rolled in with alarming speed, blocking the sun, bringing on darkness before noon. Lightning flashed, arcing into the trees in the surrounding woods, filling the air with booming thunder.

"Toby, something's coming!" said Benny.

The men heaving at LaBouche broke and ran when Abby was twenty yards away. She glanced at them, and each one of them fell dead.

"Go! Go! *Please, go!*" begged Amanda.

Abby looked down at LaBouche and sneered, then she looked at the demon with the black-scale tail instead of legs. She turned to the side and glanced at the smoking remains of the car. In three long strides, she was at its side. She flicked the heap of metal away like tissue paper and stood over Brigitta. Her shoulders rose and fell as she sighed, and she gazed up into the dark clouds overhead as though assessing the progress of the coming storm. After a moment, she turned and looked at the SUV.

"Uh, we should go," said Eddie. "You don't want to see her up close."

"No, I don't," said Toby. He lifted his foot off the brake and backed out into the road, never taking his eyes off the woman made of golden flames. She nodded at him as if she recognized him, as though she knew he remembered her, and she approved of his fear. Then she looked up at the sky and smiled.

Toby followed her gaze. "What the hell is that?" Red and black streamers of smoke whirled and twirled downward from the clouds, like two invisible stunt planes performing barrel rolls as they dove earthward.

The smoke came to rest next to Abby and coalesced into the rough shape of a woman, the red color accumulating at the top, the black filling in the rest of the body. After a moment, the smoke became flesh and hair and leather. A woman with hair the color of cherry snow cones, with creamy white skin and dressed in shiny black leather stood there, glaring at them with orange, whirling eyes.

"What is it?" asked Benny. "What is it, Toby?"

"Is it another demon?" asked Mike. "Whatever it is, I don't fucking like it!"

Toby shook his head. "That's no demon."

Eddie made a choking sound, his hands strangling each other in his lap.

"What is it, Eddie?" asked Amanda.

"Go," he whispered. "Go! Go! *GO!*" He shrieked the last word loud enough to crack his voice, and Toby lifted his foot off the brake and mashed the gas pedal to the mat.

35

LaBouche's head throbbed and throbbed, sending bolts of agony throughout his abused body. Every bit of him burned and ached and throbbed. He chuckled. *As it should, fighting a* jinn *and an* ifrit *on the same day. What kind of idiot am I?*

"What kind, indeed?" asked a woman's voice. It was the voice of a million whorehouses, a million million courtesans. Pure, unmitigated sex, an electric thrill that plugged straight into his libido.

LaBouche snapped his eyes open.

She stood over him. The goddess. She wore the skin of a pale human woman, hair colored like arterial blood, black leather everything. She was as beautiful a woman as he'd ever seen, but it was her eyes that drew him, that gave her away.

Her magnetic, orange eyes.

Lilitu, daughter of the sky, sister to night and wind and storm, he thought in reverent awe. *Our Lady Chaos.*

She stepped forward, putting one perfect boot between his legs, the chrome spike of a heel missing his sex by a gnat's breath. "Yes, motherfucker, and you *betrayed my daughter!*"

Her eyes began to spin, to whirl and twirl, orange sparks dancing into the air, spinning like whirly gigs. Her flesh began to throb, to fade in and out, in and out, as if a magical engine pulsed and pulsed, pulling her flesh out of phase for a moment, then relenting. The beautiful red-haired woman flashed and began to disappear. In her place stood something out of a nightmare, out of the worst fears

LaBouche could imagine. Made of shadows and smoke, her form was ill-defined and transitory, as though wind ripped the smoke away, only to allow it to reform and recombine with her body. For a short while, her orange eyes remained, boring into LaBouche as if she could scorch his very soul with them.

"My daughter put her trust in you, *chingado*. She desired your seed, perhaps your partnership—though why she'd stoop so low is beyond me. She would have raised you up, as I once did with Lilu." She glanced to the side as something hissed toward them. "As I did with Lamia." Lilitu bent in the middle, lowering her face to stare into LaBouche's eyes. "You betrayed her, *verraeter*! You betrayed her over what?"

The heat of her fury baked LaBouche's face as though she'd slapped plasma torn from the sun onto his cheeks. He didn't want to look at her anymore. He wanted to shrink away, to disappear, to *go back home*—anything but sit in the face of her fury.

"*I asked you a question,* puto-chulo*!*" she hissed.

"She… She had Lamia kill my mate. Truly kill her. Our children—"

She slapped him, and it felt as if a meteor had struck him. She dug long chrome talons into his cheek and pulled the flesh away from his bones. "Over an *untouchable*?"

"Yes," Lamia hissed. "Nothing more than a trollop, a walking shit-bag."

The orange of Lilitu's eyes began to dim, their spinning began to slow. Darkness crept into them as though someone had poured black ink into the corners of her eyes.

LaBouche wanted to turn away, *longed* to turn away, but his muscles didn't respond to his wishes.

"Oh, yes, *torcok*. You *will* look upon me. *You will look upon me and reap the rewards of betraying my kin, of betraying MY ONLY DAUGHTER!*" The blackness crept in and in and in, burying the orange fury.

LaBouche longed for the return of fiery fury, anything to replace the cold, soul-crushing darkness that licked at him hungrily. In her eyes, he saw every vile thing, every horrible act committed in the human world or in hell. The tortures, the rapes, the murders, the sadism, and though those very acts fed and nourished him, the images in her eyes did not. They burned him, scoured his brain with steel wool.

"Oh, yes," she crooned in a voice like the crackling of eternal flames. "You could have become like Lamia. Instead, you will become like Lilu." She leaned closer, and the images seemed to invade his mind. "I will eat your soul, *suka*, and you will feel it *forever*. Pain without end, suffering beyond that which you can imagine." She laughed, and it came out broken, as though a critical piece of machinery inside her had run astray. As suddenly as it had begun, it cut off. "You thought the others dining on you hurt, *chavo*. You will yearn for that pain."

The memory of Nicole's face flashed through his mind. "Fuck you," he spat. Something tore deep inside his body, or maybe in his soul, and pain flooded his senses. His skin began to smoke, to blister and peel.

"No," said Lilitu in an amused voice. "*Fuck you*, puto!"

Her eyes pulsed and pulsed while LaBouche screamed. He screamed more than all his victims combined, he hurt more than all the emotional pain he'd dined on for so many years, more than the sum of all the torture he'd dished out.

Lilitu smiled and sucked LaBouche's soul into the black hole at her center.

BOOK THREE: HARVESTER

Chapter 1
Saturday

I

Power crackled in the air as bolts of electricity arced from Lilitu's crouched form, piercing the scaled yellow *mazzikim* flesh she loomed over or charring the macadam. She threw back her head, laughing as she consumed the last bits of the creature that had called himself LaBouche. A betrayer, a sycophant, a fool.

A dead fool, she thought, smacking her lips. *But a satisfying snack.*

She rocked back on her heels and allowed the lifeless husk to fall to the macadam where it broke, then collapsed in a flurry of ash and dust. She wiped her hands and turned to take in the scene of the battle, her indolent gaze drifting around the parking lot, taking in the bent and broken forms of the dead humans, lingering on the bodies of dead demons.

In the road beyond the parking lot, the black Suburban roared and spun its rear tires. Lilitu lifted her face and narrowed her eyes at the vehicle, and the shrieking grew louder. "Is it true?" she mused. "Could they be so stupid?"

Behind her, Abyzou took a step. "Did you say something, Mistress?"

Lilitu cocked her head to the side and sniffed. "Are they all in the one vehicle?" She tittered for a breath, then snapped her head to stare to the northeast. "No," she murmured. "Not all of them." She stood and glanced at Abyzou and said, "You three know what to do with those I leave behind. I'm going to cut the head off this snake." She spun, a smile on her lips, and strode toward the road.

2

Three hundred yards into the trees lining the park side of the macadam lot, Dan Delo perched high in the canopy. His camouflage wouldn't fool anyone determined to find him, but the *ifrit*, the *djinn*, and Mother Chaos weren't interested in the forest.

The goddess strode toward the road, her stride long and determined. She was the most beautiful being Delo had ever seen—even wrapped in the skin of a human woman. His heart twanged as she reached for the black SUV.

He wanted to go to her, to call out for her attention, but the text he'd gotten from Chaz Welsh's phone had made him wary of Brigitta and Sally McBride—both of whom turned out to be much more than they had pretended. Not *mazzikim*, but an *ifrit* and a *djinn* guardian.

It would be better to have something for them—a gift with which to buy his way back into their good graces. His gaze jumped from Mother Chaos's divine form to the SUV, and a smile flashed on his lips.

He extracted himself from the treetop. Keeping his distance from the road and skimming just above the highest branches, Dan Delo tracked the SUV.

3

The tires of the Suburban shrieked as Toby planted his foot on the accelerator. He held the steering wheel in a white-knuckled grip, fighting to keep the SUV in the lane. "Are they coming?"

"Go!" shouted Eddie. "Go, and don't stop! No matter what, don't stop!"

"She's coming," said Amanda in a voice curiously devoid of emotion. "The redhead."

Toby glanced toward the parking lot, and for a moment, his gaze locked on the eyes of the thing walking toward them. Her eyes brightened, her irises glowing, spinning. A small smile played on her lips; the kind of smile people use when they want to tell an inappropriate joke.

He snapped his gaze away, back to the road ahead of him. The engine of the Suburban roared and whined, its tires scrabbling along the road's surface, fighting for traction.

"Oh, good Christ," whispered Amanda in the same flat voice.

"*GO!*" screamed Eddie.

A strange song began to play in the back of Toby's mind, though he was sure he'd never heard anything like it in his life. It sounded rough and raspy—as though hummed deep in the throat. The tune danced along his neurons, whole circuits coming alive at its call. For reasons he couldn't fathom, he imagined dots of color dancing on a wall.

"Do you hear that?" asked Toby, his voice sounding distant.

"Oh, shit," muttered Eddie.

"Hear what?" asked Mike.

Though he didn't want to, Toby turned his head toward the oncoming thing with red hair and orange eyes. His gaze skimmed past hers, and it was as if he'd touched a live wire. The electric sense of connection with something of vast, ungovernable power jolted him, and, at the same time, the volume of the lament worming into the back of his mind increased. The melody evoked a primal fear, the dread of something unknown, of something moving in the dark, of being stalked by a man-eater. Again, their gazes met and locked on one another. It was as if her eyes had become a powerful magnet, and his focus locked on her eyes.

Where are you heading, gringo? she asked in a sultry voice that sounded from deep inside his own mind. *Where is it you believe you can hide where I can't find you?* She tilted her head to the side, a grin broadening on her lips. *Don't you see me,* chulo?

Why are you doing that?

Doing what, chico mio? Her grin became a lopsided one, and a mechanical, monotone chuckle rang inside his mind as though she stirred his thoughts with a spoon. *Oh! The slang? It's just who I am, Tobes. You don't mind if I call you 'Tobes,' do you?* The dreadful melody playing in his mind took on a spectral wailing, a frightful, eerie quality.

Toby felt time sliding away from him, *his body* sliding away from him. He tore his eyes away from the redheaded fiend's gaze and watched his hands drop away from the wheel and his foot come off the accelerator. He struggled to grasp the wheel, to plant his right foot, and the melody playing in his mind doubled, then trebled in volume. A countermelody began, high-pitched and reedy in opposition to the throaty hum of melody. He fought to control his limbs, and the spectral lament grew stronger until agony speared through his head.

Do not try to resist me, vato. *Je ne pense pas que j'aime ca. No, I don't think I like that at all.* Inteendo?"

His hands twitched, his forearms quaking with the attempt of lifting them, but his efforts only slowed their fall toward his lap. The reedy countermelody demanded his attention. He seemed to sense it through his eyes—blotches of color dancing before his eyes. *Sorry, lady, I only speak English.*

Kei te pai tena, *Tobes. I speak all the best languages, more than enough for both of us.*

Even shaking his head seemed beyond his ability. The song wormed its way into his thoughts, unlaying every impulse, every idea. It sapped his will to resist, scrambled his mental commands to grab the steering wheel, to plant his foot.

"Toby! What the hell are you doing?" cried Mike. "She's almost on us! *Drive!*"

Toby's foot twitched, his toe pointing toward the gas pedal. His hands no longer slowed their fall, only the tips of his fingers fluttering in time to the dirge that rang in the hallways of his mind. As if beyond his control, his head lifted, taking his attention away from his lap, then turned toward *her*. His gaze snaked to her face, circling and circling its boundaries as if trying to prolong the moment. His gaze spiraled inward, toward pits of blazing orange warmth.

When their eyes locked, Toby fell away, sliding toward darkness, toward the relief from his war against the demons, toward bliss.

4

When Toby slumped, Mike had already begun to move, lunging forward, reaching for the steering wheel. When Toby disappeared with a *pop* and a *whoosh* of air, a startled yell escaped him.

"Holy fuck! Holy fuck!" shouted Eddie.

The hysteria in the man's voice—the cold slap of terror—burned through Mike's own fear, his own desire to give in to panic. "Calm yourself, partner. Here's what I need you to do. Slide over here, under my arm, and drive. I can't hold the wheel and climb over the console."

"Where did he go?" asked Eddie.

"Get a move on, Eddie! There are other demons back there who might take an interest in us!"

Eddie jumped, snapping his head to stare out the window. After a heartbeat, he scrambled into the driver's seat and took the wheel.

"You don't understand," mumbled Eddie, but he stopped shouting. He planted his foot, and the Suburban leaped forward like a racehorse coming out of the gate.

"What?" asked Mike. "What's scared you so bad?"

"She's—"

"Was that the scary lady?" asked Amanda.

Eddie swallowed hard and shook his head. "Worse."

"Scary lady?" asked Benny, dragging his gaze away from Shannon's pale face. He nudged Mike's arm and pointed at his cell phone.

Mike swiped the screen of his cell phone and punched in three digits, then turned to the window and began a hushed conversation.

Eddie drew in a deep breath and let it out all at once. "When I was a kid, my dad bought my mom this lamp." He pointed at the lamp with his thumb, staring straight out the windshield. "After a little while, it changed. All the colors, the images portrayed on the shade, they all changed, and when they did, this woman—Abby—started showing herself to me. She only stared at me and smiled her black toothed grin—her obsidian werewolf fangs. A year of fighting later, my dad murdered my mom and committed suicide." Eddie looked down at the lamp and snarled at the hateful thing at his wife's feet. "From the day my dad brought this damn thing home, my life turned hellish." He raised his head and stared at the road ahead. "All of it, the abuse my uncle dished out, the pain, and our troubles as adults..." He shivered and ran his hands through his hair. "Abby caused it all. She's my 'scary lady.'"

"But you seemed to recognize the redhead."

Amanda squeezed Eddie's forearm. "Yeah," he breathed. "She showed up two or three times with Abby. She...never did anything. Well, maybe the once, but if she did, Abby asked her to." He opened his eyes and found Benny in the rearview. "All I'm saying is this: Abby is a nightmare—the worst moment of your life magnified by about ten thousand—"

"Benny's got his own nightmare," said Mike, hanging up his cell.

"—and the redhead is worse yet." Eddie swallowed hard and scratched his head. "I don't know how, but I do. Abby commands more power than the others back there, but the redhead *dwarfs* Abby's power."

Benny threw a sharp glance his way. "How can you gauge how powerful they are?"

Eddie twitched his shoulders up and down. "It's... Look, I don't understand it, but I *do* know the limits of their power."

Benny turned his gaze to the medics working on Shannon in the space behind the seats, then looked at Mike, raising his eyebrows. "What does the ambulance service say?"

"They want us in Cuba, Eddie," said Mike. "They said the best place for them to land is at the helipad there."

"Hold on," muttered Eddie, jamming his foot on the brakes. He turned the SUV across the road and got moving in the opposite direction.

"Is what he claims even possible?" asked Mike.

"I..." Benny took a deep breath and let it out in a slow stream. "I didn't pay much attention to the story, but..." He stared at Eddie, an expression of intense concentration shrouding his face. "Yes..." he whispered. "I can almost see it." He shifted his gaze to Amanda. "Her gift is...*different*. I mean, she can peek behind their masks, but not their power. She can..." Benny gasped and let his eyelids fall shut. "I'm sorry about the baby."

A small cry escaped Amanda's lips, and she covered her mouth with her hand.

Benny's face lit up with wonder. "You fought her? Like, a fist fight? That's amazing."

Eddie nodded. "Abby came after her, and I—" A blush blossomed on his cheeks.

"You tried, Eddie," said Amanda. "You hit her with the chair."

"As much good as that did..."

"And you figured out how to get her off me."

"Listen, you two can talk about that later," said Benny. "The point is that you fought her. *Hand-to-hand.*"

Amanda gave a brief shake of her head. "So?"

Benny laughed. "So? So, she could have ripped this vehicle down the middle. Any demon could. In fact, one of them just picked up a car and smashed another demon with it."

"Abby didn't seem that strong," said Amanda in a small voice.

Benny laughed again. "And that's why it's amazing. I need to think about what that may mean."

"How did you know about the miscarriage?" asked Eddie in a cold, lifeless voice. "What kind of game is this?"

"No game," said Mike. "A demon named Herlequin kidnapped Benny, Shannon, and Toby in 1979. He fed on their terror as he chased them without mercy. They survived, and because of that, they have developed certain abilities. Toby isn't affected by their illusions. Shannon can do her own form of illusion. Benny..." He flashed a lopsided grin at the man beside him. "Benny can read minds, amongst other things."

Amanda and Eddie exchanged a look.

"What? You can believe that a demon has haunted you your entire life because of a fancy lamp, that you can see their true form, that you can assess their power through some kind of psychic instinct, but mind reading is just too hard to believe?"

A rueful grin spread across Eddie's lips, but it faded as he spoke. "Listen, we have to pass by the parking lot again. Everyone keep—"

"Are you sure that's a good idea?" asked Amanda. "What if they see us? What if they *chase* us?"

"What if they've got Toby back there? What if he's their prisoner? Do we stop?" asked Benny of no one.

Eddie's shoulders tensed. "We'll deal with that as it comes. There's no choice. This is the fastest way to the helipad at Cuba Memorial." He glanced at the medics working on the two casualties in the rearview mirror and fed the Suburban's eight-cylinder engine more fuel.

Mike peered ahead. "Benny, we might need the badass you if they come after us."

"Fine," said Benny, his voice seeming to crackle with anger. "I almost hope they do."

"The rest of you keep your eyes peeled. Catch as much detail as you can."

"But why—"

"Information," said Mike. "We are always battling an information deficit. We can't beat what we don't understand, and we need to understand who and what these new threats are—the redhead, for sure, but also this Abby and whatever Brigitta is. We need to understand their real nature."

Amanda shrugged but said no more.

"Get ready," said Eddie. He tightened his grip on the steering wheel, and though he told himself not to, he couldn't resist gawking at the demons as he drove past.

5

Even before Toby opened his eyes, he could see the quality of light had changed. The air smelled different, drier, and flintier than Western New York had a right to be. The music still wailed and cavorted in his mind, but the quiet sound of the wind cut through the melody.

He lay against the side of something warm, almost hot, and it shifted as he moved. A cascade of warm sand fell over his shoulder as the wind gusted. Toby opened his eyes.

Dirty gray clouds stretched from horizon to horizon, and the sun lit them from behind, turning everything a shade of golden-brown. Golden sand stretched as far as he could see, dune after dune after dune, without a single human-made mark. No footsteps in the sand, no roads, no buildings, no signs, nothing.

Sand shifted down over his shoulders again, but this time, without the wind. Toby leaned his head back and looked up into her orange, whirling eyes. "This won't work," he said.

She threw back her head and laughed, but not in the creepy, mechanical monotone she'd used before. She seemed genuinely amused. "Ah, Tobes... Do you know how many men have said something like that to me?"

She is gorgeous. The desert sunlight filtered through the dirty clouds and painted her with colors beyond pale cream, cherry red, and black. He shook his head, unable to trust his voice.

"That's sweet of you to think, *kisa*. But take a guess. It will be illustrative."

"A guess?"

Again, she laughed, and gooseflesh shivered across Toby's back. "A guess at how many men have said 'This won't work' to me. Then take a guess at how many were right." She stood and dusted the sand from her dress.

Toby tore his gaze away from her, choosing to view the desert's grandeur as opposed to her ravenous beauty. "All I meant—"

"No, guess. It'll be fun." She came down off the face of the dune, walking with confidence as though she'd been born to the desert. "Don't you want to have fun, *cazador*?"

Toby frowned. "I don't know what that means."

The woman waved it away. "Guess, and maybe I'll tell you."

Toby blew out a breath, savoring the spicy flavor of the air that took its place. "Ten."

"No, *chavo*. Not ten," she whispered. "More."

"A hundred, then."

She mocked him with a grin. "You're no good at guessing games."

"I don't have any idea, nor do I care what the answer is. I don't even know who you are, lady."

"Oh, Tobes… That hurts my feelings." She plunked into the sand beside him. "You can call me, Lily." She held out one dainty, pale hand as if to shake. "I already know your name. I already know *everything* there is to know about you, *cazador*."

"There's that word again."

She lifted the shoulder nearest him, almost touching his arm with her skin. He shivered at the ethereal sensation of that almost-touch. "It means 'hunter,' Tobes. It's what the *mazzikim* have taken to calling you."

Mazzikim? LaBouche had used the word in relation to the demonic hierarchy, but he hadn't had the time to explain it.

Lily arched an eyebrow at him, then laughed. "That fool?" She sucked her teeth. "He betrayed my daughter. To *you*."

"I—"

"That wasn't a question, boo. I just wanted you to understand that I knew." She leaned closer and bumped him with her shoulder as though they were lifelong lovers. "*Mazzikim* is a word of split meanings. In Hebrew, it means 'harmful spirit,' but in Arabic, it means 'mighty.' In Azerbaijani, it means 'my sweet.' We use it ironically to name the weakest, lowest caste—a pairing of Arabic and Azerbaijani. 'Mighty' because they are the weakest. 'My sweet,' because we disdain their company other than at meal time." She grinned. "But you can't distract me that easily, *chavo*. You said, 'This won't work.' I asked you two questions: guess how many have said the same to me and guess how many were wrong."

Toby let his breath wheeze out of him. "I—"

She lay a perfect pale finger against his lips. "Time for guessing has passed, *mazzikim*. I meant that in the Azerbaijani idiom. How many men have said that to me? Every man who has caught my eye. How many were correct? None of them, Toby. *None* of them." She cocked her head and stared into the distance. "Not even Lilu, though he was not a man."

The music of the desert swelled in volume until Toby thought his skull must fracture under its onslaught.

6

Eddie snapped his attention back to the road, trying to process the snippet of what he'd seen in the parking lot. The redhead had disappeared, but the other three remained as he'd last seen them: a woman with a black snake's tail from the bellybutton down, a woman made from cherry red flame, and Abby.

"Anything, Benny?" asked Mike.

"Discord. They know what the redhead is doing, but I can't…" muttered Benny. "LaBouche is gone."

"Gone?"

"As in 'no more.' The redhead…*ate* his soul."

A grim silence descended on them.

"Well, *that's* new," said Mike.

7

Toby clutched his head and groaned while Lily hummed death's own dirge, somehow humming both the low, throaty part and the reedy, wailing part at the same time—forming discordant, horrible chords that made him wish for deafness. She gazed at him while he thrashed, a faint smile on her lips. Just when he thought the song would drive him crazy, she leaned toward him and patted him on the cheek, smiling.

"It will work, *habibi*. It *always* works."

Toby lay his head back against the sand, eyes pressed shut, mouth drawn into a grim slash. "What the fuck is that?"

"What's what?"

"That song."

"Oh. Never mind that, *neshama*."

Toby opened his eyes and stared up at the golden-brown clouds. Something felt different deep inside. Something felt…open.

"Anyway, Tobes. Do you believe me now? When I say this *will* work?"

Toby drew a deep breath and blew it upward, making his bangs dance. "What I meant was the illusion. I know I'm sitting in the driver's seat of that SUV back in New York. I know this place…" He swept his arms wide. "I know this is a dream you put in my mind."

She leaned forward and chuckled. "Is that what this place is?"

"I survived an attack similar to this one before. When I was a kid—"

"First, it's not an attack, Tobes. Second, you survived a short time in the clutches of a mere *mazzikim*. I am to him as the sun is to a candle. I have but to wish it so for your life to draw to an end. Make no mistake, *motek*. I do not wish you dead. Far from it." She sat back and turned to face him, drawing one beautiful leg toward her groin, kicking the other out straight. "Third, I'm not manipulating your perceptions." She flashed a sunny smile at him. "You should feel honored. You are the first human to set foot in Akkad since I destroyed it."

Toby looked around. "Akkad?"

Lily patted the sand beneath her. "Down there, in the dark. The people of Akkad displeased me, and I buried them for all time. No human will ever find it, no human will ever give their spirits rest." As if to support her point, the wind howled across the top of the dunes.

One corner of Toby's mouth curled up. "Sure. Whatever you say."

"I do not jest."

Toby held up his hands in surrender. "I believe you."

Her face scrunched, her eyes narrowing. "No, I see that you do not. You still consider this is a simple illusion."

Toby swallowed, then forced a smile on his lips. "Uh…"

Lily's eyes whirled and whirled as he stared into them. The creepy little melody swelled in volume once again, chords smashing themselves to pieces against one another. "I am not in the habit of repeating myself. I like you, *cazador*. You have…promise." She held up an index finger. "But don't test my patience." Her voice thundered across the desert.

As if in answer, a sound like that of mighty stones grinding together hissed and spat from behind the dunes. As he watched, Lily began to change, to dissolve at the edges. The color leached out of her hair, her creamy skin faded, and the black of her dress and boots swirled and swirled into a cloud in front of her.

For a moment, Toby could see a creature out of nightmare, a being composed of the blackest of smoke, the densest of shadows, the darkest of hatreds. She pulsed, long chrome talons decorating the tips of her too-long fingers, and the edges of her frayed, wisps curling away into the air only to disappear with a *pop*. He stared, unable to look away, unable to deny what he saw.

Then, she became a column of smoke and shot upward, higher and higher, until she disappeared.

8

The Suburban's tires shrieked and slid as Eddie wrenched the vehicle into a space and slammed on the brakes. Across a double row of parking curbs, the Life Flight helicopter idled on the helipad. Mike leaped from the vehicle and beckoned at the chopper.

A trauma nurse and a doctor dropped to the tarmac from the side door and ran hunched over to the Suburban. "I'm Doctor Walker. What's the nature of the injuries?" asked the doctor, pressing her mouth to Mike's ear to be heard over the helicopter's turbines.

"Bear attack," said Mike. "And a mugging." The story had come from the combat medics, based on the wounds Shannon and Greg bore.

The doctor gave him a strange look, eyebrows quirked. "A bear attack and a mugging?"

Mike leaned toward the doctor and put his hand on the woman's shoulder. "My friend and my lover are dying in the back of this Suburban. I don't care if you believe me or not. Get to work." A rictus of anger settled on his features as the doctor looked at him wide-eyed. After a heartbeat, she nodded and stepped toward the back of the vehicle, and Mike turned to follow.

The doctor stepped up into the back of the SUV and listened to each of the medics' reports. She glanced at Mike, her eyes tracking down to the remaining bits of the black uniform that all but the Mitchells wore. Her gaze tracked to his, questions dancing in her eyes. Mike lifted his hand toward Shannon and Greg, his face finding impassive lines. With a nod, Doctor Walker turned and pushed her way between the medics.

9

Dan watched the drama unfold. He hovered three stories above the ground, in tight against the northern wall of the hospital, wrapped in cold shadow. The Trickster had looked bad, but the other one... He had looked half-dead.

The demon smiled at that assessment.

Delo waited as the helicopter took off and flew north. He paused as the somber group of would-be human hunters climbed back into the big black SUV. He waited as the SUV left the hospital parking lot and drove toward I-86.

He ascended in the column of shadows, then peeled away from the building and followed the Suburban.

10

Lily descended toward her daughter, riding the air as a fish does the currents of the sea. She regained her human form and stood staring at the three abandoned SUVs and the dead humans that littered the parking lot. She turned her head, scanning the dead *mazzikim* lying among them. Her head stopped as she gazed at the demon Lamia had killed, and her sated expression darkened.

"Come, Mistress," Lamia said behind her.

Lilitu turned, watching the snake-tailed *djinn* assist her daughter into a sitting position. Free of her adopted lower caste facade at long last, the *ifrit* burned with a bright, satisfying red. "Naamah, my dear one," she said.

Brigitta's eyes snapped open, and she glared at Lilitu. "Don't call me that! Use the name my father gave me!"

Lilitu narrowed her eyes. "I did. *Lilu* was your father, not that trumped-up charlatan!"

"Herlequin was more parent to me than anyone."

Lilitu's brows twitched, and she turned her face away, her eyes glowing and spinning with power and ire. "A *mazzikim*," she sneered.

Abyzou stepped to her side and lay a hand on her forearm. "Perhaps another time, Mistress?"

Lilitu peeked at her from the corner of her eye. "You *ifrit* always stick together," she murmured. "It was the same with Lilu."

Abyzou dropped both her gaze and her hand.

"Lamia," said Lilitu, turning her ice-cold gaze on the *djinn*. "Would you care to explain why my daughter had to face this *mazzikim* alone?"

Blood suffused Lamia's cheeks and throat. "Mistress... I..." She trembled, a rolling shiver that coursed from the top of her head to the tip of her black tail. "The *mazzikim* took me by surprise. The fury of his attack—"

"I don't believe I asked about the *mazzikim*!" snapped Lilitu.

"I was trying to explain..." Lamia's face paled as Lilitu turned toward her. "I failed you, Mistress." She bowed her head.

"Oh, come off it, *Mother*!" snapped Brigitta. "If you cared, you'd have been here instead of foisting your responsibilities on others."

Lilitu turned her head a fraction of an inch—enough so she could see her daughter—and allowed a lopsided grin to split her face. "How is it you misunderstand the ways of your own kind, Naamah?" she mused.

"I told you not to call me that!"

"It is but your name." Lilitu turned away, refocusing on Lamia. "But you'll not distract me, *mija*." She stepped forward and lay her hand on the back of Lamia's head, curling her fingers into the greenish-black hair. At first, the touch was gentle, but as she bent down to put her face on the level of Lamia's, she jerked her fingers into a fist and pulled the *djinn*'s head back. "Will she, Lamia?"

"No, Mistress. I didn't expect the *mazzikim* to act as he did. I failed to predict—to prepare for—his fury. He took me unaware."

"*And you couldn't beat him!*" shouted Lilitu in a basso voice that seemed to roll to the very edges of the earth and beyond.

Behind her, Brigitta scoffed. "The *mazzikim* have grown here—they've gained power and physical strength. Plus, he had strength born of his insane hatred of Lamia and me. I couldn't best him either."

"Ah, but you did," said Lilitu, glancing at Brigitta. "You bested him—your mistake was not ending his existence when you did." She turned back to Lamia, the planes of her face hard, her mouth set in a ragged moue. She jerked the hand holding Lamia by the hair. "The *mazzikim* beat this one!"

Brigitta pushed herself to her feet, swaying a little. She drew a deep breath and straightened her shoulders. "Leave her be!" she snapped.

Lilitu smiled into Lamia's face, then winked. She released her hold on the *djinn*'s hair and stepped back. By the time she turned to Brigitta, all traces of her smile had disappeared. "You dare command me?"

Brigitta scoffed and folded her arms across her chest.

"Oh, for fuck's sake," said Abyzou. "It's always the same with you two." She sneered at Brigitta. "Mommy didn't treat me right!" She turned and frowned at Lilitu. "And you! Always rubbing against the girl's grain! Always needling her!"

For a moment, Lilitu's face clouded over, but then she smiled, eyes whirling with humor. She threw back her head and laughed.

II

Toby gazed up into the burning sky for a long time, staring at the last point where he'd seen Lily. That he couldn't penetrate her visage scared him more than any subtle threats she may have cast his way.

Away from the constant need to move, to fight, to hunt, his mind turned inward, showing him Scott's lifeless corpse, again and again. He'd been the first of their impromptu cabal to fall. His mind turned to Shannon and Greg for a moment, and he realized the magical thinking he'd embraced—that no one would die to the demons, that there would only be victories—was pure fallacy. *I have to get back home*, he thought.

The sun remained hidden behind the gray clouds, but the heat mounted and mounted as time slithered past. As the air heated, it lost some of its pleasant, spicy aromas and gained more and more of the flinty, burning odors.

Nothing moved in the vast plain of the desert spreading itself before him. He saw no birds, no reptiles, no people, no nothing. Not even the clouds moved with the ever-present wind. Toby's throat got drier and drier as he marked the movement of the golden sun on the canvas stitched from the clouds.

Still, he waited for Lily to return. *What's the point of an illusion where I'm left alone? Where's the terror?*

12

An eerie silence fell over them as if the entire world sensed Lilitu's mounting fury. "Where is the talisman?" she asked in a voice that hissed like a volcano about to erupt.

Abyzou lifted her arm and pointed east. "It is there."

"Have you failed me, as well, Abyzou?" asked Lilitu.

"I…" Abyzou slumped and let her arm drop.

"At least they don't know its importance," said Brigitta.

Abyzou turned to Lilitu, her eyes downcast, but she said nothing.

Lilitu regarded her for a moment, her eyes spinning faster and faster and faster. Then she screamed, and the three abandoned Suburbans exploded, one by one.

13

A sigh gusted out of Toby, and even the passage of air from his lungs hurt the parched tissues that lined his throat. His thirst had continued to grow as the gray clouds dissipated, and the full force of the sun bore down on him. Judging by the sun's passage through the sky, he'd waited against the dune where Lily had put him for three or four hours, give or take.

And still, no Lily.

If I sit here much longer, I'll get heat stroke. Dehydration at the very least. I need water, shelter from the sun.

He turned his head from left to right. It all looked the same—all sand and heat shimmer, without even the hint of mirage to give him a direction to choose. He pursed his lips and let his gaze dart back and forth across the vista before him. His attention shifted from uninteresting point to point, looking for any hint of humanity, any sign of shelter.

But he saw nothing.

With a sigh, he got to his feet and fought his way up the face of the dune against which he had leaned. Lily's tracks through the sand spanned from midway up the dune's front to the bottom where they disappeared.

It's strange that her footprints remain, he thought. He cast his mind back to the nightmare of being chased through Herlequin's woods, the dog-things pounding on his trail. He didn't remember ever seeing a track there. No marks on trees, no scuffs on the roots of trees, nothing. *Strange.*

He climbed to the top of the dune and stared east, then turned and stared west. Neither direction looked any different from the other.

If what she said was true, that this isn't an illusion, and if you leave this place, how will Lily ever find you?

Toby knew he was in trouble, that if Lily chose not to come back, the chances of him living long enough to find help were slim and none. He did not understand where he was—not even which desert she'd plunked him down in—so trying to plan an escape route seemed like a waste of time. His choices were to walk in a random direction or to sit and wait.

With a shrug, Toby set off walking. *Demons lie. It's what they do. Besides, they can't teleport.*

He ignored the little voice in the back of his head that said, *Brigitta can.*

He walked along the ridge of the dune, burning in the desert sun. As the sun climbed higher in the sky, the sand seemed to get brighter and brighter, the air, hotter and hotter. He was forgetting something he'd read about surviving in the desert, but no matter how much he racked his mind, he couldn't come up with it.

The image of Lily distracted him. Her smooth skin, the graceful curves of her cheeks, her glistening lips, her long, luxurious Kool-Aid-red hair that seemed a perfect complement to her black leather dress. Her hips had been narrow and her breasts small. It was as though someone had designed her to Toby's tastes.

He shook his head and set his mind to scan the plain in front of him once more. The dune didn't run straight—it curved to the right with subtle grace—but it didn't much matter until Toby came up with a destination. And it took less effort to walk along the top of the dune where he could see his surroundings.

He walked with his mouth open, breathing in shallow little gasps as the temperature soared. Sitting at the bottom of the dune, he hadn't sweat much, but with the exertion of walking along in the loose sand, he sweat and sweat until the black assault uniform he still wore had soaked through. His thirst grew more and more demanding, shouting louder and louder in his mind until it drowned out his thoughts of home, his grief for Scott.

14

Dan pulled his archaic mobile phone from his pocket, opened it with a practiced flip of the wrist, and quick-dialed Brigitta. He arched his wings and fell into a hover as he waited for an answer. He cupped his hand over the microphone to stave off the wind.

"Hello, you have reached me," said Brigitta. "But, at the same time, you haven't. Leave your beep after the message."

A malignant grin broadened on his face. "Brigitta, this is Dan Delo. I have no idea what lies you may have heard about me, but consider this: someone warned me you were sending LaBouche to get me. After watching the fight at the park, it's clear that he was your traitor. I'm—" A long beep cut him off, and Delo cursed while he quick-dialed again. "Hi, again. Sorry about that. I'm watching the hunters who survived. I'm following them west on I-86, and I'll stick with them all the way home this time. Call me for updates."

15

No one spoke as Mike drove west on I-86.

Benny fumed in the front passenger seat. He glared at Mike every few seconds, sitting with his arms crossed over his chest. "You're wrong, Mike!"

"I don't think so, Benny."

"I want to be there when she…" He squeezed his eyes shut and set his jaw. "When she wakes! I can't believe you don't want to be there for Greg!"

"Benny, we *can't*," said Mike for the third time. "You know that, and you understand why."

"I don't care if the demons find me, Mike," Benny all but snarled. "I'll *fight* them if they come. I'll *kill* them if they try to hurt her!"

"*Think*, Benny! If we go to Rochester, if we hang out in the hospital waiting room, and *they* catch our scent, we lead them straight to Shannon and Greg. And neither of them can fight or kill anything!"

Benny's already pale face whitened further. Anger thrummed in step with Benny's pulse. He glowered at Mike. "I could make you take me there."

Mike threw a glance his way, his expression unreadable. "You could, Benny, but you *won't*. You're not wired that way."

Benny slumped in the seat. "Then let me out! I'll find my own way there."

"That's even more dangerous." Mike tore his gaze away from the highway in front of them. "Look, Benny, you helped define the protocols. SEMPRe people will meet them at the hospital. They will ensure Shannon and Greg get the absolute best care money can provide—"

"It's not the same!"

"*And* they will keep us informed. At least one of them will be a doctor in their own right."

"I don't care!" Benny slumped in the seat, his gaze turning toward the scenery flashing by. "When you got hurt, we came for *you*."

Mike sucked his teeth. "Yeah, you did. But not right away. Toby stayed with me until the ambulance came, but then he and Shannon did what they had to do. They *left* me in the care of the EMTs. They left me and got the hell out of there."

She needs me! Benny wailed.

"Right now, you are *dangerous* to her, Benny. Give it a day or two and SEMPRe will—"

"SEMPRe!" Benny scoffed. "Why do you get to decide for me?"

"Yes, SEMPRe. We set it up for a reason, and we set up these protocols for a reason." Mike grimaced. "Do you really think I *don't* want to turn north? Do you believe for one second that I like the idea of driving away while Greg—" His voice caught in his throat, and he shook his head.

"No," murmured Benny. "It's killing you—I can feel it."

Mike grunted.

"But this is the hardest thing I've ever done, Mike. And that's saying a lot."

"It's what we have to do."

"Yeah," sighed Benny. "What about Scott? Do we just leave his body there in that lot? Food for the demons?"

Mike grimaced at his own helplessness and lifted his shoulder. "We can't go back, Benny. You know that."

16

Lilitu stood in the center of the only intersection with a stoplight within the Oneka Falls town limits. Her gaze tracked from left to right, bouncing from face to face, making slow progress. With a grunt, she stalked away from the others.

Her eyes narrowed at the expression worn by one of the *mazzikim* who gawked at her. They couldn't tell her from a human woman using their eyes, but they understood her nature, nonetheless. They knew *who* she was.

The demon staring at her didn't lower his eyes, didn't express awe as they owed her. A slow, lopsided grin spread across her face. "Hello, *chingado*," she whispered as she drilled into his gaze with her own. Her nostrils flared, and above her, lightning crackled across the sky. A look of abject terror settled on the *mazzikim's* face, and his head jerked hard to the left as though he were trying to turn away.

Lilitu lifted a finger and wagged it at the demon, never blinking, never shifting her gaze. She could taste his terror as she sucked bits of his soul into her core, but she didn't want him dead. *He will serve me better as an example*, she thought as she closed her eyes. Twenty paces away, the demon's bladder let loose, but he only stood there, staring at those around him with no sign of recognition.

Lilitu spun to face her daughter. "You've screwed the pooch, here, Naamah."

Brigitta loosed a weary sigh. "*Brigitta*. And no, I didn't."

"But you have, *Naamah*." Lilitu lifted her arm out to her side and swept her hand to encompass the town. "These *mazzikim* no longer know their place. These humans…" Lilitu shook her head. "Can't you see what you are breeding here? Can't you feel the changes to both the *mazzikim* and the humans in your little town?"

Brigitta looked at the mixed groups of humans and demons, recognizing the corrupted nature of the men and women who chose to partner with the demons. "And why not? These humans have proved their worth. The demons, too."

Lilitu cocked her head to the side, a nasty smile on her lips. "Then why haven't you raised them up? Why have you pretended at being a *mazzikim*, rather than elevating the best of them?"

Brigitta dropped her gaze to the macadam with a slight shake of her head.

"Oh, of course!" sneered Lilitu. "Too busy pretending to be one of them. Lamia, too!" She shifted her gaze to the *djinn*, and Lamia whimpered. She turned to Abyzou and stared into the *ifrit's* fiery eyes. "And you," she hissed.

Abyzou inclined her head. "Yes."

"Oh, come off it!" snapped Brigitta. "Whatever has happened, it's *your* fault, *Mother*."

With a faint smile on her glistening lips, Lilitu turned once more to her daughter. "My fault, *mija*?"

Brigitta sneered, but her lips trembled. "You abandoned everyone while you played your little games in New York City."

Lilitu laughed, but it sounded mechanical, like a machine run amok, a monotone *heh-heh-heh* that never varied in rhythm or pitch, each syllable equidistant from the next. As she did, she walked closer and closer to Brigitta. When she was within arm's reach, she stopped walking and stood there laughing like a broken robot while her daughter squirmed, her gaze dancing from place to place—anywhere other than Lilitu's face.

Lilitu snapped her mouth shut, and for a few heartbeats, the mechanical laughter continued, puffing her cheeks out with each *heh*. When the laughter ended, an utter silence descended on the intersection—the car noises, the angry shouts of motorists trapped in a long line of traffic, the murmuring of people and demons on the street, all of it falling away. She lifted her hand, smiling a little as her daughter flinched. "You are right to fear me, Naamah. You have earned my wrath in this debacle. From the very first moment you arrived here, pretending to be that charlatan's daughter, pretending to be *one of them*, my anger has grown and grown. My *outrage*, my hurt."

Brigitta's gaze snapped to Lilitu's. "*Your* hurt? *Your* outrage?" She took a step closer, her fingers hooking into claws of red flame. "*YOU FUCKING ABANDONED ME!*"

"Did I, *hija mio*?" Lilitu shifted her gaze first to Lamia and then to Abyzou. "Did I?"

"Yes!"

Lilitu lifted her chin and narrowed her eyes. "Let me tell you something, Naamah…" She sighed and shook her head. "No, you won't listen." Then, as if dismissing her daughter's existence, Lilitu turned to Abyzou and clenched her jaw. "You talk to her, Abyzou. She listens to you." Lilitu raised a hand. "I've got to get back, anyway. He will walk himself to death if I don't."

Brigitta sucked her teeth and turned away.

"I'll deal with Toby Burton. You three work on corrupting the others."

Abyzou nodded. "We will see to it."

Still standing in the middle of the intersection with townspeople gaping at her, Lily smiled and turned into a bugbear of black smoke that slowly faded away into nothingness, her evil laughter echoing in her wake.

17

Shannon felt terrible—worse than she'd ever experienced in her life. At the same time nauseated, headachy, and assaulted by wave after wave of excruciating pain. The very air surrounding her seemed to attack her nerves, thrumming and stabbing at her ears. Worse yet, she was both shivering and burning hot at the same time.

She tried to open her eyes, and blistering, searing pain erupted from the left side of her face. She groaned and tried to raise her hand to her cheek, but it wouldn't lift higher than a few inches from the cold vinyl it rested atop.

"Doctor Walker? She's coming to," said a gruff male voice Shannon didn't recognize.

"Let me in there," said a woman.

Shannon's right eyelid opened, and a bright light seared her retina. It hurt as though the woman had shoved a hot poker in her eye. She moaned and tried to close her eye, and when that didn't work, she tried to turn her head, but she couldn't do that either.

"Relax, Mrs. Benjamin. Do you remember what happened to you?"

Shannon squeezed her eyes shut. The image of something dark colored and powerful charging at her flashed through her mind's eye. He'd slammed her into the Suburban, and then everything had gone black. "Something...attacked...me. Big. Claws and teeth."

The doctor gazed into Shannon's right eye, something unreadable in her expression. "Do you remember what?"

Shannon squeezed her eyes shut. All of her hurt, all of her seemed ripped apart, scattered, broken. The only thing in New York State she imagined had the ability to do that much damage was a black bear. "Black...bear."

"Uh-huh."

A machine started beeping at a frantic pace somewhere off to Shannon's left, and she sensed the doctor moving away.

"He's crashing!" the doctor said.

Who? Shannon wanted to ask. She opened her eyes, and again, only the right eye responded. She caught a glimpse of sunlight and blue sky when she rolled her eye toward her feet, but she couldn't turn her head to see anything on her left side.

The sounds of a frantic medical intervention played out on her blind side, and Shannon let her eye drift closed. *Who else got hurt?*

She prayed it wasn't Benny—from the sound of it, the chances of whoever it was surviving to the hospital seemed grim. *Benny?* She tried to send the thought far and wide, but the effort brought on a wave of agony the likes of which she'd never experienced. "Who?" she muttered.

Shannon tried to turn her head, pushing against the red thing that sandwiched her head. *Who is it?*

The flurry of activity died down, and the doctor returned to her side. She cracked her eye open and peered at the woman's face. "Is…"

"He's out—"

"He?"

"Your friend." Doctor Walker leaned closer. "Not your husband."

A sigh of relief gusted out of Shannon, followed at once by an intense sensation of guilt.

"As I was saying, he is out of immediate danger. Your friends say someone mugged him in the same park where a magic bear attacked you." Her eyebrow lifted.

Shannon blinked. "Must have been in another part of the park."

"But you know him? Joe Stephens?" She glanced around. "Is that what your friends called him?"

Shannon nodded against her restraints. "He's a friend. Can you… Can you tell me what happened to him?"

The doctor peered down at her for a moment, then turned and glanced across the helicopter. "Yes, I can do that. His attacker stabbed him between the ninth and tenth rib, and I'll bet you a steak dinner it ruptured his spleen. He's lost a lot of blood and has been unconscious the entire time he's been in my care. Your friends said his attacker clubbed him in the back of the head, and without scans, I can't speak to any potential damage there."

Shannon let her good eye slip closed.

"How do you feel, Mrs. Benjamin?"

"Horrible. I can't see from my left eye."

"It's covered in a patch. I don't want you to try opening it. I want you to stay as still as possible." She fiddled with something on Shannon's left side. "You are lucky to be alive."

"What…"

"What are your injuries?" asked Doctor Walker with a nod. "It's not a short list, however strange it might be to receive such wounds from a bear." She pointed as she spoke. "Lacerations down your sides, puncture wounds in the shoulders. The 'bear' tore the flesh from your left cheek and fractured both your cheekbone and the orbital bone of your left eye socket. You have—"

"Enough for now," said Shannon. "No more."

"The good, then. No bite marks, so no need of a rabies shot." Doctor Walker treated her to a single nod. "The thing is, Mrs. Benjamin, I don't think these wounds came from a bear."

Shannon snorted. "You don't say! I'd have never guessed…"

"Yeah. My husband says I have all the subtlety of a charging rhino." The woman smiled. "Occupational hazard, I expect."

Shannon let her right eye slide closed.

"Do you want to tell me what really caused these wounds?"

"You wouldn't believe me."

For a moment, Doctor Walker didn't reply. Then she brushed Shannon's hair away from her eyes. "It might surprise you. You see, I grew up in Oneka Falls in the seventies."

Shannon's eye flew open. Doctor Walker leaned over her, staring into her face.

Yes. I remember you, Shannon, sent Doctor Walker.

18

Why don't you do it? asked a thin voice at the back of Benny's mind. *Why do you always defer to Toby or Mike? They don't have your abilities—hell, Mike has no ability! You are more suited to making the decisions.*

Benny's lip curled at the greenery flashing by his window. The voice spoke the truth. Even as kids, even playing at *his* house, Mike always took charge. Mike was always the squad leader, the lieutenant. He had *always* expected Benny to follow Mike's orders. *I could make him go along with me this time. It would be easy.*

Then why don't you? asked the reedy voice.

He heaved a sigh and willed himself to go numb, to stop thinking, to stop arguing with himself.

Don't be weak.

"What about Toby?" Benny asked.

Mike glanced at him and lifted his shoulder. "I'm all ears if you've got an idea." He rolled the fingers of his free hand. "Can you…"

Benny heaved a sigh. "I can try, but I'm a mess, and I have no idea where to look."

"Try," said Mike with a quick nod.

19

Mike stole a peek at Benny. His friend still slumped against the passenger door, his shoulders turned so his back faced Mike. *I should say something.*

Sure, you should. You've always been so good at 'saying something,' haven't you?

The thoughts brought a shiver of fear, but also a shudder of anticipation. Mike knew the voice; he knew it well. The voice belonged to his old drinking buddy—that puppet master that lifted his arm and poured alcohol down his gaping maw.

God, I want a drink, he thought.

His mouth watered at the prospect.

20

"She's such a bitch!" snapped Brigitta, turning back toward the other two.

"Don't say such things, Mistress."

Naamah rolled her eyes at the whine in Lamia's voice. "Your Sally is showing, Lamia."

Abyzou tutted and tapped her foot. "Naamah, no—"

"I'll take it from her, Abby, because I must." She glided forward a menacing step. "But I don't have to take it from you!"

Abyzou narrowed her eyes. "Remember your place!" she snapped. "What is wrong with calling you by the name your mother gave you?"

"I repudiate that name! I reject it!"

"Such a petulant child. I'd have thought you would have matured at least a little in all these centuries."

Brigitta glowered at her. "Then turn your back on me, as your mistress has! Task this one with watching out for me again and go back to your own games!"

"Adopting their form and living amongst the *mazzikim* for such an extended time has taught you bad habits, generated weaknesses within you. You'd do well to remember who is eldest here." For a heartbeat's time, Abyzou's flames grew brighter, almost bright enough to rival the sun, and Lamia shaded her eyes. As Brigitta's own fire began to brighten in kind, Abyzou sighed. "Can you stop?" she asked in a soft voice. "Can you not try?"

"Why is it always me? Why am I always the one to stop, to try?"

"Come, come," cajoled Abyzou. "You are as my own flesh, my own daughter to me. Have I mistreated you? Name my crimes."

Brigitta stamped her foot. "You *always* take her side!"

"I *see* both sides, and I tell either of you when you are acting like a spoiled adolescent, but I try to do so in private."

"Such as now?" scoffed Brigitta.

"Yes, *Brigitta*. Just like now."

Brigitta threw a glance at Lamia, but the *djinn* had focused her attention on the pavement.

"You say your mother abandoned you. I say you also abandoned your mother. That makes you even, and it's up to you to decide whether you waste this time together, too."

"I abandoned *her*?"

Abyzou said nothing, only crossed her arms and bored into Brigitta's gaze with her own until the younger *ifrit* turned and took a few steps away. Then Abyzou turned her focus on Lamia. "How far you let yourself go…"

"I wonder how well you would have done had Hera murdered your children instead of mine." Lamia drew herself up on her tail to tower over Abyzou.

Abyzou stepped closer, and her fiery substance burned brighter still. She glowered at the *djinn*, sneering and jutting out her chin. "Not all of us were so blessed," she hissed. "Do you also need—"

"Ladies!" Brigitta shoved between them. "Remember where you are! And for my mother's sake, speak English! No one has spoken Akkadian on this planet for centuries— and never on this continent."

Abyzou stared at her a moment through narrowed eyes, then she nodded once and walked away.

"Really, Lamia. Do you know no better?"

Lamia hung her head and settled closer to the ground. "My apologies, Mistress."

21

As the Suburban passed over the state line into Pennsylvania, Benny grimaced. With each mile marker that blurred past, he felt worse and worse—as if he were abandoning Shannon, throwing her to the wolves. It didn't matter that the SEMPRe operatives had already arrived in Rochester, had already assumed his and Mike's alter-identities so the hospital could list them as family. It didn't matter that an entire tactical unit in plain clothes stood ready to surround and infiltrate Strong Memorial Hospital. It didn't matter that they carried enough firepower to repel whole groups of demons without taking casualties.

He peeked at Mike surreptitiously. The man stared out the windscreen, his eyes darting from landmark to landmark as they zipped past them. *It would be so easy.* Frustration nipped on the heels of the thought—he'd entertained the idea far too many times in the last hour and a half. It was a purposeless idea, a worthless idea.

But still, said that thin voice in his head. *You* could *do it. Mike would never even realize a change was made. You could make sure of that.*

In the backseat, Eddie Mitchell cleared his throat.

I wonder how deep their power runs, Benny thought. *Can you hear my thoughts, Mr. Mitchell?* He didn't send the words; he only thought them. He glanced over the seat at the Mitchells—both seemed lost in thought. *Should I take a peek? Could I sift their minds and know for sure where things stand?*

The answers to those questions were both in the affirmative, but Benny didn't want to invade their privacy.

22

As if no other business could thrive along I-86, bar after bar after bar blurred by as they drove west. The signs flashed with bright neon colors, colorful paintings of scantily clad women, logos of beers and whiskeys. Mike tried not to notice them, tried to ignore them when he did, but it was getting harder and harder to force his mind to skip past them.

That his mouth watered every time bothered him more than the signs, however.

It's been years! he raged at himself. *And the stress has been overwhelming many a time. So why now? Why this sudden wish to sink into the oblivion of drink?*

Having a drink or two to calm down is an age-old practice. And what would be wrong with that? Having just a drink or two?

Mike wagged his head from side to side.

"You okay?" asked Eddie. "Getting tired of driving?"

"No, I'm fine," said Mike, watching as a sign drew closer. On the sign was the image of a Viking, complete with a horned helmet. The caption read, "There are no strong drinks, only weak men." He caught himself grinning at the tagline and snarled.

23

"What?" asked Shannon.

I remember you. Doctor Walker darted a glance over her shoulder. "I grew up in Oneka Falls. I had my own disasters in 1979, but a person living in Oneka Falls couldn't avoid following what happened to you and your friends. And I remember your picture in the paper a few years ago." She pressed her lips together. *Not only because we are both from Oneka Falls.*

"Are you…" Shannon swallowed hard. *Are you going to report me to the authorities?*

Doctor Walker jerked her head back as if Shannon had slapped her. *What? No! No, of course not. No one kidnapped me and chased me through the Thousand Acre Wood as you were, but my husband, who's also from Oneka Falls, rescued me from a similar fate that fall.*

"Your husband?"

Doctor Walker nodded. "Yes. I was involved with the boy next door." She grimaced. *Only he wasn't a boy.*

A demon?

"That's what my husband says. His name's Sean. Do you remember him? Sean Walker?"

"He was older than me, but I bet…my friends would remember him."

Benny Cartwright and Toby Burton.

Shannon peered up at her, reading her eyes for duplicitousness. "Yes," she whispered.

Doctor Walker lay her hand on Shannon's shoulder. "My maiden name is Benchly. Kristy Benchly."

Shannon remembered her—a pretty blonde who dressed slutty.

"Don't worry about a thing, hon," said Kristy. "I'll take care of everything." She glanced across the helicopter at Greg. "I assume he's…"

"He's not from Oneka Falls, but he would benefit from your attention." Shannon fought the woozy feeling that was stealing over her. *He's Greg Canton, from Genosgwa.*

Kristy patted her shoulder. "I understand."

24

Naamah watched with amusement as overloaded cars sped toward the town limits. The story of her mother's little show downtown had spread like wildfire, and now the weakest of the *mazzikim* were heading for the hills. She knew it was a bad idea to let them go, that panic would only breed more panic, but she found she had a hard time summoning the energy to care.

"Are you going to allow this?"

With a sigh, Naamah met Abyzou's gaze for a moment, trying to convey boredom, then turned to Lamia. "Stop them," she said.

The *djinn* performed her unique bow—torso hunching, scaled tail slithering back to give the appearance of lowering her head. "How…*persuasive*…may I be, Mistress?"

"They are not to leave. If that means you have to eat, digest, and shit them into your garden, so be it."

"Yes, Mistress," said Lamia before slithering toward the town hall building.

Abyzou stared at her as she issued the orders, she could feel the *ifrit's* stare as though it burned.

"What now, Aunt?"

"Nothing. I like to watch you work. You remind me of myself as a youth. Why do you pretend not to enjoy it?"

Still facing away from Abyzou, Naamah rolled her eyes. "Why do you have Chris Stanton buying land for the foundation?"

Abyzou chuckled. "There's no harm in enjoying the power of command, girl. No harm in enjoying the status your caste and pedigree imply."

"At first, I thought it was a game you were playing with a pet or something. But I don't think that's all of it."

"You've always been bright, Naamah. Always a sound tactician, but I fear your time among the *mazzikim* has blunted your mind. Such backsliding is not irrevocable, provided we address it."

Naamah raised both hands to scrub her forehead. "Are you going to play games all day, or will you eventually answer me?"

Abyzou laughed aloud, filling the small downtown area with sounds of chainsaws blunting themselves on iron. "Consider this hint: your mother wants the land accessible."

Naamah squinted at the sidewalk, snarling at her shadow. "Has it come to that?"

"There's no sense leaving the circle unprotected. Plus, this way, it's ready should we need to bring more across. The hunters have been quiet of late, but they haven't quit. This morning's fun underscores that point."

Naamah grimaced but nodded.

25

Toby's gait had decayed in his slog across the burning dunes. His steps had lost their crisp precision, and the tracks trailing him like a balloon's string painted the real picture of his deterioration. His tracks appeared almost as if someone had crawled around on his knees, rather than a man walking upright. Tracks from his left and right feet drifted in and out of parallel with one another, sometimes giving the appearance that his feet wanted to travel in different directions.

His lips burned, as did his cheeks, but his forehead ached from within and without. The nerves in his throat screamed and burned and stung and throbbed. When he thought at all, he spent his energy picturing the ruin of his throat— minced meat, roadkill, hamburger.

Bleary-eyed from the brightness of the burning sun, almost blinded by the constant pressure of light reflected from the golden sand and the threat of wind-blown grit, Toby stepped wrong and pitched down the dune face, tumbling ass over teakettle for fifteen yards. When he came to rest, he lacked the strength to fight his way to his feet. His breath whistled in and out in rapid, shallow gasps. A blessed coolness descended on him, and he sighed with pleasure at the shade.

"You will die out here if you keep this up, Tobes." Her voice lilted, almost mocking in tone.

His right index finger twitched.

"The *Bādiyat al-Shām* does not suffer fools. What the hell were you trying to do? Commit suicide?"

Toby groaned.

"Ask me for water, *vato*."

Through a herculean effort of will, Toby cracked his eyelids open. Lily stood over him, one black-leather chrome-heeled boot to either side of his hips. She'd inclined her head to look at him, and her hair cascaded toward him, the sunlight seeming to ignite it into cherry red fury.

She sucked her teeth. "I can give you water, *bizcocho*, but you have to ask me for it."

Toby took a deep breath and let it sigh from him.

"Is it so hard? To ask me for help?"

I didn't give up in those three days Herlequin had me, he thought. *I didn't give in.* He groaned and rolled to his side, where he rested a moment before pulling himself out from between her boots and into a seated position. He drew his legs under him and wobbled to his feet.

Lily hadn't moved—she still stood with one foot to either side of the drag marks he'd made pulling his legs from beneath her. Her face was a study in irritation, her eyes spinning, nostrils flared. "Are you rejecting me, *chingado*?"

Toby gazed at her a moment, her features seeming to warble in and out of phase with reality. He opened his mouth to speak, but it seemed like too much effort. He shook his head.

"Then, *ask* me, *ese*. Ask me for water before you die out here."

Toby stepped past her and began to climb to the dune's ridge again.

She snapped her tongue on her teeth behind him, and the sand slithered as she turned to follow him. "Don't be stupid, Tobes. I can give you water. I can keep you alive. Just fucking say something."

It seemed to Toby that his answering her had more importance to her than the actual request for water. "Am I going the right way?" he croaked, wincing at the sandpaper feel of his tongue in his mouth.

Behind him, she sighed, and it sounded more akin to what a teakettle might emit than a human sigh. "The right way to where? But to answer your question, no, climbing to the top of the dune is not a good idea. No shade, no *chance* of shade. Going anywhere in daylight is a horrible idea, Tobes. This desert will crush you in the daylight."

He chuckled. "Haven't seen any Motel 6s. Sorry."

"Can't you ask for help, *motek*? For me? I can't do anything if you don't ask. It's the rules."

Rules set by who? Toby wondered. He stopped and turned to face her. "Point me in the right direction."

For a moment, her face worked with emotions—hope, anger, desperation, lust—then her expression hardened into a thing of granite. She stared and stared at him as the sun tried to burn them both to cinders. Her pale skin reddened as he watched.

She shrugged. "Close enough for a first step," she muttered. "But I can't let you die so soon." She turned and waved her hand, murmuring, "*Kaṣû ṭābu mû.*" The face of the dune beside her distended, forming a bowl arising from the sand. In it, water bubbled as though from out of the air. "Clean water from the Tigris, Tobes. I have made it safe to drink."

"From the Tigris? The river in Mesopotamia?"

"From the Akkadian Empire of old."

Once his eyes found the impromptu cistern, he couldn't tear his gaze away, but he heard absolute satisfaction in her voice. "And if I drink it? What will I owe you?"

She laughed, her voice burbling like a brook overflowing with spring runoff. "Nothing, Tobes. This is a gift, freely given. I give it because you have asked me for help—" He opened his mouth to object, and she raised her hand, traffic-cop style. "No, you didn't ask me for water. You asked for a direction to walk in, and for our first bargain, it is enough to satisfy the rules of the game."

"The game?"

She regaled him with a Cheshire grin. "All things are games, *chavo*."

"Who are you?" he asked in the weariest tone he could summon.

"If I believed you wanted to know, I'd tell you, but we're not there yet. For now, I'll reiterate: Call me Lily."

"Maybe I asked the wrong question," muttered Toby, staring at the water. "I should have asked what you are, not who."

Again, her burbling laugh surrounded them. "Oh, that's different. I'm the devil, Tobes. Plain and simple. Now, drink the water before it evaporates, and I have to summon more."

Toby released a sigh, and a smile crooked his lips. He sank to his knees and drank.

Chapter 2
Sunday

I

Mike tossed and turned until the wee hours of the morning. Worry about Greg gnawed at him, and Scott's death filled him with sadness, but more than either of those things, the impromptu bar his housemates kept in the living room kept him awake, screeching at him, kicking at him, scratching at his mind, his resolve.

That, and he was sweltering under the blankets.

His mouth watered just thinking about the bottles of alcohol a few steps away. Bottles of Johnny Walker Swing, Tanqueray Gin, Plantation Rum, and Skyy Vodka waited for him, taunted him.

He flung the covers away and rolled to his side. *I owe it to Greg to keep it together*, he thought. *I can't let myself go.*

The image of Greg lying bleeding on the macadam flashed through his mind. *What will one drink hurt?* The voice that uttered the thought in his mind sounded like Sally McBride's, and Mike's lip curled. *Fuck you, Sally.*

He opened his eyes to examine the clock—for what seemed like the three hundredth time since he crawled into bed. *Five o'clock. Close enough for government work. I'll make breakfast for everyone. At least that will give me something to do other than lie here awake, staring at the ceiling and thinking about drinking.*

He swung his legs to the floor and sat up, stretching and yawning.

Would an early morning drink hurt? Who would know?

2

Toby awoke as the sun woke the sky, blazing across the eastern horizon, murdering the darkness like a spear through its black heart. Overnight, the temperature had plummeted. Cold had assaulted him—invaded him—making sleep impossible until the wee hours when his exertions and exposure to the desert sun had caught up with him.

He slept in the sand, right at the base of a dune so that its eastward face loomed above him, and the dawning sun lit it like a movie screen. For a moment, shadows formed by clouds dancing in front of the sun drifted across the face of the dune, painting an abstract mural of darker and lighter shades of gold.

As he watched, the mural resolved into an image of her face—Lily's face. The image winked.

"And you expect me to believe this isn't all in my head?" he muttered.

"Yes!" boomed the basso voice of the mural. Lily's image contorted until it appeared to look down on him from the dune's face. "Because that is the truth."

"Did you watch over me all night? How cute."

With a ripping sound, the image made of shadows abandoned the face of the dune. It shrank until the walking silhouette was human-sized, then the air gave a soft *pop,* and Lily stood before him. She smiled at his expression. "*Ay, que chulo,*" she said.

"More Spanish? Don't speak a word." Toby stood and brushed himself off, more to have something to do than as preparation for the day. His calendar had only one event planned: walking. "You could have at least brought me a bagel."

"I look like some kind of waitress to you, *montro*?"

Toby shook his head. "Not like any waitress I've ever known." He glanced at her, and her thousand-watt smile almost knocked him over.

"You say the sweetest things, Tobes." Lily patted his cheek with fingers that felt as hot as lava. "Hungry?"

Toby scanned the horizon in all directions, hoping the morning light would show him something the evening light had not. "Famished."

Lily stepped closer. "Ask me."

He turned to gaze at her. Her chrome-heeled boots made her tall, even in the loose sand. Then again, the stiletto heels didn't sink into the sand. "No."

"Aw, *vozlyublenny*, don't make this hard. You're hungry, I can help. *Let* me help."

Toby narrowed his eyes. "Why do I have the feeling that your help comes at a price?"

Lily flashed a muted smile at him, then began to hum. The song made Toby's skin crawl—an eerie, mournful dirge of woe and gnashing of teeth. Her lips parted, and he could have sworn she began to hum two separate melodies at once, the notes of one lay intermingling with the notes of the other strain, forming discordant jangles in his brain.

"What are you doing?"

She tipped him a wink but didn't stop humming.

Toby squinted at her for a moment, standing still despite the urge to move, to dance, to whirl to the tempo of the ghostly elegy. As the two songs built toward a rhythmic crescendo, the melodic dissonance also increased, but instead of wearing on his nerves, it drew him in, and part of Toby listened with an intensity reserved for hunting demons. *Whatever that shit is, I can't stand around listening to it.* He had no idea where the idea had come from, but he trusted it instinctively.

He spun in the soft sand and began walking east. He walked without thinking, without plan or purpose, only walking away from Lily and her strings-attached offers of help.

His first steps were more like stumbling lurches than the smooth gait of a sober man. Despite the increasing distance, the volume of the weird songs didn't decrease. It was as though Lily walked right behind him. Prickly fear refused to allow him to look back, though he heard no footsteps following his own.

3

Anger throbbed in time with his pulse, and Benny couldn't do a thing about it. He'd tried to let it go, but as soon as he'd almost calmed down, the angry voice in his head returned. He hadn't slept a wink between worrying about Shannon and his mounting fury at Mike.

What made it all worse is that everything Mike said rang with truth. Benny couldn't think of a single thing to refute his arguments. Add to that the fact Toby hadn't come home—hadn't called, hadn't *anything*—and Benny felt isolated, alone.

He'd tried to reach Shannon's mind numerous times since they'd loaded her into the Life Flight helicopter, but either she was unconscious or too far away—or Benny's concentration was off. The reports they'd gotten through SEMPRe hadn't done much to alleviate his stress.

He flung the covers away and jerked on a pair of jeans and a T-shirt. He didn't bother with shoes or socks, despite the morning chill. His stomach rumbled, but he'd never felt less like eating in his life.

Eat, Benny. Maybe it will make you feel better.

That reedy voice in the back of his mind had grown stronger during the long, fruitless hours of the night. He was used to strange voices in his head, and he was used to distinguishing his own thoughts from those of others, but that thin voice confused him. It seemed like a part of him, but the things it said...

Hey, it's your brain, dude. Don't blame me if you're weird.

Maybe I'll make breakfast for the house. Shaking his head, Benny walked toward the kitchen.

That sounds like something a servant would do. Are you everyone's servant, or are they yours?

Mike stood at the stove, his back to the door leading to the great room. He seemed lost in what he was doing, standing with his head down, staring at the pan of eggs that burned merrily in a puddle of browned butter. Black bacon lay on a wad of paper towels next to the trash can, filling the air with the stench of charred meat.

Benny walked to the center of the room, staring at the back of Mike's head, before the man noticed him. "Couldn't sleep?" asked Benny when Mike darted a glance over his shoulder.

"No," said Mike. "Had the idea to make breakfast, but I'm screwing that up pretty good if I do say so myself." He wagged his head toward the bacon. "Never got the hang of bacon."

Benny squinted at him. *It would be so easy. Just a pruning here, a tuck there, a new connection next to it, and then Mike becomes my pawn.* He could see the steps drawn out like a circuit diagram in his mind. *Mike would never know.*

Benny took a deep breath and got to work.

4

Shannon groaned as consciousness returned. All of her hurt; all of her throbbed and pounded. She felt like puking, and her mouth tasted like the floor of the monkey cage at the zoo. A horrible pounding threatened to rattle her brains out of her head, and she thrashed for the call button for several breaths before realizing the pounding came from inside her head.

The left side of her face was covered with thick gauze, and she felt similar lumps down her sides and belly. Her wounds ached and burned at the same time, but her brain felt numb, separated from the rest of her.

She peered one-eyed at the room, which was standard hospital fare done in creamy tan and stark white. A large window showed her the early morning sun rising above the low skyline surrounding the hospital. To her left, a curtain was drawn across the room, hiding the door.

Shannon found the call button and pressed it. Moments later, a titanium-clad nurse poked her head around the curtain. "Need something, Mrs. Benjamin?"

"What day?"

The nurse smiled and came around the curtain. "It's the day after your encounter." She cocked her head to the side, her smile beaming and bright. "Was it *really* a bear?"

Shannon grunted.

"Can I get you a fresh pitcher of water?"

"How is my friend? Joe Stephens?"

"I'll have to check. Water?"

"How badly am I hurt?"

The nurse's smile turned professional. "That's something to discuss with your doctor."

"Who is?"

"Doctor Walker. She was your Life Flight physician."

"Yes, I remember."

"She took an interest in your case. Admitted you under her care."

Shannon closed her eyes and rubbed her temples. "Headache."

"I'll just bet. Can I get you some cold water?"

Suppressing a sigh, Shannon nodded. "When does Doctor Walker make her rounds?"

"I'm not sure when she will be in. She doesn't do rounds, per se. She only has a few patients, and with being on call for Life Flight…"

"I understand. Please tell her I'd like to see her as soon as possible."

"I'd be happy to. In the meantime, there's someone in the waiting room who'd like to see you. Feeling up to it?"

Benny? Shannon sent. "Who?"

"Your husband, silly. I'll go get him."

Shannon nodded and closed her eyes.

5

The twisted little clash of melodies wormed inside his head as he walked, and though Toby tried to ignore it, he found himself anticipating the song, the rhythmic changes, the dissonant notes. It was as if he'd heard the song before, as though the song had grown into his personal earworm.

"Where are you going?"

Toby flinched. The words had been whispered in his ear, like a lover's endearment. "I'm getting out of here."

"Are you sure that's the right way?"

"I suppose you would tell me if I asked you for help?"

"No. Not yet. We have things to do out here."

"Then, does it matter if I walk in the wrong direction?"

Lily laughed her mechanical machine-gun laugh that went on and on without pausing for breath for the time it took him to walk twenty paces. "It doesn't matter to *me*, *chavo*. I'm immortal."

Toby hesitated mid-step. "Are we really in a desert, then?" Lily stepped out of thin air beside him, and he felt the warm rush of the air she displaced. She was naked from head to toe, and Toby couldn't help but gawk at her.

A little smile appeared on her lips, and her orange eyes took a break from whirling and twirling so that they could sparkle with amusement. "See something you like?"

Toby gulped a breath. "Jesus Christ," he murmured.

"Not quite. I didn't care for that one. So holy, so righteous." She stroked her sides, going from her ribcage to her hips. "He could never rock your world the way I can. I'm better than any man, woman, or drug you've ever had, Tobes. I can make you forget everything that happened to you as a child—and you will thank me for it. I can give you food. I can give you water. I can give you anything you want. All you have to do is ask for it."

Toby's gaze traversed her perfect creamy skin, and while it did, his face burned as though he had a fever. Her breasts rode high on her chest, small and round and perfect. She had thin hips and long, beautiful legs.

"*Anything* you want, *papi*."

He tore his gaze away. Even her cartoon-hair seemed sexy. "You are going to get a sunburn, walking around like that."

"Want to bet?"

"Could you..."

"Don't you like me, *vato*? Am I not your type? I can appear however you'd like. Just—"

"Just ask," he said. "I know."

She lay her hand on his arm, and the first thing he noticed was the heat. The desert air was already almost too hot to breathe, but standing next to her was akin to sitting in an open-air forge. Beyond that, his body reacted to her touch as if he had been waiting his entire life for Lily to appear.

"Oh, that's sweet, Tobikins." She reached up and patted his cheek, letting her blood-red painted nails trail lasciviously behind.

"I didn't say anything," he said.

She flashed a mischievous grin and put her other hand on the waistband of his jeans. "Didn't you?"

"What the hell are you?" he gasped, fighting the temptation to lean into her and press his lips to hers with all his strength.

"Hmm. I'm going to take that as a compliment."

6

"Is there more bacon?" Benny asked, going to the refrigerator.

"Yeah, there are a couple of packs in the meat drawer."

"I'll help you with breakfast." Benny opened the fridge door and slid the meat drawer open. He grabbed two packs of bacon and joined Mike at the stove.

"Listen, Benny," said Mike. "Yesterday was…"

"Yeah, it was," said Benny. "But I know you are right."

Coward!

"I wish I weren't; I really do. This waiting is—"

"Interminable."

Mike shot him a look and chuckled. "Yes, Mr. Dictionary."

A small smile lit on Benny's lips. *Are you going to let him diminish you that way?* He cleared his throat. "This stress is getting to me. I've been arguing with myself all night."

"Huh." Mike flashed a wry grin at him. "Me, too."

"Have you heard anything new about Greg?" Benny asked.

Mike's gaze darted to the cabinet where his housemates kept a small stash of hard liquor. "No. Anything about Shan?"

Benny cocked his head to the side, resisting the urge to look at the liquor cabinet. "Need a meeting?"

Mike clucked his tongue. "Don't sugarcoat it, Benny. Just come right out with whatever you're thinking." Despite his words, Mike blushed and dropped his gaze to the pan of burned eggs. "Is it obvious?"

You could totally fix that in him. It would be easy to remove the compulsion to drink. Benny shook his head.

"At least there's that." Mike peeked at him before turning and throwing the mess he'd made of the eggs in the trash can. "I... Ever since I saw him going into that helicopter, I... The urge has come back—and it's stronger than ever. I spent the whole ride back here trying to keep from pulling over at one of the bars, trying not to salivate like one of Pavlov's dogs every time I saw a beer sign." He got a new carton of eggs from the fridge and came back to the stove.

"If you could..." Benny pressed his lips into a tight line.

"Yeah," said Mike. "If I could trade places with him, I would do so in a heartbeat."

"That's not what I was going to ask."

"No?"

Oh, for Chrissake, Benny! Don't ask him! Benny shook his head. "If I could fix it so you could drink... If I could eliminate the addiction, would you want me to?"

Mike stopped adding eggs to the frying pan and slid it off the burner before he turned to Benny. He peered into his face with an intensity that made Benny want to step back. "You can do things like that?"

Benny cut his gaze away. "I...don't know. I think so." He rubbed the back of his neck. "*Maybe.*"

"So, that bit about needing to decide my superpower wasn't as much of a joke as I thought."

"No, that was all joke. I had no inkling at the time... I'd never considered it seriously until recently."

"But now?"

Benny stole a quick glance, but Mike had his cop face on, and Benny couldn't read anything from the set of his face. *You don't need to read his expression, dumbass. Have you forgotten you can read his mind?* Benny scrubbed his fingers through his hair. *That would be rude.*

"Well?" asked Mike in a hard voice.

"It occurred to me that I *could*, that's all."

"How long have you known you could do…" Mike flapped his hands. "Whatever the fuck this is."

Benny turned his attention to the bacon. "I guess that's a no, then."

"You're damn right it is." Mike stood stock-still, staring at the side of Benny's face until it felt as though his cheek would ignite at any moment. "Have you already done something like it? To me? To Greg?" His eyelids narrowed to mere slits. "To *Shannon?*"

Do you see? Your powers are like that of a god, Benny. You don't need to justify yourself to someone who has no power at all. Anger tickled the edges of his mind. "I already answered you, Mike."

"Oh, right." Mike scowled. "It just occurred to you."

"I asked if I could *help* you, Mike."

"Would you like to 'help' me turn hetero?"

Benny tried and failed to suppress a long-winded sigh. "Forget I asked, though I would like to point out that you seemed awfully interested in whether I could teach you these tricks Shannon, Toby, and I can do."

"That's different."

Benny's laugh was sour. "No, actually, it isn't. If I knew what the circuit looked like, I could—"

"The circuit? What are we to you? Robots?"

You could be a robot, an angry voice hissed in Benny's mind. *You could be a puppet.* He shoved the frying pan to the back burner. "Not hungry anymore." He turned and stomped into the living room.

7

His pulse thundered in his throat, and he found it hard to draw breath. Lily stood there smiling at him, naked and fractions of an inch away, her body promising him pleasure beyond anything he could imagine. The desert air had dried his mouth, but his nerves turned his tissues into sawdust. "What are you?" he croaked.

She cocked her head to the side and looked him in the eye. Her magnetic eyes seemed to pulse with a regular tempo. She moved her hand to the button of his jeans, spreading her lips a tiny bit.

From within her, came the twining strains of discord he'd heard before, but where he'd been able to resist them before, standing in front of her, gazing into her pulsing eyes, the heat of her flesh baking him, he could resist no longer.

He dropped his head, and in an instant, she was pressed against him, her lips locked on his own, her hands fighting the clasp of his pants. For a moment, he wanted nothing other than to allow her to strip him, nothing more than to plunge into her and revel in the world of Lily, in the world of perfection.

I can give you anything you want. All you have to do is ask for it. The memory of her words worked on him like a bucket of ice water. He stepped back, a rueful grin on his face. She stepped closer, and he stepped back again. "No."

She dropped her head, and her luxurious candy-colored hair fell forward to hide her face like a waterfall of arterial blood. "It's okay, *kisa*. You'll get used to the idea of us being together."

The scene of her arrival to the macadam warzone where they'd fought Brigitta and the rest replayed in his mind, the black and red plume of smoke intertwining to form the shape of a woman. "I can see past the illusions of the other demons." He paused and pursed his lips. "Though I never would have guessed Brigitta had yet another hidden form."

Lily sniffed and turned away. "Naamah is her name." She snapped her fingers and was fully dressed in an instant. "And don't compare us to the *mazzikim*. It would be like me comparing you to a cow or a pig."

"Are you and Brigitta and the gold fire lady all the same kind of…"

"Naamah and Abyzou are *ifrit*. Lamia is a *djinn*."

"And what is Lily?"

"I'm the Morning Star, *cazador*."

"You're…Lucifer?"

Lily threw back her head and laughed. "Yeah, *bizcocho*. I'm the fucking devil." Her laughter echoed off the surrounding dunes, seeming to fill the entire desert. When she wound down to a smile, she patted his cheek. "Sorry about that, Tobes. I was thinking of the last person I had this discussion with. After I explained, he said, 'You're really creepy sometimes, Lily.' Isn't that *funny*?"

"And where is your friend now?" As soon as he asked the question, he knew it was a horrible idea.

All the mirth, all the reminiscence left her face as though someone had drained them out of her. The planes of her face hardened, and her mouth settled into a grim, hateful line. But her eyes were the worst.

Her pupils seemed to expand and contract, swell and subside, pulsing blackness encroaching on the orange. It seemed as though Lily fought to control it, struggled to contain the stygian darkness. "I ate his soul," she said in an emotionless voice. "He betrayed me.'"

She turned her back on him and stood staring north, her blood-red hair dancing in the desert wind.

After what seemed like a long time, Toby cleared his throat. "Sorry I brought that back to you." His voice shook with fear. The demons in Oneka Falls—the *mazzikim*—had scared him from time to time, but this was different.

Lily was different.

8

Benny shoved the door open hard enough to make it bounce back at him. He stepped out onto the terrace, letting the crisp morning air waft across his skin. *Why is Mike acting like such an ass? Yeah, his lover is away in Rochester, condition unknown, but so is Shannon.*

He walked to the edge of the fieldstone patio and stood with his toes curling into the dew-covered grass, staring out at the lake. *I could fix him. I could make him straight, eliminate his addiction. Would that be so wrong?*

His mind rebelled at the idea. To tamper with someone's mind—even with their permission—risked too much. It's not as though Benny had any training, any education. Anything he did would be a hack.

What's wrong with that?

What's wrong with it? What's right with it?

The sun painted pinks and oranges on the surface of Lake Erie, dancing on the small waves produced by the southward wind. He walked to the landing of the steps that snaked their way down the cliff to Toby's boat landing. His powerboat sat in its berth, as did four jet skis. Benny sat on the top step, elbows on his knees.

Why have power if the fear of using it is so great? Why not just wish it away. The idea was so foreign, so strange to Benny's manner of thought that he glanced around, expecting to find someone nearby. But he was alone.

He shook his head and gazed out over the water. He'd never give up his power. The very idea was ludicrous. He'd *earned* his power, and he meant to use it to one day ensure that no one else would ever suffer as he and his friends had at Herlequin and Brigitta's hands.

Is that what you're doing? Is that your goal?

Benny shook his head. *Of course!* Memories began to flash in his mind's eye. Images of him wearing a smug smile as he explained his abilities to Eddie and Amanda, of preening for Shannon, of his expression as he used his power to bat at Brigitta. *That doesn't mean anything. That isn't me.*

Isn't it?

Benny squinted down at the water. The voice in his head sounded less and less like his own. Again, he peered around the backyard of Toby's mansion on the cliff. No dark figures hid in the slowly disappearing shadows. No animals were visible, let alone animals acting contrary to their natures. There was nothing there.

Shannon?

You don't need her.

That sealed it. Benny would never have entertained such a thought. *Who are you?* he sent.

No one answered him.

9

Dan Delo relaxed in a majestic ash tree forty feet above the terrace where Benny Cartwright fumed and glared at the lake. As he walked, the bearded psychic gestured as if in the middle of an animated conversation.

She's got him, he thought. *And McBride has Richards, and all because of me.* Glee sparkled in his eyes. *This is precisely the kind of currency I needed to buy my way back into Oneka Falls. This is proof of my loyalties.*

10

Mike stood next to the rolling cart they'd fancied up to be a mobile bar. His right hand rested lightly on the bottle of scotch, his face blank, his gaze distant and unfocused. After Benny left the kitchen, a feeling of grief and sorrow had descended on him. *Greg is gone*, he thought.

He could smell something burning but had no idea what. Every time he tried to think of anything but Greg's demise, every time he tried to distract himself, an image beset him. An image of Greg in a cheap coffin, his eyelids and lips sewn shut. Every time that image flashed through his mind, Mike's grip on the bottle of scotch tightened.

He hadn't picked it up yet, though, and that was good. He fought the urge to pick up the bottle and carry it into his bedroom, fought the urge to spin the cap off and pour a gallon of the stuff down his throat.

Time enough for that after I get the call, he thought.

What call, Mike?

The mental voice belonged to Benny, and Mike latched onto it like a life ring. The door to the terrace banged open, and Benny dashed through. He glanced at Mike and shook his head. "Don't do it. It's not you."

Mike turned a numb gaze in his direction, but still, his fingers whitened around the neck of the bottle of Swing.

"Well, it is you, but not all of it. Like all that nonsense before wasn't me." Benny stepped to his side and put his hand on top of the one Mike held the scotch bottle with. "We're being manipulated."

The word jarred through Mike's psyche, waking him up, and he jerked his hand away from the booze. "Manipulated?"

"Maybe tempted is a better word." Benny shook his head. "I can't understand it. I don't sense *anything*, and I can't spot anyone, but I've got this voice in my head... At first, I thought it was my own, you know? But it... It told me to take control of your mind, to change you without your consent." Benny's eyes widened. "It told me I don't need *Shannon*."

"Demons," hissed Mike.

Benny nodded. "I think those two new ones we saw yesterday. Or maybe Brigitta and the Snake-lady."

"How?" Moving as if against a strong tide, Mike turned away from the liquor cart. "And why haven't they done this before?"

"Maybe it has to do with Brigitta's cover."

"Her *cover*?"

Benny nodded. "She's an *ifrit*—a demon of fire—but she's always pretended to be an undead demon. She was *hiding* among the demons of Oneka Falls."

"Hiding from what?"

"Don't know." Benny peered at him, his gaze boring into Mike's. "Are you okay now? I need to get my phone."

Mike turned his back on the booze cart and walked toward the kitchen. "Go. I'll throw the burnt food away."

II

Kristy rolled out of bed and yawned. Sean's side of the bed was empty—nothing new there, he often sat up all night, filling calls for research on the SEMPRe app. She pulled on a pair of blue scrubs and walked down the hall, rubbing her eyes.

She knocked on the door to Sean's office, then pushed it open. He sat hunched in front of his machine, chin on his chest, sound asleep. On the screen, the app flashed and blinked with activity from the group of researchers he spent the most time with. *Don't you people ever sleep?* she wondered. She lay a hand on Sean's shoulder. "Hon? You fell asleep at the computer again."

As usual, Sean came awake instantly. He glanced at her and blushed.

"What was it this time? Tracking down demon sightings?"

He shook his head. "In a way. A request came in last night to track down sightings of this redheaded woman. She's a demon, of course." He clicked over to his browser and played a video recorded on someone's cell phone. In it, the redhead stood in the middle of an intersection that was as familiar to Kristy as her own bedroom, an intersection in Oneka Falls. The redhead said something to a person on the sidewalk and stared at him for a moment, and as the light went out of his eyes, Sean paused the video. "She turns him into a drooling idiot and then turns into some kind of creature made of black smoke."

"They should be paying you to watch stuff like this," Kristy whispered.

"Who? SEMPRe?" He shook his head. "No, no. I do what I can because I *want* to do it."

"That's all well and good, Sean, but you have to take care of yourself. You have to—"

"Let me show you what I found!" he cried like an excited child. "There have been sightings of the entity going back decades, mostly in New York." He flipped to the research tab and scanned the new updates. "It looks like someone found older reports while I snoozed." He bent toward the monitor. "Wow... Look at all this."

Hiding her smile, Kristy grunted and turned back to the hallway. "Breakfast in fifteen, Sean. Don't let it get cold this time."

"Yeah. Fifteen. Fine."

12

Shoulder to shoulder, Toby and Lily walked east. A companionable silence had fallen over them. Lily seemed lost to reminiscence, while Toby spent the time thrashing his mind for a plan, a strategy, a tactic, *anything* that might get him out of the jam that held him as tight as a jealous lover.

The sun climbed higher, and the temperature rose with it, though because of the dry, baking heat Lily emitted, Toby didn't notice the ambient temperature. Not until it was too late.

His vision doubled, and a chill ran down his spine. His head pounded, and with each beat of his heart came sharp pain as if someone drove a spike through the top of his skull. His skin felt hot and dry, and his stomach twisted and turned in his guts. Pulsing nausea assaulted him along with the nastiest taste he could imagine flooding his mouth.

He staggered and would have fallen thirty feet down the face of a dune if Lily hadn't grabbed his arm and held him upright. She squinted and scoured his face and neck with her gaze.

"Thanks," he said.

"You've got heat stroke, Tobes." Lily sucked at her teeth. "*Mea culpa, mea culpa, mea maxima culpa.* I hadn't planned to let you go this far so soon. I was distracted."

Toby closed his eyes, wincing at the pain in his head.

"It's not too late, *habibi*. Even this, I can fix. I can create a cool palace for you to rest in, a pool of water to cool you, a feast to sate you, the choicest wines to soothe your throat."

A lopsided grin formed on Toby's lips. "Let me guess. All I have to do is ask."

"Yes," she said in a fervent hiss. "Ask me, *papi*. Ask me."

Toby chuckled and let his head hang forward.

"Do it, Toby. Let me help you. Even if it's only the once, just do it. This isn't how your time on Earth should end—lost in the Syrian Desert, alone, baked to death by the sun." She stepped in front of him and lifted his chin with a hand that felt cool to the touch. "Let me help."

He *wanted* to ask her for help. He wanted it so bad he could taste it, but the problem was, it tasted of something nasty, of betrayal, of evil deeds done in the dark.

"Look at me, *neshama*."

"More Spanish?" The slur in his voice frightened him more than a little.

"No, the language is far older than Spanish. It's a language suitable for the setting."

Toby shrugged and gritted his teeth against the surge of nausea that followed.

"It's Hebrew. It means 'soul' or 'spirit.'"

"Interesting," he murmured.

"It's used as a term of endearment between lovers, Tobias. That's what I…" Her voice trailed off until the wind blew it away. She began to hum the melody and countermelody she'd hummed before, all spectral lament and eternal dirge.

"The desert song," he mumbled. His knees went watery, and he staggered into her, but his added weight didn't faze Lily. It was like stumbling into a wall of granite.

The song continued, and something inside Toby's head loosened, opened. He closed his eyes, and colors danced on the inside of his eyelids. Bright colors: cherry reds, oranges, silver; they all intertwined in an elaborate movement that seemed too complex not to be random, but at the same time, they looked …*designed*.

"Yes," she crooned. "The desert song. I like that title." The insane discordant battle between the melody and countermelody continued unabated despite Lily using her vocal cords for speech.

"How do you do that?"

"Do what, *kisa*?"

"Hebrew?"

"Russian for pussycat." She smoothed the hair away from his forehead while stroking the back of his neck with another hand. Another set of arms held him in a tight embrace.

"How do you talk and hum two different songs at the same time?"

"That's easy, Tobes. Even humans can do something like it with practice. Though, in fairness, the cultures that developed this ability did so in imitation of me." She peeled one of his eyelids open and squinted at him. "Ask me, *ese*. Ask me before it's too late."

Toby tilted his head back, eyes closed, and exhaled. The desert song continued to play, seeming more a product of wind and weather on stone than a human throat.

"*You must ask me, Tobias!*"

"You demons... Always in my life... Ruined it. Ruined everything."

"*Ask me!*"

He fought against her multi-armed embrace, shoving at her hands when he could, settling for shoulders and forearms when he couldn't. More arms wrapped around him, more hands grabbed him, and still, she stroked his hair and the back of his neck.

"Ask me, Toby, and I'm yours. I'll be yours, and you'll be mine, forever and ever, amen."

Fingers tugged at his clothing, palms rubbed against his skin, legs wrapped around him, breasts pressed against his chest, skin on skin, her nipples as hard as diamonds. "Do it, Tobes. Do it, do it, do it." She ground her hips against him and groaned. "Oh, ask me, *motek*. Ask me, ask me, *ask me!*"

The world tilted, and Toby thought he was falling, though he landed on something soft and welcoming instead of hot sand. He came to rest with the lightest touch he could imagine, as though some giant had laid him down carefully.

Lily sat atop him, legs astride his hips, and her multitude of hands continued to stroke him, to caress him. "Ask me," she begged.

He could feel her hovering above him, ready to stab herself down on him, to envelop him. To allow it would invalidate everything he'd ever done in his life: escaping from Herlequin, fighting his first demon, tracking them, *hunting* them, killing Herlequin, fighting Brigitta—all that would be rendered like fat in a frying pan.

But he *wanted* her anyway, wanted to give in, wanted her to cocoon him, to succor him, to make him *feel* something again.

13

"Sean!"

He straightened and looked over his shoulder. "Yeah?"

"I've been calling and calling. Didn't you hear me?"

"Sorry. But you've got to see—"

"Come eat, Sean. Right now."

"But you said I have fifteen minutes."

"Yes," she said, squinting at him. "And that was *twenty-five* minutes ago, knucklehead."

"Oh…" He pushed himself away from the computer desk. "I didn't realize."

"No duh. Get your butt in here and eat your breakfast." She shook her head. "I'd say, 'before it gets cold,' but it's already too late for that."

"Mmm, cold eggs," said Sean.

"Eggs? No. Cold pancakes and bacon."

"You've got to read this stuff, though, Kristy."

"*After* breakfast."

"Yeah. You know how I said there were reports of the redhead going back a couple of decades?"

"The redhead?"

"Yeah, you know. The new entity, the one in the video. Anyway, she goes back a lot farther than that. One researcher even found ties to Hitler and Stalin!"

"She must be old."

"Well, she's a demon. The research around the Nazi party even points to the idea that Hitler was possessed by her. Now, we know possession is largely mythological, but evidently, this chick has ways of getting men to do what she wants."

"Oh, I'll bet," said Kristy as she swatted his rear-end. "I bet she can get her man to the breakfast table on time."

"Yeah. Sorry. Anyway, this entity spent a lot of time with Hitler. She even ran Bad Tölz for a time. There's even this quote…" He stopped and turned, but Kristy pushed him toward the kitchen. "Yeah, okay. Sorry. There's this quote attributed to a close friend of Hitler's that basically says, 'Hitler will dance, but the music is my own,' or something like that." Again, Sean paused walking, and again, Kristy gently shoved him toward the kitchen. "Yeah, sorry. Sorry. Breakfast, first." He headed back down the hall. "Did I tell you about Stalin?"

"*After breakfast*," said Kristy.

"Yeah. Sorry."

14

Benny ran up the stairs, taking them two at a time. As he passed the door to the guest room, Eddie Mitchell came out and nodded a greeting. "Can't stop," said Benny. *Something's come up. Meet us in the kitchen.*

Behind him, Eddie gasped at the mind to mind contact. Then came the sound of a door opening. "Amanda, get up and get dressed. Something's going on."

He slid through the door to the suite he and Shannon shared, his gaze sliding across her things arrayed on her dresser, and he felt a pang of loss, of impending grief. *But I don't know anything yet.*

Yes, you do. You know that if she isn't already dead, I will send soldiers to search the hospitals until I find her. Then she will die, *I can promise you.* The mental voice hit him like a tsunami of acid, burning everything it touched and leaving an oily, slick residue behind.

Get the fuck out of my head.

Temper, temper, Benny-boy. Your brother was never half as much of a pain in my ass as you were. Are.

Brigitta! Though no conscious answer invaded his mind, he did hear something like an echo. *Naamah? Is that your actual name?* Again, no answer came, but Benny didn't need a confirmation. He'd seen the change in her form, seen LaBouche literally beat the skin off her, but he could imagine her no other way than as she'd appeared before them as Herlequin burned back in Thousand Acre Wood, a zombie wrapped in black, rotting skin.

His phone lay on the nightstand on his side of the bed. He'd forgotten to plug it in, and the battery display read eleven percent. He snarled at himself and his innate ability to forget the most important things. *If I miss my proxy's call because of a dead battery, I'll throw myself off the cliff.* He snatched the charger and the cord and ran back to the kitchen.

He plugged the phone in and lay it on the granite countertop for a moment. Eddie and Amanda stood side by side at the sink, washing a few pans by hand. "Something has happened this morning," he said.

"Already told them." Mike sat at the table with his head in his hands.

"It was Brigitta, Mike. Her real name is Naamah."

Mike lifted his head and met his gaze for a moment, then ducked his head again.

Benny glanced at the Mitchells. "Gotta warn you, cooking breakfast seems impossible this morning."

"We've got it," said Amanda. "And we are professional breakfast burners, so don't you worry." She smiled and tossed him a wink.

A pang raced through Benny's guts. "Shannon would have loved you," he murmured.

"She *will* love me," said Amanda. "Don't borrow trouble." She turned back to the sink and began scrubbing one of the frying pans.

"I don't think the demon in my head is Brigitta or Naamah or any other name you want to call her. It almost reminds me of... But that's crazy. Anyway, the voice tempting me is more self-assured than she ever was."

"Who?" asked Benny.

"I don't know, but if I had to guess, I'd say the voice belongs to Sally McBride."

Benny stared at him blankly for a moment before shaking his head. "No matter who it is, there's a question we need an immediate answer to."

"What's that?" asked Eddie without turning.

"How do they know where we are?"

"Why do you think they do?" asked Mike.

"Did you get the feeling that McBride was in your head?"

"Well, yeah. I mean—"

"I don't mean 'talking to you in your head.' I mean right there inside your skull with you. Did she seem to read your mind? To see what you saw?"

Mike sat back in the chair and dropped his hands. "Yeah, I think so."

"Doing that, seeing someone's surroundings, getting inside their head, all that takes a lot more effort than sending a thought at someone. I'm not saying they have to know where we are to do it—I mean, they're demons, right? But *I* would have to know the location. I'd have to travel there in mind—a kind of ethereal projection—to get that kind of access." Benny stared at Mike. "I think they are here. Their minds, I mean."

"But how could they know where we are? We've been in this house for *years*. If they knew our location, they'd have come in force a long time ago."

"My point," said Benny with a quick nod. He turned and stared at the Mitchells. "So, how do they know *where* we are?"

Without turning, Eddie said, "You can stop looking at us like that. I'd bet you all the money we have that it's because of that *goddamn* lamp."

Amanda nodded and turned to face him, resting her bum against the sink. "She could always find us. She followed Eddie for *decades*. She convinced him to rebuy the lamp after his aunt sold it away. It's *important* to her."

"More than just important," said Eddie. "It's like... It's like a handle. Abby—" His voice cracked, and Amanda rested her hand on his shoulder.

"She used it to cause us harm, to try to manipulate us into fighting each other, into breaking up." Amanda's expression turned fierce. "*Fuck her.*"

"What the hell is that lamp?" asked Mike in the most burned-out voice Benny'd ever heard.

"It's supposed to be a Tiffany," said Eddie. "But the shade changes whenever the fuck it wants."

"Changes?"

Eddie nodded and gave up the pretense of washing dishes. "When my dad first brought it into our house, it was aquamarine with dragonflies on the bottom. When Abby started haunting me, it was midnight blue and dark purple with these funny electric blue fish. And you saw it as the redhead came. Red background with a snake, a tree, and a bird."

"And this morning? What does it look like now?"

Eddie glanced at Amanda and shrugged. "We left it in your garage."

Benny turned and sprinted for the door that would lead him to the garage. "We might have to destroy it."

"We hate the goddamn thing," said Amanda.

On his way past, Benny grabbed Mike's arm. "Come on!"

The four trailed out to the garage, and Eddie pointed at the cardboard box they'd stored the lamp under. He blushed. "We..."

"We thought if the lamp were covered, she might not be able to find us."

Mike stepped forward and kicked the cardboard box off. The lamp sat on the concrete floor. Its shade looked nothing like what Eddie had just described. The shade matched the color of the deep ocean, greens tinged with blues and blacks. Two images adorned it. The first depicted a giant black snake that encompassed the bottom edge, and the second stood proudly in the center of the shade—an image of an angelic woman, though her feathers were done in black, and she was sheathed in crimson red flames.

"That's yet another new scene," muttered Eddie. "Why am I not surprised?"

"Interesting," Benny said. He flipped the box back over the lamp and turned to the others. "Can't hurt, right?"

"We've got to get out of here," said Mike.

"I don't think so." Benny moved to the big bay doors and pressed the button that opened one of them. As the door rumbled upward, he waved his hand at the drive. "If they were coming, they wouldn't have wasted the darkness. They'd already be eating us."

"Eating us?" asked Amanda.

"Yeah," said Mike. "They feed on humans—some on emotion, some on flesh."

"That explains a few things," said Eddie with a grim nod.

"So, what do we do?"

When Benny turned to face them, a smile—his first real smile since finding Shannon broken and bloody—lit his features. "That's easy. We find out everything we can about this damn thing."

15

Shannon didn't know the man who peeked around the curtain at her. It didn't surprise her that SEMPRe had members she'd never met, but it surprised her that the man they sent knew almost nothing about *her*.

"Oh, Shannon!" he said with raw grief pulsing in his voice. "What did that old bear do?"

Shannon grimaced. "Tore me up pretty bad."

"Doctor, uh... Doctor Walker said you'll be okay in time."

"Yeah? I'm not so sure." She squinted at the man—a man who looked nothing like Benny. Shannon supposed it might be a demon in disguise, that they'd found Greg and her already, but she didn't see the point in having someone pretend to pretend to be her husband. *If he was a demon, wouldn't he be killing me by now?*

The man cocked his head and gave it a negative shake. "Shan, do you remember my friend Joe?"

"Of course."

"He was stabbed yesterday. You two shared a helicopter ride."

"I know," said Shannon.

"He began bleeding in his brain in the night. They had to go back in this morning." The man walked closer. "It looks bad."

"Will he..." She couldn't finish the question, not even in the privacy of her own mind.

"He's in good hands," the proxy said. "I know his surgeon. Top notch."

"I thought he was only stabbed? Why is he bleeding in his head?"

The man shrugged. "Rick says he was also clubbed."

"Rick? That's his surgeon."

The proxy widened his eyes and treated her to a stern look. "No, hon. Rick Michaels. You remember him. Joe's husband?"

Shannon let her eyelids sink. "Yeah," she murmured. She cast her mind back to the battle in the parking lot, all the way to the beginning, and tried to follow it through until Greg was struck down. But her memory didn't go that far. The last thing she remembered was fooling the pack of lesser demons and getting hit by what felt like a meteor.

"It's okay, Shan. Don't worry about old Joe. He'll pull through."

She heard the words as she teetered on the edge of unconsciousness, and she wanted to reply, but before she could, she slept.

16

Toby awoke in the shade of a silk pavilion, which matched the color of Lily's hair to perfection. More silk lay beneath him, and the softest pillow he'd ever slept on supported his head. A cool breeze wafted across his bare chest, and he smiled at the sensation. For a while, he'd forgotten what it felt like not to be hot.

He could smell water—*actually smell it*—along with meat cooking on a grill. He heaved a sigh and rolled on his side, his back to the desert beyond the open wall of the pavilion.

Lily knelt in front of the small grill on the other side of the tent, her back to him. Her perfect, naked back. Her hair cascaded along her spine like the velvet curtain in a fancy New York theater. Light shimmied across her hair, catching highlights and shadows, seeming to reflect the image of the pavilion as if her hair were a mirror.

"That smells good," he croaked, and when he did, his lips split, sending shockwaves of pain shimmering through him. "Ow, that hurts."

"You were silly," said Lily without turning. "You let things go too far."

Toby had no memory of anything that happened after he admitted to himself how much he wanted her. He had no recollection of asking for her help—or of having sex with her for that matter. *Does it count if I don't remember it?*

Why wouldn't it? asked Lily's voice in his mind, but he wasn't sure if it was his own mind that supplied the words or if she actually spoke to him, mind to mind.

"Uh, please don't take this the wrong way…"

Without getting up, Lily turned to face him, knee-walking in a half-circle. The sight of her almost took his breath away. A half-smile flirted with her lips. "You don't remember?" She ran the backs of her fingernails down the side of her trunk. "You don't remember this?"

Toby drew in a deep breath. "I remember wanting you very badly. I'm not sure I'll ever forget it."

Lily laughed, and it sounded like a thousand glass bells. When she stopped, the desert song took the place of her ringing laughter.

"Did we…"

"Shh, *bebe*." She put a perfect finger across her lips, the lacquered nail so glossy it looked perpetually wet. "You passed out."

Toby sat up and groaned at the woozy feeling that washed through him. He waved a hand at the tent, at the barrel of water in the corner, at the grill. "Did I ask you for this?"

She smiled and turned back to the grill. "Have some water, love. You need it."

"But did I ask for your help?" Toby looked toward the barrel of water, but he made no move to drink, though the tissues of his mouth and throat seemed to cry out for rehydration.

"Have you had goat before?" She shifted to glance at him over her shoulder, exposing the side of a perfect breast and the nipple at its crown.

"Uh…"

She grinned. "It's not fair, I know, but a girl has to use what she's given to best effect."

He tore his gaze away from her and crawled toward the water barrel. "If I didn't ask for your help, and I drink from this, does it… Am I…"

She treated him to another bell-like laugh. "Even if you asked me, you are not in my thrall. You don't *owe* me anything, Tobes. I don't want that. I want you to *choose* to be with me." She peeked at him again, her orange eyes twirling with intensity. "No matter what."

A copper dipper lay on the silk next to the water barrel, and Toby filled it and drank, squeezing his eyes shut at the pleasure of the sheer sensation of water trickling down his throat. He needed time to think, to consider all the things she'd told him. *I'm still not even sure this is happening. This could all be a mind-fuck like the ones Herlequin loved to throw at little kids.*

At the grill, Lily scoffed.

"Sorry?" said Toby, refilling the dipper. "Did you say something?"

She clucked her tongue and shook her head. "Be careful, *vato*. I don't like being compared to *mazzikim*. And that particular one and I have history." She removed skewers of meat from the grill. "I hope you are hungry. I think I've made enough for six or seven people."

The thought of swallowing food made him wince, but the odor of the grilled meat set his mouth to watering. "That smells awesome."

"Come," she said. "Lay next to me, and I will feed you."

"Um…"

She rolled her eyes at him. "It's just food, Tobes. I like feeding my mates."

"Mate? Then we—"

"Relax. It's a figure of speech." She wagged her eyebrows at him. "A girl could get to like this amnesia game. What shall we play it about next?"

Toby crawled to her side but didn't recline. "If you don't mind, I'll feed myself for now."

She looked at him through slit eyelids but flashed a sunny smile. "Don't be so careful to avoid allowing me to help you that you end up with less than nothing, *kisa*."

He picked up a skewer, pulled a piece of the grilled meat off the end, and popped it into his mouth. He bit down, and the hot, succulent juices squirted into his mouth. He grinned at her as he chewed. "Tastes like beef."

She smiled, but it didn't reach her eyes. "So I've been told."

"Can I ask you a question?"

She spread her hands to her sides.

"You don't eat—at least not like this. Right?"

She nodded.

"Then how come you know how to cook?"

She turned her head to gaze out at the desert. "I've been here for a long time. I was…" She stole a peek at him, then turned back to the desert. "I was *invited* to come here by a culture yours barely remembers, though it was undeniably the cradle of all the world's civilizations."

"Sumer?"

She chuckled. "Close, but no cigar. An Akkadian mystic was the first to bridge the void, the first to call. His invitation intrigued me, so, along with members of my house, we came." Lily dropped her head. "The temptations proved too much for Lilu. He betrayed me."

"I don't understand who Lilu is."

She lifted her chin and gazed into the deep blue sky. "And you don't have to."

Toby popped another morsel of the grilled goat into his mouth. "This is really good, Lily."

"I'm glad you like it." She stood and walked to the edge of the pavilion, standing silhouetted against the blazing desert sky.

"I don't really understand who any of you are. We…" He glanced at her, noting the set of her shoulders, the tilt of her head. "We interrogated one of the demons from Oneka Falls—"

"*Mazzikim.*"

"*Mazzikim*, then. We interrogated one of them a few years back."

Lily spun on her heel to face him, her face unreadable, but her eyes spinning faster than he remembered. "And?"

Toby wagged his head to the side. "I got the feeling he told more lies than truths."

"And?"

"He told us about you. We didn't know it at the time, he said something like 'the most powerful among us' came—"

Lily snorted, wearing a lopsided grin.

"—and opened a passage for the rest of them. That you made it possible for them to come here."

"And?"

"And *who are you*, Lily? Why are you here? What do you want?"

She threw her head back and laughed, a harsh, mechanical sound that echoed through the desert. In the distance, some animal screamed a challenge in response. She froze, head back, gazing at him from the corner of her eye. It was a freaky thing to see—more like a giant lizard, a Komodo dragon perhaps, staring at her prey than a woman staring at a man. "I don't think you are ready for those answers, *chavo*. They would hurt your little head."

A frustrated sigh gusted out of him. "You are clearly not the same as the *mazzikim*."

"Why thank you," she said in droll tones.

"I can see them," he said. "I mean, *really* see them. Their illusions don't work on me."

"Yes, I had heard that."

"But with you…"

"But with me, you can't?"

Toby shook his head. "All I see is…*perfection*. I can't see through to what you really are."

"*This* is what I really am. At least at this moment."

"And the smoke? The black and red smoke that came from the clouds back in New York?"

"That was what I really was at *that* time." Lily stepped closer to him, and her black leather minidress and matching chrome-heeled boots congealed around her from the air and held out her hand. "And now, I am dressed. No illusions, just leather." She cocked her head. "And my daughter? Could you see past her visages?"

Toby smiled up at her and got to his feet. He took her hand, caressing the backs of her knuckles with the pad of his thumb. "Brigitta? Sure, she—"

"Her name is *Naamah*!" Lily snapped, fire dancing in her eyes, mouth warped into a sneer.

Toby found he'd taken a step back, the silk wall of the pavilion pressed against his back. "Sorry. We've only ever known her as…by the other name."

Lily nodded, and some of the anger left her expression.

"I could always see past her visages. At least, I thought I could. Back there in the parking lot, LaBouche—"

"That *fool*."

"Uh, yes. He peeled Naamah's rotting skin off, and crimson flames and nothing else lay beneath it. I'd never seen past the undead skin."

"She is an *ifrit*, not a *mazzikim*. What you saw before the battle with the traitor was not her true form." Lily flashed an enigmatic smile.

"And her changes, her rotten flesh, that was as real?"

"Yes, though it was only skin deep."

"But she could affect true changes, no? I mean, she turned LaBouche into a yellow magpie once."

"Did she?" Lily sounded bored, her tone flat, emotionless.

"So, is it true? Did your coming here open the way for the others?"

Lily shrugged one perfect shoulder. "I grow bored of this, *cazador*. I have things to do." Without another word, she disappeared with a *pop* and a gust of warm air.

But the food, water, and shelter remained. With a shrug, Toby sank to his knees and continued eating the grilled goat. It tasted too good to let it go to waste.

17

Shannon slept in fits and starts all morning, and none of it satisfied her exhaustion. By noon, the pain meds had worn off, and she ached all over—if not from a bruised or fractured bone, then from a laceration. If not from a gash, then from an abrasion or bruise. If not from any of those, then from overtaxed muscles.

By the time Kristy Walker finally came in an hour after the nurses tried to push lunch on her, Shannon was done with the hospital, done with her injuries, and *done* with the nurses telling her to wait for this, wait for that. "Get me out of here, Kristy," she said by way of greeting.

"I know, I know. Hospitals are about the worst place to recover from anything. Too much hoopla, too many people walking around." She approached the bed and patted Shannon's forearm.

"No, I mean it. Get me out of here before I lose my mind."

"Soon, hon." Kristy stepped to the overbed table and put her laptop on it, moving the untouched tray to the chair at the foot of the bed. She flipped open the screen and scanned Shannon's chart, then snapped it closed. "Everything looks as I expected. You're doing well, Shannon, and as soon as we get more fluid into you, I'll see about discharging you. *But* you will need in-home care, and about that, I will not budge. That's probably not a surprise to you."

Shannon nodded, trying to keep the disappointment off her face.

But I imagine SEMPRe can help there.

Shannon looked at Kristy. "I was beginning to wonder if my memory was playing tricks on me. But why would you think I have—"

No. It seems like it is a surprise side-effect of having a demon for a boyfriend.

"—anything to do with this SEMPRe thing."

"Must have been something your friends said." Kristy cocked her head to the side and smiled. *Who else would be behind it?*

"My surprise was different. But we can talk about that after I get home." She turned her face toward the window. "And Greg?"

"*Joe* is out of surgery."

"And?"

"He's in recovery. The bleed was a bad one, but they've got it stopped."

"*And?*"

Kristy drew a deep breath and let it out all at once. "His prognosis is guarded at this time, Shannon. His recovery will be long and difficult."

18

"I don't know about this, Benny," said Mike.

The two men stood outside their newly rented storage space on the outskirts of Erie. A delivery truck drove back up the alley between rows of garage-like storage units toward the exit. A logo reading, "The Safe Place" was emblazoned on its back and sides.

Benny pointed his chin at the back of Mike's Cadillac. "We have to do something with it. And it's better if it's not where we are. Right?"

"Yeah, I have enough of the temptation bit."

"Me, too. Let's get it in the safe."

Mike opened the trunk of his Cadillac and lifted a cardboard box. "Do we remove the box or put it in as is?"

Benny tilted his head to the side, staring at the box for a moment. "Hmm."

"Let's leave it in. What can it hurt?" Mike turned and entered the four-foot-by-six-foot storage area. Their new safe sat in the very back, its massive refrigerator-sized door hanging open. Mike put the cardboard box inside the safe, closed the door, and spun the dial. "I sure hope you memorized the combination."

Benny tapped his temple with his finger. "It's all right up here."

"I have to tell you, Benny… I feel out of my depth here. I have no idea what we should do."

"Well, the first thing we need to do is find out what the hell that lamp is."

19

Delo shrank back into the shadows as Mike Richards drove his Cadillac to the main gate. It wouldn't do for them to see him. Not after all the trouble he'd taken to keep an eye on them for thirty-six hours.

With one side of his mouth curled upward, Delo dialed Brigitta's number once again. When Brigitta herself answered, his grin broadened.

"Delo," she said.

"Mistress. The talisman is stored in bay 19 of the You Lock It Tight self-storage yard in Erie."

"Good work."

"Would you like me to retrieve it? It would be a simple matter." When she spoke, Dan could hear her smile in her voice.

"Not at this time. Let them think they have the advantage. For this, all is forgiven."

"I never betrayed you, Mistress."

"Oh, I know that, Dan. I meant this cloak and dagger bullshit you undertook instead of explaining yourself and coming to our aid at the park."

"Oh." His voice sounded petty and weak, and he *hated* it. "Yes, thank you."

"Can you stand to keep watch over their house for another day or two? Things are in flux at the moment."

"Of course, Mistress. I'm yours to command."

"Unless you think I'm mad at you," she said.

His heart thudded in his chest, but the teasing quality of her voice reduced his fear. "I didn't think. I—"

"Relax, Dan Delo. I'm teasing you."

"Of course, Mistress."

20

Sean rubbed his gritty, burning eyes. He hadn't slept at all the previous night. He hadn't left his computer chair since the call for research came in. The call's priority code was the highest Sean had ever seen, and it bore the coded marks of one of SEMPRe's founders—a mark Sean knew belonged to Benny Cartwright.

In the previous nineteen hours, Sean had examined the detailed photographs of the lamp, including the maker's marks on the bottom of its stand. The request had said to ignore the shade, to even ignore the colors, which was how many Tiffany lamps were identified—the antique coloring, the patina.

The maker's mark had also proved problematic. It wasn't one associated with Tiffany, and what was worse, the mark bore no characters of any alphabet the researchers could recognize.

Sean believed it was cuneiform, something old. It was a long string of marks that almost looked like chicken scratch. He'd copied it to a blank sheet of paper so he could see it all in a line. It read:

He took a photo on his phone and texted it to an old anthropology professor at his alma mater, hoping she could translate it. Next, Sean uploaded the picture into the SEMPRe app and sent it off, searching for similar images.

He sat back and stretched. His eyelids seemed to weigh twenty pounds apiece, and he longed to shut them. He stood and stretched more, then turned to go to bed.

He had just laid his hand on the doorknob when his phone played its email chime. The email was from his former professor. It said:

"Easy. This says, 'Hail Lilitu, Bearer of Chaos.' You were right about the cuneiform. Akkadian cuneiform to be precise."

He turned back to his computer and sat down, reinvigorated. He passed the translation on to the other SEMPRe researchers, then started poking around the web, looking for the phrase.

21

Toby had waited throughout the day for Lily's return. Then he had waited through the evening and through half the night. Still no Lily.

He'd learned his lesson about walking during the day and about dehydration and heat stroke. The water barrel Lily had left seemed bottomless. No matter how much he drank, it remained full.

The same was not true of the grill, however, so by the time he gave up and decided to get some sleep, his stomach felt like someone had dug out his innards with a melon scooper.

She'd left him shelter, water, and the means to cook food, but no food, and perhaps worse, nothing at all to do. Toby had spent the day ruminating in his own thoughts, playing the shoulda-woulda-coulda game, racking his brain for memories of what might have happened the previous morning.

Toby didn't know what to do next. It seemed reckless to set off blindly again. It seemed *stupid* to leave the only water source he knew of within six thousand miles. But sitting there, alone in the desert, while who knew what was going on back in New York, well, it seemed...*irresponsible*.

Bādiyat al-Shām Lily had called it. The Syrian Desert. Toby didn't know much about it, but what he knew gave him pause. He knew it stretched from Syria through Iraq, Jordan, and into Saudi Arabia, where it merged with another desert. He had no idea where in that vast area he was.

He moved to the water barrel and drew another dipper of water, swishing the cold liquid in his mouth before he swallowed. His stomach growled; water wasn't what it wanted. He moved to the edge of the pavilion and stared out into the desert.

Despite how silly it would be to leave a water source that seemed infinite, Toby couldn't stay there. His friends back in New York would be continuing the fight, and he *needed* to be there.

If Lily doesn't show up by nightfall, I'm leaving without her.

He snapped his tongue against the back of his teeth and sneered at his own bravado. The truth of it was that fear of the desert's killing power had sunk its teeth deep into Toby's flesh.

He no longer wondered if the desert were real because it didn't matter. Real or all in his mind, it still had the power to kill him. Lily had proved that to him.

But she'd also proved something else.

Toby's life depended on remaining in Lily's good graces, and she had no compunction about leaving him to his own devices—all of which seemed likely to kill him.

He wondered yet again whether Shannon and Greg had survived, whether Mike had gotten the rest of them out of there and back to safety. His memory showed him Scott's broken body, and he began yet another round of shoulda-woulda-coulda.

Chapter 3

Monday

I

She appeared in the center of the intersection, evoking the screech of rubber and the crunch of bent sheet metal as a car swerved into the wrong lane to avoid her. Lily smiled at the driver and tipped him a wink—though both wink and smile were ugly, malignant. With a flick of her fingers, she sent the car careening up onto the sidewalk, its rear quarter panel smashing the big plate glass window of Mel's You Need It store. The driver froze with both hands locked on the wheel, his gaze stuck on Lily, his lips quivering.

"*Ay, que chulo,*" she sneered. With a flip of her vermilion hair, she turned and walked up the double yellow lines painted in the center of the road. She gazed straight ahead, not acknowledging the open stares and whispers of the people and *mazzikim* out and about in Oneka Falls.

Her thing with Toby Burton wasn't going as she had planned. Her charms had worked on him, but not to the extent she considered a success. She'd spent the last sixteen hours walking the streets of New York City, trying to lose herself in her memories, but Toby's resistance lurked in the back of her mind, spoiling everything.

The worst part about it was that Lily couldn't figure out the source of his strength. He was a male, and all males should be putty in her hands. It wasn't fair that he could resist her.

"Mistress?"

Lily came back to herself with a start. She stopped walking in favor of just standing in the middle of the road, arms akimbo, staring off into space. *This won't do. This won't do at all.* She turned toward Abyzou. "Where is Naamah?"

Abyzou extended her arm and swept it toward the glass door with the words Oneka Falls Town Hall emblazoned on it in gold leaf. "She's inside, Mistress. Come, I'll take you to her."

Lily narrowed her eyes and studied the *ifrit*. Concern was written in the set of her flame-borne features. Lily motioned Abyzou to proceed and followed her into the building.

Abyzou led her to the office of the town manager and pushed through the closed the door without knocking. Naamah sat in a chair that was twice again too big for her, swiveled to face the floor-to-ceiling picture window, staring out at the maple tree that grew in the lawn. The shrapnel of broken decorations and tchotchkes lay in the corner, and every surface inside the office had been swept clean as though Naamah had gone from place to place, flinging whatever had rested there into the corner.

"I suppose these trinkets must serve *some* purpose," said Lily.

Without turning, Naamah said, "Must everything I do become fodder for one of your speeches?"

"Don't—" began Abyzou.

"Can we not?" Lily strutted into the room and sat in one of the empty chairs across the desk from Naamah. "Can we forgo the normal mother-daughter tit for tat? It wearies me."

Naamah's only response was a snort.

A sigh gusted from Lily. "Tell me the others have been handled."

As slow as a glacier, Naamah spun in the chair to face her mother. She lifted one eyebrow. "Don't tell me that the great Lilitu has failed."

Lily grimaced and turned to Abyzou with a long-suffering expression on her face.

"Neither Naamah nor Lamia succeeded, Mistress."

Stone-faced, Lily nodded. "And the talisman?"

"I don't know how they figured it out," said Naamah. "We gave no clue, and yet as soon as Benny Cartwright caught on that I was in his head, they hustled the talisman away."

"Why isn't this good news?" asked Lily. "Why haven't you sent someone to retrieve it?"

Naamah took a deep breath. "Wherever they took it, I can no longer feel it."

Again, Lily turned to Abyzou, this time arching her eyebrows.

"Don't look at her! You don't need her confirmation that what I say is true, Mother!"

Lily turned a wry expression on her daughter. "I merely wanted to know if Abyzou could sense it. She has a special link with the talisman, after all."

Abyzou crossed one arm made of golden flame over the other and gave herself a little hug. "I can *touch* it, Mistress. I can enter it. But they put it in some kind of container, and that, I can't breach."

"And that doesn't make any sense to me," said Naamah. "If you can touch it, enter it, then why can't you say where it is?"

"Abyzou and the talisman share a chthonic link. It isn't a thing of this universe."

Abyzou uncrossed her arms. "Yes, I touch the talisman as though traveling through a tunnel. It serves me as a doorway back into this realm."

"So break out of the tunnel when you are near." Naamah closed her eyes and rested her face in her hands. "I wish things could go back to how they were."

"Wish in one hand and shit in the other. See which one fills up first," said Lily.

"Helpful, as always, Mother."

Lily pursed her lips and scowled.

"If you want to be helpful, tell me what to do next—" Naamah swiveled her chair and returned to staring out the window. "—because I don't have a clue."

2

Toby woke to the sound of the pavilion walls flapping and snapping. Outside, the wind carried streamers of sand aloft, then flung the sand earthward once more. Dark, angry clouds covered the sky, obscuring the sun.

Lily hadn't shown up by nightfall, and he'd found a bevy of excuses to stay another day and night—not the least of which was the fear of leaving the water barrel behind. He'd tried to lift it, but it weighed too much.

His stomach grumbled, hot and painful as though someone had stuck him with a fireplace poker. He'd taken a brief exploratory walk late in the previous day, hoping to find plant life—cactus at least—but all he'd found was sand and more sand.

Toby got up and walked to the water barrel. He submerged the copper dipper, then lifted it to his mouth. *The water even tastes good, but I've got to find something to eat.*

He knew he could survive without food for a long time. Far longer than most people thought. Plus, he'd had a lot of water—at least a gallon—and that had staved off some of the hunger. Even so, he felt good. No headaches, no nausea, nothing.

Which isn't to say that I wouldn't destroy a juicy filet mignon right about now.

The wind gusted, snapping the walls of the pavilion tight and flinging sand in through the opening. He had nothing to block it with, but at least it opened onto the face of a tall dune.

How am I going to get out of here? I've got to get back to New York.

He turned his back on the growing storm, already sick of looking at it.

I wonder if calling her name would bring Lily? Toby frowned at the thought. *But that would be like asking her for help, wouldn't it?*

3

Benny sat in the La-Z-Boy recliner while Eddie and Amanda sat on the couch. Mike stood opposite them, squinting down at the screen of his phone.

"This is amazing," Mike said. "It says here the first news clipping about the lamp is from 1895. That was the year that

Tiffany created the first of his lamps, but there is no record that Tiffany created this one. The maker's mark doesn't match any of his known marks."

Benny rolled his fingers in a hurry-up gesture. "Keep reading. It gets even more interesting."

Mike glanced at him, then nodded and returned his attention to his phone. "Holy shit," he murmured.

"*Exactly*," said Benny.

"What?" asked Eddie.

"The maker's mark shows up on a Victorian lamp in the 1850s. Before that, the researchers found a record of it on a pair of decorative brass candlesticks that date back to an estate auction in 1793."

"That's *insane*."

"There is more," said Mike. "According to this report, an ornate gilt bronze candelabra appears on a shipping manifest for a Portuguese ship sailing out of Lisbon in the early 1500s. The ship's destination was Porto Seguro in Brazil."

"There is more, but that's enough to paint the picture. This lamp has traveled the world."

"But you said the maker's mark appeared on candlesticks and a fancy candelabra. So it wasn't *this* lamp, just the mark."

"I'm not so sure," said Benny. "This isn't a random marking. In fact, one of the researchers went so far as to have the cuneiform translated. It says, 'Hail Lilitu, Bearer of Chaos.' That's not something someone would stumble upon."

"Then what?" asked Eddie.

"I think the lamp has been remade, again and again. It was probably separated out into its constituent parts, and then the metals were melted down and recast into a new form. The glass was probably used as decoration, no matter what its form."

A deep frown spread across Amanda's face. "But why? Why not make something other than a lamp? Something that wouldn't have to be remade?"

Benny cocked his head to the side. "I have no idea, but I think it's clear: the materials used to make this lamp are important at the very least."

"Then let's *destroy* it."

"How?" asked Mike. "Since it's not limited to any one form, if we melted it all down into slag, then we're left with a magical lump of slag, and the demons go on as they always have."

"Dissolve it in acid," said Eddie.

"Are we then left with a vat full of magical acid?" asked Benny with a smile.

"Who knows? It isn't as if it came with an owner's manual."

"What if we throw it down a bottomless lake or one of those trenches out in the ocean?"

"Okay," said Benny. "But how do we know what happens if we get rid of it? What if the demons only need it to exist for them to stay here?"

"On the other hand, what if it's the only thing on the planet that can hurt them?" asked Mike.

Eddie threw up his hands and let them slap against his thighs. "Then what do we do?"

Benny pursed his lips. "That is an excellent question." He met Mike's gaze. "I sure wish Toby was here."

"All of them," Mike murmured. "I wish we knew *where* Toby was."

"If wishes were fishes…" said Amanda in a singsong voice.

"Then I guess we have to wait. The researchers digging into the history of the lamp might turn something up."

"How likely is that?" asked Eddie.

"If it were one or two people? Not likely at all. Greg set up this human search engine thing, though, so it isn't just one person, it's a lot of people, and they're working twenty-four hours a day." Benny slid forward to sit on the edge of the recliner's seat. "In the meantime, we can discuss your abilities."

"It's better than sitting here, twiddling our thumbs." Eddie cocked his head to the side. "But going back to this human search engine thing for a second."

"Yes?"

"Can they look into something for us?"

"Absolutely," said Benny.

"We got this letter the day Abby appeared in our kitchen." Amanda held the letter out to Benny.

He took it and read it. When he finished, he handed it to Mike. "I take it the letter is some kind of scam?"

"That's what we thought. We certainly never agreed to sell our house to anyone."

"And what is this Stanton Growth Fund?"

"It's an investment fund. Right now, the fund is hot—the manager is a guy named Chris Stanton. He's become a recluse—often shutting himself up in his office for days at a time—and through some process no one understands, he has had ridiculous success picking investments with long odds and big payoffs."

"That's interesting," murmured Benny. "I helped Toby do the same thing. It would be interesting to see this guy's trades. But I'll ask the SEMPRe researchers to look into this land grab thing." He swiped his phone open and entered what he wanted into the app Greg's team had created. "Shouldn't take long," he said.

4

Lilitu snorted and rolled her eyes. "Well, I can tell you what we shouldn't do, and that is to sit here moaning and wailing while allowing our enemies to entrench themselves."

"You don't say! If only I had thought of that!" Naamah snarled, glowering at her mother.

"Mistresses, *please*—" began Abyzou.

"Why is it you always seem to need my help, and yet you always find a way to make it my fault?" Lilitu stood and paced to the picture window.

"Mistresses! Stop this!" snapped Abyzou. "This stupid infighting accomplishes nothing. Our situation is dire, and yet, here both of you sit sniping at one another as you always have. Well, let me ask you something: what has this cat fighting ever gotten you? Has it ever weakened either of your positions; has it ever softened either of your hearts? Why must you persist in this childish game?"

Lilitu had stepped halfway to the picture window and turned to face Abyzou, her eyebrows arched. "Please, Abyzou. Don't check your punches. Tell us how you really feel."

Naamah snorted. "Is that the most you have ever spoken to me at one time, Abby? Should I call for water? Because your throat must be parched."

Wearing a wry smile, Lilitu stepped closer to the golden *ifrit*. She put a hand on Abyzou's shoulder. "It's been hard for you, hasn't it? Always having to stand between us, to referee our petty arguments."

Abyzou said nothing, only closed her eyes and sighed.

"It must feel hopeless," said Naamah.

"Perhaps we do take things too far, Naamah."

The vermillion *ifrit* nodded but squinted at her mother.

"To business then, with all 'petty cat fighting' tabled. For now."

"Agreed," said Naamah. "You said the talisman is in a container that you can't penetrate?"

"Yes. I can only find it in the Chthonian realm. From there, I can slide my awareness inside the talisman, and through it into the dark space in which they've placed it."

"Correct me if I'm wrong, Abyzou, but you used the talisman as an anchor for your...*family* projects. But isn't it also true that you can locate your subjects even in its absence?"

"Once things have progressed past a certain point, yes."

"And were those your subjects in the black SUV?"

Abyzou cocked her head to the side. "Two of them, yes. The pair that arrived late for the party."

"But they did leave with the hunters?"

Abyzou nodded.

"Then it stands to reason that they may be with them still. Can you locate them?"

Abyzou dropped her gaze to the ground, but not before Lilitu glimpsed her wan expression. "Mistress..."

"Oh, I see. They have not yet reached that point?" asked Naamah.

"It's…" Abyzou winced and swallowed hard. "They… That is, Eddie hasn't…" She gave up speaking and scowled at the carpet.

"Eddie hasn't what?"

Abyzou raised her gaze to meet Lilitu's. Her face was locked in a rictus of shame, her eyelids fluttering as though she had something in her eye. "He has *resisted* me!"

"Ah," murmured Naamah.

"I understand. Despite our best efforts, sometimes things take a turn. It's not your fault, dear one." Lilitu turned and stared out the window. "But still, there must be some way we can find them. Even if it is only one of them, we can drag the truths from him." Lilitu turned back to face Naamah and Abyzou, raising her arms as if to hug them both. "From time to time, we all may find a human with a spectacular will—enough willpower to resist us—but no man can resist *all three of us.*"

Despite her shame, Abyzou smiled.

"True enough," said Naamah. "There's something I should add."

"Yes, *mija?*"

"I know where the talisman is."

Lilitu sucked her teeth. "Then why this charade?"

"It's an object lesson. I know where the talisman is because of a very inventive *mazzikim.* I wanted you both to see that they are more than cattle. They can help us."

Lilitu turned her gaze on Abyzou, and after a few breaths, both giggled like schoolgirls.

"They *can.*"

"Yes," said Lilitu, trying to stem her laughter. "I'll grant you that your pet *mazzikim* has saved us a bit of work, but we would have found it in any case. He did nothing we couldn't do ourselves."

Naamah turned away with a sour expression on her face. "I'll send a *mazzikim* for the talisman." She glanced over her shoulder. "Unless you feel they wouldn't be helpful."

5

Toby stood in the center of the pavilion, looking out onto the maelstrom of sand and wind. He had never minded being alone; in fact, he *needed* his alone time. But at the same time, his current situation nagged at him.

The walls of the pavilion whipped to and fro, fighting against the stakes that held the silk down and wrestling with the wind. Toby looked around, taking yet another inventory of the materials he had on hand—the materials Lily had left for him. It didn't seem likely that a silk pavilion would withstand the massive winds that he suspected accompanied a sandstorm. Yet again, he found nothing that would help him escape the storm.

Overhead, thunder boomed, and lightning lanced into the sand far out in the desert. Toby shrank away from the opening, away from the fury of the storm, then laughed at himself. *It's not as if this silk tent will offer me more protection than being outside.*

Toby had never liked thunderstorms, and this new, drier version was no exception. Eddies of grit swirled through the opening, dust devils in miniature, and they danced around before losing their lifeline to the wind outside and collapsing back to mere dust. The taste of alkaline filled his mouth, and the odors of desert musk and cactus assaulted his nose.

Sand cascaded down the face of the dune that partially sheltered the pavilion and piled up inside the door. *If the storm keeps going the way it is, it's going to bury me in this little red tent.*

Toby stood in the center of the tent, watching the sand pile up at the entrance, watching as the sky got darker and darker, Lily's name dancing on his lips. Accompanied by the booming sound of the storm's displeasure, lightning marched across the desert toward him.

But still, Toby dithered. *Do it, Toby,* a voice in his mind said. *Do it, do it, do it.*

He wanted to be somewhere else—*anywhere* else—and he knew of only one way he could escape the growling storm. *Calling her name aloud will bring Lily in a heartbeat. No one could blame you; the storm is becoming more and more dangerous.*

Toby didn't trust that voice in his head. It didn't sound like himself.

But he *wanted* to trust it.

6

"I never realized that I had this ability, you understand. It wasn't until we came to that parking lot that I'd ever seen any of these…"

"Demons," said Benny.

"Okay, sure. I've never seen any demons before yesterday morning—excluding Abby, of course, though I didn't realize she was a demon. Dr. Erikson spent a lot of time and effort convincing me that she was a fabrication of my own mind."

Benny's expression soured. "Ah, a psychiatrist?"

"Psychologist."

"Same thing." Benny waved it away. "But now you know better."

Eddie nodded. "Now we know better, but I can't help thinking I'm going to regret this new knowledge."

Benny wagged his head to the side and grunted. "Yeah, unless we can figure out how to beat them, we'll all regret knowing them."

"Well, that's reassuring," said Amanda with a grin.

7

"Shannon?"

She groaned and opened her eyes. Shannon ached all over, even the parts of her that the demon had missed. But as she came fully awake and remembered she could be discharged if she felt up to it, she put on a happy face and ignored the aches and pains.

"Shannon?" asked Kristy from the foot of the bed. "Are you awake?"

"Yes. And before you ask, I feel great and am ready to go home."

Kristy laughed. *Nice try, Shannon.*

"I thought I'd imagined that," murmured Shannon.

"Nope." Kristy put her laptop on the overbed table as she had in earlier visits and scanned through Shannon's chart. "I have someone outside in the hall. It's my husband, Sean

Walker. He is one of the researchers—or whatever you call them—at SEMPRe. He'd like to meet you."

"To meet me?"

"He wants to say hello." Kristy glanced at the open door leading to the hall. "He says he needs to talk to *all* the directors. Something about the lamp."

"The lamp?" Shannon shook her head and frowned.

"He can explain better than I can. Is it okay?"

"Yes, of course." Half of Shannon's face was hidden by a bandage, but the wounds beneath were already knitting together—if the itch was any measure of progress. "My God, this itches."

Kristy flashed a small smile. *I've done my best to accelerate your healing.*

"You—"

Kristy turned and strode to the door. "Come in, Sean, but remember what I said."

"Yes, dear. 'Don't get over-excited, don't wear your patient out.'"

He strolled into the room, his gaze resting lightly on Shannon's face. "Ms. Bertram?"

Kristy moved to the door and swung it closed.

"Hello, Sean," said Shannon.

He hit her with a dazzling smile. "Yes, hello. Before we start, I want you to know how much I admire you. You and the others."

Shannon hitched her shoulders and flip-flopped her unhurt hand on the bedspread, then grimaced at the pain that lanced through her upper back. "Nice to meet you."

"Yes, nice to meet you. Did Kristy…" He turned and glanced at his wife, who nodded. "Okay. I'm part of your human search engine effort. Your husband put out a call for research about the lamp, and—"

"Ho. Hold up. What lamp?"

Sean again peeked in his wife's direction. "The Tiffany lamp?"

Shannon shrugged.

"I..." He hesitated, looking down at his feet. "Well, there's this Tiffany lamp we were asked to find out about, and I've found out a lot." As he spoke, his voice grew stronger, less unsure. "I found this mark—a maker's mark—that indicates the lamp is not a Tiffany at all, but rather a clever forgery. Or maybe it's a copy, I don't know. The craftsmanship is—"

"Sean," prompted Kristy.

"Yes, uh-huh. Sorry. This maker's mark turns out to be cuneiform—*Akkadian* cuneiform—and it translates to 'Hail Lilitu, Bearer of Chaos.' Does that mean anything to you?"

Shannon shook her head, her gaze leaping from Sean to Kristy and back again. "I don't understand any of this."

"Well, the lamp appears to have been crafted in the late 1890s, but there are records of other, more primitive lamps bearing the same mark stretching back through recorded history. And what's really strange is that all these lamps were constructed from the same three materials—bronze, lead, and glass. In the cases where the lamp's design doesn't require one of the materials, it's used as decoration. I believe that the old version of the lamp is melted down, and the materials are reused to create the new one."

"Okay," said Shannon.

"What we really would need to know for sure is to perform a chemical analysis. For example, we can date the bronze by testing for the amount of zinc used in the alloy."

"Zinc."

"Yeah," he said, nodding. "Modern bronze uses a lot, ancient bronze uses none, or very little. It's interesting, really, that this—"

"Sean," said Kristy.

"Right, okay. The phrase. Remember I said the maker's mark is Akkadian cuneiform? I thought searching for the phrase online might yield fruit, so I did that. Searched online."

"Okay," said Shannon.

"Yes, right. The phrase 'Hail Lilitu, Bearer of Chaos' doesn't occur with any frequency in modern texts. Well, it appears in some prayers purportedly used in witchcraft, but other than that, there's not much." He rocked on his heels, smiling. "But when you go back, I mean really dig into ancient writings, it shows up a lot. Especially in Akkadian, Sumerian, and Babylonian myths."

"I don't know anything about this. If Benny asked you for this, he's the one who needs to hear it."

"I… That is, I thought you could relay the information—"

"No, that won't do," said Shannon, shaking her head. "I won't remember all that, and the others will have many questions that I won't be able to answer."

Sean glanced at Kristy. "Well, uh…"

"You two can drive me home," said Shannon. She beamed a smile at Sean. "I'm going home today."

"Oh, uh…" Again, he looked to his wife, who watched Shannon closely.

"Yes," said Kristy. "Okay."

"Good," said Shannon. "Before we go, I want to see Greg."

"He's in the ICU. They won't allow you to visit."

"I can't leave without seeing him for myself. Mike will expect nothing less, and I owe them both many times over."

"The hospital won't—"

"Yes, they will. After you've told them he's my only living blood relative."

A little grin settled on Kristy's lips. "Fine." She shooed Sean out of the room. "This lady needs to get dressed. Go find a wheelchair."

8

The storm continued to grow, continued to hurl lightning closer and closer to the pavilion, and continued to sandblast the unsheltered sides of the silk tent—which by some miracle named Lily, withstood the onslaught. Thunder and the howling wind battled for dominance, as did arguments in Toby's head for calling out to Lily and not calling her.

He dithered, first turning his back on the raging storm, then facing it again, and always, *always*, arguing with himself. He had prepared himself to die years before when he first started stalking demons, but he hadn't prepared himself to throw his life away uselessly, buried alive by desert sand. But still, he couldn't force himself to call on her, to beg Lily for help. It felt like a betrayal, a betrayal of his friends, a betrayal of all the work he'd done to rid the world of demons.

He cast his mind back—more to distract himself than for any real desire for self-reflection. He remembered all the missed opportunities: the potential girlfriends, the chance at a *real* life, of a family—all sacrificed at the altar of ridding the world of Lily's kind. He'd been alone since he turned eighteen, and Toby thought that was what he wanted, but then everything changed when he rekindled his friendship with Benny and Mike and built new ones with Shannon and Greg.

With Scott.

Toby squeezed his eyes shut—and not only to protect them from the blowing grit. *Ah, Scott!* His loss felt like a ragged hole torn through Toby's guts. He'd only known the man for three years, and they'd spent much of that time ruffling each other's feathers, but still, Toby felt his loss keenly.

He opened his eyes and looked around the small tent. He'd already done it, again and again and again, but he scoured the interior for something to *do*.

But there was nothing but a cold grill, a barrel of water, a copper water dipper, and a few silk cushions.

Nothing.

9

"Pull over for a minute, please," said Shannon. "Somewhere under cover, if you can." She pressed her face against the window and peered skyward.

"Under these trees?"

"Better than nothing," she said, "but if you can find an overpass or a fuel stop with a covered island, that would be better."

"Uh, okay. I'll find something like that." His eyes peeked at Shannon in the rearview mirror. "Are you going to be sick or something?"

"What? Oh, no. I want to disguise the car in case anyone followed us from the hospital."

"I haven't noticed anything," said Sean. He turned his head and peered behind them through the corner of his eye.

"Sean, love, watch the road," said Kristy in a well-worn, but calm voice.

"Oh, yes."

"Sean, can you see them?" Shannon asked.

"See them? Yes. Sort of, anyway."

Kristy smiled at her husband. "As a child, Sean figured out how to see past their disguises by 'not looking' at them." She chuckled. "He's tried to teach me, but I can't let go enough to make it work."

"What do you mean, 'not looking?'"

"Well, as a kid, a deputy named Karl Munnur attached himself to my mother and me. At the same time, a kid named Leif Lawson attached himself to Kristy. But it wasn't a kid and a deputy sheriff, it was a demon. He was yellow and looked like a gorilla. See, I had—"

"LaBouche," Shannon breathed.

"LaBouche? Karl never used that name."

"Lee LaBouche was the partner of one of my friends in the State Police. But in reality, he was a demon that Toby described as 'banana yellow and built like a great ape.' He had a large mouth filled with shark teeth."

"That's Karl, all right. At first, I couldn't see him, but there was something off about him. He… He kept bringing up my father—who died in Vietnam. And when he did, I would catch him staring at me with a sort of greedy expression from time to time."

Tell her about the dreams.

"Oh, right. The dreams. I started dreaming about a yellow monster, and this one time, when I was sick, I woke to find Karl staring at me, and he made a veiled threat. In my dream, he was always after Kristy, and in one of them, he wore her skin like a cape. He—"

"You never told me that," said Kristy.

Sean glanced at her and ducked his head. "Yeah. I didn't think you needed to know about that one." He switched his gaze to Shannon in the rearview mirror. "Anyway, one night Karl had set Kristy up for a…" Again, he peeked at his wife.

"Leif was selling me to old men," Kristy said. "He was pimping me out. He had me hooked on drugs and got me to do all sorts of things."

"Yeah. Anyway, I was out for a walk one night and saw Leif driving Karl's car, so I followed him. Long story short, I interrupted his plans and broke Kristy out of there. After that, Karl was gone, but I'd see this other old car following me or driving by the house. One night, I had this dream that Kristy was in trouble. That Denny Cratchkin was going to hurt her."

"Dennis the Menace?"

"The same," said Kristy.

"When was this?"

"December of 1979. You'd already…"

"Sure," said Shannon. "I remember Denny going to juvie around then."

Sean nodded. "Yep. That night I had the dream, he broke into her house and tried to brain her with a hammer."

"Tell her about how you saw Karl outside your house."

"Right, okay. So, I woke up from this dream where Kristy was being raped and hurt, and I knew she was in trouble. Back then, I didn't know *how* I knew, I only knew it was true. I peeked out through my blinds, and there was this car down the road. A Ford Galaxy that I'd seen around. As hard as I tried, I couldn't see the driver, too many shadows, not enough light, whatever. As I turned away, I caught a flash of yellow in the corner of my eye."

"LaBouche."

"If you say so. Anyway, I messed around until I got my brain to avoid zeroing in on the yellow with my eyes. I let my peripheral vision do the work."

"And that's harder than it sounds," said Kristy. "I never could get the knack of it."

"I'd like to try something," said Shannon.

"Sure, okay," said Sean.

"Find a place where you can park that hides the car from above."

Sean turned in to a self-serve carwash—the kind where drivers had to get out and spray their cars with a pressure washer—and pulled in to one of the bays. "Now what?" he asked.

"Get out and go around the side of the building."

"Er…why?"

"Go along, Sean," said Kristy.

"Yeah, okay. Sure. Be right back." Sean climbed out of the car and walked around the wall into another bay.

Shannon squeezed her eyes shut and tried to change the appearance of the car. Her pulse throbbed in her veins, and her head felt as though it might explode, but it worked. "Okay, call him back."

Kristy blew the horn, and Sean came around the corner then froze. He backed up and looked in the neighboring bay, then came back to the bay they were in. "What's going on?" asked Kristy.

"To him, this bay looks empty."

"What? How can you—"

"I can hear my loudmouth wife," Sean said, "but I can't see her." He turned his head to the side as if to look away but froze there for a moment. When he turned back, a broad smile decorated his face. "That's neat!" He walked unerringly to the driver's side door and climbed in. "How do you do that?"

"You could see us? Using that corner-of-your-eye trick?"

"Sure, yeah."

"Interesting," said Shannon with an exhausted sigh.

"Yeah, okay. Once I saw you that way, the illusion no longer worked."

"Even more interesting."

"Come on, Sean. My patient is getting tired. Let's get her home."

"Right, sure. Okay." Sean started the car and drove on.

10

As twilight fell, the storm began to abate. The pavilion still stood, though the entrance was flooded by drifts of golden sand. Toby filled the dipper with cold water and slaked his thirst, but there was nothing to mitigate his hunger.

It's time to decide, he thought. *I can't sit here waiting for a demon who may never return. On the other hand, I can't leave my only water source behind.*

He stooped by the water barrel and wiggled his fingers around its base, trying to find purchase. But a band of slick copper wrapped the bottom of the barrel, and he couldn't shift the barrel far enough to slide his fingers underneath. If she had left rope or had the pavilion been one of canvas rather than silk, he could've fashioned a sling and carried the water barrel on his back—heavy or not.

He put his shoulder against the barrel's lip and pushed, rocking the barrel onto its rearward edge. He slipped his fingers underneath and tried to lift the barrel using only his arms and shoulders. He could move it, but picking it up so he could walk wasn't going to happen.

I could call her. It doesn't mean anything. It's not an admission; it's not a pledge to serve her. Toby pulled his fingers out from underneath the barrel and slowly lowered it back to the ground. *I should just do it and be done with it.*

Yes, do it. What could it hurt?

II

Dan flew in a circle above the driveway. He'd adopted the look of a sparrow, and since the hunter was otherwise occupied half a world away, he could afford to fly out in the open.

Out on the road, a car slowed, then turned into the gravel track that led to the asphalt pad near the garage and house. He peered at the driver but didn't recognize him.

In the house, someone whooped, and the front door banged open.

12

As Sean turned on the twin-rutted track that led to Toby's mansion on the cliff, the front door of the house slammed open, and Benny came sprinting out. "*Shannon!*" he cried. He sprinted up the drive to the car and ripped the back door open. "Shannon!" He dropped into the seat next to her and made as if to hug her but pulled back at the last minute. His gaze zipped here and there, cataloging her injuries while Shannon grinned at him.

Mike came to the front door and looked out, his shoulders slumped and a dour expression on his face.

"Drive on, Sean," said Shannon. "I have to talk to Mike."

"Right, yes." Sean pulled up in front of the house and killed the engine. Benny jumped out and ran around to Shannon's side, opening the door for her and offering his hand.

Kristy watched for a moment, then turned and punched Sean in the shoulder. "You never do that for me!"

"Get mauled by a demon and I will."

She arched an eyebrow at him.

"Uh-huh, okay. Not funny. I take it back, O mysterious powers of the multiverse."

Shannon gestured toward Mike, and Benny helped her hobble to the door. She held out her good hand, and Mike took it.

"I'm happy to see you, Shan," he said.

"I saw him, Mike. I made them take me to him so I could see him with my own eyes."

Tears sprang into Mike's eyes. "And?"

Shannon squeezed his hand. "It's touch and go. He..." She chewed her lip and winced as she pulled one of the lacerations. "He had an aneurysm that they had to repair, and he's still unconscious." She turned her head. "Doctor Walker can tell you more, but he's *alive*, Mike."

Mike nodded soberly, his gaze locked on the couple as they got out of the car. "Is that..."

"Sean and Kristy Walker," said Shannon.

"From Oneka Falls. Yeah. I knew Sean, and *everyone* knew Kristy. Come on in." Mike turned and led the way to the living room. "Do you know about Scott?" he asked over his shoulder.

"Scott?"

Benny sucked his teeth. "Scott's gone, honey."

"Gone?"

"What do you remember?"

"The demon." Shannon shuddered and leaned closer to Benny.

"Right. The demon charged you, and Greg tore him off. He was struggling to hold him when Mason Harper came up behind him and..." Mike slumped into a recliner, shaking his head and wiping at his eyes.

"Scott ran to help. He shot Mason, then shot the demon attacking you." Benny helped her onto the couch and sat beside her. "The demon turned on him and—" Benny's voice hitched, but he took a deep breath and went on. "And it killed Scott, honey."

"Oh, my God," Shannon murmured. She looked around with tears blurring her vison. "Where's... Don't tell me Toby..."

Benny shook his head. "We don't know. Do you remember the two new ones?"

"The two new whats?"

You were in and out of it. Two new, super powerful demons joined the fight, and we had to run. One of them took Toby right out of the driver's seat of the Suburban. Mike and Eddie kept us from crashing, but only just."

"Eddie?"

"Yeah. Eddie and Amanda Mitchell. Eddie's been haunted by one of the new demons—the one made of golden fire—for all of his life."

"Since I was seven," said Eddie from the top of the stairs.

"Sure, okay. And you owned the lamp?" asked Sean advancing toward the stairs as though he wanted to sprint up them and interrogate Eddie.

"I did. I still do, I guess."

"That's why I'm here."

"Sean's one of our researchers," said Shannon. "He's found something."

All eyes turned to Sean. He blushed under the scrutiny and looked out the picture windows at Lake Erie.

"He's also got a neat trick for seeing the demons. Could come in handy since Toby's missing. *If* we can learn how he does it."

"That won't be a problem," said Benny. "Both Eddie and Amanda can see them, too."

13

He had dithered most of the evening away, first arguing against calling Lily's name, then switching it up and supporting it. And now, with the moon directly overhead, he had only a few hours to travel. He still had no way to carry the water barrel, and still he could not determine the best direction in which to walk.

She had come for him last time. She had come in time to save him from dying of exposure, and she'd given him water without forcing him to ask. Perhaps if he set off, she'd come again, save him again.

Don't be an idiot. She's an archdemon, a demi-goddess, feared by the demons in Oneka Falls. Why in the hell would she care whether Toby Burton lives or dies?

Toby shifted his weight from foot to foot, staring at the long shadow the pavilion painted on the sand in the moonlight. He couldn't remember the last time he had been so torn by a decision. "Oh, this is ridiculous!" He'd always taken pride in the fact that he could make good decisions quickly, but it seemed that ability had abandoned him as surely as Lily had. *And now, I'm talking to myself aloud. Perfect.*

He stepped out of the pavilion and climbed the dune that had sheltered him from the worst of the sandstorm. At its peak, he turned a full circle, his gaze darting from dune to dune, following an unbreakable line that marched toward the horizon. "Which way do I go?"

For a moment, that spooky dirge he had first heard when Lily had kidnapped him out of the moving Suburban came to him on the breeze, but it died with the dying of the wind. An odor wafted toward him. A scent that filled his mouth with saliva.

He turned and dropped his attention to the pavilion below him. He couldn't see into the silk structure from the top of the dune, but he didn't need to. The red silk tent was lit from within, and it glowed like a bed of coals.

Lily was back, and she was cooking him dinner.

Toby tried not to acknowledge her, tried not to sprint down the face of the dune into her presence.

He tried and failed.

14

Benny relaxed into the sofa, his eyes glued to Sean Walker as the man repeated what he'd already told Shannon at the hospital. Shannon sat at Benny's side, leaning her head on his shoulder.

"And as I told your beautiful wife, the phrase occurs in the ancient texts and legends of Akkad, Sumer, and Babylon. The name Lilitu seems to be used interchangeably with the name Ardat Lili."

"This is fascinating, but I don't see how it—"

"A few more minutes," said Sean. "That's all I ask."

Benny tilted his head to the side and stared at Sean for the time it took him to draw three deep breaths. "Okay."

"Yes, okay. Right. The legend goes all the way back to Akkadian mythology. It seems Lilitu was the wife of a demon named Lilu, and the pair were somehow tied to a disreputable priest. Lilu disappeared, but references to Lilitu appear even in the Judeo-Christian belief system, though they name her Lilith."

"Okay," said Benny.

"Oh, that's not the best part." He opened his phone and swiped through his pictures. "Take a look at this." He held out the phone, and on the screen was the photo of an ancient pottery bowl. The inner surface was crowded with something written in a strange language, but the figure at the bottom of the bowl drew Benny's undivided attention. It depicted a woman.

A woman wearing a black dress. She had bright red hair and orange eyes.

"Holy shit," muttered Benny.

"Yes, exactly. The language is Aramaic, and it dates back to the sixth century."

"What does the inscription say?"

"It's an incantation against evil." Sean looked at each of them. "An evil named Lilitu."

"And that's who took Toby?" Shannon asked.

"Yes."

The room started to spin, and Shannon grabbed Benny's hand. "I feel sick." She squeezed her eyes shut against the spinning, but it was no use. She fell into Benny's lap, and everything went black.

15

"Ah! The intrepid explorer returns," said Lily as Toby burst through the entrance of the tent. Her eyes twinkled, and one side of her mouth curled upward.

Toby stood just inside the entrance, panting from his exertion of slogging through the loose sand and staring at her. The eerie melody was back, though at low volume, like mood music at an upscale Manhattan restaurant.

"Cat got your tongue?" Lily's voice lilted with amusement. "Come in. Sit down. We have much to discuss, but we can do that while I cook." Tilting her head, she peeked up at him. "I assume you won't say no to more goat?"

Toby's jaw worked, but he said nothing. The truth of it was that he felt immense gratitude that Lily had returned, and he didn't want to admit it. He didn't want her to know anything about it.

The volume of the dirge increased a little, one ethereal strain following the next. Toby shook his head from side to side. "Where is that music coming from?"

"Do you like it? No human has played my melodies for thousands of years, though some have heard it."

"It's terrible." Toby thought she might be offended, that he might anger her with his blunt assessment, but Lily only smiled.

"It *is* great and terrible, but the music is also steeped in power. *My* power."

"Can you make it stop? I find it…distracting."

Lily's smile grew broader. "Can I make it stop? Of course I can, but that isn't your question."

Toby sank into a crouch and arched one eyebrow at her. "No?"

"No. Your question is: *will* I make it stop. And so far, it seems the answer to that is in the negative." She glanced down at the grill and turned the skewers of meat roasting atop it. "Come closer, Tobes. Sit next to me. Sit close enough to brush against my flesh."

Toby found it incredibly difficult not to rush to her side, to stop his hands from racing across her form.

Lily took another quick peek at him, then chuckled, and her clothing disappeared. "Tempted?"

Toby's jaw worked, and once more, he didn't trust himself to speak. *My God! She is beyond perfect! Her skin is like cream and her proportions… If ever a woman could embody perfection, that woman sits naked in front of me cooking my dinner.*

Lily threw him a wink. "*Ay, que chulo, papi.* I've made you speechless." She stood and faced him, letting the light from the grill dance across her flesh.

Lust was like a physical thing within Toby, like a wild tiger refusing to be contained. Without meaning to, he crawled a step closer, his gaze riveted on the candy-red triangle of hair below her navel.

"Come to me. Do it, *habibi*. Take what you so clearly want. Come to me and take me."

Her words danced across his mind like a brush fire, burning as they went, and leaving charred remains behind. Half of him wanted to leap across the distance between them and bury himself in her, but the other half... The other half *knew better*. Even so, it was a struggle to keep himself from dashing to her.

She looked at him and waited, her expression solemn. No further words were needed, no further enticement could top what she'd already offered. As the seconds ticked by, she cocked her head to the side, and her bright orange eyes seemed to twirl and twirl and twirl. The mournful lament that she claimed as her own music grew louder and louder.

Toby had been to the beach once. He had stood just past the line where the water met the sand and luxuriated in the feeling of the sand being sucked from under his feet. Kneeling in the tent, with Lily six feet away, naked and waiting, felt much the same. He felt himself slipping away and was as unable to resist her pull as the sand was able to resist the tide.

Ever so slowly, a bright, sunny smile spread its wings on Lily's lips. She lifted both arms, her hands open, welcoming.

Toby fought with everything he had, used every trick he learned throughout his mostly celibate life to defeat the urge within him.

"You've denied yourself for so long, Tobias," said Lily, and it was as if she spoke directly into his brain, foregoing the air between them. "All those years...the *decades* during which you refused to allow anyone to get close, during which you refused to allow yourself to even think of a lover." She beckoned him with both hands, arms still held straight out as if to pull him in. "It was such a needless sacrifice."

Toby tried and tried to turn away from her gaze, but it was as if her eyes were magnetic and his own were cast from iron. He commanded his head to turn away, but his muscles refused to obey him. He pushed with his arms, trying to force himself back, to leave the tent, to leave her temptations behind, but his hands didn't even twitch where they lay on his thighs.

Lily opened her lips a minuscule amount, and the creepy little elegy grew in volume yet again. The countermelody and the melody continued their eternal dissonance, filling him up from the soles of the feet to the crown of his head. She winked, and Toby began to hear voices buried in the music. They chanted and sang in a strange sounding language that was as unlike anything Toby had ever heard as Lily was as unlike any woman he'd ever known.

The vocals bombarded him, swirled around his head, infiltrated his ears, and wormed their way into the core of him. He felt...*different*...unwound, somehow.

Lily's eyes flashed as she brought her arms to her sides, and her face and neck flushed as she brought her hands up to cup her breasts. "Oh, please come to me, Tobias."

The urgency in her voice rumbled through him like an earthquake, reducing his wall of self-control to rubble. His shirt came off with a mere flick of his wrist, and Lily's smile turned warm and inviting. He crawled to her on his hands and knees, and he thought it correct to go to her that way.

She reached for him, and her blood red fingernails trailed across the skin of his chest. For the first time, Toby noticed her nails were filed to sharp points, but he no longer cared about such things.

She wrapped her arms around him, and he was lost in her scent, the feel of her, the delicious red of her hair. She angled her head, and his lips sought hers.

16

Shannon awoke with difficulty as though cotton encapsulated her brain, impinging on her ability to think, to choose, to act. She groaned, and a hand rubbed her shoulder. She cracked open one eyelid and found Benny leaning over her, catching her eye.

It's okay, Shan, Benny said in her mind. *Rest all you need to.*

She tried to push herself into a seated position but to no avail. She felt horrible—nauseated, woozy, and weak. The demon's comprehensive attack had taken its toll, and her body demanded more rest.

"Shouldn't she go back to the hospital?" asked Benny. "She seems so fragile."

Shannon groaned and mumbled her disapproval.

"No, she's fine. She's no doubt exhausted from the long trip from Rochester," said Kristy. "To assist her healing, she needs rest—peace and quiet—and you can't get any of that in a hospital."

"And you're sure?"

Shannon heard the worry in Benny's voice and wanted to comfort him, to tell him she was okay and would improve by morning. She longed to do all those things but didn't have the energy.

"Yes," said Kristy.

"If she needs rest—*real* rest—and the quiet to do it, she should be in our bedroom. Can I move her?"

As she tried to muster enough power to send her thoughts to him, she descended into unconsciousness once again and dreamed Toby was lost in the desert.

Chapter 4
Tuesday

I

The odor of broiling meat brought Toby awake. Outside the tent, the sun baked the golden sand, and the desert smelled of flint and dust and sage. He turned his head and pushed himself up on one elbow. Lily knelt in front of the grill, her back turned. A pang of guilt stabbed through him, and he squeezed his eyes shut.

"Oh, no, *motek*. Don't play that silly human game."

The warm, heavy air inside the pavilion felt good against his skin. The heat of the sun, mitigated by red silk, relaxed him. *What's done is done*, he told himself.

"Yes, Tobes. That's right."

"This…" He flopped back on the silk cushions and stared at the roof of the tent. "I don't…" He grimaced. "You…"

"Relax, *vozlyublenny*. It isn't as if you signed a contract in your own blood. Passion…it affects us all." She lifted four skewers of meat from the grill and placed them on a wooden platter, then turned to face him, holding out the dish for him to choose from. "Plus, I'm gorgeous."

"I never asked—"

"Shh. There is no need." She laid the platter on the ground between them. "Eat, Toby. I know you want to, and you know you *need* to."

"And you? Don't you need to eat?"

She treated him to a lopsided smile, her eyes as lazy as a cat's. "All living things must eat."

Toby reached for a skewer and ate a morsel of goat meat from it. "I'm not sure that's an answer."

Chuckling, Lily put her arms behind her, locked her elbows, and leaned back. "I eat. Does that satisfy you, *kisa*?"

"Just not goat?"

"No, not goat. I *can* eat it, but it does nothing for me. I derive my sustenance from other things."

The meat soured on Toby's tongue, and he frowned at the platter between them. "Fear. Degradation. Anger."

Lily's laugh was lilting, but it sounded forced. "Do you eat the same things as monkeys?"

"No, of course not. But—"

"The *mazzikim* are to me as monkeys are to you. Their needs are not my needs. I could sustain myself on those emotions if it came to it, just as you could sustain yourself on insects and tree bark if you must. Nevertheless, it isn't what suits me."

"And what is it that suits you, Lily?" Toby said in almost a whisper.

She tipped a wink at him. "That would be telling."

Toby pulled another morsel of goat meat from the skewer and popped it into his mouth. He chewed it, studying her face. "No, this is a serious question. One of your monkeys fed on my friends and me. LaBouche fed on both the torture of Scott's family and what that did to Scott." He squeezed his eyes shut against his grief. *Scott!*

Lily lifted one delicate shoulder and wagged her head side to side. "And should I hold you responsible for something a monkey does?"

Toby set the skewer of meat back on the platter. "No," he said. "But maybe the analogy ends there." He drew his legs up and stood looking down on her, his face a study in gravitas. She returned his gaze but said nothing. "Well, thanks for everything." Even saying that much made him want to cringe. He turned and strode from the pavilion, his back ramrod straight, and the devilish music seemed to swell from every grain of sand, every dark shadow in the distant rocks with Toby as their focus.

"Oh, come on, *kisa*. Don't be this way."

Toby scoffed but stopped walking.

"Listen to me a moment, will you? Put aside your judgments. Come."

He peeked over his shoulder and saw her standing in the pavilion's opening, the play of sunlight on her pale, perfect skin, the obsidian shadows from within the tent at war with the light, her red hair shimmering as if alive. As he looked on, she lifted a hand and held it out to him.

"Hear me out, Tobycakes. Hear me out, and if at the end you still wish to go, I will return you to New York."

Feeling foolish, standing naked in the hot desert sun, he turned and faced her. "Promise?" Even as he said the word, he cursed himself for a fool, for a child believing in daydreams and fairytales. *What use is a promise from a demon?*

Lily dropped her arm and looked at him with a frank expression. "I keep my word, Tobias. And, yes, I promise to take you back after you've heard me out." She glanced up at the sky, then returned her gaze to his face. "Now come back into the shade before your...tender parts...get a sunburn." She allowed her gaze to trail lasciviously down his chest and stomach, lingering on his groin. "That would be a shame, as I have much desire to use them for...other purposes this afternoon."

Toby walked toward her, and as he did, she backed farther into the stygian interior. He crossed the threshold and stopped, sun blind. Somewhere in the darkness, Lily began to hum, adding yet another countermelody to the music on the wind. As he heard her voice in the mix, something inside him rolled over.

Her hand came to rest on his right bicep, as light as a hummingbird. Fingers caressed his left thigh, as cold as marble. Another hand cupped his right buttock, and yet another snaked around his waist. He could still see nothing, not even the grip on his bicep, but he could feel her darting tongue sliding across his chest, slipping up his right side, in his ear.

And still, the music wailed on.

2

Smells of breakfast dragged Shannon into wakefulness. The cotton had cleared from her mind, but the sickening, dull thudding of a horrible headache had replaced it. That only added insult to injury, though. She hurt all over.

She moaned as she sat up, rubbing the sleep from her eyes. The clock on Benny's side of the bed read 8:33 a.m., and the state of her bladder reinforced that she'd slept long enough. She swung her legs out of bed and swayed upright. The wooziness she remembered from the night before touched her momentarily. She squeezed her eyes shut and shook her head a little—enough to clear it, but not enough to cause massive waves of sweeping pain crashing around her head. After washing herself as best she could in the sink and changing into clean clothes, Shannon followed her nose down to the kitchen.

"Shan, go back to bed. I'll bring you a plate," said Benny.

"No, I'm okay, Benny. I was exhausted last night—not only from all this—" She waved one hand at the left side of her body. "—but because I used my ability to hide the car."

"I don't want you pushing yourself. It's better to rest and get healed up to one hundred percent than to push it and have to start again."

Kristy, Sean, Eddie, Amanda, and Mike sat at the long kitchen table, and Shannon took a seat next to Mike. She took his hand. "Any news?"

Mike shook his head and gazed into his lap.

"Shan?" said Benny with a note of exasperation in his voice.

"Yes, Benny, I heard you, but I'm done with bedrest."

"Shannon, listen to—"

"Benny?" She said his name without rancor, without reproach, but he blushed, nonetheless. "It's okay. *I'm* okay—or at least I will be soon. If you don't believe me, ask Kristy." She turned her gaze to Kristy, willing the doctor to lend her support.

"How about this, Benny: I'll keep a sharp eye on Shannon, and she will promise to go to bed when I say so."

"Shan?" asked Benny.

"Yes, I promise."

"Well… I still don't like it, but I guess that will suffice." He turned back to his cooking.

"I had the strangest dream," Shannon said. "I dreamed Toby was trapped in the desert somewhere. Way out in the wilderness. It seemed like he had water and maybe a little food, but other than that, he had nothing."

Without turning, Benny nodded. "I've had similar 'Toby trapped somewhere' dreams since Saturday night. The first had him adrift on a golden sea. The next night, I dreamed he stood atop a glacier and couldn't find a safe way down."

Benny turned and began spooning scrambled eggs on everyone's plate. "None of the dreams give me a handle on where he is, though. I tried to reach out to him through the dream last night, but something blocked it."

"This Lilitu."

"That would be my guess."

Sean cleared his throat. "Last night, before you, uh… Yes, well, last night I was about to tell you about the incantation we found at the bottom of that old bowl. Would you like to hear it now?"

"Sure," said Shannon, resting her head on her crossed arms. "I'm listening, it's just too bright in here."

Sean hesitated, and Shannon imagined him looking at Kristy to see if it was okay to continue. "Yes, okay. This incantation written in Aramaic appears on numerous bowls from Babylon. The incantation starts with the maker's mark phrase, which out of context seems almost respectful, but reading it in the context of what follows may be mockery or disdain. It says: *'Hail Lilitu, Bearer of Chaos. Hail Lilitu, Harvester of Sorrow. Hail hag and ghoul, I adjure you by the timelessness of Tiamat, by the power of Shamash, and by the magic of Ea, here is your divorce and writ and letter of separation, sent through the will of Marduk.'* These bowls would be buried upside down below the foundation of the house it was set to protect."

"I assume those invoked are Babylonian gods?" asked Mike.

Sean nodded.

"What was this Lilitu to inspire such fear?" asked Amanda with a note of wonder in her voice.

"Yeah, okay. Right, so the mythology surrounding Lilitu is incomplete at best. Some cultures treated her as an individual entity, while others took the name 'lili' to mean female night spirits. But what seems consistent across all the various versions is that Lilitu can change her shape. She was said to adopt the form of a beautiful woman to seduce a husband away from his wife, or to take the role and appearance of the husband to seduce the wife. In either case, her goal is always to conceive a child, but once the child is born, Lilitu becomes hostile to the other natural children of the couple. And once that happens, she kills all the children but her own."

The harsh sound of Eddie clearing his throat filled the kitchen. Amanda had turned away from Sean a bit and sat staring at the floor. "That sounds a lot like Abby."

Sean leaned forward. "Abby?"

"Yes, she's made of golden fire, and she has tormented me my whole life. She drove my father to kill my mother and then commit suicide. I'm pretty sure that she went to work on my aunt and uncle after that. I—"

"She admitted to killing our unborn child," said Amanda in a harsh, ringing voice. For a moment, no one moved, no one spoke, and the only sound in the kitchen was from the bacon frying in a pan on the stove. "We needed one of those bowls." A single tear rolled down her cheek.

Eddie put his arm around Amanda and pulled her close. "After that, she focused on trying to drive the two of us apart. She wanted us to fight, to *physically* fight."

"But we showed her," said Amanda in a small voice.

"We did. We stuck it out, we refused to fight, to argue even. We chose to honor our commitments to each other, and our lives have been better for it."

Amanda turned into Eddie's hug and wrapped her arms around him. "That's right. No matter what she tried, we stood up to her."

"But Amanda's right. Everything I know about Abby says that incantation should have her name in it rather than Lilitu's."

Sean pulled on his lower lip. "Yes, I can see why you might say that. But the mythology says Lilitu is the mother of the *ifrit*, succubi, and incubi. That the succubi and incubi imitate her nature."

"Great. All we need is two of Abby," grumbled Amanda.

"You said Lilitu was dressed like a slut?" Shannon asked Benny. "A pale-skinned knockout with a sexy dress and boots?"

Benny nodded.

"Is she trying to seduce Toby, then? Why would she? He's not married, he has no children."

"Why do any of these demons do anything?" murmured Mike.

"To eat!" snapped Benny. "They all do these horrible things to get at the kind of food they like best! Herlequin said something to me when he had me in the woods. I was pissed, and I mean insane with it. I refused to play along, and he tried to threaten me. He said something akin to: 'I like the taste of your fear best, but anger will do.'"

"And LaBouche..." began Mike. "What he said to Scott."

"'I was only thinking about my own needs, my own wants.' Something like that," said Shannon. "And he didn't mean only fear. He liked taunting Scott, really rubbing his nose in his loss."

Sean gasped. "Karl Munnur did the same to me."

"Who?" asked Mike.

"From what Shannon said, Munnur was LaBouche's identity before he became LaBouche. He dated my mother and used to spend a lot of time with me. He'd bring up my dead father at least three times a week, and I'd catch him looking at me with greed in his eyes."

"And what he did to me," said Kristy. "He demeaned me, degraded me—or rather, he encouraged me to do those things to myself."

"He fed on it," murmured Shannon.

"Yes," said Benny. "Each demon we know anything about has expressed a favorite emotion, and it seems the more complex the demon, the more complex the emotion they prefer." His eyes grew full and round. "What if she feeds off leading good people astray? What if she's the ultimate temptress?"

"Then Toby is in real trouble," said Shannon in a mournful voice. "We have to find a way to help him."

"If it isn't already too late," murmured Mike.

3

"No," Toby breathed. It took every bit of his willpower, every bit of his self-control to say the word. Phantom hands slid across the planes of his body, ghostly fingers danced across his skin, ethereal tongues stroked and licked and caressed.

His nerves twitched and squirmed as if on fire, and he shivered with pleasure. "No." The word was barely audible, even to him.

The haunting music danced in the darkness around them, the volume growing, melody and countermelody racing toward a crescendo, the staccato rhythm increasing in tempo. Through it all, his flesh shivered, longing for her embrace.

"No." He wasn't even sure if he had spoken the word aloud, and Toby wasn't sure if he could repeat it if he had. He squeezed his eyes shut, teetering on the edge of giving in. "You said you wanted to tell me something."

The sensation of multiple tongues gliding over his flesh departed, leaving only one that painted saliva circles over his carotid artery. The multitudes of cool fingers disappeared, leaving only palms on his skin, and they too decreased in number until only two remained.

With a deep sigh, Lily's tongue came away from his neck, one hand left the small of his back, and the other slid down to his wrist, pulling him over to the cushions. "Fine," she breathed. "But I've never seen a man so adamant about rejecting sex. If it weren't for what you'd already done, I might suppose you to be homosexual." Her grip on his wrist loosened, and as she withdrew her hand, her fingertips trailed fire across his skin. "If that's the problem, I can as easily be a man."

Toby shook his head, trying to clear the daze from his brain. "No, don't change *anything*."

"Aw, Tobycakes, you say the sweetest things." Fabric rustled on his left. "Come on. Sit down, and we will talk."

His eyes seemed stuck, still blind in the shade of the pavilion, but he crawled toward her voice, and when he felt her hand on his shoulder, he sat. "Okay."

"I first came here in the reign of Sargon. I was summoned by a twitchy little priest named Utukku. He was as arrogant as he was bold. He wanted what every man wants and more. His avarice was legendary."

"I'm not sure—"

"Hush, now, Tobes. Let me tell it in my own way." She hesitated a moment, as if waiting for him to object, then went on. "His timing was good—there was upheaval back home, and I was tired of it. He wanted magic, a creature of magic that would bolster his power. Most of the *seraph* heard his entreaties—"

"Is that the name of your kind?"

"—and most shunned his pleas. Lilu was amused by the audacity of 'the little runt,' as he called him. I desired distraction, so I played along with the fool.

"But he was clever. He offered me more than a distraction from the petty jealousies and foolish battles of the *seraph*, he offered me release from it. He offered me an invitation to visit this realm, to live here." Lily chuckled, and it sounded like two steel-hulled ships grinding together in a windstorm. "He thought he could *bind* me. Can you imagine? He was arrogant, as I mentioned, and full of his own 'power,' which was nothing to speak of.

"But still, I played along. I stood inside his ridiculous circle of salt—his summoning circle—and played the dumb, cowed demoness the silly man expected. I came naked, and his lust was obvious. It took only five minutes to convince him to break the circle of salt and come to my arms.

"I admit to a certain curiosity about the world, about the men and women in it, and he was eager to please me, though inept and inadequate to the task." Her hand snaked out of the darkness and came to rest on his thigh, sending a shiver rippling up and down his body. "Unlike some I've known since." She almost purred the sentence, sounding as close to his ear as a person could get without climbing right on inside his ear canal. "But still, Akkad wasn't home, and no *djinn*, no *ifrit*, no *mazzikim*, and most of all, no *seraph* could bother me here.

"After a time, I grew somewhat bored with Utukku's pettiness. I told him I needed to be among my own kind. I promised to leave him and return home unless he taught me the secrets, the magic he'd used to bridge the two realms. He seemed happy to reveal his hard-won knowledge, like a puppy happy to do a trick at his master's call.

"I used his incantations to summon Lilu, and this time, he came, intrigued by the time I had spent here. I promised him worshippers, a source of sustenance much more enjoyable than that of the *mazzikim*, the *djinn*, or even the *ifrit*.

"Once here, Lilu wanted blood, and Utukku was more than happy to accommodate him. He waged war for the sake of violence, and Lilu was there, dining on the death of mortal men.

"While the two were away, I summoned my faithful maid Lamia—a *djinn*, mind—and later, I brought one of my acolytes to this world. An *ifrit* named Abyzou. We three had a merry old time among the Akkadians. Great fetes where thrown in our honor—we were goddesses, you see.

"But the temptations of the flesh led Lilu astray, and we quarreled often. He grew jealous of my status in the temples of Akkad and conspired with Utukku to banish me." A mournful sigh escaped her. "What he didn't realize is that Abyzou, Lamia, and I had created a place for him in our burgeoning pantheon among the priests and priestesses of Akkad, but we'd kept it secret from him, intending to surprise him." Lily drew a deep, ragged breath, taut with emotion, and the suppressed promise of violence and death.

He *betrayed* me, you see? That, above all else, I cannot abide."

"And you banished him?"

A harsh chuckled filled the darkness surrounding them, and Toby shuddered at the menace it contained. "No, *vato*. I didn't send him home as you do these petty *mazzikim*."

"Then, what?"

"I consumed his soul, Tobycakes." She said it as though she said nothing more frightening than a morning greeting. "I sucked it into myself, and Lilu was no more. What's more, Lilu could *never* come back. He's dead, truly dead.

"But enough of Lilu and ancient times. None of this is what I wanted to tell you, only what was needed to be told to lay the foundation." She fell silent, and the music swelled as though to fill the void left by her silence.

"What is that music? It makes me feel so…*strange*."

A fresh, dry hand emerged from the darkness and patted his cheek, pointed fingernails trailing across his skin as she withdrew her hand. "I've been here for all the millions of days since then, searching for another to stand by my side. From time to time, I've found suitable candidates and invested heavily in their causes. Some were small men with small ambitions, others were grandiose men with huge ambitions. Adolf Hitler was one such, and Joseph Stalin another. I grow bored in the company of grandiose men quickly. Or perhaps they grow tired of me because they usually stoop to betrayal before the others.

"That's what my time here has been: one betrayal after another. And civilizations rose and fell while I wept with bitter loneliness. Even my own child shuns me, preferring to pretend to be a *mazzikim* than taking her rightful place at my side."

"Brigitta?" he whispered.

"*Naamah!*" she snapped in a voice like thunder.

"We thought… She pretended to be one of Herlequin's daughters."

"Yes. More to spite me, though she claims it was to honor the charlatan himself."

"She's the crimson-flamed one from the parking lot?"

"An *ifrit*, yes."

Toby remained quiet for the space of twenty breaths, thinking about what she'd told him. "But—"

"You, Toby Burton, are a suitable candidate."

"Me?" Surprise rendered him muddle-headed.

"You. I can give you power, Toby. I can change you at a fundamental level, make you immortal. Together, we can rule the world, we can make this planet tremble at our wrath, beg for our succor. You can be a king by my side, a god, and I, a queen, a goddess."

Outside, the wind blew, and the sun beat down on the desert as though light and sand were mortal enemies. Toby stared out at the desert for some time before speaking. "I don't know what to say. I've never been one to lust after power. And…" he turned his attention back to Lily. "And I have this previous commitment, you see."

"Banishing the *mazzikim*."

Toby swallowed, fighting the dryness in his throat. "I don't think I could be happy, knowing they ran free, using—no *eating*—people."

Lily cocked her head to the side and stared at him for a moment, then inclined her head and allowed her long red hair to cascade in front of her face. "The *mazzikim* mean very little to me."

"And before I committed to anything, I would have to understand *your* nature. We can start with what you eat."

A sigh gusted out of Lily, and she turned her head to stare out into the desert as Toby had a few minutes before. "Why is it you humans are driven to complicate everything?" She chuckled, though it was not an amused sound, and returned her attention to Toby's space. "I am attracted to you, Tobes. And it's quite obvious that you are attracted to me." She flashed a lopsided smile at him and directed her gaze to his manhood. "Is that not enough?"

"It's true that I am attracted to you, Lily. As a woman, you're perfect—you tick every box I have. But I know that isn't your true form."

She arched an eyebrow at him. "Oh, you do, do you?"

"It stands to reason," Toby said.

"Ah. Then tell me, *cazador*, what is my true form?"

Toby frowned and crossed his arms. "I admit I have no idea. How could I know? You've already told me you can assume any form you want."

"Then why assume that this form is not my own?"

"The *mazzikim*—"

"I am not one of the *mazzikim*!" she snapped, and fire danced in her eyes.

Toby looked away and dropped his arms to lay across his knees like some yogi entering a meditative state. "I understand that, Lily. You say the *mazzikim* are as different from you as monkeys are to me, but I only have experience with your *mazzikim*. Well, the *mazzikim* in Oneka Falls and your daughter."

"Then you must take my word on it." She drew a deep, calming breath and let it whistle out between her teeth. "This is not going as I had planned."

"What in life ever does?" Toby smiled at Lily, and they chuckled together. "You say that the time you spend here has been one betrayal after another, and yet you would have me choose to be by your side without knowing who you really are? I'm not casting blame on you, but don't you think that might contribute to the painful ending of your relationships?"

Lily leaned across the platter filled with cooling meat and patted him on the cheek. "Sometimes, we are all too close to the problem to see the easiest solution." She sat back and gazed into his eyes. "What you say may be true, but..."

"But you don't fully trust me, either."

"You *are* committed to banishing my worshipers. You said it yourself."

"*Worshippers*? But you said the *mazzikim* mean very little to you."

Lily smiled at that and put her hand on Toby's knee. "Part of what attracts me to you, *chico mio*, is your cleverness. Let me raise you up. Or at least let me show you how it could be. Let me show you everything."

Toby allowed his gaze to meander across her body, fighting the lust it stirred within him, but drinking in the sight of her naked form. It was a tempting idea, spending every waking moment with a woman as beautiful and as willing to go *au naturel* as Lily. The power she offered him didn't tempt him—except that it might allow him to solve the problem of Oneka Falls once and for all.

But the rest of it... He wanted what she offered more than he'd ever wanted anything else.

4

"Benny?" asked Sean. "Do you have a second?"

Benny's gaze tracked to where Shannon lay on the couch with her eyes closed, then bounced to Sean's face. "I—"

"Go, Benny," sighed Shannon. "Kristy will keep track of me."

Benny gave a curt nod. "Let's go out on the deck."

They walked out onto the plank deck, and Sean closed the door behind them. "I have an idea. I didn't want to say anything in front of the others and get everyone's hopes up…"

"What is it?"

"Akkad seems to be the first place Lilitu is called out—though they called her Ardat Lili. This maker's mark on the lamp is Akkadian cuneiform. The cuneiform on the incantation bowls I looked at was Babylonian—which means it was made between two and five hundred years *after* Akkad fell."

"Okay," Benny said with a shrug.

"The earliest reference to Lilitu we have is from Akkad. Call it 2300 BCE. Four thousand years ago."

"I'm still not seeing your point, Sean."

"Establishing the frame of reference is all. Why would the Lilitu myth originate in Akkad if she was around earlier? Remember that the maker's mark is Akkadian, too."

Benny twirled one finger in a circle and glanced over Sean's shoulder at Shannon through the glass door.

"What if the Akkadian language is itself *special* to these demons?"

"Special how?"

"I don't know, but I'm willing to bet that the incantation bowl thing started in Akkad, too. I bet it started because Lilitu posed a genuine threat to Akkadians."

"Or Lilitu and this Abby."

Sean nodded.

"Say I believe that, where are you going with this?"

"What if we can build our own incantations?"

"I'm not sure—"

"We could research Akkadian magic. Look up all their curses, and their versions of the incantations like on the bowls. Their *magic*, in other words."

"Magic." Benny allowed the word to roll around inside his head, picking up impressions of stray thoughts the way Silly Putty picked up images from the funny papers. "But magic isn't real. What these demons do seems more like telepathy or mind control. Herlequin said as much to me. He said our perceptions were easy to manipulate."

"Heinlein said, 'One man's magic is another man's engineering.'"

"Yeah, and Arthur C. Clarke said, 'Any sufficiently advanced technology is indistinguishable from magic.' What's your point?"

"What if we can derive *syntax* and *semantics* from these magic spells and incantations?"

"Then we could make our own." Benny sighed. "But that doesn't mean they would work."

"Maybe not, but isn't it worth a try?"

Benny cocked his head to the side and stared at Sean for a few minutes. "Maybe so. See what you can do, but I also want more information on that lamp."

Sean nodded and pulled his smartphone out of his pocket and began to thumb-type furiously. "And I'll check on the land grab thing while I'm at it."

5

Lily stretched, and it was full of languor and lasciviousness. "I do love it when you look at me with lust in your eye, Tobycakes. You can see me like this every moment until time itself breaks and space becomes a true void. All you have to do is say yes. Not even that, you have only to nod."

Toby closed his eyes and drew a deep breath in through his nose. Having her so close, her scent enveloping him, her delectable flesh within arm's reach, made it difficult to withstand her temptations. "Lily, I *need* to know."

Silence fell between them for a moment, and then Lily began to hum, but not as she had when she accompanied the strange desert music. Instead, the melody evoked a shivering fear within him. After a moment, Toby realized she was humming more than one note at a time, making mournful, dissonant chords, and his resistance began to crumble.

"No."

Lily smiled and nodded her head, continuing to hum her haunting melody.

"No." Toby tried to stand, tried to lurch away from her, but Lily's smile only widened. "No, Lily! Not like this!"

Without seeming to move, Lily was in his lap, one hand stroking his cheek. She lifted her chin and hummed directly into his ear, and the music crawled inside his brain.

"No," he murmured.

Lily's lips brushed against his ear, sending a cascade of pleasure shuddering through him. "Yes," she said without breaking the melody, and he could resist no longer.

6

"Benny, we have to find a way to help Toby," said Shannon in a sleep-clogged voice.

The nap was supposed to do her good, and Benny needed time to think—time away from all the new faces, all the new demands for decision-making that Toby usually provided.

He also wanted a reprieve from the expression on Mike's face—the grief, the sorrow, but also the jealousy. Benny understood how Mike felt. He imagined he might feel the same way if the Walkers had brought him home and left Shannon in the hospital.

"I don't see how, Shan."

She pushed herself up until she could sit with her back against the headboard, and her legs kicked out straight. "I know. I don't see how, either, but…" A sigh gusted out of her. "He's in trouble, Benny. *Bad* trouble that makes his run-in with Herlequin look like a camping trip. What's worse is that he doesn't seem to *know* how close the danger is."

Benny leaned against the headboard, mimicking her position and sliding closer. "How do you know these things, Shannon?"

Her attention leaped from the bunched-up comforter on her lap to his face for half a second, then she looked away. "I had this dream…"

"Another lost-in-the-desert dream?"

Shannon picked at the pattern of stitching that decorated the comforter. "Yeah. In the dream, Toby was in the desert, but this time it was like he was on a camping trip." She lifted her gaze to his face. "But it's a camping trip with the devil. It's like the forty days and forty nights in the Bible."

"Wrong desert," said Benny without knowing why.

"What?"

"Jesus was tempted in the Judean Desert. That's not where Toby is."

Shannon stared at him for the time it took to take two calm breaths. "How do you know?" she asked quietly.

Benny chuckled at that. "I have no idea, cupcake." He drew a deep breath and blew it out and up hard enough to make his bangs jitter. "It's like there's something in the way. Something blocking me from knowing *where*, but they forgot to block knowing where he isn't."

"That's great news! Come on!" Shannon swung her legs off the bed and pushed herself to her feet with a groan.

"Shan, you need to—"

"Benjamin Cartwright!" she snapped. "Tell me to rest one more time, and I'll be visiting *you* in the hospital."

She said it with such vigor that Benny couldn't help but laugh. After a moment of glowering at him, Shannon's face softened, and she joined in. "Yeah, okay, but lay off, alright?"

Benny nodded and stood up. "Where are we going?"

"Computer," Shannon said as she strode toward the door.

"What for?"

"Because, silly, there are maps and pictures of every desert in the world on the internet."

"Ah!" Benny said with a smile. "You are too good for the likes of me, Shannon Bertram. Beautiful, sexy as hell, and smart! How did I get so lucky?"

"I sometimes ask myself the same thing." She winked at him over her shoulder, and the two shared another laugh.

7

Mike walked into the living room. His hair was mussed, and his eyes burned and stung from too much sleep. And too much grief. Eddie and his wife had vacated the living room, leaving Kristy and Sean to their own devices. "Evening," said Mike.

"Have a nice rest?" asked Sean, his attention glued to the screen of his smartphone.

Kristy Walker lay her hand on Sean's thigh and squeezed. It was supposed to be subtle, but Mike had spent too many years as an investigator to miss something like that.

"What?" murmured Sean, then he glanced at his wife and reddened. "Yeah, uh-huh." His gaze crawled up to meet Mike's. "Sorry. I get too involved with interesting problems. They call it 'hyperfocus.'" He hooked his thumb at Kristy. "Doctors, you know."

"It's okay," said Mike, turning to stare out at the twilight dancing on the waves of Lake Erie. "What's so interesting?"

"Yeah, okay. Benny wanted more information on the lamp. Well, that and we're doing a special project trying to collate all the instances of Akkadian prayers, magic, or incantations."

"Why?"

Sean bobbed his head. "Benny thinks the lamp is important."

"No, why the prayer search?"

"Right, okay. I had the idea that if we can determine the syntax and semantics of Akkadian incantations, we could fashion our own spells."

"Spells?" Mike's gaze darted to Kristy's, then returned to Sean, but the man had turned his attention back to the screen of his phone.

"Absolutely, yes." He thumb-typed furiously for a moment, then jumped as Kristy poked him in the ribs. "What? Oh, sure. The spells. It seems that Akkadian magic is important to these bigger demons. The maker's mark was what started me on this path, but also, the mythological history of the one called Lilitu. It starts in Akkad."

"Sean thinks that if we can learn the *hows* of these incantations, we might be able to fashion our own."

Sean flashed a perplexed look at his wife. "Honey, that's what I've been saying."

She grinned a little and patted his forearm. "Yes, but I said it aloud and without all the fluff."

Shaking his head, Sean shifted his gaze back to his phone.

"But you mentioned Benny's request first." Mike moved to the La-Z-Boy and sat. "What about this lamp is so interesting?"

"Uh-huh, yeah." Sean lifted his head, but his gaze remained glued to the phone for a few moments, his eyes rolled down comically until his position made it impossible to see the screen. He began to lift the phone, but Kristy put her hand on his wrist. He shot a look of pure irritation at her.

"The lamp?" she said.

"Yes. Okay, right. The lamp. Sean scrubbed his hands through his hair and then down the sides of his face. "I think the last report went back to the 1500s?"

"The shipping manifest from Lisbon."

"Exactly, yes. But that was yesterday morning. I was out of pocket all yesterday—well, you know that—and spent most of today on the other project. I was reading the latest report on the lamp a moment ago."

"Good God, husband! Spit it out."

"Right, right. My personal physician also says I have a tendency to blather on endlessly about excruciating details." He smiled at Kristy, then turned back to Mike. "Okay. They've found more information on the lamp's recent history—from Lisbon forward. We almost have the complete history from Portugal until today."

"Anything interesting there?"

Sean wagged his head side to side. "Sort of. Almost every time a family has owned the lamp, tragedy befalls them. The children die—most often in childbirth, but sometimes murdered by their fathers or mothers. Frequent reports of both miscarriages and abuse."

"Nasty," murmured Kristy.

"Yes, uh-huh. But worse than that, when the lamp is owned by a single person, there is almost always a slate of unsolved murders in the area."

"So either wife-beaters and family murderers or serial killers?" asked Kristy.

"Like Owen Gray in Oneka Falls," said Mike in a weak voice. "And Mason Harper in Genosgwa."

"And don't forget Denny Cratchkin," said Sean in a cold voice.

"Yes, I'm sure there are plenty of others." Kristy shivered and rubbed her upper arms.

The question is why," mused Mike. "Why bother with mortals at all? Demons feed off negative emotions…maybe the demon driving these things feeds on anger or jealousy?"

"Maybe it's the lamp itself that drives people to these things."

Mike shook his head. "The demons are always behind everything."

"Maybe one of the demons feeds off something more complicated. Obsession, say. Or whatever it is that drives serial killers."

Mike grinned at Kristy. "You might be right. Just because the demons on the low end of the scale feed on base emotions doesn't mean ones at the other end of the scale do the same." Mike tented his fingers and tapped his lower lip with his index fingers. "We know very little about Naamah." He chuckled. "Even less than we thought if we count how she looked on Saturday after LaBouche got done with her. But we do know that both Mason Harper—*Abaddon*—and Owen Gray were her pets. Maybe she's behind their actions."

Sean shook his head. "Not behind them. *Feeding* off them."

"What if…" Kristy shook her head.

"No, tell us," said Sean.

She glanced at Mike and blushed a little. "This is probably stupid, but what if she feeds off twisting them to their lowest nature?"

"Corrupting them?"

"Sure," she said with a nod. "Suppose that's possible?"

Mike shrugged. "Who knows? We keep making the mistake of thinking we understand them, and every time we do that, something happens to blow our 'understanding' out of the water."

Sean inclined his head, glancing at his phone. "We can speculate all night and never know if we are correct or way off base. Let me tell you the rest."

Mike made a beckoning gesture.

"Okay. Before leaving Lisbon on a ship in the early 1500s, it bounced around eastern Europe, from auction to auction, house to house, as an elaborate gilt candelabra. Guess who owned it before that?"

"I give up."

"Tomas de Torquemada."

"I should know who that is, but I hated history class," said Mike.

"Torquemada ran the Spanish Inquisition from 1483 to 1498. Guess who he bought it from?"

"I don't know," said Mike.

"Radu cel Frumos, the successor of Vlad III of Wallachia."

"Vlad…" Mike sucked his teeth. "If you are telling me this lamp belonged to Dracula, I'm going to scream."

"Well, don't do that. But it appears on an inventory of both Vlad III's possessions and his father's, Vlad Dracul. Vlad II received it as a gift from his mentor, Sigismund of Luxembourg."

"And I suppose there is a neat timeline all the way back through history? One crazy sadist to the next?"

Sean shook his head. "Maybe, but we don't have that timeline yet. Sigismund received it as spoils after he tried to liberate Constantinople in the late 14th century, but where it came from has eluded us for now." Sean cleared his throat. "Before that, what we know of its history is like a stone skipping across the surface of a smooth lake. We know Caligula had a decorated oil lamp that bore the maker's mark around 50 AD, and before that, Nebuchadnezzar II was painted holding another decorated oil lamp in the early 500s BCE. There are numerous references to his madness, which developed after his mistress left him."

"Let me guess. King Nebuchadnezzar's mistress had red hair and wore black."

"Not this time," said Sean. "His mistress did wear black, but her dark blue hair moved like a viper's nest, and she was rumored to be a sorceress. She was by his side as he ransacked kingdom after kingdom. He's the same guy that threw Daniel to the lions."

"Nice," said Kristy.

"That's not all—remember when I told you guys about the incantation bowls? I showed you one that had the redhead in the bottom?"

"Sure," said Mike.

"Well, it seems the incantations inscribed on them were also used during a cleansing ritual. An exorcism, if you will. The conclusion of which ended in the smashing of the bowl."

"I'm not sure where you are going with this."

"Yeah, okay. So, we have this lamp that bears an incantation of welcome to this Lilitu. What if we destroyed the lamp while performing one of those exorcisms?"

"That—"

Somewhere upstairs, Benny whooped. A moment later, he came sprinting down the stairs. "We found him!" he shouted. "We found Toby!"

8

When Toby awoke, the evening had bared its claws. Lily wasn't at his side, and panic buried his ability to think. He thrashed to his feet. "Lily!" he cried.

"Calm yourself, *habibi*. I'm right outside."

Relief washed through him, as crisp and refreshing as a mountain stream. Something felt…off…within him, and he frowned. He couldn't put his finger on it, the mysterious wrong feeling that persisted through his relief. He cocked his head, listening for Lily's footsteps.

Then it hit him. The thing that felt wrong was the lack of the faint strains of Lily's badlands threnody. For the first time in what seemed like months or years, no melody haunted the empty spaces in his ears, his mind. "It's gone," he murmured.

"Did you say something, *kisa*?" She walked to the open wall of the pavilion, her orange eyes whirling, her lips glossy and red. She smiled at him and cocked her head to the side.

"No, nothing."

She chuckled and waved her hand at the desert behind her. "Shall we walk?"

"Sure. My muscles feel tight, wound up. I need to stretch them out."

She treated him to a knowing smile and turned away from the pavilion. She lifted an arm and pointed. "That way is east. It leads to nothing but more desert all the way to the sea—what modern geographers call the Persian Gulf. To go that way would mean a long, long walk for not much reward." She turned ninety degrees and pointed south. "To the south, there is nothing but the Arabian Desert until you reach the shores of the Arabian Sea." She lifted her other arm and pointed in the opposite direction. "To the north is the land that was once Akkad. Sumer. Mesopotamia."

"The cradle of civilization." Toby exited the pavilion to stand by her side, their shoulders and arms almost touching. An electric feeling raced across his skin at her nearness, and he couldn't resist stealing a quick peek.

"If you keep looking at me like that, *bizcocho*, we will not leave tonight."

Toby turned his gaze toward the north as the hot blush crept from his neck to his cheeks. "And that leaves only the west, and the Mediterranean Sea."

She turned to him and came up on her tiptoes to brush her lips against his cheek. "There can be a thousand million nights for us to do what you're thinking," she crooned in his ear.

He didn't trust himself to speak, so climbed the dune face to its peak, casting his gaze north, trying to imagine what it must've been like in the days when Lily had been summoned.

Behind him, Lily loosed a deep-throated chuckle, and then came up to stand at his side. "Have you decided?"

"Which way should I go?" Even as he said the words, a lump of icy fear formed in his throat at the thought of leaving Lily and walking away.

"Aren't you just the sweetest thing," crooned Lily. "But I will go with you. I doubt you would survive on your own."

Toby turned and looked down on the pavilion. "I guess I can decide on a direction while I pack everything."

Lily laughed and swatted him on the shoulder as if he'd told her a funny joke. She snapped her fingers and the pavilion was gone.

"Illusion, then?"

Lily winked at him. "That would be telling."

"You said before that if I heard you out you would take me home."

Lily's expression sobered. "I did, and I will."

"Is there more, then?"

"Tobycakes, sometimes you act the child. Let me show you. Let me show you how it would be if you chose life by my side. Let me show you the wonders of the world that would come into being, the world that you and I would create together."

"And in which direction does that lie?"

Again, Lily snapped her fingers, and he was clothed in the manner of the Bedouins. She wore her black leather dress and accompanying black leather boots with chrome heels that somehow managed not to sink into the loose sand. "Let's go north."

"And you will answer my questions as we walk?"

Lily stared at him for a moment, her expression utterly devoid of any human emotion Toby could identify. Her eyes whirled and seemed to pulse. It was difficult, but Toby maintained eye contact through it all. Finally, she sighed. "As you wish."

9

"Where?" asked Mike, coming to his feet and thrusting his hand into his pocket for car keys.

Benny shot a glance at Shannon. "You're not going to like it. He's somewhere in the Syrian Desert."

Sean looked up, his brow wrinkled. "You know that desert is like two hundred thousand miles square, right?"

Mike's shoulders slumped. "Why do you think he's there?"

"Something is blocking Benny when he tries to use his telepathy to find Toby, but they forgot to block him checking to see if Toby *isn't* in a place. Because of my desert dream, we checked all the deserts in the world, and by process of elimination, found him."

Sean smiled, wrinkling his nose. "What a clever solution."

"Okay, so Toby's in Syria," said Mike. "What do we do with this information?"

"He's in the Syrian Desert, but that spans borders— Syria, Jordan, Saudi Arabia, and western Iraq."

"Fine. What do we do with this information? We can't send teams there for obvious reasons."

"No, we can't do that," said Benny. "But I can go there."

Mike shook his head and held up a hand to stop Benny. "You can't go there either and for the same reasons."

Benny grinned. "But I can, Mike. And in perfect safety."

Mike frowned, and his forehead wrinkled. "How?"

"Don't you remember what I used to do in Millvale? How I used to travel?"

"I thought…"

Benny laughed and clapped Mike on the shoulder. "You thought I was hallucinating. I wasn't." He glanced at the others. "Call it astral projection or spirit walking. I can travel places with only my mind."

"Neat trick," said Sean.

"And why do you think that will be safe?" asked Mike.

"Because no one can see me. I don't need a passport or anything."

"Don't you think this Lilitu thing will see you?"

The memory of visiting Owen Gray's cell flashed through Benny's mind. Naamah had looked directly at him and had threatened him in his astral form, even if she hadn't carried through with it. She had somehow sent him spinning back into his body with a flick of her fingers, and that gave credence to her claim that she *could* see him and cause trouble for him.

Benny dropped his gaze. "I'll stay hidden."

Mike turned his attention on Shannon. "And you're okay with this?"

Shannon closed her eyes in a slow blink. "Toby's in trouble, Mike. Desperate trouble, and he needs help—even if it's just a link to another human mind."

"And what's to stop Lilitu from taking Benny as well?" asked Kristy.

"I won't let her," said Benny. "I held off Naamah during the fight. I'm stronger than even I knew."

10

They walked side-by-side as the moon rose in the east, and for a while, they didn't speak. Their arms brushed from time to time, and on each occurrence, a thrill raced through Toby.

"What is it that keeps you here, Lily?" he asked when they stopped and sat to rest.

"As I said, I keep my promises."

"I don't mean *here* here." He threw his arms wide. "I mean what keeps you here on Earth. Why not go home?"

"Do you want me to leave?"

Toby's stomach tightened, and a grimace distorted his face.

"*Ay, que chulo*, Tobycakes." Her voice was soft, but her eyes danced with mischief.

"I just mean that you said your life here has been a series of betrayals. Why not go home? Why not find another *seraph*, another…"

She arched an eyebrow at him. "Another like Lilu?"

Toby opened his mouth but couldn't find his voice, so he settled for nodding.

Lily shook her head. "No, I've traveled that road, Tobes. I know where it ends." She stood and whirled in a circle, arms outstretched, head thrown back, eyes closed. "But here, here everything is new, even after four millennia." She stopped spinning and stood facing him. She inclined her head and looked down at him. "Your race has the capacity to change, to perform feats of novel magic, to achieve things that are beyond even the *seraph*."

"But how can you be happy? Unless I'm wrong, you are the only one of your kind here."

She flapped a hand at him. "There have been sweet times along with the bitter. The betrayals…" She shook her head, and her hair seemed to float as if she were underwater. "They hurt, but I survived them."

"Is it enough to merely survive?"

Lily pressed her lips together. "You ask so many questions, Tobycakes. You overthink everything to death."

Toby cocked his head. "I'm not sure that's a bad thing."

She dusted off her hands and turned away. "Are you rested?"

"Sure." Toby pushed to his feet and set off walking north once more, and Lily fell in at his side. After a hundred paces,

Toby glanced at her. "You said you would answer questions as we walked—and I'm curious about you. I don't mean to give offense."

Lily's head was down, and she didn't lift it. "Curiosity aside, don't your questions have an ulterior motive?"

"Well, you *did* ask me to spend eternity with you."

"And knowing why I prefer to stay here rather than return home provides you a necessary insight for answering the question?"

"I…" Toby rubbed his nose with his index finger. "To be frank, I don't understand your nature. I don't understand why you've brought me here. I don't understand why you dangle yourself in front of me like a carrot, and… And I wonder what the stick is." Toby scrunched his eyebrows together. "Meanwhile, I have no idea what's happening to my friends, or what's happening with the *mazzikim* and Oneka Falls."

Lily sucked her teeth, then blew her bangs with a gust of air. "Always with the *mazzikim*," she muttered. "I dangle myself before you like a carrot, and all you do is fret and worry about Oneka Falls!"

They walked in silence for a few minutes. "I can't help it. It weighs on me like a yoke does an ox. Cleaning up Oneka Falls seems like my calling, what I was put here to do."

"Your calling? Your calling is to be by my side, Tobes. To walk with me through eternity. The *mazzikim*, your friends, Oneka Falls—all of that is of little importance in the long run."

"It doesn't seem that way to me, Lily. Put yourself in my shoes. Imagine there was a threat to your pet *djinn* and your *ifrit* acolyte. If I said it was of little importance, would that change how you felt? Wouldn't you still believe you owed them something?"

She turned her head to the side, her gaze mapping his face. "Then, if the *mazzikim* were gone, it would be easier for you to decide?"

He lifted his shoulders and let them drop. "It would at least eliminate that worry. But what about your daughter? What about the other *ifrit* and the *djinn*? Can you call them off my friends?"

Lily met his gaze head-on, and her eyes seemed to flash like emergency marker lights. "All are bound to me. All owe me an oath of fealty. There is no question whether Abyzou would obey me, and left to her own devices, I have no doubt Lamia would, as well. But Naamah..." She shook her head a little. "My daughter is headstrong. In the end, she will obey, but she might resist."

Toby nodded once. "How would you get rid of the *mazzikim*?"

"Doesn't matter. Why should you care, so long as they're gone."

"Only curious."

"Don't your people have a saying? Curiosity killed the cat?"

"Yes," said Toby, chuckling.

"Yes." Lily began to hum her ghastly little tune, and a shiver raced up and down Toby's spine. After a moment or two, the song filled his mind like white noise, and he could think no more.

11

"What do we do while you are off gallivanting through the astral plane?" asked Mike in a light voice.

Benny sat in one of the La-Z-Boys, reclined as far as it could go. "Keep my body safe so I have something to come back to."

"Once you travel, can we talk to you?"

"If it's an emergency. To hear you, I'll have to shift my mind back here, and that will increase the chance she will sense me."

"Can't you link with me?" asked Shannon. She came to stand near him and lay a hand on his shoulder.

Benny smiled at her and patted her hand. "I could, but that would expose you to Lilitu should she try to follow my path." He shook his head. "No, it's better if I isolate my mind."

"What do we do in the meantime?" asked Mike again.

"Keep working on the lamp and the Akkadian magic angles. A confrontation is coming—whether we like it or not—and we'd best be prepared to fight these more powerful demons."

"I'm on it," said Sean.

"Good. And I hope your wife will babysit for me."

Kristy looked at him, wide-eyed. "I wasn't aware—"

"He means me," said Shannon. "He wants you to make me rest."

"I was doing that, anyway. You're still my patient."

Benny smiled and closed his eyes. Images of heat shimmering over golden sand began to flash through his mind at an ever-increasing pace. He watched closely, looking for a red tent or footsteps in the sand.

12

Toby came to himself with a start and nearly stumbled down the face of the dune on which he stood. Lily grabbed his arm to steady him, and her grip was like steel. "Thanks. I must have…"

"Yes. The wasteland has that effect from time to time, *kisa*." She patted his shoulder. "Nothing to fret over."

His mouth and throat burned as though he'd swallowed something hot, and his tongue lay in the bottom of his mouth like a dead snake. He couldn't summon enough saliva to spit the taste of flint and dust from his mouth. His back ached as though he'd been swinging a sledgehammer for hours, and his feet screamed at him with each step. "How long…" he grated. He tried to clear his throat, but it was too dry. "Water?"

Lily flashed her dimples at him. "I thought you'd *never* ask." She snapped her fingers and the water barrel appeared on the dune beside her. She handed him the copper dipper and waved at the barrel. "Help yourself, *chavo*."

He should have been wary of her response, but at that moment, he didn't care. Toby fell to his knees and sank the dipper deep into the barrel. Pulling it out, he sloshed water all over the golden sand. He sucked the liquid down his throat and plunged the dipper again. After his second drink, his mouth and throat cooled. "How long have I been out of it?"

"Oh, I don't know." Lily gazed at the horizon to the north. "To tell you the truth, I was so intent on my own thoughts that I didn't notice." She hunkered down and turned to face him.

"Thinking about what?"

Lily sighed and allowed her shoulders to slump. "My past. The choices I've made." She raised her gaze to his and stared at him. "Choices about who and when. Choices like the one you would force on me."

"Ah," said Toby. He returned his attention to the water barrel and dunked the dipper once more.

"Things draw to a close, Tobes. I'll need your decision."

Toby squeezed his eyes shut, dropping his chin to his chest. "I…"

"Before you finish that thought, I have something to show you." She waved her hand at the ground beside the barrel, and the pavilion appeared. "You'd best lie down."

"Oh, I see where this is going." He wagged his eyebrows at her. "At least I hope I do."

"That's sweet, *habibi*, but there's no time for that now. Lie down and close your eyes."

With a small shrug, Toby did as she asked.

13

The desert music woke him, creeping into his sleeping mind like an assassin in the night. He smiled, no longer thinking the melody was eerie or mournful or haunting. It just was.

An enviable state of being, *he thought.*

Toby opened his eyes to a vast stone room. He lay on a soft mattress amidst a pile of silk cushions. His flesh rippled with goosebumps as a chilly wind danced across his skin. He turned his head to the side, and there Lily lay, her body as perfect a promise of heaven as had ever existed.

Even in her sleep, she smiled at his thought.

He got out of bed and wrapped the loose white silk robes around himself, then stepped into his thick-soled leather sandals. Toby walked to the window cut through the stone wall and gazed out on the miracle of the desert. He peered right and left, then stared for a long time at the single road that stretched away through the sand and heat-devils dancing upon it.

Pilgrims packed the road.

He wasn't sure how he knew they were pilgrims, but he did. He also knew why they would risk such a journey through the unmarked desert: they all desired their own deals with the devil.

The pilgrims came from all over the world and represented every race, every creed, and every religion. Lily held no office, bore no rank, but still, everyone came to her— even so-called world leaders.

"What's got you thinking such thoughts, Tobes?" she asked from the bed.

"Oh, just watching the pilgrims on the road."

Behind him, the bedclothes rustled as Lily climbed out of bed. "I know they distress you, motek. *Shall I send them away for today?"*

Deals with Lily were dangerous. As they should be, *he* thought. Bargains with her came with strings attached, and oft times contained a trap for the unwary. She excelled at getting what she wanted.

Years he'd spent by her side, watching her slowly wrest the real controls of the planet from those leaders who came to her for help. He couldn't remember if there were any hold outs or not—because it just didn't matter. The major powers had succumbed to her charms early on, and Lily had de facto control over a wide margin of the population.

"And why should that not be?" she asked, sounding a little grumpy.

"A man needs his own head space to think, Lil."

"Then learn to think more quietly. I can't help it if you blather along at top volume."

"Sorry," he said.

"Say what you will," she said with a sigh. "But you must admit that my reign is much more peaceful than when humans were in control. There are no wars, no conspiracies to manipulate via the media."

"That's true," he said.

Toby... The word echoed along the corridors of his mind like a thief, an outsider, an assassin.

"Did you say something, Lil?" Toby turned to face her, smiling at her nakedness.

"No." *Her attention scoured the room—no doubt she'd lost her dress again.*

She'd never caught on to Toby hiding it. It was a—

Toby! Can you hear me?

"Yes, I can hear you, kisa." *She stopped her search and looked at him.* "What is it you need?"

"Hmm?" Toby cleared his throat. "Oh, nothing. Just thinking out loud again, I guess."

She smiled at him and returned to her search.

Toby, listen to me! You are in trouble! Lilitu is more dangerous than even Herlequin and his damn dog-things! We need to get you out of there!

Toby had closed his eyes and staggered back against the wall at the power of the words slamming into his head. When he opened his eyes, Lily stood only a few feet away, crouched forward, staring at him as though he'd grown a third arm.

"What was that?" she growled.

"I don't know. It... I..."

She stepped closer to him and peered into his eyes. "Is someone in there with you, Tobycakes?" Her voice sounded light and musing, but it also contained an iron edge. She took another step and sniffed him as if checking him for body odor. "There is, isn't there?"

Don't say anything. I'll hide.

"There are...words...in my head," he said. "I don't recognize them as my own."

"We can skip the audience," she said, peering into his eyes. "Perhaps you and I should—"

"No, it's nothing. My mind running away with me, I guess."

She stared at him for a long moment, then nodded. "Will you come to the audience with me, then?"

Sitting through another audience was the last thing Toby wanted to do, but he nodded, nonetheless. The smile she flashed at him was payment enough for a few hours of boredom.

"Let's go," she said. "Give me my dress, or I'll go naked." Her eyes danced with mischief. "Wouldn't that make the pilgrims blush? Can you imagine the shock value?"

Toby grinned and pulled the black leather garment from under the mattress on his side of the bed.

"You can have it back after we deal with the morning," she said. "Though you might have your hands full when it comes off again." She stepped into the dress and zipped it up, hiding all her delights from him. She turned and flung open

the double doors that had been carved from thick ebony timbers as if they weighed nothing.

Toby followed her, his gaze going to the elegant oil lamp ensconced in an alcove near the door. Cast in bronze, it bore bits of candy apple red glass and decorative embellishments done in lead. The glass seemed to glow with an inner light, and for a moment, the pattern of light reflected on the walls entranced him.

Toby... What's gotten into you?

The words seemed weak, meaningless, and the voice sounded far, far away. Toby took one last smiling look at the lamp and followed Lily to the audience chamber. They passed no servants, no guards, no priests or priestesses. Lily needed none of those things—people worshipped her regardless.

You're in grave danger, Toby! Listen to me! I'm your oldest friend.

Lily is my oldest friend, *Toby thought. He mounted the dais a step behind Lily and sat in the gilt throne next to hers. They sat at the same level and were the same distance from the steps.* Equals, *she had said.* We are equals in this.

The crowd of supplicants filling the other half of the room had gone silent as they entered. Toby's attention drifted from one face to the next, trying to guess what boon they wanted from Lily and what they would have to pay for it.

Because they always had to pay.

14

Benny pulled back from Toby's mind, reeling with confusion. Toby's mental state was almost like a dreaming man's, but there was a lucid quality to it.

He hovered near the top of the pavilion, looking down at his friend's sleeping form. Toby was alone in the tent, but he definitely wasn't alone in his mind.

No, *she* was with him.

A feeling of helplessness swept through him. Benny had nothing to counter what he'd felt in Toby's mind. His friend would have to cooperate, to fight with Benny, but it seemed like he *wanted* to be where he was.

15

At first, the audiences had offered a mild form of entertainment, but watching the naive or weak-willed humans walk into Lily's traps with their eyes wide open grew tiresome. The entertainment value to Lily seemed undiminished, almost higher *than when the audiences had started.*

Toby watched her for a moment, ignoring everything else. She sat leaning forward on her throne—not quite on the edge of the plush seat, but close. Her orange eyes whirled like they often did when she grew excited. Her lips were parted, and every once in a while, the tip of her tongue peeked from between them.

As the pilgrim kneeling in front of her lifted his head to look at her, she flashed a ten-thousand-watt smile. "Yes," she said. "What you wish for is possible, but it isn't easy. There would have to be a quid pro quo."

"Anything! You have but to name your desire."

Lily nodded and tipped her head to the side. "Be sure you remember this promise. When I come to you and ask for my favor, remember you promised me anything I desired."

"Of course, Mistress! Of course."

Toby kept his expression neutral. They always make this ridiculous mistake. It's as though they don't quite believe the stories that brought them here in the first place. *He studied the man's joyful expression with a modicum of wonder and a lot of disdain.*

Lily glanced his way and flashed a happy, victorious smile at him. "Then we have a bargain." *She waved him back, but the pilgrim stood there, looking around in the manner of a child separated from his parents.*

"Is there no…"

"No ritual? No dark meeting at the crossroads around midnight? No contract signed in blood?" *Lily threw back her head and laughed, but from the mechanical quality of it, Toby knew she'd grown bored at last.* "No need for any of that. I know what you've promised me and what I've promised you."

"Yes," *said the man as he stared fixedly into her eyes. He stepped back, then remembered himself and bowed.*

"That will be the last one for the morning session," *Toby said. He stood and extended his hand to Lily. She smiled at him and squeezed his hand as he drew her to her feet.* "Enough for today?" *he whispered to her.*

She wrinkled her nose and nodded. "I'm full." *She led him out of the audience chamber and turned to face him.*

"Full?"

"Yeah. Full to here with these petty concerns." She lifted a hand over her head.

"Why do you allow this? Do you enjoy it?"

Her only answer was a vague smile.

"And what will you ask him for?"

"The last one?" She arched an eyebrow at him.

"Yeah."

She gazed at him for a moment, then nodded. "Sometime during the next year, I will ask him to kill his political rival. The murder will occur in public, in full view of CCTV, and he will be captured immediately by the police."

"You know all this already?"

Lily smiled her crocodile smile.

"And I suppose the rival is a previous pilgrim?"

"Not him. His wife. She's reneged on her promise."

"Punishment, then. What task did you set for her?"

Lily turned and walked up the hall.

"Lily?" he asked.

She shrugged without turning to face him. "Never mind, Tobes."

The music of the wind and dunes increased in volume for a moment, blocking everything, even his thoughts. When it slid back into its accustomed place in the background, Toby felt changed, altered on some fundamental level.

But he no longer cared about the politician's wife.

16

Benny didn't know what to do to help Toby. He could feel something working at his friend's resolve from within, something that Benny seemed powerless to counter. Toby's body lay stretched out on the silk cushions but without any of the telltale movements or noises expected from someone merely asleep.

If Benny hadn't known better, he might have thought Toby was dead. But he wasn't dead… It was as though he'd gone spirit walking himself.

Benny looked to the west, in the direction of home. *Should I go back*? *If I do, can anyone help*? He sucked his teeth, dithering between the choice of hanging around, hoping to learn something, and going back home for help in finding a way to help Toby fight.

17

Sean found Eddie out in the garage, puttering around, looking at the tools and lawn equipment. "Bored?" he asked.

Eddie spun to face him, eyes wide.

"Sorry," said Sean. "I kind of snuck up on you there, didn't I?"

Eddie chuckled and blew out a breath. "No worries. I was thinking about doing some lawn work or something. Anything, really."

Sean cocked his head to the side. "The researchers have found something out about your land deal."

"Oh?"

"Yeah. It's not just your house. Everyone in the neighborhood got a letter like yours."

"All from the Stanton Growth Fund?"

Sean nodded.

"That's weirder yet. Any idea why?"

"It seems the Stanton Investment Group has long term plans for the ultra-wealthy and institutions. One such institution is called 'The Circle.'"

"The Circle? Never heard of it."

Sean offered him a lopsided smile. "It's very secretive. It's located in Oneka Falls."

Eddie lifted an eyebrow.

"Yes, uh-huh. An Abby Cho is named as the director."

Eddie grunted. "Lots of people are named Abby. Could be a coincidence."

"Maybe, sure. 'Cho' is one way of pronouncing the Zhou surname."

"I don't get it."

"Sure, okay. Have you ever heard the legend of Abyzou?"

Eddie shook his head, his mouth as dry as bone meal.

"It goes back to the Akkadian empire, as does Lilitu. She has many other names: Gylou, Alabasandria, Byzou, and Apsu, to name a few."

"Okay," Eddie said with a shrug.

"She's the demon these ancient civilizations blamed for miscarriages and infant mortality."

The blood drained from Eddie's face. "Abby," he murmured.

"Yes, uh-huh. Sorry to upset you, but I thought you should know."

Swallowing his emotions, Eddie nodded. "But why? Why buy up my neighborhood?"

"Right, okay. That section of land used to be part of the Seneca Nation's traditional lands. It was stolen from them in the late nineteenth century. It was considered a sacred site—a place of great magic."

"I don't think I like where this is going."

Sean bobbed his head. "There are legends about the land—that using 'the magical language,' wizards and witches could call horrible beasts to do their bidding."

"You think there's something to all those legends?"

"Summoning horrible beasts? It seems too much of a coincidence to be otherwise."

Eddie sighed and slumped his shoulders. "We'd better go tell the others."

18

Toby came back to himself bit by bit. He sat in the solarium, staring out at the desert, and he had no idea the time, or even if it was the same day he'd attended the audience with Lily. His brain felt wrung out, blank, and not even static echoed in the hallways of his mind.

"Lily?" he called.

Toby! Toby, listen to me! None of what you are seeing is real!

There it was again—that nagging voice that had so distracted him before. Something about the voice sounded familiar.

That's right, Toby. I'm Benny, your life-long friend.

Benny Cartwright? *he wondered.* But the real Benny is dead. The voice is only the result of the strain, the stress—

The pressure of what, Toby? What has you so stressed out? If this dream of a life gone wrong is reality, why are you stressed?

Toby shook his head to dislodge the harrying voice. The music of the wind and sand swelled in volume, and a half-smile descended on Toby's lips like a vulture on roadkill.

Don't do that! Don't call your own doom!

My own doom? *Toby stared out at the golden sand.* If Lily were here, she'd know how to get rid of these troublesome thoughts.

If things are truly how you wish them to be, then why do you need a distraction from what I say?

The blissful melody of the desert was right there; all he had to do was reach for it, and it would obliterate his doubts, his nagging voices. But he didn't reach for it, and he didn't know why *he didn't, though it seemed of tremendous importance.*

It's because she keeps wanting you to ask for help. She says it's the rules driving it, but it isn't. You already know the real reason she wants you to ask her.

"Because it's a binding action," *Toby murmured.*

"Did you say something, *kisa?" asked Lily.*

Toby jumped—he'd thought he was alone. Lily stood in the doorway, her radiant beauty eclipsing the stern beauty of the desert.

"Oh, you say the sweetest things, Tobes." She strode forward and reached out to pat his cheek. But as her fingers grazed his skin, she froze.

And Toby froze along with her. Everything froze, the tiny wind-devils dancing across the dunes, the sand kicked from the top of a dune by the wind, the passage of the sun in the sky.

"What's this?" she hissed, and the ground trembled with her rage.

19

Free at last, Dan Delo thought. He slid his phone back into the zippered pocket of his fanny pack, then cracked his knuckles. He took a moment and stretched as best he could forty feet up in a tree.

He swooped out of the ash tree in the backyard, angling his wings so he'd crash through the double French doors and right into their living room. *Fools think they are safe here? I'll teach them otherwise—starting with the damn mind reader.*

Chapter 5
The Last Day

I

Benny snapped out of his trance and lunged upright in the recliner. "Fuck!" he cried.

Sitting on the couch opposite him, Mike raised an eyebrow. "What happened? Did you—"

"They're coming!" Benny flipped the lever that dropped the footrest of the La-Z-Boy and flung himself at the gun case standing in the corner.

"Benny—"

"They're almost here! Lilitu caught me and...and..." Benny's gaze had frozen on the face of the wall clock hanging opposite the French doors. It read: 7:13 p.m. "How did that happen?" he muttered.

"Benny, what's the matter with you? First, you thrash like a madman during your trance or whatever, and then you freeze and start snoring. Then, after *hours* have passed with you barely even breathing, you start moaning and carrying on, and now, this." A one-sided smile curled Mike's lip. "Either get hold of yourself or share some of whatever you're smoking."

"What?" asked Benny, pausing halfway to the gun cabinet. "Hours?"

Mike started to nod, but the French doors that led to the terrace exploded inward, showering them both with dagger-sharp shards of glass and spears of shattered wood.

2

Every time Sean blinked, a hot, scratchy sensation accompanied it. He'd been staring at a computer screen all day, scouring paranormal sites, archeology sites, any- and everywhere that purported to have information on Akkadian religious beliefs and magical practices—there was a surprising amount of knowledge about both. Most of the incantations included demons—summoning them or exorcising them, and for so many references to exist, the ancient Akkadians must have believed they had need of magical protection from demons in their midst.

He assembled a syntax of sorts and found a nifty little website that translated English into phonetic Akkadian. He uploaded his report and transferred a few of the more promising incantations to his phone.

He yawned and pushed back from the computer desk, and as he did so, his stomach gurgled and rumbled. He thought he'd probably missed lunch, at least, but perhaps dinner, as well. He stole a quick look at his watch and discovered it was past seven in the evening. He turned back to the office door and spied the sandwich Kristy had no doubt brought him.

He smiled and took a gigantic bite out of the sandwich.

Downstairs, glass and wood shattered, and it sounded like something big—like the French doors to the terrace. Sean dropped the sandwich back on the plate and ran for the stairs.

3

Dan Delo snapped his wings once, then again, halting his forward motion. He furled them and dropped to the ground, not five feet from the mind reader. One of the unchanged humans stood across the room staring at Dan open-mouthed. *He's no threat.*

He turned all his attention on the mind reader and took a deliberate step toward the puny man, baring his talons and smiling to show his fangs. It was a display that, more often than not, inspired pure terror in his victims.

But this time, the mind reader barely glanced his direction before lunging for the corner.

Laughing, Dan intercepted him with a brutal kick to the head. The mind reader dropped like a sack full of rocks.

4

As the plain looking man launched a brutal head-kick at Benny, Mike's sleep-addled brain finally caught up. As Benny dropped to the ground, Mike jumped up on the coffee table and launched himself at the intruder.

Sean Walker stumbled to the railing of the balcony overlooking the living room. He cocked his head to the side in a strange manner and scanned the room. "Only one!" he shouted. "Big purple bastard."

The demon glanced at Sean, a sneer on his lips, which turned into an angry grimace as he saw Mike diving at him.

He swatted at Mike in midair, knocking him through the smashed French doors and out onto the terrace.

Mike hit the ground rolling, but that did little to dissipate the force of the demon's blow. He lay there a moment, sucking in oxygen, curled up and holding his ribs, and staring up at the sky.

5

Doors slammed open down the hall from the little Juliet balcony, but Sean didn't succumb to the temptation of looking to see who was coming and who was running away. He tried to hold the purple demon with his gaze.

Eddie slammed into the balcony beside him, breathing hard. "Oh, shit," he muttered. "Benny!"

Amanda Mitchell hadn't paused for a look—she'd already reached the bottom of the staircase in four leaping steps. Without pausing to think, she threw herself at the demon in a textbook-perfect cross body block.

"Amanda!" Eddie yelled as he raced toward the stairs.

The demon spun to face them, a broad smile stretching his lips. He held his arms out wide and beckoned with his fingertips. As Amanda closed in, the demon flapped his great wings twice and flew to intercept her.

6

"I've got to get out there!" Shannon shouted in Kristy's face. "Benny is—"

"You can't help, Shannon!"

"I *can*! I've done it before!"

"No," Kristy shook her head, standing with her back against the door.

"*Your* husband is out there, too!"

Kristy shook her head. "I can't let you go out there. If your injuries—"

"Oh, you stupid woman! What good is my health if the demon kills us all?"

Kristy half-turned her head to listen through the door but didn't move otherwise.

7

The slight woman squawked as they collided, her head bouncing off his pectoral muscles. He wrapped his arms around her and drew her from her feet. He beat his wings, stirring the loose papers on the coffee table.

"Amanda!" the man racing down the stairs yelled.

The woman in his clutches fought, kicking and punching.

"Stop, or I'll drop you," he rasped.

"Please do!" she snapped, lunged upward in his grasp, reaching for his eyes.

He flew toward the Juliet balcony, ascending as he did. His gaze locked on the weak-looking man who just stood there, holding up his phone like some looky-loo at a crime scene.

Using one hand, he squeezed the woman's wrist, grinding her delicate bones together. She moaned, but not as she should have. Her bones should have fractured, but they didn't.

He pulled his head away from her and stared down at her. "What are you?" he murmured.

"I'm the girl who's going to kick your ass!" she snapped.

8

Sean stood at the railing, unmoving except for his eyes, which twitched back and forth between the screen of his phone and the big purple demon. *It's foolish!* he told himself. *I have no idea if these incantations are anything other than superstitions run amok.*

But the big brute held Eddie's wife clutched to his chest as though they were lovers, and Sean had to do *something*!

His gaze flicked to the screen and then back at the demon, whose eyes roved Sean's face, also flicking back and forth to the phone. When their eyes met, the beast winked and sneered.

Hovering opposite the balcony, the demon switched his grip to free one hand. He bared his talons, never taking his gaze off Sean.

"No!" Sean looked down at his phone, then lifted his free hand above his head. "Ninurta, *aiālu annāši da'ānu,*" he chanted. Outside, the wind rose to a shriek, and shadows rushed from the horizon to cover the terrace.

"Prayers will not help you," said Dan Delo. He rested his talons on Amanda's neck. "Should I rip out her windpipe or tear her carotid artery and let her bleed to death?"

"Nergal, *aiālu annāši kišpē*." The wind blew against the house, rattling the windows in their frames, gusting in through the wreck of the French doors and making the magazines on the coffee table dance.

"Those names mean nothing to me, fool. Old monsters from the tales we tell our children."

Sean swallowed against the fear bubbling in his throat. "Ereshkigal, *abāru agannû alû!*" he shouted. The wind raced around the living room, dumping books and magazines to the floor, ruffling Benny's hair, shoving Eddie against the wall.

Dan Delo froze within arm's reach of the balcony, his taloned hand poised to rip into Amanda's flesh, but he didn't move. He didn't even twitch as he fell.

"*Anāku atta ašāpu!*" The wind howled, sending the coffee table skittering into the couch.

The muscles across the demon's back began to twitch and spasm, but he was still there, still holding Amanda tight against his chest, despite her best efforts. Sean glanced down at the phone again, the yelled, "*Anāku atta ašāpu ina irkalla!*"

Outside, thunder jangled, and greenish lightning danced across the sky. The demon moaned and foam spilled from his mouth.

"*Anāku atta ašāpu!*" Sean repeated.

The demon collapsed to his knees, groaning and gurgling, losing his wrestling match with Amanda at last.

As she scrambled away, the fiend squalled and thrashed, kicking furniture, ripping the carpet with his taloned feet.

Sean stared at the beast, willing it to die, to disappear. He was so intent on his efforts that he never heard the front door bang open.

9

Toby blinked and blinked, his eyelids moving as fast as a hummingbird's wings. Red silk fluttered in the dry wind above him. "What a dream," he said.

"There's no more time for fucking around, *motek*. I'll have your answer now."

Toby dredged up enough spit to swallow. "My answer…" he murmured.

"Yes. Your answer to my proposal. Your answer to the question of whether what you just saw, what you just *experienced* was to your liking. An answer to the question: Will you stand by my side forever?"

He turned his head to find her standing in the darkest corner of the tent, black dress and boots blending with the darkness, her red hair blending with the color of the pavilion. Her eyes glowed, casting an eerie orange pall over everything.

He had to fight to form the sentences he wanted to say. Well, *needed* to say if not wanted. "If it were just you and me, Lily, I would—"

"I can make it so," she said in a voice like that of a child expecting a disappointment.

"I don't even know what to say to that." As inexorable as gravity, something tugged at him. Something pulled at his core, his personality, his mind...his *soul*. "Why are there demons in Oneka Falls?"

She jerked her head back and stared at him without blinking. "That doesn't answer my question."

Toby let his grit-encrusted eyes slide shut. "It's corruption, isn't it?"

"What?"

"What you eat. Corruption." He opened his eyes and locked his gaze on hers.

"Some of the time, yes." She stepped forward, leaving the shadows behind. "Other times, I eat differently."

Toby nodded once. "Souls. Like Lilu."

"Does any of this matter?"

"Why are there *mazzikim* congregating in Oneka Falls?"

Lily shrugged with one shoulder and turned her profile to him. "They are like herd animals, these *mazzikim*. They gather together, fearing danger, fearing the *seraph* will find them."

"And yet many of them leave the herd," Toby mused. "Is it because of that lamp?"

Her gaze sharpened, focus twitching from eye to eye. "I don't have time for this, *chingado*. Events demand my attention." She snapped her fingers. "Your answer! Now!"

Toby opened his mouth to speak, then hesitated.

Pain blossomed behind Benny's eyes as he rolled to his side. He had no memory of how he'd ended up on the ground. He lifted an exploratory hand and felt the massive knot forming on the side of his head, groaning at the dull ache touching the bump caused.

Wind shrieked and howled around him as though he'd awaked in the eye of a tornado. Papers, books, and magazines flew around the edges of the room, borne aloft by the maddened wind.

Eddie was pressed against the wall near the foot of the stairs. The man's gaze was locked on the demon, who lay in the middle of the room, frozen as if in flight. Sean stood in the little balcony at the top of the stairs, holding one hand above his head like an evangelical preacher calling on God to heal someone. In his other hand, he held his phone.

The front door slammed open. After a breath, the two *ifrits* and the *djinn* from the parking lot battle charged into the room.

Naamah stabbed her finger up at Sean. "Do *not* finish that incantation!" she yelled. "I forbid it!"

Post the incantation! Benny sent at him. *Then finish it! They can only kill us once.*

Sean glanced his way but kept his lips firmly closed.

Naamah turned in a slow semicircle, following Sean's gaze. "Ah," she said and grinned. She advanced into the room, her eyes skewering Benny.

Mike! Run! Mike, get out of here! Get the lamp!

II

Benny's voice rang inside Mike's head like a klaxon, and he slapped his hands over his ears as if it would help. He rolled to his knees and darted a look through the shattered French doors, jerking back as Lamia turned to look out.

He thrust himself up and bolted for the corner of the house, lunging around it and pressing his shoulders to the wall.

"Mike? Is that you? What's the matter, hon? Are you hung over again?" Her voice sounded closer and closer with each question.

It's well and good to tell me to run, Benny, but...

Don't come in. Naamah, Abyzou, and Lamia are here. You've got to keep the lamp from them.

He peeked around the corner of the house. Lamia stood on her tail a few steps from the house, her scales rasping against the pavers with each and every movement, no matter how small.

One small problem, Mike thought.

On it.

After a moment, Lamia charged to the opposite side of the house and raced around the corner.

Go! Go, Mike!

He bolted around the corner and sprinted for the steep stairs that led down the cliff face to the dock.

12

Benny kept part of his mind focused on Lamia, creating one noise after the other for her to chase, while Naamah advanced on him. She came at a languorous pace, hips made of cherry red flame swaying back and forth.

"Ah, Benny," she crooned.

He turned his gaze on her and dimpled. "Hi, Brigitta. Or should I call you 'Naamah?'"

"It won't matter in a few minutes, so call me whatever your heart desires," she said, keeping the pleasant expression on her face, but unable to keep the edge out of her voice. "My father should have split your skull and dined on your brain."

"We all lament on missed opportunities from time to time," he said. *Shannon, get away if you can.*

13

"We *have to* get out there, Kristy! They can't handle all those demons at once."

Kristy glanced over her shoulder as though she could see through the door and walls, then turned her gaze back on Shannon.

"What good is any of this if they all die?"

Kristy turned her back on the room and cracked the door open. Down the hall, Sean gestured for her to stay hidden. "Sean says we should stay put," she whispered.

"As any husband would say to any wife. You've seen what a single demon can do." She swept her hand down her left side. "And the one who did this was relatively powerless compared to the *ifrit*. We don't have to fight, not overtly."

Kristy dithered, turning her gaze back and forth between Shannon and the door. "*If* we go out there, you are not to go past Sean's position. No matter what happens."

"Sure. Anything you say."

14

Abyzou smiled at Eddie and floated toward him, her feet hovering an inch above the carpet. With lips drawn from golden flames, she flashed a rapacious smile and showed her black-toothed grin to him once more. "Hello, Eddie. Do you like this body?"

Her smile grew broader, and dark shadows coalesced around her. "Or would you prefer something more familiar?" Dusky flesh encapsulated the flames and long blue-black hair sprouted from her head.

"I don't care what you look like!" he snapped.

She continued talking as though he hadn't spoken. "I underestimated you, Eddie. I see that now." She paused her inexorable advance and glared at Amanda. "Your love for the sow is strong. Perhaps I should remove that obstacle with my own hand this once."

"Leave her alone!" Eddie cried.

With a smirk, Abyzou turned to face Amanda.

15

"*Psst!*" whispered Kristy.

Sean stood transfixed at the balcony rail, one hand still held above his head, his phone in his other hand. His pallor wasn't good.

"*Psst!*"

Sean darted a glance in their direction and gave a minute shake of the head. A grimace settled on his features, and he tossed his phone at Kristy's feet.

She scooped it up and looked down at the screen, then showed it to Shannon. She led Shannon into the study and closed the door behind them.

"This might be our only chance," whispered Kristy. "Can you tell Benny?"

Shannon chewed her lower lip. *Benny*? *We need the lamp!* She listened with all her worth, but if Benny replied, she couldn't hear it.

16

Hurry, Mike! Lamia is catching on to my little tricks. Shannon says we need the lamp to have a chance.

Mike scrambled aboard the speedboat tethered to the floating dock. The engine fired at once, and Mike let it warm up at idle while he dealt with the mooring lines. As he pulled the last of the ropes aboard, Lamia appeared at the top of the stairs and hissed at him.

After putting the boat in reverse, he gunned the throttle, and the boat sprang away from the dock. *If you can hear me, Benny, I'm on my way.*

17

Abyzou paced toward Amanda, her gaze locked on the woman's face. Her smile grew as she drew closer, and hatred burned in her eyes. She flexed her hands, then folded them into tight fists. "We never got to finish getting to know one another."

Amanda backed away, matching Abyzou step for step. "I know you well enough," she said.

"So catty!" said Abyzou with a laugh. She glanced over her shoulder and winked at Eddie. "I bet she's a wildcat in the sack, too."

"You've always wanted me," Eddie said. "Leave her alone, and you can have me."

"Oh, Eddie. How little you understand me," said Abyzou. She turned her gaze back on Amanda. "Besides, this will be fun."

As she sprang, an invisible force batted her away. She squawked and slammed into the wall hard enough to smash through the sheetrock.

"You stop that," Naamah hissed at Benny, taking two quick strides to slap him hard.

In the moment of stunned silence that followed, Eddie sprang at Abyzou.

18

As Mike approached the parking area of the You Lock It Tight self-storage lot, he scoured the place with his gaze and grimaced at the demons loitering in the yard. A slow grin spread across his face as he drove past.

You were right, Benny. Again.

He skidded to a halt in front of a non-descript warehouse a mile up the street. The rollup door squeaked as he opened it, letting the afternoon light bathe the safe inside. But before he could pull the car inside, his phone chirped with a message from Shannon.

19

"You stop that," Naamah hissed at him. She took two quick steps to Benny and slapped him hard enough to drive him to his knees.

Ears ringing, Benny shook his head to clear it and focused on Naamah, sending a wave of force at her as he had back in the parking lot. She staggered back, hissing with anger. Her face contorted, and the flames that made it seemed to burn brighter.

She set her feet and shoved back, slamming Benny into the wall. A malicious grin decorated her lips as she advanced on him, applying more and more pressure until it seemed sure that Benny's spine would snap.

20

"Those foolish girls! They're going to ruin everything!" hissed Lily under her breath as she gazed to the west. She turned her attention to Toby and snapped her fingers. "No more time, Tobes. Make your choice."

"I…" Sweat beaded on his upper lip, his brow wrinkled. "You said you would take me home if I—"

"And so I shall! Now, answer me!" she snapped.

"Take me back to my friends, so I can tell them my decision," he said, blinking rapidly and staring at his feet.

"Does that mean—"

"Let me tell them in person. Help me to make them understand."

Lily smiled wide and snapped her fingers.

21

Mike flung open the safe. The lamp glowed and pulsed, its shade flickering from blue-black to red and back again. He didn't want to touch it, didn't even want to look at it.

He ran to the metal table in the rear of the warehouse bay and grabbed the welder's insulated gloves and his goggles, then put on the gloves and grabbed the lamp, carrying it back to the table. He wanted to smash the thing to bits—but Shannon had been specific. He needed to do things in the right order, or it wouldn't matter.

He lit the acetylene torch and fed it oxygen, then dipped the bright blue flame to cut the lamp in half. As the bronze body of the lamp grew soft and started to run, Mike read the words from the glowing screen of his phone.

"*Ereshkigal, anīna!*" he chanted.

He felt foolish speaking the gibberish aloud, but he did it anyway. The blue flame from the torch danced on the surface of the bronze, as if hungry to devour the lamp.

"*Ereshkigal, aiālu mar mazzikim!*"

The air in the storage bay grew oppressive, burdensome, and smelled of flint and sage. He opened his mouth to speak the next line, and the thick, flint-flavored air rushed down his throat as if to choke him.

"*Ereshkigal, aššunu ina irkalla naḫāsu!*"

He fought to get the words out, struggling against a wave of pressure as though he were speaking underwater. As the blue tongue of flame cut through the body of the lamp, the ground rumbled as if warning of an impending earthquake.

22

They appeared on the terrace of his house on the shore of Lake Erie, and the humidity in the air jarred him after his time in the desert. Toby raised his eyebrows at the smashed French doors. "I guess they started the party without us," he said.

Lily said nothing, only squinted into the house. She stepped closer, cocking her head as if to eavesdrop.

"Mistress!" said Lamia, coming up from the steps leading to the dock. "You have returned." Lamia's cold gaze settled on Toby. "It worked, then?"

"Yes," said Toby, returning his gaze to the house.

23

Benny groaned, sinking deeper and deeper into the wall while Naamah glared at him. "You killed my father," she hissed, her expression crumpling with murderous rage. She lifted him by the front of his shirt as if he weighed nothing, smashing more sheetrock with his head.

Eddie jumped on Abyzou's back, wrapping his legs around her middle. She screamed in rage and spun in ever-tightening circles, trying to dislodge him. She swatted at him over her shoulder.

Dan Delo lay on the floor in front of the Juliet balcony, his muscles twitching and jerking as though seizures wracked him. The ground rumbled, and he sat up straight, shrieking as if on fire.

Humans and demons alike froze in the middle of whatever they were doing, then turned to stare at the purple beast.

Delo sprang to his feet, but his legs didn't hold him, and he collapsed forward on his face, screaming. He thrashed on the ground, his hands and feet flopping uselessly.

When he disappeared with a pop, Naamah turned on Benny once more and growled. "*What have you done?*" she demanded.

24

Mike pointed the torch at the lead holding the pieces of glass into the shade. The lead melted much faster than the bronze, and colored glass rained to the floor. Mike squinted at his phone, then nodded to himself.

"*Lamia, anāku kāšim qirītu pašāṭu!*"

More glass fell to the floor, shattering on impact. *I hope this hurts, McBride. I hope it hurts a lot, you meddlesome bitch!*

"*Lamia, anāku atta ašāpu!*"

Again, the ground rumbled as if in warning of things to come, but Mike forged on. The air seemed oppressive, though it was neither hot nor cold.

"*Lamia, ina irkalla naḫāsu!*"

With the shade cut apart, he turned the flame on the chunks of glass, heating them until their color was lost to the glowing gold of liquid crystal.

"*Lamia, anāku atta ašāpu!*"

25

Lamia shrieked and grabbed her head as if it were about to explode. Her wide eyes stared at Lily as the *djinn* began to froth at the mouth. She tried to speak, but Toby couldn't make anything out of the hodge-podge of nonsense syllables.

"No!" hissed Lily.

With her black-scaled tail twitching, Lamia fell to her side with a crash and began to convulse.

Lily dropped to her knees next to her but stayed well back. "I won't abandon you, Lamia. I won't rest until you are back at my side."

Lamia disappeared with a loud, wet ripping sound, and Lily turned an enraged expression on Toby. "*What have your friends done?*"

Toby could only shrug.

26

Naamah stood close to Benny—close enough that each breath he took smelled of her. She held him by the neck, his feet kicking uselessly in midair. She stared into his eyes, anger brimming in hers. "And Lamia?" she asked. "Mother will be cross with you, and I, for one, can't wait to see what she does to you."

Summoning what saliva he could, Benny spat in her eye, smiling as she jerked her face away. "Your mother might be next!" he shouted. "Or maybe you, yourself, you insufferable cow!"

"Maybe so," she said in a reasonable voice. "But I'm not gone yet." With that, she flung Benny into the corner across the room, then lurched after him to grab him again. "Which bones should I break first?"

"Good God, demon. You and your lot are as bad as a bunch of James Bond supervillains!"

"What? What did you say?"

"With all your talk, talk, talk. Always explaining what you are going to do before you do it." Benny scoffed with a bravado he didn't actually feel.

"Of course!" she said with a chuckle. "We don't feed on your pain, Benjamin. We feed on your *emotions*—fear being one of them." She shook him like a ragdoll, and his teeth snapped together on his tongue. She lifted him high over her head and threw him as hard as she could.

27

With most of the glass melted into incongruous puddles, Mike turned back to the bronze, this time attacking the upper body of the lamp with the torch's blue tongue.

"Abyzou, anāku kāšim qirītu pašāṭu!"

The lump of bronze writhed between shapes, at one moment looking like the body of a snake, then the trunk of a tree.

"Abyzou, anāku atta ašāpu!"

The ground rumbled, and thunder pealed overhead. A hard grin spread across Mike's face.

"Abyzou, ina irkalla naḫāsu!"

He had no idea what the words meant, or even if he were pronouncing them correctly, but maybe it didn't matter. Perhaps his intent was what mattered.

Not that he really cared. If the shaking ground meant what he thought it did, he would dance naked in the mall to keep it happening until all the demons in the world were roasting in the pits of hell.

"Abyzou, anāku atta ašāpu!"

28

What had begun as an attack to distract Abby from Amanda had turned into a bronco ride. No longer even thinking of trying to hurt the demon, Eddie hung on for dear life. Amanda tried to help, tried to stop her from spinning, but Abby brushed her aside.

Then the ground rumbled for the third time, this time accompanied by a harsh, ugly peal of thunder, and Eddie fell to the ground. Amanda rushed to his side.

"*NO!*" roared a basso voice on the terrace.

He snapped his gaze to the hole where the French doors once stood and thought he saw a flash of red.

29

Mike played the torch across the bottom half of the lamp, melting it even as it tried to shift from snake's tail to tree stump and back again.

"*Naamah, anāku kāšim qirītu pašāṭu! Naamah, anāku atta ašāpu! Naamah, ina irkalla naḫāsu!*" He chanted the incantation as quickly as he could.

The ground thrummed with the power of the incantation, and when thunder sounded again, Mike thought he heard a scream along with it.

"*Naamah, anāku atta ašāpu!*"

30

Naamah stalked across the room, staring daggers at Benny. A visceral hatred pounded within her, coloring everything she saw, every noise that reached her ears, every breath she took.

Lilitu rushed into the room and grabbed her. "Not you! They can't send you—"

The ground began to shake, and Naamah threw back her head and wailed.

"No!" screamed Lilitu. "*I FORBID IT!*" The volume of her cry rattled the windows of the house.

Behind her, Toby stepped through the broken doorway in time to watch Naamah fade away into nothingness.

31

This last part is the most important, Mike thought. He flipped the mass of melted bronze over to expose the maker's mark. *She said there can be nothing left of this.*

"*Lilitu, anāku kāšim qirītu pašāṭu!*"

He drew the tip of the flame across the line of cuneiform, heating the metal until it glowed.

"*Lilitu, anāku atta ašāpu!*"

The words now sounded familiar, as though he'd always known them but had forgotten them. Despite their familiarity, they grew harder and harder to speak.

"*Lilitu, ina irkalla naḫāsu!*"

He dipped the torch closer to the bronze base, painting the cuneiform with its blue flame, watching the edges of the engraved words growing soft and beginning to run.

"Lilitu, anāku atta ašāpu!"

32

Lily stood with her shoulders slumped. Her expression was filled with sadness, with grief, and with anger. Her flesh seemed to fade in and out, pulsing with the passage of each breath. The speed of the pulses increased until she flickered like a loose light bulb. Then, the woman he knew as Lily was gone.

In her place stood a creature built from black smoke and shadows. The structure of her face bore a resemblance to her human features, but any similarities ended there. She stared at Toby in silence.

"This doesn't have to be the end." She raised both chrome-taloned hands to Toby, as though beckoning him for a hug. "It's not too late, Tobes. You can come with me."

Toby dithered, shifting his weight from foot to foot. A part of him wanted to go to her, to be enveloped by her presence, to join her, yet another piece of him was terrified by the prospect. Even so, he found himself inching in her direction.

Do it, Toby. Do it, do it, do it. Memory whispered the words in his mind, and Lily smiled.

"Don't do it, Toby!" cried Shannon.

"Don't do it," echoed Benny in a wisp of a voice. *Don't do it.*

Toby squeezed his eyes shut. "In 1979, I listened to a little voice that cajoled me to 'do it,' and it almost cost me my life. Herlequin couldn't hold a candle to you, Lily. He was as an ant in the path of a charging lion."

"Then—" Lily took a ghostly step forward.

He shook his head and lifted his hand like a traffic cop commanding someone to stop. "No, let me say this. You are magnificent in almost every way, and there will always be a part of me that is sad that I had to turn you down."

The room was silent for a moment, then Lily hitched a sob and turned away. "So be it," she muttered in a voice devoid of humanity. "Perhaps you were right, back there in the desert. This place…" She raised her hands to encompass the world. "It breeds unhappiness." She turned back and stared into Toby's eyes. "I will go then. But I will come back one day. There is always someone willing to pay my price in exchange for my favors. Someone will call to me across the void. Someone will offer me a place here." She dropped her gaze and stood with her arms hanging at her sides. "If…" She swallowed hard. "If you change your mind, there's a place you can go, Tobes. It's in New York, near Genosgwa. You needn't find it with any precision, just being in the right area will suffice. It is near your new friends' house." She gestured at Eddie and Amanda as she faded to translucence, her eyes growing wild. "Enter the circle and call to me, *motek*. Ask me to come, and I will."

She looked Toby in the eye, her expression flat and lifeless. She held that position for the space of five heartbeats, then an unfelt wind ruffled around her indistinct edges, pulling curls of smoke away. This time, instead of the smoke rejoining her body, it faded into nothingness.

Toby shuffled to the upended recliner and set it to rights. He stood in front of it for a moment, staring straight ahead but seeing nothing. Finally, his knees unhinged, and he sat. He buried his face in his hands. He couldn't bear to watch her go.

When Toby raised his head, Lilitu was gone, and the world was free of its last demon.

33

They gathered at Eddie and Amanda's house three days later. The group already felt like life-long friends, and it was to be a celebration—after a final ritual.

Down in the basement, Eddie had already jackhammered a large hole to expose the black soil beneath. Mike had to carry Greg down the stairs, while Eddie brought his wheelchair, but Mike didn't mind in the least. Greg was alive and getting better every day.

"Are you sure this will work?" asked Benny.

Sean Walker nodded. "Sure, uh-huh. I can show you the research if you—"

"I'm sure you are right, Sean," said Benny. "It's just jitters."

Sean nodded once and set the box he was carrying on Eddie's workbench. He peeled back the flaps and exposed the clay bowl. He lifted it out and showed it to everyone. The exterior was plain, undecorated, but the interior was full of cuneiform inscribed in a circle down to the bottom. In the center was a hand-painted image of Lilitu.

"And you're sure the cuneiform is correct?"

"Benny," said Shannon in a tight little voice. "Cut it out."

"Sorry," Benny murmured, squeezing her hand.

Sean grinned at him and nodded. "It's correct." As Benny nodded, he stepped down into the hole Eddie had dug. He held the bowl up over his head as if offering its contents to the rest of them. "Make a circle," he said. "You'll have to say it with me, so Kristy has notecards for everyone." He met each of their gazes—all except Toby, whose gaze was on the ground. "Once we start, we can't stop until we are finished, so if you have second thoughts, say so now."

No one said a word.

"Toby?" Sean asked quietly.

For the briefest moment, Lily's dissonant desert song played in Toby's mind to the exclusion of everything else. He raised his head as though it were the hardest thing he'd ever done. He looked Sean in the eye and nodded.

"Okay," said Sean. "Ready?" Sean flipped the bowl over and set it on the ground. He lifted his foot and held it over the upended bowl.

Sean brought his foot down and smashed the bowl. Eddie helped him climb out of the hole as Mike stepped forward with a brown paper sack in his hands. He upended the bag, dumping two lumps of bronze, several clumps of fused and melted glass, and a handful of lead nuggets.

Sean nodded, and together they chanted the Akkadian words inscribed on the interior of the bowl. Words that meant:

"Hail Lilitu, Bearer of Chaos. Hail Lilitu, Harvester of Sorrow. Hail hag and ghoul, I adjure you by the timelessness of Tiamat, by the power of Shamash, and by the magic of Ea, here is your divorce and writ and letter of separation, sent through the will of Marduk."

The sky rang with violent thunder, and the earth below them rumbled and shook as Lilitu's link to the world shattered.

When the noise faded away, a shroud of silence descended on the basement. After a moment, Toby broke the silence with a sigh, then turned toward the stairs.

"What now, Toby?" asked Benny.

"Now we go back to Oneka Falls and make sure the spell Mike cast sent every single *mazzikim* back to Hell."

"It did," said Greg. "And with Lilitu gone, they won't be coming back."

Toby nodded, a look of infinite sadness and loss etched into his face. "I want to be sure." He shrugged, not looking at anyone. "Plus, all of this started there for us, not in this basement."

Without another word, Toby trudged up the stairs, and his family followed him.

I hope you've enjoyed this series. If you in the mood for another spooky read, please check out my *A Rational Man* series. You can view all three books on Amazon (please note that if your local Amazon marketplace supports series pages for Kindle ebooks, all three links will point to it): Book 1: Wrath Child: https://ehv4.us/4wrathchild, Book 2: Black Bags: https://ehv4.us/4blackbags, and Book 3, Devils Dance: https://ehv4.us/4devilsdance. For my complete bibliography, please visit: https://ehv4.us/bib.

To be among the first to know what I'm up to and when the newest book I write goes live, please join my Readers' Group by visiting https://ehv4.us/join. Or follow me on BookBub by visiting my profile page there:

https://ehv4.us/bbub. Or, if you prefer to stick to Amazon, you may follow my author page: https://ehv4.us/amausa.

Books these days succeed or fail based on the strength of their reviews. I hope you will consider leaving a review—as an independent author, I could use your help. It's easy (I promise). You can leave your review by clicking on this link: https://ehv4.us/2revolc.

AUTHOR'S NOTE

Written on the completion of Blackest Crow:

Here you are again, friend. A guy could start to think you're stalking him…but, what the hell, you seem like good people!

I can see the conclusion of this series as plain as day, and, truth to tell, there's a part of me that doesn't want the story of our intrepid demon hunters to draw to an end. A part of me thinks the account should span at least a few more novels, but for now, I can't find the thread that will take us to them.

That's not to say the last book planned marks the end of *The Bloodletter* tale. I mean, the possibility exists Mr. Story will call on a fine gentleman named Noah to make a boat, and then… At the same time, Mr. Story might inform me the tale continues. You never can tell with that guy.

But the last planned book marks the end of the tale *for now* at the very least. I know a bit of what happens in the last two or three hundred pages of the series, but I can't see what happens in the final fifty with any kind of precision. There *will* be a satisfactory ending to the story.

People may perish. Demons *will* die, and not the "Oh, gee, I'm sending you home" way of dying. At least one more demon will die dead. Mr. Story keeps hinting the hunters are not safe, either, as you may have worried when this book ended with Greg in the hands of two twisted, serial-killing human rats.

You see, friend, surprises have patiently waited in the wings for their time in the sun, and not all of them are pleasant. Our fiendish friends have been keeping things from us. Quite a lot of deadly things, to be honest, and many of those secrets are itching to leap off the page at you.

I hope you survive them.

Hell, I hope I do, too.

Written on the completion of *Nightshade*:

To quote Dave Mustaine again, "Somewhere there's a reason why things go like they do." Approaching the end of this novel, I found myself reflecting on the nature of the series as a whole and asking myself whether I am ready for this series to end.

It's a strange feeling to be excited about something but dread it at the same time. I've gotten used to Toby and the gang. I've grown to enjoy fleshing out the demons of Oneka Falls. Plus, *Harvester* brings Lily to the tale, and she has a way of messing everything up (she and Mr. Story are related, I think), and she absolutely hates to lose.

It's easy to dive down the rabbit hole into their world, to escape the aches and pains of my own for a bit. I'll miss writing this series when it's finished, but on the other hand, I've got a lot of ideas kicking at the back of my teeth.

What comes next (at the conclusion of *Harvester*)? I wish I knew. Usually, the ideas sort themselves into a nice ordered queue, and I take the first one and run with it. This time, the ideas are an unruly mob, stacked up behind the gate, screaming their fool heads off. I think there might even have been a fist fight in the back.

Whatever I write at the end of this series, I hope you'll be there with me.

Written on the completion of Harvester:

For Supergirl, Real Sig™, and me, this year started off horribly. I found out about a nasty little disease I'd never heard of. Supergirl learned how well she can juggle *everything*—including a full-time job, our entire life, and keeping me sane during the worst pain I've ever experienced in my life.

We muddled through it, though it meant having a significant gap in my publishing schedule. I'd planned to write a stand-alone same-universe book, then write the rest of *The Bloodletter Saga* story.

As fate would have it, I took a different path—the path you've just finished reading. The best parts of that stand-alone book ended up incorporated into *Blackest Crow* and *Nightshade*—Eddie Mitchell's story line.

This is the point where you should stop reading if you are the kind of reader that jumps to the Author's Note first. Spoilers incoming!

Lily made her grand debut in the title novella (*The Devil*) for my collection of shorts (*Devils: A Collection of Devilish Short Fiction*), and I must admit, I fell in love with the character. Her reckless evil, her silly nickname fetish, her obvious abandonment issues, even her brutal vengeance, they all made her so much fun to write. I spent a lot of time thinking about her and how she fit in to the Oneka Falls story, and it seemed like a perfect fit until I realized that she would kill our heroes without batting an eye unless her emotions got in the way...

It was Lily that led me to the solution. Lily likes to tell people she's the devil, and she certainly has the chops for it. When I explored how Lily might deal with a group of demon hunters hassling her daughter, a lot of things fell into place: LaBouche's demise, why Brigitta/Naamah would hang out with the *mazzikim*, why Abyzou would care about a silly lamp, the three parts of this novel I call "the temptation of Toby, Mike, and Benny."

But the thing I couldn't bring myself to do is permanently end the story here, and this ending works better, anyway. After all, the devil is always waiting for the next sucker who wants to make a deal.

"What's next?" you ask.

It seems this year will end as it started. I found out a few weeks ago that the avascular necrosis I had in my left hip had jumped to the right hip, and that I had a subchondral fracture of my right femoral head. It's not as bad as the left, and thankfully, the left has remained stable since the middle of the year.

So, yeah, what's next?

I know for sure that there will be a new series (and think there may be two) rolling out in the first quarter of next year. The first series is an urban fantasy delivered with short novels, and the second is another old-school series of horror novels of the longish variety. Then again, I've also got a post-apocalyptic story kicking at my temples, another dark fantasy, and a more "straight-up" serial killer story line.

To find out my plans before most everyone else, keep your eye on social media—either at my blog: https://erikhenryvick.com or in my Facebook group: https://ehv4.us/fbog.

ABOUT THE
AUTHOR

Erik Henry Vick is an author who happens to be disabled by an autoimmune disease (also known as his Personal Monster™). He writes to hang on to the few remaining shreds of his sanity. His current favorite genres to write are dark fantasy and horror.

He lives in Western New York with his wife, Supergirl; their son; a Rottweiler named after a god of thunder; and two extremely psychotic cats. He fights his Personal Monster™ daily with humor, pain medicine, and funny T-shirts.

Erik has a B.A. in Psychology, an M.S.C.S., and a Ph.D. in Artificial Intelligence. He has worked as a criminal investigator for a state agency, a college professor, a C.T.O. for an international software company, and a video game developer.

He'd love to hear from you on social media:

Blog: https://erikhenryvick.com
Twitter: https://twitter.com/BerserkErik
Facebook: https://fb.me/erikhenryvick
Amazon author pages:
    USA: https://ehv4.us/amausa
    UK: https://ehv4.us/amauk
Goodreads Author Page: https://ehv4.us/gr
BookBub Author Profile: http://ehv4.us/bbub